"I ASK YOU, KAID,
DID THE GOD SPEAK TO YOU?"

The tips of Kaid's ears twitched as he answered. "The God spoke to me, Father Lijou, but *which* God, I'm unable to tell you."

"Then I'm not alone," Lijou murmured. He roused himself, capturing Kaid's gaze with his own. "Kaid, I truly believe that for the good of Shola, you, Carrie, and Kusac must go to the Fire Margins, *and return alive!*"

Kaid remained silent, his ears tilting fractionally in anger.

Lijou leaned forward, grasping him by the forearm and shaking him. "Do you hear me? You *must* go to the Fire Margins, no matter what!"

Kaid nodded once. "I hear you," he said, his voice barely audible. "What is the Fire Margin ritual, Lijou? What is it a test of but faith? To succeed you need to put your life in the hands of the Gods, Vartra in particular."

"No one knows what you need to do to survive, Kaid. No one *has* survived according to my records at Stronghold."

"How much truth do you think there is in the legends that telepaths once fought as well as any Warrior?"

"The Sholans in the new Leska pairs fight."

"They're reverting to type, Lijou. Those who walked the Fire Margins before were telepaths who couldn't fight; who lost their faith in the capacity of the ritual that took them back to the Cataclysm to return them to their own time. It's no wonder they didn't return."

"Will you go?" demanded Lijou, hands clenched so tightly Kaid could see the whites of his knuckles showing through his pelt.

"To the Fire Margins? I haven't lost my faith, Lijou," said Kaid. "Yes, I'll go. The God told me we have an appointment there. . . ."

FIRE
MARGINS

LISANNE NORMAN

DAW BOOKS, INC.
DONALD A. WOLLHEIM, FOUNDER
375 Hudson Street, New York, NY 10014

ELIZABETH R. WOLLHEIM
SHEILA E. GILBERT
PUBLISHERS

First Printing, November 1996
4   5   6   7   8   9

For Tal, who started it all.
And
Mike, for all his support during the dark years.

Special thanks must go to two people:

Judith Faul, who has lived through
just about every scene with me.

And, of course, my editor, Sheila Gilbert,
who has the rare gift of being able to accompany
me on my journeys to Shola.

SHOLA
(AS SEEN FROM APPROACHING SHUTTLECRAFT)

VARTRA'S RETREAT
DZAHAI VILLAGE
STRONGHOLD
FERRAKI HILLS
DZAHAI MTNS.
KYSUBI PLAINS
LAASOI
SONASHI VILLAGE
ALDATAN ESTATE
VALSGARTH ESTATE
NAZULE BAY
RHIJUDU VILLAGE
TAYKUI FOREST
NYACKO PASS
FYAK'S LAIR
SHANAGI (CAPITAL CITY)
GHUULGUL DESERT
MAIN SEAPORT
LYARTO PLAINS
JYUBA LAKE
MISHOI ISLAND
SPACEPORT

Prologue

"Approaching the trading world now, General M'ezozakk," said his navigator.

"Inform Priest J'koshuk that his skills are needed," said M'ezozakk, watching as the planet grew larger on the main view screen.

"No need, General, I'm here," said the priest, stepping out of the bridge access corridor. Behind him the door ground noisily as it closed.

"Hasn't anything been done about that damned door yet?" M'ezozakk demanded testily, ending on a sibilant hiss of displeasure.

"No, General. Maintenance and engineering are monitoring the hull patch continuously lest it is breached again. We can't afford to lose any more . . ."

"I don't want excuses," snapped M'ezozakk, his crest rising as he turned to look at the First Officer. "I want results! If it isn't fixed within this shift, I'll throw you to J'koshuk to play with!"

The officer's skin paled visibly, his tongue flicking out nervously as he glanced at the carmine-robed priest who now stood to the left of the General.

"I'll see to it personally, General," he said, ducking his head down in a low bow of obeisance.

"Do so." M'ezozakk turned back to the screen. "Wait," he said. "On your way, see that the captives are cleaned up. We need to get a good price for them. Make sure that they understand this, because if they don't cooperate, I'm sure J'koshuk could spare a few last moments with them."

"Yes, General," said the officer, beginning to sidle toward the exit.

"We're within communications range, General," ventured the crew member manning the comm unit.

"You realize our information regarding this world is minimal," said J'koshuk quietly, leaning toward the General "I can't be sure that the language we have on our data banks is their universal port language."

M'ezozakk turned his unblinking gaze on the priest. The vertical slits narrowed slightly. "Are you telling me you don't think you can communicate with these . . . savages?"

"By no means, General," said the other, his tone more conciliatory. "I don't yet know just how . . . basic . . . that communication will be."

"Your position gives you many privileges, J'koshuk. Should I, on your advice, have detoured to this world and be unable to accomplish our mission, those privileges can be rescinded. I believe Mzayb'ik has ambitions . . ." He left the rest of his sentence hanging.

"If I cannot communicate with these barbarians, General, then none of Mzayb'ik's ambitions will help you," said J'koshuk, his own eyes narrowing as he bowed his head slightly to the General.

"If you can't make yourself understood, then his lack of knowledge would hardly be an impediment," M'ezozakk said smoothly.

"We're being hailed from the planet's surface, General," the comm interrupted politely.

M'ezozakk relaxed back in his seat. "Are the cargo shuttles ready?"

"The shuttles are ready, General," said his security officer. "Shuttle One awaits your command for the automatic launch. Shuttle Two is fueled and ready. It awaits the crew and captives."

"The comm is yours, J'koshuk. I'll watch with interest while you negotiate with these beings," said M'ezozakk waving his hand lazily in the direction of the main viewer. "Open a channel to the surface," he ordered his comm officer.

J'koshuk bowed again, barely concealing the mixture of anger and fear on his face.

Let him hate me, just as long as he also fears me, M'ezozakk thought.

*   *   *

The cuboid sat at the back of the room, beyond the reach of the four Sholans. The Valtegans hadn't been about to let the unclean bodies of their captives go anywhere near their holy object. They'd lived alongside it for weeks, its brooding presence reflecting their mood just as it reflected the light. Just why they'd been kept there, Jeran had never been able to figure out. He had noticed that the ordinary troops on this vessel were even more afraid of the cuboid than of them. That was another puzzle. Why should the Valtegans fear them? Four half-starved and beaten Sholans chained to the floor hardly represented much of a threat to them, surely.

At first, Miroshi had tried to work out what the cube was. The mental exercise had diverted her thoughts from anticipating the next session with their tormentors. It had been futile, though. There was little she or any of them could glean from its featureless surfaces. It just *was*.

A short time before, the Valtegans had come and taken it away, carefully hauling it from the room on its obviously frictionless base. With it gone, they'd all felt easier. It was as if a weight they hadn't realized was there had been lifted from them. He still felt a sense of unease about it though, as if it was connected to them in some way he didn't understand.

The sound of the door opening roused Jeran from his reverie. It was all he could do to raise his head, ears facing forward, and look toward the noise. He saw the priest first, then the five armed soldiers behind him. He let his head fall back to the deck floor as the priest hissed out an order.

They wanted all of them this time. Usually they were taken singly. Maybe the damned lizards had tired of their uncooperative captives and their nightmare was finally about to end. Death held no fear for him any more: death meant freedom from their torturer, J'koshuk.

His body tensed, waiting for the kick or the blow—or even the shot that would finish him. Instead, he was grasped by the neck and hauled to his feet. A yelp of pain escaped him as the nonretractible claws dug into his flesh. So much stronger than the Sholans, they made no effort to temper that strength when handling their captives. His uniform jacket was stripped off him then, just as abruptly, he was released. Naked apart from his pelt, he staggered, trying to keep his balance, but he was too weak to stand. The heavy chain attached to the rigid metal collar round his neck dragged at him, pulling him down to the floor again.

He'd barely had a chance to see the same had been done to his three companions when they were hit by a jet of freezing water. Claws extended, his feet scrabbled against the metal-plated floor as he tried at least to get up onto his haunches. He'd expected to be killed, but not by drowning! Turning his head away from the stream of pressurized water, he bit down hard on his lower lip, trying not to yell curses at them in the few words of Valtegan he'd managed to pick up over the weeks they'd been on board.

Turning back to look at the others, he saw that even Miroshi had roused herself enough to try and keep her head free of the water. Their captors had quickly realized she was the most vulnerable member of the group and had targeted her for their special attention. What they'd done to her would have been despicable even had she not been a telepath. Her mental scars, like those on her body, might never heal.

Jeran's chain was just long enough for him to reach her and while the water was playing on the other two, he crawled along the floor toward her. The jet hit him again. Ears plastered flat to his head, he held her close, turning his back to take the worst of the torrent of water, lending her what little strength he had in an effort to keep her from falling back down to the deck.

The water stopped suddenly, gurgling as it flowed down the drains to the reservoir. He let Miroshi go, not wanting to add to her pain by continuing to touch her. As he turned back to the guards, one of them stepped forward and threw a bundle of cloths at him. Jeran grabbed at them instinctively, managing to catch them before they fell onto the wet floor.

The guard snapped an order at him. Confused, Jeran shook his head, blinking as he wiped his forearm across his eyes. The officer at the door spoke and the guard stepped forward. Leaning down, he snatched a cloth back from him and began rubbing it across his own arm.

The officer spoke again, this time addressing Jeran briefly, then they all turned and left.

Tesha looked over at him. "What did he say?" she demanded, curling her tail, which now resembled a piece of old rope, protectively round her haunches.

Jeran handed two towels over to her. "We're to dry ourselves."

"Even I got that!" she said acidly, passing the other to Tallis.

"I didn't get it all, but it had something to do with us being put down on this planet we're orbiting in exchange for . . .

supplies, I think," he said, hunkering down beside Miroshi again.

She stirred, taking the towel from him.

"Can you manage?" he asked.

She nodded, beginning to wipe the cloth along her arms.

"So why the cold shower?" asked Tesha, shivering as she began to rub herself.

"Don't want the goods to be seen covered in matted fur and dried blood," said Tallis bleakly as he made an equally half-hearted attempt to dry himself.

"There was an implicit threat concerning J'koshuk," added Jeran.

"He's selling us," said Miroshi, speaking for the first time in days. "He said if he doesn't get a good price, he'll give us back to J'koshuk."

Tesha broke the silence that followed. "Well, what do we do? Make a break for it so that they kill us, or go down to this world like tame rhaklas?"

Jeran began to dry himself, trying not to knock the scabs off the half-healed wounds. His fur was matted into the cuts on his face and arms but there was nothing he could do about it.

Before he could answer, the door opened again, this time to admit the ship's medic, flanked by two guards, one carrying a tray holding four beakers.

"Eat," said the medic as the guard came over with the tray. "Been cooked. Need eat. Soon you leave."

A beaker was thrust at Tallis. Reluctantly he took it, sniffing the contents. "It *has* been cooked," he said, surprised. "It's some kind of stew, not raw meat."

Jeran was given his. It wasn't worth the beating that would ensue if he refused it. He raised the beaker to his lips.

As he drank, the medic came over and deftly grasped his arm, pressing the hypo gun against it, then he was gone. A brief surge of giddiness, then almost immediately he felt a warm glow spread through him.

"It's some kind of sedative," he said, watching Miroshi flinch as the lizard touched her. There was no point in objecting.

The guard collected the empty beakers then followed the medic out, leaving the soldier with his rifle trained on them.

Tesha sat down suddenly. "I don't feel so good," she said faintly.

Jeran looked up, seeing her inner lids beginning to show at the edges of her eyes. "You'll be all right," he said, aware that he should be feeling more concerned than he was. With an effort, he kept his mind on what he wanted to say. "You know their drugs do strange things to us, especially you. It's not lethal. They wouldn't kill us like that. There's no amusement for them in it."

"If you focused your thoughts, you'd be able to control the effects of the drug," said Tallis.

"I can't, you know that," said Tesha, wrinkling her nose. The skin visible around her eyes had an unhealthy greenish tinge.

"You just won't . . ." began Tallis.

"Stop it, both of you!" said Miroshi tiredly, sinking back onto the floor. "Must we fight among ourselves? All we've got left is each other, and we may not even have that for much longer! In Vartra's name, shut up!"

Jeran moved over to Tesha, the chain dragging behind him. "Leave it, Tesha," he said quietly. "Just ignore Tallis. Being telepaths, it's been worse for them. Every time they've been touched, they've been mentally tortured, never mind what they've done to them physically. It's only when they use drugs on us that Tallis and Miroshi can feel they're fighting back."

"I know," she muttered, leaning her head against his shoulder. "It's been bad for all of us. What do you think our chances of being rescued are?"

"If they know we're missing, they'll make an effort to find us, but from the size of those craft we saw around Szurtha, I'd say they'll have a lot more to worry about than the four of us."

"They're coming back," said Tallis, ears flicking in distress as he moved closer to the other three.

CHAPTER 1

As Kusac opened the door to the staff lounge, he caught the tail end of their conversation.

"You gave him the right to decide, Kaid," Rulla was saying. "No one made him choose Stronghold." Hearing the door open, he looked up.

Kaid sat at the table reassembling his rifle.

"What's going on?" Kusac asked, watching Rulla's eyes flick from him back to Kaid.

"Everything's under control, Liegen," Kaid replied blandly, snapping the power pack into place. "There's nothing for you to be concerned about."

Kusac could feel the tension in the room. Something wasn't right. He shut the door behind him, mentally scanning Rulla's surface thoughts. "Where's Vanna?" he demanded. "I know this concerns her. Where is she?"

"She's paying a brief visit to Stronghold," replied Kaid, getting up and turning to face him. "I'm on my way to collect her now."

"Stronghold? What in the name of all the Gods is she doing visiting there at this time of night?"

"That's what I intend to find out," said Kaid, his voice grim as he picked up his rifle. "I'm afraid one of my people took her there." He walked toward Kusac, stopping in front of him, obviously waiting for him to step aside.

"I'm going with you," said Rulla, getting up and moving over to join him.

"No, you're not," said Kaid, throwing a glance at him over his shoulder. "You could be concussed after that blow on the head. You'll remain here. I'm going alone." He looked back at Kusac. "Excuse me, Liegen."

Kusac shook his head. "I want to know what's going on. Who hit Rulla? Vanna's been kidnapped, hasn't she?"

"You can't go alone," insisted Rulla. "It could be a ruse on Ghezu's part to get *you* to Stronghold."

Kaid snorted in disgust.

Kusac could feel himself getting angry. "No one's leaving here till I know exactly what's going on!"

"Liegen, I haven't got time for this now," said Kaid, his ears giving the faintest flick of annoyance. "It's already over an hour since Vanna was taken."

Kusac leaned back against the door. "Then you'd better tell me now why Stronghold's suddenly so interested in Vanna—and us." He watched Kaid's eyes narrow as the other male sized him up. "Remember your oath," he said quietly.

"I don't need you to remind me, my Liege." Kaid's voice was emotionless now. "You have your Leska to look after. She's still very weak."

"Dammit, Kaid!" Now he was really angry. "You two woke me with all the mental noise you were making, and that despite the psychic damper in our room! Luckily Carrie's still sedated. Vanna's one of my people—as are you. I want to know what's happened, and I want to know now!"

"I haven't the time, Liege. T'Chebbi's waiting outside in the aircar." Kaid's tone was equally implacable.

Abruptly Kusac reached behind him and pulled the door open. "Then tell me on the way." He turned and headed down the corridor toward the side exit that led to his family's private vehicle park.

He'd barely taken half a dozen steps when he heard the sound of feet behind him and his left arm was grasped firmly.

Trying to bite back the yelp of pain that rose to his lips, he turned round, his good arm unconsciously going up to cradle the wounded one.

"Liege, you can't go," said Kaid. "You're injured. I did no more than touch you and you're gray with pain. You'd be a liability to me."

"Liege is it now, Kaid?" Kusac kept his tone light as he attempted to move away from his bodyguard. "Then release me, and stop wasting more time."

"Yes, it's Liege now, since you chose to remind me of my oath." His eyes flicked across Kusac's face. "What the hell's got into you?" he demanded. "This isn't like you at all."

"Maybe not," replied Kusac, breathing more rapidly to try

and ease the pain from his shoulder. "You told us it was over, that the last assassin was dead, and now we find that we still have enemies. It's time we started not only looking after ourselves, but also our friends. Carrie and I've faced death too often recently, Kaid. It doesn't hold any fears for either of us anymore. We won't hide behind you or anyone else again."

"It's not that simple, Liege." Kaid let go of his arm. "This may be why Dzaka took Vanna to Stronghold—to flush you out and bring you there after her. Particularly as he knew you'd spent the night together."

"Then we'd best not keep them waiting." Kusac turned again toward the exit.

"Liege! I can't protect you *and* fetch Vanna back!" His tone was exasperated.

"Rulla," Kusac said over his shoulder, "How's your head?"

"I'll survive, Liegen," said Rulla.

"Good. You'll accompany us."

"Yes, Liegen," came the satisfied reply.

Kaid let out a low rumble of anger as he stepped yet again in front of Kusac. "You still don't understand. If I arrive at Stronghold accompanied by you, Rulla, and T'Chebbi, it'll mean a showdown that we can't afford at this time."

Kusac stopped again, staring Kaid straight in the eyes. "A showdown, Kaid?" He cocked one ear forward. "Why should there be a showdown because I arrive with an escort to collect my friend Vanna?"

"Vanna didn't go voluntarily."

"I gathered that when you mentioned Rulla had been hit on the head," said Kusac dryly. "When I left her a couple of hours ago, Vanna had no intention of going anywhere but the Guild. I can also tell you that she's probably unconscious, in a shielded area, or they've given her a psychic suppressant. What else should I know, Kaid? How about telling me why Stronghold's so interested in us."

Kaid's eyes narrowed again. "Very well, Liege," he said abruptly, moving aside and drawing Kusac forward by his good arm. "The Brotherhood wants to get full guild status. To do this, they need to recruit you and any other mixed Leska pairs. They have the facilities and staff to train you there."

"Why would the Brotherhood have facilities for telepaths?" Then realization dawned. "The missing talents!"

Kusac stopped in his tracks and looked at Kaid with the beginnings of understanding.

Kaid nodded.

"You're the people the Telepath Guild has missed—the ones with the minor Talents!"

"Some of us have more than a minor Talent, Liegen," said Rulla mildly. "We just aren't telepaths."

"All along, the Brotherhood's been gathering in those people. Why, Kaid?"

"That's what we are," said Kaid. "Every one of us."

"Every one of you? Then telepaths who can fight aren't new."

"Yes, *you* are," said Kaid. "That's why Stronghold wants you. They have no telepaths among their active members."

"They want to recruit us?"

"You and Carrie—perhaps. Vanna and Brynne, definitely. They think they can control them more easily than you."

Kusac gave a short, derisory laugh. "They don't know Vanna!"

"No, they don't," said Kaid, his mouth opening in the ghost of a smile.

"Dzaka is the one who took Vanna to Stronghold," said Rulla.

"He'll regret it," said Kaid, his voice barely audible.

Kusac gave himself a small shake, trying to dispel the chill Kaid's comment had caused. He started walking again.

"Stronghold wants full guild status so they can challenge the Telepath Guild's power in the World Council," said Kaid. "They can't achieve guild status unless they can prove they have a skill that is unique to them."

"Us."

Kaid grunted in reply as they emerged into the cold predawn air of the park. An aircar, its engine gently humming, was waiting for them. He passed his rifle to Rulla, clambering into the pilot's seat that T'Chebbi had just vacated.

Kusac joined him in the front, leaving Rulla to accompany T'Chebbi in the rear passenger area.

"I won't be used by the Brotherhood any more than by the Telepath Guild," said Kusac in a low voice as Kaid took off, heading northwest for the Dzahai Mountains.

"I know, but the Brotherhood mustn't realize that yet," said Kaid, equally quietly.

Kusac looked thoughtfully at him. He touched the edges of Kaid's mind with the usual result: a quiet stillness. Carrie was the only one who really sensed Kaid, and then only on their Link days when their abilities were enhanced. Now, thank Vartra, she was asleep, but her help would have been useful.

"You can't break formally with the Telepath Guild unless you have the protection of Stronghold," said Kaid. "Esken won't tolerate it; he can't afford to. If you still intend to follow the path of En'Shalla, you need to buy time, to wait until Carrie's recovered. It's dangerous enough when you're healthy."

"I know," said Kusac, his tone short. Putting their lives in the hands of Gods he barely believed in and certainly didn't trust would not be an easy step for him to take.

"If you turn down Stronghold's offer, you'll be placing my people in a dangerous position."

"Explain."

"If you refuse Ghezu and Lijou, they'll recall all the Brotherhood members I've got guarding you," said Kaid, banking to the right to compensate for the gusting wind.

"The threat to our lives is over now though, isn't it, Kaid? Surely we don't need so many people."

"I think we do. Let's just say I prefer being overcautious. Also several of them wish to break from the Brotherhood and join you and your people. If they're recalled, they'll have to disobey Stronghold and we aren't ready for that yet."

"The showdown you were discussing. I don't understand why they'd want to join us in the first place."

"Because of Kaid," said Rulla, leaning forward. "You only know one side of him. Before he was 'retired' from the Brotherhood, he had quite a following, especially when it came time to elect the new Leader."

"Enough, Rulla," said Kaid sharply, banking the vehicle against the wind and causing them all to clutch their seats.

Kusac turned to look not only at Kaid but at Rulla as the other male picked himself up from the floor. "You were a contender for Leadership of the Brotherhood?" Already he was reassessing his opinion of Kaid. A lot of things were beginning to fall into place.

"I was chosen," Kaid admitted reluctantly. "It's part of my life that belongs in the past. Rulla and others won't let me forget it. I think they're fools to risk their lives with us, but they're entitled to make their own choices. That's why it's wiser to agree to the Brotherhood's offer for the time being, until you're ready to step outside the guild system. That way you can break publicly from the Telepath Guild with the protection of the Brotherhood, who can then claim what they want—full guild status."

"They give us their protection in return for our support in breaking Esken's hold on the World Council," said Kusac.

"As you say. He's using fear of himself and his Telepath Guild to coerce the weaker Council members to vote his way. They're too afraid to speak up against him, and those who do have an idea of what's happening can't prove it."

"What about my father? He can't know anything about this. I know fear wouldn't stop him speaking out against Esken."

Kaid looked at him briefly. "I assume he knows nothing. The Council members Esken controls presume all the senior telepaths are involved. They aren't going to risk their lives by asking one to find out."

"By all the Gods, Kaid, if this is true it mustn't be allowed to continue! How could Esken claim he was afraid of us abusing our Talents when he behaves like this? What of Governor Nesul? Where does he fit into this?"

Kaid flicked his ears in a shrug. "Like the others, he can do nothing. Who'd believe him? Telepaths are vital to every level of life. No one could afford the chaos that would result if this came to light. No, Ghezu and Lijou's solution is the best. They have enough on Esken to play him at his own game. Remember, the majority of telepaths, even those in senior positions, are ignorant of what's happening. Most of Esken's manipulation is at the Council level."

"How did you find all this out?"

"I keep my ears open, and I have my contacts," he said.

"You must have," said Rulla. "Even I didn't know this."

"I've always hated politics," muttered Kusac, sitting back in his seat.

"You are the politics," said Kaid. "You and your Leska, along with Vanna and Brynne and the others like you, are the heart of this matter. With you as Telepath Guild members, Esken has what he's never had before. A private army, guild-bound to him, and the rest of the Council will know it. He'll be able to play his power games on a scale he never dreamed of before. The military? 'Sorry, my Telepath pairs aren't ready to be freed from their Guild commitments yet, however . . .' Use them, Kusac, instead of letting them use you."

"I get your point," sighed Kusac.

* * *

Meral stood safely out of reach at the foot of Garras' bed before pulling back the covers. Cautiously, he reached out to draw a claw tip along the pads on the sole of the sleeper's foot. The resultant kick just missed him as Garras landed in a crouch nearby.

"It's me, Meral," he said.

Garras straightened up. "What is it?" he asked, keeping his voice low as he cycled his side arm back to standby.

"I woke early so I went for a walk. There's a scouter in the main yard, one from the estate. The scents were fresh, and I'm pretty sure one of them was Vanna's."

"Vanna's? What the hell's she doing here?" Perplexed, Garras wrinkled his nose.

"I don't know. I didn't try to find her, I came straight back to tell you. I don't think anyone saw me."

"You did well," said Garras, turning to grab his jacket and belt from the chair. "Let's check it out. Remember the mental exercises I taught you. Keep your mind as still as possible. There're several people here capable of picking us up, and if it is Vanna, then Lijou will be awake."

They padded silently down the corridor, keeping in the shadows until they reached the main staircase. Garras held Meral back. "Remember, if we meet anyone, I'm taking you on an early morning training session."

Meral nodded and, trying not to clench his feet against the sudden cold of the stone stairs, followed Garras as silently as he could.

* * *

Dzaka's head came up suddenly and he looked toward the large curtain-covered window. "We're being watched, Father Lijou," he said.

Lijou looked over in his direction, raising an eye ridge.

"Two males," Dzaka said, shaking his head. "Their minds are too still to pick up any emotions."

"Kaid." Ghezu said the word like it was an oath.

"Not Kaid," said Lijou. "There hasn't been time, and Dzaka would know him." He turned to Vanna, feeling a flare from her mind. "Garras?" He turned back to Dzaka. "Is Garras here?"

Dzaka flicked his ears in assent. "He brought a male called Meral to enroll him in the Brotherhood."

"So, I have ex-Brothers sponsoring new members, have I?" Ghezu noticed Vanna's slight movement from the corner of his eye. "I think not, Physician," he said, turning to her. "You'll remain here for the moment. Dzaka, bring Garras and Meral here, if you please," he said.

"Immediately, Leader Ghezu," he said, bowing his head toward him before going to the door.

"Physician Kyjishi," said Lijou, returning to his chair beside Ghezu's desk. "Let's go over what you told us about these Valtegans."

Vanna leaned forward across the desk. "I want to know when you're going to let me return to the Aldatan estate," she said angrily. "I've told you what I know. When Kusac and his parents realize I'm missing, they'll be far from pleased!"

"But that's what I'm waiting for, Vanna," said Ghezu. "I want Kusac here. Since you refuse to join us without discussing the matter with him," he said, spreading his hands expressively, "we must wait for him to come to you."

"That's why you had me brought here!" she said. "You aren't interested in me, it was Kusac you wanted all along!"

"Could Kusac have identified the bones?" asked Lijou. "I doubt it. We needed you to do that. The fact that we only have to sit and wait for Kusac to arrive as well is a bonus."

"And if he doesn't come?"

"Oh, he will, my dear," purred Ghezu. "He will."

Dzaka padded silently along the corridor toward the stairs down to the south garden. He could sense that Garras and Meral had reached the floor below. He stopped, waiting till he felt them approaching the bend in the stairs, then he spoke.

"Garras, it's me, Dzaka."

There was a profound silence for the space of three heartbeats.

"Where's Vanna?" Garras demanded, cautiously coming into sight.

"She's with Father Lijou and Leader Ghezu," he said. "I've been sent to ask you to join them. Everything is fine," he said reassuringly. "You won't need your gun," he added, turning to move back into the corridor as they began to ascend the last flight.

When he reached the top, Garras looked him up then down before reholstering his side arm. "What's she doing visiting them at this ungodly time?"

"They needed her advice on a medical matter," Dzaka said as Meral drew abreast of him. "You'll be able to ask her yourself when we reach Leader Ghezu's office."

They walked in silence to Ghezu's door. Dzaka opened it for them, then stood back to let them enter first.

As he did, an arm snaked across his throat, arching his body backward. At the same time he felt the touch of steel just under his ear. He didn't struggle.

"You betrayed my trust." The voice was flat, carrying only a faint hint of the cold fury underneath.

Breathing was difficult with Kaid's arm pressed hard against his throat.

"I didn't touch the Human or Kusac," Dzaka gasped.

Kaid pressed the point of his knife hard against Dzaka's skin until it just penetrated his flesh. A drop of blood swelled at the tip and began to roll down the blade. "Vanna was in my care, too. You know that."

Icy fear ran down Dzaka's spine as he realized his life was poised at the end of Kaid's knife. "You'd kill me."

"If it was anyone else, you would be dead now."

"Where's your trust, foster-father?" he whispered. "Are you the only one due it? Do I deserve none?"

Abruptly he was released. "If you've played false with me, you'll live to regret it, Dzaka," said Kaid. "There'll be no swift death for you."

Dzaka put his hand up to rub the blood from the small wound on his neck before stepping into Ghezu's office.

"Tallinu," said Ghezu, getting to his feet as Kaid entered. "What a pleasant surprise! I send Dzaka for Garras and he finds you as well. And Liegen Aldatan! Will wonders never cease?"

"Good morning Leader Ghezu, Father Lijou," said Kusac with a curt nod to the two males. He stopped just inside the door, flanked by Rulla and T'Chebbi, Kaid standing beside him. "I trust that the emergency has been satisfactorily dealt with, Vanna, because I'm afraid we'll have to leave almost immediately."

Vanna had risen to her feet the moment she'd seen Garras. "Is Carrie worse?" she asked Kusac, moving swiftly to stand beside her mate.

"She's been in a great deal of pain for most of the night," he said. "I'm afraid the medication you left hasn't given her any relief." He looked over to the desk where Lijou and Ghezu were still standing. "I'm sure you understand that my mate's needs must come first."

"But of course, Liegen," said Lijou with a courteous bow. "We won't delay you any longer. I hope the Liegena will recover quickly."

"Before you go, Liegen, I need to have a few words with you," said Ghezu sharply as Kusac turned to leave.

"A moment only, Leader Ghezu," said Kusac. "Don't forget I feel the full measure of the pain that Carrie's suffering, and I won't let it continue any longer than is absolutely necessary."

"We've heard you're dissatisfied with the Telepath Guild because of their treatment of Vanna and her Leska, as well as yourselves."

"You've heard right."

"We'll offer you sanctuary, here at Stronghold, Liegen Aldatan."

Kusac looked in astonishment at Ghezu. "As far as I'm aware, we don't need sanctuary, thank you, Leader Ghezu."

"Let me explain," said Lijou, stepping forward. "What my colleague means is that we are offering you membership in the Brotherhood."

"Ah, yes. Kaid mentioned something of the sort to me on the way here, didn't you, Kaid?"

"Yes, my Liege," said Kaid, hand resting lightly on the stock of the pulse rifle he wore slung over his shoulder.

Lijou frowned. "It's a pity you haven't more time, Liegen. No offense to your . . . adjutant, but he doesn't have all the facts at his disposal."

"On the contrary, he pleaded your cause most eloquently."

Lijou's eye ridges almost disappeared in his surprise. "Really? Then perhaps you'd be willing to discuss the matter in detail?"

"Oh, I don't think I need to delay my decision, Father Lijou," said Kusac, his tail tip beginning to sway lazily. "As

I said, my time is short. All I need to know is why you want our membership. Kaid obviously could not tell me that."

Kusac, despite his tiredness and the continuing pain in his shoulder, was enjoying this little interchange with Lijou. He had him at a distinct disadvantage, and Lijou knew it.

He watched the Head Priest of Vartra's eyes narrow as he folded his hands in the pouch at the front of his black robe. He was playing for enough time to think of a suitable reply.

"If Kaid hasn't told you about Eksen's dealings on the Council then he's not the person I remember from ten years ago," Ghezu said abruptly.

Lijou brought a hand out of his pouch and waved him to silence. "Leave this to me, Ghezu. Liegen, we need to challenge Esken on the Council. We need to show the Council members he's terrified into compliance that we can stand between them and Esken. To do this, we need seats on the Council, and to get those, we need to be a guild. If you join the Brotherhood, then they can't deny us guild status. In return, you'll be Brothers, with all the protection that entails. We have the facilities here to train mixed Leska pairs like you, not only in telepathy, but also in combat. And should we need any extra teachers, I'm sure we'd have no lack of volunteers from the other guilds. Will you accept our offer?"

"Your proposition is certainly attractive, but we'll need to talk further on this," said Kusac. "Not now, in a few days' time."

Lijou nodded. "As you say, Liegen. The Liegena's health must come first. When will you let us know your decision?"

"When I'm convinced that changing guilds is the right thing for us to do," said Kusac, turning away again.

"Will you also reconsider our offer, Physician?" Lijou asked Vanna.

"If Kusac and Carrie are joining, then I will," said Vanna, casting a quick look in Kusac's direction.

As they began to file out, Ghezu called to Dzaka. "Dzaka, I want you to remain for the time being," he said. "I'm sure Leigen Aldatan has enough people that he can spare you."

In the hallway, Kusac stopped and looked at Kaid. He'd been standing beside them during their confrontation. Dzaka's answer was easily heard.

"I'm sorry, Leader Ghezu, but I'm oath-bound to protect the Liegena, and she hasn't released me from my oath. I have to return with them."

"Let him go, Ghezu," said Lijou, his voice sounding tired. *Stop playing your games with him and Kaid,* Kusac heard him sending.

"Go," said Ghezu, suppressed fury in his voice.

Dzaka joined them in the hallway, shutting the door behind them. Kusac saw his eyes go to Kaid's back as the other started walking. Whatever it was that was wrong between them, it went deep.

No one spoke until they were in the aircar, then Vanna turned on Kusac.

"Just what the hell are you doing here?" she demanded. "Have you looked at yourself recently? And what are you doing leaving Carrie if her condition's worsened?"

"Vanna," he said tiredly, "Carrie's fine. She's still asleep. We had to get you out of there and that was the best we could come up with."

She made a noncommittal grunt as she reached out and began to unbuckle Kusac's belt. "Pass me the medikit please, Garras," she said. "Your shoulder's begun to bleed again, Kusac."

He put a hand over hers, stopping her. "Leave it till we get back."

"No way, Kusac," she said, ears flicking in anger as she pushed his hand aside and pulled his belt free.

"Physician, Liege, I can't leave till you're seated," said Kaid, turning round to look at them.

Garras placed the kit on the seat beside her, then returned to his own seat beside Kaid.

"I said it can wait, Vanna," said Kusac, irritated by her insistence, trying to push her hands away as she reached for the seal on the front of his jacket.

"You're the one delaying us, Kusac," she said, looking him straight in the eye. "Once your jacket's off, we can sit down. You can't afford the blood loss, you know that. What weakens you, weakens Carrie."

With a muttered oath he undid his jacket, trying to ease himself out of it.

"You're an ungrateful, bullying jegget, Vanna," he said, submitting ungraciously to her help. "We've come all the way out here to rescue you, and what do you do? Start ordering us around! I wonder how you put up with her,

Garras!" He sat down on the seat, sliding over to leave room for her.

Garras glanced over his shoulder at him but diplomatically said nothing.

As she laid his jacket on one of the vacant seats, Vanna looked toward where Kaid and Garras sat. "I am grateful, Kaid," she said quietly before picking up her kit and rejoining Kusac. "What happened to make your shoulder start bleeding again?" she asked as she cut the soiled dressing free.

"My fault, Physician," said Kaid as the craft rose above the tops of Stronghold's towers. "When I tried to stop him accompanying us, I grabbed him by his injured arm." He banked away from the early morning sun, heading back to Valsgarth.

"Well, you didn't succeed, did you?" she grumbled, deftly wiping the blood from Kusac's shoulder wound with a sterile pad before spraying on a coagulant. Taking out a fresh dressing, she bound it up again.

Kusac leaned back in the seat, closing his eyes. His shoulder ached and Vanna's attentions made it worse.

He'd hoped that once Carrie's Challenge was over they'd be left alone to have some peace, instead of which, they were now at the heart of political maneuvering between their guild and the Brotherhood. Something unresolved was niggling at him, then he remembered what it was.

"Why did they want you at Stronghold, Vanna?" he asked as he felt the slight sting of the hypo gun against his arm.

"Physician," said Dzaka from behind them. "I think it would be wiser to say as little as possible for the present."

"Don't start trying to order me around, Dzaka," said Vanna coldly as she finished packing up the small medikit. "I haven't forgiven you for what you did. Had you told me why Lijou and Ghezu needed to speak to me, I'd have agreed to go. Your methods were totally unprincipled and unnecessary."

"I've a bone to pick with you, too," growled Rulla, reaching out to pull Dzaka back from Vanna.

"What did they want?" asked Garras, turning round to look at her over the top of his seat.

"They've found a complete Valtegan skeleton in one of the ancient cities," she said.

"What?" Kusac sat up again, his tiredness pushed aside by the enormity of what she'd said.

Stunned, the others looked at each other.

"How the hell did it get there?" asked Garras. "You knew about this, Dzaka, and didn't tell us? The Valtegans killed your mate and cub down on Szurtha and you said nothing of this? Just what's going on in that head of yours?"

"Dzaka knew nothing about the remains until we got there," said Vanna. "That much was obvious when Lijou uncovered them to show me. They've found bones before but this was the first time they'd been able to remove a whole skeleton before Esken's Guild priests destroyed the site," she said.

Kusac was stunned. He didn't know which news rocked him more—that Master Esken had been destroying alien remains in the ruined cities, or that centuries ago there had been Valtegans on Shola.

"The bones aren't modern," she continued. "Lijou has had them dated tentatively back to the days of the Cataclysm."

"Did you know about this, Kaid?" asked Kusac. "Is this part of the reason why they sent you out to the *Khalossa*?"

"This is news to me, Liege," said Kaid. "I've never picked up so much as a whisper concerning this."

"Did any of you know about it?" demanded Garras, looking at Rulla and T'Chebbi who sat in the back on either side of Dzaka. They shook their heads. "Dzaka? What did you know about this?"

"Nothing. I didn't even know the Brotherhood had been visiting ruins," he said.

"What did they tell you?" Kusac asked Vanna.

"They wanted me to identify the bones. All they knew was they were alien, not Sholan. They had no idea they were Valtegan."

"I know the miners recover the refined metals from the ruins," said Kusac. "I also know that our Guild sends a priest to bless the sites and protect the miners from danger, but I had no idea they were finding remains there. I thought it was only rubble and metal. I think the Telepath Guild's activities at ruins need to be investigated thoroughly to see what else is being destroyed."

"Liege, there are several important matters for us to discuss," said Kaid, turning his head toward them so his voice carried. "We're all tired. May I suggest that we get some sleep when we get back to Valsgarth and hold a full debriefing later in the day?"

Kusac nodded. "We'll meet in the second-floor lounge at twelfth hour."

Kaid reached out and held Dzaka back as the others left the aircar. "You and I have some talking to do," he said grimly.

Dzaka nodded and waited for him to complete the vehicle's power-down, then preceded him out into the garage area.

Kaid pointed to the exit for the garden. "That way."

Silently they walked across the greensward until they were out of sight of the house, then Kaid rounded on the younger male, grasping him by the throat and pinning him to the nearest tree.

"You took one of the people I'm sworn to protect into the gravest danger. You put my Liege's life and that of his Leska at risk when he insisted on accompanying us." Kaid's voice was low with anger, his ears as stiff and vertical as the fur surrounding his neck and head. "You owe me an explanation."

Half choking though he was, Dzaka didn't dare move. He could tell by the coldness in Kaid's eyes that if he made one false move, it would be his last.

Kaid could feel the hunter-sight beginning to set in as his vision narrowed till all he could see clearly was Dzaka.

"Can I help?" he heard Garras ask quietly.

Kaid ignored him. "I'm waiting," he said, tightening his grip till his claws just pierced Dzaka's flesh.

"Why should I justify my actions when you aren't prepared to trust me?" wheezed Dzaka.

"Because if you don't, you won't live to regret it," said Kaid softly.

"Answer him!" said Garras, coming forward to stand beside his friend.

Kaid watched Dzaka's eyes flick to Garras then back to him. For the first time he saw stirrings of fear in them. Good. It was time Dzaka realized he couldn't presume upon their past relationship—his actions had taken him beyond that. He tightened his grip fractionally.

Dzaka's hands made an involuntary movement as if to reach up to pull Kaid's hand away, then he froze.

Kaid could feel the younger male's blood pounding under his hand, and the sharp smell of his fear.

"I . . ." Dzaka began to cough.

Kaid relaxed his grip slightly, letting him catch his breath.

". . . was ordered to get Carrie or Vanna, preferably Vanna, to Stronghold," Dzaka said. "Knew she'd be safe." He broke off, unable to prevent himself from coughing again.

Kaid felt Garras' hand touch the middle of his back in warning. It took all his self-control not to turn around and lash out at him, so close was he to the edge of the hunter/kill state.

"They only wanted to talk, persuade her to join the Brotherhood. Knew they couldn't afford to kill her. Wouldn't have taken her otherwise."

"He's telling the truth," said Garras.

"Keep out of this," snapped Kaid. "It's my business."

"Mine, too. He took my mate, Kaid," said Garras, his voice equally angry.

Kaid watched Dzaka's eyes begin to glaze as he passed beyond fear into sheer terror.

"First time you've been on the receiving end, isn't it, Dzaka?" Kaid said, his voice as quiet and cold as the earth in deep winter. "How d'you like it? You really think you can second-guess me? Play me at my own game? Ghezu wants you to think that. Oh, you're good, no two ways about it, but not that good."

Kaid's mouth opened in a grin that never touched his eyes. "Ghezu forgot to tell you one thing, Dzaka. He and I have played this game before and each time it's cost him dear in lost Brothers. You want to be another statistic in his feud with me? Because if you step on my tail again, *I will kill you!*"

Dzaka's eyes rolled back till only the whites showed. "Ask Vanna! I meant her no harm! Told her she'd be safe, that I wasn't kidnapping her!"

Kaid took a deep breath, forcing back the darkness at the edges of his vision, forcing his fur to lie flat. As he released Dzaka, his free hand came up in a powerful open-handed blow to the other's head, sending him spinning across the grass to land in an ignominious heap at the foot of a nearby tree.

He began to walk over to where Dzaka lay but Garras was there first, pulling the younger male to his feet and delivering an equal blow to the other side of his head.

"You go near Vanna again, Dzaka, and you'd better hope

Kaid gets to you before I do," snarled Garras, hauling him upright by the scruff of his neck before letting him go. "You understand me?"

Staggering, Dzaka held onto the tree trunk, nodding as he wiped the blood off his face onto his shirtsleeve. As Kaid came over, he looked up at him, fear written in every line of his body.

"You wanted to choose, Dzaka," Kaid growled, coming to a stop. "So choose now. If you're with us, it's all the way, no turning back. If you aren't, then get the hell out of my sight and off the estate."

Dzaka wiped his face again, trying to stop shaking as he did so. "You'd trust me to stay?" he asked.

"You're alive, aren't you? If you stay, then you earn my trust from here on in," said Kaid. "You could have come to me, told me what you planned to do, but you didn't. I told you, trust works both ways."

Dzaka forced his ears upright and took a shuddering breath. "I'll stay," he said, looking Kaid straight in the eyes with an effort.

Kaid nodded. "We'll see you at eleventh hour. You'll be given your assignment then." He turned abruptly away from him and began walking back to the house.

Garras caught up with him. "*Can* we trust him?"

"He'll be watched. One more slip and he's dead, and now he knows it."

"I thought you were going to kill him back there, that's why I followed you," said Garras, matching his pace to Kaid's.

"I came close. I needed his explanation first. Vanna wasn't harmed and she wasn't out after his blood for taking her to Stronghold. Had it been different . . ."

"Damn Ghezu!" swore Garras. "If it weren't for him, Dzaka wouldn't be involved with us! Why the hell has he got to keep playing his mind games with the two of you? What's he still got against you?"

"Don't worry, Ghezu's tally is adding up. There'll be a reckoning between us before this is over," said Kaid as they reentered the garage on their way to the house.

Kaid knew what Dzaka faced. He'd had over thirty years of training and indoctrination from the Brotherhood. Talk was easy, it cost nothing. But if Dzaka really wanted to leave and join them, he'd break free of that conditioning.

He'd been trained to question, to rely on his own judgment—especially because he was a special operative like himself and Garras. They'd done it: Dzaka could. And if Dzaka succeeded, then he'd never need to doubt him again.

* * *

A chill wind swept across the spaceport, bringing with it the aroma of cooking from the stalls in the spacers' shantytown. Jeran stirred, lifting his head clear of the straw till he could see. Around their pen, the night was coming alive. Lights and flickering torches illuminated the darkness, lighting up the traders' row so that visiting spacers could see the goods offered for sale.

Nearby, the door to a local tavern was flung open, sending a gust of ale-scented warm air straight into his face. A burst of sound, the raucous voices calling out in languages he couldn't understand, then it was cut off as the door swung closed again. Nearby he could hear the sound of a ship taking off from the spaceport, going home with its cargo, while they were left marooned on an alien world. With a low moan of distress, he lay his head back down on the foul straw.

The wooden bars of the pen began to vibrate as the keeper, yelling loudly, hammered at them with his club.

Around him, Jeran heard the others begin to stir.

"What is it?" mumbled Tesha, her voice thick with sleep.

"Can you tell what he wants, Tallis?" Jeran asked as he pushed himself upright, blinking furiously to clear his eyes of the straw dust that Tesha had raised.

"I'm not a high grade telepath, Jeran, I keep telling you!" Tallis' voice was a low snarl of anger. "We've only been here a few hours. It takes months even for the grade ones to understand an alien mind!"

"Stow it, Tallis," said Tesha, hauling herself out of the straw. "We know your limitations; you never stop reminding us of them."

"Miroshi's the expert," muttered Tallis. "Not me."

Jeran turned and began feeling through the straw, trying to locate the last member of their group.

"I'm here," she said, her voice hardly audible through the din the keeper was still making. Her hand closed round his as she began to sit up.

She looked frail, worse than she had aboard the ship. Jeran helped her, remaining at her side, shielding her from the keeper.

"This seems to be their world, Miroshi," he said, flicking an ear toward the keeper. "If you can read them, pick up their language, it would help us all." He hated himself for having to ask her but he had no option.

"Tallis, give me your hand," she sighed, leaning against Jeran. "I need your energy if I'm going to try to read them."

As Tallis shuffled over, Jeran turned to look out through the cage bars at their tormentor.

It was the keeper, but this time there was someone else with him. A younger person, cleaner than the other—he could smell the perfume from here—with his hair hanging tidily to his shoulders. He wore less fur on his face than the other, and what he had was trimmed to match his mouth and jawline. The clothing was better quality, richer and brighter in hue. Everything about this one spoke of a male of importance and position on this world.

He could feel Miroshi beginning to work now. Not a telepath himself, he had enough sensitivity to give him an inkling of the world Miroshi and her kind lived in. He felt her pull on his energy, too, then suddenly his mind was flooded with information and it was done. All three of them felt drained and weaker, but now they understood these strange, partly furred aliens.

"Hey, what about me?" muttered Tesha, keeping a wary eye on the two people outside their cage.

"Tallis, you can do that much," whispered Miroshi, closing her eyes.

The unintelligible shouts from the keeper began to slowly resolve themselves into words as Jeran struggled to understand what was being said.

"Not U'Churians?" the younger one was saying.

"No, Lord Bradogan. None of them are black, they're all different in color. U'Churians come only in black, with longer fur than these ones," the keeper was saying.

"They don't look worth the price I paid for them," said Bradogan disgustedly. "Half starved, beaten—and we don't even know for sure they're intelligent yet!"

"Oh, they're intelligent," laughed the keeper. "There's two of each in there. The males knew enough of what was going on to try and protect their women! The two smaller ones are the women," he said helpfully.

"Beasts will do that. They all look the same," said Bradogan, stepping closer to the bars. "Women should look like women, not flat-chested like them." He waved a derisory hand at the Sholans. "I suppose they're worth it to keep those damned Valtegans away. Thank God they don't come here often!"

"What do you want done with them, Lord Bradogan? They won't sell in the state they're in."

"Move them out of this flea-ridden cage to the prison. Feed them, get an animal doctor to see to them, and for God's sake, try and find out what they're good for! I want my money's worth out of those mangy carcasses!" he said, turning away.

"They'd make good pets," offered the keeper. "They haven't got much fight in them just now, but if they have, I can tame them, see that they're docile. You could sell them as pets to those Northern Lords if they're no good for anything else."

"I'll consider that when they look like a salable commodity," said Bradogan as he walked away.

"Pets!" growled Tesha. "They'd make pets out of us!"

"What's a pet?" asked Jeran.

"A harmless beast with little intelligence. They keep them to look pretty and do clever tricks to amuse them," said Miroshi tiredly.

"Talking to each other, are you?" said the keeper, leaning up against the bars. "Well, talk about this! You'd better find something that makes you worth your keep or Lord Bradogan will have your skins to decorate his floors! You play dumb with me and you'll make it worse for yourselves." He stopped and called his handlers over.

"We're moving them to the port tower," he said. "Get them collared and ready to go."

Miroshi began to whimper. "Don't let them touch me, Jeran," she said. "I can't bear their touch! So ugly and violent! Please don't let them touch me," she begged.

"I'll do what I can," he promised, knowing that there was little he could do.

The cage door opened and the first of the males came in. In one hand he held one of the chain collars that had been used on them when they'd been brought here from the landing pad. Vicious things that tightened round the throat if they didn't keep the leash slack. In the other, he held an electric prod.

The male edged forward cautiously, reaching out with the prod and gesturing to Tallis.

"You," he said. "I'll have you first."

Making a decision, Jeran carefully put Miroshi aside and rose to his feet.

"We'll come quietly," he said, stumbling over the alien words. It would take some time before their speech was fluent.

"Jeran!" exclaimed Tallis. "What are you doing?"

"Miroshi can't take any more of this treatment," he said. "They need to know not to touch her."

"What the hell ... Hey, Neban!" the surprised handler yelled, not taking his eyes off them. "These damned cats can speak our language!"

The keeper swung back to stare at them. "Bring him out first," he said, pointing to Jeran.

Holding his hands up at chest level, palms facing outward to show he meant no harm, Jeran moved carefully toward the male with the prod.

"D'you want him collared?"

"Too right," said Neban. "They're even more dangerous now we know they're not animals."

Jeran ducked his head down, folding his ears flat so the chain could be slipped over his head. As it settled round his neck over the sores caused by the Valtegan collars, he shuddered. It was cold and heavy. The male backed out of the cage before tightening his grip on the leash and pulling Jeran out.

The collar tightened, choking him, making him cough. As he stumbled forward, he put his hands up to the noose, trying to loosen it so he could breathe.

"Leave it," the handler snapped, about to touch him with the prod.

Neban slapped his arm away. "No need," he said. "Not unless he gets violent. So you're the leader, are you?" he said to Jeran. "I'm glad you decided to cooperate. You see, the more you cooperate, the better the price I get for you, and the better price you fetch, the better owner you have. Understand?"

Still holding onto the noose, Jeran nodded. "We've got

skills," he said. "We're a space-going people ourselves. You could ransom us. Our people will pay to get us back."

"That's not up to me," said Neban. "My job's to get you trained and fit to sell, that's all. You cooperate with me, and you'll get well treated. You don't, and . . . Well, I reckon I don't need to tell you since you've experienced Valtegan hospitality." He grinned, mouth splitting sideways as he showed his teeth.

Jeran stepped back in shock. Immediately the noose tightened again, choking him until he loosened it.

"Right, get the others out," Neban said, turning back to the cage. "Unless you want to tell them to walk out?"

Holding onto the collar's loop, Jeran turned to his friends. "If you don't come out yourselves, they'll use the prods," he said. "Tallis, help Miroshi."

Tesha was next out, stumbling as she stepped out onto the hard concrete pavement. A chain noose was immediately slipped over her head and she was dragged clear of the exit. Clinging to Tallis, Miroshi staggered out, holding onto the cage doorway for support.

"What's wrong with her?" demanded Neban, reaching out to pull her away from Tallis.

"Don't touch her!" exclaimed Tallis, trying to fend him off. Two prods hit him simultaneously and he collapsed to the ground mewling and writhing in agony.

"Please, leave her," said Jeran, forcing himself to remain still. "She's a telepath. When anyone touches her, she knows their thoughts. The Valtegans hurt her badly—she can't stand being touched again."

"Mind readers?" exclaimed Neban, letting his hand drop. "How many of you are mind readers?" he demanded.

"Only two," answered Jeran. "Tallis is the other." He pointed to where Tallis lay on the ground curled in a fetal position, moaning.

Neban grunted. "She ill?"

"No, just weakened by their mental brutality. All she needs is food and time for her mind to heal. Let me carry her," Jeran said. "She can tolerate my touch."

"What about him?" Neban pointed at Tallis.

"They weren't so hard on him. He's stronger than Miroshi."

"You," said Neban, pointing to Tesha, "You help him. Put the collar on him."

Tesha took the collar from the handler, and bending down, slipped it round Tallis' neck, then helped him to his feet.

The prod shock was beginning to wear off now, and though still in pain, Tallis was able to stand.

Neban turned back to Jeran. "You can see to the other woman," he said, handing him the last collar.

Jeran looked at his handler, making sure the leash was slack before he stepped over to Miroshi.

"They'll let me carry you," he said quietly as he slipped the loop over her head. "If they see how weak you are, it might ensure us better treatment."

She nodded, shivering as he had when the chain fell round her throat. Putting her hand up to touch it, she looked up at him. "This is it, isn't it, Jeran? We've no chance of being rescued, have we? We're going to die on this Godsforsaken world, aren't we?" Tears began to fill her eyes.

Jeran bent to pick her up. She hardly weighed anything, he realized with a shock. "Don't give up hope, Miroshi," he whispered. "They'll not give up on us, believe me."

"Have you looked at the sky?" she whispered, her mouth close to his ear. "I don't recognize the stars, Jeran! If we don't know where we are, how can *they?*"

He had no answer to give her as he turned round to face Neban.

CHAPTER 2

Konis Aldatan, blithely unaware of the incidents spanning the early hours of that morning, hesitated before switching off his comm. For no reason he could fathom, he keyed in Kaid's number.

A few moment's delay, then his son's aide answered. "Clan Lord, what can I do for you?"

Konis hesitated, wondering if he was about to make a fool of himself. "Ah, Kaid," he began, his ears betraying him by the faintest flicks of embarrassment. "Governor Nesul has appointed me to be in charge of anomalous Leska pairs, like my son and Carrie. My work will be based at the Telepath Guildhouse in Valsgarth. I'm about to go there now to notify Guild Master Esken in person of the Governor's appointment, and . . ." He faltered, unsure how to phrase his request.

"T'Chebbi will be ready to accompany you within five minutes, Clan Lord," said Kaid. "Shall I have her meet you in your office, or would you prefer her to bring an aircar to the main entrance?"

Konis could feel the tension flow out of him as Kaid spoke. "Tell me I'm being foolish, Kaid," he said abruptly, watching the other for signs of his reaction.

"I wish I could, Clan Lord," said Kaid. "Unfortunately, I think you're wise to have an escort of T'Chebbi's caliber. Your appointment will not be . . . popular in certain circles. While I don't think for an instant anyone would seriously attempt to harm you, it might be as well if I found you a permanent aide to help you in much the same way as I help your son and bond-daughter."

He agrees with me! thought Konis as he stared at the impassive face before him. *What is happening to us when I'm afraid to visit my own Guild without an armed escort?* He felt the fur on his neck and shoulders start to rise. With an effort he pushed his anger aside. It served no useful purpose at this time and would only distract him from the business at hand.

He nodded. "See to it, if you please, Kaid." He paused. "It seems we could do with someone in charge of security for the whole household," he said bitterly.

"I would consider that a wise decision, Clan Lord," said Kaid, one ear flicking in agreement. "My own duties prevent me from taking on such a responsibility, but I can certainly find someone with the expertise you require."

"The world's gone mad," muttered Konis, half to himself.

"No, Clan Lord," said Kaid. "The world is finally beginning to come to its senses."

Konis looked sharply at him but as always, Kaid's features and mind were impassive. "Have T'Chebbi meet me at the front," he said. "Contact your person and have him take charge of security. Keep me informed of what's needed."

He cut the connection, staring at the screen for several moments before he shook his head and got to his feet.

T'Chebbi brought the aircar down in the parking area by the medical center.

"We'll leave the vehicle here until I've checked up on those kitlings," Konis told her.

T'Chebbi nodded, securing the instrument panel before getting up. "As you wish, Clan Lord," she said.

Konis glanced back at her as he stepped out of the aircar. "T'Chebbi, as my aide, I expect you to talk to me, to offer advice, and to deal with Esken's people if they start troubling me, not to just stand there like some threatening statue! You do know the protocol, don't you? I presume Kaid wouldn't have suggested you otherwise."

T'Chebbi's nose wrinkled, then her mouth opened slightly. "You want me to *be* your aide for today?" she asked.

Konis frowned. "Isn't that what I've just said?"

She nodded. "As the Clan Lord wishes," she said, her tone this time holding an undercurrent of amusement.

As she stepped out of the aircar, Konis looked at her again, wondering briefly if Kaid had made an error in judgment. She looked like exactly what she was—a bodyguard.

To start with, she only came up to his shoulder. Icy gray eyes, now with a glint of humor in them, regarded him calmly. Her pelt, longer than usual for most Sholans, was a brindled color. It was contrasted by her long, dark hair which she wore in a single, thick plait. Like Kaid, she was of Highland stock.

At the entrance to the medical unit, T'Chebbi held the auto-doors open for Konis to enter while she glanced round the waiting area. At the reception counter, again she preceded him.

"Clan Lord Aldatan wishes to see the cubs brought in from the Ghuulgul desert three weeks ago," she said. "Where are they?"

The nurse on duty opened his mouth in shock, staring at T'Chebbi dressed in her active Brotherhood grays. A long knife mounted on a shoulder baldric was visible just above her shoulder, and at her waist hung a modern energy pistol.

"The Clan Lord waits," she said, her voice dropping to a low rumble.

"You can't go in dressed like that," he said, eyes flicking round the room, looking vainly for a superior to deal with this problem. "We don't allow weapons in here. This unit is part of the Telepath Guild, you know."

T'Chebbi leaned forward to pick up the comp pad that lay in front of him.

"Hey, you can't do that! That information is confidential!"

A couple of keystrokes and she had the information she needed. "Not from the Clan Lord," said T'Chebbi, sliding it back across the counter to him. She turned to Konis. "I know where, Liege," she said, indicating a door to their right.

Konis followed her down the main corridor until they came to a junction to the left. As they turned down there, T'Chebbi fell behind him moments before he heard the sound of running feet.

"Third door on the right, Liege," said T'Chebbi. "I'll stay outside."

Somewhat nonplussed, Konis nodded, and increasing his walking pace, was in the room and closing the door behind him before he heard the raised voices.

At the center of the room, sitting on a large floor cushion, were the kitlings. Two small faces looked up curiously at him as he lowered his mental shield. He needed to pick up all the information he could from them before the hospital staff interrupted him.

"Hello," said the young female.

Konis moved farther into the room, squatting down on his haunches so his face was level with theirs. "Hello," he

said. "You're . . . Jinoe?" He turned to look at the young
male. "And you're Rrai, aren't you?"

Hazel eyes, large in the narrow face, looked warily at him.
Rrai nodded, trying hard to prevent his ears from folding
sideways with apprehension as he pushed himself upright.

"You're the Clan Lord, aren't you? They're saying you
shouldn't be in here," he said with a faint grin as he inclined
his head toward the door.

"You want to know if we're better, don't you?" Jinoe
asked. "Mostly it just itches now, it doesn't hurt."

He looked back at the young female. Like her Leska, she
was wire-thin, her dark eyes large and full of . . . a soul-deep
hurt . . . something no young one should know.

He'd hardly framed his next question in his mind before
they cautiously and rather stiffly got to their feet and turned
round for him to examine their backs. His reaction to the
partly healed cuts caused by their flogging was so well concealed that Jinoe, concerned at the time he was taking,
turned round.

"It's all right, isn't it? They said we were healing well,"
she said, an anxious expression on her face, ears twitching
apprehensively.

"You can sit down again, cubs," said Konis gently,
reaching out with his fingertips to touch Jinoe's cheek in
reassurance. "They're telling you the truth. Your backs are
healing beautifully."

While they sat down, Konis deftly probed round the edges
of their minds, trying to gauge the depth and nature of their
Link. What he found puzzled him. This was no ordinary
Leska Link.

Jinoe reached out to touch Konis. "Your son is the one
with the Keissian Leska, isn't he?" she asked.

"They think we can't hear them, but we can," said Rrai as
he cautiously lowered himself to the floor again. "They think
our Link is like your son's."

"What's she like, the human?" asked Jinoe. "Is she like us?"

"Ah . . ." Konis was momentarily stuck for words. "Quite
like us," he said.

"But no tail," said Rrai, flicking his across both his and
Jinoe's laps.

"No tail," agreed Konis, trying to stop his mouth from
opening in a smile.

"Can we get to meet her?" Jinoe asked, regarding Konis soulfully.

"Quite probably," he said. "Who's teaching you to understand your Link?"

Rrai shook his head. "No one. They come and test us, then get us to mind talk to them . . ."

". . . And send pictures to them, but no teaching," added Jinoe. "Are we doing it right?"

"I'm sure you are," he said, mentally drawing on them, trying to get more information. "What else do you do? Have you got a comm?" he asked, looking round the sparsely furnished room. The floor was scattered with large, soft cushions. At least the unit was making some concessions to their desert lifestyle.

"A comm? Why would we have a comm?" asked Jinoe, her nose wrinkling in surprise. "Only Clan Leader Ghomig has one."

"So you can learn or be entertained," said Konis. "With a comm you can access the library and have any book you want—stories or books of knowledge. Or listen to the storytellers on the entertainment channels."

"Can you get us one?" asked Jinoe.

Konis touched her face again fleetingly before he got to his feet. "I'll see one is brought to you as soon as possible. I have to go now, but I'll be back to see you before I leave," he said. "I'll start teaching you myself."

Rrai grinned, tail tip flicking with pleasure. "That will be good," he said. "Oh, they've sent for Khafsa. He'll be mad at you for coming in. We aren't allowed visitors, not even my mother," he said sadly.

"I can deal with Khafsa," said Konis, suppressing his anger at the insensitivity of the staff looking after the two cubs. "I'll also make sure your mother gets to visit you every day. I have to go now, but I'll call in before I leave to make sure they've brought you a comm unit," he said, turning to go.

"Thank you," said Rrai.

In the corridor, T'Chebbi was glowering at the two orderlies in front of her.

Konis lowered his ears in anger and advanced on them, eyes narrowed and teeth visible. "I'm going to see Master Esken. In two hours I will return and by then, these cubs had better have a decent-sized comm unit installed and working.

You will also contact Rrai's mother and tell her she can visit the cubs daily from now on. Do you understand me?"

"But Clan Lord, Physician Khafsa is in charge of them and . . ."

"I want no excuses!" Konis snarled. "How dare you treat those two young people as if they were laboratory animals! I will hold you personally responsible if my orders have not been carried out!"

"But Physician Khafsa . . ." began the other.

"Can await my return!" Pushing them aside, he strode down the corridor. T'Chebbi at his heels.

He was seething with anger. "T'Chebbi, use your wrist comm to contact my home and request that Physician Kyjishi access the Telepath Guild's medical records of those two cubs now. She's to use the comm in my office."

Ahead of them, Physician Khafsa, accompanied by an orderly, was waiting for them. As Konis and T'Chebbi swept past them, the physician reached out to touch him.

"Clan Lord . . ." he began.

As Konis flinched in anticipation of the contact, he caught T'Chebbi's movement from the corner of his eye. Khafsa was sent spinning backward till he hit the wall.

"Don't presume to touch the Clan Lord," hissed his aide over her shoulder. "You know the law!" The brief interchange hadn't even caused T'Chebbi to break her stride.

Quick on the heels of Konis' uncharacteristic flash of pleasure at the doctor's discomfiture came the knowledge that a few months ago, this situation could never have occurred. Or could it? For people like Khafsa to behave in this fashion, there had to have been a gradual assumption of powers and authorizations outside the norm. He had the horrible feeling that fur was being rubbed from a raw spot, revealing the infected sore beneath. He pushed the uncomfortable thought to the back of his mind. If that was so, then time would tell.

As he approached Guild Master Esken's office, he saw Senior Tutor Sorli standing waiting outside. Well, it was no more than he expected. His anger alone had been enough to announce his presence to the ever-vigilant Esken. Konis stopped beside him.

"Clan Lord Aldatan," said Sorli, crossing his forearms in front of his chest and bowing low. "We are honored by your

visit. Master Esken asked me to wait for you and inquire
whether you would drink c'shar with him."

"Not c'shar, coffee," he said, watching Sorli's startled
expression. Time for him to state where his own loyalties
lay—with his family. "I'm sure you have some. Please
ensure it's of the correct strength."

Sorli stilled his ears as he reached for the door handle.
"Your aide can accompany me to the staff lounge while you
are with the Guild Master, Clan Lord."

"My aide will remain with me," said Konis in a tone that
brooked no argument.

Again the startled flick of Sorli's ears. "As you wish, Clan
Lord," he murmured, opening the door for them.

The Guild Master looked up from his desk as they entered.
"Konis. How nice to see you," he said, getting to his feet and
coming out from behind his desk. He gestured to the comfortable seats by the fireside. "Please, sit. Apart from seeing
our new Leska cubs, what brings you to the Guild?"

As T'Chebbi took up a guard position by the door, Konis
reached inside his overrobe taking an official document out
of his inner pocket. "This is from Governor Nesul," he said,
sitting down on the single chair opposite Esken's usual one.
"It's my official appointment as Consolidator of the Specialized Leska Unit."

Esken turned the letter over in his hands, making no
attempt to open it. "So, the Governor has given our work
here official status. And he wishes you to be the titular head.
That's no bad thing. It'll give public credence to what we're
doing."

"On the contrary. The Governor was most insistent that I
be the *actual* head of the project, in charge of the teaching of
our new Leskas with enhanced abilities."

Esken raised a questioning eye ridge. "Perhaps I had better
read his letter," he said. Inserting a claw tip beneath the seal,
he neatly sliced through it. Opening it, he took his time
reading the contents.

Konis waited, hiding his impatience. Nesul had said he'd
tell Esken personally. Had he taken the easier option and left
the Clan Lord to do it?

There was a knock on the door and Sorli entered, carrying
a tray with two mugs on it. He set it down on the table
between them and left.

Esken's nose twitched as he smelled the coffee and Konis

smiled to himself, knowing the Guild Master had got his point.

Meticulously, Esken refolded the letter, placing it carefully on the table before picking up his drink of c'shar. "The Governor must have made an error," he said. "This is clearly a Telepath Guild matter and should be dealt with internally."

Konis picked up his mug and took a small sip of the beverage. He controlled a slight shudder at the bitterness of the drink. He wasn't fond of it, but it never tasted this bad when Rhyasha made it.

"Unfortunately not," he said. "It involves Alien Relations, not to mention the High Command, of which I'm also a member. The Governor felt it vital that someone aware of the politics involved in these cross-species Links head the project. Someone versed in diplomacy and also a telepath should be able to deal more easily with the majority of the problems that seem to be occurring between our two species."

"I've no objection to your being involved in the project in your official capacities," said Esken, returning his mug to the table. "We, on the other hand, have a tradition of educating *all* the telepaths, including the Leska pairs. In fact, as you well know, we are the primary center on Shola for training Leskas. We have decades of experience in producing well-balanced, competent Leska pairs. What makes you think you can do any better? This isn't your field, after all."

"I'm aware of that, Esken," said Konis dryly. "On the other hand, my son and bond-daughter, not to mention Physician Kyjishi, have all sampled your methods. The Governor and I both agree that a change of direction is needed, and that is best achieved by having a new outlook from the top down."

Esken stirred his c'shar. "Being the first, naturally, they have had a few problems along the road to helping us understand the nature of this new Link. Now that we know what we're dealing with, I'm sure things will advance more smoothly."

"I intend to make sure they do," said Konis, his tone silky as he lifted his mug again. "I trust you'll follow the Governor's instructions and have an office made available for me. One of the first-floor interview rooms would do nicely. I also intend to have close ties with your medical section through Physician Kyjishi."

Konis watched Esken, picking up the betraying signs of tension in the muscles surrounding his eyes and nose.

The Governor would have enjoyed this meeting, he thought. *It would have made up for all the times Esken has railroaded him during Council meetings.*

"An office, will, of course, be made ready for you," said Esken. "However, you'll not take it amiss, I trust, if I check with the Governor first?"

He hopes to browbeat Nesul into retracting the appointment! I think my next call had better be to the palace.

"By all means, if you don't trust the written instructions of our government," said Konis. "In the meantime, I'll want a copy of all your files to date on the new Leskas, including the proposed education program for the Humans that will bring them in line with their new partners. I'll also want files on the three anomalous Sholan Leska pairings, including medical data. I'm most concerned about the handling of Jinoe's and Rrai's case. Their education hasn't even started yet, and they've been deprived of any contact with the outside world. Why was Rrai's mother prevented from visiting them?"

"We wanted to separate them from the desert tribal influence," said Esken. "I want to be sure that none of the religious teachings and attitudes of that mad priest of theirs remains with them. To work properly as Leskas they need to see each other as equals, not with one subservient to the other." His voice was cold.

Konis felt the Guild Master quickly suppress a spark of concern. He could feel the change in Esken's attitude toward him. For the first time the Guild Master was having to defend his actions, and he didn't like it. Esken couldn't hide behind the sanctity of "Guild Business" with Konis, a fellow guild member who actually outranked him. Perhaps Nesul was cleverer than they'd all realized. In giving him this appointment, he'd placed the only person who had sufficient authority to wrong-foot Esken right in the heart of his empire.

"That particular case is outside your province, Konis," he said. "There's nothing anomalous about their Link—except the fact that they're so young."

"You think not? Well, perhaps you're right," said Konis,

stroking his chin thoughtfully. "Still, it'll do no harm to check the files and run a few extra tests."

Esken took another drink, obviously savoring his c'shar before he spoke again. "That won't be possible, I'm afraid. They're being returned to Laasoi Guildhouse this afternoon." There was a smugness about him as he relaxed back in his chair, smiling slightly. "On the other matters, once I have Governor Nesul's confirmation of your appointment, you will have my full cooperation."

Konis' ears swiveled forward in anger. "I resent the implication that the document I gave you is a forgery," he growled.

Esken's shocked reaction was genuine. He hadn't expected Konis to speak so frankly.

"May I interrupt, Clan Lord?" said T'Chebbi from her position by the door. "Settle it now. Contact the Governor on this comm."

"Do it," snapped Konis.

"I don't think that's necessary," Esken began, but Konis cut him short.

"Do it, T'Chebbi," he repeated. "Sit down, Esken. You've made this a matter of honor—my honor. I want it resolved immediately."

Master Esken sat down again: he had no option but to do so. His bluff had been called and they both knew who had lost.

"I'm through, Clan Lord," said T'Chebbi a few minutes later.

"Continue with the call. Explain to him that Master Esken isn't satisfied with the official letter of appointment, he wishes to confirm it personally."

He sat and watched Esken's jawline tighten in anger, knowing he'd made himself a powerful enemy. It mattered not at all now, he realized, because Esken had made an enemy of him and he was every bit as dangerous and powerful—if not more so. While he waited, he reached out mentally for his son, rendering him speechless with the nature of his request. Then T'Chebbi was turning the comm around so the Governor could see them both.

"You disturbed me for a matter as trivial as this, Esken?" said Governor Nesul, allowing his ears to twitch in obvious displeasure. "You have my personal verification of Clan Lord Aldatan's appointment. I hope this isn't the start of a trend, Esken. I won't have my meetings interrupted by you every time you disagree with one of my decisions! You have my orders. See you give the Clan Lord all the help he needs. This new unit is effective as of now. You know my opinions concerning your handling of the matter of the mixed Leskas. You failed. It's time for someone else to try. Konis, I'll expect an initial report from you within the next twenty-six hours. Good day."

As T'Chebbi returned the comm to its usual orientation, Konis turned back to the Guild Master.

"I have some business to attend to, Esken," he said, getting to his feet. "I know it'll take your people an hour or two to set up an office for me, so I'll be back just after second meal. Thank you for your hospitality," he added dryly.

Esken inclined his head politely but Konis could see by the tightness of his jaw muscles just how displeased he was. But why? Surely Esken was letting this get out of proportion. He remained silent and thoughtful until they were in the aircar once more.

"Where to, Clan Lord?" T'Chebbi asked as she started the vehicle.

"To Shanagi," said Konis, coming out of his reverie. "I think it's time I visited some old friends."

* * *

It was late morning by the time Carrie gradually realized she was awake. She reached for Kusac, panicking when her hand couldn't find him even though her mind could.

"I'm here," he said, instantly moving closer till his body touched hers. He felt her mind, linked so closely to his, absorb the happenings of the last few hours.

She turned her head slowly, resting her cheek against his chest. Weariness still held her in a warm, comfortable blanket, drawing the strength from her, robbing her of any curiosity.

Kusac looked down at his human life-mate, seeing the paleness of her skin and the dark shadows that surrounded her eyes. She was so small, so fragile compared to his people. Careful of her injured arm, he gathered her close. She'd nearly died only a few days ago—he was still afraid of losing her. Gently he nuzzled her neck, rubbing his cheek against her jawline.

"I wondered how long you were going to sleep," he said. "It'll soon be time for second meal. You must be hungry."

"I couldn't eat anything," she said.

"You've got to try, cub," he said. "You lost so much blood, you need to build yourself up so you can replace it."

She made a small noise of denial. *I want to rest,* she sent.

There was a peremptory knock at the door, then it opened. Kaid stood there. "Your pardon, Liege, but Vanna sent me for you. The kitlings have arrived and she needs your help." He hesitated. "She also gave me strict instructions to bring the Liegena down for first meal."

Kusac eased himself away from Carrie and sat up, looking at Kaid in surprise. The other gave a brief nod and flick of his ear to indicate a conspiracy.

Carrie opened her eyes and looked up at Kusac as he glanced back at her uncertainly. "Don't go," she said. "I need you here. I don't want to go downstairs."

"I have to go," he said, his hand caressing her face briefly as he began to rise. "The kitlings will need me."

Her eyes followed him as he walked over to the wardrobe to find a clean tunic. She watched the sunlight streaming in from the balcony play on his dark fur as he reached into the cupboard and chose one from the pile on the shelf.

His pelt seemed to ripple as he hauled the garment over his head. Flattening his ears, he ran his hands through the longer hairlike fur that grew on his head and down the sides of his neck in an attempt to impose some kind of order on it.

He turned back to the wardrobe, and hunted briefly through her clothes, finally pulling out one of her long robes, then turned and handed it to Kaid who now stood inside the room.

You must be getting better, he teased her. *If ever looks could speak!*

Looks are all I'm capable of, she sent. *Even thinking of anything else is tiring.*

He laughed for the first time in many days. "You'll have your work cut out for you," he said to Kaid. Returning to her side, he leaned over her, his hands smoothing her hair from her face, his nose cool against her as his tongue flicked her cheek gently.

Reaching up, she caught hold of his arm. "Kusac, I don't want to go downstairs!" She could feel the panic beginning to rise. "It's too soon after . . ." Her voice broke and she stopped, distressed by her inability to stop the tears that were beginning to flow.

"The funeral was two days ago, cub," he said quietly, squatting down so his face was level with hers. "You've got to begin to live again. Coming downstairs will be good for you." He reached out and wiped away the tears that were silently spilling down her face. "You can't hide up here. Our family wants you to be with them so they can help ease your grief." Slipping his hands behind her head, he kissed her, a Sholan kiss, his teeth gently nipping at her lips first.

She clung to him, feeling the first faint stirrings of their Link's compulsion as she returned the kiss.

He let her go, trying to steady his breathing. *The magic's never far from us, cub.* His hand cupped her cheek as he took her fingers to his mouth, running his tongue and teeth gently across their tips.

"I must go. Mother says she has some light food ready for you. She's missed having you around. She says with Taizia back at the Telepath Guild, there're too many males in the house!"

He stood up, letting her go with obvious reluctance. "I'll see you downstairs," he said, then turned and left the room before he changed his mind. He sent to Vanna, appalled at how fragile Carrie still looked and felt. She'd seemed better the day before!

She's not as bad as you fear, replied Vanna. *You're still comparing her to our females. Having no fur, her skin shows the marks of her suffering more obviously than we would.*

Listen to Vanna, his mother's firm tone told him. *She's your physician, either you trust her or you don't.*

I trust Vanna, replied Kusac, heading along the upper landing to the main staircase. *She knows that, it's just that . . .*

I'll contact Jack Reynolds, came Vanna's wry mental tone. *I know exactly how well you trust me.*

I do! he objected, making his way downstairs. *It's just that . . .*

She's dearer to you than life, I know.

"She is my life," he said simply, joining them in the entrance hall.

"Here's the aircar now," said Rhyasha. "I'll leave you two to welcome them. My first responsibility is to my bond-daughter." Reaching out, she briefly touched her son's face.

"Carrie will be fine," she said. "With so many of us caring for her, how could it be otherwise?"

Carrie turned her head, looking toward where Kaid stood a little distance from the end of her bed.

"I'd have thought they'd send Chena," she said.

"Chena's having a much deserved sleep," said Kaid, placing the robe on the bed before coming round to her side. "There's no Sholan reason for them to send a female to help you." He raised an eye ridge at her. "Is there a Human reason? All I intend to do is help you put the robe on over what you're wearing now."

"I don't want to go, Kaid," she said. "I can't face anyone."

He sat beside her. "Everyone downstairs has been up to see you since yesterday," he said. "Where's the difference in you going down to see them? You're returning their concern for you, thanking them for caring. They aren't going to add to your grief by talking about your lost cub."

"You have," she said, her voice unsteady again as her hands clutched at the blankets.

"Only because you're afraid to face her death yourself," he said, reaching out to take one of her hands in his, holding it still despite her attempts to twist it away from him. "Feeling grief for her is normal. By facing it, you'll take the edge off it till it no longer hurts so much. Be thankful you have feelings. Without them, the world would be a colder place. Now come on, sit up so we can get you dressed to go downstairs." He gave her hand a slight squeeze before releasing it and getting up.

"You never say comfortable things, do you, Kaid? You live in a world of harsh realities, and you expect me to do the same," she said, looking at him as she tried to push herself one-handedly up into a sitting position. Even through the strong analgesics, the effort hurt her.

"If you can do that, then you're unlikely to be taken unawares. The loss of your cub means more to you than it does to anyone else, even Kusac, but only just," he said, turning to pick up her robe. "The cub was part of you, a part you weren't sure you wanted at first. Because of that you feel guilty now you've lost her. You're afraid her loss is your fault. It isn't," he added, turning back to her as she pushed the covers aside awkwardly, favoring her injured arm in its sling. "Kusac's afraid it's his fault because he had a vision of the fight going wrong and his fear made him call out your name as Rala cried the Death Challenge on you."

"It wasn't his fault."

"I know, but you can't both keep taking the whole blame on yourselves and denying that the other was involved. Neither of you is to blame. I knew from the first your cub wouldn't survive; it was ordained."

"You *knew?* How?" she demanded.

"The Brotherhood has always been close to Vartra," he said ambiguously, helping her put her good arm through the sleeve of her robe. "Even an expelled member like me."

"Visions? You have visions?" she asked incredulously as he helped her take her injured arm out of the sling, then guided it carefully through the other arm of her robe.

"Now and then," he said, placing her arm back in the sling and adjusting it round her neck.

"The God told you about me?"

"Not in so many words," he admitted, swinging her legs around till they hung over the edge of the bed. "It only began to make sense when I heard that one of our telepaths had a Leska Link with a Human."

"What else do you know?" she demanded, watching him for any telltale movements that would give away his thoughts.

"Nothing," he said, reaching down to pull the two halves of her robe together so he could close the seal.

"You wouldn't tell me even if you knew," she said in disgust, looking up at him.

He blinked, then looked away from her for a moment. "No, I wouldn't," he said, bending down to scoop her up into his arms.

Aware that he was suddenly ill at ease with her, she reached up with her good arm to pull at his ear. "Look at me, Kaid," she said. "I won't bite you."

He looked down at her again. "I never thought you would," he said quietly.

"You're a strange person," she said, letting her hand slide down to touch his cheek. "So many dark stillnesses surround your mind, yet I *know* you've sent to me. Are you . . ."

"You can pick up anyone's strong thoughts, Liegena," he said, interrupting her as he began to walk toward the open door. "Yes, I've *thought* in your direction when you've needed me. Don't read more into it than there is."

Carrie tried to relax against him as he carried her downstairs, letting the rhythm of his movements and his breathing lull her. There was more to him than he wanted her to know, of that she was sure. When she'd heard Kaid mind speak to her, Kusac had been unaware of him. That in itself was unique. Then there were his visions regarding her, before he'd even been aware she existed.

A wave of utter exhaustion swept over her. She closed her eyes, unable to keep them open any longer. Later. She'd think about it later. It was too much of an effort right now.

He felt all the tenseness suddenly leaving her body as she rested her head against him. He almost sighed with relief but stopped himself just in time. She'd caught him unawares on this occasion, probing a little too deeply for his comfort. He'd have to watch her: what she knew, Kusac knew at exactly the same moment, and between them, they were too damned sharp.

His mouth twisted at the irony of his situation. Vartra gave him visions of a future that must be, then placed him at the heart of the matter, where he would be at his most vulnerable. Oh, yes, here he could help shape matters, but he could also be discovered—by her. Rhyasha's kitchen door was ahead of him and it was with relief he tapped on it.

Choa, Ryasha's cook, opened the door to him. "You've managed to bring her down!" she said, mouth opening wide with pleasure. "Come in, in, come in! We've a chair all made ready for her." She stood back, giving him room to enter, then followed after him, hovering in case she was needed.

"Over there." She pointed to the soft chair that had been placed at the far end of the table. "Put her down gentle, now. Is she sleeping? Poor little thing, with all she's been through. We'll get her better, never fear." She bustled past Kaid as he gently lowered Carrie into the chair.

Choa picked up the lightweight rug from the chair back and placed it over Carrie, tucking it in around her legs, then looked up at him. "You can leave her with us now. She'll be safe. With your folk tramping all over the house and round the estate, a jegget couldn't get in!"

"I'll stay nonetheless," said Kaid, moving backward out of her way.

Choa sighed loudly. "Then you'd best get down to the other end of the table out of my way. You can help yourself to c'shar, I'm not running around after you." She turned back to Carrie, dismissing him.

Rhyasha came in from the main preparation and cooking room next door. She looked toward Kaid, mouth opening in a friendly smile, ears flicking forward in pleasure.

"I knew you'd be able to bring her downstairs," she said. "It's a brave person that would even think of arguing with you!"

"You're both tyrants," said Carrie, opening her eyes and looking tiredly from one to the other. "You abuse me terribly."

"Only for your own good, cub," said Rhyasha, gently patting Carrie's hand as she sat down beside her. "Choa, please fetch Carrie's meal."

Carrie stirred. "I'm really not hungry," she protested. "I'm just tired. I'd rather sleep."

"I'm sure you would, cub, but we can't let you," said Rhyasha. "Your body, as well as your mind, has been badly traumatized. You have to eat, cub, or you won't have the energy to heal yourself. That's why you feel so tired. You'll make the effort for me, won't you? After all, you don't want me to have to ask Kaid to feed you."

Kaid's strangled growl of protest made Carrie look back over at him. His ears were laid back and his eye ridges met in a frown.

She chuckled despite herself. "It might just be worth it," she said.

"Good," said Rhyasha. "You've got your sense of humor back at least. Now, from today on, you're going to come downstairs and be with us. You can have a sleep after you've eaten, either in the lounge or in the garden, but there'll be no more staying up in your rooms brooding."

Carrie could see and feel Rhyasha's determination. Like everything else, it exhausted her. She bowed to the inevitable. "Yes, Rhyasha," she said as Choa returned with her food.

*   *   *

Kusac joined Vanna by the vehicle park entrance just as Meral turned off the aircar's engine.

"Any idea what all this is about?" he asked her.

"None. I thought you'd know."

"No. All Father said was he'd tell me when he returned. I

think the general idea's to keep the kitlings in the main house until Kaid's security expert has his surveillance equipment set up, then they'll be moved in with one of the estate families."

"Whatever it is, it spells major trouble if your father thinks we need all this extra security. Has it anything to do with last night?"

Kusac shook his head as he watched Garras help the two kitlings out of the aircar. "I didn't have time to tell him."

The two young Sholans were dressed in oversized purple tunics that made them seem even younger than they were. They moved stiffly, obviously still in some discomfort from their injuries. Garras stopped to pick up the smaller one, the female, and as they slowly crossed over to where Kusac and Vanna waited, the boy reached out to hold onto Garras' free hand.

Kusac stepped forward to meet them. "Hello, Rrai, Jinoe," he said. "I'm Kusac Aldatan and this is Physician Vanna Kyjishi. I hear you're coming to stay with us."

The young male nodded. "Garras said we were. He also said that my mother would be coming, too." He looked around, ears and tail flicking anxiously. "Is she here yet?"

"Not yet," said Kusac. "She shouldn't be long now. Shall we go up to your rooms and get you settled in while we're waiting for her?"

Jinoe nodded.

"Please," said Rrai. "Why are we coming to stay here?"

Seeing Kusac hesitate, Vanna stepped forward to take Rrai by the hand and lead him into the house. "You don't want to stay at the hospital any longer, do you? Since you can't go back to your Tribe, we thought you'd like to come and live here. The grounds are huge and there's lots of space for you to play in—and other younglings to play with."

"Will we have to be in separate rooms?" Jinoe asked.

"No, you'll be in the same room," said Kusac, walking beside Garras so he could continue talking to her. "You'll have a suite of rooms. That's a bedroom for you two, one for your mother, and a large room for playing in. You know all about your Link days, don't you?"

"Yes," said Rrai, eyeing him cautiously. "That's when they come and do lots of tests."

"Well, there'll be no more tests on your Link days," said

Vanna, her tone outraged. "You'll be left in peace from now on."

Picking up Jinoe's concern, Kusac added, "You can call us if you need us, or if you just want company, but you won't be disturbed on your Link days unless that's what you want."

Are they still virgins? he sent to Vanna. *Have they been allowed to pair yet?*

Vanna threw him a wry look. *Not yet. They're on medication to suppress their libidos until they're a little older. It appears to be working, probably because of their age.*

They'd walked deeper into the house and were now going up a smaller staircase that led to the rear courtyard area.

"You're the telepath who has the Human Leska, aren't you?" Rrai asked, looking up at Kusac. "Can we meet her?"

"Of course, but not yet," he said. "She got hurt in a Challenge and is too ill to see anyone at the moment."

"Tell her I hope she gets better soon."

"I will," said Kusac, stopping beside Vanna.

"Can you give Jinoe to Kusac, please, Garras?" she said, turning to her mate. "I think it best if we take them from here. I'll see you downstairs shortly."

Garras handed Jinoe to Kusac who took charge of her rather gingerly. "I'll see you later," he said, his hand touching his mate's cheek gently before he left.

Vanna opened the door and led the way in, Kusac following her. As soon as he was inside, he realized where he was.

"It's the old nursery," he said, recognizing it with a shock. He froze, his mind going numb as he remembered why this wing had been reopened.

Kusac! Vanna sent sharply. *Don't let the kitlings pick up your distress! It's not just Carrie that has to come to terms with the loss of your cub, you need to as well.*

He took a deep breath to steady himself, then set Jinoe down on her feet.

"Kusac will show you round," said Vanna. "A food and drink dispenser has been installed in your room so you don't need to worry about meals on your Link days. Do you know when your next one is?"

"In two days," said Rrai, letting go of her hand to wander over to the window that looked out on the gardens.

"Do we have to stay in?" he asked, half turning back to her.

"No, you can go out when you want, so long as you take a den-mother or your mother with you," she said, following him over to the window.

"This isn't like the hospital," said Kusac, making an effort to concentrate on the two kitlings. "This will be your home."

"Will it be better than home?" asked Jinoe in a small voice. "Home wasn't very nice."

Kusac looked down at her. Large brown eyes looked up at him from a small face that was so thin it looked pinched. The purple tunic drowned her, adding to her air of frailty. Her light tan pelt was thin and patchy around her face and scalp, testifying to her lack of proper diet and her recent ordeal.

Gods, Vanna! She's no older than my sister Kitra! he sent, reaching down to touch the kitling's face reassuringly. *How could that priest justify beating these children like that?*

I know. They're safe now, though. You show them where everything is while I get my medikit. I want to give them a quick checkup.

"It'll be better than home, Jinoe, that I promise you," said Kusac. "Would you like to meet my sister, Kitra?"

* * *

Twelfth hour came and, as agreed, they met in Kusac's rooms. There was c'shar and coffee on the lounge table, and while they waited for T'Chebbi and Dzaka, the others helped themselves. Kusac prowled restlessly between the room and the balcony overlooking the front garden. Despite what Vanna said, he was more worried about Carrie than he wanted the others to know. Their Link had become fainter since the morning and he was suffering none of her symptoms. It almost felt as if she was separating mentally from him. The worst part was there was no one to whom he felt he could go for advice. They were the first; what they experienced was becoming the rule for all mixed Leska pairs.

T'Chebbi arrived, and quietly brought Kaid up to date on her trip with the Clan Lord to the Telepath Guild.

Dzaka was the last to arrive, the cut on the side of his nose and the swelling around one eye causing raised eye ridges from some of the others.

"We're all here, Kusac," said Vanna at last, sitting back in her chair and cradling her mug of coffee in both hands.

Kusac returned to his seat and perched on the edge of it.

He looked round the small group. There was Vanna and Garras, Kaid, Rulla, T'Chebbi, Meral, and Dzaka.

"Brynne should be here," he said abruptly. "He's as involved as the rest of us."

Vanna stirred slightly. "He'll pick it up through me," she said.

He nodded. "Very well. I'll have to speak for Carrie as she's not well enough to be with us. There are several issues to discuss. The first directly involves Carrie and myself. We intend to leave not only the Telepath Guild, but the guild system completely."

As he'd anticipated, a stunned silence greeted his remark. To be guildless was to live on the margins of society, to belong nowhere.

"I won't have us treated like laboratory specimens any longer. The God willing, we'll have more cubs," he continued quietly, looking down at his hands, "but they'll never be subjected to the scrutiny of any guild. We've had enough. Neither Esken nor the Brotherhood will use us. So we've decided we're going to walk the Fire Margins."

He let the silence lengthen till he could stand it no more. Looking up at the people in the room, he shrugged. "That's it. You're free to do what you want, you're none of you bound to us any longer unless you want to be. Vanna," he looked over at her and Garras. "You'll have to do what you think best."

"I'm not staying either," she said, putting down her mug. "But to walk the Fire Margins! I don't know much about it, but even I've heard enough to know how dangerous it is."

"It's tantamount to committing suicide," said Dzaka quietly. "No one in the last ten generations has walked that path and returned. Even the Brothers won't try it."

Kusac looked over at him. "I know. But I've been researching all the En'Shalla rituals, and it's our only option."

"There's no point in asking you if you're prepared to risk your lives on something as insubstantial as this, because I know you are," said Vanna grimly, her ears flicking back in anger. "You never do things by halves, do you, Kusac? It's all or nothing! Why? Why risk everything when you both have so much to live for?" she demanded.

"If they succeed, they'll have won their liberty," said Kaid. "They'll be beyond all guild and civil laws, subject only to Vartra Himself. But above all, they'll not be outcasts. At the end of the day, it's their only logical choice."

"You're in favor of this?" Vanna rounded on him. "You're advising him to do it?"

"Yes. They'll do it no matter what we say or do. I've seen it."

"Ah," said Rulla, his voice a low purr of contentment as he settled back in his seat. "I *was* right! You *were* working toward a goal Vartra had shown you!"

"It will happen," said Kaid calmly.

"And has Vartra shown you whether or not they survive?" demanded Vanna, her voice reaching a hysterical note as her hands tightened on the arms of her chair. "Has He done that? No! I thought not! Damn the Gods! Damn the guilds! Damn all of you who're encouraging them to kill themselves!"

Garras reached out to put a restraining hand on her arm, but she pulled away, leaping to her feet and beginning to pace the room.

"Why? Why do you have to do this?" she demanded, stopping in front of Kusac, her tail lashing angrily from side to side, ears turned sideways and flicking repeatedly. "For once take an easier option, Kusac! Carrie damned near died a few days ago, and your unborn daughter *did!*"

She squatted down in front of him, putting her hands on his knees and looking him squarely in the face. "Let's leave the Telepath Guild, yes, but the rest? Dammit, Lijou's offer holds more hope than this!"

Kusac had flinched at her comment about their lost cub; now he reached out to cup her cheek in his hand, his eyes looking into hers. "You've got your own life, Vanna. You have Garras, and your own Leska, Brynne, as well as a child on the way. It's time for you to choose your own way and leave us to ours. You heard Kaid. It will happen."

"Don't wrong-spoor me, Kusac!" she said, batting his hand away. "You believe in the Gods as much as I do! If you've had enough of life and want to commit ritual suicide, why not say so and be done with it! Why this charade?"

"It's not a charade, Vanna," he said patiently. "I believe we'll succeed. I don't intend for us to die."

"You infuriate me, you . . . you . . . Ah!" She sprang to her feet and spun away from him to the other side of the room, pelt bushed out round her head and tail. "Someone talk some sense into him, he won't listen to me!"

"Your decision affects all of us, Kusac," said Kaid, leaning forward. "I have no intention of leaving you. Apart from Garras, the others belong to the Brotherhood and they are subject to Ghezu's orders. If they remain with us against Stronghold's orders, they face death. Ghezu will have them hunted down and killed."

"Let him try," said Rulla, his voice a deep rumble of menace. "I've told you that I intend to leave and follow you."

Kaid cast an exasperated glance in his direction. "Enough, Rulla," he said.

"What's to talk about?" said T'Chebbi, looking hard at Dzaka. "I follow you. When Stronghold stoops to placing undercover operatives among us, we're all at risk. Even on the streets of Ranz they trusted me." She turned her head away from Dzaka to look at Kaid. "You knew. You chose me for your Liege and Liegena. I stay."

Kusac glanced from T'Chebbi to Kaid, suddenly curious about her past. Ranz, one of the towns nearest to Stronghold in the Dzahai Mountains, was still infamous for its street gangs. As he looked, Kaid's right ear gave the barest of flicks in acknowledgment to her.

Rulla gave a bark of laughter which Kaid ignored.

"There's the matter of accepting Lijou's offer first," said Kaid. "If we're to curb the power of the Telepath Guild, it has to be done through the Brotherhood. Agreed you need to break from your guild soon, but until you're ready to walk the Margins, you'll need the protection that belonging to the Brotherhood will give you."

"When Lijou claims that the only guild that can realistically accommodate us is the Brotherhood, he's not being altruistic, he wants to use us as much as the Telepath Guild does," said Kusac.

"Brynne asks what's the difference between being used by Ghezu and Lijou and being used by Esken?" said Vanna to Kaid. "They're each as bad as the other." She glanced at Dzaka. "They both resorted to kidnapping and drugging us. How would it benefit us to change guilds?"

"The type of change Kaid is suggesting is unheard of," said Kusac. "Telepaths with medical talents also become members of the Guild of Medics, but their main guild remains the Telepaths. What he's suggesting is breaking completely from one guild to join another. There's no law that says we can't do that, but it's rarely done. There'll be opposition to us, and possibly legal action taken against us by Esken."

"Of course Lijou and Ghezu are using you," said Kaid. "The Brotherhood wants full guild status but they can't petition for that unless they can prove they possess a specialized skill belonging to no other guild. You, as fighting telepaths, represent that skill. If the move is made publicly, during the next All Guilds Council meeting, then there is little Esken can do but accept gracefully as you apply to be released from the Telepath Guild to join Stronghold. Then the Brotherhood can be awarded its full guild status. As I said, membership in the Brotherhood will protect you from Esken and the Telepath Guild."

"Lijou is offering us an alternative to being guildless," said Garras. "We must avoid that if at all possible."

"If you leave your guild and remain guildless, first you lose your profession," said Kaid. "Never again could you be legally employed as telepaths. Your guild companions will turn their backs on you; you would cease to exist as far as they were concerned. At one stroke you'd have severed contact with everyone you'd grown up and worked with. Second, your clans could choose to support you on their estates, but pressure would be put on them to turn their backs on you as well. You'd be total outcasts. I know. I've been there."

He stopped, looking round them. "Should you join the Brotherhood, even if only temporarily, you'd have their protection for as long as you remained members, and Esken could do nothing about it. If you survive the Margins, all that changes. You can stay in your guild yet be answerable *only* to the Order of Vartra, through the Head Priest, Father Lijou— not Ghezu. In the Brotherhood, the two disciplines are separate. The last option is to stay with the Brotherhood."

"Whatever else you decide, Vanna, I'd advise you to leave the Telepath Guild," said Kusac, looking over to where she still stood at the far end of the room. "You know what Esken did to you and Brynne on your first Link day. I don't yet know what he did to the kitlings my father had brought here, but obviously it was enough to convince him they were safer with us than with the Guild. Our family is headed for trouble with Esken irrespective of what I do. If you're still a member of his Guild, he may try to be revenged on us through you."

"Lijou said they have the facilities to help us train in both disciplines at Stronghold," said Vanna, moving back to the group. "What exactly did he mean?"

Kusac looked across at Kaid, catching his eye. "Tell us about the forgotten talents, Kaid."

Kaid nodded slowly, ignoring Dzaka's startled movement. "What you're talking about touches the heart of the Brotherhood," he said. "For as far back as our records go, we've recruited from three main sources. One is the Warrior Guild, the second is from wherever the Brothers find a Talent. The mountains breed a lot of the type of people we're looking for. We want people who first and foremost can fight, then we look for their Talents, their psychic talents. The third I'll tell you about later."

Kusac heard Vanna's sharp gasp of surprise. "Go on," she said.

"We have as wide a range of talents as the Humans do, only until now the Telepath Guild had forgotten they existed. They were so intent on their breeding programs to produce more and stronger telepaths they ignored any other gift. Every Brother can fight and is Talented in some way. The others have said I can speak for them," said Kaid, glancing round his people. "T'Chebbi has an extremely well-developed sense of impending danger. She can even pinpoint its direction. Rulla senses moods and whether people are speaking the truth." He indicated Meral. "We're in the process of assessing Meral's gifts but a sensitivity to people and his surroundings is what drew our attention to him." He stopped, looking pointedly at Dzaka.

"I'm an empath," Dzaka said with obvious reluctance.

Kaid raised an eye ridge.

Dzaka gave a low rumble of annoyance. "I'm also one of the special operatives hired by the Telepath Guild to assess rogue talents," he snapped. "As were Kaid and Garras."

Shocked, Kusac looked toward Garras.

"Truth time, Kusac," the once-Captain of the *Sirroki* said quietly. "Yes, Kaid and I worked together assessing telepaths with Talents that were uncontrollable, or who were themselves mentally unstable. Often they had to be terminated on the orders of the Telepath Guild. When we could, we recruited them for the Brotherhood where they were taught how to control their gifts. Termination was the last resort. We saved as many as we could, though Esken knew nothing about it."

Kusac could feel the blood draining from his face. His ears insisted on lying flat against his head as he looked from Garras to Kaid.

Vanna was as stunned as he was. He could see the look of disbelief on her face, feel the denial in her mind as she sank slowly into the nearest empty seat.

" 'Observe, assess, recruit, or destroy,' " quoted Kaid softly. "People like us are needed. There's no one else who can work outside the law to protect Shola, and believe me, in some cases, termination was the only solution. This is the third source of members for the Brotherhood. A young male telepath, one of your father's generation, a Contender for heirship to the Sixteen Clans, was involved in an accident in which he received severe head injuries. It was thought that he had made a full recovery, but several months later, he relapsed. He began to broadcast telepathically. It was totally involuntary, the ravings of one who was obviously mad, but like the insane, he had the strength of ten. No one could get near him. Two medics were lost before it was realized he was capable of killing with his mind. Warriors couldn't get near him. He had to die, there was no other option. That left only us. The Brotherhood took him, but not without mental and physical scars to the operatives."

"In our time, we managed to save almost as many as we had to kill," said Garras. "When we recruited, that person was dead as far as the rest of Shola was concerned. Granted they could never leave Stronghold, but they were alive and sane, and they were a working part of our Brotherhood, helping in some cases to train others."

Kaid sighed. "Truth time, as Garras said. When he called me, asking me to come out to the *Khalossa* to protect you, he knew it was a double-edged mission that I undertook. He knew we might have to face the reality that your Link to Carrie would make you both unstable. It was very unlikely, but it was a possibility. Then the Brotherhood contacted me, forcing me to accept the same mission by calling in a debt of honor. Your mother wanted an operative to protect you both and see you delivered safely to Shola, and at the same time

Ghezu ordered me to assess you and take appropriate action."

"You have no idea of the powers that have been ranged against you on the *Khalossa* and on Shola," said Garras. "The Telepath Guild were terrified of the consequences of your Link on their carefully constructed power base here. You were a threat to them of potentially massive proportions. Because of your identity, you couldn't be killed without a major investigation, and likewise you couldn't just disappear. Neither, of course, could Carrie. Mito came to me within the first few days after we got back to the *Khalossa* telling me she'd been approached by someone asking far too many questions about Guynor's accusations against you and Carrie. I knew then we were in for trouble and that you had to be protected from any more people like Guynor, and from any authorized evaluation which could neglect to take into full account what happened on Keiss. So I sent for Kaid. The kind of protection Kaid gave you can't be bought, even from him."

"But you just said that you knew there was a chance Kaid would kill them," said Vanna, a stunned look on her face.

"We'd just spent a great number of days in the foulest, most cramped conditions ever experienced by Sholans. If that didn't break Kusac or Carrie, then I reckoned nothing would," said Garras, avoiding eye contact with her. "There was a much greater risk of them being killed by those dissidents."

Kusac finally found his voice. "This assessment, is it over now?"

Kaid looked at Dzaka. "My mission for the Brotherhood was over by the time I was injured in the scouter crash," he said quietly. "I gave Ghezu my assessment then."

Dzaka sat motionless, staring straight ahead. Kusac could feel the tension behind his facade of calm. He was being torn in too many different directions. What Kaid was telling them were matters for the Brothers only.

"My assessments has also been given," he said finally, his tone clipped as if the words were being forced from him. "My current orders are to continue observing you, continue assessing Physician Kyjishi and her Human Leska, and report on Kaid's movements."

Reaction swept through the little group. Meral and T'Chebbi

hissed their anger, Garras nodded his head, and Kaid . . . relaxed. A small moan of fear came from Vanna.

"Aren't we rather tempting fate if we join the Brotherhood?" Kusac asked. "Doesn't it make it that bit easier to kill us? Apart from breaking Esken's power on the Council, I see no reason for us to join."

It was Dzaka who answered. "No, Liegen. They need you all alive if they want to use you to achieve full guild status. They don't dare kill you now. They need as many mixed Leska pairs as possible to prove it isn't just a phenomenon."

"And Kaid? Why are they watching him?"

"That's personal between Ghezu and myself, Liege," Kaid said smoothly before Dzaka could answer. "It doesn't affect anyone else."

From the corner of his eye, Kusac caught Dzaka's slight start of surprise as his shield dropped briefly. So Kaid was covering something for him. But what?

"Physician Kyjishi . . . Vanna," said Kaid, looking directly over to her. "Believe me, you have nothing to fear from either the Brotherhood or anyone in this room. You are far too valuable to everyone alive, and I intend to see you stay that way."

Vanna looked over at Garras. Kusac noticed that the skin visible on her face was gray with shock.

"You're nothing but killers, cold-blooded, highly trained killers who use their psychic talents to track down their prey," she whispered.

"That's enough, Vanna," snapped Kusac. Abruptly he got to his feet and went over to one of the cupboards opposite. Opening it, he grasped a bottle by the neck, and caught hold of several glasses. "Kaid, I need another couple of glasses please. Vanna," he said, returning to the table and setting down the glasses, "It's my turn to tell you to grow up. You knew damned well what Garras was when you found Kaid injured in the *Khalossa*'s sick bay. The fact that you're back here at the estate rather than still drugged at Stronghold is due to him and Kaid and the others in this room."

Kaid got up and collected the extra glasses, bringing them back to the low table.

"I had no idea that . . ." Vanna began angrily.

"Be honest with yourself, Vanna," Kusac said, interrupting

her. "You made me face some harsh realities. Now it's your turn."

Vanna subsided.

He had been unsuccessfully trying to get the cap off the bottle. With an exclamation of annoyance, he handed it to Kaid. "You open it. I think we all need a drink," he said, wiping his hands on his tunic.

"Terran brandy?" said Kaid, looking at the bottle briefly first.

"Keissian," Kusac corrected, accepting the opened bottle. "A present from Jack Reynolds." He poured a healthy measure into each glass, giving them to Kaid to hand round.

Finished, he glanced up to see Vanna sitting looking abstractedly at hers. He went over to her, lifting it up to her mouth. "Drink it," he ordered.

She looked at him, her green eyes brimming with unshed tears. *We've been used and lied to by them both,* she sent.

He refused to answer her. "Drink it," he said again, tilting the glass. "Take it all in one swallow."

She didn't have a choice as the liquid was spilled into her mouth. She began to cough, the tears now streaming down her face.

Kusac moved away from her and downed his own drink. It hit the back of his throat like a blast of heat, making him gasp. Then the liquid reached his stomach and its warmth began to spread through him. He sat down abruptly, feeling more than a little light-headed.

Pieces of the jigsaw were beginning to fall into place now, crystallizing his thoughts. This meeting had achieved all he hoped it would. Inexorably, like some sea barque of old, they were being driven toward some preordained distant shore. Leaning forward, he began to laugh as he refilled his glass.

"Kaid, tell Ghezu we won't join the Brotherhood, but we will appear to do so. He can prepare his application for guild status, but our public support will cost him."

Kaid's ears cocked forward in curiosity. "What will it cost him?"

"A permanent alliance with the Brotherhood. I want a specific number of Brothers, including those in this room, permanently released from Brotherhood duties and permanently transferred to my staff. I'm sure between you and Garras you can put together a shopping list of the people we'll need. Think big, Kaid, we're planning for the start of a new Clan, an

En'Shalla Clan of Brothers, of Human and Sholan Leskas—
and their cubs," said Kusac.

Kaid's mouth dropped in a slow grin, then he leaned forward and refilled his glass. Now Kusac's mind was working in the right direction! Vartra had chosen well: he had the makings of a good leader.

"To the En'Shalla Clan," said Kaid, raising his glass briefly before drinking.

Kusac turned to Vanna. "I need you to put together a medical team," he said. "Rather than recruit now from either of your guilds, liaise with Kaid and start training some of the Brothers as nurses and technicians."

"No need," said Kaid. "All Brothers are trained paramedics."

"Even better. Get him to suggest a staff for you. Check out that ni'uzu virus, see if it had anything to do with altering our genes. Father told me the two cubs had been exposed to it before their Link formed. Run standard DNA checks on all our Brotherhood personnel who were exposed to the virus. We need to know if this new strain of virus has had any effect on them. You'll also need to check out any new Leska pairs, Sholan or mixed."

Vanna had come out of her reverie and was even showing some interest in what Kusac was saying. "I'll need to continue working at the Telepath Guild for the time being," she said. "It's the only place that has the equipment I need. Once we make our move, I'll have to have access to another lab."

"It'll be seen to," Kaid assured her. "Meanwhile, keep Garras and one other guard with you at all times. I'll see about requesting the extra personnel we need. Rulla, I'll need your help. You're more up to date than I am about the current members of the Brotherhood." He turned back to Kusac. "We're going to need a priest, one who knows the En'Shalla rites. May I suggest your friend Ghyan?"

"Ghyan?" Kusac frowned in surprise. He had no idea Kaid knew Ghyan.

Kaid nodded. "He's well versed in the old rituals and loyal to you."

"In that case, I'll speak to him myself."

"I think we should bring this meeting to a close," said Kaid. "It's time those on duty got back to work, and I've a couple of jobs that need to be done." He stopped and turned to Vanna. "Your pardon, Physician, but I take it that you have decided to throw your coin in with ours."

"I won't join the Brotherhood," she said, "but I can live with an alliance. Brynne agrees with me, though he says he'll continue living with the Terrans at the Guild."

Kusac nodded. "At least now we know in which direction we're headed. You and I can work out the rest later, Kaid. If Brynne's determined to stay with the Terrans, there's not a lot we can do about it beyond making sure he's always accompanied by one of the Brothers."

"T'Chebbi, Lhea's currently watching Carrie. I want you to relieve her. Tell Lhea to be in the staff lounge in fifteen minutes for a briefing from Garras on our current status. Meral, get me a copy of the duty roster from N'Zulhu. Tell him I'll meet him at the seventeenth hour in the staff lounge and he can fill me in on his security arrangements. That's all," Kaid said, dismissing them.

As they filed out, Garras hesitated at the door, waiting for Vanna. Kusac saw this and sent mentally to her.

Vanna, go with him. Don't despise him because of what he is. Just remember how gentle he is with you, and how his skills have kept us both alive.

She made no answer and he saw Garras turn to leave on his own.

You knew what he was months ago, Vanna! Why punish him for his past? This isn't worthy of you. He knows you're lying to yourself, remember that! At least talk to him about it, you owe him that.

She got to her feet. "Garras, wait. We need to talk," she said.

Kaid waited till they'd gone. "So we play the Brotherhood at its own game, eh?" he grinned.

"It seems the best way," said Kusac. "It also enables us to get your people legitimately employed with us without them having to leave the Brotherhood. Naturally, we'll have this agreement down in writing so neither Ghezu nor Lijou can demand them back at a later date."

"That would be wise," agreed Kaid. "About the new clan, I presume you've checked out the legalities."

Kusac nodded. "If we prove we've walked the Fire Margins, we can set up a new clan. Then our Brotherhood members can leave and join us legitimately."

"Where do you plan to locate this clan?"

"This land is my mother's, the Aldatan land. South of here, adjoining it, is the Valsgarth estate, my settlement as heir. There's already a villa there that's being made ready for us at the moment, and the remains of the estate houses. As soon as Carrie is fit to move, I had planned to take her there to recuperate. It's time we had our own home, and our own lives," he said, getting to his feet. "We could locate the new clan there. Where is Carrie, by the way? I don't want to wake her by sending."

"In the main lounge, sleeping on the daybed," said Kaid.

"I want to call in on her before I find my father. I need to know why he wanted the kitlings brought here."

"Your father also requested a bodyguard this morning when he visited the Guild. I sent T'Chebbi with him. She said the attitude of the medical staff toward him bordered on the aggressive. She was glad she was there."

"That's bad," said Kusac.

"Esken wasn't much better," Kaid said, accompanying him to the inner balcony. "He was patronizing and insulting—just within the bounds of the acceptable, until he refused to accept the Governor's appointment without checking with him first. Your father insisted on calling Nesul, who proceeded to give Esken an earful! T'Chebbi also said your father probably had us collect the kitlings because Esken said he was moving them the next day."

"Gods, where are we headed if this continues?"

"I think Esken's rattled because he now realizes your family poses a threat to his control of the Council. With your father working with the new Leskas, it leaves him little or no room to conduct illicit experiments on them to find out their potential. He's going to have to move them if he wants to stay in control."

"I wonder if Esken realizes that in crossing swords with my father he's taking on a major government department, not just one male."

"If he doesn't, he'll soon find out," said Kaid as they made their way down the main staircase."

Vanna joined Garras in the corridor. "We'll talk in our rooms," she said, turning to go upstairs.

Garras followed her. He could tell she was still deeply upset about his past. He sighed. He'd been too long in the world outside Stronghold. He'd never bothered about anyone's reaction to his profession in those days—especially a female's, but then the females who were interested in the

Brothers weren't like Vanna. And he'd rather have her than any number of those from his past.

Once in the privacy of their lounge, Vanna turned to him.

"Before you begin, Vanna," he said, forestalling her, "please sit down and listen to what I have to say."

She opened her mouth in protest, then closed it and sat down on the settee, looking up at him.

"You didn't know me during my days in the Brotherhood," he said, sitting opposite her. "I joined, as we all do, because Vartra called me. I trained hard and became one of the best at what I did. Kaid and I teamed up early on. As Brothers all we have is the God, our oath, and each other. Lasting friendships outside Stronghold are frowned on, and are virtually impossible anyway."

He stopped for a moment, trying to gauge the effect of his words on her, but he couldn't. "What we did had to be done, Vanna. If we hadn't done it, someone else would. It's not an excuse, it's a fact. We were thorough, making sure our targets were beyond our help before we took the decision to terminate them. Others weren't so particular. When we killed, our kills were quick and painless. I've only known one that wasn't, and that was when Kaid killed Chyad. Nothing will make me ashamed either of what I was or what I did in those days, Vanna. It's part of who and what I am." He fell silent, hoping she could understand.

She looked away from him and down at her clasped hands. The silence lengthened until he got to his feet. He felt numb inside and was grateful for it just now. Later the loss of her would hit him.

"Where are you going?" she asked sharply.

"I'm leaving," he said. "If what I was is more important than me, then obviously there's no point in my staying."

"I didn't say that."

"You don't need to, Vanna. I know when I'm not wanted." He turned toward the door but before he reached it, she got to her feet and grabbed hold of him.

"Don't go!" she said. "Don't leave me alone, Garras. I need you!" The previously unshed tears were now rolling silently down her face. Her hands reached out to clutch him, relaxing only when he wrapped his arms round her.

"Don't frighten me like that again, Vanna," he said, his voice muffled against her face as he held her close, letting her scent and the warmth of her body against his push back the fear of losing her. "I can't undo my past, it's made me what I am today. I've waited too long to find you."

"I know," she said. "So have I, Garras. You're what matters to me, nothing else. It was just such a shock . . ."

"Enough," he said, nuzzling her ear. "We're still together."

CHAPTER 3

Kaid was off duty for a few hours. Returning to his room, he lay down on his bed hoping to catch up on some rest but he found his mind too active to allow him to sleep. Fragments of the God-Vision which had begun all this kept flitting through his thoughts. It had started when he'd heard the voice of Vartra telling him there was a pair in space, a Leska pair, who carried within them the key to the future.

Trying to recapture more of his vision, he let his mind roam back to that night. When the flashback came, it came suddenly and with as much force as the original vision.

He saw two figures—mere shadows within the temple—flames encompassing them as they tried to reach safety. Flying debris filled the air as the roof began to collapse. People were running everywhere, desperate to escape. The dancing flames picked out the two crouching figures, highlighting them briefly, then the images were gone, leaving him as shaken as when he'd experienced it the first time. Now, however, he knew without a doubt that the smaller figure had been the Human, Carrie.

What little the Brotherhood knew of the Cataclysm told them that it had been a time of fire—even the sky had been blazing according to their records: the records that were composed of the dreams and visions of former members from ancient times. Hardly a reliable source, but it was all they had. These records went on to say that after the firestorms, the earthquakes had come. Tidal waves from the coast had swept across the land, resculpturing it into new shapes. The thick, black clouds encircling their world had then released their burden of water onto the land below, destroying what little had remained of their civilization.

The dangers involved in the Fire Margins ritual were far greater than he'd thought possible if what he'd seen was true. Would Carrie and Kusac be subject to the dangers of the world he'd glimpsed? Could the Cataclysm destroy them as easily as it had destroyed so many Sholans over a thousand years ago? Was that why hardly anyone had survived the ritual?

What he'd read about it emphasized the fact that everyone who'd reached Vartra by walking the Fire Margins had died, their minds trapped somewhere in the far past while their bodies suffered the same fate at Stronghold or Vartra's Retreat.

It wasn't until now that he'd begun to realize what that part of the vision meant. Yes, he'd seen Kusac and Carrie traveling the Margins, but Vanna was right, he hadn't seen them return. He'd been the one advocating taking that path, the one telling them it was the only answer, and now he was doubting the wisdom of his own advice. Was Vartra calling them only to destroy them? He'd wondered that before the Challenge and somehow they'd managed to survive. Everything was leading them toward the God: if it was meant to be, then nothing he did would matter one way or the other. They would go, and Vartra would decide whether they returned.

He turned over, exhausted by the strength of the memories, hoping sleep would claim him, hoping it might bring another vision, this time a happier one.

* * *

It was mid-afternoon by the time Konis returned home. His mood was thoughtful. As they approached the perimeter of the estate, he was surprised out of his reverie when T'Chebbi was challenged over the comm for their identity. He waited while she reeled off an arcane code and they were given permission to enter.

"What was all that about?" he asked her.

"Ni'Zulhu, the new head of security," she replied. "We've been allocated passwords to use whenever we approach the estate."

"Isn't that a little excessive?"

T'Chebbi turned her head briefly in his direction. "We're taught at Stronghold that the only effective security is total security."

Konis grunted. Rhyasha was going to be none too pleased.

He'd have to have a word with Kaid. This level of security could bankrupt the estate very quickly.

Rhyasha was in her office and her mental greeting was very welcome as he made his way there to join her.

"How's Carrie?" he asked, sitting down beside her. "I sensed Kusac's concern the moment I arrived."

Rhyasha handed him a mug of c'shar and settled back in her chair. "We could hardly get her to eat anything today," she admitted. "All she wants to do is sleep. If she's the same tomorrow, then I'll be concerned. Vanna says it's to be expected after all that she's been through. She's taken the precaution of contacting Dr. Reynolds on Keiss and is waiting for him to get back to her."

She stopped, unconsciously tapping her claw tips on the arm of her chair.

"For the moment it's Kusac I'm concerned about. The last few months have matured him mentally, but emotionally and physically, he's still a young male whose hormones are not yet stable. He's in control of his feelings, but only just."

"Is he suffering any of Carrie's tiredness?"

"None. The opposite in fact. He's unable to relax at all. The loss of their cub has hit him as hard as it hit her. Then there's the demands of their Link. Thank the Gods that Carrie is free of them for the moment, but he isn't."

"It looks as if this Link of theirs has stripped away most of his training," said Konis thoughtfully. "We're going to have to assume this will happen to all our people who have a Human Leska. A new system has to be devised, one that doesn't rely on the assumption that our males will remain in control of themselves and their talents."

"Kusac will be able to help you on that, once he's got over their loss. Meanwhile, he needs something less demanding to absorb his interest and tire him out. Bringing those kitlings home was inspired," Rhyasha said, leaning forward to touch her mate's hand. "Just what he needs. He can help them settle in, start teaching them. He'll be able to find out if their Link is anomalous in any other way. Kitra can help him."

"Interesting use of the word help," he said. "Kitra's not much older than those two. I have to admit I didn't bring them home for Kusac's benefit. I brought them home because Esken was doing exactly what you predicted he would do. He was treating them as impersonally as jeggets in a maze. Do you know the young male's mother hasn't been allowed to see him for nearly a week? And on their Link days, the medics were intruding on them, demanding that they complete barrages of tests! It can't be allowed, Rhyasha, that's why I brought them here. He hasn't even started training them yet!"

"I assume Esken didn't agree to your moving them," she said, her mouth opening in a faint smile. "Did you inform Ni'Zulhu that he could expect Esken or his people to arrive at any time to retrieve them?"

"Ni'Zulhu? Ah, our security controller," said Konis, with an embarrassed flick of his ears.

"That was another little addition to the family you didn't tell me about," she said gently.

Konis' ears flicked again. "There wasn't time, Rhyasha. It wasn't even a rational decision . . ."

"Konis, it's all right. I have no objections. I would have preferred to have known before he arrived, that's all. Have you any more surprises for me?"

Konis shifted uncomfortably in his seat and looked away from his wife's amber gaze. "I know that I should have consulted you as Clan Leader first, and for that I do apologize. I've also asked Kaid for bodyguards for all of us."

"Another intuitive decision?" she asked, raising an eye ridge.

This time Konis could hear a touch of ice in her voice. Never before had he gone over her head in matters concerning her Clan.

He looked up, meeting her gaze this time. "Yes," he said. "I asked T'Chebbi to accompany me this morning and frankly, I'm glad I did. Without her, I wouldn't have been able to see Jinoe and Rrai, and I'd have had to put up with Esken's insulting attitude regarding my appointment as head of the Mixed Leska Project."

His wife's face softened but retained a worried look.

"Are we actually in conflict with Esken now?"

"Oh, assuredly. He'll not forget that I've humiliated him in front of a Brother and Governor Nesul, or that I've taken the kitlings from him."

"That shouldn't be enough to put us at risk from him. What could he do to us? Surely he wouldn't approach the Brotherhood, would he? I can't remember when the last political assassination happened. It has to be over fifty years ago."

Konis leaned forward and put his hand over Rhyasha's. "Of course he wouldn't! Apart from anything else, all our security people here are Brothers. I'm probably being utterly paranoid, but . . ."

"Better that than we're found wanting if we need it," she murmured. "How do we deal with Esken now?"

Konis sighed and sat back in his chair. "I'm working on it," he said. "For the moment, I'll get what I can in the way of files and other data from him. Hopefully Vanna managed to download the kitlings' files before Esken was alerted to their disappearance. I think we're going to have to stop any mixed Leska pairs living in the Guild for their own safety. All Esken needs to do is spirit them off to another guild-house, then say they're in quarantine or some such thing. I'm afraid I have to say that I can no longer trust our Guild Master."

"Our Human bond-daughter has brought about a greater change in our culture than either of us anticipated," said Rhyasha.

"Maybe, and maybe all this has been sitting under the surface of our lives waiting for her arrival," he sighed. "I must inform Governor Nesul that I have the kitlings."

Though he wanted to join Carrie, Kusac knew he had to speak to his father first. He had to be told what was happening to the ruined cities and about the presence of Valtegan remains dating back to the time of the Cataclysm.

Discovering that Konis was busy talking to his mother, he went in search of Carrie but was waylaid by Kitra and the kitlings. When he finally managed to leave them, he headed straight downstairs to the lounge.

Carrie was asleep on the settee. Kaid was sitting in the garden just outside the open doorway, keeping an eye on her and the immediate grounds. He looked up, flicking an ear in greeting as Kusac entered.

Going over to her, Kusac tucked the blanket more securely around her before perching on the edge of the seat. Leaning forward, he touched her forehead with his fingertips. It felt cooler than usual, and she was still so pale! She didn't stir.

Getting up, he went to sit on the step with Kaid. "Did she eat much?" he asked.

Kaid took the stim-twig out of his mouth. "Only a few mouthfuls," he said.

"I'm worried about her, despite what Vanna and my mother say."

Kaid chewed on his twig for a minute or two before answering. "Are you picking up any symptoms from her? Is her state of health affecting you at all?"

"No, and that's part of what's worrying me," said Kusac, pulling at the grass. "It's as if she's barely there, Kaid."

"Is she blocking you out again?"

"No. She hasn't got the strength to do that now. Vanna's convinced she's reacting in a Sholan way—the way one of our females would if she'd suffered what Carrie's been through in the last few days."

"What do you think?"

"I think this is atypical for either Humans or Sholans. I believe she's just giving up."

"I remember you telling me your father said he was worried for her sanity, and that was before the Challenge," said Kaid. He poked at the end of his twig for a moment, then bit off a few rough bits of bark. "Taking a sentient's life for the first time affects us all differently, Kusac," he said, still looking down at the twig in his hands. "Remember the first time you killed—three Valtegans, wasn't it? Remember your reaction. As well as her injuries, and losing your cub, she's also trying to come to terms with the fact she took another person's life and maybe believing she's paid for her death with the death of her cub—a life for a life. I know what you're going to say," he looked up at him, ears swiveling forward, "she's killed Valtegans, but they weren't people to her. Sholans are."

Kaid's wrist unit began to emit an alarm tone. He raised his eye ridges at Kusac, then activated the receive function.

"Alpha 1 to Base. Come in Base."

"Base here," he said.

"Striker 3 has requested permission to land. We have a visual. I've directed them to the open ground beyond the front of the house."

"Alpha 1, who's aboard Striker 3?"

"Physician Jack Reynolds, Base, at your request."

Again Kaid looked quizzically at Kusac. "Confirm his identity, Alpha 1."

"Did you send for Jack?" asked Kusac.

His aide shook his head. "Not me. Who, then? If it is him."

"Alpha 1. Here is a visual of the Physician."

Kaid looked at the tiny comm screen. A small but perfect representation of the Human physician was there. "Liege, confirm this is Jack, please," he said, holding out his wrist.

Kusac looked. A sandy mane of hair topped Jack's unmistakable bearded face. "It's him."

"Alpha 1, identity confirmed. Allow access."

"Confirmed, Base. Alpha 1 out."

Kaid put away his stim-twig. "They'll have landed by the time we walk round," he said.

"I take it my mother isn't expecting him," Kusac said, as overhead the sound of powerful engines could be heard.

"None of us are."

"This on top of all the other major upheavals today! My mother's really going to love us!"

"The doctor doesn't have to stay here," said Kaid placidly. "He'll automatically be granted Medical Guild status. He could stay at that guild."

"That's not a sensible option. He'll be much safer here."

The door opened, making both of them half-rise as they looked into the interior of the room.

"I swear this house becomes more like Chagda Station every hour!" said Rhyasha, her tone cool in the extreme as she swept into the lounge followed by Konis. "Who is it this time?" she demanded.

"Dr. Jack Reynolds," said Kusac, getting to his feet as she came toward them.

"Physician Reynolds?" she said in disbelief. "Who sent for him?"

"I've no idea, Mother," said Kusac. "It wasn't either of us."

"Then who?" she asked.

The same idea hit them all at the same time, but it was Rhyasha who said it.

"Taizia! When I get my hands on that cub . . . ! Her actions will be seen to be condoned by me, the Clan Leader. Damn the child! She's compromised our clan! Doesn't she realize that inviting an alien from another world isn't the same as inviting a friend from another clan over for a hunt!"

"How can Jack's visit compromise us, Mother?" asked Kusac, baffled. "He's a personal friend, why shouldn't he visit, even if he is from another species?"

"She's right, Kusac," said his father. "I didn't stop to think of the repercussions on the clan of having the kitlings brought here."

Kusac turned to look at him.

"Not to put too fine a point on it, I kidnapped them, Kusac," he admitted with an embarrassed flick of his ears. "I'll have to contact Governor Nesul and hope he backs up my actions. If not, we could be in for trouble from Esken if he chooses to pursue the matter."

"How can he pursue it? The kitlings want to be here, their mother will agree to that. You haven't moved them here against their will."

"Esken had other plans for them," said Konis.

"What?"

"He was going to have them taken to the Laasoi Guild-house so we couldn't study them. He didn't want me finding out that their Link is more like yours than the normal Sholan Leska links," said Konis.

"Dr. Reynolds arriving without official clearance makes it look even more like we think we're above the law. We could even be accused of allowing a Human physician to experiment on Sholan cubs. Just think how that could look on the newscasts!" his mother said.

She pinned each one of them with her icy glare, making sure they all felt her quite justifiable anger. "I have no personal objections to the kitlings being here or the Human Physician coming to treat Carrie, but I will not have the clan compromised again by anyone. Kaid, go and greet the physician on our behalf. Assure him he'll be staying here as our guest. Bring him to my kitchen, not here. I don't want Carrie disturbed yet, not that an earthquake would wake her at the moment!" She gave a snort of derision, making the silver beads plaited into her hair jingle. "Put him up at the Medics Guild indeed!"

She turned to Konis. "You had better go and talk to the Governor. Get Physician Reynold's visit cleared and do what you can concerning the kitlings and Esken. We might yet stave off any vote of censure from the other clans."

After a quick glance in the direction of the still sleeping Carrie, Rhyasha moved to the nearest chair and curled up in the depths of its bowl-shaped seat with a sigh. A moment's rest was what she needed.

Kusac realized her reaction was justified. He'd gotten so

used to seeking outlandish solutions to their problems that
he'd forgotten the strict protocol which defined the lives of
those who lived on Shola, and had at one time been as
natural to him as breathing.

He shifted from one foot to the other, unsure what to say,
wanting to defend his sister. Her actions might have been
unwise, but in light of Carrie's current condition, they were
very fortuitous.

His mother sighed again. "Sit down, Kusac. You've
enough to concern yourself with looking after Carrie. I'll see
to Taizia. I know why she did it—she felt responsible for
Carrie's injuries because she'd suggested the Challenge. I'll
not be too unkind. Are we expecting any more visitors that I
know nothing about?"

Kusac sat in the chair opposite. "None that I know of." He
hesitated. "We're headed for trouble with Esken and the
Telepath Guild, aren't we?"

"It looks like it." She closed her eyes and rested her head
against the back of her chair.

I'm sorry, Mother, he sent. *If it hadn't been for me having
Carrie as a Leska, then none of this would have happened.*

Kusac, let me say this one last time, then never *mention it
again! I have never been more proud of you than when we
stood in your suite on the* Khalossa *and you told me that the
Human female wearing your torc was your Leska and your
future mate. In those moments, I knew that you'd listened to
all I'd tried to teach you about life and honor and responsibility.* She opened her eyes and stretched out her hand to
him. *A lesser male wouldn't have stood by his Leska and
fought for her the way you did.*

Kusac rose and went to her, taking her hand in his as he sat
on his haunches beside her chair.

*She's my bond-daughter, Kusac, your life-mate. She's car-
ried my first grandchild.* When he flinched, she leaned forward and held his face in both her hands. *Yes, you lost your
child, but she'll have more, Kusac. You're my son, of my
blood; when she shared that blood with you, you became
one. She's part of our clan now as surely as if she'd been
born to it. I love her too, Kusac!*

She gave him a gentle shake, then tugged at one of his
ears. *I know how you feel at this time, but it still doesn't
excuse you doubting how I feel about her. She is a jewel in
our clan, someone rare and precious. If trouble with the*

Guild is what it costs for you to be together, then trouble is what we'll make! With a last affectionate caress, she let him go and sat back again.

"If Esken is going to threaten to move any new Leska pairs, mixed or not, to another guildhouse, then I fear we must find them somewhere else to live."

"I've thought of that, Mother," said Kusac. "You know that my villa on the Valsgarth estate was being made ready for us to use? If we opened up the estate again properly, renovated the existing houses, built new ones, it would serve the purpose. Perhaps Father can still work with them at the Guild during the day, with access to all the medical and testing equipment there. We can make sure they'll be safe there by assigning each pair one of the Brothers to guard them. And when they return to the estate, our security will protect them."

"That's another point," she said. "Security. Who's paying for all this?" She waved her hand vaguely in the air. "All day Ni'Zulhu has had people tramping around the house, measuring, drilling, sawing and painting, setting up his various devices. And it's not just restricted to the house. The whole estate is having ground sensors planted round the perimeter, and he's taken the old gatehouse as his 'command center.' Boxes and crates have been arriving all day. At this rate, we'll be bankrupt before the end of the week!"

"Kaid's arranged for the military to fund it," he said. "They can try out their new equipment here and protect us at the same time."

"He has been busy on our behalf," said Rhyasha dryly. "Does he consult with you first, or does he always use his own initiative and tell you later?"

Kusac hesitated. "Kaid's unique, Mother. He's always acted independently. It's his strength, and possibly his weakness. I do trust him implicitly, though."

"Hmpf! Well, try and break him of the habit. Your Physician will be here in a moment," she said as the low whine of the engines changed pitch. "Let's leave Carrie in peace for now."

*   *   *

"He's done what?" Esken couldn't believe what Khafsa was telling him.

"I have no proof it was the Clan Lord, Master Esken," said Khafsa. "Garras was recognized. He's Vanna Kyjishi's mate and they're both currently living on the Aldatan estate. It could be that Kusac Aldatan is behind this."

"Not likely, considering his father was here this morning and questioning me about them," said Esken grimly. "Thank you for telling me." He switched off his comm and turned to Sorli. "Damn Konis! The last thing I needed was him working against us! There's absolutely nothing I can do about this, and he knows it!"

"With respect, Master Esken, I did warn you against drugging Physician Kyjishi and the Human, Brynne Stevens. That's what's brought this to a head," said Sorli. "She's too close to Liegen Aldatan to have taken such action."

"What's done's done now," snapped Esken. "I've got to keep control of those mixed Leskas. When's the ship due in with Interpreter Zhyaf and his Human Leska?"

"It arrives at Chagda Station in two days, Master."

"Get in touch with Leader Ghezu at Stronghold and request an escort for them. I want them brought straight here."

"Yes, Master. Do you want them met at Chagda or at the spaceport?"

"Chagda. Let's not take any chances on Konis getting them first."

* * *

"Oh to have been there when Esken discovered they were missing!" chuckled Governor Nesul. "Yes, Konis, I'll provide you with the authorizations you need to house the anomalous Leskas at your son's estate." His mood changed, becoming serious. "We need to talk, Konis. Tonight."

"Of course, Governor," said Konis, frowning slightly. This was most unusual. "What time do you want me to arrive?"

"Not here. I'll come to you. Twentieth hour. No fuss, Konis. I don't want it known I'm coming."

"Very well, Governor. I'll see you at the twentieth hour." As Konis saw Nesul reach to turn off his comm, he remembered something. "Oh, ah . . . We have extra security on our estate now, Governor."

Nesul raised an eye ridge. "Fortuitous considering the situation," he said, then cut the connection.

Konis cleared his screen thoughtfully. The Governor, coming here for private talks? There was obviously more to this guild business than met the eye.

* * *

The door to Lijou's private study swung open. Ghezu stood framed in the doorway.

"We've got a problem," he said, shutting the door behind him.

Lijou blanked his comm screen with a sigh. He'd always found Ghezu difficult to work with, but lately he'd been worse. His lack of concern for anyone's privacy was one of his least appealing characteristics.

"What is it this time?" he asked tiredly, sitting back in his chair and folding his hands in his lap.

Ghezu gave an angry growl as he came farther into the room. "Don't trivialize me, Lijou. We're balanced on a knife edge at the moment. One wrong move and we could lose everything that Stronghold has worked toward for generations."

"I'm as aware of that, Ghezu, as you are. Now, tell me the nature of this particular problem."

"I've been requested by Valsgarth Telepath Guild to provide an escort for Interpreter Zhyaf and his Leska. They arrive at Chagda Station the day after tomorrow." He moved over to one of the chairs by Lijou's desk and sat down.

Lijou frowned. "Why do they want an escort from us? Usually the Warriors provide one in these circumstances."

"They want to be sure the pair arrive at their Valsgarth Guildhouse. I had to prise out of Sorli the information that they're afraid that Clan Lord Aldatan's people may get there before the Telepaths and take the Leskas directly to the Aldatan estate."

"Now why would they think that? Have you checked on the current rumors from the palace?"

"Naturally," said Ghezu. "What do you take me for?"

Lately, an idiot who can't control his temper and sees everything as a confrontation! Lijou thought, but repressed it hurriedly lest one of the Brothers pick it up.

"What did you find out?" *By Vartra, it's like pulling teeth from a krolla!*

"Governor Nesul has put the Clan Lord and AlRel in charge of the Mixed Leska program, and Esken isn't happy."

"Really?" Lijou sat forward, unclasping his hands and placing them on his desk. Out of sight of Ghezu, his tail flicked.

"That surprised you!" said Ghezu, leaning forward on the desk. "I don't mind telling you it surprised me, too. Seems our Governor has been looking for a way to curb Esken for some time."

"That's hardly news," said Lijou, dismissing it with a wave of his hand.

"There's more. It's rumored that the Clan Lord apparently spirited two Leska cubs out of their Guild medical center to his estate. Seems Konis Aldatan doesn't trust Master Esken either."

"Now that is extremely interesting! So both our Governor and the Clan Lord see the need to separate the new Leskas from Esken and the Telepath Guild."

"Events are moving faster than we predicted," said Ghezu. "Having AlRel in charge of the Leskas doesn't make life any easier for us." Absently, he picked up one of the carved blue-white crystal ornaments on Lijou's desk.

"They still need to belong to a guild," said Lijou thoughtfully, "and with them at the Aldatan estate, they'll be exposed to the influence of the Aldatan cub, Kusac, and kept out of Esken's way. That is definitely to our advantage."

Ghezu grunted noncommittally. "Maybe. We still haven't had a firm undertaking from him to join us yet."

"Then I'll have to pursue that, won't I? What do you plan to do about Esken's request?"

Ghezu put the crystal down and flexed his claws impatiently. "What can I do?" he asked. "If I refuse, what reason can I give? We've said we'll accept protective contracts for the mixed Leska pairs. But if I comply, we're taking them exactly where we don't want them to be."

"A dilemma indeed," said Lijou. "Perhaps in this case, the best course of action is to be direct. Contact Kaid and get him to confirm these rumors of the Clan Lord's appointment, and his . . . ah . . . acquisition of these cubs." He gave a low chuckle.

"What's so funny?" demanded Ghezu, picking the crystal up again and tapping it on the desk.

"The idea of our Clan Lord kidnapping anyone!" smiled Lijou.

"I fail to see the humor in it," said Ghezu testily.

"Ghezu, Ghezu," said Lijou, shaking his head in mock solemnity and reaching forward to take the ornament from him. "You mustn't be so serious. You should learn to see the inherent humor in most situations. You'll build your own funeral pyre at this rate." He placed the crystal flower in front of himself, out of Ghezu's reach.

"Fine. At least I'll get to choose where it'll be! So, I ask Kaid to confirm the rumors: what then, Master Planner?"

"What did you tell Sorli?"

"That I'd check my rosters and see who I have free."

Lijou leaned back again, steepling his fingertips together. *Why can't he see the obvious solution? Ghezu's slipping: this obsession with Kaid and Dzaka is beginning to make him lose his grip.*

"It occurs to me that if the rumors are true, and Clan Lord Aldatan is indeed in charge of the Mixed Leska Project, then you have no problem," he said.

Ghezu glared at him. "It's our problem, Lijou, not just mine! We both have the same goal here."

"As you say," said Lijou, flicking an ear in grudging agreement, at the same time castigating himself for once more baiting Ghezu. He knew he shouldn't, but the Brotherhood's temporal leader was so irritating that baiting Ghezu occasionally was all that kept him from really losing his temper.

"If the Clan Lord is really in charge," said Ghezu, realization dawning at last, "then I have to report this request to him and have it ratified."

Vartra be praised! Lijou thought irreverently. "Exactly."

"I'll just be unobtainable if Sorli calls back, and hopefully they'll assume we'll send the escort on their behalf."

"Which we will, but to deliver the Leskas to the Aldatan estate," finished Lijou.

Ghezu nodded, getting to his feet. "I'll contact Kaid now."

* * *

"Dr. Reynolds," said Kaid, inclining his head as the doctor emerged from the Stealth craft.

From the top of the ladder, Jack squinted down at the brown-furred Sholan. "Kaid? Yes, it is you. I'm still not very good at recognizing individuals, but I'm getting better."

Turning round, he carefully climbed down the vertical ladder.
It was with relief that he felt firm ground under his feet.

"It may be fast," he said, stretching his arms and back,
"but, by God, it's cramped!"

The copilot lowered a net containing the doctor's luggage.
Kaid gestured the house attendant who'd accompanied him
forward to catch it.

Before he turned to follow Kaid into the house, Jack raised
his hand in farewell, then took his medical case from the
attendant.

The doctor's gaze darted in every direction, taking in the
white and terra-cotta architecture of the house. "Quite palatial, isn't it?"

"It's old," said Kaid, leading him up the entrance stairs
into the inner cloistered courtyard. "One of the oldest estate
houses on this continent."

As they entered the hallway, the sight of the murals
stopped Jack in his tracks.

"They're superb," he said, gazing at the frescoes of Sholan
hunters. "Is the whole house decorated like that?"

"Some areas are," said Kaid, leading him on again.

The water from the fountain in the courtyard played across
the colored rocks, babbling merrily down into the pool. From
above came the sound of children's voices.

"Large family?"

Kaid looked at him, mouth open in amusement. "We have
quite recently added two cubs to the household," he said.
"They arrived today. They're a Leska pair about of an age
with my Liege's sister, Kitra."

"Are we going to see Carrie now? How is she?"

"The Clan Leader asked me to bring you to her kitchen
first. The Liegena is sleeping in the lounge and she doesn't
want to disturb her yet," said Kaid, leading him out of the
sunlight and down a long corridor. "As to how she is, Physician Kyjishi will tell you."

The door ahead of them opened and Kusac came out.
"Jack, thank the Gods you're here," he said, holding his hand
out to the Keissian Human. "I hope your journey wasn't too
uncomfortable?"

"I managed," Jack said, remembering as he briefly
touched fingertips with him that telepaths were uncomfortable if touched by anyone except close family or friends.

Kusac, however, would have none of it, and took Jack's

hand in both of his. "Thank you for coming," he said before releasing him. "I'm worried about her, Jack. Mother and Vanna think I'm overprotective, but I think they're forgetting that she's still a Human, too, no matter how Sholan she's become."

"We'll see, lad," said Jack, face creasing into a smile. "Between us, we'll soon have her up on her feet again."

"Come and have some coffee. Kaid's told you that you're staying here with us?"

"No, he hasn't mentioned that yet," said Jack, looking round for him. "Where's he gone off to?"

"Back to Carrie. We don't leave her alone," he said, leading him into the kitchen.

"Physician Reynolds," said Rhyasha, rising to greet him. "It was good of you to come so far at such short notice."

"Oh, it was nothing," said Jack, returning her finger-touch greeting. "D'you think I'd pass up an opportunity to visit your home world? There're more than enough doctors on Keiss to go round now, and they don't think much of the likes of me. Say I'm too parochial."

"It's their loss. Please, sit, and be well come to our home," she said, indicating a chair. "You remember Vanna, of course?"

"How could I forget a colleague?" he said, nodding in her direction, another broad grin splitting his bearded face. "I hope I'm not stepping on your toes, lass."

"Not at all, Jack," said Vanna. "In fact, I'm glad you're here. I need your advice on some other medical matters."

"With pleasure," he said, easing his slightly rotund frame onto the bench seat at the table.

Rhyasha placed a mug of coffee in front of him and gestured to a plate of cookies. "Please, help yourself. Third meal is a few hours away yet."

The other door opened and Konis came in. "Rhyasha, I've got an important meeting here tonight, I'm afraid . . ." His voice trailed off as he saw Jack.

"You must be Kusac's father," said Jack. "I can see the strong family resemblance."

"You're the Keissian physician who saved my son's life, aren't you? We are in your debt, Dr. Reynolds. I hope you enjoy your stay with us." He paused. "I'm sorry to appear rude, but could you excuse us a moment? Rhyasha," he said, turning to his wife and touching her on the shoulder to draw her attention. "I need to talk to you."

"Do excuse us," said Rhyasha, getting to her feet.

As they approached the door, it opened.

"Clan Lord, I'm sorry to interrupt," said Kaid, "but Leader Ghezu of the Brotherhood is on the comm. He needs to speak to you on a matter of some urgency."

"It's going to be one of those evenings," said Konis, ears flicking with annoyance. "Will you come with me anyway?" he asked Rhyasha. "Whatever he has to say to me can be heard by you."

"They're popular all of a sudden," said Vanna as the door closed behind them. "What do you bet it concerns the cubs, Jinoe and Rrai?"

"I don't think so," said Kusac, remembering what Kaid had said earlier—much earlier—that day. "I think that several different political factions have just realized our family holds the focus of power now. This is likely to be only the beginning."

"Sounds like I've arrived at an interesting time," said Jack, sipping his drink. "Any chance of filling in the details for me?"

Kusac's wrist comm buzzed. "What did I tell you?" he said.

"Liege," they heard Kaid's voice say. "There's a call for you from Ghyan at the temple."

"I'll take it upstairs. Patch it through for me, please," he said, rising. "Sorry about this. I'll only be a few minutes."

Left alone with Vanna, Jack looked across the table at her. "Well, now, how about telling me how Carrie is? That's why I'm here, after all."

"Jack, how long can you stay?" she asked. "I mean, what are your current orders?"

"I'm not in the military, lass, I'm very definitely a civilian. What is it you have in mind? This has to do with more than just Carrie, doesn't it?"

She flicked her ears in assent. "Apart from any other considerations, it'll be easier to carry on our research for a common contraceptive for the Leska pairs if we're both working in the same lab, not strung out across light-years of space."

"I'd be delighted to stay longer, but I don't want to impose on the hospitality of this good family."

"If I can sort out the accommodation side, could you stay indefinitely? I need someone with your experience and knowledge of Humans to help me. The number of anomalous Links is increasing, and shortly, I'll be unable to cope with the workload alone." She looked down at the table, not wishing to meet his gaze. "Also I'm pregnant by my Human Leska, and I'd like you to deliver my child. For various reasons, I don't trust anyone else to do it."

Jack looked at her in surprise. "I'd be honored my dear, but . . ."

"I'll explain it all later, Jack, I promise," Vanna interrupted, looking up again though still not meeting his eyes. Before he could say anything further, she said hastily, "I think we should go and look at Carrie now."

"Certainly, my dear," he said. "Kaid told me you think Kusac's being overprotective, so what is it that's got him and Kusac worried?"

"I don't know what's got Kaid worried, but Kusac's being overanxious, as would any male of his youth in these circumstances," she said, getting up and leading the way out.

* * *

"Ghyan," said Kusac, "this is a surprise, but a welcome one. What can I do for you?"

"Can you come over to the temple tonight?"

"Tonight? Why?" He wrinkled his nose in surprise. "Is something wrong?"

"No, nothing like that," his friend assured him. "One of the senior temple officials has asked me to contact you. There's a matter he needs to discuss with you."

"With me? Who is it?" Kusac was puzzled. He knew of no reason for the Priesthood of Vartra to contact him. Surely his plans to take the Fire Margins ritual weren't already known?

"I can't say more, Kusac. It is important. Can I expect you at the eighteenth hour?"

"Ah . . . Yes, I suppose so," he said reluctantly. "Are you sure there's nothing wrong?"

Ghyan opened his mouth in a faint smile. "I'm sure," he said. "How's your life-mate? She looked so tiny and frail at the funeral. I'm concerned for her."

Kusac's ears flicked back in worry. "Her wounds are

healing, but not her spirit. She's growing mentally distant from me, Ghyan. Even Kaid's concerned about her."

"Kaid?" Ghyan was obviously startled.

"Yes, Kaid. What's so strange about that?" frowned Kusac.

"Nothing. I just wouldn't have expected him to be so sensitive to her condition," his friend reassured him.

"How do you know him?"

"Vartra's Priesthood is ruled from Stronghold by Father Lijou, Kusac," said Ghyan.

"So it is," said Kusac thoughtfully. "One tends to forget that." So Kaid and Ghyan had had dealings with each other, had they? "Very well, I'll be there," he said. "Until then."

"Till then," echoed Ghyan.

Kusac decided this time he had to talk to his father. He still hadn't had a chance to tell him what had happened at Stronghold that morning—both of them had been so busy— and his father really should have been informed. Maybe he'd be free now.

Checking with Vanna on his way downstairs, he was told to stay away from Carrie until after she and Jack had examined her. Sighing, he continued on to his father's study.

He knocked on the door and waited. His mother answered, opening the door only a crack.

Not now, she sent. *This is too important to interrupt. Later.* Her fingers brushed his check, then she was gone and the door was closed again.

Frustrated, he headed back to the kitchen. Kaid was there. He looked up as Kusac entered.

"T'Chebbi's watching her," he said. "Physician Reynolds and Physician Kyjishi are with her."

Kusac regarded him speculatively for a moment, then, picking up his empty mug, went over to the hot plate to refill it.

"We're going out tonight, Kaid. At the eighteenth hour," he said, resuming his seat at the table.

"Where?"

"The temple," he said, watching him carefully over the top of his mug as he took a drink from it. "Ghyan has been asked by one of the senior priests to arrange a meeting with me."

"It'll be with Lijou," said Kaid, pulling his stim-twig out of his pocket. "I've just been talking to Ghezu. He wanted confirmation that your father was heading the Mixed Leska

Project and that the two cubs from the Telepath Guild were here."

"Why would he need to know that?"

"Esken's requested an escort for Interpreter Zhyaf and his Leska. He wants to be sure they reach his Guild. Ghezu's discussing this with your father now."

Kusac nodded, then glanced across at the timepiece on the wall. "Vanna and Jack have been in with Carrie for quite a while. What's taking so long?"

"It's her first contact with the life that she had on Keiss in a long time, Liege," said Kaid. "She must have missed him. Can't you sense what's happening?"

"Not really. It's confused," he said, putting his mug down. "I don't like this, Kaid. It's as if we're losing everything we had." He got to his feet, beginning to pace, tail flicking from side to side in agitation. He could feel her sudden distress. Ears flicking flat and sideways, he headed for the door only to find Kaid there before him, barring his way.

"Let me pass," he said, trying to move the older male aside. "She's upset. She needs me."

"No. Let her be upset with him. He's the nearest thing she has to her own Human family," he said, refusing to move. "If she really needs you, you'll know. Now sit down and wait till they're done."

"By Vartra's fire, Kaid . . . !" he began angrily.

"Dammit, Kusac! Stop acting like a youngling! You're only a year from adulthood, you should be able to control your pheromone responses to her. You're going to be the Clan Leader of a new clan, you can't keep overreacting like this! You don't have to prove anything to her—she knows how well you can look after her, she knows you'll be a good father to her cubs, and you know you don't have any rivals for her. So, in the name of Vartra, calm down!"

Blinking in surprise, Kusac took a step backward. He'd never seen Kaid so agitated before, and no one had spoken to him like that for a long time. He took a deep breath, forcing his heart rate down and trying to release the tension from his body. Kaid was right. He wasn't thinking straight. If she'd really needed him, she'd have sent. She was probably telling Jack about their cub. That was good, she needed to speak to another of her kind about their lost daughter. He pushed aside the grief that threatened to sweep through him, too.

This was no time to think of himself. Carrie was the important one.

"If she can speak to Physician Reynolds about your cub, then that's to the good. She was terrified that Humans would react badly to the news of her pregnancy, so the fact that she can talk to Jack about it shows she's beginning to mend," said Kaid quietly. "They shouldn't be much longer now."

Kusac nodded slowly, ears beginning to rise again as he turned and walked back to the table.

"I think you and Carrie would both benefit by learning our mental exercises," said Kaid, keeping an eye on him as he sat down again. "It's how we control not only our gifts but our bodies. We learn litanies to help to focus the mind in times of crisis. In fact, all of you could benefit from them. Why don't you ask Ghyan to visit you here daily and teach you?"

"Is it like the meditation Dzaka was teaching Carrie on the *Khalossa?*"

"Yes, the same. Ghyan knows it too and he teaches it at the temple. We've long thought that all telepaths could benefit from adopting some of our training methods. Those we recruited certainly became more stable once we'd taught them to meditate." He paused as a thought struck him. "You were helping Sorli put together a schedule for training the new mixed Leska pairs, so why not learn our methods and incorporate some of them in that program?"

"I have to admit I've never met anyone with such effective self-control as you," said Kusac. "It's almost impossible to read your body, let alone your mind."

"Oh, I have my less controlled moments like anyone else," said Kaid with a faint smile. "At least give our exercises a try. They were very effective for Carrie."

Kusac flicked his ears in assent. "Why bother Ghyan when Dzaka's here already?" he asked, watching for Kaid's response.

"Of course, if that's what you wish," said Kaid, looking down at his mug. "You and Carrie as well as the cubs could work with him, but I doubt either Vanna or Brynne will have anything to do with him now."

"Why the animosity between you two?"

"I wouldn't call it animosity," said Kaid, taking a drink.

"I would."

Kaid shrugged. "It's personal."

"I think as your Liege, I'm entitled to an answer," said

Kusac softly. "Anything that could affect your relationship with the people working here is my concern."

There was a long silence. Kusac kept his eyes on his aide's averted face. At last Kaid sighed and nodded.

"When I had to leave the Brotherhood ten years ago, he wanted to come with me," he said reluctantly. "I wouldn't let him and he still resents it, that's all."

Kusac frowned. "Why should your leaving affect him? I don't see the connection."

Kaid said nothing as he swirled the dregs of his drink around the bottom of his mug.

"Why should your leaving affect him?" Kusac repeated patiently.

"He's my foster-son," said Kaid very quietly.

"He's what?" Kusac was stunned. "How did that happen?"

"He was found abandoned outside Stronghold's gates. Occasionally the Brotherhood will admit cubs, though they aren't usually left on our doorstep in the depths of winter. I agreed to bring him up, that's all," he said, looking up at Kusac as he raised the mug to his mouth and drained it.

"That's why you were so angry when he took Vanna to Stronghold."

"I treat him no differently from anyone else."

"I didn't say you did," said Kusac.

Kaid changed the subject. "Lijou will want to see you tonight to extract a firm commitment from you to join the Brotherhood. He'll also want you to go to the All Guilds Council meeting to back their application for full guild status." His ears cocked forward quizzically. "What do you intend to tell him?"

"What we discussed earlier."

"I wouldn't mention the Fire Margins ritual yet. The fewer that know, the better."

The kitchen door opened and Jack, followed by Vanna, came in.

Kusac's attention switched immediately to them. "How is Carrie? What's wrong with her?" he demanded, half rising, torn between wanting to hear what they had to say and rejoining her in the lounge.

"Physically, she's healing well," said Jack. "But psychologically . . . You and Kaid were right about that. We think that the depression she's suffering is caused by a hormonal imbalance. Her body's still manufacturing all the hormones that tell her she's pregnant, when of course she knows she isn't." Jack sat down. "Vanna and I have been studying the hormones not only of Humans and Sholans, but of the mixed Leska pairs, too. The end result we hope will be a contraceptive for the Leska females of both species so they can have a choice whether or not they conceive—and help people in Carrie's situation." He stopped, aware Kusac's parents had returned and were listening.

"Go on, Physician Reynolds," said Rhyasha.

"There isn't much more to add," said Vanna. "We're still only correlating data at this point."

"This depression she's suffering, do our females suffer from it also?"

"Not as badly as we Humans do," said Jack. "At the moment, all we can do is try and keep her spirits up and get her interested in something—anything—other than her loss."

"Is this life-threatening?" demanded Kusac.

"Not of itself, but it can lead to a sense of desperation where the patient can become mentally unstable and harm herself."

"I was concerned about the state of her mind before the Challenge," said Konis.

"It's going to take a lot of patience and care to nurse her through this because I doubt we'll have anything ready to use on her for quite some time."

"Could putting your data through a larger comm unit speed up the process of correlation?" asked Konis. "Because if it would, the one in my study accesses the main government one. I can get permission for you to run your data through it from here."

"That would help, certainly," said Vanna, looking more hopeful.

"Clan Leader, if I might make a suggestion?"

"What is it, Kaid?" Rhyasha replied.

"There's a Healer in the village nearest to Stronghold. She's good. Send for her."

"I didn't know any Healers lived outside the Telepath guildhouses," said Konis in surprise.

"She isn't a recognized Healer," said Kaid.

"Recognized or not, it won't do any good," said Vanna. "We tried Healers on both of you during the Guild tests. They were unable to tune in to either of your minds in order to work."

"She'll be able to."

"What could happen if we have to wait for Carrie to improve on her own?" asked Kusac.

"It's not a question of what could happen," said Jack uncomfortably. "It's just not predictable."

"If she continues to cut herself off from me, she'll die," said Kusac flatly. "It would put both our lives at risk and I'm not chancing that. I know to my cost just how strong her mind is. Send for the Healer now."

Kaid looked at Rhyasha. She nodded briefly. "Have her brought here."

"Rhyasha, she's an unregistered Healer," objected Konis.

"Who's going to know?" she asked, her voice rising in exasperation. "Look around you, Konis. In the last few days, my home has become a high security enclosure housing armed guards, members of the Brotherhood, a Keissian Human and two kidnapped kitlings. My son has an alien Leska as his life-mate, she's just miscarried my first grandchild, and our main adviser is a renegade Brother! What difference could one unregistered Healer make?" Her ears flicked back as she got to her feet, planting her hands on the table and surveying them all.

"Send for the Healer, Kaid. Konis, you take Physician Reynolds to my office, I'll be along shortly. Vanna, you need to sort out if Brynne needs to be moved out here for his own safety before you join us. Kusac, you go and see to Carrie. I'm going to organize Choa and the third meal!" She stopped. "Who's feeding all our security staff?" she demanded of Kaid.

"The military are paying for our security, including maintenance of all their personnel, Clan Leader. They're completely self-contained. They even have their own caterer at the gatehouse."

"The Gods be praised!" Rhyasha said, turning her back on them and heading for the inner kitchen area. "Something in all this mess that isn't my problem!"

* * *

Dawn was approaching, but not fast enough for the two desert males chosen to watch the priest. They shivered, drawing their cloaks tighter about themselves. On the cold stony ground, wearing nothing but his pelt, the priest began to move again: small, jerky movements accompanied by a repetitive low whining.

The younger one looked nervously at his companion. "How much longer will it take?" he whispered.

Leaning forward from his sitting position on the higher rocks, the other squinted through the blue predawn light at the outline of the priest below. "As long as it takes, lad," he growled. "First time you've sat in on a vigil?"

L'Seuli nodded. "I've just been released from service in the Forces."

"It's not so bad. He's been out since dusk, so it shouldn't be much longer now," said Rrurto.

"How can he survive this cold? He's got nothing, no clothes to protect him." He shivered again.

"He's the Sun God's prophet, that's how, lad. The fire of the sun burns inside him, protecting and warming him."

"Is he really Kezule's prophet?" L'Seuli asked after a long silence.

The older one's head whipped round sharply, but not as fast as the blow with which he hit L'Seuli across the head. He went spinning from his perch on the rocks, down the decline to where the priest lay. Rrurto watched, waiting while the lad picked himself up, scuttling away from the priest before climbing back up to his post.

"The next time you ask that could be your last," he said. "You don't question the Word of Kezule. Had I been one of the Faithful, my claws would have left you permanently scarred, perhaps blinded for life. Watch your tongue, lad." Rrurto's tone was not unkind.

"I'm sorry," L'Seuli muttered, picking up his fallen head cloth and rewinding it. This time, instead of wrapping the loose end round his neck for warmth, he tucked it up under the headband, letting the chill air cool the heated side of his face.

Movements from the priest drew their attention.

"He's not in our world, lad," said Rrurto. "When he's like this, he's walking with the Gods and demons. It's them he sees, not us."

"The Gods be praised," L'Seuli said fervently.

"Praise Kezule," corrected the other, turning eyes glittering like stones in the cold half-light toward him. "There is only one God—Kezule—and his Prophet lies before us. Remember that, and you might live long enough to sire cubs.

It's all changed now, and the Faithful don't allow you a second chance. He's prophesied the return of the Cataclysm," he said, nodding toward the priest, "unless we stop worshiping the false Gods and live the way Kezule says we should."

"The demons! The demons brought their fire raining down on us because of the mind-poisoners! They must die with the demons!" the prophet howled, his voice gathering strength as he leaped to his feet, shaking his fists at the lightening sky.

"Kezule will punish you! All disbelievers will be destroyed by His Holy fire! See! Even now He sends it to cleanse the world anew! The demons will return because of the mind-poisoners, the disbelievers! They'll return to kill again! Kezule, protect us who serve You faithfully!"

As the sun rose over the dunes, the priest collapsed, his body falling to the ground.

The watchers continued to wait as the sun rose higher in the sky, its light banishing all night's shadows.

"He'll have to come round soon," growled the older male. "The aircars fly over here looking for us. We need to get below again."

"What do we do with the prophet? Do we wake him?"

"The God's always wakened him in time before," Rrurto replied, his voice concerned as he shifted his position on the now uncomfortably hot rocks. He squinted up at the sky. "It's later than usual. Maybe we should fetch one of his Faithful."

"The ones dressed in yellow? Should I go for them?" L'Seuli half rose in anticipation of the answer.

"Wait, he's moving," said Rrurto, grasping him by the arm and pointing to the prophet.

Down on the baking rocks below the watchers, the prophet stirred, lifting his head and looking myopically up at the sun. Momentarily, it dazzled him. At his throat, the green stone set in its collar of gold glinted. He blinked his eyes several times, washing away the rime of sand with his tears.

Pushing himself up, he felt the heat in the stones beneath him for the first time. He'd been gone longer than usual. No matter, the God had spoken to him, he had His message for the people.

Shakily he got to his feet, looking round for his watchers. They were already making their way down the decline toward him. The broad gold band that circled his wrist was paining him. Easing it upward, he rubbed away the grit that had gotten underneath it and waited.

He was handed his robe first, then, when he'd wrapped himself against the heat of the day, they gave him the water. He drank deeply, letting it run down his sore and parched throat. His walks with the God tired him more each time but what he saw, what he heard! That made up for it. He alone could tell his followers what the God had shown him.

He handed the empty skin back.

"We must go in now," he said. His voice had returned to the usual deep tone that captivated his listeners. "It's time for the Word of Kezule to speak to His people."

He turned and strode through the sand toward the nearby outcrop of rock. There, hidden from the casual gaze, was the entrance to their lair.

The watchers followed, each wrapped in his own thoughts.

Chapter 4

From her chair in the shade of the nung tree, Rhuna looked him up then down. Kaid towered above her. Though his brown eyes regarded her calmly, knowing him as she did, the set of his ears betrayed his uneasiness in her presence. Hair of a darker brown than his pelt was swept back between his wide ears, falling in graduated lengths, blending with the hair at the sides of his neck till it reached his shoulders.

Under his utilitarian sleeveless jacket, a short tunic, bordered with black, covered his torso. Below it, the well-muscled thighs testified to the fact that he'd kept in shape over the past ten years.

She grunted and looked back to his face. "So you're wearing the Aldatan colors now," she said. "What is it this time, Tallinu? Haven't you stopped hiding from yourself yet, eh? Still ashamed of your past?"

"You know I don't call myself that any more, Noni," he said. "I've not come on a personal matter."

She snorted, extending her right index claw and tapping it on the arm of her wooden chair. "You never do. At least you still have the manners to come in person, unlike some of the other mountain Brothers, but not to drop those barriers." Her eyes narrowed, the ridges meeting on her brow. "Female troubles again? What happened this time?"

He frowned, weighing in his mind whether it was worth arguing with her.

"It concerns a female," he said at last, his tone short, "but not me."

She snorted again, and with a flick of her ears, gestured with her hand to the lawn beside her. "Sit, sit. You're giving me a crick in the neck looking all that way up at you," she grumbled.

He sat, and she felt his uneasiness build until he took out a stim-twig.

"So she's with somebody else, is she? When will you learn, Tallinu? Go find a female of your own. It's about time you did!"

"I don't want or need one, Noni," he said defensively.

Rhuna gave a low rumble of laughter. "Sure you don't! You're not really chewing that stim-twig, are you? It's just something to hold, isn't it? You forget I know you too well! Now, who is she and what's wrong?"

As he began to collect his thoughts, slowly a realization of the situation started to build for her. Round the arms of her chair, her hands tightened until the knuckles showed white through her fur and her claws had sunk into the wood.

"Tallinu, do you realize what you've done? You've let her touch you—change you!" Her voice was low, vibrating from deep down in her chest. As she looked at him, flames seemed to flicker around and across his body. Beside him were shadow-shapes, two of them, their forms seeming to dance in the golden-red flames. A low sound, halfway between a moan and a howl, escaped her. She could almost feel the heat of those flames, hear them crackling—then her vision began to fade.

"In Vartra's name, Tallinu, why her? Why choose her?" she moaned as her eyes once more focused on the male sitting at her feet. "Their fire could destroy you! Have you any idea what you've gotten involved in?" she demanded, her voice growing stronger. "Vartra's bones, boy! What possesses you these days?"

Kaid's nose creased in worry. "Noni, I don't know what you're talking about! What did you see?" he demanded. His tail began to flick rhythmically.

She peered at his face, beginning to nod her head slowly. "So you haven't realized the full extent of it yet. You will," she said, ears swiveling round to face him.

"Noni, what did you see?" he asked again, his voice reflecting his urgent need to know what the future had shown her.

"It's the Aldatan cub's Human Leska, isn't it?" she said abruptly, hoping to divert him. "I heard she'd been hurt."

Kaid sat back on his haunches. "You don't know the half of it," he said. "She lost her cub—a Sholan cub. I need your help for her."

"They've been touched by Vartra," she whispered. "She's been singled out by the God. You want me to heal her?"

"I *need* you to heal her," he corrected. "Will you come

with me to Valsgarth? She's slipping into death, Noni. She barely eats—spends her time sleeping ... We could lose both her and her life-mate."

"I don't leave home, you know that," she said, sitting back in her chair. "Bring her to me."

Kaid looked up at her, ears flicking. "I can't. She's too weak to travel."

"Then I'll not see her," she said with finality .

"Noni, Grandmother—you must," he said, leaning toward her again.

"Must, Tallinu? There's no must about it! I will not leave here to enter the telepath town!" She pushed him back with her foot. "Bring her to me—without her Leska."

Kaid got to his feet and began to pace round the small garden, tail flicking every now and then.

Rhuna watched him, narrowing her eyes against the sun. Her head moved in a tiny nod of approval. Good, his control was slipping. Now she would learn more.

He rounded on her. "I can't bring her, he'd never allow it—especially not without him there! I thought since you know what's at stake, that you'd come," he said. "If we let them die, it could disrupt our treaties with Keiss and Earth."

"That's not what you fear most."

"There's the God! You said she's been touched by Vartra. We have to help her!"

"There's that, of course," she agreed.

"Dammit, Rhuna! What more can I say?" he demanded angrily, stopping in front of her.

"Whose cub was it, Tallinu?" she asked, head cocked to one side. "Who was the father? Was it you?"

He went rigid with shock, mouth gaping, ears tilting backward.

Not his, then, she thought with satisfaction. *Not his. But I touched a nerve there!* The growl came from low in his throat as his ears involuntarily flattened sideways. His pupils dilated and his lips pulled back in a snarl of pure rage. Then he was gone.

Rhuna sat there, waiting, watching, as the sun slowly began to sink lower behind her tree, casting dappled patterns of shade across the green robe she wore. The insects chirred louder as the day grew cooler. An attendant came to ask if she required anything, but she waved him away, telling him to go home for the night. *Tallinu will be back, it's just a matter of time,* she thought as she nodded off.

She sensed him return but continued to feign sleep till he spoke.

"I'll ask, Noni." His voice was barely audible.

"She needs to come here, Tallinu. I won't go to her," she said, opening her eyes to look at him. He was sitting on his haunches in front of her again. "Bring her here alone. Just the two of you."

He looked away, unwilling to meet her gaze.

Rhuna gave a rumbling laugh. "What's wrong, boy? Looked into one too many of the dark corners of your soul? About time some sunlight got in there! You can't face the truth? Have you begun to realize some of what's happening to you?"

"The God knows I didn't choose it, Noni! What do you think I am? A fool? I'm not the same person who came to see you about a female all those years ago." He turned his head back round to face her. "Yes, I was young, and fool enough then to think I could have something in my life that was normal. How was I to know?"

His eyes closed in anguish at the memory. She could feel it, the waves of shock and regret—and a deep fear of it ever happening again—whatever *it* had been!

"How was I to know?" he whispered. "No, I daren't touch her, Noni, nor would I if I could. She's my Liege's bonded life-mate. The child was his, not mine. How could you think otherwise?"

"I had to know," she said simply. "There is a bond between you, I can feel it. I need to know its nature."

"It's not just me," he said, taking a deep breath. "It's Garras, too, though it was slightly different for him. It was his female who found a Human Leska. What's happening, Noni? What are these Humans doing to us?"

She didn't need eyes to know the confusion he felt and the plea for help that was written on his face.

"Is Vartra just playing with us? Are we no more than His toys, an experiment He'll toss aside?" he asked, and she knew he voiced one of his deepest fears.

"Bring her to me," she said, pronouncing each word slowly. "Life goes in threes, Tallinu. It's no mistake you're all linked. I was told by my grandmother, and she by hers before, that long ago—after the Cataclysm, after the time of fire—things were thus. There was always someone to guard them, to be with them—as one of them." The images she'd been shown as a girl began to come to her mind, replaying themselves, putting a faint overlay of shapes between her and Kaid.

"Most often it was two males and one female," she said. "A Triad for mutual protection. The Telepaths and the Warrior—linked."

The shapes wavered then were gone as the memories of the images given to her all those years ago also faded. She blinked, refocusing on the here and now again.

"Go and fetch her," she said, pushing herself up stiffly from her chair. "There isn't much time left. I'll be ready when you return."

"What if Kusac wants to come?" he asked, on his feet almost instantly to help her.

He was pushed firmly away. "Leave me alone, Tallinu, I can manage! I'm not in my dotage yet," she snapped as she turned toward the house. "You'll have to convince him to stay, won't you?" She laughed, a low rumble of malicious glee. "Call it the ultimate test of his trust in you. Why not? You're doing the same to Dzaka! Now go! I need time to prepare for her."

"Vanna says moving her won't do any harm," Kaid said, distinctly uncomfortable as he watched Kusac pace round the ornamental garden.

"She's not going without me," Kusac said.

"Then Noni won't see her. I have to take her alone."

"Noni? Is she your grandmother?" demanded Kusac. "Why can't I go with her? Why does she need to see her alone?"

"She's not my grandmother, that's just what we call her," said Kaid, trying not to let his exasperation show. "Liege, you trust me to guard her, surely you can trust me to take her to the Healer."

Kusac frowned. "Of course I trust you. It isn't a matter of trust!"

"Then what is it, Liege? Tell me, because we're wasting time!"

"I want to be there!" said Kusac, stopping in front of him. "If anything goes wrong, I *have* to be with her. If she dies, so do I. I *need* to be there—to die with her if that's what has to happen! Can you guarantee that she won't die there, alone, without me? Can you guarantee that won't happen?"

"You know I can't, but it won't and we both know that," he said quietly. "What's more important, Liege? Carrie, or your need to be with her?"

Kusac's internal struggle was visible on his face, and took no talent at all to read. He was torn between what was best for Carrie and his natural desire to be with her.

"Take her then," he said finally, ears flicking with distress at being placed in such a situation. "Remember, you'll have both our lives in your hands."

Kaid crossed his forearms over his chest and bowed, hiding his relief. "Thank you, Liege. I know the level of trust you're placing in me. I'll contact you as soon as I have news."

"I know you will," Kusac sighed. "I'll take T'Chebbi with me when I go to meet Lijou at the temple," he said, changing the subject.

They walked back through the garden to the lounge. Kaid watched as Kusac went over to the daybed to pick Carrie up. Vividly, the memory of the last time he'd seen her lying limply in someone's arms came to him. He'd been in the corridor on the *Khalossa,* watching as Askad, Rhian, and Vanna rushed her to Kusac's room, trying to save both their lives. Now here they were again.

"Have you got an aircar ready?" Kusac asked, then answered himself. "Of course you have. You don't leave anything to chance if you can avoid it, do you?"

"I try not to, Liege," he replied, following them out into the hallway.

Kusac stopped, turning round to look at him. "Kaid, please stop insisting on calling me Liege. In Vartra's name, don't be so formal! I need to know that you'll act for me as a friend, not an employee. I'd feel better if you'd call me Kusac like everyone else does."

Kaid nodded slowly. "Very well, Kusac, but not in public. Then you must be my Liege."

Kusac started walking again. "Public doesn't include my family and our friends, Kaid."

"If that's what you wish," he agreed, following Kusac into the gathering darkness.

In the aircar, he waited while Kusac placed Carrie on the

stretcher bed, then stepped forward to fasten the safety straps, double-checking that none of them rubbed against her.

She hadn't stirred, remaining deeply asleep. Kusac bent to caress her cheek, laying his face alongside hers, then straightened up to look at Kaid.

"Take care of her," he said.

"*This* is the Human female?" said Rhuna, looking down at the bed where Kaid had laid her. "*This* tiny being?" She snorted as she moved her chair beside the bed. "You might at least have chosen a full grown one!"

"She's full grown enough to have lost a cub," Kaid growled. "And I didn't choose her. There's nothing between us."

She glanced up at him as she sat down. "You'll have to face your fears soon, Tallinu. If you don't, they'll continue to control you. Now go and light that incense and the candles so I can begin. We've lost enough time already." She turned away from him and took an egg-shaped crystal from her pocket.

While Kaid busied himself doing her bidding, Rhuna took hold of Carrie's hand. Instantly she was aware of the Link to Kusac and with a tart thought in his direction, she cut him out, isolating the three of them from him. She smiled slightly to herself. For all his mental strength and ability, he wouldn't be able to break her shielding because it didn't respond to brute force. The more he tried, the more insubstantial it would seem to him.

She relaxed, letting her mind roam alongside the Human female's, finding it surprisingly close in feel to her own people's. Gradually she felt herself matching the girl's rhythms, minds and hearts beating together as one.

Tallinu had been almost right; she was asleep, but it was deeper than was normal—more a retreat from the world. Rhuna could feel the hurt and guilt caused by her cub's death, but there was more. She frowned, releasing Carrie's hand to touch her face instead. Vague images were there, drifting like smoke on the wind.

Rhuna tried to grasp one, but it eluded her, dissipating as if it had never been. With a mental shrug, she returned to where the sleeping Carrie was hiding from the world and began to gently insinuate herself into the Human girl's thoughts.

Carefully and slowly she worked, healing first the mental

pain caused by Carrie's fear of her half-Sholan, half-Human child. That done, she began on Carrie's self-imposed guilt, rebuilding her shattered confidence, assuring her that neither she nor Kusac had been responsible for their cub's death.

It seemed to take an age, and Rhuna had to wryly admit to herself that she wasn't as young as she used to be, but finally it was over and Carrie lay sleeping normally.

She sat back in her chair, eyes closed, her hands holding the warm crystal in her lap. "I should have used the damned dampers," she muttered to herself.

"Noni, your drink," said Kaid quietly, holding out a glass of water for her.

Her eyes flicked open and as she took the glass from him, she tossed the crystal at him. Automatically, his Warrior's reactions made him reach up and catch it. She watched in satisfaction as he yelped, almost dropping it.

"Hot, isn't it, Tallinu?" She gave a short hiss of laughter before taking a long drink. "Get a damp cloth and wipe her face and hands. It was tiring for her, too, poor little thing. It's been a long time since I needed to work as hard as that."

"Your crystal," he said, holding the now cool gemstone out to her.

"Keep it," she said abruptly. "Since you can't have her yet, have it."

Kaid frowned. "I don't need . . ."

"Go and get the cloth!" Rhuna snapped, taking another drink.

Pocketing the crystal, Kaid went to the bathing room and came back with a damp towel. He bent over Carrie, gently wiping the sweat from her face before lifting her hands one at a time. Finished, he looked up at Rhuna.

"Did you succeed?"

"What d'you think I am, Tallinu? An amateur?" she frowned at him. "Of course I succeeded! Her wounds I didn't do too much for because it was more important to heal her mind, but they should heal faster now."

"Thank you, Noni," he said. "I'd better contact Kusac. He's been trying to reach me for the past two hours."

"That long, huh? Ah, well. She's the first alien I've worked on. Go and tell him she's sleeping and you'll return her in the morning. When you come back, put the damper on. I'm keeping her mind shielded from him tonight."

"He won't like that."

"Doubtless," she said dryly, "but it isn't up to him, is it? When you've finished, we'll eat."

While he was outside at the aircar making his call, she got to her feet, moving stiffly across to the light sensor. She was blowing out the candles when he returned.

"There's stew on the stove and bread in the pantry," she said, sitting down at the table. "Once you've brought it over you can either eat first or wake the girl. She's slept enough, she needs to eat now."

"I'll wake her first," he said, tail flicking as he headed for the pantry.

Gradually the sounds resolved themselves into voices and she realized she was awake. Automatically, she reached for Kusac and found nothing. Her eyes flew open and she pushed herself up on her good arm, looking around in fear. Then she saw Kaid standing at the foot of the bed.

"Where am I? What's happened to Kusac?" she demanded, a distant part of her mind noticing how weak her voice sounded.

"Everything's fine," Kaid said. "You were ill so I brought you to a Healer. Kusac knows all about it. He's back at the estate waiting for you. Noni wants to keep you here overnight. I'll take you back in the morning."

"Noni?" she asked as Kaid came round and helped her sit up.

"That's me, young Human," said a voice from the other side of the room.

Kaid stood aside so Carrie could see her.

Sitting at the table had to be the oldest Sholan Carrie had ever seen. The iron-gray pelt was still flecked with its original brown, but the hair, worn in a single thick plait, was snow-white in color.

"Hmpf! I'm not that old, child," Rhuna growled.

"I beg your pardon," Carrie stammered, schooling her thoughts and her expression as she realized she'd been broadcasting. "Where am I?"

"In my home," said Rhuna, turning back to the stew pot to ladle out three bowlfuls. "You may call me Noni. Tallinu, give her her stew. It's time she ate. No male likes a female who resembles a skeleton, child." She held one of the bowls out to him.

Carrie watched Kaid go over to the table to collect her

meal. The rich aroma of the cooked meat drifted up to her as
he returned with it and held it out to her.

"Eat," said Noni, waving her spoon in Carrie's direction.
"I've done all I can for you, it's up to you now."

Her stomach growled with hunger as Kaid sat on the bed
beside her.

He handed her the spoon. "I'll hold the bowl," he said.

She nodded her thanks, dipping the spoon into the thick
meaty gravy, then putting it in her mouth. "Where's here?"
she asked around her mouthful.

"A village near Stronghold, in the Dzahai Mountains," he
said. "How do you feel?"

"Hungry," she said, shoveling in another spoonful. "In
what way was I ill?"

"We couldn't get you to wake or eat," said Kaid.

"You started to sleep yourself away, child," interrupted
Rhuna. "You'll have more cubs, never fear. That one was
never meant to be. Ask Tallinu. He knows."

Carrie looked at Kaid, a wary expression on her face.
"You told me before you knew I'd lose the baby."

His ears flicked in irritation. "I hoped you wouldn't lose
her," he said.

"But you thought I would. You said you'd had a vision."

Rhuna gave a low laugh. "Go on, Tallinu. Tell her. I want
to hear it, too!"

He shrugged. "I had a God-Vision," he said. "It was enigmatic, as they all are. It's only when I see events happening
that I know they're part of the vision."

"You could have warned me!"

"What could I have said? I only knew it was likely your
cub wouldn't survive, not how she would die."

Unusually, she could feel something of his distress at
being put on the spot like this.

"Don't blame him, child," said Rhuna suddenly. "Visions
can confuse more than inform you. Eat your stew, then sleep.
Tomorrow Tallinu will take you home."

Carrie looked from one to the other. Kaid's mind was once
again as still as usual, and Noni met hers with an amused
tone to it.

Eat, the old female sent to her.

Noni had turned in as soon as they'd finished eating. She
was sleeping in the guest room, leaving Carrie her bed in the

living room. Kaid had made her comfortable, then wrapped himself in a couple of blankets and lay down on the settee. The light had been left at a dim glow for her.

Carrie's sleep was restless and troubled. Gradually the gray mists that seemed to dominate her dreams these days parted and dissolved to reveal a stone hallway.

The faint noise she could hear resolved itself into a knocking at the door. As she watched, someone rushed forward to open it a crack, letting in the three figures that waited outside.

She strained to see who they were but the hallway was too dimly lit for her to see clearly. One was female, she realized as she saw a flash of amber eyes framed by a mass of thin beaded braids. The female moved forward, the beads in her hair chiming as she passed out of sight.

Her attention was drawn to the second figure—a tall, dark male who seemed somehow familiar. The light guttered as the wind from outside blew the candle flames.

"Shut the door! We don't want to advertise ourselves," said the younger male who brought up the rear.

"You got here safely?" the one who met them asked of his tall visitor. "We heard shooting."

"We're here, aren't we?"

"Patience, Rezac," said the tall one to him. "They're merely concerned. We got caught on the edges of a skirmish down in the valley."

"Did you bring the data?" The question was asked urgently as the group turned to walk along the echoing stone corridor.

"We brought it, and the training schedule we've worked out," said the tall one. "It's still trial and error. Few of them can do it. They're too sensitive to the pain."

"How many can?"

A silence, then, "Only one so far."

"So we've suffered for nothing. There is no answer, no help." The voice sounded hopeless.

The tall male was briefly illuminated by the candle-light. What she could see of his face was tired and worn.

"I was never looking for a solution," he said. "We need to rethink our approach, that's all. If we see it as defeat, then we will lose."

"No good ever comes from playing God! We were stronger before this!"

"Enough!" said the voice she recognized as Rezac's. "You'll have us defeated before we've begun to fight!"

"Fight? What have we got left to fight with?"

"Ourselves," said Rezac, abruptly clutching his side as he stumbled against the wall. A smear of blood was left on the stone.

"You've been hit!" the female exclaimed, turning back to grasp hold of him. "That's why you blocked me out!"

"It's nothing," he said, his voice fading out as the blood began to course from beneath his hand, running down his thigh.

Someone was screaming, Carrie realized as she tried to fight her way clear of the weight that was clinging to her limbs. She had to get free!

"Carrie, stop it! Stop screaming! It's me, Kaid!" said a voice close by her ear.

"Let me go! I can smell blood!" she cried, trying to push him away with her sound arm. "We've been attacked! We have to leave!" For a wonder, the screaming had stopped.

"Carrie, you've been dreaming. It's not real," he said, tightening his grip on her. "No one's been hurt, we aren't under attack."

Gasping for breath, Carrie strained against his encircling arms. "They shot him! He's bleeding! Why is there always blood wherever I go?" Her voice had dropped to a low moan as, exhausted, she slumped against him. "Please, God, no more blood. No more fighting and hurting, I can't take any more of it," she sobbed.

"It's all right, Carrie," said Kaid awkwardly as he relaxed his hold on her. "It was a dream, nothing more."

"Ha!" said Rhuna from the doorway. "A pretty picture indeed! It's about time you let yourself feel again, Tallinu. You won't find a female who wants a male carved of ice."

"Leave me alone, Noni," he said sharply to her. "You've no call to talk to me like this."

"Hmpf!" she said, making her way into the room toward them. She reached out and put her hand on Carrie's shoulder, using it to establish a rapport with her.

"Hush, child," she said. "I know what you saw. It was a

dream, nothing more. I've had that one myself a few times. The people are long gone now."

Carrie raised her head. "You've seen it, too?" she asked incredulously.

Rhuna nodded, squeezing Carrie's shoulder gently before letting go and turning to walk toward the nearest chair.

"I've seen it, as did my mother and her mother before her," she said, sitting down heavily. "It's always the same, like a storyteller's tale told over and over again."

"You haven't told me this before," said Kaid accusingly. "You know my interest in this type of dream."

"Had you stayed longer in the village before leaving for the city, you might have learned much that would have been of use to you," said Rhuna tartly. "But no, you chose to go your own way, same as you always did when you were a cub! Wouldn't listen to anyone, would you? Look at where it's got you! Confused, that's where!"

"But dreams are dreams," said Carrie, rubbing a hand across her eyes. "They can't remain for other people to dream them."

"They're not exactly dreams, child, more like memories left in the stones of the buildings and the mountain itself. At least that's what we think."

"Memories? How can memories be held in stones?"

Rhuna shrugged. "I don't know. I'm only a humble village healer, not one of your smart Guild-trained Telepath Healers."

Carrie didn't miss the sarcasm in Rhuna's tone. Where she rested against Kaid's chest, she felt the growl begin deep inside him.

"You don't fool anyone, Noni," he said. "The only reason you aren't Guild-trained is because you hate the Telepath Guild."

"Too right," she retorted. "Esken's cast in the same mold as his predecessor! Both of them hypocrites! Esken twists good people out of true in his desire to rule the Council. He doesn't do it all himself, oh no! A bribe here and a threat there, to make sure they vote the way he wants. Then there's the ruins. He's "blessed" more ruins to date than any three of his predecessors did! Yes, I know all about him."

"Why?" asked Carrie, the terrors generated by the dream now forgotten. "Why does he destroy the ruins?"

"Told you. Power. Telepaths were feared after the Cataclysm, some folk even thought they'd caused it. Like his predecessors, he doesn't want people poking about in the ruins, bringing back memories of those days and their fear of Telepaths. He doesn't dare let it be known how powerful he is on the Council lest that awaken those old fears, too." She pushed herself stiffly to her feet. "I'm going back to bed now. I suggest you do the same. You shouldn't have any more of those dreams tonight, but if you do, just remember, those times are long gone."

"When were those times, Noni?" Carrie asked.

"Because of the fighting, we think round about the time of the Cataclysm or just after it," she said. "Once the guilds were established, things began to settle down pretty quickly. As far as we know, there hasn't been fighting on Shola on that scale since then. Now, good night. I need my sleep, even if you don't." Rhuna headed back toward the bedroom.

She stopped at the doorway and looked over at them, raising an eye ridge.

Kaid hurriedly released Carrie, moving slightly back from her. "Don't say a thing," he said, his tone cold as he looked at Rhuna.

"Me, Tallinu? What would I say?" Rhuna gave a small laugh as she left the room.

Kaid turned back to Carrie. "It's late, Liegena," he said quietly. "You should sleep peacefully now."

Carrie lay back on the pillows, pulling the covers up around herself. "Kusac said that Ghyan was interested in the dreams, too. Do you think they're all stone memories of the past, Kaid?"

"Perhaps," he said, getting up. "It would certainly be worth talking to Ghyan about them. If they are from the past, perhaps they'll make more sense when we've collected several of them." He moved away from her toward the settee.

"Kaid, could you sleep nearer me, please?" she asked. "I don't care what it was, it frightened me. I'd like you close in case I have another one."

Kaid hesitated, looking from the settee to the bed. "I don't think that's necessary," he said.

"Please."

"If you wish," he sighed, going over to fetch his pillow and blankets. He returned and began spreading them on the floor at the side of the bed.

"I didn't mean on the floor," she said, looking down at

him. "This bed is huge. There's plenty of room for you to lie across it at the bottom."

There was plenty of room. The bed was made for Sholans who averaged about two meters while she was only just over a meter tall. He picked up the pillow and put it at the foot of the bed, then sat down.

"Thank you. I'm not used to being alone," she said, her voice trailing off as she began to fall asleep.

Kaid lay down, his back against the footboard of the bed as he wrapped the blankets around himself. Something hard was digging into his side. It was that damned crystal! He shifted slightly, trying not to disturb her, but it didn't ease the discomfort. Slowly, carefully, he eased himself farther onto the bed, trying to lie on his back to take the pressure off his side.

Carrie began to make small, restless, movements, stretching out her legs till her feet touched him. She stopped then, and with what sounded like a purr of contentment, settled down again. He froze, unable to move now. Even through the thick covers, he was hypersensitively aware of the warmth of her feet against him. He waited till he heard the slow breathing that told him she was deeply asleep before he tried edging away from her. Once more she began to stir. Quickly he moved back to where he'd been, only to find his rapid movements had brought the crystal back underneath him again, making it dig in even more sharply than before.

Cautiously he sat up, making sure his legs remained in contact with her feet. Putting his hand in his pocket, he brought out the offending crystal. It seemed to come alive in his hand, warming with the feel and the scent of Carrie. Hurriedly he replaced it. Noni had left a semblance of the Human girl's presence in the crystal. What was the old she-jegget up to? he wondered angrily. And what the hell was he supposed to do with this damned crystal? At least tomorrow they'd be gone, and there'd be no further opportunity for Noni to play any more of her mind games with him.

He tried to settle down but found it nigh on impossible, so aware was he of her presence, and of the crystal in his pocket. Resorting to his litanies, he at last found something of the peace he sought.

*   *   *

An acolyte led Kusac and T'Chebbi down the corridor to the priest's private quarters. Ghyan opened the door, gesturing to them to enter.

"You surprise me, Liegen Aldatan," said Lijou, the Leader of the Priesthood of Vartra as he turned around to face him. "I was sure you'd bring Kaid with you."

"Kaid's busy," said Kusac shortly, touching Ghyan's hand in greeting as he walked past him to sit in one of the easy chairs. "You asked me to meet you here. What is it you want?"

"Sister T'Chebbi." Lijou nodded a greeting to her as she remained by the doorway on duty. "I'm disappointed that you feel the need for a Brotherhood escort in my presence," he said, moving to sit opposite Kusac. "Aren't you afraid of a conflict of interest?"

Kusac lifted his lips in a grin that was half Human, half Sholan, and watched the Head Priest wince at his display of teeth. "Not at all, Father Lijou. T'Chebbi is contracted to me from the Warrior side of the Brotherhood, not the religious side." His voice held the echo of a gentle purr. "Now, what is so important that it brings you from Stronghold at this time of night?" he asked, relaxing back in his chair.

"This conversation would perhaps be better conducted without an audience," murmured Lijou.

"I have no objections to Ghyan and T'Chebbi being present. We obviously both trust them or we wouldn't be meeting here, would we?"

"Very well, Liegen. The All Guilds Council meets in six weeks. We need to know now if you plan to support us by joining the Brotherhood."

"What's our support worth to you, Father Lijou?" asked Kusac. "What would you give to be counted as a full guild?"

Lijou frowned. "I don't understand you. What do you mean, 'What would I give'?"

"How important is our support to your cause?"

"It's vital. Without your support we have no claim."

Kusac nodded. "I just wanted to remind you, because if you want our support, it will cost you. You see, we've considered our position from every angle and we don't think it's to our advantage to become members of the Brotherhood. You'd use us for your ends, just as Esken has tried to do."

Kusac watched Lijou's eyes narrow. "So what are you suggesting, Liegen Aldatan?" he asked.

"I'm suggesting a permanent alliance with the Brother-hood. All legally drawn up, of course—and secret. As far as the world at large is concerned, we'll become members of the Brotherhood and give you our public support at the Council meeting."

"In return for what?" asked Lijou.

"Your releasing from their oath certain named Brothers to me. They'll have been approached and will be willing to join us. I feel very strongly that telepaths who can fight shouldn't belong to any one guild. They should be an independent force in Sholan politics, a force that can't be bought or used without their consent."

"They'll never grant you guild status of your own," said Lijou.

"We aren't seeking it," said Kusac. "We're quite happy to be thought of as Brotherhood members, so long as the reality is somewhat different."

"Now why would you want independence from the guilds?" Lijou's tone was thoughtful as he clasped his hands on his lap. "Clan reasons? The new breed of children?" He stopped, the realization hitting him. "It's the children, isn't it? You want them protected. The guilds can't help you, but the clans can." He paused. "No, not the clans, a new clan! You're planning on starting a new clan," he said, cocking his head on one side and looking carefully at Kusac.

"Why should you think that?" asked Kusac. "Nothing could be farther from the truth." Too late he felt Lijou's mind gently touch his.

"Dear God, you're going to try the Fire Margins ritual!" Lijou's voice was hushed with fear as his hands grasped the arms of his chair. "In Vartra's name, Kusac, you'll kill your-selves! It's madness to even think it!"

Inwardly, Kusac cursed himself. He should never have come tonight, he'd known he wasn't up to a meeting with Father Lijou. With his mind as distracted by worry over Carrie as it was, there was no way he could maintain ade-quate shielding against a telepath of Lijou's caliber. He hesi-tated, mindful of Kaid's warning, wondering if there was any point in trying to bluff it out.

He shook his head slowly. "There's no point in trying to deny it now. It isn't madness, Lijou. It's the only path for us, and it's the one we will take. It's been ordained."

"Kaid! He's behind this!" said Lijou, his fear turning to

anger as he sat forward in his seat. "Ghezu was right after all!"

"Kaid may have been expelled from the Brotherhood, but he still follows your God, Lijou. You should respect that in him," said Kusac. "It's none of his doing. Vartra Himself has shown him what will be."

"Has he told you what the survival rate is among those who manage to get there?" demanded the Head Priest. "None! That's how many!"

"He's told me, but we won't be used, Lijou, either by you or Esken," warned Kusac. "Think of the politics in this. You'd be allied to a Clan of En'Shallans—the Brotherhood of Vartra allied to those who've walked with Vartra. Think of the respect you'll receive. Think of how it will strengthen your position as the leading religion on Shola." Kusac dropped his voice slightly. "Think of the edge it would give you over Ghezu."

Lijou shot an angry look at him from under lowered brows. "You've got it all worked out, haven't you? Religious power if you survive the Margins, and temporal through the Brothers you request. You'd owe nothing to anyone!"

"An alliance is an alliance, Lijou," said Kusac softly. "We'd be working together for the same ends: to break the power of Esken on the World Council."

"There's more at stake than just Esken," said Lijou. "I doubt it's occurred to you yet, but we also face a threat from the Terrans. Once they admit telepathy exists and start training their people properly, with their multifaceted psychic abilities, they could surpass us as the Alliance's telepaths. They have a valuable contribution to make, but they're not fit to take a major role in interspecies politics. They're a threat to the power balance, one which the Chemerians could well try to exploit given half a chance. As a species, we Sholans need to change, to evolve, if we're to stay ahead of the Terrans. We can't do this if we continue to follow Esken's restrictive policies."

"I certainly wouldn't support the swift elevation of the Terrans onto the Allied Worlds Council," said Kusac. "Neither would my father. As you say, they still don't believe in their own abilities, let alone ours. They're also technologically backward and paranoid, totally unsuited to a position of such power at this time. Everything I've heard from my parents suggests they will be kept as junior members of the

Allied Worlds Council for a long time to come. They aren't even used to belonging to a multispecies society yet!"

"We're in accord on this, then," Lijou nodded. "If we agreed to an alliance with you, then you'd be willing to publicly request permission to join the Brotherhood at the Council meeting?"

"Yes. We'll stand beside you in public and back your request for full guild status—once we've signed the agreement," said Kusac. He hesitated momentarily. "There is one more thing we need from you."

"Training in the Fire Margins ritual."

"Yes," said Kusac. "I'm not a fool, despite what you think, Lijou. I don't intend to throw our lives away on this ritual. I intend us to survive it."

Lijou nodded. "Very well. Ghyan knows all there is to know about the rituals. He'll teach you, won't you, Ghyan?" he said, turning to look at his priest.

"I think this is ill-considered madness . . ." Ghyan began.

"You'll make all the records you have regarding the rituals available to Liegen Aldatan, and give him and his Leska your personal tuition, won't you?" Lijou interrupted in a voice that brooked no argument.

"Yes, Father Lijou," said Ghyan in a subdued tone. "Have they chosen a third member yet?"

Kusac's ears swiveled round to face his friend as he turned his head toward him. "A third?"

"There are always three," said Ghyan. "A Leska pair and a Warrior to guard them."

"They have their third," said Lijou. "Kaid. He's admirably suited to the job. Since the God has told him they will walk the Margins, then he should be the one to walk with them. To my mind it seems he was chosen before they were."

Kusac turned to look at Lijou. He could sense the other's amusement at the choice of Kaid—he made no effort to hide it.

"The negotiations seem a little one-sided to me," said Lijou. "Since I will have to convince Leader Ghezu to accept this proposal, my support for you comes with a condition."

Kusac looked at him with grudging respect. That Lijou would make his own demands hadn't occurred to him.

"The Brothers' Oath of Allegiance is made not just to Ghezu, but to me as Head of the Order. They *are* the Brotherhood of Vartra, after all, and I'm Vartra's prime

representative on Shola. I will persuade Ghezu to release the
Brothers from their oaths to him, but I will not release
the Brothers from their Oath to the God. However, I am prepared to second them to you. Had any of the previous Triads
succeeded in returning from the Margins, they would have
been subject only to Vartra and his Order. I'm only asking
what is due. Stay within the religious side of the Brotherhood, as priests. You'll find Shola will accept your people
more willingly if they see that you're accountable to one of
the guilds. That's *my* price, Kusac."

"They'll think that anyway, Lijou. They won't know that
we've never really joined the Brotherhood."

"You'll have to join, Kusac, then your proposed alliance
would exonerate you from your oath to Ghezu—but not to
me. I want an alliance, too, one that will remain. If you call
yourselves the En'Shalla Brothers, then it'll be known where
your loyalties lie."

"What's to stop your Order demanding that my people
submit to tests or arranged marriages for breeding programs,
Lijou? How would it benefit us to remain with you and the
priesthood?"

"You'd be En'Shalla. We'd have no jurisdiction over such
areas," said Lijou. "Ask your friend. Ghyan is my deputy, he
knows the laws. Presumably you trust him to tell you the
truth."

Ghyan stirred as Kusac looked at him. "He's telling you
the truth. If you disagree with the Order on any issue, you
have access to the usual neutral appeal channels. As for the
benefits to you, you'd be legitimately able to practice not
only as Telepaths but as Warriors, without owing allegiance
elsewhere. You can't afford to let your people be outside the
guilds, Kusac. We know you have principles, but in times to
come, others may not. You're talking of setting up a powerful group of people, with far-reaching abilities—we've no
idea how far-reaching they will be—and having nothing to
prevent them taking the law quite literally into their own
hands. They'd have the ability to read minds and the skills to
kill. A far too powerful combination to be left unchecked,
my friend."

"I'll need to think about this," said Kusac. He could see
that the points they were raising were sound, ones he'd
thought of but as yet had not come up with any solution.

"There's no time. What I'm suggesting is, shall we say,

unethical?" said Lijou, picking up a crystal ornament from
Ghyan's desk and examining it.

"Independent of Ghezu," murmured Kusac, watching the
other carefully. He knew Kaid's mind concerning the Warrior Leader, but Lijou. . . ? Here he was, acting independently, putting himself on the line. All it took was for one of
them present in the room to mention this in the wrong quarters, and if the Head Priest survived long enough, he'd be
cast out of not only the Brotherhood, but also the Telepath
Guild, even though traditionally he owed that Guild nothing.

"Very well," he said. "What do you want in surety?"

Lijou looked at Ghyan. "Type a transcript of our agreement, Ghyan. I want it signed and witnessed now."

"Very well, Father Lijou," said Ghyan, activating his comm.

"You'll excuse me implementing our agreement here and
now, Kusac, but as I'm sure you appreciate, I can't afford for
any details to become public knowledge."

"I understand," nodded Kusac. "And for the agreement
with Ghezu?"

"We have an agreement."

As they waited, Lijou broke the silence. "I have just such
an ornament as this on my desk, Ghyan. Very nice. Of local
origin, is it?" he asked, putting it back.

"Yes," said Ghyan, handing Kusac the document. When
he'd read it through carefully, he accepted the stylus and
leaning on his friend's desk, signed it then passed it over to
Lijou.

"You've made a wise decision, Liegen Aldatan," said
Lijou as he affixed his signature to the agreement. "I think
you'll find that Kaid will support your actions tonight."

"I make my own decisions, Father Lijou," Kusac replied
stiffly.

"I know, but the approbation of one you respect does
matter," replied Lijou, mouth opening in a gentle smile.
"The official Brotherhood view of Kaid doesn't agree with
what I've heard from the people who knew him. Though a
loner, he was respected by most of his colleagues, despite
the erratic end to his career with us. He was attached to the
religious side for many years, you know."

Kusac raised an eye ridge. "You didn't know him
personally?"

"Barely. I was appointed during the last year he was there.
Those were troubled times for him, I'm afraid," he sighed.

"From all accounts, you couldn't have a better mentor. Vartra knew what he was doing when he sent you Kaid."

"You surprise me," murmured Kusac. "I thought you were involved in choosing him."

"Was I?" said the priest, his tone bland as he handed the document back to Ghyan. "I forget. Keep this safe, Ghyan. It mustn't fall into the wrong hands."

Lijou got to his feet. "Have your document of alliance drawn up and delivered to us at Stronghold and we'll sign it. All I ask is that you delay your ... trip ... until after the Council meeting. Don't forget to append the names of the Brothers you wish permanently assigned to yourselves. I take it they will include all those currently working for you?"

"Yes, I believe so," said Kusac. "We don't intend to take the ritual until Carrie is fully recovered in any case."

"A wise decision," agreed Lijou, folding his arms in the pouch at the front of his robes. "Till we meet again, Liegen. It's been a pleasure doing business with you," he said, bowing his head before he turned and walked toward the door. He stopped and waited for T'Chebbi to open it for him, then swept out into the dark corridor.

Ghyan let out a hiss of anger as he sank into one of his own chairs. "What the hell are you trying to do, Kusac? Commit suicide? How could you even think of taking the Fire Margins ritual!"

"Don't you start, too," Kusac said tiredly. "It's the only way we can avoid being used by the main guilds. If we belong to ourselves, we're free of the lot of them."

"At what cost? It will likely kill you!"

"Not according to Kaid."

"And that's another point! You can't take Kaid with you. It has to be someone you can trust, and I wouldn't trust him if he was the last Sholan alive. He's devoid of any feelings ... he lives only for duty."

"You're wrong," said Kusac, sitting back in his chair and closing his eyes. "I trust him implicitly. He's with Carrie at the moment. He's taken her to some Healer up near Stronghold. She isn't improving, Ghyan, she's getting worse. Sleeping all the time and refusing any food." He paused. "Kaid has feelings, we just can't sense them."

Ghyan snorted. "Convenient!"

"Excuse me, Liegen," interrupted T'Chebbi, making both males look toward her in surprise.

"Know I'm speaking out of turn, but Kaid is the right choice. Has the gifts you need for your third. He'd die rather than let you down."

"I know, T'Chebbi," said Kusac, opening his eyes again. "I don't doubt him."

"You realize that all three of you have to work together, become a Triad, your minds linked to each other?" said Ghyan. "He'll have to be at least on the edges of your Leska Link with Carrie. Can you let him into such an intimate position?"

"If that's what it takes, yes," said Kusac, getting up from his seat. "I want our cubs to grow up without fear of being taken from us in the night by some guild determined to study them. If we're En'Shalla, they won't dare touch either them or us." He took a deep breath, forcing himself to calm down. "I need your help, Ghyan. Search out the books that tell about the ritual so that at least we can read them in preparation for starting our training as soon as Carrie is fit."

Ghyan nodded reluctantly. "I still think you're mad, but look at what you've already achieved with the help of Vartra," he said quietly. "You've married your Human Leska, and though you lost your first cub, you will have others. These things I would also have said were impossible."

"You did, my friend," said Kusac with a faint grin as he reached out to touch Ghyan on the arm. "You did say they were impossible. I have to leave now. I'm expecting news from Kaid any time."

"Take care, Kusac," said Ghyan, as he watched them leave. "I'll find the records you need and contact you as soon as I've got them. You realize that the agreement you signed with Father Lijou means that all our resources are at your disposal now, don't you?"

"I didn't, but thank you for telling me. Good night, Ghyan."

"Good night."

* * *

Taizia mentally checked the house again. No one was up but the guards, and she'd already avoided them. Silently she padded down the staff corridor to Meral's quarters. Hand on the door lock, she hesitated briefly. No point in losing her nerve now. Any day her father, as Lord of the Sixteen Telepath Clans, could inform her he'd found a suitable life-mate for her—a male to father the child who'd lead the Aldatan Clan after Kusac. Well, she had other plans, at least for her immediate future.

It had to be tonight. The time was right, and she had the opportunity. Taking a deep breath, she pressed the palm lock.

Silently the door slid back, allowing her to enter. She waited a moment, letting her eyes adjust to the change in light levels.

Meral was asleep. She could see him lying on his back, the covers tangled round his legs, his breathing low and even. Her mouth opened in a grin. He wouldn't stay asleep, she intended to see to that!

Pressing the shoulder seals on her tabard, she let it slip to the floor. Stepping out of it, she approached the bed, tail gently swaying, ears pricked forward to catch the slightest sound. She knelt beside the bed, listening for any change in the rhythm of his breathing. She needed the element of surprise for her plan to succeed: the more drowsy he was, the better.

Leaning over him, her dark hair falling down in front of her shoulders, she reached out to touch his chest, enjoying the softness of the longer fur that grew there.

He started, awake instantly, his hand closing on hers, claws pulled back at the last moment. "Taizia? What're you doing here?" he asked, his voice groggy with sleep. "I thought you were staying at your guild."

"I am, but I thought I'd join you tonight," she purred, sliding her hand out from under his and continuing its journey across his chest, then under the covers to his lower belly.

Blinking the sleep from his eyes, Meral reached up for her, pulling her down into the bed beside him. "I'm glad you did," he murmured, beginning to nuzzle and lick the under-side of her neck and jawline as he untangled himself from his bedding.

She extended the claws of her other hand, drawing careful patterns on the inside of his thigh, feeling his belly muscles tighten as he began to respond to her. Her tail curled round his leg, the tip gently moving against him.

His claws were out now as he pulled her closer, matching her body to his as he began to nip less gently at her cheeks and mouth.

Taizia reached for his mind, projecting her sensations to him, surprised when she found him responding mentally.

Now was the moment of decision for her. Resolutely she suppressed the muscles that would prevent her conceiving and increased the power of her sending so he'd not notice the change in her scent. Chances were he wouldn't recognize it anyway as she was sure he'd never fathered a child before, but this night she wasn't prepared to take any risks.

The onslaught of sensations was too much for him, and with a low sound somewhere between a growl and a purr, he flipped her over onto her other side, grasped her hips from behind and pulled her down onto his body until they were joined. Within moments he'd climaxed and Taizia knew her plan had worked.

They lay like that for several minutes, Meral trying to apologize for his urgency and at the same time trying to find the words to ask what it was that she'd done to make him respond so quickly.

Her conscience began to twinge, and as she turned to face him again, it was with a great deal more gentleness that she began to arouse and reassure him.

The pale light of morning stole through the window hangings as she rose from his bed, content yet at the same time frightened of what she'd done. They'd both face the censure of their families for her night's deeds, but as she quickly donned her tabard and slipped from the room, she knew this was the only way they could stay together. The crime of conceiving a cub outside a three- or five-year bonding contract with one's partner carried heavy social penalties, not to mention legal ones, but she'd thought it through and decided that for her, at least, it was worth it. As for Meral . . . her conscience pricked her again, but she ruthlessly subdued it. In a few weeks it would be too late to do anything about it, then she could tell Meral.

The thought that he might not wish to sign a bonding contract with her, cub or no cub, flitted through her mind briefly, only to be dismissed as she padded through the still silent house to the garage. He'd be angry, but she knew he'd also be pleased. To have a bond-mate from one of the oldest telepath families on Shola prepared to carry his child was no mean achievement for any male.

Squaring her chin to the world, like a shadow she slipped between the aircars into the grounds where she assumed a four-legged stance. Minutes later, she'd cleared the gardens and was heading for the vehicle that lay concealed in the woods to the east side of the estate.

"The Liegena Taizia Aldatan has just left, Lieutenant Ni'Zulhu," said the guard watching the perimeter screens.

The officer at the rear of the gatehouse's main control room nodded. "Very well. Make sure you log the departure time. What's her heading?"

"Back to Valsgarth, sir. I presume she's returning to her guildhouse as Kaid said she would."

"Keep one of the cameras on her till she leaves the vicinity," said Ni'Zulhu.

"Yes, sir."

* * *

The Chemerian Ambassador sat facing Commander Raguul of the *Khalossa*. On either side stood his Sumaan guards, dwarfing him with their height and bulk. Concealed in his hand the Ambassador held a computer data cube.

"Commander, between our species, trade has been good, no?"

"You could say that," agreed Raguul, sitting back while his adjutant filled two small silver goblets with the aromatic wine that was a major Sholan export item to the Chemerians.

"Many lucrative generations exchange goods. All benefit. Sholans and Chemerians both. We know some items you keep to selves, but we do same."

"Ambassador Taira, we operate a free-market system," said Commander Raguul stiffly. "The goods available to you are the same as those available to all Sholans and the Allied Worlds. What you are suggesting is against the spirit of our agreements."

Taira regarded him unblinkingly for a moment. "We keep species-specific items only. No use to Sholans or others." He broke eye contact again, blinking rapidly as he waved a thin long-fingered hand in the air. "But no matter. That not what I come to speak of."

Commander Raguul's eyes narrowed as he regarded the Ambassador. The Chemerian had requested this audience, which was unusual in itself. Normally Raguul would receive a peremptory summons to the Ambassadorial quarters, a summons that he would decline equally bluntly while issuing an appointment for a meeting in his office. This time that had not been the case.

Gently he tapped a claw tip on his desk. This current tour of duty, quieter now that the Valtegans had been driven from Keiss, had more than its share of problems even without the added abrasive presence of Ambassadors from the Allied Worlds.

The Chemerian began to look uneasy, his large eyes blinking rapidly. He leaned sideways, speaking briefly in Sumaan to one of the huge reptilian bodyguards that always stood at his side.

"Ambassador wishes lights lowered," the Sumaan said using the same basic Sholan, the lingua franca of space.

"Certainly," said Raguul, gesturing to the adjutant.

The lights were lowered until it was sufficiently dim for the Chemerian's comfort.

"Now lights no longer pain me, I continue," said Taira. "Excuse bluntness, Commander, but am instructed to tell you of planet Jalna situated in farthest reaches of our territory. Occasionally we trade there—with natives, and others."

"I don't remember hearing of that planet before, Ambassador," said Raguul, his tone deceptively bland. "Is this world one you've recently discovered?"

"Have been aware of it for some time, Commander," admitted Taira, looking down at the cube in his hands. "Existence been kept to ourselves because of dangerousness of planet."

"In what way dangerous, Ambassador Taira?" Raguul purred, noting the nervous twitching of the Chemerian's large rounded ears, and enjoying his obvious discomfiture. It was only rarely that he had the upper hand with Taira. Leaning across his desk, he offered the Ambassador one of the small silver goblets of wine.

Taira made a dismissive gesture, blinking his eyes several times.

"Planet is dangerous for several reasons. First, is a barbarian backwater—even more barbaric than Shola." His tone was disparaging.

"I'm sure it couldn't be that bad," murmured the Commander, trying to keep his mouth from twitching.

The Chemerian inclined his head slightly, stretching his spindly neck to the point where Raguul irreverently wondered if it would snap under the sheer weight. He had learned the hard way that it was essential for him to have a sense of humor when dealing with these people, otherwise their innate arrogance and paranoia only gave him colic.

"Is worse," the Ambassador said, with a rare flash of directness. "People are warlike and quarrelsome. Have only basic idea of what is for mutual benefit. Just spaceport is open to traders, rest of planet is proscribed zone controlled by local Overlords."

Carefully placing the cube on the Commander's desk, Taira edged it forward with one of his small nonretractile claw tips, still avoiding eye contact. "Here is all our data on planet. Several species trade there, none you have met."

Raguul leaned forward in his seat to pick up the data cube. His good humor had totally evaporated. "Why do your people have trade agreements which don't involve us, Taira? The Allied Worlds are on war alert, guarding our common frontiers against any possible threat from the Valtegans. This is apart from the trade treaties between our people. Yet you purposely conceal the existence of a world where not only you, but several unknown species all trade! Where is trust and good faith, Ambassador?" demanded Raguul. "This planet's very existence could have a bearing on the whole issue of who the Valtegans are and where they come from."

Taira straightened in his chair, glowering at the Sholan. "Not need to know about Jalna before this," he said angrily. "Our business private, no concern of yours till now! Trade items for us, species-specific. Inappropriate you use! Be content we telling you now."

"I think we should be the judge of what concerns us," growled the Commander. "What exactly do you acquire from Jalna, and why are you suddenly telling us about it now?"

Ambassador Taira looked away and shifted uncomfortably in his seat. The robes covering his lightly furred body rustled loudly in the silence.

"Not your concern," he said abruptly. "What concerns you, and why am ordered to give you data cube, is fact that during last few weeks, missing Valtegan battleship visit planet. Two shuttlecraft land, one in spaceport, one in mountain range in proscribed zone where crashed. Other returned safely to battleship and left."

"I need hardly ask if you followed it."

"You think we mad?" He sounded offended as he looked up, his eyes blinking slowly as he forced his ears to remain open. "We sensible race, not go looking for trouble! Our Sumaan reported Valtegans traded peacefully with Jalnians, then left. One, perhaps you say several, of trade items were Sholans."

Commander Raguul, taken totally by surprise, managed to control the flicking of his ears that would have betrayed his interest to the Chemerian.

"Sholans, you say? I don't see how that could be possible."

"You have no records of who actually killed on your colonies. Is not impossible Valtegans took prisoners," said the Ambassador, blinking and shifting uncomfortably in his seat.

"We observe Jalna for some time because of illegal drugs traffic to one of our worlds. No evidence yet found of identity of smugglers," Taira continued.

"Do you know how many Sholans were left on Jalna?" asked Raguul, toying absently with the cube.

The expression on the large pale-furred face was reproachful as the Chemerian Ambassador once more looked up at the Commander.

"Of course. Four. Two are telepaths."

Commander Raguul sat back in his chair, regarding the Chemerian. "I've never known you to give us information for free, Ambassador Taira. What are you hoping to gain in return for this news?"

"Information is gift this time," Taira said, looking him squarely in the eyes. "Have concerns on several counts. First time Valtegans seen in our sector. We know Chemer's troops of Sumaan mercenaries give us adequate warning system and degree of protection, but still we feel uncomfortable about sudden appearance of your adversaries in heart of our home worlds."

"They're hardly our adversaries, Ambassador," objected the Commander, taking a sip of his drink. He didn't need to be a Telepath to know that the Chemerian thought he was gaining the upper hand.

"We know as much about them as you. The few Valtegans we captured on Keiss went catatonic the minute we started questioning them and despite everything we did, died within a few hours. Not even our Telepaths were able to sense anything from them. All any of us know for sure is that they're not at war with any of the Alliance Worlds. I suppose we can assume they aren't in conflict with the worlds that trade at Jalna?"

"Correct," said Taira, straightening up in his chair and folding his hands in his lap. "Your data on new Leska pair shows them mind reading Valtegans on Keiss. Why you not utilize their talents on prisoners?"

"We did. While they were still on the *Khalossa*, we captured our first live Valtegan and had him brought off planet. All they found out is what you've already been told: that the Valtegans are fighting far from here, and they were using this sector as a bolt-hole when they discovered Keiss."

"Others captured. Why they not interrogate them?" demanded Taira.

"The team, Kusac and Carrie, had been posted to Shola by that time. There was no point in sending for them as the prisoner they questioned also died."

"Still, you not request their presence," said the Ambassador, frowning.

"Our policy decisions are not your affair," replied Commander Raguul, sitting forward again and allowing some of his anger to show. "I don't see your government consulting us on certain of your decisions, Taira, like keeping Jalna a proscribed world."

"May be I speak hastily," said Taira, blinking rapidly and looking away from Raguul as the edges of his ears threatened to fold over again. "We not wish Valtegans to learn location of our home worlds. Are concerned what information Valtegans obtained from captive Sholans before selling on Jalna."

"Jalna deals in people?" Raguul was stunned.

"Told you Sholans were trade items. Jalna is barbaric world, they deal in any commodity. We have scruples, they have not. Valtegans get information, then sell Sholans."

The Commander growled softly. "I would be careful what you say, Ambassador," he warned, beginning to get legitimately angry. "No matter the cost, our people would not betray us." On the table, his claws began to flex outward.

"Caution could lead to us anticipating the worst," admitted the Chemerian hastily, averting his gaze again, ears this time folding over at the edges in fear. "Perhaps reflection shows Shola not so backward after all. Am sure they not tell Valtegans anything."

"I'd be damned careful about accusing our people of crimes against the Alliance if I were you, Taira," said Raguul, his voice menacing as his claws began to tap his desktop.

"Have message for you from Government on Chemer," said Taira hurriedly, trying to change the topic. "Have decided it advisable for agents to land on Jalna. They discover what can about Valtegans—why suddenly appear and depart our sector of space, what wanted there, who at war with."

"*You* have decided, Ambassador?" purred Raguul. "Are you perhaps sending a couple of your own people? If so, I'm sure Shola has no objection to that."

Taira was totally taken aback at the suggestion. His fear of Raguul vanished and he almost rose out of his seat in indignation. "Out of question," he snapped, eyes wide and ears once more fully unfolded. "Chemerians not risk themselves on such mission! Gravity and light on Jalna prohibits even thought of such outrageous notion!"

"Yet you are willing to have us to send our people down to such a dangerous planet," growled Raguul.

"Movement on ground difficult for arboreal beings, logical that ground dwellers go," Taira protested. "Agents need be unremarkable among locals. We not. To investigate crashed ship and try discover why it in proscribed zone, need to work outside spaceport. If agents had special skills, would be their advantage."

By now Raguul was irritated beyond concealment. "What precisely are you requesting Ambassador?" he asked sharply, annoyed with the roundabout way that the Chemerians—Taira in particular—conducted all their business.

"Three different species trade with Jalna, but native population is Terran in appearance. Among traders is species not unlike Sholans in appearance. None like Touibans or Sumaan. Our mercenaries cannot move freely except within spaceport zone." Taira hesitated. "We feel team made up of Terran and Sholan able to gather information we all require. Team that includes Telepaths who probe Alien minds, and fight, is best."

The Commander took a deep breath. "Now we have it," he said. "You want Kusac and Carrie to go down to Jalna."

"Data you make available to us shows are admirably suited for job. Chemer government wishes them sent." His tone was almost pleading.

"That will be impossible," snapped Raguul. "I take it you aren't aware that Carrie Aldatan has been injured and will be unable to do anything for at least several weeks?"

"Government will be highly disappointed, but of such importance is matter that we delay until she recovered. Can brief them on situation," he said hopefully.

"I can't do even that," said Commander Raguul. "They're unreachable at present. Apparently they're recuperating somewhere on Shola and only their families can contact them. Clan Leader and Clan Lord Aldatan are refusing to pass on any messages." He stood up, indicating the interview was at an end.

"I will notify the military headquarters on Shola of your request, Ambassador Taira. I'm sure they, like myself and the Allied Worlds Council, will want this matter expedited as soon as possible rather than left until the Aldatans are available."

"This matter of great priority!" said Taira, his voice beginning to rise again in anger and distress. "I report your lack of cooperation to Allied Worlds Council. Pressure be brought in quarters to ensure we have them on Jalna soonest possible! Is Sholan duty to protect vulnerable peoples of Allied Worlds!"

"You are at liberty to contact whom you wish, Ambassador," said Commander Raguul, nodding to his adjutant to open the door. "Now if you will excuse me?"

Angrily the Ambassador signaled for his bodyguards to help him to his feet and with the briefest of nods to the Commander, hobbled out of the office to the comfort of his mobile chair.

Once they had gone, the Commander sat down and turned to his adjutant.

"Turn those damned lights back up!" he snapped. "What did you pick up from Taira? What's that tree-climbing, fruit-eating, double-dealing little runt up to?"

Myak raised an eye ridge at the Commander. "Species prejudice?" he murmured.

Raguul shot him a dark look, then grinned. "You're

damned right!" he said. "You name me anyone who likes working with the Chemerians."

"They have a different outlook from us, Commander," said Myak. "While I was in a light rapport with him, virtually everything he said and did was consistent with the way his species views life."

Raguul began to growl. He picked up his goblet, draining the rest of the contents.

"However," said Myak hurriedly, "he was acting out of character at times. It was very evident from the turmoil in his mind that he was most unhappy at being the one chosen to reveal his people's duplicity over Jalna. His anger was fabricated to cover the embarrassment."

"Anything else?" demanded Raguul, picking up the second goblet. He noticed the Telepath's glance. "It settles my stomach," he growled.

"Nothing, Commander. The rest is as he told it. The Chemerians want our mixed species Leskas to investigate on Jalna partly because they genuinely believe that they stand the best chance of survival on the planet, but also because they want to see how they perform in the field as agents. The Ambassador believes Jalna to be every bit as dangerous as he said."

"Hm. You'd better raise Clan Lord Aldatan on the comm," Raguul said.

"Is that wise? Wouldn't it be better to let it go through official channels?"

"No. If it goes through channels we've no chance of getting a message to Kusac and Carrie. If they're the ones best suited to the job, then we need them."

"I'm not part of the military Forces, Commander," said Clan Lord Aldatan frostily. "You've made your request but you cannot order me to do anything. My son and his life-mate are still on sick leave, and will remain undisturbed until they're declared fit. Good day." He cut the connection.

The Commander stared at the blank screen and cursed loudly. "Get me the Sholan Councillor for the Allied Worlds," he said, "and a cup of c'shar. I want those four Sholans off that Godforsaken world as soon as possible! When you've done that, get this cube into the computer and scan it for me. I want a summary of its contents yesterday."

"Yes, sir," said Myak, catching the cube as the Commander

threw it to him and deftly sliding a glass of multicolored liquid in front of him.

Raguul eyed it with suspicion. "What the hell's that?"

"Your stomach medicine, Commander," he said, keeping his expression bland. "You said you wanted it to be made more interesting."

CHAPTER 5

At first light, Kaid was up. What little sleep he'd had had been haunted by God-Visions to the point where he wasn't sure if they were real or merely dreams.

He'd seen the statue in the temple at Stronghold rise up and walk the corridors—but had it been a dream, a vision, or autosuggestion caused by Carrie's dream the night before? Was everything he'd seen merely a replaying of ancient memories as Rhuna had said?

Sighing, he headed out to the aircar to call Kusac.

"She's fine, Liege," Kaid reassured him. "She ate well last night, and Noni will make sure she has a good first meal before allowing her to leave."

"She threw me out mentally last night," he grumbled. "Ask her to turn the damper off, will you?"

"May I suggest that the Liegena might be better persuaded to eat if she knows she can't reach you till she leaves?"

Kusac growled. "I'll be waiting," he said and signed off.

Kaid lit the ancient stove and made himself a cup of c'shar, then sat there nursing it, deep in thought, until Rhuna came in.

"Got a mug for me, then, Tallinu?" she asked in her usual gruff voice. "Dry as the Ghuulgul desert, I am."

He got up and went over to the stove to pour her a drink, bringing it back and setting it down in front of her.

She flicked her ears in thanks and sat sipping it for a few minutes.

"The Human slept all right, then," she said.

Kaid roused himself. "Yes, she did."

"She slept better than you did, at the bottom of her bed."

Kaid ignored her, taking another mouthful.

"So you're to be the third one, are you?"

He frowned. "What d'you mean?"

"Ah, got your attention now, have I?" She laughed gently and took another sip of her drink. "That's the bond between you," she said. "You'll be the third, joined to him by her when they take the En'Shalla path through the fire."

"Don't talk rubbish, Rhuna," he said. "They're not taking the En'Shalla path, and even if they were, they wouldn't choose me."

"Don't contradict me," she snapped. "I know what I see! I tell you, you've been chosen since before you met them; you know you have!"

"I don't know what you're talking about." He tried to remain aloof from her, not wanting to be drawn into her game this time.

She leaned forward, one taloned finger poking his arm. "Don't give me that, Tallinu. You know damned well what you saw, and I know what I saw! You'll walk the Fire Margins with them, like it or not."

He moved his arm away, reaching into his pocket with his claw tips for the crystal. He placed it on the table in front of her. "I won't be part of your plottings, Rhuna. I know you left something of her in this, and I don't want it. What do you think I am? Some lovesick youngling to be molded to fit your vision? Forget it!"

The crystal lay between them, the light sparkling off its translucent blue depths.

Rhuna raised her eye ridges. "It isn't mine anymore, Tallinu. It's yours—and hers. Keep it. You may need it some day." She gave a little laugh as she rolled it back toward him. "Enjoy it. It's all you'll have of her until after the first En'Shalla ritual."

The ovoid crystal came to rest against his hand, making the fur there stand on end.

"See? It knows you!" she laughed.

He moved his hand hurriedly away from it. "You're babbling, Noni. It's only static. I don't want either it or her. I told you, she's life-bonded to my Liege."

"Take it up, Tallinu, she's waking," said Rhuna, sitting back and nursing her mug. "She mustn't have it. It's yours now."

Behind him, he heard the bed creak as Carrie began to stir.

"Take it up," she urged. "It would be wrong for her to see it yet."

"I told you . . ." he began angrily.

"Kaid? Is that you?" came Carrie's sleepy voice from the other side of the room.

"Pick it up, you fool!" hissed Rhuna, leaning forward urgently. "For her sake, if not yours! She mustn't know it exists yet!"

Angrily he picked it up and thrust it into an inner pocket of his jacket, baring his teeth at Rhuna as he did so. "I'll not be party to your plots, Rhuna!" he snarled. "I don't know what you hope to achieve with this, but it won't make me go to the Fire Margins with them!"

Rhuna laughed softly. "It won't be me that makes you go, Tallinu, it will be Vartra."

*　*　*

Konis tried to smother a yawn. He, Nesul, and Kusac had talked till late the night before, not least about the unbelievable news that Valtegan remains had been found on Shola. Almost as stunning had been the disclosure that the Brotherhood had only just managed to rescue the bones before Guild Master Esken's special priests had "blessed" the site—using a massive charge of explosives—thus destroying any chance for the ruins to be examined by anyone else.

Then this. He'd been dragged out of bed at dawn to attend a special meeting of the Sholan High Command—and not even on Shola, but on the *Rynara*, tethered in orbit at Chagda Station.

"There you have it, my colleagues," Commander Chuz, president of the Sholan High Command was saying. "All the information the Chemerians have given us on Jalna."

Drawn back to the meeting, Konis stirred in his chair. "Have they given us any data on the other species that trade there?"

"None, Clan Lord," said Commander Chuz, reminding himself that the Sholan in front of him, though a good twenty years younger than anyone else in the room, was nevertheless the head of Alien Relations and the elected representative of the sixteen Telepath Clans on Shola. He also possessed a Talent second to none—unless rumors of his son's abilities were to be believed.

"Have they indicated whether or not they intend to do so?"

"They are collating what data they have at present."

"Our priority is obvious," said General Naika, leaning forward and tapping his stylus on the table. "We get our people out of there as soon as possible."

"While our people are important, General, there are more issues at stake here, not least of which is first contact with several new species, none of whom we've met before. This matter has to be handled carefully," said Konis Aldatan. "We have only the Chemerian view of the Jalnians, and I think no one here would disagree that the validity of the Chemerian view on any species is questionable, given their racial paranoia." As he finished talking, he looked over at the Governor, getting a brief ear flick in reply.

"I agree," said General Raiban. "We need firsthand experience of these people. One doesn't go into enemy territory without spying out the land."

"Before we go any further, I think you should be apprised of the information that was brought to my notice last night," said Nesul. Four heads turned to face him.

"General Raiban, I believe this falls under your jurisdiction because news of this must not be allowed to leak out from this meeting."

"Oh, do get on with it, Nesul," snapped General Naika. "You're holding the proceedings up enough without all this cloak and dagger stuff."

"Last night, I was informed of two very disturbing facts. First, the Telepath Guild, under the direction of Guild Master Esken of Valsgarth, is purposely destroying any ruins. Second, in doing this, he's destroying evidence of the presence of Valtegans on Shola around the time of the Cataclysm. Whether he's aware of the Valtegan remains is not known."

"So the Brotherhood got in before us," said Raiban softly, nodding her head.

"You knew?" demanded Naika, rounding on her, his ears flicking angrily.

"We suspected," she said. "Until now, we had no proof. Talking of which, who corroborated this piece of intelligence?"

"My son and his physician, Vanna Kyjishi, as well as several others on my son's staff," said Konis. "If anyone should know what Valtegan remains look like, it's them."

"What the hell is Esken up to?" asked Chuz. "As far as I understood it, he has the ruins blasted to prevent any unstable structures falling on our miners. Apart from the remains of metal goods, I understood there was nothing of interest in the ruins."

"Esken, like his predecessor, has actively fostered a lack of interest in our distant past," said Konis. "The general idea is that by ignoring that period of our history, the old fears of Telepaths won't ever surface again. By and large, I'm sure neither he nor his people are aware there are Valtegan bones lying hidden in our ancient cities."

"Well, it's got to stop now," said Naika firmly, again tapping his stylus on the table in front of him. "I want excavations starting immediately. We need to know a damned sight more about the Valtegans than we do now!"

"No," said Governor Nesul quietly, leaning back in his chair. "We do *not* want a big exposure of Esken's crimes, imagined or otherwise. That's one good way to panic every Sholan on this planet. It's having that effect on you, so how much worse will it be for the uniformed public? We keep it quiet for now. Konis and I have made arrangements to deal with it and when it's been discussed with General Raiban, then you'll get your first report on how things are proceeding. Incidentally, how goes the research at Nijidi Science Station? Any clues concerning the nature of the weapon or weapons that were used on our two colonies by the Valtegans?"

"They've reached no conclusions yet," said Raiban. "Unfortunately, they know more about what wasn't used than what was."

"I thought that research had priority," said Nesul. "Why is it taking so long, General? Our people want answers and after all this time, you've still none to give them."

"We're dealing with a totally alien technology here, Governor," said Raiban sharply. "We don't even know what we're looking for, and we might not recognize it when we find it! I'm due another update from Nijidi tomorrow. Hopefully they'll have some news for us then."

"I think we should get back to the matter in hand," said Commander Chuz. "Raiban, are you happy collaborating with Konis and Governor Nesul on the matter of the Valtegan remains?"

Raiban flicked her ears in assent. "It's waited for fifteen hundred years, Commander, it'll wait a few more hours. We aren't in imminent danger of attack from the Valtegans whether or not they've been here before. I'll have a proposition to put in front of you by the time I hear from Nijidi."

"In that case, we'll return to the matter of Jalna. It's now even more important for us to get as much information on the Valtegans as possible."

"What about a straightforward approach?" asked Governor Nesul. "We could open negotiations with them as a new species, explain the situation and offer to trade for information."

General Raiban gave a snort of laughter. "And just what language do you suggest we speak to them in, Governor?" she asked. "Just because we're the largest military presence in the Alliance, and our language forms the basis for interspecies communications, doesn't mean that the same is true of Jalna. Would they even understand the concept of cooperation? We know they sell people, an idea totally alien to us. What other major differences are there between our species? Accepting a Chemerian's word on anything is like relying on a blind man to describe a sunset!"

Nesul was fighting to keep his ears erect despite his anger.

"For those of us who are regularly involved in the complexities of dealing with other species, it's easy to forget that not everyone is aware of the problems we face," said Konis, inwardly sighing and wishing for the thousandth time that intelligence officers were actually picked for intelligence. Raiban was well known for her bluntness and her ability to alienate people. One could respect her, for she had an excellent information gathering network, but liking her was another matter.

"If we go into this situation without enough information, we could jeopardize the safety of our people," said General Naika, looking round the assembled heads of the Forces. "The more we discuss the matter, the more convinced I am that it should be a covert operation, backed by force if necessary. It may not be possible to negotiate the return of our people, and in even attempting that we may lose the opportunity to effect a rescue by alerting the Jalnians to our interest in them. I say we need a lot more information before we can make a considered decision."

Commander Chuz made a note on the comp pad in front of him before looking up.

"Then we are agreed. This is an intelligence mission."

Heads nodded in agreement all round the table.

"The next item concerns who should be sent. As well as requesting us to deal with the matter, the Chemerians have specified whom they want to investigate the situation on Jalna, and I have discussed the matter in some detail with Clan Lord Aldatan. At this moment in time, it is impossible to comply with their request for the Clan Lord's son and his Leska to go to Jalna. Therefore, as an interim measure, we must send someone else."

Konis let most of this wash over his head.

Gods, Kusac, he thought, *did you ever in your darkest nightmares dream what problems your Human Leska would bring to you and to us all as a family?*

He could remember it still, the call in the middle of the night from the *Khalossa*. Kusac, his face set and determined, looking older and thinner than when he'd last seen him the previous year. *My Leska is a female Terran, not a Sholan.*

Then he finally brought her to the estate on Shola. He'd no longer been the youth who'd left a year before, but a grown male, defiant and proud of his alien Leska, the female who wore his torc.

Vartra knows why it happened, Father, but if I had the choice, I'd choose no other.

Like the rest of his family, Konis had grown to love her, almost too late. Vartra be praised that she hadn't died of her wounds, else they'd have lost Kusac, too. Now, scant days after that ill-fated Challenge, the Chemerians demanded that Kusac and Carrie be sent to a new alien world and risk their lives to find out why a Valtegan ship had landed there.

Konis dragged himself back to an awareness of his surroundings.

"The reasons the Chemerians want Konis' son and his Leska to go to Jalna are actually sound," Commander Chuz was saying. "The Terrans have a variety of Talents other than telepathy and because of Kusac's Link to the Keissian female, Carrie, he has acquired several of her abilities. Just how many we're not sure as the Guild is still processing some of the data from their tests." Chuz glanced down at his notes before continuing.

"The particular Talent that interests us most at present is the one that allows Kusac to fight. As you know, telepaths pick up the surface thoughts and emotions of those nearby, which is why they are unable to engage in combat. They experience the pain that they would inflict on their opponent.

This isn't so with the Keissian Telepath—nor with Kusac now."

"Legends would have us believe this wasn't always so for Sholans," said General Naika.

"Who knows?" said Commander Chuz. "Anyway, Kusac and Carrie have been training at the Warrior Guild, as you will all have read from the reports that get forwarded to you. It's this combination of abilities, Telepathy and combat, that we and the Chemerians find so interesting and that they believe holds out the best hope of a successful mission to Jalna. Given their description of the Jalnians and their culture, I can see why."

"It's utterly out of the question," said Konis flatly. "Carrie is still recovering from the aftermath of the Challenge. Not only was she was severely injured, but she suffered the mental and physical trauma of losing her cub, a trauma also shared by my son."

"We're aware of the tragic circumstances of the Challenge, Konis. I'm sure I speak for all of us when I say you and they have our sympathy," said Raiban.

A ripple of understanding noises went round the room.

"How long is it likely to be till she's fit," asked Rilgho, getting back to the business in hand.

"At least another couple of months," said Konis, "but I will not have them putting their lives at risk again. Kusac is my life-mate's heir and as a Telepath he is exempt from anything involving combat."

"His children will not succeed him, though," said Commander Chuz gently. "Hasn't your Clan Leader registered your daughter Taizia's future children as Kusac's heirs? That exempts him from the need to provide heirs for your Clan, thus freeing him to pursue the career he has chosen—one in the Forces."

"You know I'm in dispute with the military over this," said Konis, beginning to get angry. "I want his contract canceled, since when he signed it he was the only Clan heir, and not at liberty to do so."

"Which you are quite within your rights to do," agreed Chuz. "However, we're dealing with the situation as it stands now and his contract has not yet been canceled. They would be the ideal people for the job, but for two things: one, the delay caused by Carrie's injury, and two, neither of them has been fully trained as a Warrior, or as part of our Military

Space Force. They aren't ready to go out as field agents. The best estimate I could get from the Warrior Guild is that they could both be ready within two months of Carrie being fit to resume training. This makes a total delay of four months. We cannot afford to wait that long."

"So we send a reconnaissance team down first and assess the situation," said Raiban. "Then we can make a decision concerning what to do about our people. In the meantime, I particularly want further details of the Jalnians and the other species that trade there."

"It will be seen to. Are we agreed that this should be a reconnaissance mission?" asked Chuz.

Again, the murmur of assent.

"It's also obvious that we can't send Sholans to work undercover among a people that are Human in appearance, therefore we need to send down a team of Humans."

"No," said General Naika. "I am absolutely against using Humans. We hardly know this species. How do we know we can trust them?"

"In the last several months, negotiations and work with them has progressed relatively well from what my people on Keiss tell me, and from what I read in the reports," said General Raiban. "The Humans on Keiss are indebted to us for backing their demand for independence, and are just as motivated as we are to find out more about the Valtegans. I have no objections. This mission is important, but better we find out how well they can cooperate with us on a mission like this rather than on one where there is far more at stake than four Sholan lives."

"It's a calculated risk, but worth it," agreed General Rilgho.

"Konis?" asked Chuz.

"Like any species, if you choose the right people for the job, they will do it well. There is less of a species difference between us and them than with any other species in the Alliance. We have little choice anyway. There's no one else we can send. Yes, it has my vote."

"Naika, do you wish to change your opinion?"

"No," growled Naika. "I'll go on record as objecting."

"Konis, can you liaise with Raiban on the choice of personnel? You know the Keissians better than any of us at present. I feel that we need at least one telepath on the team, so we can get reports safely from them without exposing them to the danger of having their identities discovered," said Chuz, making more notes on his comp pad before looking round the table.

"Thank you all for coming to the *Rynara* and attending this meeting. We will reconvene when we've had the first report in from Raiban concerning the presence of Valtegan remains."

Raiban took Konis to her office to set up a vidiphone conference with Captain Skinner on Keiss.

Pleasantries and news were exchanged, then they got down to business. Some time later, Raiban escorted Konis to the landing bay for a shuttle back down to Shola.

"I'll choose a Telepath from among the Humans at the Guild," he said to Raiban as they left her office and headed for the main shuttle bay.

"It goes against the grain to rely on a Terran with, as we see it, an untrained Talent," he continued, wincing slightly at the chill from the hangar floor on his bare feet. "At least they've all had some Guild tuition. However, I want to know we have an absolutely reliable line of communication with the Chemerian cargo shuttles around Jalna. So for the Telepath on the Chemerian ship, I want a Sholan."

Raiban nodded. "Wise. We know we can rely totally on our own people. If for any reason the Terrans should be unable to communicate with our agent, then he or she can read their minds to get the information."

"It's not quite that simple, Raiban," said Konis, stepping through the hatch before turning round to face her. "You know our code of ethics. We never take, we ask. At least our Telepath will be able to contact any of the team and ask for the information."

"So long as it works," she said, "I'll leave the details to you. I'll be getting in touch with Stronghold later today. I want to actually see these bones for myself. Then I'll want to interview your son and his friends."

"His friends, yes, my son and Carrie, no, not even for you, Raiban," said Konis, baring his teeth in a grin that had nothing to do with humor.

Raiban put out a hand to stop him as he turned away.

"What's this Leska of Kusac's like?"

Konis frowned. "Still probing, Raiban? She's no security risk to us, quite the opposite in fact. I'm concerned for her.

She's fitting in too well with us and will have nothing to do with the Humans at all."

"Why?"

"It's never easy being the first, Raiban. You should know that."

She grimaced. "A hit," she conceded. "Your son's either a brave young male, or a fool."

Konis grinned, putting a hand out to grip her briefly by the arm in farewell. "He's no fool, Raiban. He life-bonded with her."

As he entered the passenger area, Konis saw Nesul waiting for him.

"Governor," he said, going over to sit with him. "I thought you'd have reached Shola several hours ago." He could sense the other male's anger and frustration and knew he'd delayed purposely to see him.

"I waited for you," said Nesul through clenched teeth. "I need your help."

"Of course, Governor. What can I do?"

"I'm sick of being treated by our military people as if I was some kind of congenital idiot! Dammit all, Konis, they may have positions of power and authority in space, but there's more to life than out here! They have no appreciation of what it's like on Shola, or the needs of the ordinary person. And I've no real idea of what it's like off-world," he said, his voice dropping.

"I need to know more about the broader political issues, about the different species—about everything! I don't even know what I need to know, dammit, Konis, and no one will take the time to tell me! How the hell can I rule this planet of ours properly with my hands tied by Esken on the council, and space denied to me by military personnel who seem to think I should go and make mudpies instead of being on the High Council!"

"I hadn't realized your problem was so severe," said Konis quietly. "Naturally, I'll do everything I can to help. I did give you my word on that last night."

"I know you did," Nesul said. "This is part of the same problem, one that's getting worse with every session of the High Council. There must be something you can do. What about a mental implant of the information I need? Esken would never countenance it, but you could, as head of AlRel."

Konis could feel his hopes, sense how frustrating his lack of knowledge was to him. He genuinely wanted to do his best for Shola, on a Council that he, Konis, had discovered to his horror last night was riddled with corruption.

"Very well," he said abruptly, "but you'll have to come to the estate. It's the only place I can do it other than at the Guild, and that's obviously out of the question."

"When?"

"No time like the present," said Konis as the engines started up. "What could be more natural than that we have second meal at my home because we traveled back together?"

Nesul stood up and beckoned to his aide who was standing just out of earshot. "Hanaz, I'm dining at the Aldatan estate. Rearrange my schedule please."

"Yes, Governor," said Hanaz, a harried look crossing his face. "Perhaps you've forgotten that you . . ."

"Rearrange it, Hanaz," said Nesul firmly.

* * *

Kaid's call at the crack of dawn had found Kusac awake, waiting anxiously for him to return with Carrie. At last he felt the damper field removed and he was once more in full rapport with her.

Where are you? he demanded anxiously. *How are you?*

I'm fine, but still tired, she sent. *We're on our way home.*

You feel better.

I am. Even my leg and arm feel easier. Noni is a fine Healer.

But what? he insisted. *I can sense you're disturbed about her.*

Not disturbed. She's just strange, that's all. You've picked up my dream?

Yes. I think we should talk to Ghyan about that, he sent. *You've had too many strange dreams lately.*

She could feel his hesitation. *I need to talk to you about the En'Shalla rituals,* he sent.

I know. We have to take the Margins' ritual or we'll never be free of Esken, Ghezu, or Lijou.

I still have to explain it to you, he sent. *You need to know exactly what it entails, then if you have any doubts. . . .*

What? she sent, her tone gentle. *We agreed about this several days ago. Leave it for now. Wait till I feel stronger.*

Very well. I need to find out more myself, then we'll talk. How long till you're home?

Kaid says soon.

I'll meet you.

Kusac was sitting waiting on the steps when his father and Governor Nesul arrived.

"Is Carrie not back?" Konis asked as they drew level with him.

"The Healer wanted her to stay overnight," he replied, getting to his feet. "They should be here any time now." He nodded to the Governor. "Governor Nesul."

The Governor stopped, holding his hand out to Kusac, who politely touched fingertips with him. "Liegen Aldatan," he said. "Thank you for your help last night. I'm sorry to hear the Liegena is so ill. I hope she'll recover more speedily now. When she's well, I'd like to meet her. Perhaps your father could arrange it," he said, glancing at Konis. "Something informal, a family afternoon, perhaps?"

"I'm sure that can be arranged," said Konis smoothly as he sent a brief version of the morning's events to his son.

Kusac's eyes glazed over momentarily as he tried to assimilate the meaning of the sending. "Of course, Governor Nesul," he murmured. "We'd be pleased to visit you."

"Good. I know that Leska pairs like you and your bondmate will be seen more often on Shola, and I'd like to establish personal ties with you as their leader," said Nesul, mouth opening in a smile as he turned away.

Kusac's ears flicked in surprise and he sent a question mentally in his father's direction.

Konis merely raised an eye ridge before turning to escort the Governor into the house.

It doesn't take much of a mental leap to make that assumption, he sent as he disappeared inside with his guest.

When Carrie returned, Kusac was there at the door of the aircar almost before it had landed. He insisted on carrying her up to their room where Vanna examined her and changed her dressings.

"Fresh air," said Vanna, repacking her medikit. "Take her

down to the garden, Kusac, or better still, to the coast. Let her enjoy the last of our summer while she can. It'll be winter soon enough and she needs the sunlight for her health, unlike us."

"The garden?" said Kusac in surprise.

Vanna flicked her ears in assent. "She's doing fine. Fresh air is what she needs. It'll improve her appetite. You *are* going to eat now, aren't you?" she asked Carrie, a mock stern look on her face.

"Don't worry," Carrie said. "I don't know what it was Noni did, but I feel a lot better—and I'm hungry."

"There you are," said Vanna, turning to Kusac. "I've got to go in to the Guild today, so I'll see your mother about a meal for her while you organize the garden."

"Is it wise to visit the Guild just now?" asked Kusac.

"I'll be fine. Garras and Lhea are accompanying me. I need to get started with Jack now so we can collect my files, and decide what equipment we'll need when we have to set up on our own."

"I'd forgotten Jack was here," said Carrie.

"You'll see him later today. You may be better, but I still don't want you overtired. Rest until this afternoon, and you'll see Jack when we return from the Guild."

"Say hello for me," said Carrie, lying back against the pile of pillows.

*   *   *

Lhea stayed on guard outside Vanna's office while Jack and Garras accompanied the physician inside. The door was still locked, as she'd left it, but once inside, Vanna found herself unable to access her research files. Her authorization into the main data banks had been canceled.

"Damn Khafsa and Esken! All that data lost to us! They'd no right to do that!" said Vanna, leaning forward on her elbows as she rested her face in her hands. "There's nothing I can do about it, Garras."

"Perhaps you can't," he said, reaching out to touch her head, "but I can." He raised his wrist comm to his mouth as he activated it. "Alpha 2 to Base."

A matter of seconds later, Kaid's quiet voice could be heard. "Base here. What's the problem?"

"Vanna's been locked out of the main comm. She can't access her data. Can you get the Clan Lord to clear it?"

"Stand by."

"Kaid'll see to it,' he said reassuringly. "Is there anything else we can do while we're waiting?"

Vanna sat up and turned away from her console to look up at him. "We could start a list of the equipment I'll need," she said. "If I give you the comp pad, will you enter it for me?"

"No problem," said Garras, pulling up a chair and sitting beside her.

"Jack, if you come over here with me and tell me what you think you'll need, I can explain the purpose of any of the equipment you don't recognize."

"That's likely to be all of it, m'dear," he said with a grin.

Garras got up and moved aside. "Physician, you sit here, please," he said to Jack, indicating the chair.

They'd been working for about ten minutes when Kaid called them back.

"The Clan Lord has cleared your access to the main comm at the Guild, Physician Kyjishi," he said. "Currently your data will automatically be relayed through the Clan Lord's comm here at the estate. He wishes to monitor your files for the moment, and to make sure there is a current copy of them here for you to work on should you wish to do so."

"Thank you, Kaid," said Vanna, leaning over Garras' wrist.

"Our thanks, Base. Alpha 2 out," said Garras.

Vanna sat back, grinning. "The Clan Lord doesn't hold back from the kill, does he? He's made sure that my data can't be kept from me again. I can imagine how Esken and Khafsa have taken this!" Her smile faded. "Brynne's coming, and he wants to talk to me."

"I'll get Lhea to take Jack down to the mess for a drink," said Garras. "If I stay outside it'll give you some privacy at least."

"It might be less confrontational if it was Lhea outside," said Vanna quietly.

"If that's what you want."

"No, it's not!" she said with an anger that surprised her. "But it's what I have to do!"

Garras stood up, then hesitated. "Send to me if you need me," he said very quietly. "I'll hear you."

Stunned, Vanna looked up at him, but his face was unreadable.

"I'll not be far," he said before turning to Jack. "I'm afraid we need to leave Vanna for the time being. Her Leska's on his way here."

"Ah, fine. A drink, you said? That would be welcome," said Jack, getting up and following him to the door.

Garras stopped to have a brief word with Lhea before they left. As they walked down the corridor, Brynne passed them.

"That, I take it, is Vanna's Leska," said Jack. "Not in an agreeable mood, I think."

"I'm afraid not," said Garras neutrally.

"I thought Leska Links were pleasant, something both people enjoyed," said Jack.

"Not always. Kusac and Carrie aren't exactly an exception, as most couples get along tolerably well, but relationships as close as theirs are rare—even leaving aside the peculiar closeness of their Link."

"I see," said Jack.

Garras turned to look at him. "I'm afraid you'll have to ask Vanna herself if you want to know any more about her Leska. It isn't really for me to say."

"Oh, I quite understand," said Jack hurriedly. "It was just that I assumed you were her partner."

"No, we're companions at the moment. Shortly we plan to take out a five-year bonding contract."

"A bonding contract? What's that?" asked Jack, following Garras down the stairs to the lower level where the mess was situated.

"A renewable short-term marriage." He looked at Jack again as they entered the mess. "The cub she's expecting is Brynne's. Like Carrie, she can only have his children, not mine. I'm sure she's told you this."

"Some," said Jack. "She asked me to deliver her child."

Garras' expression lightened. "I'm glad," he said. "There's no one else I'd trust her with."

"D'you mind telling me just what's going on here?" asked Jack as they approached the service counter. "No one's said anything much to me, but I've got eyes in my head and what I'm seeing is confusing me mightily."

Garras frowned. "I'm sorry, Jack. Like everyone else, I presumed you'd been told. Once we sit down, I'll bring you up to date, since it looks like you're going to be around for quite a while."

Jack grinned. "Lad, if I can wangle it, I'm not about to go back to Keiss at all!"

Brynne swept past Lhea into Vanna's office. "I'm glad to see you've had the consideration to return to the Guild," he said, his tone sarcastic. "You do realize what tomorrow is, don't you?"

"Yes, Brynne, I do," said Vanna, turning away from him back to her comm. "That's why I'm here, as well as catching up on my work."

"You're moving onto his estate." It was a statement.

"If you mean am I going to live there rather than here, yes, of course I am. After the way the Guild treated you I'd have thought you'd be glad to do the same."

Vanna suddenly found the back of her chair swung round till she faced him again.

"At least have the decency to look at me when we're talking," he said angrily. "I've no intention of living there and you know why! What do you think it would be like for me with everyone knowing you'd rather be with Kusac? I don't know how Garras puts up with it! I couldn't!"

"What the hell do you think it's like for me when everyone knows you'd rather be with *any* other female than me?" she demanded. "You haven't got a monopoly on hurt, you know!"

"Don't give me that, Vanna! You don't care for me and we both know it, so what difference does it make? I've found one of my own people, a woman, and I'm moving in with her. I just came to tell you that. And I don't need a bloody bodyguard, so call off your friends and tell them I'm perfectly able to look after myself!"

"It isn't up to me, Brynne. You'll have to talk to Kaid or the Clan Lord about that. You know all about Esken, and the danger he poses. Nothing would suit him better than to be able to hold us to ransom through you."

"I think you're all overreacting."

"You didn't think that after Khafsa kidnapped us!" she replied tartly.

"I intend to keep out of his way," said Brynne.

"Excuse me," said Vanna, turning her chair round again.

"I've got work to do. If that's all you came to say, then you've said it."

Brynne reached out and grabbed hold of her arm to prevent her moving. As he touched her, Vanna felt the faint beginnings of the sensitization to each other, and she felt it echoed in him.

"Let go of me, Brynne," she said angrily. "Our Link day isn't till tomorrow. You've no right to make demands of me now."

"Haven't I?" he said, reaching down for her other arm and pulling her to her feet. He traced the edge of her jawline with a finger, pursuing her when she tried to turn her face from him. Cupping her chin in his hand, he forced her to look up at him.

"Come on, Vanna," he said quietly. "You know you're looking forward to tomorrow. Our Link gives us something no other partners have, whether we want to admit it or not." His mind reached for hers, playing back their last time together as he let her chin go.

She found herself looking at him, finding him rather attractive with his dark wavy hair falling to his shoulders, and the bearded face that made him less Human and somehow more Sholan.

She felt her hand move up to his face, then stopped, realizing what he was doing, and snatched her hand back. "You've picked up Sholan telepath tricks," she said with disgust. "I've still got the choice today, and I don't want to be with you, so let me go, Brynne."

"That's not strictly true, is it, Vanna?" he said softly, his other arm pulling her closer. "You're carrying our child. I know you feel something for me. It may be deep down, but it's there, and you can't hide it forever."

"You're confusing biology with emotions, Brynne," she said, trying to push him away. "What I feel when we pair on our Link day has nothing to do with what I feel when I'm not driven by the Link's compulsion, and you know that. I could say the same about you."

"Maybe it's true," he said, placing his cheek on hers and gently rubbing against it before beginning to carefully nip her with his teeth.

He knew how to play the Sholan lover, she admitted to herself as she tried to suppress her response to him. It wasn't surprising, since he knew everything she knew, including how to please her—when he made the effort.

Before she realized it, she'd relaxed against him and turned her face to his. His mouth closed on hers in a kiss that belonged to the Human in him.

The anger had gone from his mind, and for a wonder, all she felt from him was a gentleness toward her, and his enjoyment of the moment. It was the first time she'd ever felt that outside their Link days, and even then it had only been transient.

He released her, stepping back slowly, his hands cupping her face and smoothing the soft, short fur. "Maybe it's true," he said again, and she felt a strange, fleeting emotion she couldn't name pass through him as he turned toward the door. "I'll see you tomorrow," he said as he left.

She sat down, building a mental barrier of the type Kusac had shown her. Behind this she could afford to be confused, and wonder what was happening between her and her Leska. Surely he wasn't coming to care for her, was he? Why would he make a point of telling her he was going to live with a female from his own species if that were the case? Or was he doing it to protect himself from her, from beginning to care about her, an alien female?

She shook her head, more confused than ever. Only time would tell. Would a caring Brynne be preferable to the uncaring one she was used to? She wasn't sure. It would certainly complicate her life to have two males loving her! Being honest, it was Garras who really mattered to her. That one night with Kusac had been good, had quieted the part of her that had wanted him before there was ever a Carrie, but he wasn't for her, and she knew it now.

She turned her thoughts to Garras, and his surprising remark about being able to receive her. Surely that couldn't be true, could it? Still, it was worth trying if only as an experiment.

Turning her mind outward, she focused on the feel of Garras' mind, then homed in on it, sending to him. She felt his acceptance, but it wasn't in the words she was used to receiving, more a feeling of confirmation. Surprised, she returned to her work, deciding she'd have to have a long talk with him about this later.

* * *

Seaport had altered enormously in the last few months, Jo
realized as she headed toward the metal tower that was the
remains of the star ship *Erasmus.* The place was getting
positively crowded since the arrival of the second wave of
colonists from Earth—not to mention the people from the
Khalossa.

The Sholans had insisted that the Humans accept their
help since, having surveyed the planet some twenty years
earlier, they actually had a prior claim. They'd refused to sit
back and watch the Humans start mining the hills and setting
up factories on the plains that would pollute not only the
clean air but the look of the world.

The terms of Keiss' membership in the Allied Worlds
were still being negotiated by Carrie's father, Peter Hamilton, now President· of Keiss, but aid had been granted to
them on the grounds that the Alliance was on a war footing
and arming Keiss was a priority. Consequently everything
had been in a state of flux for months and was just beginning
to sort itself out.

Adequate residential bases had been built on Keiss' moon
and blasting had started for the mining complex. Planetary
defense was currently being supplied by the Sholan battleship the *Khalossa*—still in orbit—and its complement of
smaller offensive craft, but Keiss needed its own ships as the
Sholan forces were already stretched to capacity.

Specialists from the Alliance had been shipped in from
every related field to get the Human colony up and running
on a high-tech level. No one could afford to wait for them to
evolve their own technology naturally. Defense was needed
now, as were the raw materials and industries to support the
nascent space-faring society.

Captain Skinner was now the Commanding Officer of
Keiss' military forces, liasing from the surface with Commander Raguul and his officers on the *Khalossa.* It hadn't
started out that way, Jo remembered. When Keiss was clear
of the Valtegans and the colonists on the *Eureka* had been
awakened, brought down to the planet and apprised of the
situation there, she and all the others involved with the
Sholans had been shouldered to the side as the newcomers
had taken over. Being fresh from the home world and therefore more up to date with Earth's attitudes, they had assumed
the positions of power on the planet.

They had reckoned without Commander Raguul though,

Jo grinned. By refusing to negotiate with anyone but the Humans he knew and trusted, he had Peter Hamilton and Skinner reinstated in positions of authority. Keiss, in his opinion, needed to be governed by those who had lived under the yoke of the Valtegans, knew the enormity of the task they faced, and were capable of making the necessary hard decisions.

It had been from Skinner's office that the summons had come, bringing her away from the prefabricated labs where she was working.

Jo elbowed her way past the people around the entrance, rubbing shoulders with Sholans and Sumaan. She hardly noticed them now, a sign in itself of the changes around her. Seaport was becoming very cosmopolitan. Not surprising, she thought, considering that the spaceport had been built a few kilometers away.

She sighed with relief as the elevator door closed. It was empty. She hated crowds. Well, she hated being jostled by strangers. It wasn't so bad with the aliens, it was the large numbers of humans she couldn't take.

The elevator came to a stop, doors opening to reveal an empty corridor. She headed to the right for Commander Skinner's office. Opening the door, she saw Davies sitting in the reception area.

"Hi there," he said. "You get a royal summons, too?"

"Yes. Any idea what it's about?" she asked, sitting down beside him.

His eyes moved toward the secretary who sat behind a large desk guarding the door into Commander Skinner's inner sanctum. Leaning sideways he began to talk very softly.

"Anders says there's been a flutter of excitement on the *Khalossa* over the last couple of days."

"Are he and Mito still together?" she asked, surprised. "I thought it would be a one-night wonder for that ambitious Sholan lady."

"Apparently not. She spent most of her leave planetside if there was a shuttle coming down, until she managed to wangle a posting out with us at Geshader."

"Interesting. Maybe I should have a chat with Anders."

Davies chuckled. "Oh, he's not the only one. There's another couple of the men with Sholan girls. Dr. Reynolds has tried to worm information out of them, but they aren't saying anything."

"But no more women."

"Only Carrie, unless you count those the Sholans call qwenes—that's prostitutes to you and me. Mito says there are a couple more mixed Leska pairs from among the telepaths who went from Shola to Earth."

"Men or women?"

"Our people? No idea. I don't think Mito had either." He looked faintly surprised. "Why?"

"Just a hunch, that's all," she said. "Anyway, this flurry on the *Khalossa*."

"Uh? Oh, they're refitting a twelve-man scouter with armaments and the capability for deep-space flight. I'd say there's a mission looming in the very near future, one urgent enough not to wait for a larger FTL passenger vehicle and escort."

"And you think it involves us?"

"Not a chance, but I think it might involve the Valtegans, and what have you and I been working on?"

"Valtegan artifacts," she said obligingly, hoping he'd go on.

"What do you bet . . ." he began but was cut off by the secretary.

"Commander Skinner will see you now," he said.

"Jo, Davies," said the Commander, looking up as they came in. "Good to see you. You've gone up in rank, too, I see," he grinned, getting up and coming round from behind his desk.

"Please, sit down," he said, indicating the easy chairs set around a low coffee table. "They're bringing some coffee for us. Bit different from the old days, eh?"

He looks tired, she thought as he sat down. His previously tanned complexion was paler now that his rank kept him mainly indoors.

They'd all been fitter during the days of the Resistance, but he'd kept his figure, not gone to fat like some of the younger men. Stockily built, with thinning fair hair and piercing blue eyes, at fifty-two he was still a fine figure of a man.

A knock and the door opened to admit an orderly with a tray of coffee and biscuits.

"Help yourselves," he said, taking his mug. He noticed Jo's quizzical glance. "Can't stand cups, you never get a decent sized drink in them. One of the many Sholan improvements I agree with."

She grinned, picking up one of them.

"I hear you're both working on the remains of Valtegan technology."

Jo glanced at Davies. "Yes, I'm in the lab over in the new part of town."

"I'm based at what's left of Geshader," said Davies.

Commander Skinner nodded. "I'm told it's a mixed team."

"Yes. I have a couple of sects of Touiban computer experts as well as a Sumaan electronics engineer," said Jo. "The Touibans are reconfiguring Sholan computers for our use and designing the programs to my specs."

"We have a couple of Sumaan working on engineering as well as helping sort through the heavier equipment," said Davies. "Their strength is a real time-saver, especially in areas where you can't fit in lifting equipment."

"No problems with the Sumaan or Touibans?"

"No," said Jo. "Why should there be? We all know enough basic Sholan for us to understand each other. At first, the curiosity of the Touibans was—disconcerting," she said with a grin, "but they've settled down as team members."

Davies began to grin.

"From the look on your face, Davies, doubtless your grapevine is still as good as ever," said Commander Skinner. "Especially now you have a line to the *Khalossa.*"

Davies' face fell.

"Come off it, man," said Skinner, smiling. "You don't think I lived and worked with the lot of you for all those years without getting to know you, do you? Or that I wasn't aware of most of the scams you and Skai were pulling? You were a tightly knit group then, the best I had. That's why I never interfered."

Jo drained her mug and put it back on the table. "Where are we going?"

Skinner's smile faded. "Jalna. A planet never contacted by the Alliance despite the fact the Chemerians have been trading there for fifty or more years. It's deep in Chemerian space."

"Why?" asked Davies.

"The Valtegan ship that was based here parked in orbit

around Jalna a few weeks ago and traded for supplies. They sold four Sholans to the natives."

"Sold!" exclaimed Jo. "What kind of people are these Jalnians? And where the hell did the Valtegans get the Sholans from?"

"The Jalnians are humanoid like us, which is why we've been asked to send a team there. As for the Sholans, they were probably picked up from one of the two Sholan colony worlds that were destroyed. You aren't going there because of the Sholans. Two shuttles landed on Jalna, one traded and left. The other landed briefly, and illegally, outside the spaceport, then crashed on takeoff. That's the one we want you to investigate. The Alliance needs to know what the Valtegans were doing at Jalna and they think that craft holds the key."

"Haven't the Jalnians examined it?" asked Davies.

"Not yet apparently. It's in an isolated area several weeks' travel from the nearest town and their tech level is virtually nonexistent. Briefly, several other species unknown to the Alliance trade at the spaceport on the planet but no aliens are allowed out of the port area. Only humanoids can travel undetected among the Jalnains."

"What about the four Sholans?" asked Davies.

"Not our concern. The Sholans are sending in another team shortly to rescue them. Information on the Valtegans is our priority. Jo, you're going because you're the Valtegan language expert. I don't think anyone else in the Alliance knows as much as you do about them."

"I know very little," she murmured.

"It's still more than anyone else," replied Skinner. "Davies, you're going along as the engineer and electronics expert. I don't need to tell you how important getting this job done successfully is to us as a species, do I?"

"No, sir," said Davies.

"You'll get a full briefing on Shola. The Jalnian culture is apparently comparable with our Dark Ages so you're going to the Warrior Guild for a crash course in the appropriate weapon skills. You can't use guns on Jalna, only edged weapons. You'll also pick up the third member of your team there."

"Who else is going?" asked Davies.

"A human Telepath is being chosen from the Guild to go down onto the planet with you. There'll be a team of Sumaan elite Warriors as backup in the Chemerian trading vessel in case you run into trouble in the port area. Your contact on that craft will be a Sholan Telepath."

"When do we leave?" asked Jo.

"At sixteen hundred hours today from the spaceport. I'm sorry it's such short notice, but the whole mission has been mounted as a matter of urgency. No one has had much warning." Commander Skinner got to his feet, Jo and Davies following suit. "We need to reach that craft before the Jalnians. Take care, and good luck."

As they traveled down in the elevator, Davies turned to Jo, letting out a long breath.

"I don't know about you, but I could do with a beer after that."

"Sure," said Jo. "I don't like the sound of Jalna. If we've got to dodge slavers as well as everything else, this could be very tricky. On top of that, we've to learn new weapon skills."

"Blow that. I'll certainly be taking a gun, and so will you if you've got any sense," said Davies as the elevator doors opened on the ground floor.

* * *

The following day found Kusac and Carrie relaxing in the small bay where his estate bordered on the main Aldatan land. Carrie was a lot better, though still very tired, which Kusac deduced was due to her using her own healing ability.

"They're bringing Jo and Davies to Shola, and you kept it from me?" said Carrie in disbelief.

"Father actually told me yesterday but I wanted to talk to him about it before telling you," said Kusac, squatting back down on the sandy beach beside her. "If you want to see them, he'll arrange for them to be brought out here secretly. He wants us out of the public eye for as long as possible, and I agree with him."

"What's going on?" she asked suspiciously, trying to push herself one-handedly up from among her nest of cushions. "Why are Jo and Davies coming to Shola?"

Kusac's arm steadied her. "Father won't tell me."

"Damn! I want to know."

"Don't worry," Kusac grinned, ears twitching. "I've got Kaid onto it. If anyone can find out, he can."

"What would they want with two Terran guerrillas on Shola?"

"Not just guerrillas. Don't forget that Davies is also a tech, so is Jo."

"Jo's also a linguist, a Valtegan specialist, and has at least some small telepathic talent," she said slowly, thinking it through.

"Valtegans?" said Kusac. "Perhaps that's the connection."

"Could be. But why here? There're no Valtegans near here, are there? I know the Guild has found bones in the ruins, but they were left there centuries ago."

"If Shola was in danger, Father would tell us instantly. We'll find out soon, don't worry," Kusac reassured her, sensing her fear through their Link.

He gave her a little shake, knowing how deep her fear of the Valtegans went despite her attempt to hide it.

"Carrie, this isn't Keiss, or the two colony worlds we lost. This is our home world. We've got the best military force in the Alliance sitting out there protecting us. There is no way the Valtegans can get anywhere near us. Not just that, we'd feel their presence if they were near Shola, wouldn't we?"

She nodded reluctantly as she leaned back against him, drawing strength from his presence.

"How's the research going?" he asked. "Are you back up to date with what you'd done before?"

"I've just finished reading through it."

"Have you found anything that could refer to the presence of the Valtegans?"

She gestured toward the comp pad she'd brought with her. "I'm checking through the last of the Telepath Clans' family records now," she said. "Most of them are genealogies. Did you know the Aldatan Clan records go back well over a thousand years?"

"I know we're one of the oldest clans on Shola, and that this land has always been ours."

"Funny thing is, all the records stop about fourteen hundred years ago, about the same time that the Valsgarth Clan died out. So I started doing some cross-referencing with the records of the other guilds. Yes," she said, forestalling him, "I did remember to use the security code your father gave us. My calls can't be traced."

"What did you find?"

"All guild records come to a stop at the same time. Or,"

she said, "to put it another way, all the records I've looked at begin around fifteen hundred years ago."

"That must be when we came out of the Cataclysm."

"Taizia mentioned it. What actually happened? Could it have anything to do with the Valtegan bones Vanna was shown?"

"I've no idea. No one knows exactly what happened, but there are records at the temple and Stronghold of dreams similar to the one that your Healer, Noni, told you about. I contacted Ghyan yesterday and he's researching them as well as the En'Shalla rituals. All that is certain is that at some time in our past, an immense disaster struck the planet, wiping out civilization as it was at the time. I'd be very surprised if it involved the Valtegans, though."

"Then what was that skeleton doing in the ruins? I suppose it's possible those remains are the only ones, but I'm sure that's highly unlikely. Haven't any ruins ever been excavated just for the sake of finding out what's there?" she asked.

"Not as far as I'm aware. They're certainly only used now as a rich source of ancient refined metals. I don't know that much about it, I'm afraid. It wasn't the province of my Guild."

"So you have a Dark Ages in your past, but one that hasn't been studied."

"As far as I know, very few people are interested in such ancient times. It's the achievements since then that concern our Guild Historians."

"This has me intrigued. Why is there no interest in your far past? Has it been suppressed? Your racial history only exists as the individual records of each guild. There isn't an overview of it. What happened that was so awful that a whole planet of people conspired to cover it up?"

"Not a whole planet," said Kusac. "The Guild Leaders, perhaps, but more than likely we're looking at the Telepath Guild again. If the priests on your world carried the burden of recording major events of the times, then likely ours did, too. They had the time and the learning to do it, after all."

"And all priests are Telepaths," added Carrie. She hesitated a moment. "An outrageous idea, I know, but what if this had been a Valtegan world and Sholans were the aliens here? If they'd overthrown the Valtegans and wanted to claim the world for themselves, then they'd suppress the past, wouldn't they?"

Kusac's ears flicked in amusement. "An interesting idea, Carrie, but we definitely evolved on this world. Look at the other species here—the jeggets for one. They may be only animals but they have a rudimentary form of telepathy. And how do you account for the fact that had this been a Valtegan world, there was no retributive action taken against us for wiping them out here?"

"Maybe it's taken them this long to find you again," she said with a grin. "I said it was only a theory, I didn't say it was a good one!"

Kusac laughed and flicked her nose gently with a finger. "Did you find out what you wanted to know about the Telepath families?"

"Oh, yes, I'd almost forgotten. There is a pattern," she said, reaching out to pull the comp pad closer. "I made my own notes which are easier to look at than flipping between the records." She touched the buttons, bringing several sets of figures and diagrams up on the small screen.

"When the records start, you can see that there were far more telepaths and Leska pairs. However, over the generations, despite a definite breeding program among the families, the numbers of Talented offspring has fallen. It's continuing to fall even today, though at a slower rate. No wonder the Guild and your father are concerned."

"I hadn't realized it was quite so bad," said Kusac. "Then along come the Terrans and now several of our telepaths are finding Leskas from your species rather than our own. If this trend goes on, in a few generations there may be no more pure Sholan telepaths."

Carrie broke the silence. "What's happened to cause the changes in our genetic structure until we're each apart from our own species? Has it been in us all along and we didn't realize it till we met?"

"I don't know, Carrie, but we'll show your findings to Father and Vanna. She and Jack have already started work on our genes, trying to find out which key ones have been altered."

"What do we do if they find a way to reverse what's happened?"

"They won't," he said firmly. He touched the bronze torc at her neck, then the bracelet on her right wrist. "You don't wear these because of our genes," he said, wrapping his arm around her.

"No, I don't," she said, smiling.

"I'm convinced, like you, that there's got to be a reason for our Link. Maybe if we dig deep enough, we'll find it. It's got to be something to do with Vartra if those dreams we've had are anything to go by."

"It may be worth finding out if the Telepath Guild has actual physical records from the past rather than this computerized stuff," said Carrie. "With every guild's records suddenly starting at around the same time, and being very detailed from the looks of the data I have here, it tends to suggest they were using a well established system. Therefore, somewhere there must be records that go back even farther. Would your father have access to any hidden files that might exist?"

"I doubt it, but Ghyan certainly has paper files on various ancient rituals. Maybe they hold something more. I'll get in touch with him tonight."

Carrie was looking out across the bay at a hill that was surrounded by the Valsgarth forest.

"What's that?" she asked, pointing.

Kusac followed her finger. "The hill?"

"No, the ruins on top of it."

"Your eyesight's very good," he said. "It's an old monastery or something. Hardly anything left now, just a few feet of old walls showing above the ground. When you're better, I'll take you there if you like."

"What kind of monastery?"

"I believe local legend has it that it was the primary one for the cult of Vartra. It's been a ruin for centuries." He stopped, eyes opening wide as he realized what he'd said. "There might be something left up there among the ruins," he said. "Esken and his people can't stop us investigating it because it's on our own land. I'm also pretty sure it's never been blasted for the same reason. Nobody's ever been in there to salvage metals and the like as far as I know, so there'd be no need."

"I wonder if the Telepath Guild House was always in Valsgarth town. I wonder if it could have started out in that monastery. Perhaps that's why priests have to be telepaths, too. What was Vartra the God of again?" she asked, squinting up at the ruin as the sun came out from behind a cloud.

"He wasn't the God of anything as such," said Kusac. "He was worshiped, and still is, mainly by Telepaths and Warriors. Some say he's the peaceful Warrior who fights only when there's a real need. He's the Telepaths' and Warriors' patron God."

"The two Guilds that are also clans," she murmured, looking back to her pad and making a note on it. "And Valtegan remains in your ruined cities. Interesting. I wonder why those two Guilds specifically. There's got to be a deeper link between them. And what were Valtegans doing here all that time ago? I think I'll have a look at the public records of the Warrior Guild, too. Then there're the dreams."

"I wouldn't waste any more time on the records," said Kusac, stretching out for the plate of cooked meat that lay between them. "I don't think they have anything to do with this genetics business, and if in the past there had been Valtegans on Shola in any large numbers, when we found them on Keiss, someone would surely have remembered seeing or reading a reference about them."

Carrie helped herself to a piece when he held the plate out to her. "Call it a hunch," she said.

* * *

T'Chebbi stood alongside her fellow Brotherhood members Nyash and Lasad, waiting for the arrival of the cruiser from Earth. On it were Zhyaf, who'd been the Interpreter for the *Rhyaki,* and his Human Leska, Mara.

A couple flanked by two Warriors, emerged from the air lock onto the deck of Chagda Station.

"That's them," T'Chebbi said quietly to her companions.

The Human was taller than Carrie, she noted, and dark-haired where her Liegena was fair. Dressed in Sholan robes, she walked close by the side of her Leska, putting her hand on his arm as they approached. When they stopped in front of them, T'Chebbi saw that she was pale-skinned with eyes of a bright, piercing blue.

The older Warrior saluted T'Chebbi as seniormost before speaking.

"Sister T'Chebbi, I presume you are the escort we were told to expect. I thought we were due to dock at the passenger bays rather than the military section. I trust you've no objection to letting me see your orders?"

T'Chebbi took the letter, sealed with the AlRel logo, from her pocket and passed it to him.

He opened it, quickly scanning the contents before looking up and handing it back to her. "Very well, Sister. Despite the changes, all is as it should be. Let me present Interpreter Zhyaf and his Leska, Mara Ryan." He turned back to his charges. "Sister T'Chebbi and the Brothers will escort you to the Aldatan estate where the Clan Lord will meet you personally."

As she stepped forward, T'Chebbi watched Zhyaf raise an eye ridge in surprise.

"Interpreter Zhyaf, if you would come with us," she began, only to be cut short by Mara.

"You're a female!" she said, her tone surprised. "I thought you said the Brotherhood were your special forces, Zhyaf. How come a female is one of them?"

"Nothing to prevent Sholan females from becoming Warriors or Brothers, if the God calls us," said T'Chebbi smoothly, seeing a brief look of panic cross the Interpreter's face. "Please, follow us. There's a private shuttle waiting for us at the next berth." She stood aside, pointedly waiting for them to move toward Nyash and Lasad.

The couple started walking and as T'Chebbi fell in behind them, she heard Mara say to Zhyaf, "That's what I want to do, Zhyaf. I want to be one of the Brothers."

"I'm afraid it's not quite that easy, Mara," said the Interpreter gently to his obviously younger Leska. "But that's all in the future. For the moment you need to get used to our home world. It's very different from anything you've seen so far."

She nodded, then turned to look at T'Chebbi again. "I heard there's more of my people on Shola. Where are they staying? Will I meet them? Zhyaf said you'd be able to tell me."

"Twenty Humans," said T'Chebbi as they walked the short distance to their docking bay entrance. "Most are at Telepath Guild. The Clan Lord will tell you more."

"Why the change of destination, Sister?" asked Zhyaf, turning his head toward her.

Beyond them T'Chebbi could see Chief Tutor Sorli

accompanied by four armed Warriors coming through the door that divided the passenger area from the military bays.

"Clan Lord will tell you, Interpreter Zhyaf," she said, moving smoothly past them to Nyash and Lasad. "Lasad, get them on board," she said quietly. "Nyash, stay with me. We'll deal with Sorli."

"This way," said Lasad, ushering the Leska pair up the ramp leading to their shuttle. Abruptly Zhyaf stopped, then looked at the group hurrying toward them.

"Sister, why are you taking us to the Aldatan estate against the wishes of Guild Master Esken?" he demanded.

"Interpreter, please board the shuttle," said T'Chebbi, closing the gap between them and herself. "Once we're on board I'll give you my orders, direct from Clan Lord Aldatan himself. He is now the head of the Mixed Leska Program, appointed by Governor Nesul."

"I must protest . . ." Zhyaf began, then abruptly stopped as he saw the Brothers swing their rifles into a ready position and form a barrier between them and the Guild party.

"Interpreter," said Lasad, crowding the pair forward, "this is no place for such a discussion. Please board now."

T'Chebbi cast a glance behind her as she and Nyash continued to back up the ramp, rifles at the ready.

Sorli and his Warriors stopped at the Base of the gangway as Zhyaf and Mara were herded on board.

"We're missing all the excitement," Mara protested, her voice growing fainter.

"What are you doing, Sister T'Chebbi?" asked Sorli, trying not to appear too out of breath after his dash across the deck. "You know Master Esken wants Interpreter Zhyaf and his Leska brought to the Guild."

"I have my orders from the Clan Lord, Tutor Sorli," said T'Chebbi, continuing her backward progress up the ramp. "Master Esken's wishes are secondary in this instance."

"Do the Aldatans now dictate what the Brotherhood should do?" he asked.

"No, Tutor Sorli. The Brotherhood obeys the wishes of the head of project. Your request had to be cleared with the Clan Lord. He wished them brought to his wife's estate."

"T'Chebbi, let's discuss this under more civilized conditions," said Sorli, signaling to his Warrior escort to lower their pulse rifles. "There's no need for us to wave weapons at each other."

T'Chebbi smiled to herself. The Warriors wouldn't fire lightly on the Brotherhood, and all four of them were looking distinctly uncomfortable.

"Not at liberty to discuss this issue with you, Tutor Sorli. I have my orders. If you wish to negotiate, contact the Clan Lord."

"Are you saying you refuse to release Interpreter Zhyaf and his Leska into our custody?"

"I am, Tutor," said T'Chebbi, feeling the slant of the ground under her bare feet changing. She risked a quick glance behind her. They were almost level with the air lock door.

"In!" she hissed to Nyash as she took the last few steps herself. "Good day, Tutor," she said, backing through the hatch.

As she did so, Nyash hit the door mechanism, sealing them off from the station.

"Good work," said T'Chebbi, reslinging her rifle over her shoulder as she turned to run into the passenger section of their craft.

"I'm not sitting down until I know what's going on," said Zhyaf, standing in the aisle, a hand on the back of the seat that Mara was sitting in.

"Interpreter, your letter from the Clan Lord," said T'Chebbi, handing him an envelope. "For you in case there was any trouble. These are my orders." She handed him a second letter. "Perhaps you could sit to read it. We need to take off before anything else happens to delay us," she said, moving past him to reach their pilot.

CHAPTER 6

"I must protest, Clan Lord," said Guild Master Esken, his brows meeting in a deep frown. "Had you told me you intended your people to meet Interpreter Zhyaf and his Leska at Chagda, then I wouldn't have bothered to send Sorli. We had made preparations to receive them here."

"I wouldn't feel so put out, Esken," said Konis, his tone silky. "As head of the project, had you contacted me when you should, you'd have been told. You can take it as understood that any new Leska pairs will be brought straight to the estate for evaluation. Those who have a normal Sholan Leska Link will be brought to the Guild as soon as possible, the rest will stay here."

Esken's expression didn't change but Konis could feel the anger radiating toward him from the screen of his console.

"As you wish, Clan Lord. In that case, I have another matter to take up with you."

"Certainly. How can I help?"

"Since we no longer have any mixed Leska pairs here, I tried to dismiss the Warriors who've been guarding the Guildhouse for the last several weeks. They tell me I have no jurisdiction over them and that their orders are to remain guarding the Guild and its grounds until told otherwise. When I checked with the Warrior Guild, they told me their personnel are taking orders directly from you."

"That's correct. While there are no Human Leskas at the Guild, there are some eighteen Terrans in residence with you. In the past, feeling has run high against Humans in some areas of the population. I'm sure you wouldn't want to find yourself in the middle of an interplanetary diplomatic incident, as you would should any Human telepath be killed while in your charge. They need to be protected. And, of course, Guild Master Esken, if one of them should form a

Leska Link, then they *will* need to brought here for the level of protection only we can offer."

Esken's anger washed over him, reaching a new high. "Is this utterly necessary?" he demanded. "As a Telepath yourself you should understand that my staff and I find the presence of Warriors in our Guildhouse extremely offensive, not only because of the mental noise and attitudes they bring with them, but also because of the atmosphere their presence creates. It's most unsettling for us all, especially the cubs."

"On the estate I warrant we have three times the number of Warriors and Brothers you have," replied Konis, his voice becoming more clipped. "You'll get used to it. We did. Fit dampers in all the rooms, Esken, then you'll get your peace."

"And just who's supposed to pay for this? The cash outlay will be ridiculous! We can't afford it, and on principle, I have no intention of fitting dampers all over the Guild to accommodate your Warriors!"

Konis lifted his shoulders in a shrug. "That's entirely up to you. However, I suggest that if you change your mind, you contact the offices of the High Command and request your funding from them. Now if that's all, Master Esken, I will have to go as I'm extremely busy. Good day."

Konis leaned forward and cut the connection. During his conversation with Esken, he'd been aware of the noise from outside but had been able to ignore it—just. Now it resolved itself into something recognizable: the kitlings and his daughter, Kitra. He frowned, getting to his feet. They weren't allowed to play on the south side of the house, Kitra knew that. Apart from any other consideration, Carrie was resting in the room immediately above his.

He strode out of his office and into the corridor, heading through the archway, calling for his youngest daughter.

"Kitra! What in Vartra's name is all this noise about! Shouldn't you be at school or something?" he demanded, then stopped dead as he surveyed the scene before him.

"I'm not to go to school, Father," said Kitra, turning round toward him. "Don't you remember? You said we weren't going to the Guild any more for the time being."

Four guilty faces were turned toward him, and one of them was human.

"Did we disturb you?" the Human asked brightly. "I'm sorry. We were just playing."

In her hand she held the end of a rope that was attached to one of the lower limbs of an old, gnarled fruit tree.

Konis took a long, slow, deep breath before answering. "Kitra, that tree is one of the oldest on the estate," he said, unable to stop the tip of his tail from flicking in anger. "It's also one of the more fragile ones. It isn't up to holding even Jinoe's weight. You should have known better. Return with Rrai and Jinoe to the play area, then go and find your brother. Ask him to meet me in my office." He looked over to the Human girl.

"You must be Mara Ryan, Interpreter Zhyaf's Leska," he said as the three younglings dashed round to the back of the house. "I'm Konis Aldatan. I hope you've found your rooms comfortable?"

"Yes, thank you," said Mara. "I'm afraid this was my idea," she said, letting the end of the rope dangle free. "Shall I untie it for you?" She turned toward the tree again.

"No, just leave it, thank you," he said, pushing her very inexpert mental probe aside. "One of the gardeners can see to it. It really is too fragile for anyone to climb. You're lucky you didn't fall."

"Oh, don't worry about me," she said brightly, a Human smile splitting her face. "I was born climbing trees."

Konis refrained from saying anything and even managed not to let his ears flick.

"Have you met your aide yet?" he asked, wondering what he or she was doing allowing all the young people outside on their own.

"You mean Rulla? He's upstairs talking to Zhyaf."

"I think it would be a good idea if you rejoined them for the moment," he said. "This is the time when we try to relax after work. Third meal will be ready in an hour or two, but if you want anything to drink or a light snack, there's the dispenser in your lounge. I take it you've been shown where everything is?"

"Not really," said Mara, backing away slowly toward the corner of the house.

Konis could feel her embarrassment. "Don't worry," he said in what he hoped was a reassuring tone. "You'll soon get used to our ways. Carrie did. I know how much of an upheaval in your life this has all been, but the worst is over now. You're not only among friends, but also with others

who have a Sholan partner. Just take your time and everything will be fine."

"Yes, sir," she said before turning on her heel and
sprinting back in the direction the younglings had gone.

Konis sighed. He remembered Zhyaf. He was a good
person and a fine interpreter, well suited to his intellectual
profession—but to have a Leska who was no more than half
his age? He shook his head as he returned to his office.
Zhyaf had been born staid and middle-aged. It looked like
Mara was going to be a handful.

Kusac joined him a few minutes later. "Kitra said you
wanted me, Father. What can I do for you?" he asked,
coming over to perch on the edge of Konis' desk beside him.

"Kitra and the two kitlings," he said succinctly, mentally
opening their private family link.

"Ah, their schooling," Kusac nodded. "I was about to
come down and see to them myself, but you beat me to it."

"Did they disturb Carrie?"

Kusac shook his head. "No, she's still sleeping. That
Healer Kaid took her to must be one of the best around.
She's really on the mend now."

"I'm glad. We've been very worried for both of you,"
Konis said, reaching out to lay his hand on Kusac's arm.

I'd be careful, Father, warned Kusac. *Tomorrow's our
Link day. Already the sensitivity's increasing.*

Konis moved his hand, smiling faintly. "I know. Is she up
to it? There are drugs Vanna can use if she isn't. I know her
system was too weak after the Challenge, but she's stronger
now."

Kusac shook his head. "No need. She's fine," he grinned,
dipping his head to one side. *We weren't sleeping all
afternoon.*

Konis gave a small purr of laughter. "The kitlings," he
reminded his son. "Among the people you requested, is there
a teacher capable of educating not just the three young ones,
but also Mara?"

"There will be when Ghyan joins us," said Kusac. "Dzaka
has been teaching them meditation and self-control techniques. Until Ghyan leaves the temple, how about letting
him start training them in combat? It would keep them busy
and out from underfoot."

Reluctantly Konis nodded. *I dislike the whole concept of
any of you learning combat. I know it's necessary, not only*

*for your own personal safety, but because it's what the High
Command wants. You know they want you all trained as special field operatives, don't you?*

Yes, we know, Kusac replied with a sigh. *If Vanna and
Brynne, as well as Zhyaf and Mara develop the same way we
did, then they'll have their elite telepath fighting force.*

I'm torn two ways, Konis admitted. *In my official capacities, I know you'll be an asset to the Forces and to Shola, but
as a parent and a telepath, I don't approve of it at all.*

*Neither do we. We haven't an option at the moment. All we
can do is go along with them and see where it leads us.*

How's the work on your estate going?

It's taking time for them to start, sent Kusac. *Before they
can begin they must assess the state of the buildings still
standing and see what's needed in the way of repairs. Once
that's done, then they'll be free to start work on the new
structures. At least all the people involved are camping out
down there rather than staying up here.*

*Believe me, Kusac, your mother and I are very grateful for
that!* sent Konis. "You're still determined to become
En'Shalla? There's nothing we can do to dissuade you?" He
looked anxiously at his son.

Kusac met his gaze. "Nothing, Father."

"Have you any idea what it entails? You realize no one has
survived the journey in over ten generations?"

"So I keep getting told," said Kusac, flicking his ears in
faint irritation. "Carrie's been using the authorization you
gave us to get files from the Telepath Guild, the Warrior
Guild, and everything she could find in the public sector on
the Brotherhood. She's trying to see how far back their
records go. We've also seen how the number of telepaths is
dropping with every generation despite the breeding program that's been going on for over a thousand years. It's
worrying."

"That's my problem, not yours," said Konis.

"Did it ever occur to you that perhaps the reason for the
decline is that our bloodlines have become too inbred?
Maybe what we need is some of the outside blood, like that
from the Brotherhood."

"You mean because of their lesser Talents?" Konis frowned.
"Surely they're not worth taking into consideration?"

"I've been told that some of their Talents are far from
lesser ones. Look at the Healer, Noni. She's got to rate as

highly as one of the best in the Guild, if not better. Think it over at least. You'll have Vanna's research shortly. I've asked her to do DNA tests on everyone who's been exposed to that virus Carrie and I had a few months ago. It'll show up the changes in our genes and tell us who's compatible with whom. I'm hoping that those who don't find Leska partners will be essentially Sholan so that we don't lose too many of our telepaths to the new genes."

"I'll ask Vanna to give me copies of all her work, including weekly updates. We should know one way or the other fairly soon. Now," Konis said, standing up, "I'm going to raid your mother's kitchen for a mug of c'shar. Coming?"

"Right beside you," said Kusac.

* * *

"You agreed to what?" demanded Ghezu.

"I agreed to an alliance with them in return for their support at the All Guilds Council meeting," said Lijou patiently.

"Dammit, Lijou! You had no right to agree to that! An alliance is no good to us! We need them as Brothers or we have no claim!" He got to his feet and began pacing between the desk and the window, tail lashing angrily from side to side.

"Ghezu, you're not listening to me," said Lijou. "I've just told you that publicly they will be seen to join us. Only we will know the reality."

"You haven't the right to make decisions like that on your own," snarled Ghezu, stalking over to the less formal seating where the Head Priest sat.

"I'm the only one clearheaded enough to see that we weren't going to get anything more from him!" Lijou's temper broke. He'd had enough of making allowances for Ghezu's increasingly unbalanced behavior. "Stop letting your prejudices rule your thoughts and actions! For Vartra's sake, Ghezu," he continued more quietly, "we're on the brink of a new era for the Brotherhood. Let's make the best deal we can with them and ensure we get our full Guild status. That's surely more important than any other consideration."

Ghezu flung himself down on the settee opposite Lijou, glaring at him. "He only wants twenty-five of my best operatives, Lijou! It's all right for you! He doesn't want your best lay priests!"

"On the contrary. I'm losing Ghyan and four of my religious Brothers—five people I can ill afford to lose, considering there are fewer of them than your warriors in the Brotherhood. Don't be so blind, Ghezu. Think of what we're gaining."

Ghezu growled deep in his throat. "I know who's behind this, it's Kaid! And he's not having Dzaka, that's final!"

Lijou sighed inwardly and closed his eyes for a moment, silently offering up a prayer to Vartra, asking Him to make his colleague see some sense.

"Let Dzaka go, Ghezu," he said. "You've had your fun from all accounts. Kaid has come near to killing him because of you. Surely that's enough to satisfy any revenge."

"You know nothing about it, Lijou, so don't presume to make my mind up for me," Ghezu snapped. "It's not Dzaka I want."

"By the sword of Vartra, Ghezu! What the hell did Kaid do to you all those years ago to make you hate him so much?" demanded Lijou, sitting forward in his chair. Then he sensed what it had been. "A female? All this over a female? Gods, Ghezu, don't you think you're getting this completely out of proportion?"

"Stop reading my mind, Lijou, it's none of your damned business!" he growled, getting up and heading back to his desk to pick up the offending document.

Lijou turned in his seat, following him with his eyes. "Whatever it was, it was long ago, Ghezu. It's time to let it go."

"Like hell it is! They can have everyone except Dzaka," he said, taking up a stylus and scoring through one of the names before signing the document with a flourish. Tossing the stylus back on the desk, he picked up the agreement and stalked across to Lijou, thrusting it into his hand.

"Here, take it! It's not time to let go my revenge, Lijou. I can't wipe out thirty-five years of waiting and hoping to find her again just like that, even if you could. It's time to have my reckoning with him for two reasons. Now she's finally been located, I find out she's dying. I can never have her now, but I'll be damned if he does! Somehow he'll find out where she is and go to her. I can't live with that again."

Lijou took the document from him. "You should be caring

more for her approaching death than plotting revenge
because she preferred him to you. Where's your compassion
gone, Ghezu? You never used to be like this. What's it all
got to do with Dzaka anyway? Why involve him in your
schemes? Only a couple of months ago you said Kaid was
once a friend. What's suddenly changed to make you want to
destroy him now?"

Ghezu turned away. "He's thwarted me at every turn since
this business began, Lijou. The Brothers that knew him
before—and some of the newer ones, damn him—want to
follow him! It's beginning all over again, as if he'd never
been away!" Angrily he turned back to his colleague.

"I've led the Brotherhood well. You know it's prospered
under me. The day I was appointed Loed's successor, they
all gave me their loyalty. Then he turns up again. A flick of
his ears and it's all forgotten. I won't have my Leadership
challenged by him, Lijou!" he said, his tail beginning to lash
angrily from side to side again.

"He's not challenging you, Ghezu, you're imaging it,"
Lijou said in what he hoped was a placatory tone.

"If you can't see it then you're blind! Everyone else can.
Look at what he's demanding through that damned Aldatan
cub! He's got some of my best people completely under his
own rule—his own Brotherhood, Lijou! He's making his
own territory, Challenging me on *my* ground! And I'll never
forgive him for what he did to Khemu!"

"What did he do?" The question was asked before he
could stop himself.

"He didn't care about her, he just used her. He paired with
her once, then never again, leaving her so damaged by the
experience that she wouldn't look at another male outside
her family. Nothing I said or did made any difference. I tried
to find out what had happened, but the one time I saw her,
she refused to tell me. So did Kaid."

"It was their business, not yours," said Lijou. "You hadn't
the right to interfere."

"I had!" He spun round again, teeth bared in an angry
growl. "I wanted her, too! And I wouldn't have treated her
like he did! She was from a good family, Lijou, not just one
of the village females. She shut herself away, wouldn't talk
to anyone. Her betrothal was called off because she refused
the mate chosen for her. They told the Clan Lord she'd died
in a mountain accident, but he was the only one that believed

that! Her family disowned her because of her behavior. After
a year or two, she ran away and just disappeared."

"Then how did you find her?"

"I had our people keep a lookout for her. She's living at
Rhijudu, with one of the desert tribes. She has one of those
damned wasting diseases; she won't last till the winter."

The emotions Lijou felt from Ghezu were strange, owing
more to anger and revenge—against both of them—than to
love. That had withered and died long ago, to be replaced
only by jealousy and hurt pride. He also sensed Ghezu's
anger that she'd not responded to the glamour he'd tried to
use on her. Lijou felt appalled that Ghezu had sunk so low as
to use his Talent to make a young female want him.

Ghezu turned and walked back to his desk. "I won't tolerate him any longer, Lijou. Dzaka's younger and faster than
him—and has good reasons to hate him," he said, sitting
down. "I want him to kill Kaid. I'll make sure he does." His
voice had dropped, becoming silky with the contemplation
of his final revenge.

"Ghezu, you're mad," said Lijou, getting up from his
chair, sickened by the other's attitude. Their talk had
devolved into a hate session. There was no point in him
remaining, nothing of any use could be accomplished now,
and his continued presence was only fueling Ghezu's desire
for revenge. "Dzaka won't kill Kaid."

"Do you want to bet on it?" asked Ghezu as he watched
Lijou walking to the door.

"No!" Lijou snapped. "I want you to give this foolish idea
up! It's beneath you—a scheme born of utter insanity! Leave
Dzaka alone to make his peace with Kaid, and, for Vartra's
sake, leave Kaid alone, too! I was only appointed the year
you expelled Kaid, but I've seen you do enough damage to
both of them these past ten years or more. What you did
before that, I don't know, but I do know that if you pursue
this course, you're more likely to come out of it dead than
Kaid is!"

He shut the door firmly behind him, taking a deep breath
of the clean air in the corridor. Not only was Ghezu heading
rapidly toward insanity, but the feel of his darkening soul
was like a miasma of evil. Something had to be done about
him, and soon, before he destroyed Stronghold in his desire
for revenge. A sudden conviction hit Lijou like a punch in
the gut: Kaid had to survive to walk the Fire Margins. Why,

he didn't know, but the conviction that he must was already growing stronger.

* * *

It was the following day when Kaid got a call from Ghyan requesting him to go to the temple in Valsgarth. When he arrived, an acolyte led him out of the ancient building and into the gardens where Ghyan and some half a dozen younglings were picking redberries from the bushes.

The priest looked up as soon as they stepped through the archway from the temple precinct. Handing his basket to one of the youths, he made his way back through the bushes toward Kaid.

"Thank you, Sonjhi," he said, nodding his thanks to the young female as she moved off to join the others. He turned back toward the temple.

Kaid followed him in silence. Ghyan wasn't happy—it took no talent on his part to know that.

Once inside, the priest went to his desk, indicating that Kaid should sit on the chair opposite. He handed him the envelope that lay there.

"That's the agreement, as arranged, between Liegen Aldatan and the Brotherhood. It's been signed by both Lijou and Ghezu. When your Liege has signed both copies, return one to me and I'll see it reaches Stronghold," he said.

"They agreed to all the people we wanted?" asked Kaid, putting it away in his inner jacket pocket for safety.

"Not all. Ghezu refuses to release Dzaka."

Kaid's ear flicked briefly in annoyance. "I rather thought he might," he sighed.

"I've also got some information on the En'Shalla rituals," Ghyan continued, handing him a data cube. "It includes the transcripts of the last two attempts made to reach Vartra through the Fire Margins some thirty years ago. Both were unsuccessful, but the words of the officiating priests were recorded."

"Thank you," said Kaid, pocketing the cube and moving to get up.

"Haven't you got anything to ask?" Ghyan demanded, face creasing in a frown.

"Excuse me?" Kaid looked at him in surprise.

"Lijou says you're to be the third—to make up the Triad

necessary to follow the Fire Margins ritual. You do know there needs to be three, don't you?"

Kaid's eyes widened in shock. "You're wrong. He can't have said that."

Ghyan nodded, obviously not pleased. "I hope both he and Vartra know what they're doing," he growled. "Have you any idea what it entails?"

"Some, and I'm not doing it," Kaid stated flatly.

"I told you, you've no choice. Kusac's agreed. By Vartra, Kaid," he said angrily, "You'd better start living up to the job! You have to be part of their Link, in rapport with the Liegena so Kusac can sense you. As the Warrior, *you* have to guard them from any physical and spiritual danger! You need to keep a clear head and watch what's going on around you as they'll be too involved. You need to *care* what happens to them or none of you will return! Do you think you can learn to do that, Kaid?" he asked sarcastically. "Learn to care? You'll have to if she's going to accept you— if Kusac is."

"Stop it, Ghyan," said Kaid, turning away from him and getting to his feet. "You've no call to preach at me. I know how to do my job, but I've told you, I'm not going."

Ghyan reached out across his desk and grasped his arm, holding him back.

With a snarl, Kaid rounded on him just as the priest suddenly released him, his ears flicking back and staying there in shock.

"Don't touch me!" Kaid could feel the blood pounding in his head and knew that the priest had felt his anger. He had to be more careful, his control was slipping too often these days. He took a deep breath.

"You misjudge me, Ghyan," he said, speaking more slowly. "If I'm to help them, I have to keep some objectivity. Only then can I see their best course of action. You know that like all the Brothers, I was a lay-priest in my time. I still follow our God. If He's called me—truly called me—then I'll go with them."

"You've been chosen," stated Ghyan, rubbing his palm against the side of his robe. "You've obviously got a strong enough Talent to do the job. Read the data. You'll need to get closer to her, on a personal level. She needs to trust you almost as much as she trusts Kusac because she'll be the link between you and him. If she trusts you, so will he. It's all on the cube. See that you read it, Kaid."

"I'll read it," he said, turning and walking to the door. "You've been chosen, too, Ghyan. You're on the list of people we need at Valsgarth. Kusac's opening up the old estate for the mixed Leskas to live on. We'll need a real priest, not one of the Brothers, to teach the cubs."

"I know all about that so don't think to divert me, Kaid. There's more," said Ghyan, coming out from behind his desk.

Kaid stopped, his hand on the door lever. "Well?"

"The bond you'll share with her is the same as any telepathic link, only weaker. Weaker because you aren't a telepath."

"Get on with it, Ghyan," snapped Kaid, annoyed at the way the priest was still standing in judgment over him. None of this was his doing. Vartra knew he hadn't looked for it.

"The bond will grow until you're drawn to pair, then it's sealed, completed so you can work as a Triad. Sort your mind out, Kaid, or you'll never get close enough to her. For the God's sake and theirs, try to care about her!" he said earnestly. "If you hurt her in any way, Kusac will quite literally have your hide."

Kaid shut his eyes, leaning against the door, glad that his back was to Ghyan. There was no way he could do this. Pair with Carrie? It was impossible. He felt a rising tide of panic which he ruthlessly suppressed. Ghyan must not know how he felt—no one must know. He felt hounded. First the visions, then Noni. Now this.

"He'll likely try to have it anyway," said Kaid tiredly. "He does know about this aspect of the En'Shalla ritual, doesn't he? He agreed, knowing this?"

"If he doesn't, he will when he's read the data."

"You'd think Vartra would have had the sense to choose a Sholan pair, wouldn't you?" said Kaid, attempting to sound more like his usual self as he opened the door. "Humans with their confused morality and odd religions aren't the likeliest candidates for any of our rituals."

"We're all in the hands of the Gods, Kaid. Frankly, I don't know why Vartra picked you either." Ghyan's reply was sharp. "I haven't forgotten our last talk, before the Challenge. Perhaps He's chosen you to teach you compassion— He knows you need some!"

"You presume too much, Priest," growled Kaid, opening the door. "What I do or don't feel for them is not your concern!"

He walked along the narrow dark corridor, cursing under his breath. With any other female, he'd just approach her and after some talk, ask her to spend time with him, then let nature take its course. At least that's what he'd done before . . . Khemu. He was sure customs hadn't changed that much in the last three decades. But he couldn't do that with her. Afraid as she still was of Terran reactions to her marriage with Kusac, she'd never understand he meant no insult to her. And Kusac? He was so protective of her, so strongly tied to her every thought and action! If they intended to take the En'Shalla path to the Fire Margins, then someone would have to be the third, that was an inescapable fact. Why him, though? If they did achieve a Triad between them, what effect would he have on it—and them?

His senses suddenly began to swim, and, dizzily, he stopped, leaning against the wall for support as the corridor before him seemed to lurch and then vanish.

He stood on the darkened edge of a brightly lit field. Around him the immense shadows of cargo ships loomed out of the night, their access ramps glowing golden in contrast to the intense white of the surrounding illuminations. Kusac stood beside him and he could feel the rage his Liege was directing against the small group of people ahead of them. He shifted his stance, accommodating the weight in his arms, looking down to see if she was all right.

Once more, his surroundings seemed to lurch, then he was back in the corridor, his cheek pressed against the cold stone walls. With him came the memory of the pain he'd read on Carrie's face and in her mind, and the way she'd been clinging to him.

Closing his eyes, he took a deep breath while he searched his memory for an appropriate litany—but there wasn't one for what he'd just experienced.

*   *   *

Jo's and Davies' first port of call had been the *Khalossa*. Their stay couldn't have been briefer. In line with current policy, they stopped only long enough for a crash course in the orientation program on Sholan culture and language given to all visiting Humans. They still needed to practice the skills and experience the culture for themselves, but it saved months of time and many potential misunderstandings.

Then they embarked on the adapted shuttlecraft. Seven days later they docked at Chagda Station, the mercantile and military space station in orbit around Shola. The regular shuttle service delivered them to Valsgarth, home of Shola's main Telepath Clan, the Aldatans, and the largest Telepath Guild town.

They were met by Telepath and Warrior Guild personnel who were there to escort them in a private vehicle to the Guildhouse.

It was early afternoon and as they looked down on the crowded streets below, Jo turned to the Telepath beside her.

"No ground vehicles?" she asked.

"Only the Chemerians' powered chairs," she replied. "All deliveries of goods are made in the early morning before the stores open for business. Vehicles arriving at Valsgarth at any other time wait in the goods area at the spaceport till the next day."

"Where are we going now?" asked Davies as the craft rose, then banked slightly to clear a high wall.

"Here. This is the Telepath Guild where you'll be welcomed by Clan Lord Aldatan. From there you'll go to the Warrior Guild where you will stay during your time with us."

"Kusac's father," Jo said quietly to Davies.

As the craft set down in the large courtyard it sent clouds of dust billowing up around it. The students caught in it scurried away, coughing and choking.

As the dust settled, Davies leaned forward over the seat to talk to Jo.

"The place is built like a fortress," he said, nodding toward the huge wooden doors that stood open at the entrance to the Guildhall.

"Our past included a time of superstition and fear, just as yours did," said the female beside Jo.

The extent of the building, which reached in places to the height of three or four stories, was palatial. The ancient central hall had been added to over the centuries, expanding that

modest building into a rambling complex. Despite this there
was a harmonious look and feel to the whole.

"It's at least a thousand years old," agreed the female as
she moved to get up.

They were ushered into the ground floor room that served
as the Clan Lord's office.

"Well come," said Konis, getting up to greet them. "So at
last I meet some of the Terrans who worked with my son and
bond-daughter. Please, be seated." He indicated the comfortably padded chairs. "Hot drinks are on the table in front of
you. Would you prefer some of your coffee or our c'shar?"
he asked, indicating the two sealed jugs.

"Coffee, please," said Jo, glancing at Davies for confirmation as she sank into one of the chairs. A look of surprise and
pleasure crossed her face.

"I'm sure the chairs are a most welcome change after the
scant comfort on our military shuttles," said Konis, sitting
down again.

"I regret having to break your journey like this. I'm sure
you want to reach your final destination as soon as possible,
but I wished to see you first. Not least of all you, my dear,"
he said, watching Jo carefully as his mind gently touched the
edges of hers.

Surprise made her tense.

"Why did you choose to keep your Talent to yourself and
remain on Keiss?" Konis asked.

Jo looked at Davies in panic, then back to Konis.

"You're mistaken," she said. "I'm not a telepath. What on
earth gave you that idea?"

"As Clan Lord, I know the mental feel of every telepath on
this continent, my dear. When a new Talent is born, I know.
Before your shuttle landed outside the town, I sensed you
and knew you had an untutored Talent. You keep it walled
away, using only a fraction of its true potential. Why?"

Jo frantically tried to think of a reason that the Clan Lord
would accept, but he forestalled her.

"So you worked in the Valtegan cities, too," he said.
"Then it's no wonder that you desensitized yourself. But
why continue to hide it now?"

"I like my job," she said, a note of desperation creeping
into her voice. "I don't want to give it up to be a Telepath."

"It's your Talent that helps you be the linguist that you
are. It gives you the insight into understanding cultures for-

eign to your own. However, be that as it may," he said, reaching for the coffee jug to pour them a drink, "you are under no obligation to come here and train, my dear. The choice is yours. Even as a trained Telepath, you could continue in the career you've chosen. I'm not trying to coerce you, I was merely curious."

Jo looked relieved. "Elise and Carrie were always considered freaks because of their abilities. I don't want to be seen the same way," she said, casting another sidelong glance at Davies, who for once had the good sense to be looking in the opposite direction.

"As you wish. The third member of your group, Kris Daniels, is already at the Warrior Guild waiting for you. He's a Terran Telepath and will be the one keeping in contact with the Chemerian vessel that regularly trades on Jalna. He's well trained and capable of helping you if you have any difficulties with your Talent during your mission."

"Is there any reason why I should have difficulties?" Jo asked anxiously.

"None at all," said Konis calmly. "After all, you've been coping like this for many years, as have all the Terran Telepaths. We are merely able to help train your Talents and utilize them more fully."

He held out a mug to her. "Help yourself to whitener and sweetener while I tell you what I know of the planet Jalna and give you a brief outline of the information we have so far. You'll get a more detailed briefing from your contact on the Chemerian cargo vessel. You rendezvous with it at Chagda Station in three weeks' time."

"Three weeks!" exclaimed Davies. "How are we expected to pick up the weapons skills in three weeks?"

"The Guild Master assures me that this can be done," said Konis. "Don't worry. It's their responsibility to have you ready on time."

When Jo and Davies had departed for the Warrior Guild, they left a very thoughtful Konis behind them. He returned to his desk, sitting down and activating the display screen. As it rose from its recess, he tapped out the access codes for the data on the Terran Telepaths currently on, or in transit to Shola. Of the sixty persons on his list, thirty-three were in the Guild, two were on his wife's estate and the other twenty-five were in transit from Earth.

Of the four mixed Leska pairs, including the pair who had

died at the Guild, all except Vanna were Sholan males with Human female partners. Of the rest, there were only three single Terran females here, with another four on their way.

He keyed in another sequence giving him the personal information on the single females' backgrounds. All but one were in their early to mid-forties, the other was thirty-nine. Frowning, he stared at the screen. If the Terran, Jo, was right, then there was something here that he was missing, but what?

Coming to a decision, he took the unusual step of contacting Vanna mentally. He wouldn't afford Esken's spies the opportunity of finding out what was on his mind, so to speak. They might tap his internal communications between departments, but they wouldn't dare attempt to mentally eavesdrop on either him or Vanna. As the acknowledged Sholan specialist in Terran physiology, she would surely be able to close her teeth on what he was looking for.

Vanna, Konis here. Meet me in my office as soon as possible, please, he sent.

Coming.

Five minutes later she knocked and entered. "What can I do for you, Clan Lord?" she asked, approaching his desk.

Konis reached out for the nearest chair, hauling it behind his desk till it was beside his own.

"Thank you for being so prompt, Vanna. Come, sit down and look at this data."

Vanna sat beside him and regarded the screen. "What are we looking for?"

"These are the details of the female Terran Telepaths. Out of sixty Terrans, we only have seven females. Apart from the fact there are so few of them, there is something here so obvious I'm missing it. With your knowledge of Terran culture, perhaps you can tell me what it is."

"I hadn't realized there were so few," she said, leaning forward toward the control panel set into the desk surface. "May I?"

"Please," said Konis, moving his chair back.

She tapped a few keys, checked the files of the fifty-three males, then ordered the computer to find the common factors.

"The females are older, their average age being forty-two, the males being only twenty-eight," she said. "Apart from that, I can't see any correlation beyond the fact they come from the major cultures on Earth."

She turned puzzled green eyes toward him. "What exactly are you hoping to find? What did Jo tell you?"

"She thinks Earth is still restricting the number of telepathic females they're sending to us. Why would they do that? You know more than any Sholan about the Human culture, even if it is on Keiss, not Earth. Can you think of a reason for them to do that?"

"I wonder if age is a key factor," she said, pressing more controls. "There is a large discrepancy in the averages." Again she turned to look at him. "Being a shorter-lived species than us, they mature earlier. Clan units like ours don't exist, and they form a bond with one partner for life. They tend to remain possessive of their females, treating them almost as if they own them."

"They're shorter-lived? I hadn't realized," Konis murmured. "What is their life span?"

"Sixty or seventy seems to be the average for the males, with the females living for perhaps another ten years."

Konis blinked in shock. "So short a time?" His thoughts hung loud and clear in the silence. Were his son, and Vanna, doomed to so short a life because of their Human Leskas?

"We've changed, Clan Lord," said Vanna. "The Humans, too. Who knows how long either of us will live now? Only time will tell." She looked back at the screen.

Konis refocused his mind on the current problem. "So what Carrie faced on Keiss is not uncommon among Terrans. The females are not perceived as equal citizens but as a form of property. Presumably they don't want them in situations where they can mix freely with males, so they prevent them from coming to us."

"Perhaps they don't want them mixing with Sholan males," said Vanna. "We know they suffer from xenophobia to a greater extent than we do, so keeping them away from *our* males could be more important."

"In my dealings with the Earth delegation, I found them more xenophobic toward each other than us, but it is part of the same pattern. What of the age factor in the females? Why do you think they're older?"

They're too old for childbearing, came Brynne's thought. *No chance then for any alien half-breeds. They'll leave that to the Sholan females.* Then his presence was gone.

Vanna looked acutely embarrassed, ears flicking backward despite her attempt to keep them upright.

"My apologies, Clan Lord," she began, but Konis silenced her with a wave of his hand.

"No need, Vanna. I know how difficult things are for you, and Brynne's insight has been most useful."

She looked back to the screen. "Yes, Clan Lord," she said, her voice barely audible.

Konis frowned at her. "You're forgetting my name," he said gently. "No more Clan Lord, please." He looked back at the screen. "It looks like Jo was right. The Terrans are restricting the Telepaths they send us." He leaned past Vanna to key in more data.

"At least the ones we get here are in the main people with genuinely useful Talents," he said, reviewing the screen. "These are the ones that have been vetted on the *Rhyaki* before being sent here. I hear there've been a great many sent to the ship who've had only the delusion of having a Talent."

Vanna looked questioningly at him.

"Because telepathy isn't recognized on Earth," said Konis, "the people have developed a subculture of their own based mainly on their abilities to foretell the future or to contact the deceased. The Tutors on the *Rhyaki* complain that for every three people with a genuine Talent, they're sent twenty who have nothing of any use to us, far more than one would expect in a random sample. They feel sure the Terrans are aware of this.

"It seems I've been too engrossed with our new Leskas," said Konis, his ears beginning to lie flat with anger. "It's time I involved myself more in Alien Relations. I think another visit to Earth is called for, one with full Ambassadorial status, to inquire into their selection procedure for suitable Telepaths. I'll speak to Commander Chuz and Governor Nesul about it today," he said, switching his comm off. "I want another batch of people sent out here as soon as possible, and it had better include more younger females! These Terrans are as devious as the Chemerians. Thank the Gods we are dealing with people we know on Keiss. That at least goes smoothly," he said, turning to Vanna.

"Changing the topic completely, what's the state of the ni'uzu epidemic here? Have you managed to find a workable vaccine yet?"

"Not yet. Since Carrie and Kusac first caught and mutated it, it won't respond to our vaccine. So far it only appears to be affecting the single telepaths. Existing Leska pairs seem to be immune, yet we can't find what it is that gives them the immunity. It's not just our Guildhouse either, the other fifteen Telepath Guildhouses have been similarly hit. In fact there have been several deaths directly linked to the new strain of ni'uzu."

"Why only telepaths? I don't suppose it could be some Terran virus, could it?"

Vanna shook her head. "Unlikely. The DNA mapping of the Humans is far enough advanced for us to rule that out. So far we can't trace the cause, but even when they've recovered, it's leaving many people weak and ill for several days."

"Have you got all the facilities and staff you need?"

"Yes, Clan Lord."

Konis frowned.

"Yes, Konis," she amended, feeling self-conscious at the use of his personal name.

"Right," he said, getting up. "Keep me informed, Vanna. I want to know if there are any more deaths due to this virus and if it leaves those who've contracted it with any enhanced abilities or altered genetics. I need to go and see the Governor now."

* * *

After more than two decades of life in the military, Kris, the telepathic member of their team, came as something of a shock to Jo and Davies. The shoulder-length fair hair held back by a plain suede headband, the T-shirt and jeans, and the bare feet in open leather sandals all firmly proclaimed him a civilian, despite the Sholan uniform jacket he carried. However, as their days at the Warrior Guild merged into weeks, they realized the differences between the soldiers that they were and the Warriors they needed to become.

This Guild had never turned out obedient ranks of soldiers; traditionally they fulfilled a totally different role. They trained males and females to fight with any available weapons, including their natural ones; to search out the enemy's weaknesses; to assess and plan tactical advantages; to survive and ultimately win in the most extreme circumstances. In short, unless they were Warrior-trained first and foremost, there was no way junior officers could gain access to the upper echelons of the Sholan military.

The three of them found that they were expected to be able to act independently of each other yet mesh instantly into a tightly knit unit when the need arose. Without a conscious decision having ever been made, Jo found herself being regarded by the two males as the natural leader.

Their training included not only the traditional Sholan swords and daggers but also modern energy weapons. Unarmed combat, too, both Sholan and Human style. The knowledge of the existence of new martial arts had caused an immediate demand—diplomatically rephrased as a request by the Alien Relations Department—from the Warrior Guild for practitioners to be sent to Shola. They had not been long in arriving.

Though Jo and Davies had years of experience in guerrilla warfare on Keiss, Kris had more than a head start on them at the Guild, having been training there regularly since he had arrived on Shola some five months earlier. Despite his time still being divided between the Warrior and the Telepath Guilds, he never completely lost that lead. By the end of their three weeks on Shola, the bonds of trust that had been forged between them were strong and they knew they were as ready as they would ever be for their mission on Jalna.

Almost before they realized it, they were at Chagda Station, boarding the *Summer Bounty,* the Chemerian merchant ship of Chijuu Liokso. Like all Chemerian vessels outside their home worlds, it was run by the Sumaan, the only species the Chemerians trusted, and then only because the heavy worlders and they had no common needs.

Jo and Davies didn't meet the last member of their team until they were ushered into the lower level crew lounge. Because of the fever still raging through the Telepath Guild, the Clan Lord, Konis Aldatan, had delayed his choice until one of those he had short-listed for the mission had recovered.

Vyaka was her name. Of average height for a Sholan female, she was stockily built with an air of competence about her. Her coloring was light gray with dark bands round her tail and tipping her almost-tufted ears. The hair between her ears was dark and worn short, the military style fitting in with the sleeveless Forces jacket. Unusually bright green eyes regarded them steadily while Kris and Jo felt her feather-light mental touch at the edges of their minds.

She held her palm out toward Kris in greeting. "You must be my contact on Jalna. I'm Vyaka, from Alien Relations. The Clan Lord thought someone with my background would be best suited to your needs." She turned to the other two. "You must be Jo, and you, Davies," she said, offering her palm to Jo who hesitantly returned the gesture, knowing that her Talent had been acknowledged by the Sholan female. To Davies, Vyaka inclined her head.

"I'll show you to our quarters," she said, walking past them to the door. "This level is the one used by Chijuu, the Chemerian. We have the two passenger cabins."

The three Terrans followed her back out into the corridor, past the lift shaft to the two cabin doors. Vyaka stopped, turning to Jo. "I thought you'd prefer to bunk with me. The Terran females I met at the Guild were no different from us in enjoying some time away from the company of the males." Her mouth opened in a broad Sholan grin.

"Sure, suits me," said Jo, smiling back.

"In which case," said Vyaka turning to Kris, "that's your room next door. You'll find the toilet and shower through the door at the rear. We'll meet you back in the lounge in five minutes." She placed her palm on the door mechanism.

"Oh, no," groaned Jo as she looked in through the open door. "Now I've seen it all! First it was curved beds, now it's bowls in the floor!"

"You haven't seen the crew quarters," said Vyaka, making a noise Jo recognized as a laugh. "They sleep on heated sand. At least we have covers and a padded mattress. As for Chijuu, wait till you see his suite. He rarely leaves the *Summer Bounty* so his quarters approximate how he would live planetside." She waited for Jo to enter.

"What are they like?" Jo asked, unslinging her bag as she headed over to the ubiquitous drawer unit near the unused bed.

"The Chemerians? Difficult is the best word to describe them. The ones we meet, like Chijuu, are the gregarious ones, misfits in their society because they are willing to actually meet aliens face-to-face and trade with them. Don't worry, though," she reassured Jo, "we'll probably only see him a couple of times during the trip. He'll keep to his quarters because of the gravity. The Sumaan worlds are heavier even than Shola, and since the Sumaan run the ship . . ."

"Sounds like a fun journey," said Jo, putting the last of her possessions in the drawers.

"It shouldn't be too bad. The Sumaan will probably set their gravity nearer ours for our convenience, they're good that way."

"How do the Chemerians cope?"

"They've developed a device that allows them to have their own gravity in their quarters. No one knows how it works, and they aren't telling us. They won't even discuss it, let alone allow anyone else near it. Pity, the medical benefits alone would be worth almost any price they asked. Ready?"

Jo nodded and followed Vyaka back to the lounge area. Kris and Davies were already there. The Sholan went over to a hatchway in the far wall while Jo sat down on one of the couches.

"This area has been set up for passengers," she said. "This is the food and drink synthesizer. It works on a similar principle to the Sholan ones. It's been programmed with ten dishes which have proved popular with your people as well as several drinks, including your coffee. The menu is here," she said, pointing to a display panel above a row of recessed buttons. "Press one of these and your choice will come on the screen; press this one to confirm your selection. I take it you all want coffee?"

"Please," said Jo.

As they sat down with their drinks, several loud clanks and booms reverberated throughout the craft.

"We're under way," said Vyaka, taking a sip of her c'shar. "I think now is the time for your final briefing." She put her mug down on the low table in front of her.

"When we reach Jalna, we'll all transfer to the cargo section control room and travel down to the planet's surface. Jalna has no space station so trading takes place planetside in the spaceport. Once we've landed, the Captain will request an unloading team. They'll be Jalnians who have passes allowing them into the port area. The whole spaceport is rigidly controlled by the Port Lord, Lord Bradogan, who restricts the flow of off-world goods onto the planet. He also restricts the movements of the natives and the spacer crews. No aliens are allowed to go outside the Port town perimeter."

"So how do we get out?" asked Davies.

"We have a fake ID for each of you," she said. "While the Jalnians are unloading, I will attempt to link in lightly to one of them, then you, Kris, will link with me and hopefully be able to pick up all you can about their language and culture." She frowned briefly. "I know you've been practicing this particular skill. You Humans seem to have a talent for it. Hopefully the combination of our minds should be enough. Really we needed Carrie and Kusac for this, but it wasn't to be," she sighed. "We have to have this information or the mission has little chance of success."

Jo hesitated. "If you can give me what you do pick up, like we were given a knowledge of the Sholan language and culture on the *Khalossa,* then perhaps I can make some sense of it."

Vyaka looked at her in surprise.

"The Clan Lord said my Talent was with languages," Jo said quietly.

"Of course, you're the Keissian expert on the Valtegans! That will certainly give us the edge we need," said Vyaka.

"Vyaka," said Jo worriedly, "There isn't a problem with Carrie, is there? I thought she was doing well. She seemed all right when we spoke to her a couple of weeks ago."

Vyaka raised an eye ridge. "You were lucky to be allowed to speak to her. Since she lost her cub, no one has been allowed to contact them. The Clan Leader has been most protective."

Jo and Davies exchanged a glance.

"You didn't know?" said Vyaka in surprise. "It was widely publicized on Shola. The genesis of a new species is not something that can be kept quiet, especially when the heir of the largest Telepath Clan is the father."

"Carrie and Kusac?" asked Davies, frankly disbelieving. "That's impossible."

"Not with the mixed Leskas. Somehow a genetic drift was initiated in both of them until they were compatible. Kusac's child would have been the first but Carrie lost it when she was injured in the Challenge. Now it'll be Vanna's cub."

"Not the Vanna we know? The medic?" asked Jo incredulously.

Vyaka nodded.

"But she's not a telepath!"

"Oh yes, a wild Talent to be sure, but a Telepath nonetheless, and one with a Terran Leska."

"Good God," said Jo, still stunned by the double shock of the news.

"How many more pairs are there?" asked Davies.

"I think another two or three. But enough of that," Vyaka said, picking up her mug again. "Back to the mission. Once we've managed to pick up something of their language and culture, you'll mingle with the Jalnians in the hold. When they leave, so will you. According to the Sumaan, the guards only glance at the Jalnians' cards, they don't do a head count so they shouldn't notice there are three more of you leaving than arrived." She took another drink.

"Once outside, you'll make your way to the crash site in the nearby hills. We'll return to Jalna every week, so I'll contact you as soon as we arrive and you can pass on any information you have. Luckily there's some in-system work we can do over the next couple of months or so, trading directly in space with the other species. When you're ready to leave, you make your way back to the native shantytown outside the spaceport perimeter and we'll pick you up the same way we dropped you off. Any questions?"

"How do we find this crashed vessel?" asked Davies.

"As we approach Jalna, the Captain will scan the surface, taking images of it which he'll print out for you as a map. You've got a direction finder, haven't you?"

Davies nodded.

"Then you should be all right. Just remember that maps don't exist on Jalna yet and don't get caught with it. I'm glad to see you all wearing Jalnian clothes," she said, glancing at them each in turn. "By the time we get there you'll look like you've lived in them rather than just put them on."

Davies scratched vigorously at his upper arm. "Damned tunic is itchy," he complained. "I never did like natural wool next to my skin."

"You'll be grateful for its warmth on Jalna," said Jo. "Modern fabrics don't have the same insulation or natural waterproof qualities as this stuff."

"Smells, too," he grumbled.

"Natural oils," said Kris, speaking for the first time. "We could do with rolling in some dirt. These clothes are far too clean."

"There's plenty of dirt in the cargo area," grinned Vyaka. "You can roll about there to your heart's delight."

"What happens if we get caught by the Jalnian authorities?" asked Davies.

"We'll try to get you out the best way we can. With us we

have ten Sumaan warriors specifically here as an assault unit in the event of trouble. We won't abandon you, believe me, but it would be best if you weren't caught in the first place," Vyaka said.

"We must find out why the vessel crashed, what it was doing, and if it has anything on board that will give us a clue as to where the Valtegans come from, is that right?" asked Jo.

"That's about the size of it," agreed Vyaka.

"Is there some way we can communicate with you when you aren't on Jalna?" asked Davies. "In case of emergencies."

"None, I'm afraid."

"I'm not happy about that," he muttered.

"There shouldn't be a problem," said Vyaka. "If you stick to your cover of itinerant gypsies, then you have a reason to be out in the middle of nowhere between villages. When you find the vessel, your cover is that you're using it for shelter."

"I'm still concerned with the initial information gathering from the Jalnians at the spaceport," said Jo.

"I'll be working with Kris throughout the trip to improve his transfer skills," reassured Vyaka. "Now I know you've a Talent for languages, I'm more confident we'll get what we want."

"I do hope you're right," said Jo.

* * *

Meral had been concerned about Taizia, but since he'd received the cryptic message to meet her at The Warrior's Respite in Nazule, his worry had turned to annoyance. He'd only seen her once in the last six weeks, and then she'd just faced a dressing down from her mother because of inviting the Keissian physician, Jack Reynolds, to Shola without permission. She hadn't been in the best of moods that night. Now this.

As he entered the garden at the rear of the inn, he saw her sitting on her own at a table near the riverside.

He slid down on the bench seat opposite her, frowning in surprise when he saw what she was drinking. "Milk? That's not like you."

"I need the calcium," she said, wrapping her hands around the glass.

"What d'you need calcium for? You aren't ill, are you?" A note of concern had come into his voice.

It made Taizia feel worse than ever about what she'd done to them both. In the past few weeks she'd come to realize the enormity of her actions.

"I'm pregnant, Meral," she said quietly, keeping her eyes focused on her hands. "Remember that night I came to you in your room? I decided then."

His stunned silence lengthened until she had to look up. "It seemed like a good idea at the time," she said lamely. "I wanted to be with you. I didn't want Father finding a mate for me. It would have meant ending our relationship." She looked back down at her drink, unable to stand the stillness of his face and mind.

"I wanted us to be together—for a year or two at least. I did it, it's my responsibility. I don't expect anything from you. There's no need for us to take out a bond-contract."

Her heart sank as he got to his feet. "You needn't worry," she said, her voice almost a whisper, "I won't tell them who the father is. I won't involve you in my dishonor." A knot of unhappiness was tying itself around her heart now, making her feel ill.

He reached out, grasping her by the arm. "I want to talk to you—in private," he said, his voice low with anger.

She got up, walking beside him along the riverside toward the small bridge. His mind was still closed, no thoughts or emotions beyond his anger that would give her a clue as to what he was thinking.

He stopped when they reached it, turning round to face her.

"Kusac was right about you," he said angrily. "You're as impulsive as a cub half your age! Did you stop to think of the consequences of your actions before you decided to conceive? You don't bring a cub into the world just so you don't have to marry, or because you don't want to lose a lover! There's a little person growing inside you now! A life you've made me equally responsible for, without even asking me!"

She couldn't look at him. "I know. I'm sorry. I've said I'll take full responsibility for it—I'll say it isn't yours."

He gave a hiss of exasperation and she could see his tail flicking from side to side. "Be realistic, Taizia! Who's going to believe that?"

"There's nothing more I can do now," she said, blinking

rapidly before dashing her forearm across her eyes in an effort to stem her tears. She knew her ears were flat with distress but she couldn't raise them.

She felt him grasp her by the arm again, then pull her close before folding his arms around her.

"You damned, stupid, idiotic child," he said, lowering his face to hers before capturing her cheek with his teeth and beginning to gently nip it. "I'll not have you telling anyone it isn't mine," he growled as he moved his mouth downward to her throat. "We'll sign a bonding contract before we tell your parents. No one else is claiming our cub, Taizia."

She tipped her head back as his tongue rasped across her throat, then his teeth closed over her larynx and tightened till they marked her flesh.

"If I go home now, my mother'll know I'm pregnant," she said. "I'm not ready to face them yet."

"Where have you been staying?"

"With a friend, but I had to leave for the same reason. And the Guild's so oppressive since Father and the Guild Master fell out."

"You're not going back there," he said firmly. "We'll go to the judiciary and take out a contract today, then I'm taking you home."

"Home?" she said, startled.

He held her close again. "Yes, to my parents' estate," he said, rubbing his face against hers. "You'll be safe there until I've seen your brother and your parents."

"You can't tell them on your own," she said, pulling back from him.

"I can, and I will," he said. "If you hadn't been an Aldatan, I'd have asked you to be my mate. The God knows I wanted to, but telepaths don't life-bond to outsiders. And I'm insisting on a five-year contract. I wish it could be longer—because I love you, Taizia."

Her laugh was slightly hysterical. In her mind, she'd faced every possible reaction from him but this.

"You must be mad," she said, hugging him tightly. "I love you, too, and I wish we could be life-mates, Meral, but at least we'll have some happiness."

"Don't think about the future," he said, letting her go before they turned round to walk back to the inn. "We'll find a way to stay together. You may have to marry but you can still choose whom you love."

Her mouth opened in a smile as she looked up at him.
"Yes, I can, can't I?"

* * *

Kaid was sitting in the staff lounge when Garras came in.
"I've been hoping to find you on your own all day," he
said, going over to the drinks dispenser. "Can I get you anything?"

"Please," said Kaid, pushing the disposable mug aside.
"This one's well and truly dead."

"C'shar or coffee?"

"C'shar."

He watched Garras bring the two mugs over to the table,
putting one down in front of him before sitting down
opposite.

"Thanks," said Kaid, leaning his elbow on the table so he
could prop his head up on his hand. "How's Vanna?"

"Fine," Garras said, taking a sip of his drink. He gave a
little purr of amusement. "Carrie keeps teasing her about
looking more like a Human female now. I suppose she
does."

Kaid raised an eye ridge questioningly. "I would have said
Human females look like permanently pregnant Sholans," he
said. "Vanna does look well, though. How did Brynne react
when you signed the bond-contract?"

"Indifferently. All in all he's been acting rather strangely
in the last week or two. He's taken up with one of the new
batch of Terrans—an older man. Now *he's* a strange one. He
refuses to live at the Terran building on the Guild grounds,
and has taken a room at the Accommodation Guild instead.
Apparently Brynne has been spending a lot of time with
him. That's not what I wanted to talk about, though."

Kaid sighed and picked up his mug in his other hand. "I
know. Go on, get it over with if you must," he said, taking a
mouthful of the c'shar.

"It's about the En'Shalla rituals. You know there has to be
a third person for the Margins, don't you?"

"I know all about it, Garras. If I didn't, I'd be the only one
on the estate. Lijou told me to copy the data before giving it
to Kusac."

"Why'd he do that?" asked Garras, ears pricking forward.
"What's Lijou got to do with it?"

Kaid frowned. "You're getting too good at receiving, Garras," he said.

"I wouldn't say that. It's come in very useful on several occasions, notably when we were chasing Chyad, but you're not going to put me off my trail, Kaid. All our people are gossiping about the En'Shalla rituals. They know there has to be a third, and they're taking bets on who it'll be."

Again Kaid raised an eyebrow. "Oh? Who's the favorite?"

"The priest, Ghyan."

"He won't choose Ghyan."

"You sound sure of that," said Garras. "You're the second choice, by the way."

"Am I? I hope you're discouraging them from betting."

"You don't sound surprised."

"You know there's very little gets past me, Garras."

"It's more than that," his friend said slowly, studying his face.

Kaid looked away and took another mouthful of his drink. He could sense the way Garras' mind was working. Better to weather it out now than leave it till later.

"You've not been yourself since you came back from Noni's," said Garras abruptly. "I know what she's like, always probing at any sore spots she can find, manipulating you into dropping your guard so she can pick up stray thoughts. What happened while you were there?"

"Nothing," said Kaid, suddenly aware of the warmth of the crystal he wore hung in a small leather bag round his neck.

"What's Lijou's involvement in this?"

"I've no idea what you're talking about, Garras," said Kaid tiredly. "What's the point in all this?"

"Noni told you something, didn't she? And Lijou said the same thing. What exactly did they say, Kaid?"

Garras was pushing him, determined to find out. "Nothing that need concern you, Garras. It was personal."

"They told you that you'll be the third, didn't they? That's why you know Kusac won't choose Ghyan. Has Kusac discussed it with you?"

No point in denying it. "He hasn't spoken to anyone yet as far as I'm aware."

"If he doesn't choose you, he's a fool," Garras said abruptly. "I don't understand you, Kaid. You sit around looking morose, yet you're likely to get what you want most handed to you without any problems."

"You know nothing about it, Garras. I don't care what anyone says, I can't be the third! I've been through it with Noni, Lijou, and Ghyan! I'm sick of the whole damned thing. I hope he doesn't ask me because I'll have to refuse, and I can't tell him why!"

"Can't, or won't? Is it because of that female all those years ago? What was her name?"

"Khemu."

"Yes, Khemu. You never did tell me what happened."

Kaid sat up, ears flicking backward in annoyance. "I'm not about to do so now either."

"As you wish," he said. "Has it ever happened since?"

"No, because I haven't dared go near another female since then," Kaid snapped, angry at having to admit to even that.

Garras leaned forward, grasping Kaid by the wrist. "When he chooses you," he began.

"He won't," interrupted Kaid, trying to pull his hand away.

"*Listen* to me," said Garras, ears folding sideways as he tightened his grip. "When he chooses you, you'd better have put that demon to sleep, because if she means as much to you as I think, you don't want it happening with her! Find yourself a female, Kaid. Take the edge off this fear—now, once and for all."

"Garras," he said, his voice holding an edge of ice. "I'm warning you. Don't meddle in my life." Again he attempted to pull away from his friend, but Garras held on even more tightly.

"Kaid, he'll ask you, and you'll have to accept."

Kaid got abruptly to his feet, the chair falling over behind him as he wrenched his wrist free.

"You have to go, Kaid, can't you see that? He trusts you to look after her personally. He's already put their lives in your hands. He isn't going to choose someone else!"

"If he trusts me so much, then why has he said nothing?" demanded Kaid, stalking over to the door, his tail bushed out and lashing from side to side. "He won't ask, and if he did, I wouldn't accept!"

"You'd let them go into the Fire Margins with someone other than you guarding them?" said Garras, turning to watch as Kaid pulled the door open. "Don't make me laugh, Kaid! If you do, it'll be the first time I've ever known you to give up without a fight!"

Kaid slammed the door behind him and headed down the corridor to his room. Damn him! Garras was right, and he knew it! He was sworn to protect them, he couldn't refuse—and he couldn't accept.

As he reached the corridor that branched off to his room, he saw Vanna approaching.

"Just the person I wanted," she said cheerfully. "If I didn't know you better, I'd say you've been avoiding me. I need a sample of your blood for the DNA tests Jack and I are doing."

"I'm afraid I haven't the time right now, Vanna," he said. "Carrie's waiting for me. It's time for her therapy."

Before he could pull away, he felt the sharp prick of her test needle.

"There, it's done," she said, turning to leave.

He watched her walk away, cursing under his breath. More problems, as if he didn't have enough.

Carrie was waiting for him in the massage room next to the main bathing area.

"Hi there," she said as he entered. "I thought you'd forgotten about me."

"No, I wouldn't do that," he said, taking off his jacket and placing it on one of the benches. "Garras and I were talking, that's all. You're not usually quite so prompt."

"Kusac's at the estate lab today," she said. "He wanted to see for himself how it's all going. The main buildings we need should be ready soon, he says."

"That's good news." He rolled his tunic sleeves up as he went over to the massage couch where she was perched. The scent of her soap hung in the air. It was a special preparation made for her by Vanna's sister, Sashti, as was the small container of oil he picked up.

Carrie swung her legs up onto the table. "Sitting or lying, Kaid?" she asked.

"Lying, please. It's easier to work on your leg. How's it been today?"

"Not quite so stiff," she said, lying back on the couch. "I think between you and Sashti, not to mention Noni, you've worked a miracle on my injuries."

Kaid paused, looking up toward her head. "Would you like a cushion?" he asked. "You don't look very comfortable."

"Please."

Still holding the bottle, he went over to the cupboard by the door to get it. Returning, he handed it to her and began pouring some of the oil on his hands.

"What were you and Garras discussing?"

"This and that," he said vaguely as he pushed her robe aside and began spreading the oil over her injured thigh. "The wound has healed well, hasn't it?" he said as he carefully smoothed it over the scar. "I think you'll only have the faintest of marks in another couple of weeks."

"Mm," she said.

He looked up at her. Her eyes were closed and she seemed relaxed. "Are you all right?" he asked.

"I'm fine. I just thought I'd practice one or two of the litanies Dzaka's been teaching me."

He continued smoothing the oil into her skin, then began to gently knead the muscles at the sides of her thigh. "Which one are you practicing?"

"Right now? The one for relaxation. Then I'll go on to the one for clear thought."

He could sense the amusement in her voice. "What's funny?" he asked, beginning to work gently over the scarred area.

"You, Kaid. You're never just you, are you? Always on duty, holding yourself back. Are you like this in your leisure time too? I don't suppose I'd recognize you if you weren't."

"People spend their leisure time in different ways, Carrie," he said. "I tend to read, or . . ."

"Sit drinking c'shar in the common room with Garras and the others, if you're not out on the training ground at the new estate," she finished for him.

"It seems it's a day for people telling me how I should spend my leisure time," he said wryly. "Turn over, please."

Grabbing the wrap-over front of her robe, Carrie obligingly rolled onto her stomach and laid her head on her folded arms.

He felt her wince as she moved the damaged arm. "Still paining you?" he asked sympathetically.

"A bit," she admitted. "And before you ask, yes, I've been doing the exercises!"

"It takes time," he said, moving her robe so he could reach the back of her thigh. "You know how deep that cut was. It nearly cost you your life."

"I know," she said, and he could feel the shudder pass through her body.

"Go back to your litanies," he said. "I'll be a while yet." He knew the rhythm of his massage would relax her, it always did, and within a couple of minutes he could feel her muscles losing their rigidity and becoming supple again under his fingers.

He stopped to put more oil on his hands and began gently pushing her flesh with his thumbs, rolling them upward one after the other as he worked toward the top of her leg, then back down again. He had to be careful that the pressure he used didn't trigger his claws. That had taken a little getting used to as her skin was much more yielding and soft than a Sholan's. He had to use the more sensitive parts of his fingers so he could gauge more accurately how much pressure was needed.

The feel and texture of her skin was unlike anything he'd come across. And her scent, already overlying the aroma of the oil and soap, was something he was trying hard to ignore. The preparations seemed to enhance her natural smell, but then that wasn't surprising considering Sashti had blended them specially for the needs of Carrie's human skin. Sashti was a professional, a much sought after professional at that. Her oils and soaps fetched the highest prices around these days, and to have one specially crafted for one's own use said something for the way Sashti felt about Carrie.

"She's coming over today," said Carrie quietly.

"I though she might," he murmured, moving to work on the softer skin on the inside of her thigh. "What is it today? Just a social call on you and Vanna?"

"Mm."

She was almost purring, he could feel it through her skin. Once the worst of the pain had gone from the newly-forming scar tissue, she'd enjoyed the massages almost as much as he did. It was a time of trust and almost-intimacy between them, probably the nearest he'd ever get to her. He'd tried to work out what it was that pleased him so much and had come to understand it was simply that—her trust, and being able to touch her without her fearing him, giving her pleasure in fact. The feel and sight of her skin—something alien to him as a member of a furred race—was in itself exotic, a fascination that hadn't faded for him, as obviously it hadn't for

Kusac—or for Zhyaf, despite the fact that his young Leska, Mara, ran him ragged.

He stood back, sliding his hands from her leg. "If you'll sit up, I'll do your arm now," he said.

Carrie groaned. "Just as I was getting comfortable! You pick the worst time, Kaid!"

He grinned. "You were falling asleep."

"Rubbish! I was practicing my relaxation litany," she said, sitting up and slipping her left arm free of her robe.

"Sleeping."

"No. Relaxing. It shows how well I've learned the litany!"

"Hmm." Kaid wasn't convinced. He moved round to stand beside her, pouring more oil on his hands. "Here, you hold the bottle," he said, handing it to her.

"Hey! Careful, Kaid!" She had to grab for it as he let it go, assuming she'd catch it. As she did, she had to pull her injured arm away from him and clutch at her robe to prevent it falling. "I have my modesty to protect, you know."

His ears flicked back briefly. "Sorry. I forgot," he said, taking hold of her arm as she held it out to him again. He *knew* she wasn't Sholan, so why did he keep forgetting it? Probably because if she were, he could have approached her. Because she was human, it wasn't that easy for her— or him.

"Don't worry about it," she said, still clutching the bottle to her chest.

He reached out and took it from her, putting it on the couch beside her. "I forget sometimes that you aren't Sholan," he said.

She smiled. "I know. You've told me before."

He was just finishing as Sashti arrived.

"I'll wait for you in the main lounge," she said. "I'll get us drinks."

"I'll be about fifteen minutes," said Carrie, slipping the robe back over her arm. "A quick shower, then I'll be down."

Sashti waved as she disappeared through the door again.

"Thanks, Kaid," Carrie said as he helped her down from the couch. "You'll join us?"

"If you wish. I'll keep Sashti company till you arrive," he said, wiping his hands on a towel as she padded over to the door through to the bathing room.

* * *

After she'd left Kaid, Vanna rejoined Jack at the newly installed lab on the Valsgarth Estate. He and Kusac were sitting drinking coffee at one of the lab benches.

"Well, I like that!" she said, arms akimbo as she surveyed the two seated males. "I go up to the main house for an hour or two, and what do you two do? Nothing, that's what!"

"Vanna, lass," said Jack, getting to his feet, "we were waiting for your return. See, we even put a real brew of coffee on for you!" He indicated a mobile external heating unit with a glass beaker perched on top of it, the brown liquid contents gently bubbling. "Can I pour you a cup?"

Kusac turned away, hiding a grin as the rotund Human physician picked up a strainer and, lifting the beaker with a pair of heat-resistant tongs, poured some into a mug for Vanna.

"The comm is still crunching the data," said Kusac, turning round to pour some whitener into her mug. He looked at his wrist unit. "Another five minutes and it should be done."

Vanna came over to them, accepting the stool that Jack had vacated for her. "Hmpf!" she said, picking up the mug and tasting the drink. A smile crossed her face. "I'd forgotten it could taste like this," she said, tail flicking with pleasure.

"The ones from the dispenser units just aren't the same, are they?" said Kusac.

"Definitely not," she said, holding out a vial to Jack. "There's Kaid's sample. Once you've processed this, we've got a fair selection of DNA to compare with that of the latest ni'uzu victims. Thank goodness, it looks like the epidemic has burned itself out."

Kusac got down from his stool. "I'm going home now," he said. "Carrie's finished her therapy with Kaid, and Sashti's come to visit. When shall I tell her you'll be back?" he asked Vanna.

"Oh, for third meal," she said, sipping her drink with obvious pleasure. "I want to get the results from the DNA matching first. I hope to be able to confirm our first findings, that all the telepaths who contracted the mutated ni'uzu have had their Talents enhanced, and that these changes will be passed on to their children."

"Like us," said Kusac.

"Yes, and no," said Jack, moving round behind Kusac to take his stool. "You mixed Leskas are still unique. We think some of our Brotherhood members may just be genetically compatible with you, but we aren't sure, which is why we're running a second set of tests."

"As for all the other telepaths," said Vanna, "we know they're not genetically compatible with you at all. They're still normal Sholans."

"Father will be pleased to hear that news," said Kusac. "Have we heard anything from the Brotherhood yet? Have they had anyone else down with the virus?"

"I contacted Lijou," said Vanna, "and he says there are no more cases. Perhaps their isolation in the Dzahai Mountains has kept the virus away from them."

"They're not that isolated," said Kusac. "We know they have a fair turnover of personnel going in and out on active service, as well as several full telepaths who can't ever leave Stronghold."

"Perhaps it's taking longer to reach them," said Jack.

"Perhaps," agreed Vanna.

"I'll see you both later," said Kusac, turning to go.

"Vanna, lass," said Jack, coming over to join her at her desk. "The results have just come through."

Vanna looked up at him. "Great! Just in time. If we want to make third meal we'll have to leave in ten minutes. What's it say?"

"What we more or less expected. It's virtually the same as last time. There are some four or five of our Brotherhood friends who appear to be genetically compatible with the mixed Leskas. What's also interesting is this," he said, leaning over her to point to a section of text. "Seems we've got a couple of people here who're closely related."

Vanna frowned. "What do you mean? Who are they?" she asked, scanning back up to the top of the results. "No. They can't be," she said, looking up at him. "There's no way they're related."

Jack shrugged. "It's there in black and white, m'dear," he said. "You yourself told me he's been avoiding giving you a blood sample. I'd say that's why, wouldn't you?"

"Then he knows about this."

"Looks like it."

Vanna folded the paper over and put it down on her desk. "Gods! What do we do about it, Jack?"

"Only one thing you can do. Take his data out and make sure these results are erased. Just run a duplicate of our first program. Knowledge like this could cause them both a lot of trouble if it got into the wrong hands."

"Should I speak to him? And what about Kusac? He ought to know."

"Talk to Kaid, yes, but no one else, Vanna. The information we have is confidential, we can't go telling anyone else. You can suggest Kaid speak to Kusac, but that's all."

Vanna unfolded the results again, checked through them, then crumpled them into a ball. "Destroy them, Jack," she said, getting to her feet and handing him the ball. "Burn them. I'll see to the comm files now, I'm not leaving it till later. At least we're not linked into the main house comm yet. No one else could have seen this data. Let's keep it that way."

"Right, m'dear," nodded Jack, walking over to the sink. He put the paper down, then dug in his pocket for a lighter.

*   *   *

When Kusac had returned to the main house, Kaid excused himself to head off for a shower. He stood under the ceiling faucet, ears flattened back, face turned up to it, letting the water stream down over him while the lower jets sent their needles of pressurized water beating against him, massaging the tiredness out of his body. Tilting his head back, he smoothed his hair away from his ears and stretched a hand out for the container of soap.

At the same moment he realized it wasn't there, he sensed someone else in the room. Pulling his head away from the stream of water, he reached out and grabbed hold of the person, dragging them in beside him and flinging them flat against the back wall. His hand closed over the throat, claws out, his own body kept well back.

A definitely female Sholan shriek resulted, which he confirmed moments later when he'd dashed the water from his face with his free arm.

"Sashti! What the hell d'you think you're doing, creeping

up on me like this?" he demanded, letting her go. "That's a good way to get yourself hurt!"

Sashti stood there, the water cascading over her shoulders turning her fur black. The bushy mane of hair was flattened now, clinging in long, wet strands to her face and shoulders, and she was laughing.

"I was going to offer to join you anyway," she said, one hand going to massage her neck, the other to push her hair aside so she could see him properly. "You've just made it more difficult for you to refuse now."

Kaid spotted the container of soap lying on the floor and stepped out of the shower to pick it up. "You're welcome to join me," he said, "but don't come in unannounced like that again. If it had been anywhere but here, where I know the security is tight, you might have found yourself getting hurt. Old habits die hard, Sashti, and I'm Warrior trained."

"I'll remember," she said, holding out her hand to him. "Give me the soap and I'll wash you first."

He handed her the container reluctantly. It had been a long time since he'd shared a shower.

"Turn round," she said, and as he did so, she began rubbing the soap into his back. "How's Carrie coming along?" she asked. "She seems a lot more mobile than I've seen her since the Challenge."

"She's doing fine, said Kaid. "The scars are healing without tightening the skin. I think you'll have to look really hard to find a scar in a few months' time."

"That's good. Without fur, a scar that would be invisible for us would show up quite badly against her bare skin."

He was beginning to feel uncomfortable under Sashti's ministrations. What should by rights have been a sisterly wash was beginning to turn into more as her touch across his shoulders and arms became lighter.

"You must work out every day to keep yourself in such good shape," she said, her voice sounding quietly in his ear as he felt her body touch his.

"I do," he said.

"I thought so." It was almost a purr as she stroked her hand across the back of his neck then turned him round to face her. "I've wanted to get to know you better." The soap container was forgotten as she ran her hands across his chest, down to his hips. "We've got a little time to ourselves now,"

she said, looking up at him. "No one else is coming for a
shower before third meal."

He looked down into her brown eyes, trying not to see
someone other than Sashti. She was beautiful, there was no
doubt about that, and with a personality to match. Maybe
Garras and Ghyan were right. Maybe she was what he
needed, someone of his own age, not a skittish youngling.
She was here, and she was asking for him.

He reached out for her, putting his hand behind her head
and drawing her closer with his other arm. Her body pressed
against his was warm, and as he laid his face against hers,
her mouth closed on his cheek, nipping him gently.

His fingers clenched in her hair, and as he pulled her face
away so he could reach her, he felt the first stirrings of
desire. Leaning back against the shower wall, he drew her
with him, his mouth reaching for hers, his teeth catching
hold of her lip. As he moved on, alternately licking her
cheek and nipping it gently, her hands began to slide lower.
He could hear his heartbeat echoing inside his head, getting
faster, more urgent. Then like a sudden deluge of cold water,
he felt it begin to start again.

Pushing her away, he backed out of the shower, water
dripping everywhere. "No," he said, his voice calmer than he
felt. "I can't. I'm sorry, Sashti, it isn't you. It's me. I can't."

He turned, and grabbing his towel from the bench, bolted
for the door to the massage room.

Hurriedly he wiped off the worst of the water before
leaving, still rubbing himself dry as he went. In the privacy
of his room, he leaned against the door, letting himself slide
down it till he sat on the floor, his eyes closed.

Nothing had changed. He'd felt his control slip, but this
time he'd recognized it for what it was, and thank the Gods,
had been able to stop in time. Lifting his head, he took a
deep breath, trying to control his heartbeat, slow it down to
its normal rate. Now he knew for sure he could never be their
third, could never pair with Carrie. He couldn't bear to see
written on her face what he'd seen on Khemu's all those
years ago, and for his own sake, too, he couldn't risk losing
control. Another deep breath, then another, then he was ready
to repeat the litanies that were his mainstay.

Vanna found her sister sitting in her lounge when she
returned to the Aldatan household. "Hello there. Kusac said

you were here," she said, going over to her and giving her a hug. "Are you staying tonight?"

"No, I don't think I will," said Sashti, returning the hug. "I want to get back. I saw Carrie and had a nice chat with her, and with Kusac." She leaned down and reached into her bag. "Here you are, the oil I promised you," she said. "Don't let Garras overuse it on you," she grinned, flicking her little sister's ears as she got up and moved toward the door. "I only waited to give you this and say good-bye."

"Thank you, Sashti," said Vanna, walking her to the door. "I wish you were staying."

"Next time," Sashti promised.

"I don't suppose you've seen Kaid, have you. I need to have a word with him?"

"Not recently," said Sashti, turning away from her. "I think I saw him heading for his room earlier. I'll see you next week, Vanna."

"Bye, Sashti." Vanna shut the door behind her, a slight frown on her face. She was concealing something, but what? She shrugged. It obviously wasn't important or she'd have told her.

She changed out of her work clothes, putting on something more casual, then headed downstairs to Kaid's room.

He took longer than usual to answer her knock.

"Could I come in a moment, Kaid? I need to have a word with you."

He hesitated, then opened the door. "Come in. I've been expecting you."

"We've just finished running DNA tests on our group here," she said carefully.

He turned away from her. "You know about Dzaka."

"I'm sorry, Kaid. It wasn't our intention to pry into your private life," she said sympathetically, aware of the slow movement of his tail tip. "I came to tell you that we've erased all the data pertaining to you. We'll rerun our original program again tomorrow and use that as our final result."

She saw his ears dip in thanks. "Who else knows?"

"Only myself and Jack. Not even Brynne will be able to find out."

He turned round to look at her again, reaching out to pick up an unopened pack of stim-twigs from his desk. Meticulously, he opened it, taking one out and putting the pack

back down on his desk. "Dzaka doesn't know, and I want it
kept that way." He put the end of the twig in his mouth.

"Of course, but I think you should tell Kusac. He ought to
know about your true relationship."

"Why? What difference does it make to him that I'm
Dzaka's biological father?"

"It could be relevant later."

"If he needs to know, I'll tell him, Vanna," he said, taking
the twig out again.

"How did it happen, Kaid? How did you become his
foster-father?"

"It happened just as I told Kusac. Garras and I found
Dzaka abandoned in the dead of winter, outside Stronghold's
gates. I knew the moment I picked him up that he was mine.
Say it was blood calling to blood if you like, but I knew."

"Why? Why was he left there? What happened to his
mother?" She found it beyond understanding. "To leave him
there like that, how could she? He could have died!"

Her words hung in the air unanswered, then she realized
that had been the intention. Kaid returned the stick to his
mouth. "I'm sorry, Vanna, but that's my business, not
yours."

"I shouldn't have asked," she murmured, still shocked at
what had happened to Dzaka as a cub.

"I asked myself that for years, till I found the answer," he
said quietly. "I think we should go in for third meal, don't
you? Otherwise your worthy mate will start regarding me
with suspicion."

She grunted derisively as she turned to leave.

After their meal was over, as everyone was drifting off either
to the lounge or their rooms, Kaid felt a light touch on his
shoulder. He turned round to see Kusac standing beside him.

"I need to talk to you, Kaid," he said. "Not here, though.
Will you come to The Limping Jegget with me?"

"When?"

"Now. Carrie wants to rest so I've told her we're going out
for an hour or two."

As they walked from the parking area outside Valsgarth
into the town, Kusac could feel Kaid glancing at him out of
the corner of his eye.

"What is it?" he asked, turning to look at him.

"I never put you down as the sort who'd go out in the evening for a drink," said Kaid.

Kusac grinned, a human grin, showing his teeth. "I do a lot of things now that I never did before. And do you know what? Life is sweeter for it!"

Kaid laughed. "I know what you mean."

They'd come in by the clothing quarter, and as they walked along the busy sidewalks, the color and noise of the night began to wash over them.

Most of the stores were still open, their doorways spilling golden light onto their path as they threaded their way among the late shoppers and the early evening revelers.

"Doesn't the noise get to you?" said Kaid curiously.

Kusac shook his head. "No, not really. I was trained to block it out as a cub. I had to," he said, stepping off the curb to make way for a group of Touibans who skittered by them trilling in their high-pitched voices. "My Talent started early and was strong even then."

Kaid reached out to pull him back onto the sidewalk as a Chemerian powered chair rushed past.

"Thanks. It's busy tonight."

"A bit," said Kaid. "There's a performance by the story-teller, Kaerdhu. That's probably attracting people into the town."

"Isn't he the one who started the new technique of using a group of people on stage with him to portray the story he's telling?"

"That's the one," said Kaid, as they turned into the entrance of the inn. "Seems to be catching on with his audiences. Apparently he's booked in at the Governor's Palace later this year. A charity performance to raise money for those left Clanless after the destruction of Szurtha and Khyaal."

"When? I'd like to take Carrie."

Kaid shouldered his way through the throng of people standing by the bar until he came to the back room—the less crowded area.

"Sometime in the next two months," he said, finally able to turn round. "I'll find out for you if you like. I would quite like to go myself. I've heard a lot about Kaerdhu but never seen him."

They went up to the counter, waiting for one of the harassed bar staff to serve them.

"Why don't we get a group together?" suggested Kusac. "I'm sure Vanna would enjoy it, and Garras. Jack would probably be interested as well."

"I'll contact the Entertainment Guild office tomorrow," said Kaid.

Finally, holding their drinks, they headed over to an empty booth. Once settled, Kusac made some more small talk until they were onto their second drink.

"When you were in the Brotherhood, you were a qualified lay-priest, weren't you?" he asked, idly playing with his glass.

Kaid looked surprised. "Yes, I was. We all did some time at Vartra's Retreat with the Head Priest, but I spent several tours as a lay-brother. Why?"

"You're our main bodyguard, Kaid. You need to know where we are and what we're doing," he said, keeping his eyes on his hands. "Under the old rules of En'Shalla, as you're a qualified lay-priest, I can tell you what I intend to do and ask you to be a witness to that intent."

"You're talking in riddles, Kusac," said Kaid. "What old rules are you talking about, and what're you planning to do?"

"Even though you're no longer a Brother, under the old rules governing the Priesthood of Vartra, you remain a lay-priest unless dismissed by the Head Priest of your Order. Were you dismissed by Lijou when you left the Brotherhood?" asked Kusac, looking up at him.

"Lijou had only just been appointed Head Priest then," said Kaid, pulling his stim-twig out of his pocket and beginning to chew the end thoughtfully. "No, I wasn't. What's this all leading up to? I might still have my lay-priest status, but . . ."

"Nothing else matters," said Kusac firmly. "If I tell you of my intention to follow one of the En'Shalla rituals, then you're a witness to the fact I intend to do it."

"Intent doesn't prove anything."

"In three days we have the All Guilds Council meeting. The day after tomorrow is our Link day," said Kusac. "Tomorrow I intend to take Carrie on an En'Shalla retreat for two days. I'll tell you where so you can satisfy your protective urges by keeping an eye on the area, but I want us left alone. I want you to confirm that we did go on retreat and remained there for two days. Will you do that for me?"

"Yes, but . . ."

Kusac interrupted him again, locking eyes with him. "Carrie's fertile again, Kaid, for the first time since we lost our cub. She'll conceive on our Link day if we don't do it now. Neither of us wants to go through what happened last time. I swore then our next cub would be conceived when we chose, and would be an En'Shalla child."

Kaid nodded slowly, his eyes still held by Kusac's.

"Everything's been done the way the ritual is laid down." He broke the eye contact and grinned. "Collecting all that sweet-grass without coming home smelling of it was a job in itself!"

Kaid gave a faint grin. "I can imagine."

"So, now I've told you my intent, and as you'll be guarding the area, you can be a witness that we were in fact there for two days. That's all that's required under the old laws."

"Of course I'll be a witness to that, but why me, Kusac? Why not Ghyan? He's not only a priest but your friend."

"I'm telling you because we want you with us as our third when we walk the Fire Margins."

He watched Kaid's eyes widen with shock.

"I want you, but more importantly, so does Carrie," he said. "It's our choice. I don't care what anyone else has said about it, none of that mattered when we made our decision, least of all who had the favorite odds." He gave a half grin.

"You knew about that?"

"Of course we did! Will you do it for us?"

He looked away. "I can't, Kusac, and I can't tell you why."

"I don't care why you think you can't do it. I'm having to place our lives in the hands of a God I don't quite believe in. I want a male I can trust implicitly with us. I want . . . We want you."

"You don't understand . . ."

"I don't *need* to understand!" he said forcefully, reaching out to cover Kaid's hand with his. "You and Carrie have a rapport of some kind, I know that, I can feel it. Trust it, Kaid, as we trust you. I don't know why you say you can't, but surely you can work it out between now and when we decide to go."

"When's that?"

Kusac shrugged. "When the God tells us," he said with a wry smile. "Will you come?"

The silence lengthened until Kaid's hand began to move underneath his, turning over so it clasped his. "I'll go if the God calls me. I can't say fairer than that."

Kusac's hand tightened briefly round Kaid's before he let him go. "Thank you, Kaid. Now I know you'll be with us."

"I didn't promise!"

"Trust your God, Kaid, that's what you told me. He's got work for you, for us. Changing our world, you said. Did you really think He'd leave you out of the center of the picture?"

"No, I have to admit I didn't."

CHAPTER 7

The message had come that morning via the main house comm and was handed to Dzaka by one of the attendants.

Surprised, he opened the note, then as he scanned the words, he realized it was from Ghezu, requesting he contact him immediately.

Dzaka's first impulse was to crush it into a ball and fling it the length of his room. If he'd ever been in doubt that Ghezu was using him against Kaid, this note, coupled with the fact he'd refused to release him from his oath, proved it. Then he stopped as common sense took over. He couldn't afford to disobey the Leader of the Brotherhood, it would mark him for the rest of what would be a very short life. It was, however, an ideal opportunity to try and find out what Ghezu was up to this time. That it involved spying on Kaid yet again, he had no doubt, but despite everything, the ties that had bound him in the past to his foster-father were still strong. He was all the family Dzaka had left since he'd lost Nnya and their cub at Szurtha.

He'd shut all thoughts of her away for months, unable to cope with the aching loss. Now her image came to his mind as clearly as if she'd been in the room with him. She'd been a colleague, attached like him at the time to Lijou's staff. He'd surprised Dzaka by giving them permission to take out a bonding contract, and suggesting it be for five years, when she'd requested planet leave on Szurtha to have their cub. Normally they'd only have been allowed a three-year contract.

Their cub, Khyaz, had only been a couple of months old when he'd been recalled to the *Khalossa*. He'd been everything a father could want in a son. Alert, healthy, and already developing his own personality. Dzaka smiled at the memories of him and Nnya. Then reality returned, and with it the grief. Once more he hardened himself, turning his mind away from them and his loss.

He'd contact Ghezu and see what he wanted this time. Spreading the message out on his desk, he did his best to flatten it again before folding it neatly and putting it safely in an inner pocket.

Once in Valsgarth, he headed for the Warrior Guild Accommodation house and requested the use of their secure comm.

"Leader Ghezu," he said as his superior's image appeared on the screen.

"I've got a job for you," Ghezu said without preamble. "One involving protection. At Rhijudu, a village on the western side of the Ghuulgul desert, there's a female called Khemu Arrazo. I've reason to believe that Kaid may try to reach her. There's been bad blood between them in the past, but until now he's not known where to find her. I want you to keep an eye on him, follow him if he leaves the estate."

Dzaka sat motionless. "What are my orders if he does head for Rhijudu?"

"Do nothing unless he tries to contact her," said Ghezu. "Then you must stop him by whatever means possible. This female's life must not be put in jeopardy."

The cold knot in the pit of Dzaka's stomach was beginning to spread as he listened to Ghezu. "'Do we know the nature of what lies between them?"

"That's not your concern," said Ghezu.

Dzaka hesitated briefly before speaking again. "With respect, Leader Ghezu, I think you'd be better off choosing one of the other Brothers. My relationship with Kaid is close enough that I may not be able to conclude this job for you should he attempt to harm the female."

"Your closeness is precisely why I want you," said Ghezu, leaning forward slightly. "You're the last person he'd expect to be involved in guarding the Arrazo female, especially since you're based at the Aldatan estate with him. No one else can get close enough. Unless you have news, report to me weekly through the usual channels."

The comm went dead and Dzaka was left staring at a blank screen.

* * *

L'Seuli was aware of the sudden sense of purpose in the air before he heard the commotion caused by the Faithful and the guard as they scrambled from their bedrolls. Fyak, the Prophet, was back from his vigil earlier than expected. Like the rest of the elite guard, L'Seuli was instantly on his feet and ready.

While the Faithful prostrated themselves on the ground, their sand-colored robes making them almost invisible, he and the other guards were allowed to remain standing. The air was electric with expectation as Fyak, the Word of Kezule, entered the huge canopy that formed their communal tent.

He watched the Prophet stride to the center, stopping to survey the bowing figures of his followers. Alone among them, his head was uncovered against the sun, his mane of long tan hair flowing wildly around his narrow face. At his throat, the green-jeweled torc briefly reflected the light.

"Rise," Fyak commanded, his voice filling the expectant hush. Around him, like grass swaying in the breeze, the Faithful rose to their feet.

"Today we are in the territory of the Rhijudu Tribe. We shall consolidate our position here. Go to the same families you visited last time. Listen to their problems, their achievements, and praise them where you can. Where they have slipped back into the old ways of looking to their one-time Tribal Leader for guidance, chastise them. Remind them of the power of Kezule's wrath."

His almost hypnotic voice rolled over them, washing toward L'Seuli and the other guards. He had to force his attention away from the Prophet and concentrate instead on the male who stood just behind him, the Commander of the Guard.

"Tell them of the duty they owe to Kezule, God of Fire," continued Fyak, raising his arms above his head, hands spread out to the heavens as if in supplication. His eyes glowed feverishly. "I have visited the time of destruction! I saw the demons walking among us, spitting venom in our faces, killing our people with one blow! Beside them walked the mind-poisoners—our own people—helping them! I saw the very sky ablaze with the holy fire of the God as He came to our aid!"

Fyak paused to survey the upturned faces of his followers. The sudden silence took L'Seuli by surprise and he looked

back at the prophet. Behind him, beyond the edges of the
tent, he could see the movement of shadowy figures as more
and more of the villagers of Rhijudu gathered to hear their
Prophet speak. Glancing at Fyak's face, he saw that he was
well aware of his impromptu audience.

"Kezule will come to our aid again! He will free our
people from the slavery of the demons once and for all.
Make no mistake," he said, dropping his voice, "the demons
still walk among us—the demons and the mind-poisoners!
Search out those who talk with their minds for they are
cursed of Kezule! Bring them to me so that we can deal with
them as befits those who are traitors to their own kind!" he
said, raising his voice again. "The time of fire is near at
hand! Only those who believe will survive. Go now, and
spread the word of our God."

The Prophet let his arms fall by his sides and turned
toward the curtained-off portion of the tent that was his private sanctum. L'Seuli shook his head to dispel the feeling of
dizziness that always came over him when Fyak began to
speak. He was convinced the Prophet had to have some kind
of Talent. It was the only way he could mesmerize a crowd
like that and somehow get past his own training. But why
target telepaths as being from the same den as the demons?
And who the hell were the demons anyway?

A hand closed on his shoulder and shook him roughly,
making him jump. He looked round to see Rrurto.

"Come on, lad. We've got work to do," he said. "Stop
dreaming."

L'Seuli flicked his tail in compliance and accompanied the
older male to the edge of the tent. The crowd of villagers was
dispersing now, returning to their homes to wait for the
Faithful to call on them.

"We're on the usual duty," said the old trooper. "Mingling
in the village, ready to arrest anyone that causes any
trouble."

L'Seuli remembered their last stop with a shudder of
horror. A suspected telepath had been identified but they
hadn't reached him in time. The villagers had managed to
inflict such severe wounds on him that he'd died shortly
after.

"Don't go remembering the one who died," said Rrurto as
they ducked under the tent edge and walked toward the village walls. "That's why we're here. To stop that."

"What the Prophet does to them is almost as bad," said L'Seuli. "They're like the walking dead when he's finished."

"Aye, well, maybe, but they say life of any kind is better than death," said Rrurto. "I'm not so sure myself, but I wouldn't want the death he had. Dying fighting is one thing, but being torn apart by a mob is another."

L'Seuli turned to look at him. "What's he got against telepaths?"

"You know as much as I do, lad. You heard him. The telepaths worked with the demons to destroy us."

"Do you believe all that?" he asked, frowning.

"He's the one the God takes back to those days. What he says he sees is what he sees. Now enough talk. We got work to do," Rrurto said as they passed between the gates into the village square.

L'Seuli kept his eyes open as they walked through the narrow lanes between the houses. He hadn't seen any sign of the female he was looking for yet, but then if she was as ill as he'd been told, she'd likely be inside her home.

All was quiet for now as the Faithful had dispersed into the houses to speak to the family groups. It was easy to tell they'd been here before. Peer group pressure had worked on the dissenters in the interim, and everyone who remained was prepared to listen to their lay-priest as he or she dispensed punishment or praise for their actions over the past four weeks.

Here and there blank windows faced the morning sun—homes that were now empty because their owners had been driven from the village for raising their voices against the Word of Kezule.

"It's not right," said L'Seuli abruptly. "These houses," he indicated the empty ones, "they should have families in them. They shouldn't have been forced out."

"Keep your opinions to yourself, lad, I told you that already," growled Rrurto. "It's not about families any more, it's about couples. Some of those empty houses will be used for couples, and others will be single-sex houses where the cubs will live till they're old enough to pair, then the Faithful will choose mates for them."

L'Seuli stopped dead. "What?"

Rrurto grabbed him by the arm and pulled him on. "You heard me. It won't be families any more, only couples, with one of the Faithful assigned to them."

"When was this decided?" he asked, still too stunned to take it in properly.

"The last time the Prophet talked with the God. You missed it. You were in Laasoi getting provisions. That's what the Faithful are out there doing now," he said. "We're to stop here for a couple of days till the village has been set up right, then four of the Faithful will stay behind. When we move on, we're taking the Tribal Elders with us. The Prophet says their presence is a reminder of the old ways."

L'Seuli's mind was beginning to work now. This latest edict of the Prophet's fit in with his doctrine of one male bounded to one female for life. By destroying the structure of the family, and through that the Tribe, Fyak would control the whole of the desert community.

"It's not so bad," said Rrurto, misunderstanding his silence. "At least it's not our lot to go on the punitive mission to Sonashi village. I've done my time fighting. I don't like the idea of waging a war on poorly armed villagers. I've seen too much death and bloodshed."

L'Seuli said nothing. His time among the Ghuulgul desert people was turning into a nightmare.

Raised voices nearby drew Rrurto's attention. "Over there," he said, pointing to the street corner on his left as he began to run toward it.

L'Seuli followed, rounding the corner and almost sending Rrurto flying into the house as he skidded to a stop behind him.

"What the hell's going on?" the older male demanded of the villager standing in the open doorway.

"She refuses to get up," he said, ears flicking in distress. "Because she lives alone, the Faithful at our house said I should take her to the gathering hall where all the other infirm are being assembled."

L'Seuli's ears pricked forward. If they were collecting the infirm, then there was a chance he'd be able to see the female he sought.

"One old female's causing all this commotion?" said Rrurto in disbelief.

"I'm not old, you ignorant plainslander!" came the quiet but venomous reply. "This has been my home for thirty years, and no dirt-grubbing snit like you is going to tell me to leave it!"

"You see?" said the villager.

Rrurto gave a low growl of annoyance. "Just go in, pick her up, and carry her out."

The villager looked at him in horror. "It's not that easy," he said. "You don't know what she's like!"

"Get in there and do it," snapped Rrurto, giving him a push.

The male disappeared from sight as he stumbled inside, only to reemerge with a howl of pain amidst a shower of pots and pans and other kitchen implements. Rrurto and L'Seuli dodged aside.

"You see?" the villager said, leaning against the wall for support as he removed his head covering and began to massage the back of his head. "If you want her out, you can damned well fetch her yourself!" With that he stalked off up the street.

Rrurto stood there with an expression of disgust on his face. L'Seuli was hard pressed not to grin, and when a smirk did escape him, the older male rounded on him angrily.

"Wipe that grin off your face and get busy picking this rubbish up," he snarled. "I'll get one of the Faithful to see to this." He stalked off back the way they'd come.

L'Seuli thumbed on his rifle's safety switch and, slinging it over his shoulder, began to pick up the pans.

Finished, he stood at the doorway, unsure what to do next. "Excuse me," he said. "What shall I do with your pans?"

"Bring them in here, of course! What do you think I use for cooking? There aren't food dispensers out here in the desert, you know," she said in a voice that this time held a trace of vulnerability.

"You won't throw anything at me, will you?" he asked cautiously.

"Are you going to try and take me out of my home?" she asked in reply.

"No. I'm just going to put these inside the door."

"Then unless you try something you'll regret, I won't throw anything at you. I'm not short of ammunition, you know." She broke off to cough.

L'Seuli cautiously poked his nose round the doorway. The room smelled musty though it looked clean enough. To his right, leaning against an ancient stone cooking range, stood the female he was looking for.

The autumn sunlight, still powerful here in the eastern desert, illuminated her strong features unkindly. The wasting disease had obviously got her firmly in its clutches. The high cheekbones were almost as sharp as blades, the hollows below them and around her eyes, pockets of dark shadow. The arm that held onto the range was stick thin, the bones almost showing through the thin layer of gray fur.

Cautiously, he stepped inside, his arms full of her hardware.

"Bring it over here," she said, gesturing to the stove. "I won't bite you. I haven't got the strength anyway," she said, mouth opening in a faint grin.

He crossed over to her and waited as she took the various metal objects from him and replaced them on the stove top.

"At least you've got your ammunition back," he said.

She turned to look at him, eye ridges lowering in concentration.

"A strange thing for one of you Modernists to say." Her voice was quiet, barely audible. "Best not let anyone else hear you."

"Why do they want to move you?"

"Pass me a chair, lad. I might as well sit beside my ammunition. If I have to stand any longer, I'll fall down."

L'Seuli turned and fetched a wooden chair from beside the table. He placed it behind her, lending her his arm to lean on as she lowered herself onto the seat.

"Thank you. They want all us old and infirm together because they know that away from our families and the young ones, many of us will just give up the fight to live. We'll have no purpose in life anymore." She shrugged, leaning against the back of her chair and closing her eyes. "They want to be rid of us. With no Elders in the village, the rest are dependent on the Faithful for advice, aren't they?"

"Can't they see what's happening?" demanded L'Seuli. "Are they that stupid?"

"Yes, lad, they're that stupid," she nodded. "Four years of drought have given them a hopelessness. They don't want government handouts, what they need is hope. This Prophet gives them that. He says the drought is Kezule testing His people, hardening them for the time of fire that will come soon." She sighed. "At least he's stopped the interminable bickering and petty fighting that's always gone on among the Tribes," she said.

L'Seuli heard voices from outside. "I'd better go," he said, backing away from her toward the doorway.

"Go, and don't let them catch your thoughts, lad," she said, her voice only a thin whisper now.

Rrurto was approaching with one of the more senior Faithful. They came level with him, then stopped. "She still as belligerent?" he asked.

L'Seuli shrugged.

"I'll see if she'll talk to you," Rrurto said before sidling into the building. "One of the Faithful wants to talk to you," he called out.

"I'll talk, but that's all," she said. "He can stand inside the door."

Rrurto turned back to the street. "Go on," he said to the sandy-robed acolyte.

They waited a minute, hearing only a quiet murmur of voices from inside. The acolyte emerged again. "We'll leave her here," he said. "One dying female living on her own doesn't interfere with the Prophet's interpretation of Kezule's Will. She's more trouble than she's worth."

Rrurto nodded, and the acolyte left. "Come on," he said. "Back to the main streets."

As they walked back round to the square, L'Seuli was still thinking of the female and what she'd said. It was becoming more and more obvious that these people were utter fanatics, following some sunstroke madness of Fyak's. *Not madness,* he corrected himself, *he's too methodical, too devious for mad.*

*   *   *

Kaid rose at dawn the following day and went in search of T'Chebbi, who was on duty outside Carrie's and Kusac's suite.

"I'm going to the Valsgarth estate, T'Chebbi," he said quietly. "I need to speak to Ghyan. You know what to do when they leave?"

She nodded.

"Meral will relieve you at midday. You two and Lhea will cover them over the next two days."

She raised a curious eye ridge. "Aren't you taking a shift?"

"No, not this time."

"He's asked you," she said with satisfaction. "Knew they'd choose you."

Kaid gave her a long look. "I'm spending this time in retreat myself at the new Shrine. Dzaka's coming with me."

T'Chebbi looked away, ears flicking back and remaining there in apology. "Your pardon, Brother Kaid," she said quietly. "There's a rightness in you going."

He reached out and briefly gripped her shoulder with his hand. "It's all right, T'Chebbi," he said. "It's just that it comes as a mixed blessing for me. You know where I am if you need me."

Dzaka was waiting for him in the aircar. As soon as Kaid was seated, he took off.

"Why are you going on retreat?" he asked, banking the aircar out toward the Valsgarth estate.

"I thought we could both do with some time for meditation. I'll tell you now, since you'll hear soon enough. I've been chosen as the third for their Triad."

Dzaka glanced briefly across at him. "Was that ever in doubt?" he asked.

"I take nothing for granted," said Kaid. "Ghyan and Rulla are expecting us. If I know Rulla, he'll be planning a large first meal for all of us. I need to speak to Ghyan first, so we'll join you when we're through."

"As you wish," said Dzaka.

As predicted, Rulla was waiting for them at the doorway of the newly appointed Shrine of Vartra. Kaid and Dzaka picked their way through the still unfinished front yard, trying not to stand in the muddy ruts.

"We're getting the cubs onto that today," Rulla said, grinning at their discomfort. "At least we're finished inside. We've even taken delivery of the statue of Vartra. That arrived yesterday, courtesy of Father Lijou."

Kaid looked at him in surprise. "A generous gift indeed."

"Lijou is Head of the Order," Rulla reminded him, "but I agree. Ghyan's in his office. He asked me to point you in the right direction when you arrived." He led them into the main corridor. "Straight ahead, last door on the right."

Ghyan looked up from his desk as Kaid entered. "Good morning," he said, closing his book and getting up to come round and join him. "Can I offer you some c'shar?" he asked, gesturing to the jug and mugs that sat on a storage unit to one side of the old-fashioned hearth.

"Please," said Kaid.

"Take a seat," the priest said as he went over to the unit. "I take it you've requested this retreat to study the En'Shalla rituals," he said, adding whitener and sweetener to the mugs.

Kaid moved toward the fireplace, sitting down in one of the two informal chairs placed there. "I've already been studying them, Ghyan," he said, accepting the mug he was handed.

"Kusac's asked you then," Ghyan said, sitting down opposite him. "Since you're here, I take it you didn't refuse."

"I tried, Ghyan," said Kaid, taking a sip of his drink. "Vartra knows, I tried. Kusac would have none of it, though. Said it was what she wanted too. I need to get close to the God, to find out what He wants of me."

He could see the coldness in Ghyan's eyes when he looked at him. Inwardly, he sighed. Personally, Ghyan's prejudice didn't matter, but it would make him more difficult to work with.

"You're welcome, of course," said Ghyan. "Father Lijou is due later this morning to dedicate the Shrine. We're not on the same level as the Temple at Valsgarth town was, never will be, in fact. I'll have a small staff of acolytes, plus any of the youngsters from either estate who choose to serve some time here. In fact, the cubs that are helping outside are all from the main estate. There's still quite a lot of building work going on to extend the premises, so this isn't the quietest of times for you to be here."

"It has to be now. The Liege and the Liegena are on an En'Shalla retreat for the next two days," said Kaid, looking away from him as he put his mug down on the table that sat between them. "Kusac asked me as a lay-priest to witness his intention to make sure that the cub they'll conceive in the next two days will be En'Shalla—in the hands of the Gods."

"He has, has he?" The question was rhetorical, but Kaid could hear the amusement in his voice.

He looked up sharply, frowning as he saw the humorous look Ghyan was giving him. "What?"

"You're not the only devious one, Kaid," said the priest, mouth opening in a slight smile.

"What are you talking about?" asked Kaid.

"You know what he's doing, don't you?" Then he stopped, ears flicking briefly backward as he obviously realized Kaid had no idea what he was talking about. "You don't know, do you?" he said. "Vanna's DNA tests show that there's a chance that some of us may be genetically compatible with the mixed Leska pairs."

"So what, Ghyan? He wants to know her cub is his. What could be more natural? If you think that bothers me, you're mistaken. Last time we spoke you complained I needed to learn to care about her, now you're amused because you think I do! I suggested you as the priest for the new clan because I felt you genuinely cared about the people in your charge. We're working toward the same ends. Stop treating me as if I'm the enemy."

Kaid was letting his quite justifiable anger mask the sudden fear that Ghyan's remark had caused. He remembered Noni asking who'd fathered Carrie's lost cub. Had she seen something in the future that she wasn't telling him?

Ghyan was silent for a few moments. "You're right," he said, his ears going flat. "It was unworthy of me. I apologize. Of course I'll help you all I can."

Kaid picked up his mug again, pushing the disturbing thoughts to the back of his mind. "We've all had to put duty before our personal wishes at some time, Ghyan," he said. "If what you've just told me doesn't show you the hand of Vartra positively at work in their lives, then I don't know what He has to do to convince you. Only He could arrange the timing of everything so it all fitted together."

This time, Ghyan's gaze was curious. "Father Lijou said you were unusual."

"Did he also tell you that for good or ill, once I give my oath, I keep it?" Kaid said. "I don't give my oath lightly, Ghyan, but Kusac *is* my Liege, as is Carrie. You still see Kusac as the youngling you knew at the Guild, not the adult he's become; that's why you don't trust his judgment."

Ghyan sighed. "Once again, you may well be right. How can I help you?"

"I need time in the Shrine room, to mediate. Will this be possible? When do you expect Father Lijou?"

"About an hour before second meal. We're still finishing off decorating the Shrine room, although it's almost set up. As I said, Father Lijou is dedicating the Shrine today. He gave us our statue of Vartra. A small one, to be sure, but then the actual Shrine is too small for a life-size one. It was a most generous gesture on his part, as is his offer to come and do the dedication."

"Very," said Kaid, wondering what was behind the Head

Priest's gesture. "Considering how Ghezu views us, I'm impressed. Lijou couldn't have had an easy time justifying it to him."

"I believe our Leader is more than capable of handling the situation," said Ghyan, his tone becoming formal. "Our Order is independent of Stronghold. Father Lijou is co-ruler of the Brotherhood with Leader Ghezu, not his subordinate."

"There's no need to be defensive, Ghyan. You've not been involved in the Brotherhood's religious functions. They're somewhat different from yours, even leaving aside the fact that we're all trained as lay-priests," said Kaid. "I'll agree that outside the Brotherhood, Ghezu has no authority over the Order, but that's not the case within Stronghold. Rulla's been with you for some time now, surely he's told you something of the religious setup?"

Ghyan's ears gave the tiniest of flicks.

Kaid grinned. "Let me guess. You thought it was just his bias."

"You have to realize," Ghyan said, his tone defensive again, "that when you hear tales of the absolute head of your Order having leadership wrangles over the deployment of personnel, they do seem somewhat unbelievable."

"I'm sure they do," Kaid said, getting to his feet. "However, now you can put them in their correct perspective. Shall we join Dzaka and Rulla for first meal?"

"Yes. Of course. I'd forgotten about that," he said as he rose. "After we've eaten, I'll get Rulla to show you to your rooms."

"I'd also appreciate it if I could have a look at some of the records you've been compiling of the God-Visions and dreams experienced by Leska pairs, and the Brothers."

"You know about my work?"

"I keep my ears turned to the wind, Ghyan," said Kaid. "It may be that we can collaborate. I've had one or two visions of my own lately."

"I'll pull them out for you later today."

Rulla took them to their rooms. They were small, and though the furnishings were austere, there was a meditation mat and lamp in each of them. Dzaka elected to go with Rulla and organize the local younglings and cubs into flattening the front yard while Kaid decided to remain in his room until Lijou arrived.

The building had once been a communal school and nursery, but for now they had more need of a Shrine with the religious guidance and teaching it would provide. A school building and nursery could come later, when the estate had its own population of cubs.

Kaid spread the meditation mat on the floor, then placed the low table and lamp in front of it. Going over to the bed, he dug in the small kit bag he'd brought, bringing out a packet of his favorite incense. From the cupboard set atop the drawer unit by the window, he took out the standard flask of oil and incense bowl which he placed on the table to the right of the lamp.

He dug in his pocket for an igniter, then undoing his belt, he shrugged off his jacket and flung it on the end of the bed. Finally, he squatted down on the mat. Putting the igniter on the table, he picked up the oil flask, and as he poured it into the lamp, he quietly began murmuring the litany of Preparation.

The bronze lamp was shaped like the flower of the nung tree, symbol of hope and rebirth. The outer bowl was sculpted in the form of the nine petals that protected the inner stamen from which the three wicks protruded. Surrounding it were three ornamental filaments.

Threes again, he thought, his mind drifting as he took the charcoal out of the incense bowl. The igniter's red glow spat and crackled as it spread across the black disk. Hurriedly he placed the coal back on the surface of the sand-filled bowl. Taking a small block of incense from his packet, he put it on the table before lighting the lamp.

It flared brightly for a moment, then settled down to a steady yellow flame. He continued reciting the litany as he crumbled the incense onto the charcoal. Once more it spat and hissed, this time sending up clouds of blue smoke until the resins had melted over the surface of the block.

The heavy scent filled the small room, and as he finished the Preparation, he began the Relaxation, withdrawing his mind from the reality of his surroundings through the familiar phrases and the flickering light of the lamp. Deeper and deeper he let himself sink, until all he could sense was a gray mist surrounding him.

He waited, drifting patiently, praying that the God would be accessible today.

* * *

"How're things at the main estate?" asked Rulla, leaning back against the wall, nonchalantly chewing his stim-twig as he watched the younglings padding around with buckets of earth for the cubs to enthusiastically stamp into the wet ruts and holes.

"Things are quiet," he said. "Kaid has me doing electronic surveillance shifts at the gatehouse and accompanying Clan Leader Rhyasha and Clan Lord Konis when they need an aide."

Rulla nodded. "He's seeing you widen your experience," he said. "That's good. And Ghezu?"

"He's getting twitchy about my weekly 'Nothing to report' reports."

Rulla took the twig from his mouth. "The time will come when Ghezu asks you do to something you can't. What then, Dzaka?"

"I'll avoid it."

"And if you can't?"

Dzaka turned to look at him, his green eyes cold. "I'll have to decide at the time, Rulla."

"If you've still to decide, what are you doing here?" he demanded, straightening up, his ears giving a brief flick of annoyance. "You've had plenty of time to make up your mind."

"It's easy for you, isn't it, Rulla?" said Dzaka. "You knew what you were going to do from the first, didn't you? Never had any doubts. And, of course, Ghezu freed you from your Oath. Tell me what *you* would have done if he hadn't released you?" He looked back to where the cubs were happily sending mud splashing everywhere before continuing. "You haven't had any choices to make. I face death on every side, Rulla. Had you thought of that?"

"Don't you trust us to protect you, youngling?" asked Rulla, a sneer in his voice as he lifted an eye ridge in mock surprise. "If you wanted to leave the Brotherhood now, all it would take is asking Kaid. We'd all back him."

"Listen to yourself, Rulla," said Dzaka, looking at him again. "You'll back *him*. Not me. Hardly calculated to inspire my confidence."

Rulla gave a snort of derision and put his twig back in his

mouth. "Why should any of us back you, youngling? We don't know you, and before you say because we're guild brothers, think again. One of our prime rules is that Brothers never take opposing contracts. You let yourself be maneuvered into that position, then compounded your idiocy by not telling anyone!" He shook his head. "You give us reason to trust you, Dzaka, and we'll back *you* against Ghezu."

The younger male said nothing, returning to watching the cubs.

Rulla observed him from the corner of his eye, but Dzaka remained still, showing no emotions, neither his body nor his face giving away what he felt. After a few minutes, Rulla took the twig from his mouth once more. "If it happens again, Dzaka, tell one of us," he said quietly. "The Brotherhood looks after its own. A way out can be found. Leader Ghezu has always had a tendency to blur the lines between breaking guild policy and fulfilling difficult contracts. We older ones have found ways to deal with him. As we hear it, he's gotten worse since he brought Kaid back."

Dzaka said nothing, continuing to stare stonily ahead at the yard where the cubs' pothole filling detail had degenerated into a mudslinging match.

Rulla sighed, then pocketed his twig before turning his attention to his charges.

"Just what the hell do you think you're doing?" he roared, striding forward to the margins of the mud field. His hand snaked out to grab the nearest youngster by the scruff, holding him up until he was glaring eye to eye with him. "Look at you! I could plant next year's grain crop on you, and it would grow! What d'you think your mothers will say about the state of you?" he demanded, looking past his dangling catch to pin the other half a dozen youngsters with his glare.

"We'd finished, Brother Rulla," stammered his captive.

"Did I hear you speak?" he thundered, shaking the lad.

"N . . . no, Brother!"

"The beach is five minutes' run from here," he said, dropping the cub to the ground. "I expect to see you back here, without a trace of mud, in eight minutes!"

Rooted to the spot with fear, not one of them dared move.

"What are you waiting for?" he roared, watching his victim scramble to his feet and take off in the direction of the sea.

The others left, running for dear life. Beyond them the ten

younglings who'd been carrying the buckets of earth, rushed up, attracted by the noise. They stood beyond the yard wall, mouths open in grins.

"Did I say you were excused?" demanded Rulla, turning an angry face on them.

They disappeared on the heels of the cubs.

Rulla turned and walked back to Dzaka. "I'm going in for a c'shar," he said.

Dzaka frowned briefly. "The cubs?"

The other gave a purring chuckle. "They'll find us. They've done their work, let off some steam, now it's time to reestablish the discipline. Are you coming, or do you fancy a cold swim, too?"

Dzaka's mouth opened a fraction in a grin. "No. I think I'll pass on that one for today," he said, following him in to the refectory.

*   *   *

The mists resolved so gradually that it took Kaid some time to realize that they had. His surroundings weren't familiar. He'd expected the God's temple, instead he saw a cavern, its walls lined with spars of wood. At first he thought the two figures were engaged in some kind of highly ritualized dance, then he realized they were fighting.

His role as an observer was totally passive: he had no control over the scene before him, being unable to either move closer or shut his eyes to end it. As the scene unfolded, he realized they were fighting with knives, and that they each wore padded body armor. A practice session then, some portion of his mind observed.

The younger male was faster, quicker on his feet, darting in, then dancing back out of range. The older male, however, waited, using the minimum of energy, always meeting each attack with a deft counter. He had the experience and the patience. Then there was a quick flurry of movement from him and suddenly it was over. The younger male lay on his back, throat and belly exposed, knife held pressed beneath his ear.

As he was released, and a hand held down to help him rise, the scene faded, returning Kaid to the mists. Once more he floated in timelessness until suddenly it was ripped apart and he was catapulted into another scene.

This cavern was brightly lit, but cold. At the half dozen benches sat young adults, most of them scribbling on the pads of paper that lay there. Once more his vision focused on the same young male, whom he could now see was mountain-born like himself.

A striking female, her pelt the color of pale amber, was approaching him and he turned to speak to her. Kaid could feel the youth's intense interest in her. He spoke, then, as she turned away again, he was suddenly gripped within the young male's thoughts as everything spun sickeningly around him and her mind exploded within his.

"No! Dear God, not a Leska Link with him! Not Rezac!" he heard her cry before darkness descended on him.

It was later and they'd just left the building. Dropping onto all fours, they began to lope for the tree line, heading down the hillside. Faster and faster he ran, trying to deny what had happened while all he could remember was her reaction of hostility to what he'd been before. He knew she'd looked into the depths of his soul and condemned him without understanding. Then the world around him erupted in coruscating colors and sounds, and with a cry of impotent rage and pain, he was pitched back to the gray mists, shaking and trembling as if it had happened to him.

You thought to avoid me? said the voice he knew so well. *Think again! You and I have an appointment at the Fire Margins, Tallinu. See that you keep it.* The voice died away to a whisper, leaving behind it a faint, echoing laughter.

Abruptly he returned to the reality of his room and the glow of the lamp. No more was it a gentle anchor beckoning him to safety, now it seemed to leap and flare, casting ominous shadows around the room.

He was lying on his side, his body still shaking from the realism of his experience. For perhaps the first time in his life, fear gripped him in its claws and wouldn't let go. What were the odds that they'd have almost identical backgrounds? *Coincidence,* he told himself, and *memories from the past, nothing more. Only echoes. A replay like the one Carrie had at Noni's.*

Still shaking, he pushed himself upright, trying to remember the words of the litany to banish fear but his mind seemed frozen in that faraway time. The female—so fair, the color of Rhyasha Aldatan, even down to the braided hair. But the hatred she'd directed at him! And the male, from the mountains like him, from Ranz where you still walked with the packs or died on your own, a victim of the pack-wars. He knew what it was like, having lived there for several years when he was a youngling.

It wasn't me, he kept repeating to himself, *he was younger*—until at last he believed it. And the female wasn't Khemu, with hair and pelt the color of soft moonlight. This one had been as bright as the sun, but her mind had seared Rezac just as surely as Khemu had seared him. There lay the true horror, all the other aspects of the ancient memory adding up to that final climax. He shuddered again, leaning forward abruptly and blowing out the lamp.

He'd had his message from the God, and there was no comfort for him in it.

*   *   *

As they walked through the thinning trees toward the clearing, Carrie stopped and turned to him. "We're here now," she said. "What's all the mystery about?"

"I wanted us to have a break away from everyone," he said, reaching out to take her hand. "A couple of days on our own."

"Sounds like a good idea to me, but where are we going, and why all the mystery?"

"We're camping not far from here, and actually, I do have an ulterior motive," he admitted, then hesitated. Despite all they'd been through together, despite the love they shared, she still had that quality about her that kept him unsure of her at times.

"What is it?" she asked gently, her hand tightening round his. "You're still shielding something from me."

"Tomorrow's our Link day," he said, reaching out to touch her cheek, "and you're fertile again. By tomorrow evening, you'll be pregnant."

As he felt the shock his words caused her, she tried to pull away from him.

"Carrie, listen to me," he said, reaching out to draw her

into his arms. "Jack and Vanna haven't managed to find a
way to prevent that yet, but we still have one choice left. We
can *choose* to have this cub, to make it ours. En'Shalla, a
child of the Gods, free of all the Guilds and Clans."

"I don't believe you. How can you know I'm fertile when I
can't even tell?" she demanded, still twisting within his
embrace.

"Be still a minute and listen to me," he said. When she'd
stopped, he continued. "Believe me, Carrie, I know you're
fertile. Your scent's different for one thing. Before, so much
was happening that we had hardly any time for each other.
Now I know you better, I know the signs."

"Another cub won't replace her," she said defiantly, looking up at him, her eyes sparkling with unshed tears.

"Never," he agreed. "You know I still grieve for her, too.
Today is ours, no Link demands. It's time we moved on,
Carrie; took control of our lives rather than sat back and let
fate dictate what happens."

"I'll have no tests," she said.

"No tests, no doctors unless you want one," he agreed,
beginning to nuzzle her ear. "You don't need to leave the
estate for anything. The only Humans around will be those
with Leskas of their own." His teeth gently closed on her ear.

*Your choice, Carrie. It's what we talked about, our first
step to freedom,* he sent. *Will you choose to be the mother of
my cub?*

She could feel the tension in his mind. They might be life-
bonded, and though it gave him the right to expect her
to carry at least one cub, he was asking her the way any
young male would ask the female he loved. After what had
happened the last time, he knew it was no small thing he
hoped for.

*I know it wasn't your choice before because we didn't
think it was possible. It would mean so much to me to know
we both chose to make this cub together.*

Yes, she sent, and, *I love you,* as she felt the joy wash
through him. *I'm glad we have the choice this time.*

With relief, he felt her body become soft and pliant once
more. *There's no need for fear now. We know what to expect,*
he sent, gently releasing her though he kept hold of her hand.

"So we're camping out for two days in a cave, are we?"
she said as they moved off toward the clearing ahead.

It has to be done the old way, he sent. *It's a nice cave. I've*

*made it as comfortable as possible, even brought some food
and drink in case our hunting proves fruitless.*

"Are we going hunting, too?" she asked. "I'm glad it isn't
winter yet!"

"Yes," he said, lips curving up in an almost human smile.
"We're going hunting. If we don't catch anything, we'll have
a sparse third meal!"

"How do we cook anything we might catch?" she asked,
slowing down again as they approached the hillside.

"I've collected firewood," he said, tugging her gently
onward. "It's quite a civilized cave, honestly. Come and see
it for yourself."

He led her over to the creeper-covered rock face and
began feeling among the vines with his free hand, trying to
locate the entrance.

She hesitated, and he knew instantly what she feared.

"It is like stepping back into the past of my species, but
there's nothing to be afraid of. I'm no different out here in
the wilds than I am at home," he said quietly. He knew there
were still times when for a moment she saw him as alien.
"What have you to fear?"

Nothing, she sent, dipping her head to one side, a half-
smile on her face. She stepped past him and into the cave
mouth.

He followed, his hand automatically reaching for the ledge
inside where he'd placed his torch. Picking it up, he flicked
it on, illuminating the interior.

"It's bigger than I thought," she said, following the beam
upward with her eyes. The rocky ceiling was some six or
seven meters above them.

"It's natural," he said. "Hollowed out by the sea I
believe."

"Impressive."

He turned the light on themselves so she could see his
grin. "Daunting, you mean. Don't worry," he reassured her.
"We're camping farther back, and there's a natural flue to
the outside under which we can light our fire."

"You used to camp out here as a youngling, with Ghyan."

"That's right," he said, aiming the beam deeper into the
cave as he reached for her hand again. "I'll show you where
we're sleeping. We need to go there to collect our bows."

A few meters ahead of them was a small side chamber and

as they stepped inside it, Kusac felt the gentle draught of cool air from the surface ruffle his hair.

The torchlight fully illuminated the small chamber, its light bounced back by the seams of crystal that crisscrossed the rock face.

"Grass?" Carrie said in amazement, looking down at the sea of greenery around her feet.

"Not ordinary grass," he said, bending down to pick up a handful of it to show her. "See, it's round, not flat. It's called sweet-grass because of its scent. It's part of doing it the old way."

She took some from him, sniffing it gingerly.

"Traditionally, we males would find a den for our mate and line it with sweet-grass," he said. "It's supposed to possess special qualities."

"Oh?" she said, letting the grass fall back to the ground. "What are they?"

"You know the type of thing," he said evasively, his tail swaying gently from side to side as he stepped further into the chamber. "Aids fertility, helps in childbirth, the usual things. It probably won't affect you, as I expect it's species-specific." Seeing the bows and quivers propped against the far wall reminded him why they'd come into the sleeping cave. He was reaching for them when Carrie touched his arm.

Leave them till later, she sent. *And no, it doesn't matter if it's me or the grass,* she added as he turned round to face her.

We'll miss second meal, he sent.

We can eat later. Reaching for the buckle on his belt, she lifted her face up to his.

The torch still held in one hand, he put his arm around her, letting the fingers of his free hand run through her hair.

Gods, cub, you haven't been like this since before . . . his thought faltered.

. . . the Challenge, she finished for him.

Since then, he agreed, lowering his face to hers and gently nipping her lips before kissing her Terran-style. *It's good to have you back, cub. It's been too long since you felt this relaxed with me.*

It's in the past now. Let's leave it there, she sent, returning his kiss as she dropped his belt to the ground and pressed open the front seal on his tunic.

Let me put the torch down, he sent, trying to gently push her back.

"Sod the torch," she murmured, her hands running across the silky fur that covered the front of his body. Reaching behind herself with one hand, she took the torch from him and let it fall to the ground.

The beam flickered crazily then steadied as it landed on the deep layer of grass.

As he bent and swept her up into his arms, he felt the tension begin to build in the muscles of his lower abdomen and groin.

"I've never known anyone like you," he said softly, kneeling on the grass before putting her down gently on the pile of furs that lay nearby. "A touch, a kiss, and you have me as aroused as any youngling with his first female. You do it every time."

She lay there looking up at him as he leaned over her and deftly untied the sash she wore round her waist. His amber eyes glittered in the reflected torchlight and as he unsealed her tunic and pushed it aside, his hair brushed against her cheek.

Do I still make your heart beat faster? he asked, his hand cupping one breast as his mouth gently closed on the other.

"Oh, yes," she whispered, reaching down to touch his ears and hair. "As fast as yours does."

One hand closed in his hair, clutching it as his teeth and tongue began to work their magic on her. Then his body was touching hers, his fur like velvet against her bare skin. The sensations began to build inside her, higher and higher till they broke, leaving her shuddering with pleasure as he released her and gave a deep purr of amusement.

"Stop teasing me," she moaned softly, reaching down for him, but her hand was batted away as he continued.

"No more." She trapped his hand with hers. "I want you *now,* Kusac."

Then he was there, within her, part of her.

En'Shalla, Carrie, he sent as she arched her body against his. *Say it, say En'Shalla. The cub we're making is in the hands of the Gods.*

"En'Shalla," she whispered, pulling him closer. "We're one, in the hands of the Gods."

As always, their minds fused, each of them experiencing the other's pleasure mingled with their own. Around them, the scent of the crushed grass rose, filling the air and making it even more difficult for him to keep the self-control he needed.

Your decision as well as mine, Carrie, he sent. *This time we choose to make our cub, our daughter.* Then, with both their minds focused on that thought, he let his control drop.

She could feel it, like currents ebbing and flowing through their bodies and minds: a convergence of potentialities. Then mentally they reached out and grasped their choice and she felt a power like that of the gestalt surge through them. Their shared world exploded, the heightened sensations different from anything they'd experienced before, and for a brief moment—so brief that later she doubted it—she felt a third presence join with them only to vanish in the pleasure of their shared climax.

Afterward as she lay clasped safe in her life-mate's arms, she knew that their daughter had been conceived. The arm that held her cradled against his chest was unlike hers with its covering of black fur. Across her legs she could feel the gentle weight of his tail, and the feather-light touch of its tip as it rose and fell slowly. She turned her face to look up at him, feeling the warmth and silkiness of his fur against her skin. His face with the high cheekbones and bifurcated mouth was humanoid but not human, nor were the amber-colored eyes that regarded her solemnly.

She reached up to stroke his cheek. "Kashini," she said as a quiet contentment filled her. "She's called Kashini."

With relief, he released the breath he hadn't realized he'd been holding. "Kashini," he agreed, lowering his head to kiss her. This time he knew she wouldn't fear their child: this time she had faced the reality of his alienness and had accepted the fact that the cub she was carrying was only part human. This cub she'd chosen to carry. He thanked the Gods that he was a telepath because there was no way words could convey to her what he felt.

* * *

Lijou sat at his desk looking out across the valley to the Kysubi plains. Already he could begin to see the seasonal changes in the trees far below. He heard a scratching at the door and with an effort pulled his attention to his office.

"Enter."

The door opened to admit his second-in-command. "Excuse the interruption, Father Lijou," he said, "but we've had a disturbing message from one of our Brothers at the Laasoi Guildhouse concerning the situation in the Ghuulgul desert. I thought you should be told immediately."

Lijou nodded and gestured for the gray-robed Brother Vusho to enter.

He approached the Head Priest's desk. "Support for the self-styled priest, Fyak, is growing faster than we anticipated, Father," he said. "Vray sends that they've lost another telepath to them. Brother Chay. He was killed . . . most horrifically," he said, his ears lying back along his head in obviously great distress.

Lijou rose and went round to Vusho, taking him gently by the arm and drawing him over to the informal seats.

"Sit, Brother Vusho," he said. "Take a moment to regain your composure. I take it you picked up the details of Brother Chay's death."

Vusho nodded briefly as he sat on the edge of the chair.

Lijou went to the heated c'shar unit and poured them both a drink. Returning to Vusho, he handed him a mug. "Drink it," he said, sitting down opposite him and taking a mouthful himself.

With a shaking hand, Vusho put the mug to his mouth and took a sip. "He was torn apart by the villagers," he said softly, tears beginning to roll unheeded down his face. "How could they do that? How can they inflict such pain on another person?"

"Fear and hate are powerful motivations," said Lijou. "Fyak preaches both."

Vusho looked up at him. "Is there any news of Raza and Shi?"

"Nothing good," said Lijou regretfully. "This Fyak managed to burn out the area of their brain that processes their telepathic talents. There's nothing we can do for them. They're still comatose and likely to remain that way. If our medics at Valsgarth can do nothing for them, then it's just a matter of time."

"What about Noni? Can't she help them?"

"Noni?" Lijou said in surprise. "Is she still alive? She must be nearly a hundred and thirty by now!"

"Could she help?"

Lijou took another drink, regarding Vusho thoughtfully. "The Brothers still go to her?"

Vusho's ears flicked assent. "Those from the mountains would rather see her than our physician or medic," he said candidly.

"Does she still refuse to travel?" Seeing Vusho's ears flick again, he continued. "It would mean bringing them back from Valsgarth in IC units and all that entails, including asking Esken to release them to us. Relations between us and the Guild are not the best at the moment," he mused. "In the end, Noni may be able to do nothing either."

He sat for a moment, deep in thought then, coming to a decision, put his mug down. "Contact Valsgarth Medical Center on my authorization and familiarize yourself with the details of their cases, then go to Noni and tell her. See what she says. There is no point in bringing them here if she can do nothing. We haven't the facilities for caring for them long-term, they're better at Valsgarth if that's the case."

Vusho's ears pricked up and forward. "Father Lijou," was all he could say, all he needed to as his mind conveyed the rest.

"What other news is there from Lassoi?" Lijou asked.

"Fyak's support grows," said Vusho, taking a drink. "Every day he takes more of the desert people on as his Faithful."

"Faithful?"

"Disciples, his inner priesthood, for want of a better word," explained Vusho. "He surrounds himself with a guard made up of the older males, veterans of the constant inter-Tribal skirmishes. There was a battle a few days ago at a village called Sonashi."

"A battle?" Lijou's eye ridges lifted in surprise.

"The Sonashi were decimated," said Vusho. "There hasn't been such ferocious action between the Tribes in the last thirty years."

"Hmm. I wonder if it was just a battle. Could it have been a disciplinary action? Perhaps the Tribe wanted nothing to do with Fyak and his followers."

"I don't know, Father," said Vusho. "There have been reports of a few refugees arriving at the Laasoi Guildhouse. That's where we got what little information we have. Unfortunately they aren't saying much at all."

Lijou shifted in his seat, his long robe rustling as he

moved. "Contact Brother Vray again and have him question these refugees more thoroughly. Since they've come to us for sanctuary, they can tell us what they know. Tell him to order the return of our remaining two priests from the desert areas as a matter of urgency. I won't have our people endangered any longer. The risks are too high."

"Guild Master Esken still has telepaths in the field."

Lijou gave a hiss of exasperation. "Then he's a bigger fool than I thought! There's nothing we can do, I'm afraid, Vusho. My next worry is how long the Guildhouse at Laasoi will be safe. They're too near the desert for comfort. I'll have to contact Mentor Nishou myself about that. Thank the God that his Guildhouse is for us, not Esken!"

Vusho nodded, setting his empty mug down on the low table between them before getting to his feet. "I'll see to those matters straight away, Father," he said.

Lijou stood too, his hand going out to touch Vusho on the shoulder. "Your sensitivity does you credit, Brother Vusho," he said gently. "You can only do so much to help and no more."

"I know, Father Lijou," he said with a sigh. "Sometimes that side of my Talent is more of a curse than a blessing. There should be another report in by the twenty-third hour tonight. I'll bring you the news when it reaches us."

"No, Brother Vusho, you won't," said Lijou firmly. "You will be sleeping. The Brother on duty can bring me the news. I need you rested if you're going to see Noni tomorrow and hopefully bring our Brothers home from Valsgarth. There's no one else I can entrust these tasks to. I will be at the new Valsgarth estate for much of the morning. If you need me, have a message sent."

"Yes, Father Lijou."

As Vusho approached the door, Lijou called out again. "How is Leader Ghezu today?"

Vusho didn't turn round. "Those of us who have to deal with him go in pairs, Father. The Warrior Brothers make sure there is always an extra senior Brother at all training sessions. For the moment, Vartra smiles on us as Leader Ghezu is busy researching the Brotherhood's Warrior records for some reason."

"Let us pray that He continues to smile," said Lijou dryly. "May Vartra walk with you, Brother Vusho."

"And with you, Father."

* * *

Parallel rows of mats covered the floor of the new Shrine. As he followed the mixture of Aldatan estate members, Brothers, and younglings in, Kaid looked around for Dzaka. Catching sight of him sitting to the rear of the hall, he headed in his direction. Squatting down on the mat beside him, he flicked an ear in greeting.

"I thought you'd still be at your meditation," said Dzaka, keeping his voice low.

"I didn't want to miss this," Kaid replied, looking up to see Lijou emerge from behind the curtain at the opposite end of the hall.

Circling round the unlit right-hand brazier, the Head Priest stopped in front of the plinth bearing the statue of the God. Lijou looked round the assembled people, his jaw dropping in a wide smile. "It's gratifying to see so many of you here today," he said. "And to see among you some familiar faces. Greetings to you all. We are well met in the presence of Vartra."

Kaid and Dzaka joined in the reply. "Well met, Father Lijou."

"From Stronghold, I have brought with me the traditional gifts," said Lijou. "Fire, incense, salt, and water. Let the torch be brought before our assembly that we can light the fires of truth and clear thought once more in our hearts."

Kaid glanced sideways, seeing Ghyan enter from the rear of the hall carrying a blazing torch.

The flames flickered in the dimly lit hall, sending shadows dancing as Ghyan walked slowly up to where Lijou stood between the two braziers.

Lijou accepted the torch from him and stepping to the right-hand brazier, lit it first. The flames leaped upward, crackling and dancing as if alive. Moving to the other brazier, he touched the torch to it. A second time the flames leaped high before settling down.

Handing the torch to Ghyan, Lijou once more took his place in front of the statue.

"Let the incense be brought to sweeten the air and aid our meditation."

Rulla entered this time, bearing a casket. As he

approached Lijou, he lifted the lid, presenting him with the open box.

From it Lijou took a handful of the resinous granules and stepping toward the first brazier, threw some into the heart of the flames. They flared up brightly, spitting and crackling as a cloud of sweet-smelling smoke began to billow upward. He repeated this with the second brazier.

Rulla closed the casket and stood back, parallel to the statue, on the opposite side from Ghyan.

"Let the water that sustains our life be brought that I may add my gift of salt to it," Lijou said, taking a pouch from his pocket and holding it aloft.

The female who entered carrying the bowl of water was one of the Brothers newly come from Stronghold. Vaidou was her name. Kaid had seen her from a distance before, but as she drew level with them, he looked more closely at her. Her coloring was fair, almost as fair as the female he'd seen in his vision. A mane of amber-colored hair lay around her shoulders, making the black of her robes seem darker than it was.

She approached Lijou, who poured the contents of the pouch into the bowl. Taking the knife from his belt, he held it in both hands and proceeded to slowly stir the contents of the bowl with it.

"Let the water of life and salt of the earth be conjoined and purified," he said. Removing the knife, he wiped it meticulously on the empty pouch, then returned it to its sheath before taking the bowl from Vaidou. As she stepped back beside Ghyan, Lijou turned to the statue of Vartra and bowing, placed the bowl on the plinth at His feet.

"Bless us who are here today, and bless this Shrine which we dedicate to You." He bowed once more before turning back to the assembly. "Before you pass in front of Vartra to give Him your offering of incense and to receive His blessing, let us take a few minutes to make our own prayers to Him."

There was a little shuffling as people resettled themselves before lowering their heads.

Do you really see and hear us, Vartra? thought Kaid as he let his chin drop against his chest. *Has the weight of years passed turned You into a God? If You're listening, I need to know why. Why are You playing with us, shaking up our comfortable lives, sending us the Humans with their seduc-*

*tive talents that they don't believe exist? What's it all for,
Vartra?* In the silence, he thought he heard the sound of distant laughter.

He jerked upright in shock, knocking Dzaka on the elbow
as he did so. His foster-son's hand caught hold of him,
steadying him as he swayed slightly.

"Are you all right?" whispered Dzaka, a concerned look
on his face.

"I'm fine." He took a deep breath and tried to relax. The
vision he'd had just under an hour ago was still affecting him
more than he'd realized. "I'm fine," he whispered again. "I
came out of my meditation trance a little too quickly, that's
all."

Dzaka let him go, still keeping a thoughtful eye on him.

Everyone else was stirring now, beginning to get to their
feet. Dzaka stood, holding out his hand to Kaid, who hesitated before taking it.

"Thank you," he said as they fell in at the back of the
queue waiting to pass in front of their God.

As they came level with Rulla, in turn they reached out to
take a pinch of incense from the casket to throw on the braziers. Kaid recited the ritual words under his breath, then
stepped forward to put a fingertip in the bowl of water at the
feet of the God.

Finding himself eye to eye with the statue, he hurriedly
looked away, dabbing the water on his forehead.

"Bless me with the gift of clear thought," he said mechanically as his legs moved him down the hall to the exit where
the light of day and the fresh air waited for him. The heavy
scent of the incense was beginning to make his head ache.

The dedication of the Shrine over, Lijou thanked Rulla and
Vaidou before accompanying Ghyan to his office.

"How long before the Clan Lord arrives?" he asked the
priest as Ghyan handed him a mug of c'shar.

"Not long, Father," said Ghyan, sitting down opposite him.

"How goes things with Liegen Aldatan and his bondmate? Any idea if they've decided when they'll take the Fire
Margins ritual?"

"None. It hasn't been mentioned. Kusac's been studying
with me for an hour or two most days over the last month,"
said Ghyan. "He's more at ease accepting the presence of
some higher being that we call Vartra, so that's at least a step

in the right direction. The meditation techniques work as
well for him and the other Leska pairs as they do for
the Brothers, you'll also be pleased to know. Actually, at the
moment, Kusac and Carrie are on an En'Shalla retreat."

Lijou raised an eye ridge.

"Kusac wants their cub conceived in En'Shalla," he
explained.

"Their cub?" said Lijou. "There's to be another so soon?"

"I don't think they have a choice, Father," said Ghyan,
picking up his mug. He hesitated.

"You have a question, Ghyan?" asked Lijou, watching the
younger male carefully. "How can I help you?"

"I know it's presumptuous of me, but *why* did you choose
Kaid to be their third? He's totally wrong, Father," said
Ghyan, ears flicking as he rushed the words out before he
lost his nerve. "He thinks only of his duty. He doesn't care
for them!"

Lijou took a drink, then set his mug down before
answering the priest. "You still have a lot to learn about
people, Ghyan," he said. "Vartra has chosen Kaid, not me.
As for him not caring, you haven't looked deep enough.
Don't rely on your Talent for everything."

"I don't, Father," said Ghyan, ears flicking in acknowledgment of the rebuke. "He came to me, telling me not to dissuade the Vailkoi Clan from the Challenge. He cared nothing
for the risks Carrie and Kusac faced!"

"He did as I ordered, Ghyan," said Lijou.

"You?"

Lijou could plainly hear the shock in his voice. "Yes.
Ghezu and I both gave him his orders. We needed the public
proof they could both fight. Our bid for full Guild status
depended on that proof and now we have it. I'm sorry she
lost the child, but there is more at stake than the life of an
unborn cub and her parents."

"But to use them for political ends . . ."

"No," interrupted Lijou. "They *are* the politics here! Their
very existence, not to mention that of the cub, challenged the
order of our society. We had to have the proof. As for Kaid, I
suggested him because he *does* care. Even Ghezu realized
he'd become personally involved—with the female. I'm surprised you missed it. The God knows, I wish Ghezu had!"
He sighed and shook his head. "I need to speak to Kaid. I

saw him at the dedication. Can you ask him if he'll spare me a few minutes of his time?"

"He's here on retreat himself," said Ghyan.

"Is he, by God! And you said he doesn't care?" said Lijou, ears pricking forward. "They may have more of a chance than I thought."

Ghyan's ears went back parallel to his head in embarrassment.

"Ah," purred Lijou. "You did notice then. And I imagine you . . . shall we say, drew attention to it?" He made a noise of disapproval. "Why is it so many people have no idea how to handle someone like Kaid?" he asked. "The simple answer is, you don't. Someone like him is best given a summary of what you want, pointed in the right direction, then left to get on with it. His talent is in his unorthodox approach. Now, go and get him for me, please. I must speak to him before the Clan Lord arrives." Taking a mouthful of his drink, he sat back in his seat and looked at Ghyan.

"Yes, Father Lijou," he said, getting to his feet. "Kaid may be meditating . . ."

"He's not," said Lijou, cutting across him.

Ghyan was back within five minutes. Lijou watched Kaid as he entered. The angle of his ears and tail was exactly what it should be—politely curious—none of the disquiet he'd sensed in him earlier.

"Thank you, Ghyan. Would you mind indulging me a little longer? What I have to say to Kaid is personal."

"Certainly, Father Lijou."

As Ghyan left, Kaid moved over to sit opposite Lijou, looking at him expectantly.

"Ghyan tells me you've agreed to form a Triad with Kusac and his mate," Lijou said at length.

Kaid sighed. "I've been given no choice in the matter."

Ears pricking forward, Lijou looked sharply at him. "The God has spoken to you?"

Kaid hesitated, obviously unsure what to say.

"I've been looking at the records kept in the temple at Stronghold," said Lijou, his voice low enough that Kaid had to lean forward to hear it. "I know you were a lay-priest during the time the Leadership was being decided. You were one of the few to whom the God spoke regularly, weren't you?" Lijou didn't wait for an answer. "My predecessor, Father Jyarti, thought so highly of you that he proposed you as the new Warrior Leader. He wrote that you not only combined the best of both disciplines, but you truly heard the words of Vartra. I ask you again, did the God speak to you?"

The tips of Kaid's ears twitched as he answered. "The God spoke to me, Father Lijou, but *which* God, I'm unable to tell you."

Lijou let his breath out in a sigh and sat back in his seat. "Then I'm not alone," he murmured, more to himself than Kaid. He roused himself, capturing Kaid's gaze with his own. "We have very little time, Kaid. The Clan Lord and General Raiban are due here any time. To show my good faith, I have a warning for you. Watch Ghezu. He's become obsessed with revenge on you for an incident in your youth. It had to do with a female. He's located her again, in a village at the edge of the Ghuulgul desert. He'll draw you there, then have you killed. I'm afraid I have to say he's teetering on the edge of insanity and will likely fall over it any day now."

Kaid sat there, obviously stunned by his disclosure.

"I'm telling you because I truly believe that for the good of Shola, the three of you must go to the Fire Margins, *and return alive!*"

Kaid remained silent, his ears tilting fractionally outward and to the side in anger.

Lijou leaned forward, grasping him by the forearm and shaking him. "Kaid, do you hear me? You *must* go to the Fire Margins, no matter what! Don't let Ghezu lure you into the desert. This is far more important. The mixed Leskas and their cubs *must* be independent of both Esken and Ghezu!"

Kaid nodded once, righting his ears. "I hear you," he said, his voice barely audible.

Lijou released him. "I need something from you in return," he said. "I need to know what you really believe about Vartra. Jyarti trusted you, recorded many of your visions in a private journal which I discovered some time ago. You were the one he trusted most, his right hand. Your visions didn't stop because you were expelled from the Brotherhood, we both know that, so what was it you saw today?"

He waited, hoping that hearing about the female and Ghezu's mad schemes of revenge would shock Kaid into being incautious.

"Memories. I saw memories trapped in stone and crystal,"

said Kaid, his voice as expressionless as his body was now.
"Carrie and Noni have seen them, too, up at Stronghold. We
all have."

Memories in stone and crystal? He hadn't time to ask him;
perhaps he could speak to Noni later. "What else, Kaid? I
need to know what else you've seen and heard."

"Vartra. I've seen him in the memories." Kaid's voice was
a whisper, his eyes looking beyond. "Not a God then, only a
male like us."

"What else? There's more." Lijou was inches from Kaid
now, desperate to hear every word.

Kaid's eyes refocused. "The God. Vartra. You know it's
Him, Lijou," he said softly, locking eyes with him as he
moved back.

"Kaid, Jyarti trusted you. Give me your trust," said Lijou.
"I can't take anything away from you, you have nothing left
to lose. Would I warn you about Ghezu if I wished you
harm? All I've read and heard and experienced myself points
in the one direction. I need to see if another, such as yourself, has reached the same conclusions as me. I *cannot* ask
one of my Order: I cannot ask them to face the conclusions
I've drawn!"

"Yet you ask me," said Kaid. "I have things I hold dear,
Lijou. My faith is one of them. Shortly I will be putting not
only my life, but that of my Liege and his mate, to say
nothing of their unborn cub, at risk because of my faith in
Vartra. Would you shake it after what you've said about the
importance to Shola of our going?"

"No," said Lijou, closing his eyes briefly as he sat back. "I
wouldn't do that. I apologize. I should never have asked
you."

"What is the Fire Margins ritual, Lijou?" Kaid asked after
a moment's silence. "What is it a test of but faith? To succeed you need to put your life in the hands of the Gods,
Vartra in particular."

"No one knows what you need to do to survive, Kaid. No
one *has* survived according to my records at Stronghold."

"What if those who went expected to find a God and found
a living being no different from us, what then? The shock of
facing the disintegration of all they believe could make it
impossible for them to return from the world of the past. It
could kill them, couldn't it?"

Lijou opened his eyes again, looking at Kaid with renewed interest. "It could."

"So many centuries of prayer, from the strongest minds on our world, all directed toward one mortal person. Could that, blended on top of an existing deity, make a person into a God?"

Lijou could feel his heartbeat pounding in his ears. "If you believe the old tales of tapping into the psychic energy of our forefathers, yes, it's possible."

"How much truth do you think there is in the legends that telepaths once fought as well as any Warrior?"

"The Sholans in the new Leska pairs fight."

"They're reverting to type, Lijou. It can be done. Those who've walked the Fire Margins before were telepaths who couldn't fight, who expected a God and found a male no different from themselves; who lost their faith in the capacity of the ritual that took them back to the Cataclysm to return them to their own time. It's no wonder they didn't return."

Lijou watched Kaid get to his feet.

"I can hear your visitors," he said, turning toward the door.

"Will you go?" demanded Lijou, hands clenched so tightly on the chair that Kaid could see the whites of his knuckles showing through his pelt.

"To the Fire Margins? I haven't lost my faith, Lijou," said Kaid, turning round briefly as he reached the door. "Yes, I'll go. The God told me we have an appointment there."

CHAPTER 8

"And was Raiban satisfied once she saw the remains?" asked Rhyasha.

"She was convinced they weren't Human or Sholan," said Konis, reaching for another cookie. "She's taken a couple of the smaller bones to be analyzed at the Nijidi Science Station. You know, dated and so on."

"You'll spoil your appetite," his mate warned. "Third meal's only an hour away."

"No chance of that," he said, nibbling at the edge of his cookie. "After missing second meal at the Shrine, I'm starving. I must say I didn't expect Lijou to break ranks with Ghezu like this. It's worrying."

"I'd be more worried if he hadn't," said Rhyasha candidly. "Does he really think Ghezu will ask that the joint leadership of the Brotherhood be set aside in his favor?"

"He must think it possible or he wouldn't have asked me to block it. He's right, too. A Guild that combines the talents of Warriors and Telepaths should be ruled by both disciplines."

"Mm," said Rhyasha, cradling her mug in both hands as she took a drink. "There's certainly more going on at Stronghold than meets the eye."

Konis sighed. "It's Kusac's involvement with them that worries me."

Rhyasha reached out and put her hand on her mate's. "Our son's no fool, Konis," she said. "He's told us the agreement between him and the Brotherhood has been signed and witnessed by Ghezu as well as Lijou. In two days' time, he'll be free of the Telepath Guild and the Brotherhood both. He has us, his Clan, to back him until he takes the Fire Margins ritual. As well as that, he has the backing of the Forces. Look how much they've put into ensuring our estate is well protected to keep not only him and Carrie safe, but the others as well."

"That protection can act as a prison, too," said Konis.

"Not when the people who protect us are all looking to Kaid and Kusac as their leaders."

"I don't like it," he said, ears flicking in concern. "Too much lies in the control of one person that we hardly know. What if something should happen to Kaid? And what about this ritual? No one has survived it so far. We could still lose them, Rhyasha," he said, his fingers curling round hers.

"I feel your fear, and I understand it," she said gently. "We have to trust, Konis. Trust that Kusac, and Carrie, know what they're doing. There has never been a Link like theirs before. Together they are more powerful than any Leska pair within your experience, remember? Then there's Kaid. They've chosen him to make up their Triad. They've trusted him with their lives many times. If they trust him, why shouldn't we? His own life is at risk, too, and he doesn't strike me as having a death wish."

"I hear what you're saying, Rhyasha," he sighed. "I suppose what bothers me about Kaid is that with most people I can pick up a general understanding of their characters without trying. With Kaid, there's nothing. Nothing at all."

"You're telling me?" she said, taking her hand away as she put her mug down. "I've found quite a few of the Brothers are like that. Garras and Ni'Zulhu to mention only two. You feel what they want you to feel, nothing more, but are they any less trustworthy for that? Don't we hide behind our Talent?"

"You've got a point," he agreed.

"Are you going to finish that cookie or not?" she asked, tweaking it out of his lax grip.

"Yes, if you give it back to me," he said with a faint grin, reaching for it.

"What are you planning on doing tomorrow? Who have you still to see before the Guild meeting?"

"I need to see Nishou over at the Laasoi Guildhouse. Lijou's extremely worried about the situation in the desert concerning this self-appointed priest, Fyak. He feels that the Guild should evacuate all nonessential personnel, leaving a couple or so there with a group of Brothers to protect them so we can continue to get up-to-date information. There's several refugees there at the moment and I need to talk to them. Pretty soon we could have more than small tribal wars on our hands. All it needs is for this Fyak to get too ambitious, and we could have them pouring over the Nyacko Pass into the plains."

"Have you tabled this for discussion at the Guild meeting?"

"Yes. Governor Nesul and I worked on the agenda last week. Nearly every Guild has sent in their proposals except for the Brotherhood, of course, and Esken."

"That was to be expected. There's only a sham of civility toward you and Nesul left in him," said Rhyasha. "Nesul seems to be relying on you more and more now he knows all telepaths are not like Esken. Who can you definitely count on to vote for the Brotherhood?"

"The vote to allow Kusac and the others to change guilds is the crucial one. If they lose that, the Brotherhood can't request guild status."

"So who will support our son?"

"Myself, Vizoen of the Artificers Guild, possibly Vyaku of Communications, Fryak of Manufacturing, and Rhayfso of the Warriors. Nesul himself and High Commander Chuz of the Forces, predictably," he said with a small chuckle. "He'll probably be able to sway Tayangi of the Civil Protectorate our way, and there's Nadu Kayal of the Priests, but they're sub-guilds and may not be allowed to vote in this matter. Even if they are, neither Ghezu nor Lijou will be allowed to vote as a sub-guild master because of their interest in the outcome."

"It's nice to know we still have strong ties with the Artificers," she said. "A fair proportion of our unTalented clans-people have gifts with the arts. I'm glad they're with us. You have nearly half of the main Guild Masters."

"If we can get a majority of them, then it needn't go to the full vote of forty-five," said Konis.

"Is there anything Esken can do to prevent the proposal being presented to the Council?"

"Not really. He can't be seen to do anything about it. He has his own people to back him, but I think we'll have the edge. I want to see Vyaku tomorrow. I'm sure I can talk him round to our way of thinking."

"That one's a tree-rhudda!" she said with a small noise of disgust. "No backbone unless he knows he's backing a sure winner."

"Perhaps you could lean a little on him," said Konis

hopefully. "After all, he's used to dealing with both of us in Alien Relations. It would save me some time tomorrow."

Rhyasha groaned. "You only want me to do it because he keeps inviting me to spend some time with him!"

Konis grinned. "Look on it as your contribution. You never know. You might find you want to take him up on his offer after all!"

"With him? I'd rather den with a nest of tree-rhuddas! Enough of this. Have you heard from Taizia in the last day or two? She's not at the Guild and when I checked with her friend, she'd just packed up and left."

"No, I haven't. Not since the row over sending for Jack. Are you worrying about her?"

Rhyasha drummed her fingertips on the table. "Concerned rather. She doesn't normally sulk for so long after a row. I hope she hasn't done something stupid."

"If she had, she'd have done it immediately after the heat of the row," said Konis reassuringly. "If she's been seen around the Guild and staying with a friend up until a day or two ago, then it's highly unlikely that it's more than that she's gone to stay with someone else. I'd have suggested Meral, but he's based here."

Rhyasha sighed. "I expect you're right. The house seems empty today now that most of our guests have moved out to Kusac's estate. Even Carrie and Kusac aren't here just now."

"We've still got Vanna and Garras as well as our Keissian medic," he said. "And Zhyaf and Mara. At least she and Kitra are quieter now that we've got Jinoe and Rrai settled temporarily on our estate with his mother and a foster family."

"I don't know what we'd have done without Dzaka and Ghyan. They're still keeping them busy, thank Vartra! Mara's almost as much work as Kitra, and Zhyaf's no help at all! He spends most of his time shut up in their rooms pretending she's nothing to do with him! It isn't as if he's old, Konis, he's of an age with us! He's had seven stress-free weeks here to come to terms with events. I think you should have words with him. I've tried talking to Mara with no result. I'd have asked Carrie but . . ."

"No. You're quite right. Carrie shouldn't be involved in this just because Mara's human. I'll get Vanna to have a word with her and I'll see Zhyaf myself this evening, after third meal."

* * *

The Terran building within the Telepath Guildhouse grounds was virtually self-contained. The upper two floors were given over to personal living quarters while the ground level contained the communal areas. A mess had been built where they could eat food cooked on the premises rather than from the dispensers that had been installed in each living room. There was also a lounge and a couple of recreation rooms.

Brynne was sitting in one of those lounges nursing a coffee when Terry came in.

"I thought you were here," he said. "I saw Lhea outside."

He grunted and raised his mug to his mouth. "She's part of the problem."

"What's up?" asked Terry, sitting opposite him. "Had another row with Sara?"

"Terminal this time," Brynne muttered. "As if I haven't enough to cope with without her demands and tantrums."

"Hey, I know you don't like being followed round by Lhea or Maylgu, but it's better than Khafsa and Esken getting their hands on you again, isn't it?"

"Yes, dammit!" he said with anger. "They're also a constant reminder to her of Vanna, and she hates Vanna! I couldn't get it through her thick head that I had no choice over whether or not I had a Leska—until yesterday."

"Mmm?"

"I sent to her during our Link day," he said.

"You what?" asked Terry.

"You heard," Brynne said, looking up at him. "I sent to her."

"I bet that made you popular with both of them."

"You could say that." He pulled a pack of cigarettes from his pocket and lit one, inhaling deeply. "Vanna hit the roof, and left me with a few claw marks to prove it."

"I wouldn't like to get any Sholan female angry with me, let alone that lady," said Terry.

"Especially when you're being intimate." Brynne winced at the memory. "She's got a bloody powerful kick."

"Well, let's face it, Brynne. How would you feel if she was with Garras and sent to you? It's flouting how you rate her as a lover."

"Trouble is, no one's matched her," said Brynne morosely. "Sholan or human. It's the damned Link. It spoils any other relationship because on the physical level, there *is* no comparison."

"Don't tell me you're finally getting attached to Vanna," said Terry. "It's about time! She's dealt fairly with you from the start, you know, and you haven't exactly been pleasant to her. It's not easy for her, being the only female expecting a half-human child. She's never made a fuss about it. I've got a great deal of respect for her."

"Don't rub it in," said Brynne testily, flicking the ash off his cigarette into the ashtray. "If you think that much of her, go and proposition her yourself! She won't mind. After all, she's got three of us already, what's one more?"

Terry reached across the table and grabbed Brynne by the front of his sweater, pulling him across the table toward him. "I'd watch what you say about her, if I were you," he said quietly. "If I wasn't sure you know it's not an insult to Sholans, I'd land you one. You cause your own trouble, Brynne. What the hell's wrong with you? Can't you admit to yourself you could care for an alien female? Get a grip on yourself before you lose the few friends you've got left." He released him and, getting to his feet, walked out of the lounge.

Somewhat shaken, Brynne took another drag on his cigarette. It wasn't like that. He hadn't meant to insult either of them.

The last couple of times he'd stayed longer with Vanna than usual, remaining in their Leska quarters for most of the twenty-six hours rather than leaving as soon as he was able.

What insanity had possessed him the day before, he didn't know. He'd been feeling good about himself and about her— strangely he usually did on their Link days. He'd only meant to let Sara know how the Link compulsion felt.

Vanna had been soft and warm in his arms. Her body was losing the hard muscular lines, just beginning to grow the gentle curves of her advancing pregnancy. They could both feel the presence of the child now, a male. She was carrying his son. He'd felt closer to her at that moment than he ever had to any female and as they joined for the last time that day, he'd reached out for Sara, bringing her mentally into their Link. It had been stupid and insensitive of him, but it hadn't been done maliciously, as both females believed.

Unable to react any other way, Vanna's hands had tightened on his back, her claws suddenly puncturing his flesh. As the pain began to bite, they were swept beyond such considerations.

How dare you! she sent immediately afterward. *I'm no qwene to enjoy an audience, especially when it's your Companion!* As her hands had pushed him away, her feet had come up to contact his upper thighs in a double kick that had sent him flying off the bed to collide with one of the chairs.

"Get out of here!" she'd hissed, her face a mask of fury as, four-limbed, she leaped to the end of the bed, tail lashing and canines showing.

"Vanna, I didn't . . ."

"Get out!" She'd begun to growl, a low, ominous sound that made his blood run cold. He was suddenly reminded that she was all feline, and fully capable of killing him with one swipe of her hand.

He reached out and grabbed his clothes from the floor, backing up till he felt the door behind him. It opened, sending him sprawling backward into the lounge. As it shut, he realized he was trembling with fear.

Hurriedly, he pulled his clothes on, wincing as the materials abraded his claw-scored back and lacerated thighs. Still keeping his face to the bedroom door, he left, only turning round once he was in the corridor.

He'd gone straight back to the rooms he'd shared with Sara, and in the bathroom, had undressed again. The wounds on his legs were deep and still bleeding as he eased himself out of his jeans. The blood was slow and sluggish to be sure, but it was startlingly red against his skin. Feeling rather sick and dizzy, he sat down suddenly on the floor.

He was still there, dabbing futilely at the cuts with a towel, when Sara returned. He heard her banging about in the room and called out to her.

"Sara, I think I need Dr. Reynolds," he'd started to say, but she flung open the bathroom door and cut him short.

"You bastard!" she'd said, picking up his toothbrush and flinging it at him. "How dare you send to me when you're screwing your alien whore! Your things are in the corridor. Don't bother coming back!"

"Sara, I'm bleeding . . ."

"I don't give a damn! Go and bleed somewhere else! If she

did that to you, it damned well serves you right! Now get out
of my bloody flat! I never want to see you again!"

"But, Sara!"

She'd left and returned with Lhea. "You're in charge of
him. Get him out of here," she snapped. "If he's not gone in
five minutes, I'll call Security and have him thrown out!"

Impassively, Lhea had squeezed past her and knelt beside
him. "They are not serious," she said, examining the lacera-
tions. "If it pains you to put your clothes back on, come as
you are. Physician Reynold's office isn't far."

He'd balked at walking through the center trouserless with
bleeding wounds on his thighs, and had struggled back into
his clothes while Lhea used her wrist comm to call for
someone to collect his belongings.

Jack Reynolds, now officially the Terrans' doctor, had not
been sympathetic either. In fact he'd torn a strip off him
while he stapled the edges of the worst cuts together, then
sprayed them and the ones on his back with sealant.

"What kind of man d'you call yourself when you treat a
woman like Vanna this way?" he'd demanded, pressing the
hypo gun to Brynne's neck. "Neither Garras nor Kusac will
stand for much more of this, you know. Nor will I," he said,
fixing a steely glare on him. "You should think yourself
lucky, Mr. Brynne Stevens! There's many a man, Sholan and
Human, who'd like to get as close to Physician Kyjishi as
you do! Many a young Sholan male would give anything to
have her carrying his cub! That means a lot to these people.
It should mean as much to you. Now get out of here, before I
forget myself!"

He'd left, his silent shadow padding behind him as he
headed for his favorite tavern until he felt up to returning to
the Guild and sorting out new living quarters.

His coffee was cold and his cigarette finished. Sighing, he
got up and squashed the end in the ashtray before heading for
the town.

* * *

"This takes me back," said Kusac, raking the last of the
four mud-cased carcasses out of the embers of the fire. "Do
you remember? It was the first time we'd shared food."

"How could I forget?" she asked, leaning against him as he cracked it open.

"You've no idea how worried I was that you'd be afraid of me."

"I think I realized who you were from the moment I found you in the garden," she said, accepting the piece of meat he held out to her. "D'you know what I remember most? Your eyes," she said, looking up at him as she licked her fingers. "I'd never seen eyes the color of yours before."

"I remember when we tried to find the rest of my crew," he said quietly. "The feel of holding you for the first time, the smell of your scent, and when our minds linked."

"It seems so long ago now. We've come a long way," she said.

"You don't have any regrets, do you?" he asked, handing her another piece of meat.

She waved it away. "I'm full now, thanks. No, I don't have any regrets. Those I thought I had were only caused by the fear of what was happening to us," she said.

Kusac licked his fingers before putting his arms round her. "It's our time now," he said, nuzzling her ear. "We're a family again. No one can use us for a long time to come. Our cub is too important to us to risk her. This time I'm going to see you're properly looked after. Nothing's going to come between us again."

"We've still got that Fire Margins ritual to do," she said, resting her head on his arms. "That's worrying."

"We can do things that no one else on Shola can even imagine," he said. "The two of us combined are more powerful than any other Leska couple who've tried the ritual. And we have Kaid with us."

"So we have." She sighed. "Let's hope your God knows what He's doing. The timing is all wrong as far as I'm concerned. I'd rather have gone before I was pregnant again. I don't suppose we can leave it till after?"

"We'll go when we know the time is right," he said. "Vartra's your God, too, you know. My belief is enhanced by yours. Maybe your pregnancy is also necessary. Maybe it'll give us yet another edge toward succeeding."

She nodded, putting her hand up to try and stifle a yawn. "Maybe."

"You're tired," he said, letting her go. "Let's get some sleep. We've enough food in for tomorrow, so we can just

relax and enjoy our day." He held out his hand, helping her
to her feet. He kicked some loose earth from the cavern floor
over the fire, reducing it to a tamed glow.

"The Leska link takes precedence," said Viaz, turning
to look at her. "The cubs you will bear will be Rezac's,
that's why your link to him has formed."

"No!" Rezac spat the word out.

"You'll find it impossible to deny the link," said Viaz
gently.

"I'll choose not to conceive," stated Zashou flatly. "I
won't have cubs, Mentor."

"You do have the choice," agreed Viaz, "but you'll find
that eventually you'll want his cubs. It's a biological
imperative."

"Viaz," said Rezac, his voice dangerously low, "you'd
better do something to break this link because it's
obvious neither of us wants it."

"There's nothing I can do, Rezac," Viaz said, meeting
the angry young male's gaze calmly. "It's the will of the
Gods. You're linked now for life."

"Then I'll deny the link! Dammit, she's got a husband
to give her cubs, she doesn't need me!"

Zashou looked over at him. "Don't flatter yourself that
I want you either, Rezac," she said, her tone sharp and
biting as her ears swiveled to the sides of her head.
"You know nothing but violence and killing! A fine mate
you'd make any female!" Anger and hate exploded
from her mind, touching them all, spiraling Carrie to
another time.

The wind blew cold across the wasteland to the rear
of the enclosed cargo storage lot, bringing with it the
promise of more snow. Underfoot, the ground had been
turned to slush by the tramping feet of the distributors.
Now it was frozen solid, making the ground uneven and
painful to walk over.

Tallinu stood beside Chertoi, trying not to shiver as
they watched the leader of the Fleet Pack come toward
them, his second obviously as twitchy as he was.

They stopped ten meters away, on the edge of the
designated neutral zone.

"You wanted to talk, so what you got to say?"

Koszul's voice was a low growl as he stood there, his pulse rifle cradled at a ready position across his chest.

"We've lost people same as you," said Chertoi. "Good pack members. We fight, we expect death to come to us sooner or later. We know the risks. This last killing, though, was bad. It's got to stop."

Koszul snorted in contempt, tail swaying angrily. "You're telling me? Your people killed the cub. You've killed two of my pack as well! The killing will stop, all right—when we've wiped you out!"

Chertoi shook his head. "Not us. Whoever it is wants you to think that. When we found our people, it looked like your pack had done it. Someone is trying to get us to kill each other. Trying to start a pack war."

Aware that something wasn't right, he filtered out the speech, listening only for key words as his eyes scanned the other pack, then his own. Not there. He looked further, beyond them into the night, then as he turned his head toward the container lot, he saw a slight movement from behind a pile of rubble.

"Sniper!" he yelled, raising his rifle at the same time as he rammed his leader aside.

His shot lanced out, lighting up the darkness so the fleeing shape was briefly visible. He'd missed, but by then he was racing after the killer. Several shots flared around him as both packs reacted to the threat they thought he posed. He dodged the ruts in the frozen snow, feeling the space between his shoulders twitch in anticipation of a hit. Mercifully it didn't happen. The rubble was ahead. He leaped high, feet barely touching the ground, then he was over and pounding after the retreating shape.

He brought his rifle up, aiming purely by instinct, and fired. His quarry yelped and stumbled, but continued running. Out in the rough, the going was more difficult as tussocks of frozen grass almost invisible in the dark, grabbed at his toes, threatening to trip him. With a growl of annoyance, he slipped the rifle across his shoulders and with an easy movement, switched into a four-legged run.

He made better speed and was less visible to his target now. This close to the ground he could also follow the scent. Dodging between the low bushes and patches of tall grasses, he knew he was gaining ground. He could hear the heavy breathing, labored and erratic now, could smell and feel the fear. Gathering himself, he leaped, catching her cleanly in mid-back, bringing them both tumbling to the ground.

She twisted and writhed under him, trying to break free. With a powerful blow to the side of her head, he stilled her. She slumped limply under him. Panting slightly himself, he rolled off her still body and got to his feet, squatting down on his haunches for a moment to catch his breath.

He got to his feet, unslinging his rifle again, and bending down, grasped hold of her by the back of her jacket, pulling her up enough to see her. The ears were narrow and long, her face the same. Her coloring was tan and unremarkable, as was the short fuzz of hair on her head and neck. Lowlander, probably from the desert regions. He hissed angrily as he noticed the silver disk set in her left ear. One of the Runners. That figured. Kill off a few of the Fleet and the Claws, make it look like they were killing each other and you had a pack war. While they were occupied slaughtering each other, the Runners took everything. Not original, but effective.

He dropped her again and fumbling for the belt round her waist, unfastened it and pulled it free. Pulling her arms behind her, he lashed them together before retrieving her rifle and slinging it across his back.

Finally he reached down and clawed up a handful of frozen snow, rubbing it none too gently over her face till she began to splutter and come round. Grasping her by one arm, he hauled her to her feet and began to head back to the container lot.

She trudged along in silence, stumbling occasionally only to be yanked upright again. Words weren't necessary. They both knew what the outcome would be. There was no mercy for pack killers. Ahead of them, the glow from the container lot's security lights grew brighter and as they rounded the pile of rubble, he could see the two packs standing facing each other, guns drawn, waiting for his return.

He held his rifle aloft. "One of the Runners!" he yelled, pushing his captive forward.

The sentries from both packs kept their guns trained on them till he reached the space between the two leaders.

With his free hand, he pulled her ear upright. "See. A

Runner. We've both been set up by Nizoh. He's after all of us."

The female snarled and pulled her ear away from him.

Chertoi looked round at his people and signed for them to lower their guns. "Told you, didn't I, Koszul. Now maybe you'll believe it isn't us."

Warily, Koszul gestured to his second. "Check her, Lebbu," he said. "You know some of the Runners."

Lebbu stepped forward into the neutral area, approaching the female. Grasping her jaw in one hand, he turned her head one way then the other before he began to nod. "Recognize her. She's a Runner sure enough."

With a low growl, the female bared her teeth at him and spat in his face.

Lebbu's hand went back to deliver a blow that rocked even him. "Filthy tree-climbing qwene!" he snarled. Reaching for his belt, he pulled his knife free. There was a flash of silver and a howl of pain from the female.

"Always wanted a Runner trophy," he said, holding her severed ear aloft as he walked back to his leader.

Still howling, she struggled in his grasp as blood poured down the side of her head, splashing onto him.

Koszul stepped forward, beckoning Chertoi to do the same. "Shut her up," he snapped as he passed them.

He looked to Chertoi.

"Do it, Tallinu. We don't need her," he said, passing him.

He drew his knife, then clamped his forearm across her chest and pulled her head to one side. His blade slipped easily into the juncture of jaw and neck. The howling stopped abruptly. As he removed his knife, he wiped the blade on her jacket, letting her lifeless body fall to the ground. Stepping over her, he returned it to its sheath as he joined his leader.

"A joint raid on the Runners would solve both our problems," Chertoi was saying. "There'll be more trophies for all of us."

She woke screaming, babbling incoherently about packs and wars till Kusac finally managed to calm her. He'd experienced nothing of her dreams, and what he now received from her, he found just as confusing as she had.

Kaid woke abruptly, his hands slick with sweat, his fur damp. Sleep still fogged his brain and it took him a moment or two to remember where he was. Not Ranz: that was far in his past. The Rezac vision must have triggered the old memory.

Unable to sleep, he got up and padded down the corridor to the Shrine. From the far end of the room, the braziers cast a red glow on the ceiling and walls. Beyond them, the statue sat in semi-gloom. Now He seemed to brood, a sense of almost-menace surrounding Him. A shiver passed through him and Kaid wished he'd put some clothes on before leaving his room. Taking a deep breath, he walked toward the image, remembering to pick up a piece of incense.

Stepping between the braziers, he looked up at the statue while he crumbled the incense into one of them. Smoke coiled upward, making his eyes smart.

I ask you for enlightenment, and You send me more and more riddles. Why? Who is this Rezac that so resembles me? What joins us, calls to us across time? Why are you doing this to me?

He didn't expect an answer, but he squatted down at the foot of the plinth anyway, trying to still his mind until it was receptive should Vartra deign to acknowledge him. He was still in the same position when Ghyan came to make his early morning prayers.

* * *

Brynne had gone to see his friend at the Accommodation Guildhouse in Valsgarth.

Ross Derwent was a tall, lean man past his middle years. The brown hair might have been thinning on top, but the mind beneath was as sharp as the pale blue eyes that stared piercingly out at the world. He'd been among the last group of Terrans brought to Shola. He had a measurable Talent, but exactly what it was baffled the Sholans at the Telepath Guild. He claimed to be a guider of souls, one whose mission it was to walk the paths of the spirit and commune with the dead. He said he was reborn from the past to herald in the New Age of Consciousness. The Sholans merely observed him, listening to his stories and teachings, adding them to their increasing knowledge of Human spiritual and religious beliefs.

Ross opened his door to Brynne, a genuine smile of pleasure on his face. "Welcome, Brynne! I'd hoped to see you yesterday so we could continue our discussion of crystals."

"I couldn't come yesterday," he said, stepping inside the lounge. "It was my Link day. I have to be with Vanna."

"Your Sholan partner," Ross said, closing the door and ushering him over to the comfortable seats. "I appreciate your need to be with her, but if you're really serious about becoming a guider of souls, you mustn't neglect your studies. I'm sure you could have spared an hour or two yesterday."

"It's not that easy, Ross," said Brynne as he sat down. "I can't leave Vanna until the Link compulsion starts to fade. Believe me, it isn't wise to ignore it. I know, I've tried."

"Hmm," Ross said noncommittally as he went over to the dispenser. "Coffee?"

"Please."

"What I'd really like to do is take a field trip out into the nearest hills to look for crystal samples from this world. Do you know how to fly one of those little runabouts they all seem to use?"

"Yes, I can fly an aircar. It shouldn't be too difficult to get hold of someone who knows the land round this area to come with us as a guide. Perhaps Lhea or Maylgu knows someone."

"See if you can schedule something for tomorrow," said Ross, bringing over the two mugs and handing one to Brynne. "Now, tell me what you remember about crystals from our last session."

"Certain crystals have a natural resonance to specific functions, you said. Rose quartz, for instance, is good for helping control pain and for healing."

"Good. But you don't just go into a shop and buy a piece, do you? What do you have to do to it to make it work for you?"

"You have to find one that you feel an attraction for," said Brynne, sipping his drink. "You said it can be any shape, even an irregular polished stone."

Ross nodded. "Right, you've found your crystal. Now what?"

"You have to attune it to yourself. Carry it around with you or wear it. Only silver can touch it, not gold because gold can carry feelings just like the crystal can."

"What about other metals, like brass or bronze? They use those metals for jewelry here."

"They're base metals. You can't use a base metal because it contaminates the crystal—it dilutes the effect or something."

"You're not doing too badly," said Ross, putting his mug down to unwrap the small cloth-covered package that sat on the table. "I've got some crystals here and I want you to try reading them. See if you can tell me what they were used for."

Brynne looked dubiously at the older man. "I don't know if I can," he said.

"Have a try. Try and work it out for yourself. If you can't, I'll tell you how."

* * *

Rhyasha was waiting for them as they came in from the garage area.

"Well come home," she said, embracing first Carrie then Kusac. "You'll have to shower quickly if you intend to make the opening of the Council meeting. I'm sure you don't want to arrive there still smelling of sweet-grass! That would be something of a giveaway! Have you had first meal?"

"Not yet," said Kusac as they accompanied her toward the main bathing room.

"I'll have a snack ready for you to take with you. Your father has already left. There's a couple of people he needs to talk to before the meeting convenes."

"Is Kaid back?" asked Kusac.

"He's with Vanna and Garras in the kitchen eating. Don't worry. Everything's in order. Your father anticipates no real problems today. Vanna says Brynne has decided not to go with you. Like Zhyaf, he feels that there are enough of you going. Now go and shower!"

"Yes, Mother," said Kusac.

* * *

Konis was standing talking to Nadu Kayal when Esken and Khafsu, followed by Sorli, entered.

"Clan Leader," said Esken, essaying the barest movement of his head in greeting.

"Master Esken. I trust you're keeping well," said Konis. "I

haven't seen you around the Guildhouse for the last couple of weeks."

"My health is of the best," said Esken, his voice as cold as his look. "I'm kept busy with the new schedules for the Terrans. Which reminds me. I haven't seen Kitra or Taizia recently. They're falling behind in their work. If they don't return soon, they'll miss their gradings." He smiled, showing his teeth. "Now if you'll excuse me?" With that, he and Khafsa swept into the Council hall, Sorli casting an apologetic glance in their direction as he trailed after them.

"Sour-faced jegget," muttered Nadu. "How long is it until we can force him to retire?"

"Too long, my friend," said Konis quietly. "Let's deal with the Brotherhood matter first. If we win, they'll give us another two votes on this Council when the times comes to depose Esken."

"I know Lijou and Ghezu are already here. What about your son and Physician Kyjishi? Have they arrived yet?"

"Stop fretting, Kayal. They've just arrived. All is as it should be. If you continue to fret like this, you'll never last the day. There's a lot of business to attend to before we hear the petitions. Now let's take our seats. I think we're about to begin."

The Council hall was circular with a staged rostrum opposite the doorway. On the higher level, Konis saw that Sister Tokui of the Sholan Goddess cult was sitting in the Moderator's chair. Mentally he sent her a courteous greeting as he walked to his seat on the level below her.

Greetings to you, Clan Lord Aldatan, she sent in reply. *It looks like we have a full attendance today. I wonder why.* Her mental tone was dry. She knew from the agenda why so many of the sub-guilds had turned out. They smelled a challenge and wanted to witness it.

Planetary Governor Nesul and High Commander Chuz were already in their seats. They greeted him with nods. The rostrum was where those few major government figures like himself, the Governor, and the High Commander of the Forces sat. They represented the world and interstellar views that transcended the Guild system yet affected them all. Nesul, in fact, was hypothetically guildless, belonging to a guild with no voice—the Diplomatic Guild. Konis, as head of Alien Relations, was also a member and it was in this capacity that he was attending the meeting.

He looked out across the hall, his gaze immediately drawn to the two empty seats flanking that of Colony Governor Jayafa. Draped in the traditional red-stained white cloth of mourning, they were a stark reminder of the deaths of the people of two worlds.

Beyond them, in seats separated for privacy, sat the eighteen Guild Masters. Behind each sat their sub-guild leaders, close enough for them to confer with their Masters during the debates. To either side of the rostrum sat the clerks and recorders who were already busily involved with their comp pads. At the Speaker's table, the official recorder was leafing through his papers and checking his comp while the Truthsayer sat quietly, his eyes closed in meditation. The low buzz of restrained chatter filled the hall.

"Quite a gathering today," said Nesul, leaning over to him. "I see Esken isn't talking to Lijou or Ghezu. He seems quite hostile in fact," he said with a chuckle as he watched the Telepath Guild Master talking to Khafsa and patently ignoring the two Brotherhood Leaders.

"Esken will have a few tricks up his sleeve," said Konis quietly. "Remember, he's not beaten on this issue until we've won."

Chuz leaned over. "Who's seconding Ghezu's petition?" he asked. "Is it still me? I haven't heard a word from him in the last two weeks."

"He's been busy with some research, so Father Lijou told me," said Konis. "As you, say the idea is for you to second him and Rhayfso and myself to back you both."

"Damned lax of him not to have confirmed it with me," grumbled Chuz, sitting back in his seat. "Not military at all."

Nesul raised his eye ridges at Konis who gave the barest of ear flicks in return.

A chime rang out and within moments, the hall was silent.

"Today's gathering of the All Guilds Council is now in session," said Sister Tokui. "Before we begin, I ask for you to join me in showing our respect for our deceased brothers and sisters from the worlds of Khyaal and Szurtha."

The assembly took the note from her and as the low-pitched keen for the dead filled the air, all thoughts were with those who had died at the hands of the Valtegans. Two of those present also prayed for the safety of the four Sholans they hoped were still alive on a far distant world.

Their respects paid, Sister Tokui opened the meeting by

referring to matters outstanding from the last session. She
asked for the report from the Science Guild on their findings
from the samples taken from the two colonies.

Guild Master Chafsu took his place at the Speaker's table.
"We have very little to report, Moderator," he said, his tone
apologetic. "Samples of every kind of tissue, plant and
animal is well as Sholan, were taken from a hundred different locations on each world. They were transported in
sealed containers to the Nijidi Science Station where they've
been subjected to every test we could devise. We found
nothing. In almost all cases, the level of decay in our animal
and Sholan samples was already too high to ascertain the
cause of death. As for the plant and soil samples, there was
nothing present to give us a clue as to the vehicle for such
widespread destruction. We are no wiser now than when we
landed on Khyaal and Szurtha."

"You've been unable to discover anything?" asked Sister
Tokui in disbelief.

"Nothing at all, Moderator," Chafsu confirmed. "We gave
the identical report to the World Council only a month ago.
We have found nothing new since then."

"I find this worrying in the extreme," she said. "Then have
we no defense against this mystery weapon if they should
come toward either Shola or Khoma?"

"With respect, Moderator, that isn't my field," said
Chafsu, with a glance toward High Commander Chuz. "I can
say that whatever this weapon was, it wasn't deployed
against us in our engagement with the Valtegans at Keiss,
the Human colony world. Perhaps it is incapable of being
used in space."

"Vyaku of Communications, you have a question?" asked
Tokui, looking over to the standing figure.

"I have, Moderator. What is our current defense state?
How close could the Valtegans get to Shola or Khoma?"

"Commander Chuz, your field, I think," said Tokui.

Chuz looked over to the Guild Master. "The situation's
unchanged since I gave you the last press release, Vyaku,"
he said. "The Alliance as a whole is patrolling the relevant
sectors of space, and the Home Fleet is positioned at the
edges of our solar system and that of Khoma. Our early
warning satellites will give us at minimum a week's notice
of the approach of any vessels. We know that like us they
have to come out of jump outside the system, and when they

do, we'll have them before they've had a chance to confirm
their location. Neither Shola nor Khoma is in danger. Hell,"
he said, hitting his hand on the table in front of him, "we
can't find the damned lizards to fight them! Personally, I
don't think it's us they're interested in. They've completely
disappeared. They're as elusive as their damned weapon."

"Any more questions, Vyaku?" asked Sister Tokui.

"Have you been back to take fresh samples since the last
ones were so inconclusive?"

"No. As we left, the sterilization procedure was activated.
Fire was used so the dead could be honored in accordance
with all Sholan religious beliefs. If our samples showed
nothing some two or three days after the event, there would
certainly be no traces now even had we not sterilized the
planets," said Chafsu.

Vyaku nodded, then returned to his own seat as another
Master stood.

"Zadoh of the Merchants Guild. Will you still be providing escorts for the merchant ships trading within the
Alliance?"

"Mine again, I think, Moderator," said Chuz. "Yes, all the
merchant routes will continue to be patrolled for the fore-
seeable future, you need have no fear of that. The work to
outfit the Keissians with suitable craft continues and they
will soon be able to take their place with the rest of us in
keeping Alliance space defended."

"Any more questions?" She looked around the hall but no
one else rose to speak. "No? Then I suggest we move on to
the next topic."

The Petitioners' room was not uncomfortable, but it was
reasonably sparse. Upright preformed chairs, thinly padded,
stood against the walls of the room and formed three rows in
the center. They weren't the only occupants. Another two
people were hoping to change guilds, and three had unresolved complaints against specific guilds.

After they'd all been treated to the ramblings of one
male's case against the Providers Guild for insisting on
repairing a faulty entertainment comm instead of replacing
it, Kusac and Carrie's little group had had enough and they
left for the refreshment area.

They helped themselves from the drinks dispenser and
took seats in the far more comfortable lounge.

"You'd think they'd have coffee here by now," Carrie muttered, taking a sip of her c'shar.

"The Guilds are quite conservative," said Garras. "They might stock mild coffee here in another five or so years, when they're convinced it's here to stay."

Conversation was subdued as none of them felt like talking. Vanna curled up beside Garras and began to nod off and Kusac decided he wanted to get some fresh air.

"I'll stay here, if you don't mind," said Carrie. "It's a little too cold for me today."

"Cold? It's barely autumn yet," said Kusac.

"I can't be bothered," she said. "You and T'Chebbi go. I've had enough fresh air for the moment."

Kusac touched her cheek affectionately as he got to his feet. "You enjoyed our break, though."

"Oh, yes," she agreed. "Up until that pack of jeggets woke us up!"

"A nest of jeggets," he corrected her with a laugh as he and T'Chebbi left.

"Jeggets?" asked Garras, raising an eye ridge.

"We went camping over our Link day," said Carrie. "Guess who forgot to put the psychic damper on before we fell asleep? We attracted every jegget in the neighborhood!"

Garras began to chuckle. "Entertaining."

"No, it wasn't," she said tartly. "They gave me a hell of a shock, coming up under the covers and running all over us with their cold little paws! We couldn't get rid of them until Kusac thought to switch on the damper. Then they left."

"Well they would, they're telepathic. You'd spoiled their fun," said Garras, still chuckling. "They only wanted to join in. They're quite harmless."

"I dare say they are," she said drily. "If you know what they are to begin with. This was the first time I'd encountered your wildlife." She heard a faint sound opposite her and looked over to Kaid, who was suppressing a grin.

"Well at least it's raised a grin on your face," she said. "You've looked positively miserable since we met you this morning."

He shrugged. "I've had a couple of bad nights, that's all, Carrie."

"You too, huh?" She leaned across the table toward him. "I think it's time you and I collaborated with each other about our dreams and visions, Kaid. Between us we seem to be having more than anyone else."

"You've had some more?" he asked, tilting his head and ears toward her.

"Yes. The night before last, before our Link day began. I had two dreams, both of them so much clearer than any others I've had. It was as if I was actually there. I'm sure that hill has something to do with it." As she spoke, she could feel him mentally take a step back from her.

"Perhaps you're right," he said noncommittally.

"The second one was in Ranz. I'm not sure of the name of the male I saw, but I don't think it was Rezac."

"We know very few names from those days," said Kaid.

"I'll give you two more. Zashou. That's the name of his Leska. And a pack name—the Runners, I think it was."

Kaid tried to maintain eye contact with her, but couldn't. "Ranz breeds packs and pack wars, Carrie. Some of the pack names are as old as the town," he said, examining his mug.

"For a people who don't remember their history, you know a fair bit, Kaid," she said quietly.

"I lived in Ranz for a few years. You get to know the stories of the past."

"I know. Childhood is short in the mountains, especially for those who grew up at the wrong side of the hearth."

His ears flicked and he looked up sharply, but her head was turned away from him toward Garras and Vanna.

She sighed. "I wish I had her capacity to sleep anywhere. At least when she wakens she won't remember the wait."

"You'll develop that by your seventh week," Kaid said without thinking.

It was her turn to look at him sharply.

"Kusac told me why you were camping out," he said lamely. "I needed to know so I could arrange discreet security."

"Arrange?"

"I wasn't there."

"Oh? Where were you then?"

"At the Shrine for the dedication."

"Dreaming," she said, holding his gaze this time. She wanted him to realize she had heard his name in the dream.

"Carrie." Garras' voice cut across hers and drew her attention away from Kaid. "I don't want to talk too loudly. Will you come over, please?"

Casting a small frown back at Kaid, she got to her feet and joined Garras and the sleeping Vanna on the lounging chairs.

"What is it?" she asked quietly.

"If you're going to work with Kaid on the visions, I suggest you involve Ghyan. From what I hear, he's been collecting them for years for Lijou."

The midday break for second meal had come and gone before they were called into the Council hall. Not being involved in a change of Guild, Garras had to remain outside.

Chairs had been set out for them at the Speaker's table and when they had settled, the Moderator addressed Kusac.

"Liegen Aldatan, what is your petition?"

Kusac glanced up at his father before he began. His mouth felt dry with apprehension. So much depended on getting this vote to go with them. "We represent the Mixed Leska pairs. We're all of us currently members of the Telepath Guild," he said, "and we request the Council's permission to change our Guild."

"What is the name of the Guild you wish to join?" Tokui asked.

"We wish to join the Brotherhood," he said.

A hushed intake of breath greeted his words. The Moderator frowned at the delegates but said nothing as the noise subsided into silence once more.

"Why do you request such a radical change of Guild?"

"We're the Mixed Leska pairs. Each of us has a Human Leska as a partner. The traditional barriers that have prevented us as telepaths from being able to fight no longer exist for us. We're having to come to terms with a side of ourselves that we haven't been trained to deal with. The Telepath Guild isn't equipped to train our newly released aggression, and the Warrior Guild hasn't the facilities to deal with our telepathic talents. The Brotherhood, with its close connections to the Priesthood of Vartra and thus the Telepaths, offers us a single location with the facilities not only to train us in combat, but to continue our work as telepaths and to help us educate our Human partners, enabling us to better serve Shola. It offers the expertise of both guilds in one location."

Tokui nodded. "Your reasoning is sound, Liegen Aldatan."

Esken rose to his feet. "Moderator, I object to this . . ."

"Master Esken, you will have your say presently. Until then, please remain silent," said Tokui, looking sternly at him.

"I absolutely refuse to . . ."

"Master Esken, you have been warned to be silent! Sit down!" She looked beyond him to the sub-guild benches where Lijou and Ghezu sat.

"Is the Brotherhood willing to accept you as members? Leader Ghezu?"

Ghezu stood up, meeting the Moderator's gaze. "Yes, Moderator. We are more than willing to accept the Mixed Leska pairs."

"Father Lijou? Are you also prepared to accept them?"

Lijou rose. "Moderator, we are also willing to accept them. They are already members of my faith and known to me through the offices of the priest, Ghyan, who until recently ran the temple at Valsgarth."

"Very well. Let the records show that Liegen Aldatan on behalf of the Mixed Leskas has asked for a Guild transfer from the Telepath Guild to the Brotherhood, and that the Brotherhood is willing to accept them," she said, looking over to the Recorder who sat at the Speaker's table.

"Master Esken, now it's your turn," she said.

Esken rose and turned so all the delegates could see him. "I oppose the transfer on the grounds that all telepaths must owe their initial loyalty to my Guild. It is ludicrous in the extreme to even discuss the matter! If they leave, I would have no option but to forbid them to function as telepaths. There is no other guild here that would allow its members to leave yet still continue in their profession. Imagine the chaos that would result if, for instance, members of the Medical Guild asked leave to join the Building Guild and began practicing their medicine on the building sites. This could lead to the eventual breakdown of the whole structure of our society! This may be the way the Humans run their worlds, but it is not the Sholan way! I say that the Mixed Leskas are bringing alien ideas to our Council and that their petition should be dismissed on those grounds."

"Thank you, Master Esken. You may sit down. I should point out to the Council that there is a precedent. Though telepaths, the Priests of Vartra owe their primary allegiance to their Order rather than the Telepath Guild. We've heard both sides of the petition. I shall now throw the matter open to the Guild Masters for discussion," said Tokui, glancing round the hall. "High Commander Chuz, you were first, I believe."

"The Mixed Leskas are all still members of the Forces, Moderator. They possess unique abilities which may well be needed in the future, especially if we do meet up with these Valtegans. Shola needs them not only as functioning Telepaths but also as Warriors, and the Brotherhood is in a unique position to train them in both disciplines. They have our backing."

"Master Ngaiu of Administration," said Tokui, nodding in his direction.

"I agree with Master Esken," he said. "What's wrong with them staying in the Telepath Guild? We can't have them working outside their proper Guild. There's no need for them to change. I say no."

"Master Rhayfso of the Warrior Guild."

"We can't accommodate them properly at our Guild. It wasn't so bad when it was only one pair, but with three of them now . . ."

"Four," interrupted Ghezu.

"Four of them now, we haven't the shielded facilities for them when they stay with us. We've got enough problems trying to cope with the extra numbers caused by the Human Telepaths without Leskas as it is. At least they don't need dampers in their rooms. I vote yes. The Brotherhood are the specialists, let them train them."

"Don't you realize what you're doing?" demanded Esken, barely controlled fury in his voice as he got to his feet again. "If you do that, you're handing the Brotherhood guild status on a plate!"

Rhayfso rose again. "So what? They deserve it for doing the dirty jobs for all of us, yourself included, Esken! Who do you call in to defend yourselves if there's a real threat? The Brotherhood. Who tests all the new military equipment, risking their lives in craft that could easily blow up in their faces? The Brotherhood. If you ask me, it's long overdue, and it would give us nineteen guilds instead of eighteen, which would mean fewer drawn votes! You don't want it because it'll water down your power, Esken! Telepaths that don't belong to your Guild couldn't be controlled by you, could they? Don't be greedy. You've got all the new Human members, though they're sub-guilded to me, too, and I'm not

complaining. Let them change guilds and give the Brotherhood full guild status now, I say." He sat down amid an out-
break of raised voices.

"That's put the cat among the pigeons," said Carrie. "Why
did he suggest the guild status now?"

"Someone had to once Esken mentioned it," said Kusac
quietly.

"Silence!" roared Sister Tokui, hitting the bell so hard it
almost fell over. It had the desired effect as all talking
ceased.

"Master Rhayfso has suggested that the Brotherhood be
granted full guild status," she continued in a normal voice.
"He and Master Esken are both correct in saying that if the
Mixed Leskas are granted permission to change guild, then
the Brotherhood will have the right to request that status. In
fact, their request *is* on the agenda if the petitioners win their
right to become members of the Brotherhood. That being the
case, I have no option but to link the two matters together.
Recorder, let the records show my decision."

She stopped and surveyed all the delegates carefully. "I
will not have the sanctity of the Council hall broken by such
an outburst again. Offenders will be ejected and their vote
will be forfeit. I will now call for the Guild Masters only to
vote on the petitioners' request to change guilds. Those for,
please stand."

Vartra, let the vote go our way, thought Kusac, his hand
searching for Carrie's as he began to count the people
standing.

"Clerks, your total please," she said.

"Ten for, Moderator."

"Those against."

There was a short silence. "Six, Moderator.

"Those abstaining?"

"Two, Moderator."

"Thank you, Masters. Recorder, let the records show that
the petitioners have been granted the right to become members of the Brotherhood, and that the Brotherhood has
accepted them into their ranks."

"Gods," breathed Vanna, leaning forward to touch Kusac.
"I didn't think we'd do it when Esken started ranting about
guild status."

"That worked for us," said Kusac quietly. "A lot of the

other Masters dislike the way he runs his Guild. Anything that puts him at a disadvantage suits them."

"Liegen Aldatan, your group may remain for the next matter," said the Moderator, looking down at them. "Perhaps you would take seats at the end of the clerks' bench behind you?"

"Certainly, Moderator," said Kusac, getting up and bowing courteously to her. "Come on," he whispered, ushering the others over to the bench where the clerks were hurriedly moving along to make room.

"Leader Ghezu and Father Lijou, would you come forward to make your request, please?"

Lijou and Ghezu rose and took their places at the Speaker's table.

"Moderator," said Ghezu. "We formally request that the Brotherhood of Vartra be granted full guild status on the grounds that we possess a skill no other existing guild has."

"Name the skill, if you please."

"Among our members are Telepaths who can fight. No other guild possess members with these Talents."

"Who seconds your request?"

High Commander Chuz rose. "I do, Moderator."

"Since we have just dealt with the matter that gave you these members, that is not in dispute. We've also heard the arguments from Master Rhayfso and Master Esken for and against the Brotherhood being granted full guild status. That, however, is not the issue. What you delegates are being asked to vote upon is, does the Brotherhood have a skill that entitles them to full guild status rather than remaining a sub-guild of the Warrior and Telepath Guilds? Since this is likely to be a contentious vote, I will exercise my right to throw the vote open to all Guild Masters and Sub-Guild Leaders without any further discussion. Clerks, take your places as counters, please."

Kusac watched the clerks scurry from their seats to places throughout the hall.

"Those in favor of granting the Brotherhood full guild status, please stand."

I can't see to count them, Father! Kusac sent.

From where I stand, it looks like we may have won, sent Konis. *You presented your petition well, Kusac. You'll make a politician yet!*

Not funny! You know how I hate politics.

"We have the count, Moderator," said the chief clerk.
"There are twenty-eight for the motion."

We've won, Father!

I know, Vartra be praised!

"Those against, please."

The count was a little quicker this time. "Eleven against,
Moderator."

There was a flurry of movement as Esken got to his feet
and stormed out of the Council hall, followed by Khafsa.
Once again Sorli trailed after them.

"Recorder, strike two votes from the Against total. Guild
Master Esken and Leader Khafsa have forfeited their vote by
leaving," said Tokui, her voice cold. "As an aide, Senior
Tutor Sorli has no vote."

"Yes, Moderator. The total Against is now nine."

"Abstentions please."

"Six, Moderator."

"Very well. Recorder, let the records show that today the
Brotherhood of Vartra has been welcomed to the rank of
Guild. Leader Ghezu, and Father Lijou, you both now have
the title of Guild Master. Congratulations."

"My thanks, Moderator," said Ghezu. He opened his
mouth to speak again but found himself unable to utter a
word. He cast a look that was both frantic and angry at Lijou
before leaving the table.

"Thank you, Moderator," said Lijou, bowing low to her
before moving away to his seat.

Be silent, Ghezu, lest you lose all we have gained today,
came the stern thought from Konis.

Ghezu looked up at the Clan Lord, realization dawning on
his face.

*Yes, it's me you're dealing with, Ghezu. You've won Guild
status; be content with that. Your Guild needs you both.*

"Liegen Aldatan," said Sister Tokui, "your presence will
no longer be needed. Thank you for remaining."

"Moderator," Kusac bowed, getting to his feet and leading
the way to the door.

Once outside, Garras and Kaid were surrounded by them
all speaking at once.

"One at a time, in the God's name!" exclaimed Garras.

"We won," said Vanna simply. "We got permission to
change guilds and the Brotherhood is now a full Guild."

"We won?"

"Twenty-eight to nine, with six abstentions," said Kusac.

"I thought we'd lost when Esken and Khafsa came barreling out."

"No. They left because *they* lost," said Kusac.

"And the Moderator disallowed their votes for leaving," said Vanna delightedly, grabbing Garras by the arm.

"We're almost free," said Carrie quietly. "Almost there, Kusac."

"Yes," he said, putting his arm around her as they walked toward the exit. "We're almost there now."

Chapter 9

The cargo pod of the *Summer Bounty* touched down as planned on landing bay three of Jalna's one and only space-port. While the formalities were dealt with, Jo, Kris, Davies, and Vyaka pored over the aerial photographs they'd taken on their way in.

"It looks like it's winter out there," said Davies. "Do any of the Sumaan know what sort of weather we can expect?"

"The port is near Jalna's equator, so it could be similar to Valsgarth's," said Kris. "I only know the summer season, I'm afraid, and that varies between Mediterranean and tropical, depending which part of the continent you're on."

"Not necessarily. Climate also depends on the prevailing winds and ocean currents," said Vyaka. "Around the Valsgarth region, in the winter, winds from the pole cut down across the southwest bringing heavy snow and freezing temperatures. However, Captain Sharaaza says it's considered spring here, so the weather shouldn't pose too many problems."

Vyaka looked up from the map at the three humans. "There's still snow on the hilltops. Once you get up there, you'll need to guard against frostbite and hypothermia. That's why we believe the Valtegan craft hasn't been touched yet. It's been cut off by the severe winter."

"Surely they have aircars or something," said Davies.

Vyaka's ears flicked a negative. "This is an interdicted world," she said. "According to the Sumaan and the Chemerians, none of the species that trade there want the Jalnians to gain any technology that will lead to them getting off the surface of their world."

"How far is it from here to the crash site?" asked Jo.

"About sixty miles to the mountains, then you have to climb up to it," she said, pointing to the mark on the map that was the Valtegan ship. "Chances are that even if an intrepid local or two have reached and looted it, the type of data we're after is so specific it should still be there."

"What about this object they left behind? Where's it likely to be?" asked Davies.

"In the same area," said Jo, stepping back from the table and the map. "Kris, you handle the map reading. Both of you run a final check on your kit to make sure you've got everything and are carrying no modern weapons or other items." She looked sternly at Davies. "That means no lightweight portable stove! Have you both got your Jalnian coins?"

The two men nodded, then as Kris folded up the map, Davies went off to collect his kit.

"Portable stove?" asked Vyaka, raising an eye ridge.

"Just a private joke," said Jo, moving over to the chair where her small bundle of possessions lay. They were taking nothing with them that couldn't be easily carried on their backs or in pockets or belt pouches.

The status of women on Jalna wasn't known, therefore it was decided Jo was to pose as Kris' wife—with his long hair, he looked more like a native Jalnian than Davies—and if her role was contested, better that he should take the attention away from the Keissian.

A buzzer sounded in the common room.

"Time to go," said Vyaka, getting up. "Remember, try to link in to one of the Jalnians without being seen if you can. Then we'll know everything about them that we need."

All went as planned. The mind Vyaka and Kris chose was able to provide a smattering of the spaceport patois used between the space-going species and their land-bound hosts. No one remarked on their presence as one by one, they joined in with the unloading team.

The goods, packed in regularly shaped container units, were unloaded onto waiting animal-drawn carts and taken to the warehouses nearby. As night fell, the perimeter lights came on. In this world of draft animals and carts, their blinding whiteness was an anachronism. Around them loomed the immense shadows of other cargo ships, entry ports glowing golden in contrast to the floodlights.

The air was no longer chilly, it had become bitterly cold. It was with relief that they helped load the last of the crates onto the cart and joined the rest of their work force at the base of the ramp, waiting for their foreman to collect the money due them.

Davies stamped his feet, flapping his arms round his body to keep himself warm. "If it's this cold here . . ." he said to Jo, leaving the sentence unfinished.

She nudged him in the ribs as the foreman came down the ramp, pausing before the end to speak to them all.

"We'll divide out the money in the tavern," he said.

There was some disgruntled muttering, then the group of twenty-odd individuals turned and began to make their way to the gate across the other side of the field.

"What's that?" whispered Davies, nodding in the direction of a tall keep to the right of the gateway.

"The Port Lord's residence," said Kris equally quietly. "He owns the spaceport and the surrounding land."

Jo trudged on in silence beside Kris, only too aware that she was the only female present. She felt another presence and looked up, eyes meeting their foreman's. As he fell in step between her and Kris, she forced herself to remain calm. They couldn't have been discovered this soon!

"I don't remember you arriving with this group," he said to Kris.

"No. We were working on the U'Churian vessel alongside but we finished early," said Kris.

The foreman kept looking at him. "She got you into debt?" he asked, jerking his head toward Jo. "I like the idea of making her work for what she owes. Better than beating her."

"Ah. Yes," said Kris. "That's why we joined your team."

"You won't get full pay," he warned. "Only from the time you started."

Kris shook his head and shrugged. "Sorry. Don't know when that was."

"I do," he said, looking away. "You'll get paid at the tavern, after everyone else." With that, he speeded up and returned to the head of the little group.

"What was that all about?" asked Davies.

"I think he knows something's up," said Jo.

"He does," said Kris. "He's wondering why we're going to the bother of breaking out of the port when most people want to get in and leave Jalna. That's why he wants to see us."

"Well, at least we know in advance," said Davies.

They were nearing the perimeter fences now. Between

them they could see the spacers' town where the traders conducted their business while on Jalna. The smells of cooking
from the market stalls wafted their way through the fence,
making their stomachs growl with hunger.

"I'm not surprised we're all hungry," said Kris with a grin.
"We've just done several hours of hard labor! Let's hope the
food in the shantytown is as good."

"I doubt it," muttered Davies. "This lot don't exactly look
well fed. I wish we weren't excluded from the spacers'
town!"

Then they were at the gate and queuing up for the guard to
pass them through.

The guard was the picture of bored negligence. As they
passed through, ID cards held up for him to see, he barely
glanced at them. None of them were aliens, beyond that, he
didn't care. How many Jalnians given entry to the port
would want to escape back to the world outside?

"How does he know we're not smuggling off-world goods
out?" Davies muttered.

Kris pointed to the wolflike beast sitting inside the sentry
box. "He knows."

"Will he pick us up?" asked Jo.

"Unlikely. We've been mixing with the Jalnians for several hours now."

"Let's hope we smell enough like them," she muttered as
their turn came.

The beast rose to its feet and began to growl, a deep, rumbling sound. In front of him, the guard came to life, swinging
his rifle round into a ready position.

The foreman was suddenly at his side, putting a hand on
his arm. "I'll vouch for them," he said. "A container of dried
herbs split while they were carrying it, that's all. They can't
get rid of the scent till they reach the tavern."

The guard hesitated, glancing from man to beast. The
beast moved forward, sniffing at the three humans, the stiff
spines round his neck bristling ominously. Teeth bared, it
snarled.

"Papers!" demanded the guard.

They handed them over, hearts pounding as the creature
snuffled around their feet.

"Back, Dagla!"

Snarling resentfully, the animal retreated.

After studying each pass carefully and checking it against

the owner, the guard thrust them back at Kris. "Get out of here, and watch how you load the containers in future," he said.

As they started to move, the beast growled again, taking a pace forward warningly.

"I said get back!" yelled the guard, turning round and kicking at it with his booted foot.

"Hurry!" said the foreman, grabbing hold of Jo and hauling her through the gateway.

Kris and Davies followed at a run. They were through the other side of the double-fenced enclosure, and on the edges of the shantytown.

"Doesn't do to hang around by that damned beast. Gets its teeth into you and it don't let go. You're safe now. Tavern's that way," he said, pointing down the muddy walkway between the rows of rickety buildings. "Second last on the right. I'll see you there shortly." With that, he was gone.

Davies and Kris turned to Jo. She shrugged and looked down the street.

"We do what the man says. If we do anything else, we'll call more attention to ourselves."

The tavern was warm. That was where the pluses stopped. A greasy, cloying smoke, mingled with the smell of sour ale, filled the room. They pushed their way through the throng of sweaty, unwashed bodies till they reached the counter. A fat landlord, dressed in stained clothing, directed his serving wenches to the tables.

"What do you want?" he demanded, pausing briefly.

"A room and meals for three, please," said Kris.

"I'll sort the room out later," he said. "Go sit there," he nodded to the far corner where an empty table stood. "What d'you want to eat?"

"Anything. Meat and whatever."

He nodded. "It'll be over shortly. Drink?"

"Three ales."

They headed over to the table, sitting down and looking round at the tavern's other customers.

"They got our clothing right," murmured Jo. "In fact, they seem to have done a very good job."

"When they told us Jalna was backward, I didn't realize how backward they meant," said Davies.

"It's not that bad," said Kris quietly. "Here come our drinks."

The serving girl, resplendent in a stained blouse and an equally stained skirt, pushed her way over to them, throwing comments over her shoulder to the groups of men she passed.

The mugs were banged down in front of them, then she stood with her hand open, waiting.

"You pays for these now," she said.

"How much?" asked Kris.

"Three coppers apiece."

"I've got it," said Davies, digging in his pouch and dropping the money in her none too clean hand.

They were halfway through what proved to be, despite their fears, a palatable stew, when they saw the crew foreman come in and dole out the wages to his men.

"He's heading our way," said Davies. "Now we'll find out what he wants."

"What can you pick up?" Jo asked Kris.

"Not a lot. He keeps his mind quite still. He's suspicious of us, why he isn't sure, but he thinks we can be of use to him," said Kris quietly as the man approached their table.

"My name's Strick," he said, putting his tankard down before joining them at the table. "What they call you?"

"I'm Kris, he's Davey, and she's Jo," said Kris, nodding at each of them in turn. They'd decided there was no need for them to assume other names as their own fitted in with those of the natives.

Strick nodded at them. "You worked for a good four hours each, but the woman wouldn't normally get paid. How about accepting two gold for what you did?"

"Sounds fair to me," said Kris around a spoonful of stew.

Strick reached into his pouch and put two gold coins in front of him. "You planning to work here regular?"

Kris shrugged. "Maybe, maybe not. Can't say yet. We like to move around."

Strick narrowed his eyes. "You don't have the look of nomads," he said. "From the west, are you?"

Kris hesitated, spoon between his bowl and his mouth. He played his hunch. "No. From the northwest. We're heading back that way."

"Thought you was. Got that look about you. What you

doing breaking out of the port?" he asked, taking a swig from his mug. "Most folk want to break in."

"Not us," said Davies. "Like we said, we'd finished the other job and saw you busy, so thought we'd help out and earn a bit extra."

"Uh huh," said Strick, looking from one to the other. "Sure. Well, your business' yours. If you aren't leaving for a bit, let me know. Might be I could use you for work."

"We'll let you know," agreed Kris. "Where can we get hold of you?"

"I bunk here. Foremen are permanent, unless we screw up something. Most men round here just earn money to drink. You, now, you lot're different. Could use folk with brains as permanent staff. Interested?"

"Could be," said Kris. "We got some business to attend to first, but maybe we come back this way."

Strick stood up. "Well, you know where to find me," he said before leaving. They watched him join a group of men at a table near the bar.

"Interesting," said Jo as Kris began to laugh softly.

"What's so funny?" demanded Davies.

"They've got a bloody underground movement against the Port Lord going here! They think we're a unit from another group!" said Kris. "He thinks we were checking the port either to plan a possible raid, or to steal some goods for ourselves."

"They're trying to get the off-world goods distributed more fairly," said Jo.

"You've got it," nodded Kris, leaning toward them. "I also got the impression this Lord allows only his cronies to have trade items from the aliens. He uses the goods to buy their loyalty."

"In which case, that crashed ship should have caused a ripple all the way to here," murmured Jo thoughtfully. "They'll be hoping it was a trade ship, and go looking for off-world goods. So why haven't they sent an expedition from here to the site themselves?"

"That's something we'll need to find out," agreed Kris.

"There's room for a good scam here," said Davies. "If we can persuade Strick to pass us on to any contacts he has in the mountains, then we're laughing."

"And just how are we going to do that?" demanded Jo.

"For a start, we tell him we've got off-world contacts.

That we're heading up into the mountains to check this crash
out and . . ."

"Are you mad?" demanded Jo.

Kris put his hand over hers and squeezed it warningly.
"Quiet, Jo. You're drawing attention to yourself! Let's listen
to what Davies has to say."

Angrily Jo pulled her hand away from him. "Get on with
it, then," she snapped.

"Hell, we just tell them why we're here," said Davies,
grinning ingenuously. "We don't tell them we're not from
here, but we do say our off-world contacts are prepared to
pay for the information about this crashed ship. Naturally if
Strick helps us, he'll be well paid too—in whatever goods he
wants."

"Don't dismiss it out of hand, Jo," said Kris, looking
thoughtful. "Davies' suggestion has got the merit of being
simple and believable."

"What do we use to pay Strick? Have you thought of
that?" demanded Jo, her voice, though low, intense with
anger. "You *know* you haven't! Why should he believe us?
Or help us? We can't prove what we're saying is true!"

"Yes, you can," said Davies, picking up his drink. "If
you're not too principled to do it. Use your telepathy to make
him believe us."

"We can't do that!" Jo was horrified at the thought.

"There you go, then," said Davies, shrugging. "It's no
more than I expected of you, Jo. In this kind of work, you
can't afford to have principles."

"You can't violate someone's mind like that, Davies!
There have to be limits!"

"Why? We're here to find out what the Valtegan craft was
up to, and what we can about the Valtegans themselves!
Have you forgotten your time in their pleasure camps on
Keiss? The friends they killed? I haven't. I offer you a solution that's quick and easy: you want to reinvent the wheel
rather than offend your sensibilities."

Jo opened her mouth to reply but once again, Kris grasped
hold of her, this time shaking her arm quite forcefully.

"Stop it, both of you!" he hissed. "This isn't the place for
an argument! Jo, sorry, but he's right. We can't afford to
follow the Sholan telepath code here. We need to make full
use of all our resources, including my Talents."

"And what happens if he decides to turn us in?" demanded Jo.

"Why should he? If he's that committed to his cause, then he'll welcome us because of our off-world contacts," said Davies.

"He could try to hold us for ransom."

"Again, why? He'd only get a one-time payback. No, it's in his interests to help us and have our contacts in his debt. There's always the chance of more work from them."

"I don't like it!"

"Come on, Jo," said Kris, patting her arm gently. "Look at who they sent on this mission. A known scam merchant . . ."

"Thanks, Kris," said Davies.

". . . who is also good with electronics, and myself. I never told you much about my background. Let's just say I've been known to run a scam or two in my time," he grinned. "And you, with your experiences on Keiss. If we're being honest, we've been picked for the fact that we can do what it takes to get results. We don't have to like it, we just have to do our job."

Jo sat there, anger boiling inside her. Since Keiss had been liberated by the Sholans, life had changed dramatically for her. Her skills were what mattered now; not her sex. Now she could do the kind of work she loved. She'd hated the Valtegans and their pleasure cities, hated having to go there to spy on them and collect valuable information for the guerrillas. That had all been left behind. She'd been dealing straight with the world—until now.

"We're still fighting the same war, aren't we?" she said bitterly. "Nothing's changed! It's all lies and cheating!"

"The decision's yours, Jo," said Kris quietly. "If you've got a better plan, we'll use it. I don't like the thought of manipulating other people's minds any more than you do, but that's what gives us the edge on the Sholans. We're prepared to use our Talents that way if we need to. They can't because they're conditioned not to right from the start of their training."

"Dammit! All right, we'll use Davies' plan," she muttered. "Go and get Strick."

Strick followed Davies back to their table, settling himself in the empty chair.

"Said you wanted to talk. What about?"

"Order us some more drinks, Davey," said Kris. "Seems like we might have something in common, Strick."

"Oh? And what would that be?" asked the foreman, resting his elbow on the table and propping his chin on his hand.

"A wish to see free trade established on Jalna."

"Free trade?"

"Look at all the goods that come into the spaceport. Does any of it actually benefit the people? No, most of it goes into the coffers of a few greedy Lords, doesn't it?"

"It's always been that way."

The drinks arrived and Strick accepted his with a nod of thanks. "From the northwest, you said."

"West, actually."

"What really brings you to our parts?" Strick looked round their little group.

Kris sighed. "You got us there," he admitted, gently touching the edges of the foreman's mind with his. "We travel around a lot. Get to know all kinds of folk, some stranger than others, if you know what I mean."

"How strange?" Strick took another swig of his ale, his eyes never leaving Kris' face. "As strange as the Sumaan?"

"At least as strange as them," Kris agreed. Slowly he increased his mental contact, sensing, probing for an area where he could enter unnoticed.

"You weren't working on another ship." It was a statement.

There was a sudden burst of raised voices from the other end of the tavern. Startled, they all looked round, except Kris. With a sure touch, he pushed past the barrier between Strick's surface and deep thoughts. He had the contact he needed.

He relaxed now, waiting for them to turn back to the table. "You're right," he said when they did. "We came in on the Sumaan craft."

Caught as he was taking a drink, Strick began to cough, spilling ale over the table. Solicitously, Jo took his tankard from him and thumped him on the back.

"Enough!" Strick croaked, twisting away from her.

Kris felt his shock, and his almost disbelief.

"Why're you here?" he demanded. "What do you want?"

"We've a job to do," said Davies. "For our contacts."

"The crashed ship."

"That's the one," said Kris, gently steering Strick away

from thoughts of contacting his people. "The species that own the craft are warriors. My contacts need information on them. They think the ship can help."

"They want the ship?" Strick was confused. How could the ship help them?

"Not the ship," said Davies. "It has information inside it. We want the information it carries."

Strick was running through the options in his mind. There were quite a few even Kris hadn't considered. Helping them was one. He steered Strick's thoughts gently in that direction.

"If I help, what's in it for me?" he asked at length.

"They'll trade . . ." began Davies, but Kris cut him short.

"Medical supplies," he said smoothly.

Strick nodded. "Next to weapons, that's what we need most."

"No weapons," said Kris firmly, reinforcing the negative mentally.

Strick frowned and put his hand to his head, rubbing the side of it.

Kris swore under his breath. Too strong, dammit! He'd noticed. He tried to relax his hold, make it less obvious.

"Something wrong?" asked Jo, shooting an angry look at Kris.

Strick shook his head. "Thought I had a headache starting," he mumbled. "Gone now. Medicines. Yes, we need them. How do I know I can trust you?"

"You're in the port tomorrow, aren't you? I'll give you a code word to give to one of the Sumaan and he'll see you're paid. How you get the stuff out is up to you," said Kris, mentally backing off a little way.

"And in return, you want contacts at Kaladar. I can do that," nodded Strick. "First I want the medical supplies. Once I've got them, then you get my help."

"It's a deal," said Kris.

Half an hour later, they trooped upstairs to their room. The door safely closed between them and the world, Jo threw her kit down on the nearest straw palliasse.

"You overdid it with him," she said, rounding on Kris.

"It's an inexact science, Jo," he said. "We're all still learning how to use it. I didn't intend to hurt the man, believe me. I overdid it because I don't make a habit of using my Talent this way."

"Lighten up, Jo," said Davies, dropping his pack at the end of his straw mattress and flinging himself down on it. "We got the help we needed. All we have to do is hang around tomorrow till Strick comes off duty, then we're on our way." He clasped his hands behind his head, looking up at them. "I reckon you should be thanking Kris. He did a good job, and he convinced Strick not to ask for weapons. Not bad at all, Kris."

"Thanks." Kris knelt down by the remaining mattress and began to unpack his cloak from his kit bag.

"You did all right," said Jo grudgingly as she sat down on her bed. "Staying here an extra day will allow us to shop around for the provisions we need."

Kris made a noncommittal noise as he put his cloak over the mattress.

As the last one to settle down, Davies extinguished the oil lamp, plunging the room into darkness.

Try as she might, Jo couldn't sleep. She tossed and turned restlessly, wishing she was back on board the *Summer Bounty* again. At least there she could have got up and gone into their common area for a hot drink.

"What's the matter?" asked Kris at last. "Bugs biting?"

"Bugs?" she said. "Don't do that to me, Kris," she said, a note of pleading in her voice. "Tell me you're getting your own back because of what I said about the telepathy earlier, for God's sake!"

"I'm serious," he said. "The cloaks should keep the worst of them away."

She groaned. "I might as well be back on Keiss!"

"Was it bad there?" he asked after a moment.

"What? Keiss?"

"No. The domed cities."

"I never mentioned them!"

"I wasn't prying, Jo," he said quietly, shuffling his bed closer so he couldn't be overheard by Davies. "You were projecting earlier."

"They were bad," she said, her voice taut with remembered pain and lost friends.

"Sorry. I could see how using my Talent on Strick brought it back. Were you close to Elise? She was Carrie's twin, wasn't she?"

"Yes, she was. Elise and I kept each other sane when I was there." Memories she'd hoped were lost began to return. The clammy feel of Valtegan skin against hers; hands and minds that pawed and took, that couldn't understand any gentler emotions. She shuddered, trying to push them back where they'd come from.

Kris' hand touched her arm, making her jump and cry out in fear.

"It's only me," he said quietly, his hand searching in the dark for hers, then curling round it. "I didn't mean to bring back the past."

She felt his mind alongside hers, helping to nudge the memories down below her conscious mind.

"Thanks," she said, taking her hand carefully away from him. "I'm fine now. And I'm sorry I snapped earlier."

"That's all right," he said. "If the bugs get too bad, let me know. I can zap them mentally for you."

She grunted disbelievingly as she curled up again and tried to sleep.

*   *   *

"What are you doing with spades?" asked Mara as Carrie walked past her out of the house.

"We're going out to look at some ruins today and I want to do some digging," she said, stopping briefly to look at the younger girl. She felt sorry for her. There wasn't much for someone her age to do out here on the estate. Not that she'd have been much better off had she lived on Keiss, she reminded herself.

"A treasure hunt! That sounds interesting. Could I come?" she asked, getting up off the step.

Carrie hesitated. It wasn't exactly a private trip since they were taking Meral and Kaid with them, but it was the first chance they'd had in the last six weeks to have some leisure time. Mara she didn't mind too much, but Zhyaf? She could feel Mara's unspoken plea.

"Why not?" she said, giving in to her better self. "See if Zhyaf wants to come also, then tell Choa to put some extra food in for you. We're leaving in half an hour."

"Thanks!"

As she watched Mara head off at a run, Kusac sent to her.

Carrie! You were the one who persuaded me we needed this time as a break! There's a lot I should be doing at the new estate.

Don't talk to me about the estate! You come back every day covered in dust and plaster. You'll set into a statue one of these days! she warned.

I just want everything to be right.

I told you before, the builders know what they're doing, and you've got Garras out there whenever Vanna's at the lab. You don't have to see to everything yourself.

The worst's over now, I promise. Another couple of days and they'll be finishing off the house and the other main buildings. I don't need to oversee their work on the estate homes. His mental tone was even more conciliatory now.

She smiled to herself. She couldn't stay angry with him for long, and he knew it.

Mara I don't mind, but her Leska? he sent.

Zhyaf might choose not to come, she replied as she headed for the front of the house to put the spades in the aircar. *Mara's almost more isolated than I was, Kusac. I'm here, another human, and she's been kept away from me. A break like this with us is what she needs, too.*

I'll take your word for it, he sent with a mental sigh.

"I don't know what you expect to find," said Kusac, as they climbed into the aircar where the others were waiting for them. "There's not going to be much of the ruin left standing after so long."

"Aren't you curious about the building? It is part of your family's past."

"Not when it's that far back," he said, getting into the pilot's seat. "I told you, we don't have the same preoccupation with the past as the Humans."

"It's not a preoccupation," she said, sitting beside him. "It gives them a sense of continuity, and by studying the past they feel they can better understand themselves."

Kusac made a noncommittal noise and waited for Rulla and Zhyaf to get seated before sealing the door and starting up the engine.

He could feel her thoughts become still as she looked out at the scenery below. It wasn't far and within ten minutes, they were circling round to land on the top of the hill.

I want you to take it easy today, Carrie. There's bound to be a lot of overgrown rubble at the ruins and I don't want anything happening to you. No falls, please.

There are times when you are too cautious, she sent. *I'll be as careful as I usually am. You need to loosen up, stop seeing what could go wrong, otherwise life will get boringly predictable and pass you by.*

With you around? Not likely! You attract the unpredictable like a magnet! "Look, there's the ruin below us," he said, pointing toward the ground. "As I said, there's not much left. I'll set down to the rear of it. There's a sizable clear area there."

"There's more of it standing than I thought there'd be from what you've been saying," Carrie said, peering below as Kusac brought the craft down to land. As soon as he'd cut the motors and unsealed the door, she scrambled out.

"Don't go off on your own!" Kusac shouted after her. "I told you, the ruins are probably unstable and dangerous!"

"Then hurry up," she said, stopping and turning back to look at him through the doorway. Her brown eyes, the vertical pupil an amber-edged slit in the bright light, regarded him with humor. "And stop fretting over me, I'll take care." With that, she was off.

Kusac gave a small growl of annoyance as he scrambled out after her. "Keissians," he muttered.

"Carrie strikes me as being more of a Sholan without fur than a Keissian, particularly when you see her eyes," said Meral as he followed him out. "She's very like Taizia."

"Worse," said Kusac. "I wonder how much of that is due to my sister's influence."

"Almost none from what Taizia says."

"I feared as much," he sighed as they headed after Carrie. Kaid and Rulla ambled behind them with Zhyaf and Mara.

"Would either of us want a female from the Clan estates?" asked Meral, turning an amused look on Kusac. "One who only thought of duty and position and looking attractive?"

Kusac returned the grin. "Gods, no!" he said. "Think of Rala Vailkoi! Actually, I'm surprised you and Taizia are still together. Her relationships don't usually last this long." When Meral didn't answer immediately, Kusac stopped and looked at him. "You are still together, aren't you?"

"We have a fondness for each other," Meral said evasively.

"And Taizia being named as the mother of the Clan's heirs after me has upset your plans," he said quietly. "You now have the problem Carrie and I had up until three months ago. I'm sorry," he said, starting to walk on again.

They joined Carrie by the outer wall of the ruin, and waited there for the others to catch up with them.

Meral's ears flicked back, then righted themselves. "Liegen, I've something I must tell you. Taizia and I, we took your example and went to the temple. Ghyan witnessed the signing of our five-year contract," he said, the words coming out in a rush.

Kusac looked at him, his mouth dropping open with sheer surprise. He found himself unable to say anything as the young warrior before him braced himself for what he felt was the inevitable explosion of anger.

As his surface thoughts came to her, Carrie began to laugh gently. "She's pregnant! So *that's* why she's hiding with your family on the Nazule estate! I wish you both happiness, Meral."

Kusac closed his eyes, a pained look on his face. "Just wait till I get my hands on her! That cunning, conniving little she-jegget! How *could* she choose to compromise you both . . ."

"No," interrupted Meral. "The decision to sign a contract was mine, and I insisted on a five-year one. There's nothing you can say to her that I haven't already said, and more."

Kusac closed his mouth as Carrie nudged him mentally.

Leave it to him, Kusac. He needs to accept the responsibility for this. You're touching his sense of honor now.

I know, but they shouldn't have done this!

They've done no more nor less than we did. Found a way to take the happiness they want, came the gentle reminder. *Have we the right to be moralistic with them and begrudge them their happiness?*

I don't, Carrie, the God knows that. I love my sister dearly.

So tell him that!

Kusac refocused on Meral. "Stop looking so worried," he said, mouth widening and opening in a grin. "A five-year contract with my sister is enough punishment to wish on any male, as I think my parents will agree when you tell them. You do realize she'll still have to provide the Clan with heirs?"

"Yes, but she'll be mine for those five years," Meral said,

relaxing now as he realized that the anger he had expected wasn't coming.

"Bring Taizia over to stay at the villa if you wish," said Kusac. "You shouldn't have to be apart at this time."

"She'd love to come," said Meral, face breaking into a wide grin. "But wouldn't her condition upset . . ."

"No," smiled Carrie, reaching out to touch his arm. "It won't bother me. By the end of spring, our cub will be born. I would love some female company, especially Taizia's, in our house full of men. I'm glad Kusac suggested it."

She looked over her shoulder and called out to Kaid, who, having a fair idea of what they were discussing, had kept himself and the others a short distance away.

"Kaid, you and Rulla can help us explore while Kusac and Meral indulge themselves in your species' peculiar passion for genealogies."

Kaid came walking over to them. "Meral's spoken to you? His family is the Nazule Clan, Liegen," he said. "He's the second son, and a fitting mate for Liegena Taizia."

Kusac nodded. "I know, Kaid. Meral told us about his family when we were still on the *Khalossa*."

He turned to Meral. "I know your qualities as a person, and I know you're good for each other, Meral. That matters more than anything else."

Carrie looked from Kusac to Meral, seeing the latter's tail tip swaying with pleasure at the praise he'd just received. She reached for Kaid's hand and tugged at him. "Come on, Kaid. These two need to talk," she said, towing him round the low wall toward the center of the ruin.

"Over here," she called to Mara. "This is where your treasure hunt starts, Mara, though I doubt we'll find any treasure here! Zhyaf, are you coming?"

"I think I'd prefer to sit in the shade, thank you, Liegena," he said, ambling over to one of the trees that offered a broad trunk for him to lean against.

Within ten minutes Carrie was calling Kusac over to where she and the others stood in front of a large mound of rubble. At the base lay the weathered remains of a clawed foot.

"This was obviously part of a statue, Kusac," she said. "I get the feeling it was a religious one." She scuffled in the loose rubble with the toe of her boot, then bent down to pick something up. "What's this?" she asked, rubbing it against her trouser leg before holding it out to him.

Kusac took the stone from her, turning it over in his hand. "It's a piece of worked crystal. It's common all over this area. Must have been set in the statue somewhere," he said, handing it back to her.

"It's shaped like an egg," she said, holding it up to the sun and squinting through it. "What would they use a piece of clear crystal for? Could it have been an eye? How do your sculptors portray eyes in statues today?"

Kusac shrugged.

"Can I see it, Liegena? The civic statues are usually all carved from the same stone," said Kaid. "However, the ones at the Warrior Guild and the Brotherhood are a good few hundred years old and they have crystal eyes."

Carrie handed it to him and watched as he turned it over in his hand.

"It's not clear, Liegena, it's a blue white," he said, handing it back to her.

She had to grab for it as he almost dropped it in his haste to return it to her. Puzzled, she glanced at him but he was already turning away.

"You say these crystals are common here?" she asked Kusac.

"Yes. We've got several worked pieces in the house. Ancient heirlooms Mother calls them. There's an old story that says a hermit priest lived up here. Apparently he survived by carving crystal animals and flowers which he exchanged on the estate for food for himself and the wild creatures that lived up here," said Kusac. "There were seams of the same crystal in the cave lower down where we stayed, Carrie. Remember?"

She nodded, putting the piece in her trouser pocket. "I remember. I wonder what else is buried under that pile of rubble," she said, looking at it wistfully.

"Can I see it?" asked Mara.

"Later," said Carrie. "When we stop for second meal. I want to do some digging here."

"That's not a job for us, Carrie," said Kusac. "That'll take several people a day or more to uncover, and I don't know that it's worth the effort."

"Mmm," she said, drifting off toward a gap in the broken wall beside them. "You could be right. Let's see what else there is here. The story and the presence of the statue certainly substantiates that this was a religious site at some time. If we could find some more of it, we could probably tell if it was a statue of Vartra. I wonder how old all this is."

Kusac accompanied her while she wandered around the rest of the ruins. It covered quite a large area and from the distribution of the pieces of wall sticking up like jagged teeth from the ground, they could tell that it had been quite a complex building.

He could sense Carrie probing at the ground with her mind. Some of what she was picking up he could feel, but it was so subtle, so much a matter of her judgment that he was more aware of her conclusions than how she had reached them.

"I'm sensing a lot of crystal," she said at length. "It's identical to the one we found. Also large amounts of metal." She frowned, perplexed by the conflicting images.

"Probably a crystal mine under here," suggested Meral.

"Could be," she said. "Do you have a scanning device that would show up any tunnels or caverns?"

"We can get one," said Kusac. "Do you really think it's that important?"

"Yes," she said unequivocally, looking up at him. "I also want that statue uncovered. I need to know if it is Vartra. I was getting the sensation of peace and tranquillity from that area of the ruins, but not from here. If this was a monastery or a shrine, then I should be getting the same feelings here, unless the whole building had been destroyed as a result of violence. The violence would then be an overlay on the general feeling of peacefulness. Only what I'm getting here is much more mundane."

She hesitated, unable to find the words to fully explain what she was feeling. "There's a sense of aggression here that wouldn't fit with the purpose of the building if it was a monastery. It feels like the Warrior Guild—you know, controlled aggression. Couple that with large amounts of metal buried quite deeply underground and you have a puzzle that begs for an answer."

Kusac sat down on a pile of rubble. "On Keiss we were able to find the pod using our combined talents so I know it's possible to sense large amounts of metal, but feelings from the past?"

"That dream I had while I was at Noni's with Kaid," she said. "Noni said it was the rocks and stones keeping memories and replaying them in our minds while we slept. You have crystals that store electronic data, don't you? How about a crystal that stores people's memories? It would explain why my dreams in the cave were so vivid. It would also explain why people at the Valsgarth Telepath Guild have dreams only when they stay there."

"What about those we have at Stronghold?" asked Rulla. "Many of us have even seen the God walking down the corridors there!"

"Perhaps there are crystal deposits in the Dzahai Mountains, too," said Carrie.

"Lijou keeps an ornament of blue crystal on his desk," said Rulla thoughtfully.

"Can we find out if there are deposits near Stronghold?" asked Kusac.

"The miners would have records in the Guild of Manufacturers' archives," said Kaid. "The Guild of Artificers might know about it too since the crystal can be carved."

"That definitely should be followed up," said Kusac.

"I'll do it," offered Kaid.

"I knew this place was important from the first time I saw it," said Carrie as she began to wander away from them again. "It's really strange, Kusac. As if it's calling to me. I'm feeling it even more strongly now."

"Then I suppose we'd better do some excavating today," he said. "I don't suppose you have any idea why it's important, do you?"

"None, but I was right about the crystals."

"We haven't proved they hold memories yet," said Kusac warningly. "We'll have to find a way to experiment with them."

"They hold memories," said Kaid quietly.

Carried looked over to him. "How d'you know?" she asked.

"The crystal Noni used to heal you," he said reluctantly. "It retained a feel of you."

"She used a crystal? Then Noni should be able to help us find out more about the piece I've found. Perhaps we can go and show it to her."

"We could ask," said Kaid.

"Where do you want to start digging?" asked Kusac.

"Well, since we can't do anything about what's below ground without a sensor, how about we start on the mound where I found the foot? If it is a statue of Vartra, then we've got a good idea that it's worth looking further."

Kusac sighed and stood up. "Let's get started then."

Midday came and they broke for their meal, spreading the rugs outside in the partial shade of the aircar and the nearby tree. Afterward to Carrie's and Mara's annoyance, the food coupled with the heat and the Sholan's natural tendency to rest during the hottest part of the day, found them surrounded by fairly soporific males.

"I'd like to get back to excavating the statue," Carrie said, looking pointedly round at each of them in turn.

"There's no rush, Carrie, we've just eaten," said Kusac from where he lay sprawled beside her. "Why don't you rest, too? It would do you good." His tone was persuasive.

Carrie could feel his waves of drowsiness spreading through her. Firmly she pushed them back. "I don't want to rest, thanks," she said, moving to get up.

Kusac's arms were wrapped round her waist before she could move any further and she found herself gently but firmly pulled down beside him.

"You should rest, cub," he said as he tucked her body against his. "You need all your strength." His nose was cool against her cheek.

"I don't want to rest. Now we've unearthed most of the torso, I want to see what else is under the rubble," she replied, trying to break free as his tongue began to lick at the edges of her ear. *Kusac, that's unfair.* Once again the waves of lassitude from him began to wash over her.

En'Shalla, Carrie. His mental tone was almost a caress as his hand moved to the back of her head, turning her face to his as he began to kiss her. *We're in the hands of the Gods. Don't fight it this time.*

The Terran portion of her mind—becoming smaller with every day—balked not only at the too public display of affection, but also at the means he was using to persuade her to rest. Despite that, she felt herself begin to relax, responding to his closeness.

"Perhaps," she murmured softly, her fingers toying with the hair that grew on his neck, "the Gods wish us to uncover this statue, and even discover what lies at the heart of this hill. If it weren't for my Talent, we wouldn't even be aware there was anything here."

She could feel the light touch of his mind as he looked deeper into her thoughts.

Kusac sighed and released her. "All right," he said, sitting up. "You do realize that you'll only have a few weeks to oversee this, don't you? We can't afford you taking any physical risks. You really will have to take it easy, Carrie. The last thing either of us wants is you to miscarry."

"Miscarry?" said Mara, looking over at them from where she sat on the rugs. "I thought you two were married. How can she . . ."

"Mara, hush," said Zhyaf, obviously embarrassed.

"What . . . Why?"

"Carrie lost our last cub in the Challenge, Mara," said Kusac.

"*Last* one?" said Mara, looking in disbelief from Kusac to Zhyaf, then to Carrie. "You mean, *your* cub . . . I mean your *baby?*"

Then it dawned on Kusac. "You weren't told?"

"Cubs? She's having a Sholan *cub?*" Mara was rising to her feet, a look of realization dawning on her face as she began to radiate fear of what could happen to her.

Zhyaf, control her! snapped Kusac as he mentally reached out for the girl's mind himself. *Carrie, you know what to do!*

They reached but she pulled free, physically and mentally. With a strangled cry of terror, she turned and ran.

Kaid was first after her, following hard on her heels as she instinctively took the remains of a wide pathway down the rear of the hillside. Memories of Rezac's flight kept flashing in front of him and he had to keep shaking his head to suppress them and see where he was going. He stumbled on a rock and as he fell to the ground, he shifted his muscles ready to land on all fours. Angry with himself, he thrust the intruding false memories aside and concentrated on his quarry.

He gained on her and, bunching his muscles, he leaped, bringing her down, sending them rolling over and over till they came to an abrupt halt against a tree trunk.

Stunned, he pushed himself to his haunches just as her mind seemed to explode inside his in a swirling mass of wild images.

Gestalt, Kaid! Don't touch her! The warning shot through the images like a lifeline and he clutched it, letting Carrie pull him free of Mara's and Zhyaf's minds as he staggered away from the girl to collapse into unconsciousness.

He'd come round by the time Kusac and Meral reached him, both of them concerned for his safety rather than the Human's.

"Mara?" He managed to get the word out through a mouth that was as dry as the desert.

"Unconscious but fine," said Kusac, taking Kaid's jaw in one hand and turning his head so he could see his eyes.

Kaid felt the beginnings of Kusac's touch at the edges of his mind, only to feel it thrust aside by Carrie.

"Carrie says you're fine," Kusac said, releasing him. "Did you hurt yourself when you fell?"

"No," he said, trying desperately to moisten his lips with a tongue that was equally dry. "Didn't know they'd never triggered the gestalt before."

"Neither did I," said Kusac, helping him to his feet. "My fault. No one told me they'd decided not to tell her about Carrie and Vanna."

"Probably thought it would start the changes."

"They were right, but they should have known that she was bound to find out sometime soon."

Swaying slightly, Kaid pushed Kusac away. "I'm fine," he said. "See to Mara. All I need is a drink." His head was pounding but he wasn't about to admit that.

"Meral, you help him back up to the aircar, I'll bring Mara," said Kusac, turning to crouch down at the side of the limp figure of the human girl.

While Meral, on Carrie's instructions, rifled in the medikit for an analgesic for Kaid, Kusac saw Mara was settled comfortably on one of the aircar seats and covered with a rug. He left Carrie sitting with her and went to see how Rulla was getting on with Zhyaf.

"Out cold," said Rulla, looking up at him.

"Why the hell didn't you tell me they knew nothing of the pregnancies?" demanded Kusac.

"I didn't know you hadn't been told," said Rulla. "Zhyak knew, but decided to keep it from her. I suppose because of his greater experience he was able to prevent her finding out until now."

"Well, it had to happen sometime," sighed Kusac, squatting down beside him. "I just wish it hadn't happened out here."

"From what I've been told by Vanna, it doesn't make much difference where it happens," said Rulla pragmatically. "They'll just sleep it off, then wake up tired but otherwise fine."

"Well, yes, but that isn't the point," said Kusac. "Mara will have to have the whole situation explained to her, and I don't want Carrie to have to do that. Her loss is still too painfully close for her."

"I understand," nodded Rulla. "Why don't we put Zhyaf into the aircar and I'll take them both back to the house? Vanna can see to them there. You'd have to wait till I returned, but the Liegena wouldn't mind that. She'd have time to get some more digging done," he grinned.

Kusac nodded. "Do that, but take Kaid with you. I want Vanna to have a look at him. I'm not happy that he was exposed to the gestalt."

Rulla flicked his ears in agreement and getting to his feet, headed over to the vehicle. Moments later, Kaid came over.

"I'm fine. Meral can go with them," he said.

"Your mind has taken quite a shock, Kaid. It's the same as having a severe blow on the head. I'd rather Vanna checked you out. You haven't got the mental resilience we telepaths have."

"I'm fine," said Kaid determinedly. "Meral can go."

Kusac got to his feet. "I can't make you," he said. "Stay if you wish."

Rulla returned with Meral to fetch Zhyaf. Between them they carried him into the vehicle and settled him on the other bench seat, then strapped them both in safely.

"We'll see you in about an hour," said Rulla as he started up the engine.

When they'd gone, Kusac turned to Carrie. "Let me guess. Back to the statue."

"You got it," she said. "Remember those dreams we had not long after we arrived on Shola? The ones of Vartra?"

"Yes," he said cautiously. "The one most new Leskas experience."

She reached out to touch him, aware of his sudden worry that perhaps they were treading on thin ice with regard to the Gods, Vartra in particular.

"If the Gods are controlling our lives, then we've nothing

to fear from looking more closely at this. Surely They'll stop us discovering anything that should remain secret?"

"The incident with Mara and Zhyaf could have been them warning us," said Kusac.

"No," said Kaid. "That wasn't a warning. The Gods don't work like that, Kusac."

"I agree," said Carrie. "I'm sure this site is where we'll find our answers. The dreams are more prevalent here than anywhere else. Look inland across the bay," she said, pointing to the mainland town. "There lies the Warrior Guild town of Nazule, and to our left?"

"The remainder of the Valsgarth Estate, the Aldatan Clan lands and the Valsgarth Telepath Guild," he said quietly, following her raised finger.

"And between the two, this shrine to Vartra," she finished. "I don't think it's a coincidence."

"Traditionally the Warriors have been the defenders of the Telepaths," said Kaid. "It's said it wasn't always so, that at one time, telepaths could fight as well as any of us."

"What happened to change that, I wonder? It's yet another fact that doesn't fit in anywhere."

"Kaid, can you check with Lijou to find out how long ago the Warriors started official duties with the Telepath Guild?" asked Kusac.

"I can ask him," said Kaid. "I can't guarantee he'll have the answer."

"If the Brotherhood has been able to recruit all the Talents the Telepath Guild has missed, and most of those come by way of the Warrior Guild, is it possible that the Warrior and Telepath Clans were once one and the same?" asked Kusac. "That would take into account the old tales that telepaths could fight. Maybe a disease or an industrial accident robbed some of them of their Talent completely and left others unable to fight. That could have caused them to split into two distinct sects."

"It's feasible," said Kaid thoughtfully. "I don't think anyone's actually looked at that possibility. Unless it involved genetic damage, the changes wouldn't be passed on, though. They would only affect that generation."

"So what caused the gentic damage?"

"The Valtegans?" suggested Carrie. "I can't see them being here as anything but conquerors."

"But why? What brought them here, and what caused them to leave?"

"The leaving's easy. The Cataclysm. If it destroyed your civilization, one that seems to have been fairly sophisticated, then it must have also destroyed the Valtegan presence on Shola," said Carrie.

"If the Valtegans were here in our past, even if Shola suffered a cataclysm, why didn't others from their home world return afterward?" asked Kusac.

"Maybe there was nothing of value left afterward," said Kaid. "Look at the way they totally destroyed Szurtha and Khyaal. When we drove them from the Keissian system, we couldn't find a trace of them anywhere. They disappeared as if they hadn't existed. It's as if they aren't concerned with us, for now at least. I honestly think we were just an obstacle in their way so they destroyed us. The same could have been true in the past. We were there, so they used us like they used Keiss, but when we suffered such destruction during the Cataclysm, we were no longer of use."

"Or they tried to destroy Shola and failed," said Carrie. "That's a possibility, too."

"I'm not so sure about that," said Kaid. "It depends how many Valtegan remains there are on Shola, and we've no way of knowing that yet."

"They'd have been willing to destroy their own people too," said Carrie. "You weren't inside the mind of that Valtegan officer on the *Khalossa*."

"I wonder how far back the records of the past Clan Lords go," said Kusac thoughtfully. "There's been a genetic breeding program going on for the God knows how many hundreds of years, and they'd have to keep records to see none of the Clans became too inbred. Perhaps we'll find the proof of the link between the Warrior and Telepath Clans there. It's a pity the Brotherhood has always been a collection of individuals rather than families or we might have been able to link them in as well."

"We should be able to find some links," said Carrie. "I think it was you, Kaid, who told me that many of the mountain families have provided members of the Brotherhood."

"Perhaps," said Kaid, "but I don't think Leader Ghezu will give us access to the records."

"Master Ghezu now," said Kusac.

"As you say," agreed Kaid. "If you want to continue digging

through this rubble before Meral returns, we'd better get on with it now."

"A good point, Kaid. Well," said Kusac, getting to his feet and tugging Carrie up with him. "At least you've given us a starting point. If this is Vartra's statue, and the scans show refined metals beneath this ruin, then we know we're on the right track."

"But the right track of what?" asked Carrie, following him back to where the statue of a God was emerging from the rubble of over a millennium.

Once Meral had turned the engine off, he sprinted over to where they were still working.

"Kaid, there's a call on the comm for you. Came in as I was landing."

Kaid straightened up, looking curiously at him. "For me? Who?"

"A female, that's all I know. There's no visual."

Kaid handed his shovel to Meral and ran over to the aircar. Settling himself in the pilot's seat, he sealed the door before answering the comm.

"Kaid here."

"Tallinu, is that you there?" demanded Noni.

"Yes. What's up, Noni? Why no visual?" he asked, trying not to let his anxiety for her sound in his voice. "Is something wrong?"

The small screen flickered, then her image was displayed. "Think I'm going to let all and sundry see me, Tallinu? None of their business what I look like! Now listen closely to what I got to say as I won't repeat it. You know I don't like using these damned units! I got a warning for you. Remember that female you were involved with all those years ago? The one you came to me about? Well, Ghezu's found her."

"Ghezu's found her?" He suddenly found it difficult to take in what she was saying. Lijou had given him a similar warning only two days before.

"Yes. She's at a village on the edge of the desert. Rhijudu it's called. She's dying, Tallinu, of some wasting disease. She'll be dead by midwinter from what I've been told. There's nothing you can do so leave her be, you hear me? The village is full of those damned fake priests and they're killing or maiming any telepaths they get their hands on. If they get hold of one of the Brothers, Vartra help him! Death is kinder than what this Fyak does to them and the telepaths—if they survive long enough to be given to him."

"Why are you telling me this?"

"Because Ghezu's trying to get you to go to her. He wants you and her both dead, Tallinu. You mustn't go there, hear me? Let her die in peace. You got nothing to say to each other after all this time anyway! You've got to go to the Fire Margins, and you can't do that if you go chasing after her and get yourself killed—or worse."

Kaid stirred, his ears flicking briefly. "How do you know all this?"

"Ghezu's crafty. He knew you'd been here with your Human. He sent one of his folk to tell me, then I had a visit from someone who was worried, and he told me the same. He's setting Dzaka against you, Tallinu. He wants him to do the killing."

"What?" This stunned him.

"Told you. He's ordered Dzaka to kill you if you go near the village. He won't have left it at him either. There'll be others, including those Priests!" She spat the word out as if it was a curse.

"Why hasn't Dzaka told me?"

"Use your brain, Tallinu," she said. "He's damned if he does and damned if he doesn't! If he tells you, you'll go to her, then he's either to kill you or end up with a contract on his own head for disobeying the Brotherhood. He knows he'll likely die whichever way he goes."

"*Damn* him!" said Kaid, thumping his hand down on the console facia. "Why the hell didn't he come to me? He knows I can protect him! You wouldn't believe the level of security we've got round this estate, Noni! The Brotherhood couldn't reach him."

"Don't be too sure on that."

"I've survived at least four attempts on my life in the past ten years, Noni. If I can do it, I can see he's safe!"

"Is he safe from you?"

Her eyes bored into his, stripping away what they could of his barriers. He looked away.

"You'll kill him if he betrays your people once more, won't you?"

"I'd have no choice." His voice was bleak. "All he has to do is trust me."

"Why should he, Tallinu, when you don't trust him, eh? He knows you're waiting for him to slip up in some way."

"I'm not. I *want* to trust him."

"Ghezu's told him that this female is his mother."

He said nothing.

"He's told him you raped her. Used drugs on her so she became pregnant with him."

The accusation stung him into replying. "Ghezu can't know that! As Vartra's my witness, I never used drugs on her!"

She raised an eye ridge at him. "Doesn't he? Or has he made it up, like the drugs? What did you do to her, Tallinu? You never told me."

"That's none of your business, Rhuna," he snapped. "You won't goad me into telling you. It's between her and me, no one else!"

She sighed. "It's time you told him he's your son, Tallinu. Ghezu's meddling has made him hate you more, especially now he knows you didn't trust him enough to tell him that. He could be capable of trying to kill you in the belief you dishonored his mother and him. If you tell him now, it might repair the damage."

"Dammit, Rhuna, I had no choice over Khemu, you know that!" he said angrily. "I couldn't get near her after that night, her family made sure of that! The first I knew she was still alive was when I found Dzaka at the gates of Stronghold! As for telling him, I didn't dare. It was bad enough Ghezu knew I was his foster-father, I didn't dare let him know he was my real son! It was the only thing I could do to protect him from Ghezu. He's guessing, he doesn't know the truth. If he did, he'd kill Dzaka himself, you know it."

She nodded. "Like as not, now he would. His mind is diseased, Tallinu. He's not sane."

"There's been a reckoning building between me and him for years, Noni," said Kaid grimly. "By telling Dzaka those lies, he's just signed his own death contract."

"In Vartra's name, leave it till after the Fire Margins, Tallinu. Too much depends on you taking them safely there. You have to go there before you see to Ghezu!"

"I'll decide what needs to be done first, Noni," he said. "Ghezu was right in that I did dishonor Dzaka's mother, but through no fault of my own. I need to do what I can to right it with Khemu before she dies. If Ghezu's expecting me in Rhijudu, then I won't keep him waiting."

"No, Tallinu! You mustn't go! The God needs you to guide them to Him!"

He saw real panic on her face and in her voice. "What's wrong, Noni?" he asked. "Did your plans go wrong this time? But you know me so well." His voice was a low, sarcastic purr. "You should have known I wouldn't go before Vartra with that stain on my honor given a chance to clear it. If it's all meant to be, then you know I'm doing what I should."

He cut the connection and sat there trying to gather his thoughts. Khemu. Small and slim, her pelt and hair a soft silver gray. How could someone so alive be dying? He remembered when they'd first met.

The Brotherhood always used one particular tavern in the village. Khemu, from the Arrazo Telepath Clan, was one of a small group of females that found the Brothers' company exciting. She was often to be seen there, chatting to the young males who had to leave to visit the village. He and Ghezu had been part of that group. She'd played them all off against each other, but particularly him and Ghezu—until the night she'd asked him to walk her home.

Unbidden, the memory of the long-gone Rezac and his Leska came to mind. His Khemu hadn't been like her, with hair the color of the sun. No, she was like the soft moonlight, but she'd burned him just as surely as Rezac had been burned by his Leska.

A thumping on the door brought him back to the present and he leaned forward to open it.

"Everything all right, Kaid?" asked Meral.

"Yes, fine," he said, getting to his feet and exiting the craft.

"They've just found some fragments of stone that might be pieces of weapons," Meral said as he followed him back to where they were still digging. "It looks like this was a shrine to Vartra after all."

"I rather thought it might be," Kaid murmured.

Kaid returned to his room after third meal. Propped up by pillows, he sat on his bed chewing a stim-twig and thinking. There was no reason now to keep Dzaka's parentage secret from him. Ghezu might have thought he was telling him a lie, but inadvertently he'd given him the truth. There was still an element of danger for his son should Ghezu discover his mistake, but at least now he was at his peak, while Ghezu was getting older, his mind eating itself up from within with his need for revenge.

He'd tried to trust Dzaka and when the need for him to show some trust in return came up, he said nothing. It might be that he didn't want to face the truth because of the anger that lay between them. Ghezu had used that anger and turned it to hate. Perhaps in treating Dzaka the same as he would any of the people under his command, he'd forgotten the one important factor—he wasn't the same: he was his son, a fact he'd had to suppress all through Dzaka's childhood so that Ghezu would never guess the real link between the foundling and himself.

He'd checked with Ni'Zulhu on Dzaka's movements today and been told that he'd taken an aircar and left the estate, heading toward Valsgarth, or beyond. Noni had said she'd received a second visitor, one who was troubled. Maybe that had been Dzaka trying to have Ghezu's news confirmed. Noni knew everyone and everything about Stronghold, but she couldn't have told Dzaka much because she didn't know what had happened between him and Khemu—until now. She'd have said to ask him.

Swinging his feet over the edge of the bed, he sat up and called Rulla on his wrist com.

"Rulla, Kaid here. Where's Dzaka?"

"On surveillance at the gatehouse. Anything wrong?"

"No. I need to talk to him. Can you have someone up there to relieve him in fifteen minutes' time?"

"No problem."

"Don't tell him I'm on my way."

"What's he been up to now, Kaid?" said Rulla. "Are you sure I can't help?"

"Nothing's wrong. I need to speak to him on a personal matter."

"I'll see to it now. Rulla out."

Fifteen minutes later, Dzaka came outside. As he stood in front of him, Kaid could see and feel the resentment in every line of his body.

"They told me I'd been relieved of duty and that you wanted to see me."

Kaid gestured for him to start walking. They moved away from the gatehouse, heading toward the Valsgarth estate where Dzaka was living now.

"I've only asked for a temporary relief for you," said Kaid. "Noni called me this afternoon. What she said made me realize we needed to talk. You saw Ghezu today?"

"He summoned me to Stronghold. I'm still one of the Brotherhood, even if the rest of you aren't," he said, his tone sharp and bitter. "I wondered how long it would take you to come and see me. Father." He said the word as an insult.

Kaid winced instinctively, ears flicking.

"Funny how you can talk about trust so easily yet show none yourself," Dzaka continued. "Why didn't you tell me? Have you been so ashamed of me in these past thirty years that you could never acknowledge me as your son?"

"Dzaka, you don't . . ."

"Don't tell me any more of your lies! How you must have hated me all these years. There I was, an unwanted cub, a reminder of the fact that the only way you could have my mother was to drug her!"

Kaid reached out and grabbed Dzaka by the arm, pulling him to a halt. The younger male turned on him with a snarl of rage but he held on.

"Dammit, Dzaka! It wasn't like that. Ghezu's lying to you! He's using you against me again. Can't you see that?"

"Let go of me," said Dzaka, his voice suddenly cold as his eyes began to narrow.

Kaid stared at him for a moment then released him. "Ghezu's lying, Dzaka. He doesn't know you're my son. He's only guessing."

"Am I your son?"

"Yes, you are."

"Then he's not lying."

"He's only guessing, Dzaka. He doesn't know."

Dzaka's ears flicked in a negative. "You're the one lying. You drugged my mother, then raped her, and I'm the proof of it. Why else would she disown and abandon me?"

"I didn't drug her and I didn't rape her, Dzaka," he said, trying to keep his voice calm and even. He could see by the rapid, jerky movements of Dzaka's ears and tail that he was only just controlling his rage. "I told you, Ghezu's lying."

"You're the liar, Kaid! No female willingly has a cub outside a three-year contract, we both know that, just as we know the drug you used neutralized her ability to choose whether or not she conceived! You used her, paired with her once and never saw her again. You treated her like a common qwene!"

"It wasn't like that, Dzaka. Did Ghezu tell you he wanted her, too? All this is because of his jealousy. Khemu approached *me* that night. Ghezu knows because he heard her. I didn't need to drug her."

"Don't lie!" Dzaka snarled, canines showing starkly in the moonlight as he leaned forward, ready to attack. "There was no way she'd have agreed to have your cub the first time you paired!"

Kaid had to force his ears from instinctively flattening outward ready for a Challenge. The slightest move now could tip them into a fight to the death, and that was the last thing he wanted.

"What happened when we paired was an accident. Neither of us intended for her to conceive," he said.

"An accident?" Dzaka said scornfully. "Accidents like that don't happen, *Father!* You'll have to think up a more convincing lie than that!"

"It's no lie. Something . . . happened . . . between us, and she left," he said. "I followed her but she wouldn't see me. I tried several times, but each time her family had me thrown off the estate until I was ordered by Father Jyarti not to go back. Then we heard she'd been killed in an accident."

"Can you blame them? You'd dishonored their daughter— my mother! It might not have mattered that much down here in the lowlands, but in the mountains?"

"She told no one, Dzaka. Her family didn't know I was the father. That's why I *know* Ghezu is lying! What happened was between Khemu and me, and it still is. You have no right to interfere."

"*I* have no right to interfere?" he said, taking a step toward Kaid, his claws flicking out of their sheaths. "I'm her son!"

"You're also my son," said Kaid, holding his ground. "Use your head, Dzaka! Why did Khemu carry you full term if she didn't want you? She could have aborted, but she didn't." He felt the first trace of doubt enter Dzaka's mind.

"Yes, you were left at the gates of Stronghold, but when Garras and I found you, you'd not been there long. I knew you were my son the moment I held you. Why did I ask to foster you if I hated you? Think carefully, Dzaka. Who could have told Ghezu about your birth? What has he to gain from telling you all this?"

"Noni knew!"

"Noni knew nothing till today! When you told her what Ghezu said, then she worked it out!"

"Everyone is conveniently lying but you, is that what you want me to believe?" he demanded, straightening up. "Well, I don't believe you! You've already destroyed her life completely, so stay away from her and at least let her die in peace! Her family may have been too afraid of you and Stronghold to take revenge for her, but I'm not, and, by Vartra, *Father,* you'll pay for what you did to her!"

He lunged forward with such speed that Kaid was only just able to deflect some of the force of the blow, then Dzaka was gone.

As he hit the ground, pain exploded along his forearm. Then Garras was kneeling over him, swearing as he pressed hard above the wound, trying to stem the bleeding.

"I should have shot the tree-climbing little bastard when I had the chance," Garras muttered.

"You followed me," said Kaid, trying to concentrate on what his friend was doing as the world wheeled crazily around him.

"No. I sensed something was up. Now shut up, you need a medic." He raised his head toward the gatehouse and bellowed for a guard.

All those on duty shot out of the door and stood looking at them, too stunned to come forward.

"Get me a medikit now! Call Physician Reynolds at the house. Tell him I'm bringing Kaid in and that he's losing blood fast! Then get me a two-person hopper!" He turned his attention back to Kaid.

"You're not that bad," he said, moving so the injured arm was out of Kaid's line of sight. "But it'll do them good to jump!"

"Huh," said Kaid, trying to lift his head to look at his arm. "How long were you there?"

"Long enough. I had you covered. I got a shot off at him but it missed."

"You heard?" He could hear his voice becoming fainter and Garras seemed to be farther away.

"I heard," he said as the guard came running over with the

medikit. "Large pressure bandage," he snapped, holding out his hand for it.

The guard pulled the sterile wrapper off and handed it to him.

The voices took on a faraway quality and he was vaguely aware of Garras ordering the guard to contact Ni'Zulhu and mount a search for Dzaka, saying he was to be brought in alive.

When he came round he was in his own bed with Vanna checking the canula in his arm.

"How do you feel?" she asked, seeing he was awake.

"Tired," he said, closing his eyes again.

"Good. You need to rest. You lost quite a lot of blood, you know. Garras told me it was Dzaka." She hesitated a moment. "I take it you'd told him he was your son."

"Is there anyone who doesn't know?" he asked dryly.

"Not many," she said. "Dzaka's voice was a little too loud a couple of times. They don't know the details, though."

"Thank Vartra for that," he muttered. "Have they found him?"

"Not yet. It's only a matter of time, though. Why did he try to kill you?"

Kaid opened his eyes again, a slight smile on his face. "He wasn't trying to kill me, Vanna. He lashed out in anger, that's all."

"That's all? He damned near did kill you, though. If Garras hadn't been there . . ."

He reached out with his good arm, placing his hand over hers and squeezing it gently. "But he was there, Vanna. That's what counts. Now tell me what the damage is. How long before it's healed?"

"A good month, maybe two," she said. "I had to use a plasmagraft. He'd sliced you down to the bone, Kaid."

"It happens," he said, closing his eyes again.

"I'll let you sleep," she said, gently removing her hand. "Kusac and Carrie both wanted to see you but I've told them to wait till the morning."

"Whatever you say, Vanna," he murmured.

He waited till she'd gone, then cautiously sat up. The room swam for a few seconds then righted itself. He swung his legs over the bed and attempted to stand. Wobbly, but he could do it. Reaching out, he lifted the plasma infusion unit and carrying it in his good hand, he carefully made his way over to his desk. Sitting down, he put the unit on the desk and opened the bottom drawer.

Inside it he kept his own emergency medical kit. Taking the sealed tube out, he unscrewed it, wincing as the action put some strain on his newly stapled wound. He checked the contents and took out the small container of tablets. Enough for now, he thought as he took a couple of the powerful stimulants. He sorted through the contents, checking the items he needed most. He had a couple of fresh dressings, a dozen analgesic tablets, sealant and antibiotic spray, and a dozen Fastheal tablets. He took two of the latter and closed the tube. He needed more medical supplies but he could pick them up at the Valsgarth estate's new medical unit. A handheld ultrasound unit, a hypoderm, two dozen ampules of analgesic, the same of stimulant, and some more Fastheal should do it. Maybe another couple of dressings to be on the safe side.

Shutting the drawer, he picked up the plasma unit and staggered over to the cupboard, opening it and taking out his grey Brotherhood jacket. With some difficulty, he managed to pull it on. He hesitated over the plasma unit, then stuffed it into the most convenient pocket. Might as well let it finish the infusion. His medikit tube he slipped into another pocket. Pulling the ends of the belt together, he managed to fasten it then he reached back into the unit to pull out his backpack.

A wave of dizziness hit him and he had to sit down for a minute or two before he could open it. It was as he'd left it, with everything in it he might need for living rough. Getting up, he slung it over his shoulder and padded slowly to the window, thanking Vartra that his room was on the ground level. Before he left, he retrieved a slim volume from his secret cache. Stuffing it into an envelope, he addressed it to Carrie, leaving it on his desk.

Chapter 10

How he made it to the bay at the rear of the estate, Kaid never knew. The boat was still tethered at the side of the wooden jetty. A week or two later and it would have been stored for the winter. Untying the painter, he pulled the cover back enough to crawl under, and let the boat drift. The tide was going out and he knew it would carry him toward the fishing town of Raul, out of the range of Ni'Zulhu's scanners.

It took an hour or two, but he wasn't in a rush and the pain level in his arm was just enough to ensure he couldn't drop off to sleep. By the time he reached the middle of Nazule Bay, he was able to push the cover back completely and turn the power on. Within fifteen minutes he was docking at Raul.

He disconnected the infusion unit but left the canula in place. He could reconnect it later when he'd found somewhere to stop. Pulling a long coat from his backpack, he eased himself painfully into it before leaving the boat and entering the small town. Stopping at a public comm, he called one of Nazule's hire companies, asking them to bring out one of their two-person sports aircars.

The local tavern was warm and as he waited, he nursed a bowl of fish stew. He knew he needed to eat to build up his fast diminishing reserves of energy, but though he managed to force down about half of it, the rest was beyond him.

Finally the door opened and he saw the hire company agent. Standing, he beckoned him over.

"Vehicle for Rhyjidi?" the agent asked.

Kaid nodded and followed him out.

"You've hired from us before, haven't you?" the agent said. Without waiting for a reply, he handed Kaid a rigid card. "Here's the authorization card. Same as usual. Put your credit card in the slot, then that one, and you're away." He flicked an ear briefly at him, then sprinted over to the other aircar where his colleague waited.

Kaid settled himself in the vehicle, stowing his backpack on the seat beside him before taking off. The pain and the side effects of the Fastheal had reached a point where he knew he'd have to find a secure place to stop for a couple of days. His best bet was to head for the Taykui forest, some half an hour's flight from Raul.

As he came down in the small clearing, he realized his judgment was virtually shot to hell. The vertical landing was fine, but the craft bumped and jolted over the uneven ground before he brought it to a stop scarcely a meter from a patch of thorn bushes. He released the canopy and hauling himself one-handedly to his feet, looked around. At least he was under cover from any vehicles flying overhead. The area seemed quiet and he couldn't sense any Sholan presences. Trusting his instincts, he sat down and sealed the craft again, activating the opaque privacy shield.

Pushing the seat back on its tracks, he swiveled it round to face the rear. The model he'd requested was usually used by hunters and contained a living area large enough to sleep its two occupants, a basic toilet facility, and a food and drink dispenser. Nothing fancy, but adequate for his needs.

When he stood up in the living area, his head almost touched the roof, but there was enough room for him to shuck off his coat and toss it in a corner out of the way. Sitting down again, he pulled his case forward, setting it on his lap. From it he took out the hypoderm and the pack of assorted ampules he'd acquired from Vanna's pharmacy.

His hands shook as he tried to load one of the analgesics. He was burning up and he knew it. Fastheal always had that effect on him but with the febrifuge action of the analgesics, he could weather out the fever. Placing the hypoderm just above the bandage on his left arm, he pressed the trigger. The relief was almost instantaneous and he sank back in the seat, exhausted.

Pain gets you that way, he thought. *You never know just how bad it has been till it's gone.*

He put the empty ampule in his pack and took out a second one, this time an antibiotic. The last thing he needed was an infected wound. He rearranged the ampules in the order he wished to take them for the next two days, then laid the kit near at hand.

Leaning forward, he studied the dispenser. He didn't want anything, but he needed to keep replenishing his energy levels for the Fastheal to work without killing him. It was a dangerous drug, used only sparingly in emergencies, and he was using it at the maximum dose. He needed to be fit again as soon as possible. He had to reach Khemu before she died.

"Vartra be praised!" he muttered to himself. It had a protein drink on the menu.

While that was being dispensed, he staggered to his feet and pulled the rear locker door open. A couple of sleeping bags and pillows fell out. Taking one set, he pushed the other back in and returned to his chair, spreading the opened bag over it.

Retrieving the mug, he put it on the floor and took the infusion unit out. He removed the piece of bandage he'd wrapped over the canula and reattached himself to it. Replacing the unit in his pocket, he sealed the bag, then picked up the mug.

The warm drink along with the drugs began to make him feel drowsy. Finishing it, he set the mug down and fully reclined the seat, passing his hand over the light sensor switch on his chair arm.

At daybreak, his wrist comm roused him. He downed another protein drink, then took another dose of analgesics and the Fastheal.

He hovered in the fever dreams, surfacing only long enough to take the protein drinks and further doses of his drugs, at the regular and insistent urging of his wrist comm before he lapsed into semiconsciousness again.

The fever images that chased around inside his mind were of fire and flood, people fleeing in terror; of Rezac and his new Leska; of a fiery path leading to a gateway through pillars of flame; and finally of Khemu and of Carrie.

* * *

Morning came very early that day as Vanna alerted the household to Kaid's disappearance during the night. A call to the gatehouse revealed nothing. No sign of anyone leaving the estate had been noticed after Dzaka's exit.

The parcel Kaid had left for Carrie was delivered and turned out to be an account of the various dreams and visions he had experienced over the last few months.

Later that morning the missing items from the medical unit's dispensary were reported to Vanna and Jack.

"He's gone after Dzaka," said Vanna when they met in the main lounge before second meal.

"No," said Garras. "He's not gone after Dzaka. I've a feeling he knows where he is, but that's not what he's concerned about."

"Then what?" asked Carrie. "What could have been so important as to make him leave here in the state he was in?"

"It's my bet they've both gone to the same place," said Kusac thoughtfully. "Dzaka believes Kaid was lying so he doesn't trust him, but Kaïd may just have shaken his belief in what Ghezu told him enough to not entirely trust him either. Who's left that would know what really happened between Kaid and his mother?"

"Noni?" said Garras.

"No," said Carrie, sitting up as she followed Kusac's line of thought. "His mother. They've both gone to find her!"

"Possible," said Garras with a nod.

"He'll be lucky if he doesn't kill himself!" said Vanna. "The drugs he took from the pharmacy are very powerful. If he's keeping himself going on a cocktail of stimulants, Fastheal and analgesics, he's likely to burn himself out in hours not days!"

"He's paramedic-trained, Vanna. He knows his own metabolism, he won't overdo the drugs. It's not as if he didn't know what he was doing," said Garras calmly.

"Considering he's your friend, you seem very unconcerned," said Vanna. "The wound he got from Dzaka last night was serious. Not only did he lose a lot of blood, but Jack had to call me in to use a plasmagraft. There's still the chance of infection."

"He did take the infusion unit with him," said Garras.

Vanna merely grunted in reply.

"Where does this Khemu live?" asked Konis.

"According to her Clan, she died thirty years ago," said Garras. "She was the oldest daughter of the Arrazo Telepath Clan. I doubt they'd be willing to help us prove she's alive and that they lied about her death all those years ago. They're a proud lot, the Arrazos."

"Khemu Arrazo, you say?" said Konis, scratching his chin thoughtfully. "That was before I took over as Clan Lord. Still, she should be in our records somewhere. Technically dead, is she? Hmm. I'll check it out. What do you plan to do now? Just how dangerous is Dzaka?"

"That depends," said Garras. "I suggest we call off the search for him. I'm pretty sure he's headed for Stronghold or Dzahai village to check out what Kaid said. We need to contact Noni ourselves. Ghezu or Dzaka might have told her where Khemu's supposedly living now, so at least we'll know where they're headed."

"If we assume she is alive and Ghezu's told Dzaka where she is, what are the chances of him telling us?" asked Kusac.

"Absolutely none," said Garras. "He's been setting Dzaka against Kaid since he landed on Shola a couple of months ago, and before that on the *Khalossa*."

"How, and why?" exclaimed Carrie.

"By getting him to watch Kaid and report his movements back to Stronghold. As to why, well, Kaid and Ghezu fell out for a couple of months after Khemu disappeared. Then it seemed to blow over until the time came to choose a new Warrior Leader. From what I was told, what had seemed to be friendly rivalry got out of hand. I'd had to leave by then as my older brother had died and the Clan needed me. Personally I believe that Ghezu had set Kaid up by using Dzaka. It's quite possible that Khemu isn't where he's told them."

"Then is Lijou likely to know where she is? Would Ghezu have told him? Or failing that, would he be willing to find out for us?" asked Kusac.

"I've no idea," said Garras. "Kaid kept a lot to himself, so I don't know much about the state of affairs between Lijou and Ghezu, and I haven't had any dealings with them myself."

"I can help there," said Konis. "Lijou and I spoke about Ghezu. He's not happy about his state of mind at all. He feels he's walking a thin line between sanity and madness and, most of the time, madness wins. I need to go to Stronghold to see him about coordinating the final stages of the evacuation of the Laasoi Guildhouse. I'll call on him today and see what I can find out."

"Thank you, Father," said Kusac. "That would be an enormous help." He turned back to look at Garras. "So what do we do about Dzaka?"

"We can have someone near Stronghold, and Noni's keeping an eye out for him. If he turns up, they would follow him when he leaves, hopefully leading us to Khemu and Kaid."

"Shouldn't we be watching for Kaid, too?" asked Carrie.

"No point. He'll probably have traveled as far as he could last night and will be holed up somewhere till he's fit to go on. Then when he gets near where she lives, he'll hide out and watch her till he knows her movements and can approach her safely. That also allows him the time and rest he needs to finish healing," said Garras.

"Why does he want to see her again after all these years?" asked Vanna. "He's never struck me as being interested in any females, let alone carrying an undying love for one from his past. It isn't even as if she wants to see him or she'd have been in touch herself long before now."

Garras shrugged. "That's his business, Vanna, not ours. He's never spoken to me about Khemu."

"What was Khemu like?" asked Carrie.

Garras turned to look at her, an amused smile on his face. "Gods, it was years ago, Carrie! She wasn't my type so I didn't really mix with her and the others. From what I remember, she was intelligent, proud as only one of her kind could be . . ."

"Her kind?" Carrie interrupted.

"Mountain Telepaths. Up in the mountains, few of the Arrazo telepaths stayed on at the estate. Most of them preferred to live in the towns at one of the guildhouses. Those that did stay at home were very much in demand. They could pick and choose what they wanted to do. Anyway, Khemu used to tease all the males that formed her little crowd. She was a beauty," he admitted, with a sidelong glance at Vanna. "She had bright blue eyes and silver gray hair with a pelt to match. She was small, though, not much bigger than you, Carrie. I told Kaid he was a fool, but he insisted there was more to her than she let the world see. Maybe he was right. Who knows?"

"For someone who wasn't your type, you've a pretty detailed memory of her," said Vanna.

"I didn't say I didn't notice her, I said she wasn't my type," he replied. "She strung them all along, teased them too much. If she ever took anyone other than Kaid as a lover or companion, none of us knew of it."

"Well," said Carrie, getting up, "I'd like to know how Dzaka got left outside Stronghold. How could any mother just abandon her cub?" She put her hand protectively over her belly.

"Who knows?" said Garras. "Maybe she took him when she left, or maybe her family abandoned him after she died. We certainly won't find out from the Arrazos."

"We'll see about that," said Konis, his voice grim as he got to his feet. "Once I've checked out the records, I may well be starting an investigation into the circumstances surrounding Khemu Arrazo's disappearance."

"Mother sends that the meal's ready," said Kusac as he joined Carrie and his father at the door through to the dining room.

Second meal over, Konis had headed out to Stronghold with Garras.

"Dammit! I warned him, Konis!" said Lijou, pushing himself up from his chair and pacing over to the large window overlooking the Kysubi plains. "I did what I could, believe me!" He turned back to look at Konis. "Ghezu's invented this . . ." he waved his arms expressively, "tale of who Dzaka's parents were, and told him to guard the female, Khemu, as Kaid is likely to kill her!"

"Trouble is, Lijou, it isn't a tale," said Konis. "Though he doesn't know it, Ghezu told him part of the truth."

Lijou's ears flicked backward then righted themselves. "What?"

"Kaid and Khemu are his parents," repeated Konis. "We don't know for sure she's still alive."

"Oh, Blessed Vartra," whispered Lijou, his ears staying back this time as he returned to his chair. "He's set him to kill his father or be killed by him! We have to stop this from happening, Konis," he said, leaning forward.

"That's why I'm here. Have you any idea where this Khemu Arrazo lives now?"

"Yes, yes I do. According to what Ghezu told me, she *is* alive, though I didn't tell Kaid where she is because I didn't want him to go after her. He has to go with your son and his Leska to the Fire Margins! If he's killed . . ." He couldn't finish, so awful to him was the specter of them not going. "He's their best chance for survival!"

"Where, Lijou? Tell me where she is," said Konis quietly.

"She's at Rhijudu, almost at the heart of this Fyak's territory," he said. "They couldn't be going into a more dangerous area."

Konis glanced over at Garras. "What's the latest news from there?" he asked.

"Bad," said Lijou, running a hand through his hair in desperation. "The Sonashi Tribe have been virtually wiped out according to the few survivors that made it to the Laasoi Guildhouse. Fyak sent his warriors in to cleanse the village of those not willing to follow him. They say that Rhijudu has been taken by Fyak. It's policed by his warriors and the families split up into pairs who look to one of Fyak's Faithful to guide them materially and spiritually. The younglings and cubs live in single sex houses until Fyak chooses a life-mate for them, then they move into one of the vacant houses. He's breaking down all the ties of the tribes and building his own army of fanatics who worship this god of his, Kezule."

"Have you a map of the area?" asked Garras.

"No, but I can get one," said Lijou.

"Can you get it without alerting Ghezu?" asked Konis.

"Yes. He's been away from Stronghold for the last two days. I don't know where he's gone. I've just sent to Brother Nyash to bring us a map of the region," said Lijou.

"While we're waiting, I think you should tell us everything you know about Ghezu that might help us," said Konis, signing to Garras to bring some c'shar over for the Brotherhood's co-Guild Master.

"He's become obsessed with revenge against Kaid for all manner of imagined wrongs," said Lijou, his voice noticeably shaken. "His mind's become polluted by it. All he thinks of is Kaid's death, and he wants Dzaka to do it because, he says, he's the only one of the Brotherhood who could best him."

"He probably could," said Garras, "but only if Kaid holds back because Dzaka's his son. What reason did he give for this hatred of Kaid?"

Lijou looked briefly up at him before continuing. "He said at first it was because of Khemu, but it wasn't just that, it involved the Leadership contest. My predecessor told me he forced Kaid to withdraw from the final test because of something he did to Dzaka. Ghezu's conscience has troubled him since then, which is why when Kaid kept disobeying him and going his own way, he reached a compromise with him."

Again Lijou looked up at Garras, then back to Konis. "I don't know the details, but Kaid was dismissed from the Brotherhood—one of the few times that has ever happened—on the condition Dzaka remained. As you know, Kaid accepted and left. I don't think he had any option. Then, when we heard about your son and his Link to the Human, Carrie, we needed someone on the *Khalossa* to assess them."

Lijou looked down at his hands as he stopped speaking.

"Esken approached you and asked you to assess them, didn't he?" said Garras, leaning toward the Head Priest.

Lijou nodded slowly, unable to look at Konis. "He wanted them assessed, and if they were dangerous or could not be controlled by his Guild, we were to terminate them," he said quietly.

Konis' ears flicked to the side and he began to growl softly. "Go on," he said.

"It's been one of the traditional functions of the Brotherhood throughout known time, Konis," said Lijou. "How do you think the rogue talents are contained? Those who can create fire at will and whose minds have become unstable at the magnitude of their ability? Who would protect the people of Shola from them if not us?" He looked Konis straight in the eye. "When we can, we rescue those we can train. Here, in Stronghold, are about ten telepaths whom Esken would have had killed, but because of our training methods, we've been able to teach them to control their Talents. That's why we want people like your son and Carrie. We've always been the last refuge for those the Telepath Guild either can't control or are afraid of."

"Clan Lord," said Garras from the far side of the room. "Before Kaid got the message from Ghezu and Lijou, or from your wife to protect them and see them safe home, I had contacted Kaid and asked him to protect them for me. Yes, Kaid would have terminated them if they had been uncontrollable and bent on a course of conquest, but I knew them. I knew they were incapable of that, and I knew that they were good people. That's why I took the risk of calling in an old debt that Kaid owed me, and asking him to protect their lives with his."

"All these years, under my very nose, this has been happening, and I knew nothing," said Konis softly. "Nothing! No one Guild Leader should have the power of life or death over anyone, even if they are rogue telepaths with unstable Talents!"

"It wasn't Esken's word alone, Clan Lord," said Garras, returning with the c'shar. "Don't forget the influence of the Brotherhood. They were the final arbiters. If they could save a telepath, they did. I agree with you, though. Esken and his predecessors have had far too much power and they've misused it. It's time for drastic change, once the threat of Fyak is dealt with. However, this doesn't explain Ghezu's hatred of Kaid."

"It was I who insisted we use Kaid, because I had a feeling that one of the lesser operatives might terminate them out of hand," said Lijou. "Ghezu was against it, but he knew as well as I that Kaid was still the best, even after ten years outside the Brotherhood. He didn't trust Kaid, so he set Dzaka to watch him. At first it was nothing much, then when Kaid and your son had returned to Shola, he recalled Dzaka. Then he began to get more paranoid about Kaid, even though he was no longer working for the Brotherhood."

He stopped for a moment to accept the mug that Garras held out to him. "It came to a head when Kusac asked for the alliance with us and wanted the people he and Kaid chose released from their Brotherhood oaths. Ghezu saw this as the return of the days leading up to the Leadership contest when Kaid was the popular choice, not him. He felt everywhere he turned Kaid was Challenging him, and on his territory. There was no reasoning with him, and from then on, he's become more determined to have Kaid killed—by Dzaka, as an ultimate revenge."

"I wonder what Ghezu's up to," said Garras thoughtfully. "If I remember him of old, he won't be relying only on Dzaka to kill Kaid, he'll have an alternative plan."

A knock on the door interrupted them and Brother Nyash entered with the map. As soon as he'd left, Garras spread it out over the low table between them.

"Rhijudu is on the western side of the desert, in the foothills, and the Sonashi tribal land is to the north, just the other side of the mountains from the Laasoi Guildhouse. What other villages has he taken?"

Lijou leaned forward. "As far as I know, he's taken the Songoh oasis which lies here, between Rhijudu and the Sonashi, and the Lhafsa oasis in the south. The Khoesh Tribe is still untouched, as is the Kubi'h Oasis. The Ghomig nomads settlement just west of the Rozoa Mountains is where it all started, and the Kidoah nomads have joined them."

Garras nodded. "That leaves only the Shyazi nomads, the Kubi'h oasis and the Khoesh Tribe free. Fyak is gradually moving east and north. The Laasoi Guildhouse is tantalizingly near, isn't it?" he said, looking up at Konis. "Fyak may hate telepaths and be killing them, but if he had one or two terrified ones who would do anything he wished just to stay sane, what then?"

"If they had a powerful enough telepath, or a Leska pair, they could listen in just about anywhere on this continent," said Konis. "And if I were Fyak, that's just what I'd do, then head over the Nyacko Pass to take the fertile plains of Nyacko, Lyarto, and finally Kysubi."

"And wouldn't you manage it a lot more easily if you weren't having to defend yourself from the Brotherhood up in the Dzahai Mountains which overlook the Kysubi plains?" said Garras softly.

"Surely he wouldn't be mad enough to . . ." began Lijou.

"Clan Lord," interrupted Garras, "can you reach the Laasoi Guildhouse mentally from here?"

"Of course, but why?"

"Ghezu's been gone two days. Tactically, once Fyak's warriors have consolidated their win over the Sonashi, then they can use it as a base to attack the Laasoi Guildhouse. What if Ghezu's offering a noninvolvement in the taking of Laasoi if Fyak will have Khemu watched and Kaid, perhaps even Dzaka, too, taken captive if they show up? It's my bet he may even now be advising them. Contact the guildhouse, see what's happening."

Konis sat back in his chair and closed his eyes. They could see him slowing his breathing, preparing himself for mentally reaching out to Mentor Nishou.

Abruptly he jerked upright, his eyes flying open and his ears swiveling forward. "Get Governor Nesul on the comm instantly! Laasoi is indeed under attack!"

Garras was at Lijou's desk before he'd finished speaking.

"The Governor has ordered me to call the Brotherhood out immediately and send them to Laasoi Guildhouse," Lijou said, looking across his desk at them. "Since Master Ghezu isn't present, I am their Commander-in-Chief for the duration of this emergency."

He returned his attention to the comm, punching in a code. Almost immediately, a klaxon sounded throughout the building. As it blared out its summons, he and Konis were aware of the rush of anticipation as the Brothers dropped what they were doing and headed for their designated craft.

The door burst open as two figures hurried in, one of them coming to an abrupt stop as he saw Konis.

Konis' eye ridges disappeared briefly as he looked at the young male. "Brother Vriuzu," he said, inclining his head.

The Brother bowed his head briefly. "Clan Lord," he said, then turned to Lijou.

"Brother Rhyaz," said Lijou, standing up as the klaxon wailed its last note. "We have our orders from Governor Nesul. The Laasoi Guildhouse has been attacked by the renegade priest, Fyak. I'm appointing you the Commander-in-the-Field. We have no further information at present so my orders are simple. Take the Brothers there and deal with the situation. Brother Vriuzu will accompany you as our contact. The Warrior Guild will join you at Laasoi. The home fleet troops from the *Rhynara* are being recalled. Some will be deployed to Laasoi, the bulk to the Nyacko Pass. You will liaise with your counterpart from the Forces when they arrive. Dismissed."

Rhyaz crossed his forearms over his chest, inclining his head, then turned and left at a run, followed by Vriuzu.

A little unsteadily, Lijou sat down again.

"Rhyaz is a good choice," said Garras from his seat by the table.

"He's our best tactician, and no friend to Ghezu," said Lijou before looking over at Konis. "Vriuzu was recruited three years ago. Esken ordered he be terminated because he couldn't control his ability to broadcast his thoughts. His was a wild Talent, a gift that came late to him. Esken couldn't stabilize him long enough to have him taught the control he needed."

"I remember," said Konis. "His accident seemed a little convenient at the time. It looks as if your recruitment scheme worked."

"It did. In fact it paid off very nicely for us," said Lijou, getting to his feet and joining him and Garras at the small table. "We used drug therapy to calm him, then our standard meditation techniques to start the training. With people like him, our approach has to be individually tailored, not like the classes at the Guild. He's now our strongest and most dependable broadcaster. He's even been able to improve his ability to receive."

"I'm glad you were successful. How do you manage to conceal people like him from recognition? Surely sending him out to Laasoi puts his life at risk?"

Lijou smiled and shook his head. "I wouldn't put him in danger, Konis. He'll be heavily disguised as a priest. All our people learn what basic Brotherhood skills they can, even me. No one will recognize him, not even his own mother, by the time they arrive at Laasoi. Will you wait here for news, or do you intend to return home?"

"I'll wait here for news, then go directly to the Palace so Nesul knows what's happened."

Lijou nodded.

"If I may make a suggestion, Master Lijou," said Garras, "I think it would be wise for you to keep one of the Brothers you trust implicitly with you at all times from now on. We don't know how Ghezu will react to your ordering the Brothers out."

Looking thoughtfully at him, once more Lijou nodded. "I think that's a wise suggestion. I have some research that needs to be done. Having an assistant to sort through the books and so on would help matters. I'd need him with me at all times, of course, so he's on hand to take notes."

Garras opened his mouth in a brief grin. "Just what I had in mind."

*   *   *

The Laasoi Guildhouse hadn't been large, it didn't need to be to accommodate the two hundred souls that had until a few days before lived there. Now it was a smoking ruin. Large holes, their edges jagged and raw, pockmarked the walls. Windows had been blown out, and the front door was nothing more than a pile of shattered timber.

Bodies lay strewn in the rubble like autumn leaves. The smell of blood, burned flesh, and the after tang of energy weapons filled the air. Medics were checking the bodies, followed by the morgue detail

Naira and Zsyzoi picked their way through the smoldering

ruins checking for any more survivors. So far they'd pulled a couple of telepaths out of a basement storage area. They'd been in shock and had been taken to the medics, who'd dosed them with suppressants and shipped them immediately out to the Valsgarth Guild for specialized treatment.

The Warriors had arrived some half an hour after the Brothers, but by then, the raid by Fyak's people was well and truly over. Their job was mainly to help with the mop-up operation and check for survivors.

They'd all arrived too late. The Brothers had exchanged some sporadic fire with Fyak's people, but that had been merely a rearguard action, the bulk of them having moved out before they'd arrived.

Their sweep of the western side of the guildhouse completed, Naira and Zsyzoi headed back to the Forces transporter that was HQ and reported in to the officer on duty.

A camp had been set up, and when they'd been debriefed, they reported there to be allocated a sleeping area before standing down from duty. The nearby mess tent drew their attention, and having collected a mug of c'shar and a sweet pastry snack, they joined a table of mixed Brothers and Warriors.

"Any news on what's happening now?" asked Naira, climbing over the bench seat to sit down.

"We're staying here, that's what," said one of the Brothers from the far end of the table. "Setting up a permanent garrison. We're to keep the Tribesmen contained in the desert."

"Contained?" demanded Zsyzoi. "After this massacre? We should be gunning down every last one of them!"

"And start a civil war?" drawled the male next to her. "Besides, we haven't the numbers to go hunting them in their own lairs. Not here, now."

Zsyzoi muttered angrily to herself as she took a large bite out of her pastry.

"Heard the Forces troopers say most of their company have been sent to the Nyacko Pass," said Naira. "They must be expecting them to head out that way, too."

"If they want to leave the desert, that's the way to go," said his neighbor. "I don't think they'll go for it just now. As I hear it, this Fyak doesn't control the desert yet."

"Why attack here, then? It isn't a tactical point, it's not good farming land, so why bother?"

"Fyak's out to destroy telepaths," said Zsyzoi, wiping the

back of her hand across her mouth to clear away the crumbs.
"We got called in a month or two back to pull out a new
Leska pair. Kitlings, they were, that's all. He had them
flogged almost to death."

"Nice person," the Brother at the end of the table said.

"Well, he did a good job here. Luckily, most of the telepaths
had been pulled out. Only some half a dozen were left, as
well as six Warriors and four of our people. Fyak got all but
five of them, but by Vartra, it cost them dear."

"Thirty Tribesmen," confirmed Naira's neighbor with a
nod. "And we got another ten when we arrived."

"How many telepaths were killed?" asked Naira. "We
found a couple alive."

"Three bodies that we know of."

Naira looked at Zsyzoi. "Looks like they kept one," he said.

"What would Fyak do with a telepath?" asked a Warrior
from the opposite side of the table. "If he's out to kill them,
why would he take captives?"

"Depends who's missing. If it was Rhaid, then there's only
one reason. She was one of the contenders for Clan Lord last
time around. She's a powerful telepath, almost as good as the
Aldatan Lord," Naira replied. "I know she was sent here last
week because we brought her out. She was posted here to
keep our Guild informed on the situation."

"What's she look like? I came past the morgue area," said
the female Brother opposite.

"Tall. From the Northern continent—dark pelt with eyes
to match. Wore her hair in a long braid at the back."

The female shook her head. "No one like that either in
purple or other clothing. Looks like she's been taken."

"Get over to HQ and tell them," the Brother said to Naira.
"They'll need to check it out."

Naira gulped down the remains of his c'shar and poked
Zsyzoi in the ribs. "Come on," he said.

Vriuzu was sitting in the command vehicle, listening to the
latest reports from the various groups as they completed
their sweeps of the surrounding hillsides and the northern
edge of the desert. He could cope with death and the aftermath of battle reasonably well, but not so soon after the
event. The sensitivity that allowed him such accurate and
long-range mental communication, prevented him from visiting the guildhouse for the next couple of hours. Even

though he had a personal damper, the pain of the injured was
seeping through to him and it was more than he could bear.

"Do you know this Rhaid?" asked the sub-Commander.

"Yes. I've communicated with her several times since she
arrived here last week."

"Try and see if you can locate her," said Brother Rhyaz.

Vriuzu sat back in his seat and switched off his damper.
He began his relaxation ritual and a few minutes later, he
was able to send a probing thought out in the direction of the
retreating tribesmen.

He'd located them! He frowned, wincing as he picked up
the adrenaline-high they were still on after what they considered a successful mission. Blood lust was foremost in their
minds as they urged their riding beasts to greater speed.

"Some have taken trophies," Vriuzu muttered, his voice
thick with pain and disgust. "They mutilated the dead."

The sub-Commander glanced at his aide and lifted an eye
ridge. "We didn't tell you for fear of upsetting you," he said,
keeping his voice quiet. "What of the telepath?"

"I can sense a captive," said Vriuzu, shaking himself out
of his contact with the desert folk and switching on his
damper again. Almost instantly, he began to relax. "It wasn't
pleasant," he said apologetically. "I stayed as long as I
could. The captive was radiating terror, and though the mind
had the feel of a telepath about it, I can't be sure," he said.
"I'm afraid we'll have to wait till they've done a check on
the identities of the bodies."

The sub-Commander nodded. "I think we've found our
person," he sighed. "I'll send a report to Guild Master Esken.
We'll have to hope Fyak wants a telepath because while he
needs her, Rhaid should be safe, assuming she'll cooperate."

"I imagine she'll have no choice," said Vriuzu quietly.
"Our ability to experience others' pain, never mind our
own, makes us vulnerable in any military action. What do
you plan to do next, sub-Commander?"

"Our orders are to consolidate our position and guard the
pass," he said. "We're not following them into the desert
until the situation has been properly assessed. I'm afraid we
can't mount a rescue for her. It looks like we're all here for
several weeks at least."

Vriuzu nodded. "My orders are to return to Stronghold
tonight. If you need me further, you'll have to approach

Guild Master Lijou. I have duties at Stronghold I can't neglect."

"Very well. We'll have you flown back at dusk."

"Thank you, sub-Commander."

"Poor bastard," muttered Zsyzoi as they walked back to the mess tent. "I'd rather be dead than taken by Fyak."

"Well, he's got a soft spot for us, hasn't he?" grinned Naira, showing his teeth. "Ever since we took the kitlings and their mother away from him.

* * *

Ghezu had also heard the news on the comm. He was not happy, as Zhaya knew only too well.

"I knew I should have pushed for sole control of the Guild!" he raged as he drove the aircar back to Stronghold.

"Guild Master," said Zhaya from his seat beside him. "Perhaps I should land the craft. You could then contact the Guild and see what's happening."

"I don't need to contact Stronghold to know what's happening! I know what's bloody well happening! So does all the world! Why the hell couldn't Fyak have waited? He wasn't supposed to strike till tomorrow at the earliest! I'd have been back by then."

"He must know by striking a day early that he can't depend on our help."

"He's a bloody lunatic!" said Ghezu, as he skimmed the vehicle across the tops of the trees outside Dzahai village. Slim branches whipped at the underside of the vehicle, testifying as to how small a safety margin Ghezu was allowing. "His hatred and fear of telepaths is getting out of control. He's letting that overrule his common sense!"

The comm started to beep insistently. Ghezu flicked on the auto-response, transmitting his vehicle's ID to security.

"I could swear he was one himself," said Zhaya thoughtfully. "If he can burn out the mind of a telepath, he has to be one."

"Not necessarily," Ghezu replied. "His answer is that His God gave him his powers. They don't include the ability to read minds."

He was over Stronghold now, cutting the power of the engines as he hovered preparatory to landing. The comm came to life, demanding the passwords. Ghezu replied sharply. He had no patience with anything but seeing Lijou and demanding an explanation of his actions.

Around them as always, the wind swirled, buffeting them from side to side. Almost automatically, Ghezu used the attitude jets to stabilize his position, then slowly allowed the craft to sink down to the courtyard below.

As soon as they touched down, Ghezu cut the power completely. "Park it, Chyal. The rest of you come with me. I want to see Lijou now," he said, getting up and gesturing to his personal guard.

Ghezu brushed aside the two Brothers on courtyard security, ignoring their requests for identity cards. Hurrying through the temple, he stopped barely long enough to do homage to Vartra in his haste. He pulled the curtain aside and stormed through the door behind it into the corridor beyond. Stopping at the first doorway, he slapped his hand against the palm lock. The door slid back, revealing an empty room.

With a snarl of rage, Ghezu swung round and headed farther down the corridor till he came to the stairs at the end. Taking them at a run, he quickly reached the second level and started along the corridor to Lijou's office.

Wrenching the door open, he stalked in, eyes narrowed, ears folded sideways, ready to hunt. Looking across the room, he saw Lijou at the brewing unit.

"Just who the hell do you think you are, calling out the Brothers without my permission?" he asked coldly from his position in the doorway.

Lijou turned round slowly. "A decision needed to be made, Ghezu, and since you left me no way of communicating with you, I did what had to be done."

"I, and only I, will decide what is appropriate action for the Brotherhood," he snarled, pacing slowly into the room. "The Council may have said we were jointly in charge, but no one other than me shall ever give orders to my people, Lijou! You've made a grave mistake in taking that power upon yourself, one you'll never make again!"

"On the contrary, Master Ghezu," said Konis, getting up from his seat in the corner of the room. "Master Lijou did what was right and proper in the circumstances."

"You keep out of this, Konis," snarled Ghezu. "You and

that damned cub of yours have had too much to say for too long! This is between Lijou and me."

"Even before we were a full Guild, Ghezu, sole authority resided in me in the event of the Warrior Leader being unavailable in a crisis," said Lijou calmly. "This was just such an occasion. If you had left word where you could have been contacted . . ."

Ghezu growled angrily, knowing full well why he'd been unable to be contacted.

"Governor Nesul himself requested the Brotherhood, Ghezu," said Konis. "You're the nearest unit to Laasoi. Naturally he would want your people there."

Ghezu continued to growl until Zhaya leaned forward to touch him on the arm.

As his leader spun round, he diplomatically took several steps backward. "May I suggest, Master Ghezu, that we contact our people in the field and see what the current situation is?"

Ghezu took a deep breath, his ears beginning to right themselves again. "You're right," he said. "I'm wasting my time with this convocation of toothless nest-raiders!"

Konis walked to the doorway and watched Ghezu and his guards till they reached the end of the corridor. "How long has he been in the habit of having a personal guard?" he asked, turning back into the room and looking over to Lijou.

"Some three or four weeks. As I said, Ghezu's become paranoid about Kaid and anyone who knew him. His bodyguard's made up of newer members, ones who never knew Kaid and who weren't friendly toward Dzaka. In actual fact, training them is keeping him so occupied he hasn't the time to interfere with anyone else's work. All the staff and the senior Brothers are a lot happier because of their influence."

"How unstable is he? Have you been able to touch his mind long enough to tell?"

Lijou flicked his ears in a negative. "He picks up even the lightest mental touch. His main Talent is to receive, after all. What I have felt in the past has worried me, though."

"Ghezu has another Talent," said Garras. "He can mentally affect the way you perceive him so that even the most outrageous suggestions can seem sensible when you're in his sphere of influence."

"So that's what it was," murmured Lijou.

"Have all the telepaths you trust monitor him, especially

any Guild-trained ones like Vriuzu. He can't keep his mind guarded night and day," said Konis.

"No, but the dampers he plans to have installed in Stronghold can," said Lijou, his tone grim. "I've been trying to work out why he wants them."

"That could be the proof of his paranoia that we want," said Garras.

"Esken's had some installed at the Guild because I've insisted the Warriors continue to patrol the grounds and corridors at night," said Konis. "Wanting dampers installed doesn't prove anything. However, if I were you, I wouldn't delay in appointing your research assistant. In fact, I suggest you make sure there are a couple of people that you trust around you at all times."

"Now would be a good time to acquire a lover," added Garras. "One of the Sisters, even if it's in name only."

"I'm ahead of you on that," said Lijou, mouth opening in a faint smile. "I have a Companion already."

*   *   *

Carrie hadn't been sleeping well for the last couple of nights. It was nothing either of them could put their finger on, she'd just been restless and fretful. Today, Kusac had persuaded her to return to bed after first meal and had accompanied her up to their rooms. When she finally dropped off, he rose and went back downstairs.

He found Meral waiting outside the door of Konis' office. His tail was swaying anxiously and his ears were showing a tendency to flick every now and then. Kusac raised an eye ridge questioningly at him.

"I'm to see the Clan Lord any time now," Meral said in a low voice. "He's expecting me."

"About Taizia?"

Meral nodded. "He can't overturn our contract, can he?" he asked, ears flicking even further back.

Kusac shook his head. "No, he wouldn't do that. Not now, anyway," he amended, the edges of his mouth curling slightly in a very human grin. "He might have several months ago."

They heard Konis call out for Meral to enter.

"Wish me luck," said Meral, stilling his tail and ears before reaching out for the door handle.

"Do you want me to come with you?" Kusac asked.

Meral shot him a horrified look and shook his head as he opened the door. Thoughtfully, Kusac ambled off to his mother's kitchen for a snack.

The house was run very differently now from the way it had been over a year ago when he left to join the Forces. Nowadays it was much more of a home. Before it had almost been a civic building with the coming and going of all the various officials both his parents had had to deal with. Now, by contrast, virtually no business except of the indirect kind on the comm, was conducted at home. Perhaps his disappearance had rung in the changes he'd longed for after all.

His mother was finishing her c'shar when he walked in. "Where's Carrie? Still resting?"

Ears flicking assent, he sat down beside her. "Mother, I need some advice from you."

"Hmm? What is it?" she asked, reaching out absently to flick a lock of hair off his face. Her fingers caressed his cheek before returning to lift up her mug.

"Well," he said, picking up her spoon and toying with it. "Do you remember me saying that perhaps the clans have been becoming too inbred, and that might be the reason for the fall in the birth of telepathic cubs?"

She regarded him over the top of her mug. "Yes." The word was said cautiously and drawn out.

"I know you've seen Vanna and Jack's report showing that even among the few Brothers here, there are a couple who could become genetically compatible with us mixed Leskas. Given that that's the case, and we know all the Brothers are Talented in some way, then do you think there's an argument for allowing marriages between the Brothers who have a strong Talent and telepaths? I mean dynastic marriages."

Rhyasha took a deep breath before replyng. "There's certainly an argument for trying a few such bondings for a limited time to see how productive they would be. Why, Kusac? Where's all this leading? These matters fall into your father's province as Clan Lord, not mine." She stopped, putting her mug down and looking hard at him.

He looked away, finding the spoon absorbing. "I was just wondering," he said. "I haven't seen this spoon before. Have you been getting some new cutlery?"

"Kusac." He could hear the warning tone in his mother's voice. She reached out and took hold of his chin, turning his face to hers. "Out with it, scamp," she ordered, catching his eyes with hers. "What's this all leading to?"

Kusac glanced away again. "Nothing, Mother. Just a question, that's all."

"Kusac!" she said warningly, giving his chin a pinch. "Out with it!"

He looked back at her, eyes wide in feigned innocence. "Honestly, Mother, it's nothing to do with me."

"Then who? Oh ho," she said, letting him go. "It's that sister of yours, isn't it? What's Taizia done now?"

Kusac shrugged. "I really can't say, Mother."

"Can't, or won't! Let me guess," she said, her voice getting tight. "She's pregnant, isn't she? And Meral came in this morning wanting to see your father. He won't allow it, Kusac," she said. "There's no way he'll allow her to bond with Meral."

"They're already bonded. For five years," said Kusac. He reached out and took his mother's hand in his. "Mother, I want you to speak up for them. Ask Father to allow them to life-bond."

As she began to shake her head and pull her hand away from him, he held onto her more tightly. "Mother, he's of the Nazule Clan. He's their second son, and he's an honorable male. You won't find one better, nor one more able to handle Taizia. Speak for them, Mother," he pleaded, lifting her hand up to his cheek.

"Gods, Kusac!" she said exasperated. "Do you know what you're asking of me? And don't try to act like a cub at your age! It won't wash," she said tartly, pulling her hand away. "I don't know what this family's coming to! I thought I knew you and your sister, now look at you both! You, the quiet one, have a Human Leska. You couldn't be less like the youngling I knew before you ran away! As for Taizia! I never thought I'd see the day when she'd settle down enough to have a cub, let alone choose it as a way to put off an arranged marriage!"

Kusac took hold of her hand again, this time in both of his. "Speak for her, Mother. This grandchild will be pure Sholan, and both parents are Talented. There's a good chance their cub will be, too. As good a chance as with any arranged marriage."

Before she could answer, the door opened and Konis

strode in. Behind him, Kusac could see Meral hovering anxiously.

"I see you've just learned about what your daughter has done," he said. "Well? What do you think of this ... situation?"

Rhyasha took her hand from Kusac's and drew herself up as she looked over to her life-mate. "*My* daughter, Konis?" she said, arching an eye ridge at him. "Since when did *our* daughter become mine?"

"I want to know your opinion on this," he said, frowning at her.

Kusac watched his mother look past her husband to Meral. "I think," she said, her voice softening, "we should ask Taizia to join us."

Startled, Konis came farther into the room. "You can sense Taizia's presence? Meral said she was with his family."

"I believe your sister's in the shrine, Kusac. Go and fetch her," his mother said. "Meral, don't stand out there, join us. You've been in here often enough."

Kusac got up and left the kitchen, heading down the corridor to the shrine at a run as soon as he was out of sight of his parents. Taizia was already on her way to meet him.

She stopped, looking anxiously at him. He swept her up into his arms in a hug.

"Taizia! I've missed you," he said, rubbing his cheek on hers as he set her back down again. "You're looking and feeling well! In fact," he said, standing back a little from her, "you look pregnant!" He wrapped an arm around her shoulders and drew her toward the kitchen. "Mother sent me to fetch you. I take it Meral didn't know you were here?"

"No. I couldn't let him face Father on his own, Kusac, no matter how much he wanted to. What do you think he's going to say? Do you think we've got a chance?"

"I honestly don't know. I've been working on Mother, softening her up for you," he said, then they were pushing the door open.

Taizia went straight to Meral's side, her hand going down to take his.

"I told you not to come!" said Meral quietly, his voice somewhat angry. "I said I'd see to it."

"I couldn't let you tell them on your own," she said. She looked over at her father and Kusac saw her jaw tighten before she spoke. "I want him, Father. He's not a telepath, but he's got enough Talent to receive me. He's obviously got the genes, and that's what you really want, isn't it?"

Konis looked over to Rhyasha.

She sat for a moment, tapping a claw tip on the table. "You're a second son I'm told. You'd be prepared to leave your clan for ours?"

Taizia's face lit up with hope as she looked at Meral.

He looked from her to Kusac, then Rhyasha. "Yes."

Rhyasha continued to tap the table thoughtfully for a moment or two. "You have my retrospective permission as Clan Leader to bond," she said abruptly.

Konis sat down at the table and ran his hands across his ears, looking from one to the other of them.

"The world we knew is changing drastically," he said. "It doesn't belong to our generation any more, Rhyasha. It belongs to Kusac and Taizia, and their partners. In the space of less than a year we've had the first Sholan/Human Leska Link, their first child conceived, and discovered that for hundreds of years we've ignored every mental Talent but telepathy in our desire to breed more of ourselves." He sighed.

Rhyasha reached out to touch his arm, but he took her hand in his instead. Kusac couldn't believe he was seeing it. His father particularly wasn't given to public shows of affection.

"I nearly lost my son because of the female he loved," Konis continued. "I don't intend to risk losing my daughter. You can have your Warrior, Taizia. For now, I'll sanction your bonding for five years. After that, we'll review the situation. Agreed?"

They all felt not only Taizia's but Meral's mental exhilaration.

"Father . . ." She flung herself at her father, arms going round him. "You don't know what this means to me!"

"I think I do," he said, his voice droll as he looked over his daughter's head to Rhyasha. "I know another female who did the same as you to ensure she had the husband she wanted."

"Konis!" said Rhyasha, her tone one of shocked outrage. "You've no business telling them that!"

"So that's why you called Taizia Mother's daughter," said Kusac with a grin.

"If it's time for truths, I can tell you a thing or two about your father," Rhyasha began.

"Rhyasha," Konis interrupted blandly as Taizia gave him one last hug before going back to Meral. "You've a bonding ceremony to record. Don't you think you should take these two younglings and get started on it now while I work out how I'm going to justify my decision to the Clans? I've also to approach Meral's family and ask them."

"Oh, they won't refuse, Clan Lord," said Meral hurriedly. "They wouldn't have looked for such a marriage for my older brother, let alone me."

"I don't doubt it," said Konis dryly as chuckling, Rhyasha got to her feet.

"Come on, you two," she said, gathering them up and sweeping them toward the door. "You've your brother to thank for this, Taizia."

"Bless you, Kusac," Taizia said over her shoulder as they left for Rhyasha's office on the floor above.

*   *   *

Carrie had slept till she'd been called for second meal. Afterward, with Kusac busy on the new estate, she'd decided to work on Kaid's book. So engrossed was she that she failed to notice that T'Chebbi was standing at the doorway to the lounge.

"Liegena, sorry to disturb you. A vehicle's arrived from Dzahai village with a message from Noni," said T'Chebbi. "She wants you for a checkup."

Carrie looked over at her. "A checkup?"

"I know the pilot. Noni told him it was important. She wants only you."

"Alone?" she said in disbelief.

T'Chebbi flicked her ears in agreement. "Without the Liegen. I'm only the messenger, Liegena," she apologized.

"Noni shouldn't even think of asking me to go without him, T'Chebbi, and Kusac agrees with me. What's she got against him coming anyway?"

"Don't know, Liegena. You ask her. I'll go with you."

"Kusac's as displeased as I am about this. I think I'd better contact her. What's her comm address?"

"She doesn't have one. The only way you can contact her is by going there."

Carrie hesitated, finally overruling Kusac's mental objections. "I'll go, but this is the last time I'll go without Kusac."

"Has the Liegen found anything about Khemu?" asked T'Chebbi as they left.

"He's managed to locate her Clan records and is checking through them now. He says it'll take him a while yet."

The trip to Noni's was quickly over, and as the pilot brought his vehicle down in the roadway outside Noni's cottage, Carrie felt the old female's mind touch hers lightly in greeting.

Noni was waiting for them at her gate. "Don't know what you think you're doing, T'Chebbi. You and that pilot can just take yourselves off to the inn. There's no place for you useless Brothers here!" she said tartly, opening the gate for Carrie.

T'Chebbi backed away from the gate. "Peace, Noni! I'll wait here."

"Suit yourself! More fool you for preferring that aircar to the inn!" She turned to walk back to the house. "Give me your arm, girl," she said, reaching out to take it.

"Why did you want me to come, Noni?" Carrie asked, matching her pace to the elderly Sholan's. "You know I'm fine now."

"Wait till we're inside, girl," she said, pushing open the door.

As soon as she'd stepped inside, Carrie turned angrily to Noni. "You've got a damper on! Why? I demand to know what this is all about!"

"Sit, youngling," said Noni, pointing to the table. "It's not for you, it's for that mate of yours. I need to talk to you about the Margins, and Kaid, but first, let me see that crystal you found."

"How do you know about it?" demanded Carrie.

"Let me see it," said Noni, sitting down and holding out her hand.

Reluctantly she fished it out of her trouser pocket and held it out.

Taking it between thumb and forefinger, Noni held it up to the light, squinting through it as she studied it. "Sit, sit," she murmured as, finishing her visual examination, her hand closed over it and a distant look came into her eyes.

Carrie sat, waiting to see what Noni could learn from it.

A look of pain crossed the Healer's face and with a low moan, she reached out and gave the crystal back to Carrie.

"Take it!" she said, getting to her feet as quickly as she was able. Rubbing her hands together, she went over to the sink.

"What's wrong, Noni?" asked Carrie, hurrying over to her side. "Can I help you?"

"No, child. It's what you thought it was, an eye from a statue of Vartra. The impressions are stronger than I expected, that's all." She turned on the faucet and ran her hands under the stream of water for a minute or two. "You go on and sit down now. I'm fine."

After drying her hands on a towel, she moved over to her stove and began busying herself pouring out two mugs of c'shar.

"What did you find out?" asked Carrie, putting the crystal away.

"Patience," said Noni, bringing the mugs back to the table and placing one in front of her. "And keep that crystal out. We'll need it awhile yet."

Once she was settled, Carrie asked her again. "What did you find out?"

Noni took a sip of her drink. "Like I said, it's an eye from the image of the God."

"I knew it! What else did you discover?"

"These crystals can store memories and feelings," she said. "There are many in this one, as you'd expect. What I picked up was a confusion of emotions that shouldn't by rights go together. Yes, there was peace and tranquillity, but that was in the past of its existence. The later emotions are quite different." She stopped, and peered across the table at Carrie.

"Is there something wrong with the way I make c'shar? You haven't touched yours yet."

Carrie made a noise halfway between exasperation and anger as she picked up her mug and took a large swig of the drink. Noni was stringing her along on purpose. "Well?" she demanded, putting it down again.

"They conflict with each other. The feelings of anger and frustration are strongest."

"I picked up the same from the actual ruins," Carrie said nodding. "I got very little from the crystal, though."

"If you can read the stones of buildings and the land on which they stand, then you can read this crystal."

"How? At the shrine, the feelings just came to me. I didn't go looking for them."

"Hold the crystal in your hand and just reach into it with your mind."

Carrie looked at her. "What?"

"I told you, girl! Hold it and reach into it with your mind!" she repeated tartly.

Taking it in her hand again, Carrie sat back and closed her eyes. She wasn't quite sure what she was doing because when she had mentally searched the ruins, it was something she'd done without thinking. She concentrated on the crystal in her hand, probing around it till suddenly, she'd found what she was looking for.

"I see a time of darkness, of neglect, then suddenly there is light and people—many, many people. Flames leap from a bowl before him . . . no, closer than that. A bowl in his hands, I think," she said, her voice quiet so as not to lose the tenuous contact she had with the gem. "There's incense and chanting—the low, pleasing sounds of worshipers."

The scene grew, expanding to fill her mind till she could hear nothing but the chanting, smell nothing but the scent of incense from the nung tree, and see nothing but a sea of heads bowed toward her beyond the flames that gently flickered in her hands.

"There were so many then, all worshiping me. These ones were peaceful, not like the ones who lived below," she said, hearing with horror the sudden deepening of her voice. The voice continued as if it belonged to someone other than herself, leaving her terrified as it spoke words in a Sholan dialect she didn't know.

"Fire ran through their veins! They were Warriors. At the end, they fought the furless ones, dying like heroes, taking them with them into death."

Suddenly finding herself partially released from the spell of the past, she gave a low cry of anguish, putting her hands up to protect her head. The crystal fell to the floor, rolling away to stop by Noni's foot even as the old Sholan stepped over it to reach her.

"They destroyed the Shrine and me! I fragment! I am lost!"

"It's only a memory, child," Noni said, pulling her arms down by her sides and holding her close. "A memory, no more."

Carrie shuddered several times, then the tension left her body and she slumped against Noni.

"Sit, child," she said, moving her grasp to Carrie's hands as she did so.

Carrie looked up at her, blinking to try and bring her eyes into focus. She took her hands away from Noni, putting them up to her face as she began to shudder again. "He spoke through me! He took over my voice, Noni!" Even she could hear the panic in her voice.

"No," said Noni, gently lowering herself to her chair again. "Your subconscious mind copied the way they spoke and thought in those days, that's all."

"I don't like it, Noni," Carrie said, rubbing her eyes. "All these dreams and voices—it's frightening."

Noni poked Carrie's mug toward her again. "Take another drink," she said, then bent slowly down to retrieve the crystal orb from the floor. "Don't be frightened," she said. "It's other people's memories you're seeing and hearing, not yours. That painter that lives on the Aldatan estate, she sees a picture in everything she looks at, that's her Talent. Yours is to be sensitive to thoughts, amongst other things. So you pick them up from crystals like this." She put it down in front of Carrie.

"I don't know," Carrie began dubiously.

"Well, I do!" interrupted Noni sharply. "Stop working yourself into a panic over something as natural as those damned comm crystals you use every day! They store electronic information, don't they? Well, these ones," she said, taking Carrie's hand from the table and placing the crystal in her palm, "store information from our minds! I want you to keep that crystal. Wear it round your neck. Get a jeweler to put it in one of those silver cage things. Now, put it away, I've got more important things to say to you."

Holding the crystal gingerly between thumb and index finger, Carrie returned it to her pocket. Noni's explanation sounded eminently logical and already she was feeling a little easier about the whole incident. Instinctively she reached for Kusac, forgetting about the psychic damper.

"Yes, I use a damper. I need privacy for myself and those who come to me," Noni said. "You'd be surprised how many of the Brothers are sensitives if not telepaths. Now we know for sure there was a shrine to Vartra on your estate, that along with the fact that the new Leska pairs dream of the

God in Valsgarth Guildhouse, makes it pretty sure there are seams of these crystals on your land. They're also found here at Stronghold, which would account for the dreams and visions of the Brothers."

"Kusac and I camped out for a couple of days in a cave that had seams of those crystals in it. The cave was at the foot of the hill on which the shrine stands."

"I know that these crystals store memories," said Noni. "I use them for healing. I used one when I healed you. Because I was working with your mind, it picked up the essence of what and who you are. It also picked up the feelings and emotions of my helper."

Carrie looked up at her, puzzled. What was Noni getting at?

"I wanted Tallinu to be an element in that crystal."

"Kaid? But why?"

"I wondered that myself, till now," Noni said. "Part of it was because you would become a Triad. Now, with Tallinu missing, and Ghezu wanting him dead, it suddenly makes sense."

"How does it make sense?" Carrie asked. "You've lost me, Noni." She was thoroughly confused now.

"I've used that particular crystal for more years than I care to remember, but this time, I knew I had to give it to Tallinu just as it was, with both of you a part of it. His link to you is now something tangible that he can believe in every time he touches the crystal."

"Are you telling me that he can somehow contact me through it?"

"Not quite. He isn't a telepath, after all, but he can sense some of what's in it because he's also a part of it. It sensitizes him to you. It's possible that you could use it to try and locate him. Perhaps you'll pick him up anyway."

"Pick him up how?"

"You ask too many questions!" Noni growled. "Try thinking for yourself, girl! You might have dreams that show you where he is or what's happening to him. Anything's possible! Just be on your guard for any strange feelings regarding Tallinu, that's all. Who knows? After you've paired, he may be able to reach you mentally by using it himself."

She stopped talking and leaned forward. "What is it?

You've already felt something, haven't you? I can sense you thinking about it. Tell me!"

"It's nothing, Noni." She wasn't happy about anyone else being able to know her thoughts. "Just that I've been sleeping badly. No dreams or anything, just unable to sleep."

"Since he left?"

"Round about then," Carrie admitted, looking away from her as she toyed with her mug. "Noni, this pairing. I know you have a different outlook on pairings from Humans, but in my experience, all the people around me except Vanna seem to have only one partner."

"What people do in their private life isn't usually common knowledge," said Noni. "Many Leska pairs have a mate as well, and I remember times when your bond-parents had a lover or two."

Carrie looked up quizzically.

"No, I won't tell you," said Noni. "Private is private. My knowledge was legitimately come by, not gossip. What is it that bothers you about the pairing? Do you dislike Tallinu?"

Carrie could feel her curiosity. "No. He's never been anything but kind and understanding with me," she said.

"He's older than Kusac," said Noni, "but that's no bad thing. You'll not find him causing trouble for either of you."

"How could he cause trouble?" She watched Noni's eyes narrow.

"How much do you know about the Triads, girl?"

"Only what the Brotherhood and Ghyan at the temple in Valsgarth have in their records."

Noni made a noise of disgust. "They know nothing!"

"How do you know more?"

"Knowledge passed down through our families, girl," said Noni. "Our knowledge goes back further than theirs! At the time of the Cataclysm, there was a hatred and fear of the Telepaths. Many believed they caused the disaster that swept across the face of Shola, but that wasn't so. Theirs was a time when the guilds grew up out of the ruins of the past, a time when people fought to keep as many of their skills alive as possible so they could rebuild their world. Warriors were needed, and to protect those telepaths that were left, they formed Triads with the Leska pairs."

"The telepaths would have been able to sense danger."

"And the Warriors could protect them from attack," finished Noni.

"I suppose it was easier for lone telepaths to go unnoticed."

"Within reason. With people trying to loot all they could from what was left of their world, telepaths were easy to spot because of their inability to stand physical violence. So they set up their own guild and retreated to defensible places with Warriors to protect them."

"There were the Valtegans as well," Carrie reminded her.

"We've only just begun to learn of their existence in the past, we can't assume they survived the Cataclysm. In time, some of the Warriors became the Brotherhood. Perhaps they were the result of pairings between Warriors and Telepaths. Who knows? Be that as it may, these Triads had to be close, had to trust each other. Especially if there were cubs," she said quietly.

Carrie looked away, picking up her mug and taking a drink. "That's not likely in our case."

"What made you choose Tallinu?" asked Noni, sitting back in her chair.

"What d'you mean?"

"Just what I said."

"I feel I can trust him," said Carrie, refusing to look her in the eye. "He's the only other male I know well enough." She had no intention of telling Noni, or anyone else, that she'd sensed the presence of his mind several times.

"What else?"

"His touch doesn't make me want to move away."

Noni made a small, noncommittal noise.

Carrie looked up at her. "I like him! Is there anything wrong in that?" she demanded, angry at being goaded into admitting it.

Noni spread her hands expressively. "Did I say anything?" she asked. "Your reasons are good. Most people choose lovers for less sound reasons."

"I didn't say I was choosing him as a lover!" Carrie exclaimed.

"What do you think the third in a Triad is, if not a lover to one of you? It isn't a one-time tumble just so you can walk the Fire Margins! Think Sholan, girl, not Human!" said Noni, her voice sharp. "If you don't, you'll hurt them both."

"But . . . Surely Kusac doesn't want me to . . ."

"He's Sholan, girl, just remember that. For all his understanding of your Human side, if you confuse the Human and
Sholan ideals, you'll cause your mate more hurt. Tallinu
needn't mean to you what Kusac does, but treat him as less
than a lover and you'll hurt him too. Just enjoy the pairing
when it happens. It's a pleasure the Gods gifted to us, to be
enjoyed for what it is, no more. Your loyalty to your life-
mate isn't affected by that, is it?"

"No," said Carrie dubiously.

"Ha! I'd heard you Humans didn't pair for pleasure but
did it for duty and cubs. I didn't believe it till now!"

"I'm not Human," said Carrie, stung by her words.

Noni leaned forward, taking hold of her chin. "Then show
it! Trust your Sholan side, girl, and enjoy what the God gives
you!"

"My Sholan side is *male*, Noni," said Carrie, pulling herself away. "I only have Kusac's view of his world, not a
female's."

"So what? There's no difference between male and female
Sholans when it comes to that!"

"There is with Humans. What's acceptable for males, isn't
for females."

"Think Sholan!" repeated Noni. "When it comes time for
you and Tallinu to pair, what will you do? Run from him?
How d'you think he'll feel? Or your Leska? You'll shame
Kusac in Tallinu's eyes if you do! Another Sholan male
would assume your mate was an uncaring lover. Is that how
Tallinu should see Kusac?"

"Of course not! He's nothing of the kind," she said
angrily.

Noni sat back again, mouth opening in a small grin. "Then
make sure Tallinu doesn't think so. Kusac wouldn't want the
pairing to be unpleasant for you, so if he knows you've
enjoyed it, he'll be pleased."

"Yes, but . . . Our Link!"

Noni shrugged. "If he's sensible, he'll be with your friend
Vanna. You don't mind them pairing now and then, do you?"

"It's not like that!"

"Like what? You don't want them to enjoy?" Noni raised
an eye ridge in her direction.

"Of course I do, but . . ." She knew then she'd been
trapped in her own logic.

"So, why shouldn't it be the same for you?" asked Noni

quietly. "Think Sholan, child. There should be no guilt over this, only sharing pleasure. In time, Tallinu will find his own female. Trust the Gods, child. They know what They are doing."

"Kusac's said that," Carrie said quietly.

Chapter 11

Jo, Davies, and Kris had been lucky enough to find employment as guards for a small caravan heading north toward a town called Forestgate. Only a few kilometers off their route, traveling in company afforded them protection not only from the armed bands of raiders, but from the starving wolfish creatures similar to the one at the spaceport, who'd come down to the plains looking for food.

The journey was slow and uneventful. Once away from the shelter afforded by the port and the shanty houses, there was nothing to break the bitter winds as they swept across the barren snow-covered plain that stretched for miles around them. For once, Jo appreciated the fact that the women lacked any parity with the men on this world. As a female, she wasn't expected to stand sentry duty and was allowed the luxury of sleeping in the back of one of the goods wagons. Helping the camp cook also meant she had plenty to eat.

The first night, sitting round the camp fire and using the Jalnians' equivalent of playing cards, Davies introduced the other two off duty guards to the concept of a poker school and promptly proceeded to divest them of their hard earned coins. When Jo heard about it, she was livid.

"Our instructions were clear: nothing above the cultural level of Jalna was to be brought with us. That includes gambling!"

"I wouldn't worry about it," said Kris, testing the edge of the axe he'd bought at the shantytown before continuing to hone it with his stone. "I don't know of a species that doesn't gamble. All he introduced was a new game."

"That's not the point! We can't afford to draw attention to ourselves, or earn the dislike of these people! Taking their money from them in a card game is really calculated to make us friends, isn't it? Tonight, Davies, you're going to have the worst run of luck imaginable, d'you hear me? You're going to lose *all* the money you took from them! And don't try to justify keeping it," she continued as he opened his mouth to speak. "As far as I'm concerned, there is *no* justification for what you did!"

"Okay, Okay, I get the point," he said, getting to his feet. "D'you know, you're getting to sound like one of the Jalnian women as well as look like one?" Turning his back on her, he stalked off to the campfire.

Jo, arms still akimbo on her hips, stared after him.

"Though I agree with you, you might have been more subtle about it," said Kris.

Jo turned to look at him. "What d'you mean?"

Kris put the stone aside and bent down to pick up his oily rag. "Just that it might have been less degrading for Davies to not have had me here, Jo. He'd have still got the point without feeling humiliated by it. Little things like that matter you know. Give respect and you get it back."

As she stared speechlessly at him, she simultaneously heard a chittering sound and felt the presence of something alien in her mind. Frozen in shock, she watched as from the neck opening of Kris' jacket, a small white head appeared. It turned toward her, eyes bright and nose twitching as it very obviously began to scold her.

"There's a . . . creature in your coat," she said, taking a step backward and trying to keep her voice low and controlled so as not to startle it.

With a sigh, Kris laid his ax aside and reached for the animal, pulling it free. It sat upright in his hand, holding onto his fingers while it continued to chatter angrily.

"I know," he said. "It was only a matter of time till you found out. I'm surprised Scamp managed to stay hidden for so long."

"He's a *pet?* You're keeping an alien creature as a pet?"

"Calm down, Jo. He's only a jegget, he's not alien. I've had him virtually since I arrived on Shola."

Jo took another step backward and fell over the small pile of logs, landing with a thump. She remained where she was, just staring as the jegget, its scolding over, turned away from her and wound its long sinuous body around Kris' hand till it was looking up at him. With a flick of its long bushy tail, it leaped to his shoulder and settled there, curling itself around his neck.

"You brought an animal all the way from Shola to here?"

She couldn't believe what she was seeing. "Am I the only one here who has any idea of the importance of not drawing attention to ourselves?"

"No, Jo, you're not," Kris said, reaching in his pocket for a piece of dried fruit which he held up for his pet. "Scamp fits the niche of an animal that's a cross between a ferret and a squirrel back on Earth. I'd bet if he's common to both Earth and Shola, there's something like him here. It's one thing to not draw attention to ourselves, and another to be so unremarkable that we also stand out. A little idiosyncrasy like him makes us more, not less, normal."

"I felt him in my mind!"

Kris grinned. "You would. He's telepathic, like all jeggets. They're the only other species on Shola that are."

Jo watched the jegget accept the piece of fruit and sit up, daintily holding it between both paws to eat it.

The cold dampness of the snow she was sitting on finally penetrated enough to remind her to get up. Keeping her eyes on the jegget, she scrambled to her feet and moved closer.

"Are you going to give me earache for bringing him?"

"What for?" Jo sighed. "It's too late now, isn't it?"

"As it was with Davies," he said, reaching up to take Scamp down from his shoulders. "A word or two and his own conscience would have told him to lose the money tonight. It didn't need the dressing-down. Would you like to hold Scamp?" he asked, nodding to his pet. "He's very friendly, unless he thinks I'm being threatened!"

Jo moved closer. Reaching out a tentative finger, she touched the small head gently. "He's tipped like a Siamese," she said, seeing the pale brown markings on his ears for the first time.

"Not quite, but close."

Scamp leaned forward to sniff her hand as she grew more confident and began to stroke the side of his face and shoulder.

"He's cute. I didn't know Sholans kept pets."

"They don't. He's a wild one. I discovered I've got this thing with the animals on Shola. They seem to like me. Scamp I saved from a tree-rhudda that was raiding his nest. He was the only surviving baby. When he was old enough to let loose in the wild, he refused to go. I'm glad."

Jo sighed. "Do me a favor and try to keep him out of sight," she said, straightening up.

Kris laughed quietly as Scamp turned and, running up his arm, disappeared down the neck of his jacket. "Don't worry, he doesn't like crowds. He only came out because he recognized another telepath."

"Hmm," was all she said as she walked slowly off to her wagon. Kris had been right. She hadn't needed to talk to Davies like that in front of him. Sometimes she felt the weight of the responsibility of her position as leader. Now was one of them.

As she climbed on the tailgate, in the distance she heard the howling of the wolves. An involuntary shudder passed through her. In another couple of days they would reach Forestgate. After that, they were on their own in the forests where these beasts lived. She sent a prayer to any God that was listening that the wolves were all out here on the plains. According to the map they reckoned there was a good eight kilometers from the town to the end of the tree line. From there, it was all uphill till they reached the crash site.

* * *

Kaid awoke with a start, wondering why his alarm hadn't roused him. Then, as the fog of sleep cleared from his brain, he remembered. Blinking, he rubbed his eyes before undoing his sleeping bag and reaching forward for a drink of water from the dispenser.

His hand was steady; the fever was gone. A second drink and he was ready to check his arm. Removing the bandage, he could see a scab had formed on top of the wound. The flesh around it, when probed, was tender and still slightly swollen. Flexing it, he found his arm was usable. The Fastheal had worked well enough for his purposes. He reached for the ultrasound scanner and played it over his injury, checking to see it was healing from the bottom up. It was. He kept the scanner on it for several minutes before switching it off. A few days more treatment and he'd be fine.

He stood up, stretching every muscle group in turn from his ears to his tail. Gods, but he was stiff! Turning back to his seat, he began to gather up the rubbish his four days of healing had accumulated.

Sitting down, he returned his seat to the forward position and switched on the main comm, listening for the next news broadcast. It was at that point he realized he was hungry.

Getting up again, he clambered back to the rear of the craft. Examining the options on the menu, he opted for a light meal of eggs and meat, surprising himself by wolfing it down ravenously.

His gear stowed away, he returned to his seat and dug the map of the desert region out from the chart drawer. If he crossed the mountains at the Nyacko Pass, he could fly in low and land the vehicle in the arroyo near Rhijudu. It was the perfect place not only to conceal the craft, but also to use as a base. From the foothills he could observe the village and try to locate Khemu.

Activating the craft's motor, he taxied out into the clearing for takeoff. Idly, he wondered what the situation was back at the estate. They'd have called off the search by now, he was sure. Garras would have persuaded them of the futility of looking for him when he didn't want to be found. His conscience pricked him over deserting his post as Carrie's bodyguard, but he forced it into silence by reminding himself that the rest of the team had been handpicked by himself. If they weren't capable of covering for him, then he shouldn't have chosen them in the first place.

As the craft rose vertically above the trees, he also recognized for the first time that this was a fool's errand. He was risking death or capture not only at the hands of the desert folk, but also at Ghezu's. Dzaka was yet another threat. He was out there somewhere, looking for him. His conscience might bother him over not personally guarding Carrie, but he couldn't live with himself if he hadn't made the effort to see Khemu and set things straight with her before she died, especially now he knew where she was. He hadn't been lying when he told Noni that he couldn't go before Vartra with that stain on his soul.

Kaid cursed when he heard the broadcast concerning the Laasoi Guildhouse and the deployment of troops at the Nyacko Pass. It mean detouring and flying in at night, low and from the northwest. Not just that, it was a bad time to be away. The Brotherhood should have anticipated this move by Fyak, the God knew he had! Still, it would keep, he supposed. They'd all managed before he was involved, and he knew they could manage now. There were enough people around the estate to give Kusac and the Clan Lord the information they might need. He checked the position of the sun.

If he took it easy, he would reach his destination just as dusk was falling.

He was shaking with exhaustion by the time he finally let his vehicle slowly descend to the surface. A few meters away was the cave he planned to use to conceal the scouter. Turning the craft carefully, he eased it backward into the cave. A scraping, ripping noise signaled that he'd managed to catch the side of the vehicle's body work. He was too tired to care: he needed sleep and food. The engine turned off, he slumped forward across the console.

With a jerk, he came awake. Looking bleary-eyed at his wrist comm, he realized he'd slept for upward of an hour. Not good, especially when he hadn't concealed the entrance yet. Tiredly, he stirred himself. Opening the hatch, he got up from his seat and reaching back for the bush knife set in the tool section, he climbed down to the cave floor.

Outside, he chose branches from within the centers of bushes where the cut edges wouldn't be easily noticed. Some fifteen minutes later, he was back in his craft looking out through a screen of greenery.

Once more he turned his seat around, setting up the cabin as a living area. This time he wouldn't be so helpless, thank Vartra! Digging out the bedding, he set it up, then turned his attention to his grumbling stomach. He was too tired to eat by now and settled for a couple of protein rich drinks before succumbing to sleep.

* * *

Shift change time had just passed. L'Seuli and Rrurto had been newly assigned to duty outside the temple area of the cavern complex. The Prophet liked his personal guard to be made up of faces he knew. After of his last fit of ungovernable rage, Rrurto and L'Seuli had been promoted to fill the places vacated only hours previously by his latest victims—those who had been responsible for the losses incurred during the assault on Laasoi Guildhouse.

Lighting units were strung up against the sandstone walls of the corridor, their glow brightening the gloom as the two males headed deeper into the hillside. The remains of decorative carvings still lined the walls but their extreme age had rendered them almost invisible even to Sholan eyes.

As they rounded the last bend, a servant heading the way they'd just come, collided with them.

"Your pardon," the youth said, staggering to regain his balance.

Rrurto's hand grabbed him before he could run off.

"Where d'you think you're going in such a rush?" the older male demanded.

The youngling's eyes were wide with fear. "The female," he said, looking fearfully over his shoulder, then back to them. "The telepath. She's hurt. He wants Anirra to see her. Please, let me go," he said, trying to pull away.

"What'd he do to her?"

"She hurt herself when he paired with her. I must go! I've to tell Vraiyou to bring the Sun God's plant! The Prophet wants to talk to Kezule. He'll kill me if I don't hurry!" With a last squirm, the youth pulled himself free and raced down the corridor.

"Dammit! You don't use female captives like that!" snarled Rrurto. "As for what he did to Nyanga and Raylma . . ." He left the sentence unfinished.

L'Seuli flinched, feeling the skin on his back crawl at the memory of it. The two would-be tacticians had been allowed the opportunity to lead the assault on Laasoi. Their losses of forty fighters were totally unacceptable and Fyak had ordered them flogged—with a difference. They had been stunned on full power first. Nyanga had died in agony after only nine lashes; Raylma had lasted a little longer.

The punishment had been ordained by Kezule himself, Fyak had claimed, and was to be used in future on anyone who transgressed against the God's wishes. It would act as a deterrent. He was right.

"Rrurto, keep your voice down," L'Seuli whispered. "It will do no one any good if we're the next two victims."

Rrurto growled again but started toward the doorway into the temple, pausing between the twin carved pillars of flame to take up his post.

As L'Seuli took up his position, he risked a glance through the open doorway. Filling the area in front of him was the huge circular altar on which the Eternal Flame burned. He wrinkled his nose as the faint aroma of singed fur drifted out into the corridor.

Minutes later, the medic, Anirra, came rushing toward

them carrying his medikit. Rrurto stepped in front of him, barring his way with his rifle.

"Get out of my way! There's an injured person in there!" said Anirra, trying to push past him.

"L'Seuli, go check with the Prophet that he's expecting the medic," said Rrurto, grasping Anirra by the arm.

L'Seuli stepped cautiously between the pillars and through the doorway into the temple. As he entered, a blinding light filled the room, making his eyes water and blink. Instinctively holding an arm in front of his face, he looked upward for the source. In the roof of the cavern was a hole that let the sunlight stream down into the temple, hitting the polished mirror below it.

"Who are you to dare disturb the peace of Kezule?" demanded Fyak.

Still blinking, L'Seuli looked toward the voice, seeing the Prophet sitting in a large carved chair a short distance from the altar.

"The medic Anirra waits outside, Liege," he said, gripping his rifle more firmly. He was not enjoying being so close to Fyak.

"He may enter."

L'Seuli bowed low. "Yes, Liege," he said, backing out of the temple. A slight movement at the base of the altar caught his eye, and head still bowed, he glanced toward it. Lying huddled on the ground was the female. She caught his eyes, her look and the message she dared to send him, begging for a swift end. He looked away, hardening himself against her. He could do nothing for her, just like he'd been unable to help the many others who had looked at him in just that way.

Once beyond the doors, he swung round to face Rrurto and Anirra. "The Word of Kezule says he may enter," he said.

"About bloody time," muttered Anirra as Rrurto let him go.

In the meantime, Vraiyou, followed by the youth, had come round the corner and was observing them with raised eye ridges.

"I trust you don't intend to detain *me*," he said, approaching them, a small wooden casket held before him in both hands.

"No, Father," said Rrurto, standing to attention. "You may enter."

The chief of Fyak's Faithful inclined his head in gentle sarcasm as he passed between them. The youth shot them anxious looks, tail down and ears flicking as he followed.

L'Seuli exchanged glances with Rrurto. They both knew that if Fyak planned to take the sap of the holy plant then he intended to speak with the God that evening. They were in for another night's vigil in the desert.

Raised voices came from within and L'Seuli and Rrurto edged closer to the middle of the doorway in an attempt to hear what was being said, but they could distinguish no words.

"What did you see when you went in?" the older male asked quietly from the side of his mouth.

"Not a lot. He'd just had the ceiling opened to the sky and the brightness almost blinded me."

"Did you see the female?"

"Yes. She was at the foot of the altar."

"What sort of state was she in?"

"Not good."

"Where was he?"

"Sitting in some kind of carved throne."

"I know the one you mean. That throne wasn't made for folk with tails," Rrurto muttered.

"What d'you mean?"

"What I said. It was made for folk more like those demons the Prophet's always on about."

L'Seuli forced his ears and tail to stay still. He might just find out more than they'd dared hope. "The demons? You think they exist then?"

"I *know* they exist, lad. That's what keeps a lot of us with Fyak! Fear of them returning! You didn't think this place was built by us, did you? Me and my partner—the one you replaced—were on temple guard duty when they were getting it ready for some service or other. We had the chance to look round. On a couple of stretches of wall in there are carvings and paintings that have lasted better then the ones out here. You can see enough to tell that the folk in them look more like the Terrans than us."

"Like the Terrans?" L'Seuli edged even closer.

"Sort of," said Rrurto, looking at him. "They were furless like them. No hair, even on their heads, and their eyes were larger. Noses looked to be just slits on their faces. Their hands were all shown clawed so I reckon they couldn't retract them like we can."

It took all the self-control he possessed to stop himself

from reacting. "Sounds interesting. Any chance of getting a look at these carvings?"

"Forget it," said Rrurto sharply. "You go poking about around this temple and Fyak'll make raw meat of you! Besides, all you have to do is look at the walls of this corridor as we leave here. You'll be able to see their likeness now you know what to look for."

The voices suddenly got louder and hurriedly they separated. Anirra emerged and grasped Rrurto by the arm. "Get rid of that rifle. I need you to carry the female down to the infirmary for me," he said.

Slinging his firearm over his shoulder, Rrurto disappeared into the temple to reemerge moments later carrying the unconscious female, the remains of her purple robe draped around her.

Concerned, L'Seuli watched them leave. He didn't like being left alone here. He didn't trust either Fyak or Vraiyou. Ears flared wide and turned as far backward as they would go, he hovered close enough to the open doors to hear without, he hoped, being seen.

It seemed an age before his partner returned, though in reality it was only some ten minutes.

"How is she?" he whispered as Rrurto resumed his post.

"She'll live," he said, his voice, though quiet, full of anger. "She's been knocked about some, and has burns on her hands and arms where he held her against the altar."

"That's desecration!" L'Seuli hissed, shocked.

"Not when you're the Word of Kezule and you claim He told you to violate the female telepath! Just remember, we know nothing about it, hear me?"

L'Seuli nodded, keeping his thoughts to himself. If there were other old-timers like Rrurto who were beginning to see the insanity of some of Fyak's actions, then perhaps all wasn't lost. It meant that at least there was hope for the future.

They stood in silence for perhaps another half hour, aware that the brightness from the hole in the temple roof was gradually dimming. Then, as it was abruptly cut off, Vraiyou emerged.

"Come," he said to them. "We'll take the temple exit."

Glancing questioningly at Rrurto, L'Seuli waited for the other to step in front of him before following. Though he'd done guard duty during a vigil, he'd never been there at the start before.

The temple was now illuminated by the same units that were used elsewhere in the cavern complex. On his throne, Fyak sat slumped against one carved wooden arm. They could hear his heavy breathing and as they drew nearer, see that his eyes were almost covered by his inner lids.

"The drug the Prophet uses to enable him to travel to the realm of Kezule takes a heavy toll on his body," said Vraiyou, his tone urbane. "We are all grateful for his sacrifice."

"Kezule be praised," L'Seuli chanted in time with Rrurto as they waited for the senior member of the Faithful to help the staggering Prophet to his feet.

L'Seuli's mind turned to the drug Fyak had used. Underlying the odors that permeated the air in here, he could smell a sharp, almost pungent, vegetable smell, unlike anything he'd come across before. He let his eyes roam around the floor by the throne, hoping against hope that there was some fragment lying there that he could pick up, but predictably, there was nothing. He had to find out more about it—get a sample if he could. He knew most of the plant-extract drugs and this smelled like nothing he'd come across before.

As they began to walk slowly through the temple toward the wall hanging that covered the exit corridor, he took the opportunity to quickly glance round the chamber for the carved paintings that Rrurto had mentioned. He saw a blur of color on a far wall, but it was too far away to distinguish any details.

"Father," ventured Rrurto. "Would you send the lad for our cloaks? We're not blessed by Kezule as the Prophet is. The nights are sharp enough now to freeze a warrior's hands to his gun."

Vraiyou gestured to the youth who sped off in the opposite direction.

*   *   *

It had been a month or two since Konis had attended the Council of Leaders. What with one thing or another, his life had been rather complicated since his people's first contact with another telepathic species, and by his son's Link to one of those individuals.

Governor Nesul had contacted him in advance, asking that he attend as General Raiban had requested the opportunity to address the council on the issue of the Valtegans. Normally Konis' position was filled by one of his senior members of staff at AlRel and he would attend in person only when he had a report to make or his presence was necessary to the issue being discussed.

The current debate concerned another plea from Tayangi, head of the Civil Protectorate, for more resources to be allocated to combating the pockets of organized crime that flourished in the major cities, Ranz in the highlands of the Dzahai mountains and the capital Shanagi itself being prime among them.

Konis reached for his glass of water, glancing as unobtrusively as he could at his wrist comm in the process. It was nearing the end of the day's business. If Nesul intended Raiban to speak, he'd better do something soon.

Almost as he thought it, the governor interrupted the discussion.

"I've asked General Raiban to attend the meeting today because she has some news that concerns us all. Hanaz," he said to his aide, "would you ask the General to come in, please?"

A few minutes later, Raiban entered, carrying a large, flat case and followed by a Human. As Konis sat up, he was aware of the sense of outrage, and expectation, from the assembled Guild and Clan Leaders. This was going to be heated and controversial, he realized—if he'd correctly interpreted the presence of the box and the Human.

Raiban walked round the oval wooden table, stopping at the places left vacant for herself and her companion. Placing the case on the table, she looked over at the Governor.

"This is completely out of order, a breach of security," said Guild Master Mnoeshi, her ears twitching in anger. "Since when has our Assembly been open to members of other species?"

"Dr. Michaels is here by my invitation," said Nesul. "If General Raiban, head of Military Intelligence, doesn't consider him a security risk, then neither should we." He turned to look at Raiban. "General, please. When you're ready?"

Raiban nodded and as her companion sat, she leaned forward to open the case fully. As she pushed it into the center of the table, clearly visible in their nest of form-fitting padding, lay the skull and several large bones from the limbs of a Valtegan.

"These remains were found at one of the ancient city sites," she said, looking directly at where Master Esken sat, "before it was destroyed by members of Esken's Guild. They're the bones of a Valtegan who walked on Sholan soil over a millennium ago."

A stunned silence greeted her statement, then exclamations of surprise broke out from all directions as the Councillors furthest from the case rose to their feet in an effort to see it.

"I had Dr. Michaels and a team of his chosen archaeologists," she said the alien word carefully, "brought here, not only to date the bones, but because we need their skills if we're going to find out what Valtegans were doing on Shola at or around the time of the Cataclysm. If they've been here once, they may come back. They've already unleashed a weapon of devastating proportions on Khyaal and Szurtha, a weapon about which we still know nothing."

Looking Esken squarely in the face, she continued. "I think it's time you were accountable for this wanton destruction of our past. I want answers to some questions, and I want them now, Esken!"

Esken's face and ears remained impassive as he lifted his shoulders in a shrug. "I've done nothing that my predecessors haven't done for hundreds of years, General Raiban. Naturally I'll answer what questions I can, providing they don't touch on Guild secrets."

"Guild secrets be damned, Esken." Konis' voice was a low growl of anger. "My son and bond-daughter nearly died on the *Khalossa* because your medics refused his physician guild-specific medical information! We're entering a new era, not only on Shola, but out there," he gestured toward the ceiling. "If we can't learn to communicate freely with each other, irrespective of guilds, then I foresee the collapse of our people under the weight of traditions that will destroy them!"

Governor Nesul nodded. "Well said, Konis. We're in danger of remaining too planet-bound, my colleagues," he said, talking over the angry exclamations from round the table.

"We have to learn to see the whole picture. The Valtegans aren't a distant threat out in space. We've lost two colonies to them, and now we've found evidence that they've lived on our home world. Esken, I want to know why explosives have to be detonated in the ruins before the mining and salvage teams can enter. I want to know why your Guild has been spreading a doctrine dismissing our past history as unimportant, and I want to know if you knew about these remains before now!"

"I think you're exaggerating the situation, Governor. The ruins have always been dealt with in this fashion. Commander Chuz, the explosives are controlled by your people and you knew what they were being used for. Check your records and you'll see that I've only been continuing in the footsteps of my predecessors." He paused, looking round the faces turned toward him. "As for spreading a doctrine against our past—that's ridiculous, as I'm sure many of you will agree."

Konis watched as Esken looked expectantly from one to another of the people he would normally have expected to back him up. He might dislike him, but as a fellow telepath, he felt some sympathy for this public abandonment. Still, he'd only himself to blame. Coercion and threats were no way to win allies.

Finally, Clan Leader Chekoi spoke up. "I have to agree with Master Esken," he said. "I don't see how you can accuse him of trying to suppress an interest in our past. What do the achievements of our ancient ancestors matter to us now?"

"Tell me which God or Goddess you personally worship," said Nesul, looking at the comp pad in front of him.

"Excuse me?" Chekoi was obviously taken aback at the question.

"Which deity does your clan look to as its protector?"

"Nylam, God of the Hunt, but what's that got to do with anything?"

"There's a temple to Nylam in Taykui forest, near your clan's estate, isn't there? Who runs it?" He looked up at Chekoi, stylus poised.

The Clan Leader frowned. "The priest, of course!"

"Uh huh. Nickoe, who does your clan look to?" He fixed his eyes on another of Esken's supporters.

"The Goddess of Shola, the Green Goddess. Why? What point are you trying to make, Nesul?" demanded the female Sholan as she watched him annotate his pad.

As Nesul raised his head and looked slowly round his Council, Konis began to purr gently in amusement.

"I expect each one of you has sent your own and the clan cubs to your local temple, haven't you? As well as taking their turn in helping the lay-brothers maintain the building and the grounds, and assisting in the various rites and ceremonies, I'm sure they, and you in your day, have been taught by the priest in charge, haven't they?" asked Nesul, carefully replacing his stylus beside his comp pad. "Master Esken, please tell us to which guild do *all* the priests belong?"

"Mine, of course!" snapped the now irate telepath. "What's your point, Nesul?"

"Merely that priests spread doctrines, and all priests, bar those of Vartra, answer directly to you because they're all telepaths."

Konis, sensing the telltale signs that Esken was about to really lose his temper, decided to intervene. "Governor, I'm sure that Esken was only following the orders of his predecessors," he said, looking over to the beleaguered Guild Master. "You're doing exactly what every Master of the Telepath Guild has done, right back to the days of the Cataclysm, but have you ever thought to ask yourself why?"

"You all know why! The ruins are dangerously unstable, full of rooms where tons of rubble are held up by ancient rusting girders. The slightest movement could make them collapse on those within! Blasting them makes them safer for the miners!"

"The blasting will stop as of now, Esken," said Nesul, his voice taking on a hard edge. "You will also instruct your priests to encourage an interest in our past history."

"If I may, Governor Nesul," said Raiban. "I feel we need all the guilds to pool their records so a common database can be set up from which we can try to find out what our ancestors knew, if anything, about the Valtegans and their possible involvement in the Cataclysm."

"What makes you think they had anything to do with the Cataclysm?" asked Tayangi.

"I'm afraid that's classified at the moment," said Raiban. "However, I can tell you that the traditional links between the Brotherhood, the Warriors, and surprisingly, the Telepath Guild appear to be closer than we ever suspected."

"Governor Nesul," said Commander Chuz, speaking for the first time. "General Raiban's request will have to be considered an order. I consider it a matter vital to planetary defense, possibly even of important to the Alliance as a whole, that all our guilds and clans make what historical records they have available to a team of researchers to be assisted by experts in the relevant fields from our Human allies. Dr. Michaels will be one of the experts who will assist our people."

"This is some mad scheme dreamed up by a colicky pessimist after a heavy meal!" growled Mnoeshi angrily. "Why should we open our guild records to anyone? They're our business, no one else's! What good will it do the Medical Guild to know how often we service the lighting in our streets, eh? Damned fool idea, if you ask me!"

"If that's all your records hold, then why the fuss about making them available?" asked Dr. Michaels quietly. "We don't want your guild secrets, like how many grams of powdered cadduh shells make the purple dye for the telepaths. We need records that show major changes in areas like the political system, the population, health, wars . . . that type of detail will help us build a picture of your planet's history."

"Seems to me you've already made your minds up that that's what's going to happen," said Chekoi. "We'll cooperate, but I'll be damned if I like it."

"General Raiban, Governor Nesul," said Khomi. "Speaking for my sub-Guild, I would like to be involved in this undertaking. It seems to me that the Department for Intellectual Development is the natural place to start recruiting your work force. I'm sure my members will be happy to work with Dr. Michaels and his people. After all, we'll learn new skills."

"Your offer of help is accepted," said Nesul. "A committee will have to be set up to implement this project. General Raiban, you're in overall control, but I feel that as well as Councillor Khomi, Councillor Rhuha of the Environment and Guild Master Vyaku of Communications should also be involved. I suggest we schedule a meeting later this evening as the matter is urgent."

Raiban nodded. "Certainly, Governor," she said, standing up and closing the case containing the remains.

"Ah, before you leave, General," said Esken smoothly, "I'd like a closer look at those Valtegan bones. I'd like to be able to identify them if they turn up again."

"Your people won't get the opportunity to visit the ruins

from now on," said Commander Chuz. "They are now under military guard. No one will have access to them without permission. Archaeologists from Earth will be starting work on the most likely sites shortly. We need to find out as much as we can about these damned Valtegans."

Konus watched Esken's expression harden and felt the faintest trace of his anger. Catching sight of his adversary looking at him, Esken quickly suppressed it and relaxed his facial muscles. "If that is your wish, then of course I'll be happy to oblige you."

"Commander, I need a statement for the public comm nets," said Vyaku. "If you don't issue one, then the sight of armed forces personnel will create alarm."

"A statement has been prepared," said Commander Chuz. "You'll have it at the end of this Council session."

While Raiban was collecting the case and waiting for Dr. Michaels to accompany her, Governor Nesul called a break for c'shar. Konis took the opportunity to go over to Nesul, taking the now vacant chair beside him.

"I hadn't realized Raiban had got so far with her plans," he said quietly.

"Neither had I. We need Lijou in on this. Will he help do you think?"

"I'm sure he will," said Konis. "Kusac is convinced the Brotherhood holds a lot of the pieces to this puzzle. Did I tell you Carrie and Ghyan, the priest from the temple at Valsgarth, are working on the visions and dreams that telepaths and the Brothers have experienced?"

"No, you haven't. What do they expect to find?"

"I'm not entirely sure, but it's something Kaid's been encouraging. Apparently he's been taking notes for years and he left them for Carrie to use."

"Left them?" Nesul frowned. "What's happened to Kaid?"

"Nothing. He's gone off looking for someone he used to know, that's all," said Konis, suddenly realizing that perhaps it would be better for Nesul not to know where Kaid was. "He seems to think the people who see the visions are actually seeing a replay of events from the past. If they are, this could be a vital part of the picture of our past, especially as the visions all involve the God, Vartra, and it's known He was active during the years of the Cataclysm."

"How can they possibly be seeing a replay of past events, Konis?"

Seeing the owner of the seat returning with his mug, Konis got hurriedly to his feet. "I'll tell you later. What about Fyak? I thought we were going to be discussing that today."

"We are. It's next on the agenda. Commander Chuz and the High Council are meeting to discuss it tonight as well. We're going to be busy. I need you at both those meetings."

"I'll be there," said Konis, moving away as Councillor Chaidu returned to her seat.

* * *

Kusac stood at their suite's inner doorway, watching the environmental force screens being installed in the lounge and the bedroom of their new home. He was aware of his father approaching—he'd been thoughtful enough to announce his presence mentally.

Konis put his hand on his son's shoulder. "I see you persuaded Rayazou to decorate for you. She's surpassed herself," he said, looking up at the painted moonlit sky overhead. Around them, the bedroom walls had been transformed into a woodland grove where creatures of all sizes were partially concealed among lush vegetation, their eyes shining out from among the bushes even in the daylight that filled the room.

"That's why I've been watching them," Kusac replied quietly. "I don't want the walls damaged. Rayazou actually painted most of this suite and the nursery herself as a gift for us. The murals for the whole house are her designs, of course, but her senior apprentices have been working on them." He turned round to face his father.

"It's a surprise for Carrie. Luckily she hasn't wanted to come down to the estate since the building work began. Too much dust and noise, mentally as well as audibly, she says."

"I'm sure she'll be delighted with the result. Your mother's going to be wanting our rooms redecorated as soon as she sees these." His tone was rueful.

With a grin, Kusac gestured to the hallway. "They're about finished now. Shall we go over to the lab? It's the only place where we can get away from the noise and the dust and sit down. Jack's there, and possibly Garras. Unless what you have to say is private?" He looked quizzically at his father, flicking an ear in deference to him.

"No, it's not private," said Konis, following him along the

balcony to the corridor leading downstairs. "I just wanted to tell you what happened at the council meeting last night. You'd turned in before I got home." He had to raise his voice above the sound of hammering and sawing.

"Loud, isn't it? In a couple of days it'll be finished. There's only the furnishings to be put in."

Kusac took his father's arm and hurried him down to the ground level, the noise decreasing as they walked along the colonnades. "We spent the afternoon out at the ruins again. All that fresh air made us tired."

"Watch she doesn't overdo things, Kusac," his father warned as they walked across the grassy courtyard to the wide arched gateway that led out into the estate gardens. "The first quarter is the most vulnerable time for females, and we still don't know for sure that it'll be a twenty-four week pregnancy."

"We'll soon find out," said Kusac. "Vanna says her pregnancy is following the normal Sholan development. She's only got four weeks to go now."

The wide gravel front to the house had been laid and the grassed areas cut. It was beginning to feel more like a home than a building unused for several generations. Kusac turned back to look at it. Despite the rather gray sky, set with the forest behind it as it was, the white exterior seemed almost luminous. A small army of clansfolk were finishing off behind the builders. Already the windows at the front of the house were hung with the brightly colored gossamer-fine drapes that Carrie loved.

"How could she fail to like it?" asked Konis as Kusac turned back to him and they began to walk down the pathway to the newly rebuilt estate village.

"Because she also has an unpredictable Human side."

"Isn't that part of what you love in her?" Konis raised a questioning eye ridge.

"Yes, but it also drives me mad at times," Kusac admitted, albeit with a grin. "Carrie was with Ghyan at our Shrine yesterday morning. They've been collating the data on the dreams and visions experienced by many of the past new Leska pairs at the Guild Hall, and, of course, ourselves. Did you know that Lijou has been giving Ghyan information on the Brotherhood's dreams too? I suppose with hindsight it makes sense since Ghyan is the principal priest of Vartra, outside of Lijou himself. We've probably got the most com-

prehensive database on Shola regarding these phenomena—
if you don't count the mountain folk."

He waited for his father's reaction and wasn't disappointed.
"*What* did you say?" Konis demanded, stopping dead in
his tracks.

The look on his father's face said it all. "I said, we have no
records of the replayed images that we call dreams, experienced by the mountain folk, nor of the stories of the cataclysm that they pass down from generation to generation."

Konis let out a low growl and started walking again. The
lab was only a few buildings ahead of them now. "Those
mountain folk are a law unto themselves," he said. "Apart
from the odd person, they flatly refuse not only to be tested
by the Guild, but to have anything to do with us in any way.
They're almost a clan in their own right! In their own way,
they're as bad as the desert Tribes."

"I think you've closed your teeth on the problem," said
Kusac thoughtfully. "Carrie said it was a shame there were
no clan records for the Brotherhood, but there are, after a
kind: the mountain folk themselves and their communities. A
high proportion of the Brothers come from the Dzahai
region. It should be possible to ask the village elders if they
keep any family records."

"This fits in with what I want to tell you about the meeting
yesterday," said Konis. "My news can wait, though. Tell me
more."

"Carrie was over at Noni's again a few days ago. She was
told that apparently we guild folk—meaning all the guilds—
know nothing about the Cataclysm. They have tales passed
down from mother to daughter. Detailed tales."

"We need those stories, Kusac," said Konis, stopping
again. "Raiban, with Chuz's support, has brought down
dozens of Human archaeologists to study the ancient cities in
order to discover as much as possible about our past. They're
also setting up a committee to collate all the guild histories.
The input from people like Noni could prove vital!"

"I agree, but how do you propose to get her and others like
her to cooperate?" asked Kusac, reaching out to draw his
father onward toward the lab.

"Vartra knows, Kusac, Vartra knows. I don't suppose you
have any ideas?"

Kusac led the way up the path to the lab doors. The medical
and research center had been one of the first buildings

completed on the estate. Already it looked like it had been there for decades because of the layers of dust from the construction work that coated the outside.

"You could try a straightforward approach and just ask her," he said. "Father, you know we've been digging up at the old ruined shrine, don't you? Well, Carrie is convinced that there's something beneath the surface of the ruin. When she was at Noni's, the Healer confirmed that the same crystals that are found on our land, particularly in that hillside, are also prevalent around Stronghold. They both believe that the crystals store memories in a similar fashion to the way our comm crystals store data, which is why the Leskas at our Guild, and the Brothers at Stronghold, have very vivid dreams. As I said, according to Noni, they aren't dreams, they're actual scenes from the lives of our ancestors that we can pick up when asleep or in a deep trance."

His father remained silent as they made their way into the building and down a corridor till they came to the lab door. Giving a brief knock, Kusac opened the door.

Jack looked up from his bench on the other side of the room. "Hello there! To what do we owe the pleasure of this visit? Getting away from the dirt and noise again?" he grinned.

Garras flicked his ears in greeting.

"I thought you'd be with Vanna," said Kusac.

"Not likely!" grinned Garras. "Vanna's recruited her brother and Sashti to help her reorganize the furniture in our house for the third time this week! I'm staying out of the way. Her nesting instinct is too damned strong now. I've seen it all before with my sisters. She'll be like this now till she goes into labor."

Konis sat down on a stool opposite him. "I know what you mean," he commiserated. "Kusac's got all those joys ahead of him."

"Oh, he'll enjoy every moment of it. It's the first time for them, after all."

Kusac made a skeptical noise as he headed over to the dispenser. "Can I get anyone a drink?" he asked.

The chorus of affirmatives was such that Garras came over to help him. Once they were all settled, Konis turned to his son.

"Have you discussed the replays, as you call them, with Garras?"

"Yes, he has," Garras answered for him. "I'm more skeptical than Kusac is. Not being a highlander like Kaid, I don't have his belief in what Noni says. She's a bit too manipulative for my likes. Nothing's ever simple with her, there's always got to be an underlying psychological reason for every ill or injury you take to her. Having said that, when I looked at Kaid's book with Carrie, there are an incredible number of dreams repeated word for word over the years. Too many to be a coincidence. There could well be something in what Kusac says."

"What differentiates a dream from a replay?"

"The very fact that it's been experienced in the same form by more than one person," said Kusac. "They also tell you something about how the world was then. You get a feel for which is which. There's definitely a cohesive picture emerging about the days of the Cataclysm."

Konis looked over to Garras, who nodded.

"There's a distinct story there."

Konis took a drink from his mug. "What makes you so sure it goes back as far as then? They could all belong to another, nearer time."

"Vartra's inextricably linked with the Cataclysm, we're all agreed on that at least, aren't we?" said Kusac, looking round the four of them.

"Yes," said Garras.

"Kaid's research shows that the replays depict a time of war, a time of drastic change for the people who lived then. After it, society as we now know it was set up, complete with guilds and clans, and Vartra was deeply involved in bringing those changes about. What do the stories told not only by the temple but outside by the storytellers tell us about Vartra?"

"Exactly the same," said Konis.

'Which came first, though?" asked Garras. "The stories or the dreams? They could each have affected the other."

"Carrie says that according to Ghyan, it's in the records that the Leskas who had these dreams or replays, were ordered not to discuss them with anyone other than the temple priest or the head of the Order at Stronghold."

"We could argue which came first till the end of time," said Konis. "Do we have any input from the Telepath Guild?"

"Some," said Kusac. "Ghyan said that in the past Telepath

Guild Masters have requested more information on the replays or dreams than they've provided in return to the Order of Vartra. It's as if they've been researching it themselves for as long as the Order but are less willing to share their data."

"Why would the Guild be independently interested in religious matters?" said Konis thoughtfully, taking another sip of his drink. "Have they a secular reason for their interest, one they're keeping to themselves?"

"Let's assume the replays are from the Cataclysm," said Kusac, finally remembering his own drink and taking a mouthful. "We have to have a starting point. Given that, several facts can then be assumed. The Cataclysm involved some kind of warfare, whether with other Sholans or not, we don't know, but the presence of Valtegan remains dating back that far strongly suggests it was with them."

"Wait a minute," Garras objected. "Look at Keiss. There wasn't out and out warfare with the Valtegans there. They might have been visitors, traders even, back then."

Kusac gave a snort of derision. "You don't believe that any more than I do. There *was* out and out warfare on Keiss once we arrived. Only the lack of weapons and numbers prevented the Keissians from rising before. Just assume I'm right for the moment. Now, the people in the replays are in hiding, that much is incontestable, as is the fact that a person, who may well be Vartra, is involved with a group of these people and that they're telepaths. They have to be, because some of the replays involve people who have a newly formed Leska Link." He looked across at Garras who nodded.

"We also have one replay which mentions that these Leska pairs have suddenly become too sensitive to pain to be able to fight, indicating that the disability is a new one. In another replay, we find Vartra concerned for the happiness and welfare of new Leskas. He's aware of the suffering the telepaths of those days have endured, saying that too many have died, and that they've all been discovered too soon. There is almost a sense of guilt in the Vartra of the visions, as if he feels personally responsible for causing the telepaths suffering. He feels the need to justify himself, saying *I was never looking for a solution.*"

"Why would a political figure such as Vartra feel responsible for their suffering?" asked Jack. "Could he have ordered them to do something for the good of Shola that resulted in large numbers of them dying?"

"Possibly, but there's more of a sense of having had a plan in the making and that it, and they, had been discovered too soon," said Kusac.

"This all hinges on whether or not Vartra was a real person, or the personification of an idea," said Garras. "I still say you're building on sand, Kusac. More than a few of us know Ghyan is biased toward the theory that Vartra was a living person, not a God."

"We've nothing else to build on." Kusac was beginning to get exasperated at Garras' stubbornness.

"In Earth's past, heroes easily became gods in the eyes of the people who came after them," said Jack. "The outstanding abilities they showed immediately marked them out as the son or daughter of one or another of the gods—immediately with hindsight, of course," he grinned.

"What does Kaid believe?" asked Konis.

"He believes Vartra is a God, as I do," said Garras. "And that Vartra speaks to him, as He does to others."

"I know Kaid believes Vartra was a God, so do I, but I also believe he was a person! How could Kaid experience these replays without being aware that Vartra, as a person, was in them?" demanded Kusac. "He recorded them!"

"Patience, Kusac," said his father. "What about Lijou? Could he shed any light on this? Perhaps his records say something."

"Lijou's head of the Order. Of course he believes Vartra is a God," said Garras.

"I wouldn't be too sure if I were you," said Kusac. "Lijou obviously knows how Ghyan feels yet he never removed him from office. Carrie's reminding me that Kaid told her that Lijou and Ghyan were cooperating on this whole issue. If they were diametrically opposed, how could they cooperate?"

"I need to speak to Lijou personally about this," said Konis. "What you've told me, Kusac, shows that there is definitely some link between these replays, as you call them, and the past. If they can be reliably tied to the time of the Cataclysm, then that's all we need. Whether or not Vartra is a God isn't relevant to whether or not we can rely on these replays as being historically accurate."

He looked over to the Human. "I'll keep in mind what you've said, Jack. It seems logical to me that a folk hero could well become regarded as a God with the passage of time. Now, changing the topic slightly, yesterday the council, backed by High Commander Chuz, ordered that all guilds were to make their records available to a committee led by General Raiban. There will be Terrans involved too. A Dr. Michaels will help guide the committee until someone more appropriate has been brought from Earth. He's actually here to head a team of Terran archaeologists who are to excavate the ruins looking for more clues to our past, specifically what the Valtegans were doing here."

"That's going to please the guild leaders," said Garras. "I can't see them opening up their records willingly."

"They don't have the choice," said Konis. "It has to be done. We have to find out why the Valtegans had a presence on Shola during the Cataclysm."

"They're going to investigate the ruins?" asked Kusac. "I can imagine how delighted Master Esken was."

"They're choosing the five most promising sites to excavate," said Konis. "All ruins will be placed under military guard to prevent them being tampered with."

"Looks like there'll be new skills to learn," said Garras. "It's an exciting time for the young ones."

"It is indeed," said Konis, glancing at Kusac. "No one could have realized how far-reaching the impact of meeting the Humans would be on our culture. I hope we don't change too fast."

"I'm sure we won't, Father. We can rely on people like Esken and Chekoi to stop that happening." Kusac hesitated, wondering whether or not to bring the ruined shrine to his father's attention again. "Father, what about the ruins on my estate?"

Konis finished his drink before replying. "I'm sure you can rest easy on that issue, Kusac. I don't think the remains of one building will be of interest to the archaeologists."

"I'm afraid they may be. As I began to tell you earlier, on our visit yesterday, we unearthed the bulk of what is definitely a statue of Vartra. Not just that, but Carrie is sensing more of the building underground. Caverns and metal structures, she says. Several of her dreams, or replays, have been centered there, so have Kaid's. She's convinced that a group of telepaths, possibly under Vartra's command, were in hiding there."

His father swung round on his stool to face him. "Let me

get this straight. You think that you've found Vartra's primary headquarters up in that old ruined shrine?"

Kusac nodded. "Yes. It has all the potential of a concealed base, if there's anything underground as Carrie says. The feel of the ruins at one part is like the Warrior Guild, controlled aggression is how she put it. Not what you'd expect on holy ground."

"The Brotherhood has that," reminded Garras.

"This place is nowhere near as large as Stronghold. There isn't the room above ground for a large number of people to have been trained as Warriors. Believe me, the last thing I want is a group of Humans on my estate," said Kusac. "I don't want Carrie exposed to them again, especially now that she's pregnant and we're just about to move into our own home, but . . ."

"What we need is a large ultrasound scanner," said Jack thoughtfully. "Like the one down the corridor. Of course, it would need a few adjustments—a way of running it without a main power feed, for instance. And if we were lucky enough to find anything, well, I used to hunt for fossils on the east coast of England as a lad. I know a little bit about unearthing finds of archaeological interest. How are you at tinkering with electrical equipment, Garras?"

"I've had to do a few field repairs in my time," he said. "Not that I think this has anything to do with Vartra, you realize."

"Think of it as an opportunity to prove me wrong then," said Kusac, relieved that Garras was prepared to help. "Or a legitimate reason to be excused moving furniture."

Garras' mouth opened in a deep grin. "That'll do," he said.

"No need to tell the authorities unless we're sure of what we've found, is there, Konis?" said Jack. "You're just indulging an old man's whims, aren't you? I mean, what possible interest could they have in a ruined monastery?"

Kusac watched his father look from Jack to Garras then back to him as a pained expression crossed his face. "I've never met anyone more devious than your mother, till today." He shook his head, ears flicking in mock dismay. "Keep me posted on what you find. I can't see it's in Carrie's interests to have strangers living on the estate, but if you do find anything important, we'll have to tell Raiban."

Kusac nodded. "Knowing that the ruins are being worked

on will make it easier for Carrie to accept that she can't do any more digging herself."

"Until we get these two new global projects off the ground, none of us will have any idea of what is and what isn't important," said Konis, glancing at his wrist comm. "We'd better be heading back soon. When will the estate housing be finished?"

"Garras and Vanna are already living in their home, and several of the Brothers are in one of the finished dormitory houses, but that's all as yet. There will be some ten estate cottages ready by the end of the week when we plan to move in. Jack's quarters here should be ready around the same time. The rest of the cottages are further into the estate and not of such a high priority. Obviously I wanted the main area totally finished first, and the nearest fields are having their crops planted now. We couldn't have managed it without the help of Mother's clansfolk. She's even arranged for me to have an estate manager."

Konis got to his feet. "It looks like you've got everything well in hand," he said. "I'm going to head back up to the house. I'll see you later."

"You forgot to tell us what's happening about Fyak," Kusac reminded him.

"So I did. It's been decided that we're going to see he's contained within the desert region for the time being. We'll be monitoring his activities from a distance. The tribes are fiercely independent, as you know, and no good will come if we get involved at this stage. The last thing any of us wants is a civil war on our hands. Naturally, the sale of armaments to them has been stopped, but that's all for the moment. It's not what I feel we should be doing, but there's enough going on with this social upheaval without making more trouble for ourselves. Have you had any news of Kaid or Dzaka yet?"

"None, beyond what you already know, that when he reached Raul he hired a hunting aircar for two weeks."

"If he's gone off to Rhijudu then the worst thing we can do is draw attention to that fact," said Garras. "He'll contact us when he's ready. Until then, we wait."

"When he's back, I want to speak to him about that female, Khemu. Before I see Naeul Arrazo personally, I need to have all the facts," said Konis, walking toward the door. "I'll see you all at third meal."

* * *

"Nearly there," said Brynne, following the beacon into the parking area at the rear of the building. "That's it. Vartra's Retreat." He took a moment to glance down at it himself.

Nestled in the rocky embrace of the Dzahai Mountains, the Retreat was an imposing building. Built of blocks of the native stone, its gray exterior lay sprawling beneath them. From the air, it was easy to see that the original building had been of quite modest proportions, and had been added to over the centuries.

Byrnne returned his attention to the aircar and began to circle down to the vehicle park.

"We can take a look at the Retreat, then go crystal hunting," said Ross.

"Fine by me."

"What's the history behind this place?" asked Ross, as he and Brynne walked toward the entrance. Lhea followed them at a respectful distance.

"Ah. Give me a moment," Brynne said, searching through his memories. A stray thought came from Vanna.

The Retreat?

Yes. What is it?

Legend has it as a place where Vartra will answer the prayers of His worshipers. It's where you go when you really need the God's help. If you're actually interested, ask Lhea or one of the lay-priests. They'll be glad to tell you.

"Vanna says it's a place to get close to Vartra," said Brynne. "Apparently the people believe the God answers their prayers here."

"A place of pilgrimage," nodded Ross. "Very imposing. Do you think we'll be able to find anyone to guide us round it?"

"We can ask," said Brynne. "It isn't a tourist attraction, though, it's a working holy place."

"They don't cater for visitors?" Ross stopped to look quizzically at him. "You do surprise me."

"Why?"

"I'd have thought their trading instincts would have made them aware of the commercial possibilities of such a place." He waved his hand toward the massive wooden doors. "I'm sure any visitors from Earth would love to come and see this."

Brynne drew him on again and they passed into the entrance hallway. "This isn't for the curious, Ross. It's for people who believe in their God. They don't make a circus out of their religion, it's a very personal thing." He turned to look for his bodyguard.

"Lhea," he said, beckoning her closer. "Can you tell us about the Retreat?"

"What would you like to know?" she asked.

"How about starting with where we are?" suggested Ross.

Lhea raised an eye ridge. "In the entrance hall," she said quietly. "If you look at the paintings on the walls, you'll see the story of the God's life"

"Take us round them, please, Lhea," said Brynne.

She led them past a small group of curious Sholans to the first panel. "This one shows the world as it was before the Cataclysm," she said, indicating a scene showing large cities, busy roadways and airports. "It wasn't a pleasant world, as you can see by the dark clouds that sit above the scene." She moved on to the next panel.

"Looks just like Earth," said Ross in an undertone.

"I think that's the point," said Brynne. "Don't you prefer Shola with its forests and plains to Earth with its highly industrialized cities?"

"Each has its own merits," said Ross placidly.

Lhea stopped at the next panel. "Then came the Cataclysm," she said.

The scene depicted a world in chaos, with angry, boiling clouds of darkness in the sky, echoed by floods and earthquakes below. City towers were falling, and everywhere Sholans were shown running for their lives.

She moved on to the next panel. "This is our God," she said simply.

On a rocky parapet, a tall Sholan wearing a Warrior's harness was standing. Arm upraised, he appeared to be calling to them as they stood looking at the panel. Behind him, the sky was tinged with fire.

"Powerful," said Ross. "Primitive imagery always works best."

Brynne shifted uncomfortably and Lhea positively scowled.

"Excuse me," said a voice from behind. "Perhaps I can be of assistance?"

Brynne turned to find one of the Brothers standing behind them.

"News of the arrival of two Terrans travels fast," said the lay-priest, mouth opening in a slight smile. "I've been asked to invite you to visit the Guardian."

"The Guardian?" asked Brynne. He felt Ross tap his arm and turned to look at him.

"What are you talking about?" asked the older man, frowning.

"The Guardian's invited us to visit him," said Brynne.

"In English," Ross said, his tone sharp.

Brynne frowned. He was sure he'd told him in English.

"You are to meet the Guardian of the Retreat," said Lhea, coming to the rescue.

"I'm sorry," said the Brother, switching to English. "I had not realized you only spoke your own language. You must have been one of the first Humans to arrive on Shola. Nowadays everyone is given a knowledge of our language. Please, come with me."

They followed him through the inner doors into the main hall of the building, walking down the side aisle past the rows of padded mats, some of which were occupied by sleeping or meditating Sholans.

"We're a working Retreat," the Brother said quietly. "There are always those who are ill in spirit or body who need to seek the God's healing."

He led them toward the statue of Vartra, where he stopped. Taking a piece of incense from the container, he crumbled it into the glowing brazier held between the God's hands. Bowing, he stepped past it and waited for the others to follow.

Brynne felt self-conscious as he paid his respect to the God. He could feel Ross' critical gaze burning holes in the back of his head. Ross didn't agree with any of the Sholan religious beliefs and his request to come here had surprised him. Stepping over to join the lay-priest, he watched to see what Ross would do.

"Sorry," Ross said, with a gentle smile to the Brother. "This isn't my faith." With that, he stepped past the statue to join them.

Brynne tried not to glance at the Brother, but his eyes slid sideways despite himself. He saw the gentle flick of the lay-brother's ears in his direction, saying that he understood and it didn't matter to him.

Lhea took a moment or two longer to make her obeisance before she joined them. The Brother turned, and, pulling the heavy crimson drapes aside, led them into the residential area of the building.

"It's a pleasure to welcome you to the Retreat," said the Guardian, standing up to receive them.

Brynne looked round the small lounge. He was surprised to find it no different from any other he'd been in.

"It's good to have a homely anchor when one lives in a holy place," he smiled. "I'm pleased to meet you," he said, holding out his hand. "Your presence honors us. I'm Dhaika."

They touched fingertips briefly.

"You've brought a friend with you, I see. And Sister Lhea."

"Guardian Dhaika," she said, inclining her head to the priest.

"This is Ross Derwent," said Brynne, indicating his friend.

"Please, be seated," said Dhaika, indicating the easy chairs. He switched to speaking English. "What brings you to the Retreat? You're the first of our new Guild members to visit us."

"Ross asked to come. We were in the area on a rock and crystal gathering expedition."

'You've certainly come to the right place. The whole mountain range is blessed with a multitude of different crystals, depending on which part you're in. Are you looking for anything in particular?"

Brynne looked over at Ross.

"Oh, I'm interested in comparisons with Earth," said Ross. "On our world, crystals often give access to great power."

"Indeed," said Dhaika. "I'm afraid you're more likely to find that kind of crystal a little closer to home. In your comm, to be exact," he smiled. "The kind of crystals you speak of are grown industrially, not found naturally."

"Your world must be very different from ours, then," murmured Ross. "At home, natural crystals magnify natural energy, and many people can tap that power, people who are attuned to the earth we live on, and believe Her to be a living entity."

"We have such a cult here," nodded Dhaika. "The Green Goddess, we call Her."

"Not the same," smiled Ross, settling himself more comfortably. "Your Green Goddess isn't the incarnation of the planet."

"I can't say, Mr. Derwent. As I'm sure you'll appreciate, we're of a different belief here," said the Guardian gently.

"A reverence for Mother Earth should be common to us all, Guardian Dhaika."

"Perhaps, were we on Earth, Mr. Derwent. But as you yourself said, Shola is a different world." The reprimand, though gentle, was there and Brynne winced. "Perhaps a visit to Her temple at the Ferraki hills would be of more interest to you."

"Perhaps. Tell me, Guardian, do you have ley lines on Shola?"

"Ley lines?" Dhaika raised an eye ridge. "I'm unfamiliar with the term."

"Lines of power that cross the planet. They usually join sites of ancient religions."

"We've certainly got ancient religions, but as for lines of power . . . What kind of power do you mean?"

"Psychic power. You can tap into these lines and use the power."

"Interesting theory," murmured Dhaika, glancing toward Lhea. "Not one I've come across, though. Is that what brings you to our Retreat? A quest for power?"

"A search for the natural power of the planet," corrected Ross.

"Why would you want to locate such areas of power, Mr. Derwent? I must admit to being baffled as to any practical value that these lines of power could have."

"They're a source of energy when you work."

The Guardian looked toward Brynne, then back to Ross. "When we work as telepaths, Mr. Derwent, we use our own power and energy. We have no need for any outside source."

"Oh, I'm not talking about the commercial work," said Ross, warming to his theme. "I mean the *real* work, when you bless a holy site, or when you repair the damage caused to it by thoughtless youths or pollution. Then you need to draw on the power of the earth, and make use of the crystals that channel this power."

Brynne was beginning to get concerned. He was

increasingly aware of the Guardian's feelings about Ross
and the topics he was determined to discuss. It was time to
bring the discussion to an end.

"Ross, you didn't tell me you wanted to discuss this with
the Guardian," he said. "If you had, I could have told you
we'd come to the wrong temple."

"That's all right, Brynne," said Ross. "I'm sure that now
the Guardian is aware of these powers, he'll want to look
into them for himself. After all, only earth endures forever,
doesn't it, Guardian Dhaika?"

"If you allow for erosion," Dhaika murmured in Sholan.

Brynne bit back his smile. There were times when even he
found Ross too much to take seriously. Still, he'd learned a
lot that was useful from him in the few months since they'd
met him.

Dhaika rose to his feet, indicating their meeting was at an
end. "I won't keep you from your expedition, Mr. Derwent.
It's been interesting meeting you. Do come again, Brynne,
and bring your Leska next time," he said. "Sister Lhea."

They made their way back through the main temple area
till they reached the open air.

"Where now?" asked Brynne.

"We'll just have a wander round," said Ross, sticking his
hands in his pockets and strolling toward the exit. "I've
picked up a ley line around here somewhere and I'd like to
follow it. I'm sure it'll cross another somewhere over there,"
he said, nodding toward the south. "We may even find an old
shrine or something there that we can look at."

"Stronghold lies that way," said Lhea. "You will not be
allowed to visit there."

"Oh? What makes you so sure, my dear?" asked Ross.

"Stronghold doesn't allow visitors."

"I wouldn't be a visitor if I accompanied you, now would
I? There must be some business you have to do there today,"
he said, stopping and turning toward her.

"No," was her short answer.

"Brynne, that Guardian chappie said you were a member
of the Brotherhood now. What about you? They'd allow you
in, surely?"

"No way, Ross!" said Brynne, beginning to walk on again.
"I haven't been sworn into the Brotherhood yet. That place is
just not open to the likes of us, take it from me. Even if it

was, I wouldn't go there! I haven't forgotten the night they had Vanna kidnapped!"

Ross frowned. "You're being overcautious, Brynne. There's no reason why they shouldn't let us in, is there? Still, we can always try another day," he said. "Now, let's find out exactly where this ley line is, shall we? What I want you to do is be aware of the earth, feel its power under your feet. Watch for any changes in that power, because that's where you'll find the ley lines."

Lhea walked a few feet behind them, keeping her senses alert for any potential dangers. She was glad Brynne had told the old one to stop talking to the Guardian the way he had. He was always going on like that. Why he had come to Shola, she couldn't understand. Nothing was as good here as it was back on *his* Earth. She wished he'd head back there, and as soon as possible! All this mysticism rubbish he was talking was just that—rubbish. Only the younglings he told it to didn't know that. If Brynne kept company with him for much longer, she was afraid he'd end up in trouble too, and her job was to keep him out of trouble!

She sighed and shook her head. She felt really sorry for Physician Kyjishi. All the troubles she'd had with him, and now this Ross Derwent came along making more for her.

CHAPTER 12

From the safety of the bushes on the rear slopes of the village, he'd kept watch on the comings and goings of the inhabitants for several days now. He'd a good idea where she was—in a small cottage just to the right of where he was concealed. It was one of the few dwellings where the sole inhabitant was obviously ill. Once a day, in the evening, a neighbor would call with hot food. On the third day, by a stroke of good fortune, he'd heard the female call out to her. *Khemu!* she'd shouted. *I'll be late tonight! The Faithful have called a prayer meeting.*

The next day he stayed hidden till an hour after sunset when all the villagers and Faithful alike closed their doors for the night. Slowly, cautiously, he climbed down the slope to the pathway at the back of her house. Staying close to the wall, he crept along to the partially open window. He stood up, slipping his claw tips between the shutters, easing the left one outward just enough to allow him to see the interior. Across from him there was a bed with a long mound in the center of it. He waited, watching to see if she moved. She didn't: she must be asleep.

Pushing the shutter open a fraction more, he vaulted quietly to the window ledge, balancing there momentarily till he could see what was in front of him. It was the sink, and it was empty. To one side of it was a work surface, also clear of any implements. Stepping onto the surface, he leaped quietly to the floor. After a moment or two's stillness, when he knew he hadn't wakened her, he turned and drew the shutters closed.

"Who's there?" she demanded, suddenly raising herself up on her elbow and peering toward the window. "I know you're there. Show yourself!"

Kaid turned round again and stepped out of the shadows,

standing so the moonlight from the front window fell full on him. He should have known he couldn't surprise her.

Khemu sucked in her breath with an audible hiss. "Tallinu!"

He stayed where he was, unmoving. "I heard you were ill, Khemu."

"You haven't changed," she said abruptly. "How did you find me after all these years?"

"I didn't. Ghezu did."

"He's still around, is he?"

Kaid flicked an ear in agreement. "He's the Leader of the Brotherhood Warriors now."

"Huh," was all she said as she tried to push herself up into a sitting position.

Kaid came forward, reaching out to help her.

"I can manage. I don't need your help," she snapped, pulling away from him before he could touch her. "What brings you here anyway?"

"I needed to see you, to apologize for that night . . ."

"Apologize?" she said, frowning. "Just how do you intend to apologize, Tallinu?"

Shifting from one foot to the other, he tried not to look away from her. He'd forgotten how piercing her gaze could be. "It all happened so quickly. I'd never been with a telepath before, I didn't know what could happen . . . what would happen," he said, aware of how lame he sounded.

"You *knew* what you were." Her voice was unforgiving.

"Suspicions, nothing more. Dammit, Khemu," he said, trying to keep his voice as low as possible. "I knew nothing for sure! You ran off before I could speak to you—ask you what had happened! By the time I'd made some sense of it all, you wouldn't see me!"

"Vartra's bones, Tallinu! What did you expect of me? I was no older than you! We were just younglings then. You scared the life out of me! I couldn't cope with what you were—what you'd been."

"I realize that now."

"Then there was the cub. You left me pregnant, Tallinu!" Her voice cracked and broke, sending her into paroxysms of coughing.

Turning, he went to the stone water cooler by the sink and fetched her a drink. "Here," he said, sitting on the edge of her bed and handing her the mug.

Ears flicking in thanks, she took a couple of shuddering

breaths. Her hand closed over his as she took the mug from him. She sipped the drink, not taking her eyes from his face.

"Did you find the cub?"

"Yes, I found him," he replied, moving his hand from under hers so he could reach up to touch her face. "No one guessed who he was except old Jyarti who let me foster him." He let his hand fall to rest on the covers beside hers.

She handed the mug back to him. Taking it from her, he leaned forward, placing it on the night table.

"I kept trying to see you. I called at the house daily," he said quietly. "I wanted to do what was right, Khemu. Not just for your sake, but for the cub's. Why didn't you . . ."

"I'd no choice," she said, cutting him short. "My parents knew what had happened by then. They knew it was one of the Brothers and they didn't want any trouble with Stronghold. Because I refused to tell them who I'd been with, they kept me locked in my room."

Her voice had become as bleak as her eyes.

"Why didn't you tell them? Surely they guessed it was me when I kept calling?"

"Why should I tell them? You weren't the only one who came, you know. Ghezu called too," she said. "They weren't interested in who the father was, only in the fact that the betrothal arranged by the Clan Lord had to be canceled. They refused to let the world know of my shame. They told him I'd died . . . in a climbing accident," she said contemptuously. "Me, mountain born and bred, killed in a climbing accident? The Guild believed it though, as did the Clan Lord."

"They did that because of our cub?" Anger surged through him.

She put her head to one side, raising her eye ridges. "Our cub?" she said. "I suppose he is. I never thought of him as mine, only yours. They took him from me as soon as he was born."

"Why?" In part he already knew the answer. The depths that families could sink to in their quarrels were no surprise to me. Too often he and others from Stronghold had been called in to settle disputes in a manner that forbade further argument.

She shrugged. "Since I was dead, how could the cub exist?"

"What did they do with him?"

She sighed, moving restlessly, trying to get comfortable. "They gave him to the estate nursery. He grew up there, in the charge of whoever was on duty."

"I know what it's like to grow up on the wrong side of the hearth," he said, his voice betraying an anger he was finding increasingly difficult to control. "I saved him from as much of that as I could at Stronghold. Who brought him to me?"

"Some time after he was born, they sent me to a house near the Clan village. My father's punishment was for me to see the cubs every day but never be able to speak to them. When he was old enough to play outside, I could tell which cub was yours: he was always alone or being picked on. So when I finally managed to escape, I took him with me."

He caught her eyes but with a flick of her ears, she looked away. "I couldn't leave him there. All that pain and hurt in one so little. Yes, I suppose I did care for him," she admitted quietly. "I did what I could to wipe out his memories of the time on the estate so he could have a fresh start. The rest you know. My family couldn't admit I was still alive so they couldn't search for me or him."

Ever alert, Kaid heard a slight noise from behind. Ears pricked as far sideways as they could go, he urgently signed for her to be silent. Turning his head to look over his shoulder at the open window, he leaned forward, ready to spring into the shadows by the front door.

"Don't bother, Kaid," said Dzaka's disembodied voice. "Move, and I *will* shoot."

Kaid relaxed, his left hand slowly inching toward the knife concealed at the back of his jacket. He was glad the wait was over.

The muzzle of the gun appeared first, then Dzaka vaulted through the window to land on the work surface. The sound of a soft footfall and he stood in the room with them.

"Who the hell are you?" demanded Khemu angrily. "Are you one of Fyak's people?"

"No. I'm Dzaka."

She glanced from him to Kaid then back.

"He's our son," Kaid confirmed.

"You might have taught him better manners. What the hell do you mean by entering my house like that without leave?" she demanded, looking him up then down.

Their attention safely diverted for the moment, Kaid palmed his knife under a fold in the bedcover.

"I've been appointed to protect you," said Dzaka, his gun still trained on Kaid as he stepped closer to where they sat.

"By whom, and against whom?"

"Leader Ghezu told me Kaid intended to harm you because of his guilt over his actions toward you in the past."

Kaid could tell by the constant movement of Dzaka's ears and the occasional jerky flicking of his tail that his son was balanced on a knife edge. Dzaka had psyched himself up to the point where he was prepared to kill him if he thought it necessary.

"Just what did Ghezu tell you?" asked Khemu.

"He said Kaid had drugged you with faka juice so you'd go with him that night."

"Drugged me?" She looked at Kaid. "He certainly hasn't inherited *my* brains!" She turned back to her son. "Tallinu didn't drug me, youngling. How old are you now? Thirty?"

"Thirty-four," said Dzaka stiffly. "What's my age got to do with it?"

"You've known Tallinu thirty years and yet you believed Ghezu?" She gave a snort of disgust. "I didn't know I'd given birth to a fool! Ghezu's Talent is to cast a glamour over what he says. You've been duped, boy!"

The nose of the gun barrel had begun to droop and a confused look crossed Dzaka's face. "You mean he didn't drug you?"

"That's what I just said, isn't it?"

"But why did you . . . How did I come . . ." He broke off, obviously at a loss to know how to ask his all-important question.

"That's none of your business!" she snapped, beginning to cough again. "How dare you ask me that!"

Kaid realized she'd staggered Dzaka, making him doubt what he'd been told. Now was the time to push the advantage home. The risk was still there, but it was acceptable.

"I'm going to give her some water, Dzaka," said Kaid, slowly stretching out his hand for the mug. "Either use that damned gun and get it over with, or put it away."

He held the mug to her mouth and this time, when she'd done, her fingers remained curled round his and she leaned against him trying to regain her strength.

"How much longer?" he asked her softly, his other hand reaching up to smooth the hair away from her face.

"Days, a couple of weeks at most," she said, her voice barely audible. "If I'm unlucky."

He pushed aside the grief. It served no purpose now. "Tell me where your medication is and I'll get it for you."

"I've none. They won't let me have any."

He began to growl deep in his throat, ears flicking sidewards with the anger he could no longer contain. His hand tightened round hers protectively. "Are you in pain? I have something with me that I can give you."

"I can just control it," she said, pushing herself upright again. "You can't be weak in the desert. It either strengthens you or kills you. Looks like it's done both to me."

"Leave with me, Khemu," he urged. "I've a vehicle not far from here."

"No, I've lived here too long to want to leave now," she said.

Kaid had been keeping a portion of his mind focused on Dzaka and knew he was no longer a threat. He reached into a pocket with his left hand, wincing as the almost healed wound on his arm was stretched.

"What have you done to your arm?" she asked, concern in her voice.

"It's nothing," he said. "An accident. Take this." He put a small blue capsule into her hand, closing her fingers around it. "For when you choose to end it. Bite the capsule and swallow the liquid. It acts in minutes and is painless."

Opening her hand, she looked at the capsule lying in her palm. "You've just given me my freedom."

"I've one other thing to give you. Please don't refuse it." He hesitated, wishing Dzaka wasn't there. "I said I hoped to make things right. When I realized there'd be a cub, I had a bracelet made for you. I carried it with me each time I came to your estate, hoping to get the chance to offer it to you."

He saw a surprised look cross her face then felt the gentle touch of her mind against his for a moment.

"You really did," she said. "Why? We didn't love each other, Tallinu."

"I know, but I had hoped for a relationship with you, not just one night. And the responsibility for our cub was mine; I didn't want him to grow up as I did, with no registered father."

She looked past him to Dzaka. "Yes," she said thoughtfully. "Why not? I'll take your bracelet, Tallinu. Do something useful, brat. Fetch me the box you'll find on the top of that chest on the far side of the room."

Dzaka, still with a stunned look on his face, was putting his gun away. "Ghezu lied to me. Everything he said was a lie," he said, looking from one parent to the other.

"I tried to tell you," said Kaid. "Ghezu and I fought over Khemu that night and when she refused him, he got abusive with her."

Khemu nodded. "He'd heard me ask Tallinu to accompany me home. While his friends restrained him, we left." She began to cough again, bending over and putting her hand to her throat to ease the pain.

"More water?" asked Kaid.

She shook her head. "Let's get this done, then you must leave. You've been here long enough as it is. You risked too much in coming here, both of you," she said. "Fetch the box, Dzaka." She turned to Kaid. "You chose the name? *Brought-in-from-the-cold.* Apt."

"It's a traditional mountain name, one that's fallen into disuse now," said Kaid, pushing back his right sleeve so he could take off the silver bracelet that lay concealed beneath it; the bracelet he'd worn for nearly thirty-five years.

As Dzaka came over with the box and handed it to her, she grasped him by the wrist. "Stay, brat. You're a lay-priest like your father. You can witness your own legitimization." She let him go and took the box from him, laying it on the bed beside her.

"Just put the bracelet on me, Tallinu. No messing about, hear? We're long past the need for all that ritual."

As Kaid took her hand and placed the bracelet round the painfully thin wrist, he could almost see again the young female he'd known all those years ago. Her face seemed to flesh out and her hair and body fur were once more the soft luxuriant gray of her youth.

He heard Dzaka let out a gasp of shock, and the image was gone, replaced by the thin, frail female she'd become.

"Memories never age," she said, her mouth opening in a faint smile. She opened her box, taking out a bracelet only slightly narrower than the one she now wore. "You can have this one. It has my family crest on it. Wear it and damn them for me, Tallinu!" she said, reaching for his hand.

"Oh, your father'll be damned, never fear," said Kaid grimly.

"No," she said, pushing the silver circlet over his hand and down onto his wrist. "Go to him, take Dzaka with you, and show him *your* bracelet. That will break his pride more than anything."

He turned his hand over, clasping hers. "If that's what you wish. We are one now," he said.

"We are one." She released him and picked up the box to hand it back to her son. "Here, take this with you, Dzaka. Everything that's in it is yours now. You have two families, always remember that. The Arrazo and Tallinu's. Be sure to honor both, and wear my family crest for your grandfather to see!"

She froze, ears swiveling toward the door. "Go now!" She pushed Dzaka and the box away from her. "Fyak's warriors are coming! You've a chance if you leave immediately!"

Dzaka hesitated.

"Go!" said Kaid, picking up his knife and pocketing it as he rose to his feet in one fluid motion. "I'll be behind you. If I don't make it, leave without me. My craft's in the arroyo two kilometers west of here." He knew his son would be hard pressed to reach it ahead of Fyak's warriors—unless he bought some time by creating a diversion.

Dzaka staggered backward as an image of the location of the craft flashed briefly in his mind's eye.

From the street outside, the sound of running feet and low voices could now be plainly heard.

"Go, I said!" growled Kaid, heading for the door. Grasping the heavy wooden latch, he slammed it into place. Pulling his gun out, he returned to Khemu's side.

Dzaka turned and ran for the window, jumping up onto the work surface. He turned for a last look at them, then Kaid was beside him, thrusting a coin into his hand before pushing him through the opening. Already Fyak's guards had reached the door and were pounding on it.

"You'll need this. Give it to Garras. Tell him I said he was to protect you!"

Kaid had time to push the shutters together and turn back to the room.

"I'm sorry, Khemu," he began.

"Don't be. I'm glad you came, glad to have seen him . . ."

The door flew open and two warriors burst in as Kaid flung himself toward the table in the center of the room. The floor beside him ignited briefly, sending up a shower of hot splinters as he hit the ground rolling. He came up in a crouch, getting off a couple of shots before a narrow beam of light hit him on the thigh, sending pain searing down every nerve in his body. Unable to control his muscles, he hit the ground hard this time, his injured arm crashing against the table leg as he fell. His gun spun in a lazy arc across the floor to stop at the feet of the male who'd shot him. From nearby he could hear Khemu howling in fear.

"Rrurto, get the gun. L'Seuli, get after the one that went through the window," snapped the warrior in charge.

Lying there in frozen agony, all Kaid could see was the leader's clawed toes poking out beneath his tan robes as he came toward him. The feet stopped half a meter from his head. The male bent down, grasping him by the hair. His head was jerked up off the ground and pulled backward until his captor could see his face.

The mouth opened in a large grin, teeth shining in the moonlight. "We got him. He's the one the Prophet wants."

At this point, his world blacked out.

When he came round, the worst of the pain was gone though his arm still throbbed and his whole body felt as if it was tingling. Arms bound behind his back, he was propped against the side of the bed in a vaguely sitting position. Opposite him an armed guard stood on watch.

He moved his head slightly but he could neither see nor feel Khemu. He looked up at his guard. "Where is she?" he asked.

The guard jerked his head toward the bed. "Behind you. She's dead. Took some poison capsule before we could stop her."

Kaid closed his eyes and let his chin drop on his chest. At least she was beyond pain and suffering now. He hadn't been able to delay them by much, but hopefully it had been enough to allow Dzaka to reach the aircar.

"What does Fyak want with me?" he asked, remembering what his captor had said.

"You'll find out when we reach Khezy'ipik," was the short reply.

Khezy'ipik? He'd never heard that name before. Could he mean Chezy? And Fyak? Where did he fit into this? Ghezu he could understand, but Fyak? Unless Fyak was acting for Ghezu. They'd made some kind of deal that involved him! It made sense for Ghezu to have a backup plan, and how else could he reach straight into the heart of Fyak's territory?

How had they known he was here, though? There had been no guards visible. A telepath? Was Fyak a telepath? He couldn't be, that was implausible. Why would he persecute them if he was one himself? Still, stranger things happened. Likely he'd find out when they got to Khezy'ipik.

He tried to move and immediately wished he hadn't. Tendrils of pain shot through his nerves causing him to yelp involuntarily. The effects of the stunner hadn't worn off yet. He felt as if he were on fire as his bruised nervous system continued to send waves of pain along every limb, particularly his arms, against which he was leaning. Muscles jerked in reaction, trying to avoid contact with the bed behind him and he pitched forward onto the floor as unconsciousness claimed him again.

* * *

"Craft approaching, Lieutenant," said the tech-op on duty in the Aldatan estate gatehouse.

Ni'Zulhu looked up from his desk. "We're not expecting anyone at this time of night. Query their identity."

"Lieutenant, it's Dzaka! He's saying something about Kaid having been taken by Fyak's people in Rhijudu."

"Give me the link," he said, pushing the papers aside and activating his comm unit.

Dzaka's face came on screen.

"Lieutenant. Kaid's been taken at Rhijudu. He sent me here to see Garras." He held the coin up by the tiny ring set in the outer edge. "I'm under Garras' protection. I must see him," he said urgently. "Permission to land?"

Ni'Zulhu hesitated. He recognized the coin—what Warrior wouldn't? "I'll have him meet you here at the gatehouse. Permission to land granted, but our security system's alerted. Be warned not to deviate from the landing procedure."

"Understood." The screen blanked.

"Shall I call Garras, Lieutenant?"

"Call our Liege first, then Garras," said Ni'Zulhu. "Security on maximum alert as of now. If he makes one aggressive move, take the craft out."

"Yes, sir."

* * *

Garras had been on duty up at the main estate house. He and Kusac met in the garage area. Kusac didn't waste words as he grasped Garras by the arm and pointed to a couple of two person hoppers. "Meet you there," he said.

As they arrived, Dzaka was just emerging from the craft. Garras slewed to a stop, leaped off and flung himself toward Dzaka, but a curt word and gesture from Kusac sent one of the guards to intercept him.

Garras' growl of anger rose in pitch as he tried to break away and reach Dzaka. "Why are you protecting him, Kusac? He's already tried to kill Kaid once! How d'you know . . ."

"Enough, Garras," said Kusac, his eyes already on Dzaka as he got off his hopper.

He stood, his back to the open doorway of the craft, facing six guards armed with pulse rifles. His ears were flattening as he looked impassively toward Kusac.

"Where is he, Dzaka? What have you done with him?" Garras demanded.

"He'll answer to me alone, Garras." Kusac's voice, carefully pitched, brought instant obedience, rendering Garras silent and still. He'd been taught the technique but till now had never had occasion to use it. All his senses, augmented by Carrie's mental presence, were alert. Skills learned in AlRel now had a purpose.

He stepped between the guards, stopping a few feet from Dzaka. "You've brought a coin from Kaid. Where is it?" He held out his hand.

Dzaka's eyes slid from him to Garras, then back.

"Yes, I *am* the greater threat. Kaid's loyalty, like that of all our people, is to me, mine to him." Kusac's voice was a low, menacing purr as he let his ears fold against the sides of his skull. He moved his tail, letting the tip flick lazily, adding to the implicit threat. "If he sent you here with a message, then give it to me."

Dzaka's pupils dilated as, hand shaking slightly, he placed the coin in Kusac's palm. His tongue flicked out, moistening his lips. "He said to give it to Garras and tell him to protect me."

"From whom?"

Again Dzaka looked from one to the other. "From the Brotherhood, and from you."

Kusac raised an eye ridge.

"He knew you'd both prefer me dead." His voice was bleak now and his gaze didn't waver.

Kusac looked at the coin, flicking it over with a claw tip. He could feel Dzaka's fear, and his realization that Kusac hadn't yet decided his fate.

On one face the coin bore the sigil of the Warriors, and on the other, that of the Priesthood of Vartra. It was the coin they used among themselves when fulfilling a commission. Kusac knew exactly what it meant, and through his link with Carrie, he could sense from the actual coin the purpose of Kaid's last decision, that of giving it to his son as a surety for his life.

He closed his hand over it. "What happened?"

"I waited for him at Rhijudu. When he went to Khemu, I followed." He stopped. "I found out the truth, but it's not for me to say. Only Kaid can tell you what occurred between us."

Kusac caught Dzaka's tiny involuntary hand movement and followed it through to the knife that sat on his left hip. He reached out for it.

Dzaka's defensive movement, though once more checked, was more noticeable this time and around them the ring of rifles began to hum in readiness.

Drawing the blade, Kusac examined the crest on the hilt. "The Arrazo Clan. Khemu gave it to you?"

Dzaka nodded. "And the torc and buckle that accompany it."

"How do we know you didn't steal them?" demanded Garras.

"Be silent!" Kusac's eyes held Dzaka, watching for the truth in them. "Why is it that you're here and he isn't? I think you owe us that much of an explanation."

"Fyak's people were coming. He told me to head for the aircar, he'd be behind me. Then he gave me the coin and the message and pushed me through the window. I had to leave then, the warriors were at her door—were coming round the back . . . He ordered me, and she sent the image . . ." He squeezed his eyes shut for a moment. "She must've taken it from his mind." He opened his eyes and stopped speaking. He'd said all there was to say.

"They bought you the time to escape, and to tell us he'd been taken. Why do you need protection from the Brotherhood? I thought you were still with them."

"I was. I've left the Guild now. I told Ghezu personally on the comm, but I don't expect you to believe me. I disobeyed his orders. I won't survive the night if you don't grant me protection."

There was no hope left in his eyes. He expected nothing but death at their hands.

"You haven't presumed on your relationship with Kaid," said Kusac thoughtfully.

Dzaka shrugged. "It isn't relevant. It's my actions you're judging."

"Not even to save your life?"

He remained silent, eyes still meeting Kusac's.

Mind made up, Kusac turned to the guard holding Garras. "Release him," he said, letting his ears raise. Holding the hand that contained the coin out to Garras, he said, "You've been given a commission by Kaid; to protect his son. See you discharge it once Dzaka's oath has been taken." He handed him the coin. "He's also under *my* protection. See that everyone on both estates knows this."

Silently Garras took it from him.

Kusac turned back to Dzaka. "Your knife," he said, handing it back to him hilt first. "The Arrazo Clan lost its honor the day they announced your mother's death. I hope your actions in the future can restore it, Dzaka."

Too stunned to speak, Dzaka took the knife from him and returned it to its sheath.

Tiredly, Kusac turned to Ni'Zulhu. "Stand your folk down, and get that vehicle returned to the hire firm."

"Yes, Liege." At a signal from him, the guards powered their rifles down and silently returned to their posts.

"Garras?" He waited till the older male had come over to him. "Take Dzaka to the Shrine and waken Ghyan. Apologize for the disturbance, but I want him witnessing Dzaka's oath now."

"Yes, Liege," said Garras.

Kusac looked round at his one-time Captain but as Garras crossed his arms over his chest and bowed his head in salute, there was no trace of sarcasm present.

"Liege!" Dzaka was standing by Garras.

"Yes?"

"Thank you," he said, also saluting him. "I'll not give you or Garras reason to regret this."

"I trust you won't. If I can command the same loyalty,

however misplaced, that you gave to Ghezu, I'll be content." He moved away from the group round the aircar. "I'll meet you at the Shrine."

Wake Father, Carrie. Tell him what's happened. He'll know if there's anything we can do.

Why go to the Shrine for the oath? Can't you do it there? she asked.

No, cub. Only an oath taken in front of Vartra will count as far as the other Brothers are concerned. Remember, he's the only one forsworn—he was never released from his original oath.

Garras was still angry.

"I'm sorry," said Dzaka as he got on the back of the hopper behind him. "I know you'd rather see me dead, but . . ."

"You know nothing," growled Garras as the vehicle rose into the air. "If you were my son, I'd have beaten some sense into you long before now! How the hell could you believe Ghezu? You nearly killed Kaid that night, do you know that?" he said, increasing the speed of the vehicle as he banked round the bushes onto the roadway to the Valsgarth estate. "Would have, if I hadn't been there."

"I didn't intend to harm him!" Dzaka had to shout to be heard above the noise of the engine.

"You've behaved like a fool from the moment you heard he was your father! Did you stop to think how *he* felt? Imagine bringing up a son of your own, unable to admit to the relationship for fear he'd be killed outright by your Guild Leader! How would you have felt? Just think about that, Dzaka!"

Thankfully, Dzaka remained silent for the rest of the short trip. Garras knew he was speeding, and that it was still too dark to see properly, but he was angry to the core with the younger male. He also knew, being honest with himself, that part of his anger was because Kaid hadn't trusted him enough to tell him about his son. Intellectually he knew why, but that wasn't enough.

He slowed down as they approached the building, bringing the hopper down carefully. Dzaka got off and waited for him.

As Garras stepped off and turned to face him, he saw the youth square his jaw and look him straight in the eye.

"Get it over with, Garras," Dzaka said quietly.

Garras opened his mouth to deny it, then changed his mind. "What the hell," he muttered, taking a backhand swing at the side of Dzaka's head.

As Dzaka landed heavily on the ground, Garras gave a slight yip of pain and began massaging his hand.

"I've got a hard head," said Dzaka, feeling his jaw carefully.

"I should have remembered," Garras muttered, but his anger had broken, and with a faint grin, he stepped over and held his other hand out to him.

Dzaka took it and let Garras help him to his feet. "Khemu told me Ghezu's Talent is glamour. He can make anything seem reasonable when he uses it."

"He had you well and truly fooled, didn't he?" said Garras as they headed for the doorway.

* * *

The journey to Forestgate had been slow but uneventful. Their small caravan thankfully hadn't seemed attractive enough to any marauding bandits for them to risk their lives against the caravan's guards. The town, enclosed as it was by a wooden palisade, wasn't large. Dusk had been approaching as the caravan straggled tiredly through the gates and headed for the only inn.

The following day they went in search of supplies to see them on the final leg of their journey. That done, they returned to their room to check and repair their kit, and equally important, for Kris to contact Vyaka. The *Summer Bounty,* the Chemerian merchant ship they had arrived on, was in port again. She was able to confirm that the weather in the mountains showed no signs of thaw. This meant they could take an extra day to fully recuperate.

The next day, shortly after dawn, they set out toward the forest. It was bitterly cold—too cold for the luxury of speech as they trudged along in silence. Gradually the landscape around them began to change as they passed between the first of the trees. Small animal tracks weaving their way around the snow-covered tangle of bushes were all that marred the virgin surface, and as the undergrowth grew denser and interspersed with evergreens, gradually the force of the biting wind dropped.

Jo was the first to unwrap her scarf from around her face and ears. She stopped, signing to the others to do the same.

"Kris, can you check our heading?"

He nodded and pulling off his mitts, dug the various sections of their compass out of his pockets and assembled it.

"If we keep heading in this direction, we'll be fine," he said, squinting up at the pale sun above. "We've got another three hours before we need to start looking for a place to camp."

Davies groaned. "Are you planning on building an igloo? Because that's about all that will keep us warm tonight!"

Kris looked over at him, faintly amused. "Look around you," he said. "There are animal tracks—they manage to survive in this weather, so will we."

"How?"

"Lots of ways," said Jo, moving off again. "You should have tried to stay awake during the survival lessons."

That night they camped in a sheltered hollow at the center of several tangled bushes. They constructed a primitive shelter by anchoring their lightweight groundsheet to the branches above and around them, leaving enough of a space for them to see through. A small fire built in a shallow pit, heated up enough water to make warm drinks and rehydrate the dried meat they'd brought with them.

They'd underestimated how tired they'd be the day after a night punctuated by taking turns at sentry duty. Their tiredness, added to the thickening of the forest meant their progress was slower, and as the sky began to darken, they still hadn't come across a suitable campsite for the night.

"Why can't we use a bush like last night?" asked Davies, pulling his pack off his shoulders and resting it on the ground.

"Wrong kind of forest now," said Jo, leaning against a tree trunk. "Conifers. The ground's bare under them: no undergrowth worth mentioning."

Kris looked around, weighing up their options. Davies groaned as he saw him look upward.

"I'm not a bloody Sholan," he said. "They can shinny up a tree in no time flat, but they've got clawed feet to help them!"

"It's a conifer, Davies," said Jo, pushing herself away from the trunk and walking over to join Kris. "It's easy to climb. Plenty of branches."

"And that one has branches that are nearly level," said

Kris, pointing to the one ahead of them. He pulled his pack off and handed it to Jo. "I'll check it out first," he said.

They watched as he clambered up the trunk, reaching a height of some twenty-five meters before he stopped. Carefully, holding onto a thinner branch above, he began to edge along his perch. He stopped, looking down at them.

"This one's fine," he yelled. "A couple of branches intersect here. It'll give us a narrow platform where we can spend the night. Throw the rope up to me. It's easy enough to climb but there's no point taking risks."

"Up you go, Davies," said Jo.

"I don't want to spend the night in a tree," he objected, slipping the coil of rope over his head.

"I thought you'd prefer to once you'd seen the size of those paw prints," said Jo, picking Kris' pack up and moving closer to the tree.

"Hang on a minute," said Davies, hurriedly joining her. "What paw prints?"

"Didn't you see them?" she asked, letting surprise creep into her voice. "Sorry. Kris and I did. We just assumed you had too."

"What was it?" he asked, getting ready to fling the rope upward to Kris.

"We reckon something the size of a large dog—maybe even one of those we saw on guard at the spaceport."

Davies' throw went wide and he turned to her, face pale. "You're kidding, right? Those brutes don't live wild out here do they?"

"Yes, they do," she said, serious now. "It's getting dark, Davies. I think you should hurry up and get that rope up to Kris."

As if to add emphasis to her words, the air echoed to the sound of a hoarse howl that ended in a bark.

"Bloody hell," Davies muttered, running over to retrieve the rope. Hurriedly he recoiled it and, aiming more carefully this time, flung it up to Kris. This time it reached him.

Ten minutes later, they and their kit were all balanced on two broad overlapping branches. Kris had already taken some pitons out of his pack and was hammering them into the trunk.

"We'll need to anchor ourselves and the kit to the tree, unless we want to wake up on the ground."

"If there's packs of those wolf things roaming these woods,

what chance have we got of reaching the mountains safely? As soon as we get down tomorrow, they'll be after us."

"They're mainly nocturnal," said Kris, threading the rope through the straps of all three packs and lashing them securely to the piton and the upper of the two branches.

"Mainly? Is that meant to be reassuring? Anyway, how the hell do you know that?" demanded Davies.

"I read the guard at the gate. The animals are not much good during the day. They're too sleepy. Davies, stop chattering and get yourself tied onto the branch, while there's still enough light to see by. Jo?"

"I'm doing it now," she replied. "It's going to be a cold meal tonight, and no hot drink either. Davies, it's your turn for a full sleep tonight. Kris and I'll split the watches."

Somewhat mollified at the prospect of a decent sleep, provided he didn't fall out of the tree, Davies began digging another rope out of his pack.

Huddled in their cloaks, they sat with backs pressed to the main trunk.

"D'you know what I want most," said Jo, her tone taking a dreamy quality as she chewed on her piece of dried trail meat. "A hot bath. Maybe after an hour or two's soak I'll be able to get the cold out of my bones."

"The Warrior Guild has nice baths," said Kris as he broke bits off his meat ration to feed to Scamp. The jegget was huddled inside Kris' jacket, against his chest. It was too cold for him to want to do more than stick his head and paws outside. "We could go there when we get back," he said, looking over at Jo.

"Not me. I want a soft bed and a good, hot meal," said Davies. "I've got used to living in a house since the Sholans arrived on Keiss. I never did like camping out. What about you, Kris?"

"Oh, a hot bath'll do me fine too," he said lazily, turning back to Scamp. "Not that I would turn down the offer of a meal and a decent bed."

In the distance, another canine started to howl, his cry answered by another from a different direction.

Jo shivered. "I thought they said all the large carnivores had gone down to the plains."

"If there wasn't easy food there either, they'd probably return to their pack territory," said Kris, looking over toward her again. "Don't worry. We're safe up here."

*   *   *

Morning dawned, bringing with it the end of Vanna's Link day. Waking alone, she sighed with relief. Since the incident with Sara, she'd had no patience with Brynne and it was she who kept their time together as short as possible. To give him his due, Brynne had tried on several occasions to apologise but she'd refused to listen to him. He'd eventually given up and withdrawn from her. Now they talked as little as possible.

She moved cautiously, pushing her heavy body up onto the pillows by dint of carefully using her hind claws for purchase on the mattress. Twisting round onto her back, she managed to sit up. A noise by the door drew her attention and she looked up to see Brynne coming over carrying a mug of coffee for her.

"I felt you waken," he said, putting it down on the night table beside her. "I got this for you as well." He held out the plate he'd been concealing behind his back. "It's one of your favorite fruit pastries."

Vanna was about to deny any hunger when her stomach betrayed her by grumbling.

"Take it," he said, putting the plate on her lap as he sat down beside her. "I know you're hungry."

Inwardly cursing her vanished telepathy, Vanna picked up the pastry and began to nibble round the edges of it. Though her advancing pregnancy had silenced her talent several weeks earlier, it hadn't diminished the need for their Link days. Now there was no mutual exchange of memories; for her, there was nothing but the physical pull toward him.

"Look, Vanna, I think it's time we talked."

"I've nothing to say."

"I have." He hesitated briefly. "Our son is due in a few weeks. There's decisions we have to make about him."

"I've made all the decisions." She narrowed her eyes as she regarded him. Lhea was outside in the main lounge. Vanna insisted on a guard being within calling range since the incident with Sara. She hoped he wasn't going to get difficult. "Let get this straight, Brynne. He's *my* son."

"He's my son too, whether or not either of us likes it. I have a right to be involved, Vanna. I'd rather we came to an agreement."

She had no idea what he was thinking, it was as if she was blind and deaf! She stalled, taking another bite of the pastry.

"I want to stay at the estate for the next few weeks, Vanna, and I want to be there when he's born."

"Forget it!" she snapped, eyes blazing. "Males don't come into the birthing room!"

"They can, if invited."

'I won't have you there. One biological act doesn't give you the right to demand that, or anything else, of me!" She put the pastry down on the plate and pushed it aside. "I should have known you wanted something from me! It'll take a damned sight more than this to bribe me into accepting your presence!"

"I wasn't trying to bribe you," he said patiently, trying to catch hold of one of her hands. "I gave you that because I felt your hunger. I have the right to acknowledge our child as my son. I want to do that, so I need to be there when he's born."

She pulled away from him, attempting to turn back on her side so she could get out of the bed and away from him.

"You didn't want him, Brynne. You can't suddenly decide you want to be involved now, I won't have it! Your presence makes me tense. That's the last thing I need when I'm giving birth!"

He leaned forward, taking her by the arms and holding her still. "I admit it, I didn't want him, but neither did you at first. I'm not trying to take him from you, Vanna, I just want what I have a right to by law. Garras may be your mate, but he isn't the father of your child. I *will* have him Validated as my son, and I also want the right to visit him regularly. That's not a lot to ask, Vanna."

She felt vulnerable and trapped lying like this on her back. Her bulk meant that she had to lie on her side to get up, and pinned down like this, she felt like some shelled sea creature stranded upside down on the sand at low tide.

"He's a cub, Brynne," she said, staring unblinkingly up at him. "You want to be his father, then first you have to accept that he isn't a Human baby, he's a cub!"

Brynne released one of her arms to reach up and stroke her face. "Just like you," he said quietly. "I hope his pelt will be as soft as yours. He'll have to live with you on the estate, I know that. I'm not going to interfere between you and

Garras. I only want it acknowledged that I'm his father, that's all. I won't let Garras claim him."

"I wouldn't let Garras claim him either! As far as I'm concerned, he's *my* son, no one else's! Go and find a Terran female with a child to play fathers with, because you're not doing it with mine!" She pushed his hand away and began twisting round again.

"If you do that, I'll have to approach Konis Aldatan as a judge and ask him to give me my rights," he said. "I don't want to do that, Vanna."

She froze. "You'd do that? You'd humiliate us all by doing that?"

"Only if you make me. Dammit, Vanna! Sending to Sara that day was stupid, yes, but I didn't meant to hurt either of you! And there hasn't been anyone else but you since then."

"I don't believe you."

"It's true nonetheless. Look," he said, helping her sit up again, "we got off to a bad start, mainly because of Esken."

"Hah! So you say! It was your attitude that you wouldn't be forced into a relationship with any female that caused the trouble!"

"I was also automatically enrolled into your military forces because of you! I'm stuck with a long-term job I would never have chosen myself, because *you* chose it," he said. "There've been mistakes and injuries on both sides, Vanna, we can't ever repair that, but we can at least reach an understanding, can't we? Be civilized about this?"

"Why should I trust you? You've given me no reason to so far. Even now you're threatening me to get your own way in something that involves *my* body!" This new solicitude made her suspicious.

"We've a lifetime ahead of us, Vanna, and there will be more cubs, we both know that. I don't want to spend all my life fighting you. We've wasted enough time doing that already. Let's call a truce. Please."

"You don't ask a lot, do you?" she said sarcastically. "You wait until my cub's almost due, and my Talent has shut down to protect him, then you ask me to trust you! I'll say it again, why should I?"

"Because I care about you and him! Are you happy now that I've admitted it?" he demanded, his hands tightening on her arms. "Dammit, I've fought it from the start, you're right, but I wasn't ready for the relationship I suddenly had with you. Yes, I cared—I still do. You excited me from the start—everything about you was so exotic, so sensual," he said, pulling her closer and laying his face against her cheek. "You've no idea what you did to me that night in the shower all those months ago!" He turned his head, his mouth seeking hers in a kiss.

She tried to push him away but he continued to hold her, breaking off for a moment to speak.

"Don't fight me, Vanna," he said quietly. "Just this once, forget our past, think only of now."

She tried to turn her head away from him. "Our Link day is over, Brynne. Let me go."

"I know it's over," he said, capturing her ear tip briefly yet gently between his teeth. "I don't want it to be. I want to make love to you, not be controlled by the Link." His mouth moved across her cheek in a series of tiny bites as he worked his way down to her throat.

Her body shocked her by responding to his touch.

"See?" he murmured as he released her and moved his hands to open her robe. "This isn't just the Link and you know it, too."

Clutching her robe tighter round herself she tried to push him away. "You've never sunk this low before, Brynne. I don't deserve this cruelty from you," she said, a catch in her voice. "I know how huge I am, there's no need to mock me!"

"Mock you? No, Vanna," he said, pulling back from her so she could see his face. "That's why there's not been anyone else. You've never looked more lovely than you do now." His hand touched her face gently. "My feelings are no different from those of your Sholan males when it comes to my pregnant lover."

Vanna's eyes suddenly overflowed with tears and as her hands went up to hide them, Brynne for once knew exactly what to do: he gathered her close, seducing her gently with words until they made love for the first time.

* * *

Kusac was surprised when the comm chimed. They'd only moved into their new house that morning. His mother must have had it relayed through their private line.

He activated the unit. "Sub-Commander Farak. What can I do for you?" he asked, sitting down at his desk comm.

"We'd like to recall you and your Leska to active duty, Liegen Aldatan," said the Forces officer. "We haven't received a medical report concerning your state of health or that of your Leska for several weeks now. Please report to the medical center at the Nazule Warrior Guild."

"I'm afraid it won't be possible for my mate to attend, sub-Commander," said Kusac, his tone one of model politeness. "She's pregnant and since our child was conceived under the rituals of En'Shalla, she's not obliged to submit to any medical examinations. I'll certainly take the medical, but you realize that with her pregnant, I cannot return to active duty."

"Pregnant?" The officer was taken aback by the news.

"That's correct. You'll appreciate I don't wish to go into details with you, but after the loss of our first cub, we're taking no chances with this one, which is what prompted us to ensure she would be En'Shalla."

"I'm afraid I can't comment on that, Liegen. If you would report as instructed, someone will be in touch with you regarding your mate. Thank you for your time."

The line went abruptly dead.

"Trouble?" asked Carrie, coming over to join him.

He gave a small laugh as he turned round to her. "I don't think so," he said. "Nothing for you to worry about, anyway. Have you and Taizia finished exploring the rest of the house?"

She nodded. "It's huge, Kusac. Almost as large as your parents'."

"It should be, considering this used to be a separate estate in its own right. It fell into disuse several generations back when our Clan was hit by an epidemic that cost many people their lives. Those still living here moved over to the main estate and this one was just abandoned. There wasn't enough people left to run both of them." He looked around the room. "Where's Taizia? Is she all right?"

"Yes, she's fine. Just tired. She got Meral to take her home."

Kusac reached out to take her hand, urging her closer. "Do you really like our new home?"

"It's beautiful. Our rooms are just unbelievable," she said, leaning against him. "Do you remember when I first saw the stars from the *Khalossa?* The ceiling in the bedroom reminds me of that."

"That's why I chose it."

"Kitra loved the nursery. She says she wished hers had been like that when she was little."

"When she was little?" Kusac laughed. "What does she think she is now?"

"Getting older, unless I'm very much mistaken," said Carrie. "Maybe it's mixing with Mara and the kitlings that's made her grow up, but I've certainly noticed her eyeing up the young males around here today."

Kusac frowned. "I'm sure you're mistaken. She couldn't be, she's just a baby still."

Carrie laughed. "You sound like my brother! You all take longer to admit that we've grown up, probably because it makes you suddenly feel older yourselves and you think you've got to look out for us even more!"

There was the briefest of knocks at the door, then Kitra scampered in. "Jack's here with Garras. They've finished scanning the hill. Shall I tell them to come up?"

"Please. Isn't it nearly time for second meal? Hadn't you better be heading home?"

"No. Zhala said I could stay," she said, coming over to the front of the desk. "Can I stay and listen to what they've found?"

Carrie frowned. "Who's Zhala, Kitra?"

"Your cook, of course! I've met all the house attendants, haven't you? Can I stay and listen to Jack and Garras?"

"Provided your mother agrees. Call her now on the comm in the downstairs den."

"Thanks, Carrie!"

"She doesn't seem any more adult to me," said Kusac, turning round to close the comm unit, letting it slide down into its desk recess.

"Did I tell you that, a few weeks back, Taizia and I had a chat about our species differences?" she asked, her tone light as she pulled a seat over to the desk.

Kusac was instantly on his feet, taking it from her. "I'll do that. I don't want you doing any lifting, cub."

With a tiny inward sigh, she stepped back, letting him move the chair. "I'm perfectly healthy, you know," she said. "Noni confirmed it only a few days ago. I don't want to be treated as if I'm ill."

"I know you're not," he said, arm round her shoulders as he drew her over to the chair. "I'm just looking after you, that's all. Now, what were you saying about Taizia?" He sat beside her, keeping hold of her hand as he gave her his full attention. "Species differences, you say? I didn't realize you still had problems with our culture."

"I don't, now. I just decided that being female and only having a male's understanding of your people isn't exactly helpful. So we swapped. I now have her female perspective, and she has my Human one to compare with. We can help each other more now, especially as she's continuing her studies in AlRel and wants to specialize in the Terran culture."

Kusac groaned, shutting his eyes and shaking his head as his ears dipped in partially genuine distress. "How could she do this to me? What have I done to upset her? She was bad enough on her own, but combined with you—I haven't got a chance now!"

"That's not a very nice attitude, Kusac. How would you like it if I said that because you'd shared knowledge with one of the Terran male telepaths?" She stopped, her face creasing in mock surprise. "You have! And you kept it from me! Kusac, how *could* you?" she asked, snatching her hand away from him.

"Like you, I thought it would help," he said, recapturing her hand. "I didn't go to a telepath, though. I went to Jack."

"Why Jack?"

"Um, well. He was married once and has family still on Keiss," he said, ears flicking in embarrassment. "I just thought . . ."

"I know what you thought! At least I did it because of our cub!" she said. She wasn't angry, exactly, just disappointed.

"It wasn't much use anyway," he said. "I've come to the conclusion that the males of neither of our species understand their females." He sounded morose.

"Never mind," she said with a grin, reaching out to touch his cheek gently. "*We* understand *you,* so there's no problem!"

"Huh! I don't think I like that comment," he growled, leaning toward her. "Is that a Taizia or a Carrie remark?" He nipped her cheek softly before pulling her into an embrace.

"Both."

Then the door opened and Jack, followed by Garras, came in. "Looks like you were right, Carrie," he said, waving a roll of paper as he strode over to them. "There's extensive underground caverns and tunnels under that old monastery."

"Monastery?" said Kusac, letting her go with obvious

reluctance and turning to face his desk. "I thought it was only a shrine."

"We got Ghyan to send us copies of the plans for the major temples of Vartra on Shola and compared them with the ground plan of the ruin. It follows the same general configuration as those and the temple at Valsgarth, all of which are monasteries," said Garras.

"Can we use the desk?" asked Jack, hovering at the end of it, his plans poised ready to unroll.

"Certainly," said Kusac, moving the few items on it to one side.

"Hold this end down, Carrie," Jack said, laying it on the surface and pushing the roll toward the other end.

Garras stopped by the coffee table to pick up a couple of books lying there. Coming over to Carrie, he handed her one. "Use that."

He waited till the plan was lying fully spread out then placed the remaining book at the other end.

"We used the comm to construct a hypothetical elevation from the readings," Jack said, pointing to the appropriate diagram. "You can see just how extensive it is when compared to the mid-section aerial view. The plans are to scale, by the way, with the base of the hill being just over half a mile in length. There's two large caverns, connected by sloping tunnels. Looks like it might have once been a mine of some kind."

"Crystal," said Carrie. "It was a crystal mine, for these." Reaching inside her tunic, she pulled out the ovoid eye of Vartra, set in a silver wire cage and suspended from a silver chain round her neck. "They carved them into ornaments, or ground them smooth and oval to use as eyes in statues of Vartra."

Diverted, Jack reached out to hold the crystal. "May I?" he asked.

She took it off and handed it to him.

He turned to face the window, holding it up to the light.

"Hmm. Nice," he said. "Obviously some kind of quartz." He turned back to the desk, handing her the crystal. "Our readings indicated the presence of large quantities of metal, mainly in the lower chamber. Probably the remains of some mine carts."

"What about entrances to this complex?" asked Kusac, aware that Kitra had just reentered the room.

"There are two. One was obviously through the monastery itself, the other was here, at the base of the hill. A north facing exit in line with this estate."

"This tunnel?" said Kusac, pointing to it on the map. "That's where we camped, Carrie. We've been there, Jack! In fact, we were staying in a small chamber about halfway along its length!"

"What's the rest of the tunnel like?" asked Garras, leaning over the desk to see the diagram better.

"Blocked off. A rock fall I believe. Not a recent one," he added. "I played there as a cub. I'd have remembered if there had been a cave-in."

"What about the top entrance?" asked Carrie.

"There's a short vertical shaft under what would likely have been the floor of an office or some such room. It leads as you can see, to a smaller chamber and a passage to the first of the large caverns. From there another leads down to the second cavern. The one that's on a level with the entrance tunnel."

"I'd say it's definitely been used as a concealed base," said Garras.

"We've two options," said Carrie. "Either we go in at the top from the ruins, or we extend the tunnel at the base of the hill. I think going in through the tunnel is likely to take less time and bring quicker results."

"Carrie, you're not going to be involved in this," warned Kusac. "I don't need to remind you what's at risk, do I?"

"Don't be ridiculous, Kusac, I've no intention of digging out the tunnel! What kind of idiot do you think I am?" she asked. "Here I am, surrounded by six foot males, all of them stronger than me. Why should I do any digging when I've got you?" She grinned up at him, then Garras. "I don't intend to take risks," she said more seriously, looking back at her mate, "but I do intend to be there with you. If I'm not, I'm more likely to get high blood pressure from being kept away, aren't I, Jack?"

"Ah, yes, there is that, Kusac," said Jack, keeping his gaze on the diagram. "If she doesn't do any lifting or digging, there's no reason she shouldn't come with us. This first bit, now, it's likely to be just digging through a rockslide. There's unlikely to be anything much hidden under those rocks. What we need is some heavy mining equipment."

"Most of the building machinery is still here on the main

estate," said Kusac. "There are one or two devices I've seen them use for digging out foundations that might be of use to us. Some of the builders are estate members, non-telepathic clansfolk of ours. I'm sure they'd cooperate with us without reporting the extra labor to their guild."

"Can you see them about it today?" asked Carrie. "I'd like the work started as soon as possible."

"Why the rush?" asked Kusac. "I'm as intrigued as you as to what's actually there, but why do you feel such a need for urgency? Remember, Jack did warn us that this isn't an accurate view of what's inside the hill."

Carrie sat back in her seat, gathering her thoughts for a moment. "I'm convinced that this complex under the monastery is connected to Vartra. I *know* I've seen it in several of the replays, and I'm sure that Kaid's seen it too. If we're traveling back to those days, we need to know as much about them as we can find out. I think that a lot of the answers Raiban wants will be found inside this hill, including what the Valtegans were doing here."

"I'll be with you, Carrie," said Kitra, who during their conversation had worked her way round to her bond-sister's side. "I can make sure she doesn't do anything to lose the cub, Kusac. I'll help her."

Carrie couldn't help but grin as she put her hand up to stroke the youngling's head affectionately. "There you are, Kusac. With your sister to keep an eye on me, how could I possibly come to harm?"

"We'll see. I don't know which of you will be looking after the other! Well, Garras," said Kusac, looking over at him. "We're getting nearer to finding out one way or the other whether Vartra was a male like us, or a God."

"Hmm. I'll stick to my opinion a while yet," said Garras.

There was a knock on the door and Dzaka looked in. "Second meal's ready now, Liege," he said.

"We're on our way," Kusac said. "Can we keep these plans for the moment, Jack? I'd like to look them over in more detail later."

"Certainly. We've got them on my comm at the medical center. We can run off copies as we need them."

Kusac shifted the books off the ends of the document and began to roll it up. "I'll have a word with the builders later today and see if their machines can do what we want. We

might even be able to make a start tomorrow." He opened the
drawer in front of him, placing the plans in there.

As they went down, Carrie kept an eye on Kitra as she
walked alongside Dzaka, deep in conversation with him.

"I didn't know you'd assigned him to the house," said
Garras.

Carrie glanced up at him. "Still cautious, eh? You know
he's been sworn to our Clan and Kusac, just like all the rest
of you, Garras. He'll not betray us, believe me. There's too
much of his father in him. We were monitoring him all the
while Kusac was questioning him, and at the temple during
his release from the Brotherhood Oath and taking the Oath of
Allegiance to us. He still has problems to resolve, but none
of them will affect his loyalty."

"You have to understand the nature of the relationship
Kaid and I had up until I left Stronghold, Carrie," Garras said
carefully. "Warriors, especially the Brothers, often work in
pairs, close pairs. Your people have nothing comparable as
far as I can tell, so it's difficult to explain. It was a relationship that was closer than brothers, sometimes closer than
you'd be with a lover because our lives depended not only on
the trust between us, but on knowing each other's mind.
Given our Talents, Kaid and I, we fitted together like that—
still do in fact."

He stopped talking for a minute or two, then looked at her
again. "It hurt to discover he hadn't trusted me enough to tell
me Dzaka was his son, just as it hurt when I thought I'd lose
him the night Dzaka attacked him. I have to find my own
way through this, Carrie, and I can't till I've spoken to him
again—and that might never happen because he remained
behind to ensure Dzaka escaped."

Carrie reached out and took his hand. "I understand," she
said softly, feeling the hurt he was trying to control. "You're
someone special, Garras, always will be to me. When we
needed help back on Keiss and the *Khalossa,* you were there
for us. You didn't need to be, but you were, even to asking
your friend to guard us from harm. I'm honored to count you
my friend." She gave his hand a gentle, comforting squeeze.
"If I can help, even if it's only to listen to your troubles, please
come to me. You and Vanna mean a lot to both of us."

Garras returned the gesture before gently freeing his hand.
"I know, and thank you. If I seem wary of Dzaka, now you
know why."

* * *

Later that day, Kusac headed over to see his father, leaving Carrie organizing their new home with the dubious help of Kitra and Dzaka. On the way, he stopped to talk to the building foreman. Arrangements were quickly made to start excavating the tunnel the following day. Secrecy was assured by the foreman suggesting he only take clansfolk with him as they were surveying the site for the small outer estate settlement, weren't they?

Kusac was still grinning when he parked the hopper round the rear of the house. His mother was in her study upstairs. Of his father there was no sign.

"He's over at the Guild," Rhyasha said, hand hovering over the internal comm button. "Do you want c'shar or coffee?"

"Coffee, please," he said, making himself comfortable in the seat beside her. "What's he doing there?" he asked after she'd spoken to Choa.

"Another twenty telepaths have arrived, mostly Terran women this time, and two new Leska pairs. He's gone out to meet the newcomers, and bring the new Leskas here."

"Anyone we know, or are they fresh from Earth?"

"He didn't say. Now your news. I hear Dzaka's back. Did he bring news of Kaid?"

* * *

"She's pregnant again, you say?"

"Yes," said Raiban, helping herself to another mug of c'shar. "We'll have to postpone any thought of a rescue mission to Jalna until after the cub's born, I'm afraid."

"Do we have to send them? Wouldn't some other operatives serve just as well?" asked Chuz.

Raiban gave a snort of disgust. "You're the one who keeps complaining about the cost of maintaining a high level of security at the combined Aldatan and Valsgarth estates, *and* the one who wants to see some return for that outlay!"

"Of course I do! I've got the Alliance Treasury breathing down my neck; I've got to justify the outlay to them, Raiban."

"We both knew this would be a long-term project. It'll be several years before we know what the cubs of these Leskas will be capable of. At least we now have the proof that the

Sholan partner is capable of fighting without losing any of his or her Talent's sensitivity. And that, Chuz, is why we need to send them to Jalna. We need a telepath on that planet and this mission. I don't want to trust to the Terrans alone."

"Have you any new information regarding the group on Jalna?"

"Not since I sent you the latest report. We're getting a great deal of information on the planet's social structure and its winter ecology which is being passed over to the appropriate department, but with the spring thaw delayed, their progress across the plains to the mountains is slow. Now they've left the caravan and struck out on their own, they've not only the weather to contend with but also local bandits and wild carnivores."

"So we're looking at how long a delay until Kusac and Carrie are ready to leave?"

"I wouldn't have put a second team on Jalna yet anyway, but at a reasonable guess I'd say, including training time for the mission, somewhere in the region of nine months to a year."

"A year! You'll have to rethink those figures, Raiban. A delay of that long just isn't acceptable! Those four Sholans are enslaved on that world! We can't abandon them for that long!"

"Commander," said Raiban, taking another drink and replacing her mug carefully on the table that separated them. "I want our people back as quickly as possible, but we cannot send in anyone but this pair. Their telepathic skills will enable them to locate the four and rescue them. We can't send down normal Sholan telepaths! Apart from the fact that we haven't yet got a reliable way of making even one Sholan look like a U'churian, they'd be so affected by any pain around them, and so vulnerable to capture, that they'd quite frankly be a damned liability! Only these mixed pairs combine the necessary telepathic abilities with the fighting skills. Like Carrie Aldatan, Vanna Kyjishi is pregnant, and although she'll be ready to return to duty before the Aldatans, she's a medic—completely untrained in combat— that rules her out, and as for Zhyaf—" She shook her head, sighing.

"All right, all right," said Chuz testily. "Don't go on about it! But nine months to a year, Raiban!"

"Kusac can begin training now, but his Leska can't," said

Raiban. "She's some seven weeks into her pregnancy, so it will be another seventeen before her cub is born, and . . ."

"How do you know the pregnancy will be as long as a Sholan one?" interrupted Chuz.

"Information from the Valsgarth Telepath Guild medical center," said Raiban.

"If you can get information out of Esken's lot, why haven't you put someone in at the Aldatan estate?"

Raiban looked pityingly at him. "Do I have to tell you why, Commander? We may pay the bills, but every person on that estate has been hand-picked by Kaid Tallinu and has sworn loyalty not only to the Aldatan Clan, but to Kusac personally! They wouldn't tell us what time Kusac got up in the morning, even if their lives depended on it! I wish I could achieve security of that standard, I'll tell you. We may not be able to get any information from them, but we know no one else can either and that in itself is worthwhile. Now, may I continue?"

Chuz merely flicked an ear this time.

"She has another seventeen weeks to go before the cub is born, that means another six weeks till she's fit enough to start training, then approximately twelve weeks training. That's where your time has gone, providing we can persuade her to waive her mandatory maternity leave of six months."

"Has it occurred to you that she might fall pregnant again during this training, or even during this mission?"

"That has been a concern," Raiban admitted. "But it looks like the Terran scientists working with our people have come up with a contraceptive that will work on our Mixed Leskas. It's not been given a proper trial yet, but we've still got the best part of a year ahead of us. Tests will start shortly as supplies of the drug arrived today with the latest group of Terran Telepaths. They're mainly female and they're willing to take the drug if they should form a Leska Link with one of our people."

"Naika's still paranoid about this new species, Raiban. I must admit to having worries myself."

"What do you suggest, Commander? That we kill all mixed Leska pairs? That we sterilize them so there can be no cubs? We don't know what effect that would have on them since the Leska Link seems to be a biological imperative. All we can do is what we *are* doing, wait and watch. Their skills are useful to us in a way our normal telepaths aren't, namely the undercover work and the ability to fight. Anyway, they've already been useful: that ni'uzu epidemic they started only enhanced our existing telepaths' abilities, it didn't alter them genetically. The bulk of them are still pure Sholan, and the percentage of these anomalous links is small. I don't feel we need to worry."

"What do we do if Naika is proved right?"

"If the worst comes to the worst, a possible colony world has already been located where we can send them. Without space-going capabilities, they wouldn't present a threat to us for many generations." She took her mug up again. "I'm usually the one accused of being paranoid, but I honestly believe we have nothing to fear from them. If we treat them with suspicion, we're more likely to foster a *them and us* attitude that would lead to trouble."

Chuz grunted. "Well, time will tell, as you say. Even if we have to wait for the female to have her cub, we can at least start Kusac's training. Maybe with their Link she won't need to train for as long," he said hopefully.

"Commander, I have no intentions of putting inadequately trained operatives into the field, especially when it's these two! I don't like losing any of my people. She will be as well trained in her own right as her Leska."

* * *

Vanna returned home to the Valsgarth estate later that afternoon accompanied by Brynne. She'd sent ahead to Kusac, getting permission for her Leska to stay with Jack. After dropping him off at the medical center, she returned to her own home to tell Garras.

Konis arrived toward evening, as it was getting dark. With him were the two new Leska pairs. Kusac had Dzaka escort them over to Ghyan at the Shrine. They'd stay there until Ghyan had integrated them into the small community, then they'd move into homes of their own.

"We've got enough couples here to warrant getting our own teachers now," said Kusac, fetching his father a mug of c'shar.

"Thank you," said Konis, gratefully taking the mug from him. "I'll attend to that through AlRel. Just let me know if you've anyone in mind. It's getting cold now. Do you realize that the winter festival's not that far off?"

Kusac did a quick mental calculation as he sat down with his own drink. "You're right," he said. "Carrie'll enjoy that."

"Where is she, by the way? Resting?"

"No, she's in the kitchen with Kitra. They've been baking pastries. Mother gave her her own recipes." He gave a small laugh. "I hope they're edible! The first lot she made weren't."

"Of course they're edible," said Carrie, coming into the den bearing a plate of the newly cooked pastries. She held them out to Konis. "Try one."

Casting a pained look at his son, he took one from her and cautiously nibbled the edge of it. He looked over at Kusac, shaking his head with a grin. "That was unfair, Kusac! They're fine, Carrie."

"Told you so," she said, joining Kusac on the settee and holding the plate out to him. "Your turn."

"Is Kitra still in the kitchen?" asked Konis.

"Kitra? No, she went with Dzaka to the Shrine. He said he'd take her back home afterward."

"Was that wise?" asked Konis, looking over at Kusac. "Are you sure of him?"

"I trust him with Carrie," said Kusac. "He'll see Kitra home safely."

"That's not what I meant," said Konis.

"She's safe with him, Konis," interrupted Carrie. "I wouldn't have let her go otherwise. Stopping her would only have made him more interesting. Better to allow her to be in his company, then you know where she is."

"Am I missing something here?" asked Kusac, looking from one to the other of them. "What's all this sudden concern over Kitra?"

"I told you earlier, Kusac," said Carrie. "You didn't want to believe me, though. She's growing up. Look at her tomorrow, you'll see her markings are toning down to their adult coloring."

Konis nodded. "She's right. We're trying to keep a careful watch on her now to see which males she favors. We want her first lover to be someone who'll ensure it's a pleasant experience for her."

"When? I mean . . ."

"Your mother says within the next couple of weeks. I'm beginning to feel old, Kusac," sighed his father. "There's both you and Taizia soon to be parents, and now Kitra's

leaving her childhood behind. It seems like yesterday you
were all cubs. At least you and your sister are both happily
settled." He drank down his c'shar and got to his feet.

"I'd better get home. It's been a long day. I dislike my
meetings with Esken. I swear all we need for snow is him
standing out in the rain!"

After Kusac had seen his father off, Carrie turned to him.

"What will you do if Kitra chooses Dzaka?"

"She won't!" Then a moment later, "Why do you ask?"

"Because she's been following him about all day. That's
why I took them with me to the kitchen. He's desperately
trying to avoid being alone with her, and she's just as anxious to be with him. I don't think she's fully realized what
the attraction is yet. Your females certainly mature quite a
bit younger than we do."

"Ah, well, I wouldn't know about that," he said. "Kitra
with Dzaka? Gods! I don't know what I'd do, Carrie. What
should I do?" he asked, running a hand across his head in
bewilderment.

"Nothing, except accept it as graciously as you can, that's
why I'm mentioning it to you now. Your reaction will be
everyone else's benchmark for how they treat Dzaka. If you
trust him with your young sister . . ."

'I don't know if I do!"

"He was bonded before. His mate and son were on
Szurtha."

Kusac shook his head, reaching out for her. "Thank the
Gods we have to stay together," he said, holding her close. "I
don't know how he coped. Even if we hadn't been Leskas
and you'd died on one of those two worlds, I couldn't have
lived without you."

"Nor I you," she said, sharing his distress at the thought.
She let the matter of Kitra and Dzaka drop there. It was
enough that she'd mentioned it to him.

CHAPTER 13

Locked in sleep, Carrie's mind was held captive by the past till the scene before her had finished unfolding.

Half-formed images haunted Rezac, making it difficult to know what was real and what was not. Voices faded one minute and were amplified the next as he moved restlessly in his bed. The sheets were pulling at his fur, pushing it against the lie, making each follicle burn with discomfort. Every movement hurt his joints yet he had to try and move away from the pressure of the sheet.

He dreamed he was made of fire, a fire that burned from deep within him. He opened his eyes only to see beams of flame streaming from them. Devastation followed his gaze, burning and searing everything around. Fear touched him then, his own fear, and instinctively he fought against it, lashing out at it with taloned hands until he was held forcibly down.

"Get that wound dressed immediately," Dr. Nyaam ordered as the nurse staggered back holding his slashed and bleeding forearm. Nyaam continued to fasten Rezac's limbs to the bed frame as Goran grabbed for the arm that he'd managed to pull free. Maro held on grimly to the other limb until Nyaam had finished, then began picking up the scattered ice packs and replacing them around Rezac's body.

"This'll only make him struggle more," said Goran dispassionately.

"I hardly think you're qualified enough to give a medical opinion," said Nyaam, moving round beside the security chief. "He's as much a danger to himself as to us in this state."

"I know my people, Nyaam, which is more than you do. You sent for me because you couldn't control him. I've told you already, put the female in his bed."

"Don't talk rubbish," the doctor snapped. "Look at what he did to my nurse! One blow from him and his Leska would be dead, then we'd lose them both."

"He'd quiet down," said Goran. "He'd know she was there and he'd stop fighting. They're linked mentally, right? So why're you treating them separately? What have you got to lose, Nyaam? At this rate they'll both die. You can't get their temperatures down and he's exhausting himself by fighting your restraints."

"If he weren't so violent I might consider it, but look at him," said Nyaam.

Rezac, already pulling frantically at the restraining bands round his limbs, had lifted his head as high as he could and was leaning over, trying to snap at those holding his wrists.

"We haven't got a bed wide enough for both of them, even if I was prepared to countenance the risk," Nyaam added.

"I told you it would make him worse," said Goran, stepping back to allow Maro in to replace the ice packs. "He's a warrior, Nyaam. Restrain him and he'll fight all the harder against it. That's going to give him convulsions faster than a high temperature."

"Goran's right," said Vartra abruptly. "Try it. We've nothing to lose. If we can't get their temperatures down within the next hour, Rezac is certainly going to go into convulsions."

"I'm telling you, he'll kill her," said Nyaam, looking over to where Dr. Kimin was beginning to unfasten Zashou's bonds. The young female was lying semi-comatose and panting, having exhausted herself with her own struggles.

"Fix the two beds together," said Dr. Kimin. "Use the restraint straps, anything. We know nothing about these new Leska pairs. We've all seen how Zashou's condition has paralleled Rezac's, something that doesn't happen with normal Leskas. For all we know we could be making the situation worse by keeping them apart."

Maro pushed Zashou's bed over beside Rezac's while the other nurse took the restraints from Dr Kimin and dived under the beds to lash the legs together.

"I'm advising you to keep the restraints on Rezac for the moment," said Nyaam. "I think you're taking a foolish risk and I refuse to help you. However, I've no doubt you're going to ignore my opinion."

Goran began moving the ice packs from what was now the middle of one large bed, making room for Zashou to be placed beside Rezac. The sheet, dried out by his body heat, was taken off him and as he flinched away from contact with the others, he lurched briefly against Zashou. He froze, then as Zashou was moved closer so the contact was maintained, his body went into spasm.

"What did I tell you?" demanded Nyaam, grabbing his hypo off the treatment trolley behind them. "Just touching her has made him worse! Give her an anticonvulsant before she starts too! Hold him still for the Gods' sake," he said, trying to get a grip on Rezac.

Goran took hold of Rezac's head. "Hold his arm," he ordered Maro.

Nyaam stuck the needle in Rezac's arm while the two males held him as still as possible.

Almost as they watched, the spasms that wracked his body began to diminish until suddenly, Rezac relaxed and lay there limp and panting, his tongue partially protruding from his mouth.

"Give him some water, Layul," said Dr. Kimin, leaning forward to unfasten the restraints.

Nyaam frowned. "What do you think you're doing?" he demanded, reaching out to stop her. "You should be moving the female away! That's what started the convulsions!"

"For the Gods sake, Nyaam, look at his wrists!" she said, batting his hand aside with one of hers. "The leather has already lacerated him, he's bleeding. Goran's right, Rezac can't help but fight against your restraints. That's what made him convulse, not Zashou! Do something useful, pass me the dressings," she added. "We're working blind with these two, we've no idea what will help them since they're not responding to our treatment like any of the other telepaths. They're suffering identical symptoms, as if they were one person, not two." She took the dressings that Goran held out.

"I'd put money on it that they're amplifying each other's fever dreams. If they're touching, it might just give them the reassurances they need to cope with the hallucinations," she said, wiping the blood from the cuts with an antiseptic pad.

Vartra began unfastening Rezac's other arm.

"On your head be it, then," snapped Nyaam, standing back.

Kimin looked up from bandaging Rezac's wrist. "This isn't a competition, Nyaam," she said quietly. "If you want me to take sole responsibility, then I will. I have a gut-feeling that Goran is right and this will work."

Maro poured a small amount of water onto Rezac's tongue and when he swallowed reflexively, gave him a little more. When his panting began to decrease, Goran released him.

Rezac moved his head slightly, his face creasing in pain. He opened and closed his hands, automatically checking to see if they were free.

"We telepaths learn to trust gut-feelings and instincts, Dr. Nyaam," said Maro quietly as he replaced the water container, then moved round to Vartra's side and began dressing Rezac's other wrist.

Nyaam grunted disbelief. "We've got the damper on, Maro. Neither you nor Dr. Kimin can be picking anything up from him."

"We're inside its influence, Doctor," said Kimin, releasing Rezac's ankles. "Our thoughts don't escape the field, that's all."

It was Zashou who moved first, turning on her side to lie close against Rezac. The anticonvulsant had sedated him and he continued to lie still save for a slight movement of his head and the blinking of his eyes.

He fought against the lassitude, trying to make sense of what was around him. His eyes refused to focus, everything was a blur that made his stomach tighten with nausea. The touch of her body against his was somehow helping the fire in his body die down. When a damp sheet was laid over them, it no longer made him burn, and the coolness that surrounded him, except for where they touched, was welcome.

He was tired, and his eyes began to close. His arm was too heavy to move more than a few centimeters. His hand touched her, reflexively closing on her arm. Now he could sense her mind, feel his heartbeat slowing till it matched hers. All he wanted now was to join her in sleep.

Carrie woke to find herself swathed in a blanket with Kusac holding her close. Jack was sitting beside them, a con-

cerned look on his face. She was drenched in sweat and still
shuddering convulsively, though that was beginning to pass
now. Gradually she grew still, and as she did, she began to
push against the blanket.

"I'm fine now," she said, her voice hoarse. She swallowed, realizing how thirsty she was. "A drink," she said. "I
need a drink."

Jack fetched one while Kusac allowed her to push the
blanket open so the cooler air of the room could get at her
body. He insisted she keep it round her shoulders though.

"What happened?" she asked, having drunk her fill. "Am I
all right?"

Jack leaned forward, feeling her forehead. "You're fine
now," he said. "You were feverish, that's all, but it's broken
now. Probably caught a chill."

She pushed her hair back with a shaky hand. "I dreamed. It
wasn't me who had the fever, it was Rezac. The new Leskas
all took the fever and they didn't know how to treat it then."

"Carrie, you had us worried," said Kusac, touching her
face to check her temperature for himself. "You really did
get burning hot, that's why I sent for Jack."

"I tell you it wasn't me," she insisted. "Maybe he and I
were linked in too closely in the dream, but it wasn't my
fever."

"Tell us what happened," said Jack soothingly.

She put her hands up to her face, scrubbing at it before
pushing her hair back again as she tried to recall the dream.

"He had a fever and they tied him to the bed to stop him
struggling. It made him worse." She stopped, trying to catch
the images that were beginning to slip from her mind like
smoke rising from the temple burners.

"There was a warrior—Goran. He said Rezac and Zashou
should be together but one doctor didn't want that. They did
it anyway, then packed ice round them."

"What then?" asked Kusac gently.

"Their link was like ours, too close, but they were the
first." She stopped again, face creasing in concentration.
There was someone there, she had to remember who it was.
"I remember! It was Vartra! He said, *Try it. We've nothing to
lose.* They didn't know much about Leskas then, Kusac.
Why?"

"I don't know, cub," he said. "It's over now, that's the
main thing."

"Kusac's right, Carrie," said Jack, standing up. "Get back into bed now. You should sleep the night through peacefully. Call me again if you need me."

Kusac stood up, still holding Carrie in his arms. Jack pulled the cover back and Kusac laid her down.

The bed felt fresh and cool after the heat of the blanket. Gratefully she lay down and curled up as Kusac put the cover over her.

"I'll see myself out," said Jack. "Goodnight."

"Thank you for coming over, Jack," said Kusac. "Goodnight."

She was almost asleep when he climbed in beside her, dimming the light before wrapping his body round hers, his arm lying across her waist.

"How do you feel now?" he asked quietly.

"Sleepy," she said. "It wasn't a scary dream, Kusac. I was there, watching them, then inside Rezac's mind. Vartra was there. They didn't know about the new Leskas, Kusac. There were new Leskas then, ones with a link as close as ours."

"I hear you. We can record it in the morning. I won't forget what you've told me," he said, gently nuzzling the back of her neck. "Go to sleep now, cub."

"Mmm."

* * *

Fyak's warriors still used the traditional riding beasts for traveling across the desert. Carrie would have said they looked like a cross between an ox and a camel, had she seen them. Unlike aircars, they were cheap to run, supplied many of the tribes' physical needs for food and fuel, and had air inlets specially evolved to cope with the sandstorms.

Kaid, his hands bound behind his back, spent the journey between Rhijudu and Fyak's lair at Chezy pressed hard against the greasy fur that covered the creature's thick bony neck. His captor sat behind him holding firmly onto Kaid's bound hands as well as his mount's reins.

Pain caused by the stunner still jangled through his body. Pulled behind him as his arms were, the strain on his injured forearm was exacerbated by the jolting gait of the beast, and he spent much of the journey drifting in and out of consciousness.

He surfaced again as he was being hauled off the creature

and into the entrance to Fyak's underground lair. His two guards stopped only long enough for him to set his feet on the ground, then he was hustled along a sandstone passageway till they reached the main chamber. There the bulk of Fyak's experienced warriors were working on stripping down and cleaning their weapons while the others were unpacking crates of new firearms.

He had no chance to take it in properly before he was hauled off to a smaller side chamber. A large table dominated the room. Bending over it were Fyak and several older males: they were studying a map of the surrounding area.

Fyak looked up, his eyes glinting as they settled on Kaid.

"So this is the Brother that Ghezu wants," he purred, moving round the table until he stood opposite him.

Head still throbbing from the effects of the stunner, Kaid began to sway as his escort released him and moved back to the door.

"You don't look much like the feared warrior that Ghezu described," Fyak said, walking round him.

The footsteps stopped immediately behind him. "You're wounded!" Fyak's tone had changed to one of fury. "I said I wanted him brought in whole, that's why you were issued stunners! Who shot him?" he demanded of the two males. "And why is he still bound?"

"He was bleeding when we found him, Prophet," said one, drawing a knife to slit the bindings round Kaid's wrists. "The wound isn't new."

Fyak hissed in annoyance. "Get him seen to." He walked round in front of Kaid again and reached out to grasp him by the uninjured shoulder. "When you're recovered, we'll talk again." He turned to the guards. "Take him to Anirra and have his wound dealt with. Treat him with courtesy," he ordered.

His arms freed, the returning circulation only exacerbated the pain from his wound. He winced as he brought them round in front of himself, then before he had the chance to massage some feeling back into them, he was grasped firmly again and escorted back to the main cavern. This time they took him down a narrow side corridor till they came to an infirmary.

An odor of antiseptic greeted them as they stepped through the curtain into the small ward. He saw a medic rise from the bedside of one of the patients.

"Another one? Haven't you had your fill of blood yet? I'm running out of suppressant drugs to treat them with. You'll need to get me more."

"He isn't a telepath, Anirra, he's one of the Brotherhood. Fyak wants his wound seen to. Says he's to be well treated. Where d'you want him?"

"In the examination room," said Anirra, gesturing to the far end of the ward.

Stumbling as they went, Kaid was led through to the back. At last they released him. He reached out for the examination table, holding on to it to steady himself. All he wanted to do was sleep.

"Help him up!" said Anirra sharply, going over to wash his hands.

Unceremoniously, he was lifted up onto the table. He sat there, holding onto the edge, waiting.

"Well? I'm sure you've got work to do!" Anirra said to the guards.

Kaid watched them take their leave, then the medic turned to look at him.

Anirra took hold of his forearm, examining it carefully. The dried blood had stuck his shirt to his arm like glue.

"I'm going to have to cut your shirt off. It's stuck firmly. I'll only reopen the wound if I try to pull it free. Take your jacket off, please, then lie down."

Kaid eased the jacket over his shoulder, lifting his injured arm free. As he struggled to push it off his good arm, the medic leaned forward and helped him. Carefully pulling his legs up, Kaid lay down.

Anirra was reaching across him to the shelf where his scissors lay when he suddenly stopped, his hand going to touch a patch of singed fur on Kaid's thigh.

A hiss of pain, quickly turning to a low moan, escaped Kaid as his muscles clenched involuntarily.

"That's a stunner burn!"

Kaid closed his eyes, waiting for the throbbing in his leg to decrease, trying to focus on the litany for pain. The medic's footsteps receded then returned and he felt the cool touch of the hypoderm against his neck. A slight sting, then the analgesic took hold, quieting his screaming nerves. He could feel the tension drain out of his muscles, and gradually, he was able to relax his body. The pain in his arm was no more than a dull throb now, as was the headache.

"Better?" asked Anirra.

"Yes." His voice was a croak. He smelled water and opened his eyes to find Anirra holding out a beaker. He raised himself on his uninjured side and gratefully took it from him, drinking deeply before handing the empty beaker back.

Anirra set it aside, then began cutting the shirt free of the wound until only a small piece of fabric was left attached to him.

"The analgesic was strong. You'll find yourself becoming drowsy very shortly. What do they call you?"

"Kaid," he replied. Lying there, he worked on stilling his mind and beginning the litany to banish pain again as Anirra sponged the stiff cloth free of his arm. It was painful, but at last it was done and Anirra was able to remove the rest of his shirt.

"You've used Fastheal," he said accusingly as he carefully probed the edges of the wound. "How long ago did you sustain this injury?"

"Eight or nine days."

"What dosage of Fastheal?"

"I forget." He heard the sound of a hand scanner passing over his arm. Opening his eyes, he waited till the scan was complete before grasping Anirra's hand and pulling the unit closer so he could read it.

"Fastheal has to be carefully administered, otherwise you deplete the body's reserves," Anirra said, anger in his voice as he pulled himself free. "You've abused the drug to the point where this wound will take twice as long to heal naturally. The tissues are inflamed and you'll be lucky if an infection hasn't set in!"

"Vitamins and rehydration are all I need," said Kaid, letting his good arm fall back by his side. "I injured myself again trying to avoid capture, that's why it's inflamed." His eyes closed again and the world around him gradually faded.

"A month's too much. I want him on his feet long before that!"

"With respect, Prophet," he heard Anirra answer, "he's already over-used Fastheal. A second dose would be dangerous."

"Find a way!"

He heard the receding footsteps, then Anirra swearing.

"Dammit! He demands the impossible of me! Get him set up with catheters and canulas—I'll have to do a sleep cure."

"Yes, Doctor."

A sharp prick in his arm, a slight feeling of pressure, then nothing.

His sleep was uneasy, haunted as it was by images. Pillars of flame stood before him, calling him to pass through them but he retreated, unwilling to enter the world of fire and devastation he knew lay beyond. Unable to wake properly, he felt his body being moved, examined, then probed by sharp implements that brought momentary pain.

Against his chest he felt a sensation of coolness, a burning with no fire, no pain. He grasped at the crystal he wore round his neck, holding onto it through all that long night, anchoring his reason to it as the one solid object in his world.

He awoke abruptly, eyes open, body tensed, hands ready at his sides. He could sense no one else present. The room was unfamiliar. The soft light of an oil lamp on the night table cast a gentle glow on the sparse furnishings and the sandstone walls of the room. As well as the bed in which he lay, there was a small chest against the wall, a stool, and a woven rug.

The air smelled reasonably fresh but he sensed the faint scent of the medic, Anirra. He pushed himself up, then realized he was resting his weight on his injured arm—and it didn't hurt.

Sitting bolt upright, he examined the wounded forearm. All that remained was a hairless line of bright pink scar tissue. Incredulously he explored the scar with a cautious fingertip. A little sensitive but nothing more.

He remembered the second hypoderm. He'd been drugged then, but for how long? Running his hands through his hair he realized it had grown by perhaps a couple of centimeters. More than a night, that was certain. A month? Had he lain here drugged for the last month?

Throwing back the covers, he climbed out of bed. On the chest he could see his uniform jacket, his belt, and a fresh shirt. As he walked over to them, he realized that there was none of the weakness in his limbs that he'd have expected if he'd been unconscious for so long. Not a month, then. For all Anirra said, he must have used Fastheal. That would account for the hair growth.

As he was buckling the belt, the door opened, admitting one of the desert people complete in tan robes and head covering.

"Good morning. We've been waiting for you to waken. A meal awaits you, then the Word of Kezule has commanded that you be brought to him. Please, follow me."

"One moment," said Kaid. "Who's this Word of Kezule?"

"The Prophet Fyak," said the male, turning back to frown at him as he held the door open. "You are his guest. It's due to his generosity your wounds have been treated."

"How long have I been here?"

"The Prophet will answer all your questions in his own time," was the placid answer.

As he followed the warrior into the main cavern, Kaid smelled food and realized he was hungry. Tended cooking fires glowed in one corner and nearby, empty packing crates formed crude tables and seats.

A large plate of eggs and cooked meat with a couple of slices of bread on the side was handed to him by a female who kept her eyes firmly turned from his. As he made his way to the nearest table, his companion collected two mugs of c'shar, then rejoined him.

While he ate, Kaid assessed his surroundings. Definitely no chance of escape, the cavern was far too busy. They might be treating him as a guest for now, but he was no less a prisoner for that. He glanced again at the female by the cooking fires. She was serving a couple of the warriors with c'shar and, as with him, she kept her gaze firmly fixed on her task, never looking at the males.

"If you're wondering what a female is doing outside her home, she's too old to have cubs so Fyak ordered her to cook for us. There are a few like her who'll never be given a mate, but then they chose to live alone in the first place. That one came from the Laasoi Guildhouse. She reckoned herself a warrior. Not any more." He grinned as Kaid looked back at him. "She knows better than to raise a hand against any male now."

Kaid grunted noncommittally and finished his meal.

"I'll take you to the Prophet," his companion said, getting to his feet.

They walked across the cavern to the room where he'd first been taken. This time, Fyak was alone except for one guard—from the look of him, the commander of that unit.

Fyak looked up as they entered.

"I see you're in better health now," he said. "I hear your wound is fully healed."

"My thanks, Prophet," said Kaid, aware that the male who'd accompanied him had remained and was standing behind him, against the door. "I hope I haven't imposed on your hospitality. Perhaps you'd be so good as to tell me how long I've been here?"

"Time is irrelevant," said Fyak, resting his elbows on the desk in front of him. "You remember me telling you that Guild Master Ghezu is interested in your whereabouts."

"I don't remember much about our last meeting, I'm afraid," said Kaid.

"It seems Ghezu wishes me to deliver you into his—tender care. Have you any idea why he should want this?" Fyak's voice was a gentle purr as he raised a questioning eye ridge.

"None," said Kaid, aware of Fyak's minute examination.

"Strange." Fyak rested his chin in one hand, his sleeve falling back to expose the broad gold bracelet he wore. "I assume it involved the dead female in some way since Ghezu said we'd find you at her house."

Kaid shrugged, maintaining a disinterested facade. In reality he was using it to justify looking round the room, gleaning all the information about Fyak that he could. His gaze kept returning to the bracelet. There was something about it, a familiarity he couldn't explain. Where had he seen its like before?

Fyak frowned, sitting up and putting his arms on the desk. "I think you owe me a few answers in return for my hospitality," he said sharply. "If I hand you over to Ghezu, your fate will not be as pleasant as it could be if you remained here."

"We have an old score to settle," admitted Kaid, bringing his attention back to the prophet.

"Perhaps I shan't tell Ghezu I have you. Maybe I have another use for you," said Fyak, sitting back in his chair, his arms stretched along the armrests, claw tips gently tapping the wood. "I have a proposition to put to you, one that is infinitely more attractive than being Ghezu's unwilling guest."

"What kind of proposition?" asked Kaid.

"I don't entirely trust Ghezu's promise of neutrality. I need someone capable of training my people properly. He said you were the best of the Brothers, and I've no reason to doubt that in view of his dislike of you. I want my fighters not only to be able to stand against the Brotherhood if necessary, but to be able to withstand the minds of the telepaths."

Kaid considered him for a moment. "It depends on the individual fighter. Not everyone can learn that skill," he said. "As for combat, you've already got seasoned fighters here. Why do you need me to train them? And anyway, why do you want them to learn the mental disciplines against telepaths?"

"That's my concern," said Fyak. "I've told you all you need to know for now. Will you accept my offer, or would you prefer to be handed over to Ghezu?"

Kaid mentally ran through what he'd learned so far. A captive female warrior from the Laasoi Guildhouse reinforced the newscast he'd heard several weeks before. It might have been Fyak's first move outside the desert: it certainly wouldn't be his last. If he wanted his warriors trained to a higher standard, he was planning a larger campaign where he knew he'd be up against a better trained force—possibly including the Brotherhood. That suggested he had an agenda Ghezu knew nothing about. Then the anti-telepath training: that meant he expected to be dealing with telepath guildhouses again.

He tried to envisage the local geography. What was Fyak after? The Tribes. He was attempting to unite all the tribes before taking his warriors over the pass into the fertile lowlands to the west. If he managed that, there'd be no stopping him. Fighting against fanatical warriors who could emerge from the forests, attack the estates in the plains, then disappear again almost without trace, was a terrifying thought. And Ghezu had embroiled the Brotherhood in this! *Vartra, cast his soul into the deepest pit of hell,* he prayed.

"Well?" demanded Fyak. "What takes you so long? I'd have thought it obvious my offer was more attractive."

Kaid shrugged. "When do I start?" Time was his ally. With enough time, he could discover the details of Fyak's plans and maybe even escape.

* * *

It had taken several days work to dislodge the rockfall at the base of the monastery's hill. Ahead of them, the tunnel began to open up, then it was once more clogged with dirt and debris. Outside the tunnel entrance, the pile of rubble and earth was steadily growing, and the builders were getting anxious to return to their official Guild work.

This left Kusac with only his group of twenty-nine Brothers, a good proportion of whom were on guard duty at any given time. Ni'Zulhu and he arranged the shifts so there were always eight people digging at a time. With all the electronic surveillance on the combined estates, during the day the duty rosters were light enough that they could cope. Everyone's spirits were lifted a little when they'd excavated enough of the cavern entrance to see another sloping tunnel off to their left, obviously heading upward into the secondary, and larger, cavern complex.

Kusac's return to the Forces semi-active list meant a resumption of his training sessions at the Warrior Guild in Nazule. Not so for Carrie. Thankfully there had been no more dream replays but she found herself glad that the work at the hill was going slowly as she didn't have the energy to stir far from the house.

With Garras working on the dig, and Kusac at Nazule with T'Chebbi, she kept Vanna company. She didn't want Vanna to be left alone for any length of time now that her friend was in the last two weeks of her pregnancy. The first day she went round, Vanna took one look at Carrie and requested protein supplements from Jack for her.

"I know this is an En'Shalla cub, Carrie," she said, "but your body just doesn't produce enough of what the infant needs from you. Vartra Himself would approve of you taking supplements." Fussing over Carrie made Vanna fret less about herself, and Carrie stoically put up with it.

Brynne had decided to help the diggers and though relations between him and Garras were civilized, they were not good. By an unspoken agreement, they worked on different teams.

It was discovered that the upward tunnel had less rubble in it, being only partially filled with the detritus of over a thousand years. The team digging there were making good progress when two weeks into the work, the first finds were made—in the main cavern.

"Hey! Bones! I've found bones!" yelled Rulla, grabbing hold of the protruding end of a piece of ivory-colored material.

"Don't pull at it like that!" exclaimed Jack. "It's fragile, you'll . . ."

With a yowl of surprise, Rulla went flying backward, grasping a knuckle-ended piece of broken bone in one hand.

". . . break it," he finished with a sigh.

"Sorry. How was I to know it would break so easily? I thought bones were bones."

"Not when they're over a thousand years old, they aren't," said Jack, going over to take the piece from him. "Where did you find it?"

Rulla scrambled up, dusting off his jacket as he answered. "Over there." He pointed to the spot where he'd been working.

A crowd quickly gathered round Jack as he used a small brush to gently remove the earth around the rest of the bone, all the while explaining how and why he was doing it.

Finally, the rest of the bone lay exposed on its bed of soil. "Well, there you have your first lesson in archeology," said Jack, brushing the loose earth from around it, "and your first Valtegan leg bone."

"Valtegan?" demanded Garras. "Are you sure?"

Jack looked up at him. "I'm a physician, Garras. I know as much about your people as I do about my own. If I say this isn't a Sholan bone, and that I'm pretty certain it's Valtegan, you can be sure I know what I'm talking about."

Garras lowered his ears in apology. "I didn't mean to imply a mistake, Jack, only surprise that we'd found Valtegan remains so soon."

"Well, we'll soon know when we find the rest of him," said Jack, beginning to carefully undercut the soil around the relic. "We knew there would likely be bodies down here. If this was the entrance, then I imagine it saw the fiercest fighting."

Garras turned round to face the others. "Back to work, everyone," he said. "We know we're on the right track now." As the top tunnel team wandered reluctantly back to work, Garras bent down beside Jack. "What do you want us to do?"

"Carry on working at the face," he said. "Just make sure not to disturb the earth near me. I've no wish to be buried like our scaly friend!"

Garras nodded. "This find has given us all more enthusiasm to continue," he said. "It couldn't have come at a better time."

"This is a slow process, Garras," said Jack, picking carefully away at the underside of the bone, "and we haven't the time to take it as slowly as it needs, I'm afraid. We'll have to leave that to the professionals from Earth. We need to find evidence that this was a secret base for telepaths—anything we can that will connect this place to some of the replay dreams Carrie and Kaid have had. A lot of fascinating archeological information is going to have to be sacrificed to do that, but," he looked up at Garras with a grin, "every now and then we can take the time out to properly excavate any really interesting finds."

"Have you had any news from the archaeologists at the site in the Kysubi plains yet?"

"Not much. Just that they're on to something big—a major town is buried under all those fields. They've done their scans and are currently deciding what area they think will yield the most finds. I've a feeling their choice is more likely to be dictated by which fields are lying fallow this winter than what they hope to find in a given area! I did hear that they're coming up with large numbers of small green stones unlike any other mineral yet found on Shola, though."

"Interesting. I wonder what conditions created them, where they come from."

*   *   *

The door to Sorli's study opened, and without ceremony, Esken walked in, pausing only long enough to pull up a chair.

"Have you read the book?" he asked, sitting down opposite the senior member of his tutorial staff.

Sorli sat back in his own chair, suppressing a sigh. Master Esken had become increasingly neglectful of his staff's feelings of late. He hoped the rift between him and the Clan Lord was soon healed. Life would be so much more pleasant again.

"I have, Master Esken. It was heavy going, though. I only completed my initial analysis half an hour ago. I still need to cross-reference it to other reputable sources." He started to rise. "May I offer you a drink?"

"No time, Sorli. I'm too busy to stay long. Just give me your first impressions."

Sorli reached for his comp pad. "I came across several warnings that were to be passed on to those training for the position of Guild Master. They've been repeated by each

successive Master in turn throughout the book. It seems our
ancestors were anticipating trouble. Have you ever read this
volume, Master Esken?"

"I had a look at the book when I was training for this
Office, of course." Esken paused for a moment, obviously
reminiscing. "Suddenly having the wisdom and secrets of
many of the past Guild Masters at your fingertips is an
incentive for any trainee master to study books such as this,
Sorli." He sighed. "But I do wish they hadn't wrapped up
what they had to say in so many innuendos and mysteries."

Sorli grunted. "They give obscure a new meaning."

Esken looked at him sharply. "I hope you're not becoming
judgmental, Sorli."

The Tutor assumed a slightly outraged expression.

Esken had the grace to glance away as he said, "I'm afraid
when I first looked at them, I got mired in all that ancient
history too. I promised myself I'd come back to it when I had
time. It's surprising how closely ancient wisdoms are apt to
resemble the day-to-day ramblings of senile predecessors,
Sorli. No doubt you've already found that out for yourself,
though." He sighed. "So what were the points you considered vital?"

Sorli looked at his comp pad. "They are, Firstly, *Record
all visions and dreams pertaining to Vartra, for at times He
enlightens his Chosen with true insights.* Secondly, *Bless all
contrivances of ancient days, that they become Holy, for they
hold the Green Seeds of New Regret.* Thirdly, *Cherish and
keep close our Brother Priests of Stronghold, who were once
our Claws and will be so again.* Fourthly—and here, Master
Esken, I confess I wonder if some relevance to present times
is implied—*Be ever vigilant against the False Priest, agent
of Demons, tool of their Retribution, through whose Leadership the Griefs of our Past may yet destroy our Future.*"

Sorli paused and awaited Esken's reaction.

The Guild Master nodded. "That's more or less as I
remember it, Sorli. Don't bother cross-referencing, I've done
enough on that already. Essentially the same warnings go
back a full eight generations earlier, and forward to our
time. There are gaps, of course, but since the warnings span
them, we can assume they remained essentially unchanged.
Each Master in the records restates these warnings. My
predecessor, Myaddu, thought them no more than ancient
superstitions, but she was uneasy enough about the second

injunction for me to maintain her policy of swift and thorough Blessings of the ruins."

"Obviously there's more to it than she thought, Master Esken. Twelve hundred years; that's a long time for so many superstitions to survive. I was unaware our records went back that far."

"So was I until I looked. Combine those warnings, Sorli. What do you get?"

"I find myself thinking of Fyak." He hadn't wanted to voice his fears lest words give them substance.

Esken did not disagree.

At last Sorli looked up. "It seems, Master Esken, that we're seeing a picture of a past we never suspected until Valtegan bones were found in our ruined cities. That one factor puts all our ancient writings into a completely different context." He scanned the pad, seeking some comfort in his notes. "My opinion has to be that this past is rushing to catch up with us now. How, I don't pretend to know."

"Nor do I, Sorli, nor do I. But as I said, you endorse my own conclusions."

"Remember the references to the *'Demons of Fire'*? Fyak mentions them, often and loudly, as do his Faithful. Too much of a coincidence?" Sorli warmed to his theme. "Fyak preaches the destruction of all telepaths, blaming them for causing the Cataclysm by conspiring with these demons. He warns his people those days will return unless they follow his teachings. Our lowland people care very little about religious dogma, they scent no danger in his rantings. To them he is obviously mad. Yet the desert tribes seem susceptible; their ears are wide open to his words, insane though his notions about social restructuring seem to us."

Esken held up his hand. "You've no need to convince me, Sorli. Are you therefore suggesting that the Valtegans are the demons, and Fyak the False Priest?"

"Yes, Master Esken. Interestingly enough, the region where Fyak lairs used to be called Khezy'ipik. Our name for it is Chezy."

"Khezy'ipik . . . ?"

"Recently, in my spare time, I've been assimilating the data that the Keissian, Jo, made available to us on the Valtegan language, in case we should ever need it. That name, Khezy'ipik, has a Valtegan ring to it."

"Ah. Does it?" Esken stood up. "I think I'll have that drink after all."

While he was occupied with the c'shar brewer, Sorli continued: "We now know Valtegan bones are regularly being found at all five sites where the Terran archeologists are digging. They obviously had a reasonably large presence on Shola. Also, large quantities of green stones—the *Green Seeds of New Regret?*—have been found in areas that appear to have been exclusively Valtegan. No purpose has been found for them as yet."

"I hate to admit it, Sorli, but it might be politic to let our opposition to the digging drop. No need for a major about-face. Just let the matter quietly die." He resumed his seat.

Sorli decided it was best not to comment on his Guild Master's decision. "Do you know that I can't find any mention of where Fyak comes from? Nor of a god called Kezule?"

"To hell with him and his God!" said Esken unexpectedly. "What we're going to *do* about him is more to the point!"

"We ought to give this new information to the relevant authorities," said Sorli. "Our traditional role is to facilitate communications, after all."

"I imagine the Forces' attention is already sharply focussed on Fyak," Esken said drily. "He's attacked the Laasoi guild-house, abducted one Telepath, brain-damaged two more beyond hope of recovery, and caused the deaths of at least four others."

"Empire building?" suggested Sorli.

"Possibly, but we still have the dire warnings against investigating our past, and against demons to take into consideration. In the circumstances . . ."

"Perhaps Father Lijou is already downwind of this question?" He was reluctant to add that Ghyan, currently serving in Vartra's newly appointed Shrine on the Valsgarth estate, might also be able to help. Ghyan's connections to the Aldatan clan would only inflame Esken's feud with Konis over the issue of the new Leska pairs. That particular insult had not yet been forgotten. Then he thought of what might be at stake and changed his mind.

"Master Esken, maybe you should approach Ghyan as well as Father Lijou. Lately we haven't kept as close contact with Stronghold as, according to those ancient texts, we should; they may have a lot to tell us. Our Leskas' dreams have always been relayed to Ghyan, and I know he, in turn, sends them on to Lijou. Neither of them reports back to us unless we specifically request it."

"It looks like I'm going to contact them, doesn't it? We have to be beyond personal politics. My differences with Clan Lord Aldatan must take second place."

As Esken stopped to take a drink of his c'shar, Sorli heaved an inward sigh of relief at his decision.

"Don't talk to anyone else regarding this matter, Sorli," Esken continued, "When we have something more solid, then we can approach the appropriate people."

"Will we be making this information available to the committee collating all the guild records?"

"All in good time, Sorli," said Esken, draining his mug and getting up.

* * *

Vanna was restless today. Carrie watched from the depths of her chair as her friend got up for perhaps the fifth time and began pacing the room. Instinct, coupled with the knowledge Taizia had given her, convinced her that Vanna was likely to go into labor today. The very fact she didn't feel a need to rest was significant in itself in these latter days of her pregnancy.

"This Derwent Human is strange, Carrie," she was saying as she paused by her desk. "I don't understand him. He must be talented or he wouldn't be on Shola, but . . ." She broke off with a sigh and began pacing again, tail flicking rhythmically from side to side.

"But what, Vanna?"

"He attends the lectures at the Guild but refuses to take the tests so they can gauge his progress. He's also refused to have an aura scan, or cooperate in any attempts to chart his talents!"

"Then why is he here?"

Vanna stopped by the settee, carefully sitting down and pulling her legs up so she could stretch her gravid body out more comfortably.

"That's what I've been asking myself. I believe it may be that he's more interested in letting us hear *his* ideas. Several times he's been reprimanded for telling his theories to groups of Sholan students in the Guild refectory. He's even had the

temerity to try preaching to Guardian Dhaika at Vartra's
Retreat! If he goes on like this, they'll exclude him from the
Guild, maybe even request his return to Earth. I can't say I'd
be sorry."

"What's he been saying that's so radical?" asked Carrie,
remembering her own early clashes with the Telepath Guild
over its rigid ethical code. She watched Vanna continue to
make herself more comfortable, suddenly realizing that her
friend had never seemed so feline, so alien, as she did now.

"He's saying that our Talent is a gift from the Mother
Goddess. Not the Green Goddess, you realize, *his* Goddess,
and that we should be worshipping her and no one else."

Carrie frowned. "What's so bad about that?"

"Our work as telepaths bears no relationship to our religious beliefs, Carrie. You know that. Telling the young ones
that the two are connected is wrong, very wrong. As for
telling them which God or Goddess they should worship!
That's a very personal matter, one to be discussed with the
appropriate priests, not with someone who's a stranger to our
culture."

"You shouldn't let it worry you, Vanna. It sounds to me
like Master Esken's going to solve the problem for you. I
don't know why you're letting yourself get so worked up
about it. How did you hear about all this anyway? You
haven't left the estate for weeks now."

"Brynne's friend Terry keeps me generally informed," she
said. "As for the business at the Retreat, Brynne took Derwent there to look around. He was as embarrassed as I was at
the way the man behaved! You're right, though. You know, I
wouldn't be so concerned if it didn't involve Brynne. He's
been seeing a lot of Derwent since the day that one arrived.
Brynne told me last week that it was as if he'd had one of
those visions that we all had when we first formed our links.
He knew he had to be at the Guildhouse to meet one of the
new arrivals from Earth, and he knew the one he was waiting
for was Derwent the minute he set eyes on him."

"Stranger things have happened to us, Vanna. I'm the last
one to say what is and isn't possible."

Vanna sighed. "I know. There's more. Derwent even stays
apart from the other Terrans. He lives in a suite at the
Accommodation Guildhouse in Valsgarth. Brynne goes there
regularly to see him, and he won't tell me why! He's keeping
something from me, Carrie," she said, pushing herself up on

one elbow. "I may not have been able to use my talent for the last two months, but there's nothing wrong with my instincts and he's definitely hiding something from me! What are he and Derwent doing that I can't be told?"

Carrie eased herself out of her chair and went over to her friend, sitting on the floor beside her. Reaching up she took Vanna's hand in hers. "You're getting too worked up about it, Vanna," she said soothingly. "I'm sure it's nothing much to worry about. You and Brynne have been getting along so much better this last couple of weeks."

"That's only because of the cub," Vanna said fretfully. "I don't think he's really changed, nor does Garras."

"I'm sure you're wrong," she said. Then she sensed Brynne's arrival at the house. Dzaka had stopped him from entering and was asking why he was there.

She reached for the Terran, and as she made contact, she sensed what Vanna had been talking about. There was an area of his mind that was closed off in such a way that to Carrie at least, being of the same species, instantly drew attention to itself.

What can we do for you, Brynne? she asked.

He was surprised at her sending to him, but that passed, to be replaced by a faint sense of confusion. *I came as quickly as I could when I realized she was in labor, but I thought Jack would be here.*

As Carrie turned her attention back to Vanna, her friend's hand tightened on hers, claws extended and beginning to penetrate. She reached up with her other hand, easing the pressure of Vanna's fingers slightly.

She's just started. Get Dzaka to fetch Jack! She cut him off and reached for Kusac. *It's time,* she sent. *Bring Garras. Brynne is already here, tell him that.* She sensed her mate's affirmative rather than heard it as she returned all her attention to Vanna.

There was a surprised and pained look on her friend's face as she lay on the settee, her other hand curved protectively around her belly.

"It can't be now," she said. "It's too early!"

"Only by a few days," said Carrie soothingly. "Don't worry, everything will be fine. Dzaka's gone for Jack, Brynne's on his way up, and Kusac's bringing Garras."

"No! I don't want either of them here!" she said, snatching her hand away from Carrie to place it with the other. "It's too early, I tell you!" Her ears were laid back flat and her pupils were enormous.

The door opened and Brynne entered, coming straight over to join them. Like many of the male Terrans, he'd chosen not to dress like the Sholans, and in his jeans and coat he looked completely out of place in the Sholan household.

Vanna's body had relaxed again but now she pushed herself upright, growling. "I don't want you here, Brynne!"

"We agreed I'd be here," he said quietly, crouching down beside Carrie. "Jack's on his way. Is there anything I can do?"

"Yes, leave!" she said, batting at him with one hand.

He caught it in his, exerting his strength against hers as she tried to pull free. "Vanna, you know you agreed, and you know why I have to be here," he said. "Paternity has to be registered. It causes less problems if it's done immediately." He hesitated. "Besides, I want to know you're both all right."

Carrie decided it would be a good idea to move and began to rise to her feet.

Angrily, Vanna swung out at Brynne. Carrie felt a sudden hard blow across her chest. Her mind froze in fear as she went flying backward. Then strong arms caught her in midair, grasping her close for a moment before setting her gently down on her feet.

"Liegena, are you all right?" Dzaka's face was creased with worry as he held her steady.

She passed a shaking hand across her forehead and nodded. "I'm fine, Dzaka. Thank you," she said with feeling as she looked up at him.

He steered her toward the chair, moving his grip to her elbow as she sat down. "I'm glad I was there," he said quietly, then turned to Vanna and Brynne. "Physician Reynolds is on his way," he said.

Vanna's hands were at her mouth in shock as she looked over at Carrie. "Oh, Gods, Carrie! I'm so sorry! I didn't mean to . . ." she tried to say, but Carrie interrupted her.

"I'm fine, Vanna. No harm done," she said. "Brynne, Jack'll want to examine her. Take her through to her room, would you? It'll save him time when he arrives."

Brynne nodded. "Are you sure you're all right?" he asked.

"Yes, fine. You see to Vanna."

Lifting Vanna up despite her protests, he carried her from the room. At least the near-accident had taken Vanna's attention away from her resentment of Brynne's presence, Carrie

thought as she closed her eyes and relaxed back in her chair. The incident had shaken her more than she realized. Kusac was fretting and mentally she reassured him she was fine.

"Can I get you a drink?" asked Dzaka, hovering beside her.

"Please," she said. "A c'shar." She found the rather bland drink more palatable than coffee these days.

When Garras arrived with Kusac, Carrie could feel his hackles rising as he looked over to where Brynne sat on the settee. She put her drink down on the side table and looked from one to the other.

"Jack's in with Vanna just now. I don't want any trouble between you two. You'd better start behaving civilly to each other," she said. "I've no intention of letting either of you upset Vanna, or me for that matter, with your male posturing! You're both responsible for Vanna in your own ways, and you're both important to her. But Garras, the cub is Brynne's, and as his father, he has the right to be here."

The two males looked at her in surprise.

"Brynne, Garras is Vanna's mate, don't forget that," she said tiredly. "If you want to be accorded your rights as a father, then makes sure you give Garras his as her mate. So you can both put your hackles down now—and yes, Brynne, you have hackles just as real as Garras has!"

She could feel Garras forcing himself to relax as he padded over to one of the other chairs. Brynne . . . well, he seemed to almost disappear mentally. Kusac joined her, perching on the arm of her chair and putting his arm round her shoulders.

A short time later, Jack emerged to ask them to arrange for Vanna to be taken to the medical unit at the Valsgarth Telepath Guild.

"There's nothing to worry about, I simply want to be sure I've got the best equipment and staff to hand just in case. Carrie, I want you to stay here," he said. "You're too recognizable. If you come with us, it'll only attract the newsnets. Besides, you need to rest. Go home. You look tired out."

* * *

Dzaka was relieved shortly after Kusac and Garras joined Carrie at Vanna's home. He went up to the dig to take

Garras' place as the imminent birth of Vanna's cub brought back more memories than he could cope with.

He found the place where he'd been working before and, collecting his tools, was carefully scraping the soil away from a piece of an ancient vehicle, finding comfort in the mindless, repetitive work. The sound of a footfall close by disturbed his peace, then he recognized her scent. Kitra. He sighed. Lately he couldn't turn round without finding her behind him. Not that he minded in one way, she was a bright kitling, always asking sensible questions. But it could be damned inconvenient having her following him at times.

"Lo, Dzaka," she said, squatting down to one side of him. "Thought you'd be up at the villa with Carrie. Jack took Vanna off to the medical center to have her cub."

He flicked an ear in greeting. "Is Vanna all right?" he asked, stopping what he was doing to look round at her.

"I think so. Jack said to Carrie that he wanted her to be safe, she didn't really have to go. Do you think she'll be all right?" There was a worried frown on her face.

"I'm sure she'll be fine," said Dzaka reassuringly. "She's got plenty of experienced physicians round her at the center."

"I suppose," she said.

He returned to his scrapings, hoping she'd wander off and find someone else to talk to.

"What's that?" she asked, her hand coming between him and the piece he was working on.

"A piece of a road vehicle."

"Road vehicle?"

"They didn't have aircars back then, Kitra," he explained. "Their vehicles ran on wheels."

"There's writing on it," she said, her hand once more coming between him and his work. "What does it say?"

"I don't know yet. I haven't uncovered enough of it to show all the letters."

"I could help," she offered. "It would be finished twice as quickly."

He stopped and looked round at her eager face. A wide-eyed amber gaze looked up hopefully at him.

"Please."

He found it difficult to say anything but "All right." He reached for the brush and handed it to her. "Here you are.

You start brushing all the loose soil off that piece there, while I carry on digging it out."

They continued working for about an hour, chatting companionably, until someone yelled, "C'shar! Come and get it!"

"I'm thirsty," said Kitra. "Are you? Shall I go and get us a drink?"

"No. You stay here, I'll get them," said Dzaka. "I could do with stretching my legs. I'm a bit bigger than you and I've been sitting cramped up for too long!"

Kitra laughed, watching him get up and stretch before he ambled off to where a c'shar urn and mugs had been set up.

As he waited in the small queue, he felt a tap on his shoulder and turned round to find Rulla behind him.

"I'd be careful, if I were you, Dzaka," he said. "Playing fast with the Liege's little sister. Not a good idea."

Dzaka frowned. "Don't be ridiculous," he said, turning away from him. "She's barely more than a cub. What do you think I am?"

"I think you're presuming on our Liege's good nature, that's what."

"Look," Dzaka said, turning again. "She's a child! She's the one that's following me around!"

"Then stop encouraging her," Rulla growled, grasping him by the arm. "She's the same age as that young Leska pair from the desert, she's old enough! We've seen how she looks at you, so just make sure you leave her alone, hear me? There's a couple of us watching out for her. You touch her, we'll know about it."

Dzaka prized Rulla's hand off his arm. "You've really taken a dislike to me, haven't you, Rulla?" he said. "Why? I've done nothing to you. If you think you can use Kitra as an excuse to have a row, think again! Anyone who'd stoop that low is beneath my contempt. Kitra's as safe with me as if she were my own daughter!"

"Hey, Dzaka! Your turn," said T'Chebbi.

"Just watch your step," warned Rulla as Dzaka turned to answer her.

T'Chebbi handed him two mugs, looking past him at Rulla. "Say hello to Kitra," she said pointedly. "Rulla forgets himself at times."

Dzaka turned to leave, only to find his way blocked by Rulla. "Remember what I said."

"Get out of my way," snarled Dzaka, sidestepping him and heading back to where Kitra was sitting.

She took the mug he offered her. "Thanks."

He sat down, keeping his back to the cavern wall so he could see everyone. "It's getting late, Kitra," he said. "Might be sensible to drink your c'shar and go home."

"It's not that late, and Mother knows I'm here. I told her I was coming to see you."

Dzaka began to feel uncomfortable. He raised his mug, taking a mouthful of his drink. "When you're over at the villa, where do you tell your mother you're going?" he asked, almost afraid to hear her answer.

"I tell her I'm going to see my brother and Carrie, of course," she said with a small frown.

Dzaka began to breathe more easily.

"And you," she added with a grin.

The mouthful of c'shar went down the wrong way and he began to choke on it.

"Are you all right?" she demanded, putting her mug down on the ground and moving closer. She began to hit him repeatedly on the back.

He twisted away from her, coughing. "I'm fine, Kitra. Honestly. I don't need any help."

She squatted back, looking at him in concern. "Are you sure?" she asked. "Your eyes are watering and your face is scrunched up."

He rubbed the back of his hand across his eyes and began to laugh. "Yes, I'm fine, little one. Now, come on. Finish your drink and head back home. It's going to be dark soon."

She reached for her mug again. "Won't you walk me back?"

"Not this time, Kitra. I want to finish this first," he said, waving a hand in the direction of his partly exposed vehicle.

"You're going to be here very late," she said, glancing over at it.

"I don't mean finish digging it *all* out," he said. "Just the lettering."

"Oh," she said quietly. "I thought we could have finished it together." She paused, then added, "I like helping you. You're one of the few people who don't treat me like a child. The others won't see that I've grown up now."

Acutely uncomfortable and aware that he was being observed, Dzaka thought furiously for a suitable answer.

"I like talking to you, too, Kitra. I'll tell you what. Tomorrow morning I'm off duty. How about you come over to the villa and I'll have a weapons practice with you? You enjoy learning how to use a sword, don't you?"

"I'd like that," she said, brightening up.

"Oh, I forgot to tell you, T'Chebbi said hello," he added.

"T'Chebbi?"

He nodded. "She doesn't think you're still a cub, does she?"

Kitra shook her head. "T'Chebbi doesn't say much of anything to anyone."

"Well, she speaks to you, doesn't she? And she wouldn't waste her time on a cub."

He got a long look in reply. "Dzaka, don't patronize me," she said. "If you don't want me around, just tell me."

Oh Gods! he thought. *Now I've done it!* Then anger hit him. He'd managed to hurt her feelings because he'd been concerned at what Rulla had said.

"Kitra, you want to come and talk to me any time, you do it, d'you hear me?" he said, reaching out to touch her cheek. "I'll leave this bit of my digging until the next time you can help me." He got to his feet and held out his hand to her. "Come on. I'll walk you home."

She looked up at him, surprise written in the set of her ears. "You will?" she asked, taking his hand and letting him help her up.

"Yes, I will," he said firmly. Bending down he picked up their mugs. "Let's give these back to T'Chebbi on our way out."

As they turned to leave her, T'Chebbi caught Dzaka by the arm. "Be careful coming back," she said quietly.

"I will," he said.

*   *   *

The afternoon was made even longer because they were waiting at home, but as night fell, Garras called them to say that Vanna was well, and the cub, a male called Marak, had been born safely, though Jack wanted them kept in overnight for observation and tests.

"What's he like?" asked Kusac, who'd taken the call.

"What we expected, predominantly Sholan, I'm thankful to say. It makes it easier for me as Vanna's mate. Had he been more Human, Brynne might have felt he should be more involved in his upbringing than we want—maybe even have tried to take him away from us. Apart from that, it's difficult to describe how a cub this young looks, Kusac."

"Try." He needed to know.

Garras sighed. "Small, very small I thought, but Vanna says they're all that size at first. His pelt is pale just like Vanna's—you know, that lovely beige color like the sand out by Nazule Bay. His eyes aren't open yet, won't be for another five days. The specialist at the center said it's still too early to see any difference between him and a pure Sholan cub."

Kusac didn't know whether to be relieved or not. Their cub ought to be the same, which meant she'd look like his people. But how would Carrie feel about that? At least Vanna was now holding a child that looked like her, who would grow up with two Sholan parents, not one Human, the other Sholan.

"You worry too much, Kusac," said Garras gently. "Carrie will cope better than you think."

"Why the tests?" he asked, feeling guilty that he'd let his worries intrude into Garras' news. "He's all right, isn't he?"

"Is Carrie there?" Garras asked quietly.

"No. She's sleeping in the bedroom."

"Because he's a mixture of Sholan and Human, Jack wants to be sure there aren't any defects. There's possibly a heart murmur, but it could just be an echo that's common with newborns. Don't mention it to Carrie though. We don't want her worrying about her cub. Don't you go worrying either," he added.

"Perhaps I should have let Vanna do a post mortem on our cub after all," he said.

"No, you did the right thing, Kusac. I would have done the same."

"It's too late now to regret it anyway. But Vanna? You say she's fine?"

"Tired, that's all. Jack said he wished it could be as easy for Humans as it was for her. Vanna wanted me with her after all, and Tutor Sorli himself came over to register Brynne as the father, so he's happy. Considering he didn't know that Marak would look so Sholan, he took it well."

"We'll come and see her tomorrow," said Kusac, shaking

himself out of his morbid concern. "Tell her we'll ask the Green Goddess to look after her and her cub."

"She'll appreciate that. Till tomorrow."

* * *

Rhyasha persuaded Dzaka to join her for a cup of c'shar and a plate of cookies in the family kitchen. He was puzzled by her sudden interest in him, but too polite to refuse. Consequently, it was dark before he started back, carefully choosing to return by a different route. He was within a few hundred yards of home and the illuminated main street when he sensed he was being followed. Growling softly to himself, he considered his options. Not good, he was in the open. He could make a dash for the lights, but that course didn't have much dignity attached to it. This was something that wasn't going to go away. There would be more times like this, when Rulla and his particular friends decided they didn't like what he was doing. As well face it now as later.

Turning so the lights were behind him, he backed off to the nearest tree, scanning the grounds in front of him for his attackers. He could feel Rulla's anger and resentment washing over him. He blamed him for his father's capture, and while he couldn't do anything to help Kaid, he could hurt the one he considered responsible.

Rulla stepped out from the shadows of a nearby bush. "You couldn't take a warning, could you, Dzaka?" he said. "You use people, do you know that? You used Kaid to get away from Fyak's lot, and now you're using Kitra to get close to our Liege."

Dzaka frowned. What was he talking about?

"You want to make a place for yourself, somewhere you'll be safe from Kaid when he returns, is that it?" He moved closer, tail swaying rhythmically, ears flattening ready to fight.

A movement to his left caught his eye. He risked a quick glance. One of the estate guards Rulla had been keeping company with lately.

"Are you afraid to Challenge me then, Rulla?" he asked. "Is that why there's the two of you? Can't be sure you can take me alone?"

"Count again, Dzaka," purred Rulla. "There's three of us. And no, I'm not going to Challenge you. This isn't worthy of

a Challenge. This is a warning. Stay away from the cub.
She's too young to be used by the likes of you."

As Dzaka saw a third person join the other two in front of
him, suddenly another figure loomed up out of the night. He
recognized the scent. T'Chebbi. She stepped up to his side.

"You fools," she said, putting her hands on her hips and
regarding the three males with utter scorn. "You know
nothing, Rulla. You talk lots, say nothing! She's not child, is
Kitra. You males are stupid when it comes to us!" She gave a
bark of laughter. "That little one will chose who she wants,
and soon! You won't stop her. Now go, before I tell the
Liege you break your oath to him!"

"I'm breaking no oaths, T'Chebbi!" Rulla hissed. "This
has nothing to do with you!"

"Has. Our oath is obey our Liege. He says Dzaka protected. What is protection worth when his liegemen attack
each other, huh?"

"She's a child, T'Chebbi! He's trying to seduce her!"
Rulla protested.

"Not a child," she insisted, shaking her head. "You aren't
at the villa. You don't see her follow him. She's hunting
him!" She stepped forward in front of Dzaka. "You want I
get the Liegena? You ask her about his sister?"

"Don't be ridiculous," muttered Rulla, looking away.

"Ridiculous? You are! Go home. Leave them be. They sort
it themselves, not you! Unless you want a Challenge with
me!" She growled, one hand going to rest on the long knife
at her belt.

Dzaka moved to stand beside her. "T'Chebbi, I can handle
this," he began.

She pushed him back. "You stay there. Kaid won't be
pleased if you're hurt. He'll only fight Rulla and those two."
She faced Rulla again. "I tell you for the last time. The
Liegena knows what happens. Kitra and Dzaka meet at the
villa. Not your concern," she said, taking another step
toward Rulla. "Now go!"

Rulla turned to look for his friends—and found himself
alone. He began to back away.

They watched him turn and head for the Brothers' house,
waiting until they saw him go in. Dzaka turned to T'Chebbi.
He didn't quite know what to say. For the second time that
day, he'd found support in an unexpected quarter.

"He feels too much for Kaid," said T'Chebbi, starting to walk toward the lights.

"Feels too much?" asked Dzaka, keeping pace with her.

She looked at him. "He wishes he was you. Kaid's son."

"Ah, I know what you mean."

"You like Kitra?" she asked as they approached the villa.

"She's a nice child," he said.

T'Chebbi began to laugh gently.

"What is it?" he demanded.

"You're in for a surprise," she chuckled, a look of pure mischief the likes of which he'd never have expected to see lighting up her usually somber face. She headed under the archway into the villa's grounds, leaving Dzaka standing bewildered outside.

He broke into a run, catching up to her as she walked round to the side door. "Why did you help me?" he asked, taking her by the arm to slow her down.

"Told Rulla why," she said.

"Yes. Apart from that. I mean earlier," he stammered.

She stopped and regarded him seriously. "You're Kaid's son. Like him, but different. I should have known someone like you when I was Kitra's age," she said. "I didn't. It was too late when I met Kaid. Early hurts don't ever go, Dzaka." She turned and walked into the house, leaving him to follow in his own time.

* * *

Kaid had been working with Fyak's warriors for nearly a week now. The desert tribes were a law unto themselves and actually enforcing the conscription into the Forces of all eighteen year old males was virtually impossible, especially when dealing with a large population of nomads. So very few of the desert army of around five thousand souls had ever seen military service, and those who had tended to be in Fyak's elite bodyguard. They were not included in his training schedules.

He'd split them into units a couple of hundred strong, each one in the charge of the most experienced warrior. He'd brief the newly appointed officers at the start of the day, then go round the individual units, keeping a check on standards.

Apart from their weapons, the overall tech level was low. The labels and signs on the packing crates had been obliterated but Kaid knew they'd been illegally acquired. Nothing he saw was overt enough to confirm his gut-feeling that Ghezu was involved, but by playing for time like this, he might just come across the proof he wanted. As yet, he'd had no chance to escape. He might as well be in a cell for all the freedom he actually had.

Their lack of military experience meant he could manage the training in such a way as to give an advantage to the Forces in any future engagement. Their normal operating procedure was that on sighting the enemy, the base was immediately contacted so coordinates, enemy numbers and other vital information could be passed on. They had three mobile field-comm units—old fashioned but in good working order, and one base unit as their main means of communicating with their HQ.

Kaid set up a corps of signalers and advised them that waiting till an engagement was over meant more detailed information could be given. He also impressed on them that in the event of a comm failure, it was vital a message be dispatched immediately to let the base know what had happened. The old practice of using a mirror to reflect sunlight was reintroduced, as was the sending of basic smoke signals. Beyond that, he kept his training methods to standards commonly used by the Brotherhood. If, in building up their endurance, he demanded they carry heavier loads or run farther than the Brothers would, it was only because Fyak wanted them ready as soon as possible.

L'Seuli watched him from a distance with interest. As an elite guard, he didn't train with the rest. He saw the flaws immediately and waited to see who else would spot them, or complain about the unrealistic goals Kaid was setting. No one did. The fact that the Brotherhood could perform these tasks meant that Fyak's males would die in the attempt rather than admit Kaid's standards were beyond them. L'Seuli was content just to watch and wait.

During a training session Kaid was overseeing, a delivery vehicle flew in, landing close to the mouth of the lair. Since the Laasoi raid, the Forces had kept the Sonashi and Nyacko passes heavily patrolled and set permanent garrisons there. All legitimate arms deliveries to the desert regions had been halted, and presumably vehicle manifests were being checked at the ports before they were allowed to take off in an effort to ensure no illegal shipments were made.

Kaid didn't see Zhaya climb down out of the vehicle, but Zhaya saw and recognized him. He stopped dead, watching as the warriors Kaid was working with struggled round the obstacle course. He moved back into the lee of the transporter, continuing to watch as one of the males stumbled and fell with heat exhaustion despite the time of year. He had to be carried off, one ankle already very obviously swelling.

Zhaya, swearing under his breath, waited no longer and headed into the main cavern. He accosted the first male he came across, demanding to be taken to Fyak.

"The Prophet is in the temple praying, and cannot be disturbed," said the guard. "I'll take you to Vraiyou."

He followed the warrior across the main cavern past the cooking area to a doorway. His guide stopped, knocking before entering. "Brother Zhaya wishes to talk to you," he said, bowing low.

"Tell him he may enter," said Vraiyou.

Zhaya pushed the guard aside and stalked in, letting the position of his ears and his lashing tail convey his anger.

"Is this how your master keeps his agreements, Vraiyou? By harboring wanted males? It's a good job *we* at least honor our contracts!"

Vraiyou finished what he was writing before turning round on his seat to look at him. "Brother Zhaya, what a pleasant surprise. You brought the latest shipment of 'grain,' I take it? It's good of Master Ghezu to take such a personal interest in us."

"Don't bother hiding behind polite conversation, Vraiyou. You agreed to have Rhijudu watched and if Kaid turned up, to take him into custody and inform us. Instead of which, I find him training your people! Just what the hell are you playing at?" he demanded, eyes narrowing and ears folding even flatter.

"The Prophet was told that we could benefit from his skills for a few days before handing him over to you."

"He's not even under guard out there, Vraiyou! He's wandering around as if he owned the place! And just what do you think he's teaching your fighters? He's exhausting them to no purpose! In the few minutes I was watching them, I saw one fall and sprain his ankle. How many more have been injured trying to carry impossible loads?"

Vraiyou's eye ridges met in a frown. "Excuse me? Are you saying he's purposely working them into a state of collapse and injury?"

"What would you call it?" Zhaya demanded. "He's sabotaging your troops under your very noses! He's treating you like the fools you are, Vraiyou!"

Vraiyou rose to his feet in one fluid motion. "Come with me," he said, his robes billowing around him as he stalked from his room into the main cavern. They headed back toward the exit, detouring by a group of the off duty elite who were drinking c'shar.

"Rrurto, L'Seuli, come," he ordered before continuing out into the area in front of the lair's entrance.

They halted by the vehicle, which was all but unloaded by now, and watched the troops under Kaid's instruction. As if aware of their presence, Kaid turned round briefly to look at them.

"He seems unconcerned by your presence," observed Vraiyou.

"He doesn't know me."

"Tell me what they're doing, Rrurto," the head acolyte ordered.

"Endurance. He's getting them to run an obstacle course in full kit," the older male answered.

"Is their load excessively heavy?"

"That's not something I'm qualified to judge, Liegen. I have no experience of the Brotherhood's training methods, and it's a long time since I was in the Forces."

"Would you have them carrying that much?"

Rrurto hesitated. "No, Liegen, I wouldn't. And there's no need for them to be dressed in heavy winter clothing yet."

"L'Seuli? You've lately come from active duty."

"No, Liegen Vraiyou, I wouldn't either."

"How many have been injured in the last two days?"

"Six, Liegen," replied Rrurto. "And about as many down with heat stroke."

"Arrest him. Take him to the Prophet's room and wait for us," Vraiyou ordered, his voice a low growl of anger. "Zhaya, we'll handle it from here. The unloading is complete. I suggest you return to Stronghold now. You'll be contacted in good time."

Zhaya opened his mouth to argue, then saw the set of Vraiyou's ears. This was no time to argue over priorities. "I'll inform Master Ghezu," he said.

"You do that," said Vraiyou shortly.

Kaid was released by the guards as soon as they entered Fyak's office. They stood behind him, blocking the doorway. He didn't have to wait long before Fyak and Vraiyou, followed by the commander of the guard, entered. With them was a female. Kaid recognized her as Rhaid, the telepath who had been taken from Laasoi guildhouse.

Fyak went straight to his desk. He stood behind it looking dispassionately at Kaid. "You've betrayed my trust. Why? Are you so anxious to become Ghezu's guest?"

Kaid sensed the movement from behind before he heard it. Turning to keep all three guards in view, he backed a few steps away from the desk.

"I won't help you take the lowlands, Fyak."

"You disappoint me," said Fyak. "Still, if I can't trust you to train my followers, perhaps I can get some information about Stronghold from you. There's still time for us to come to an agreement. I believe there are several hidden entrances to the mountain fort. I want to know where they are."

"There may be no love between me and Ghezu, but I'll not tell you how to get into Stronghold."

Fyak gestured to the female. "Rhaid, how strong are his convictions? Am I likely to persuade him to cooperate?"

She raised her head to look at Kaid for the first time. He felt the touch of her mind against his, but knew she couldn't read him. He saw the confusion on her face as she realized that she was unable to penetrate his mental shields.

"I can read nothing, Liege," she said.

"Nothing? How can you read nothing?" demanded Fyak, turning to look at her.

"His mind is closed to me, Liege."

Quick as the movement of a snake, Fyak cuffed her round the side of her head, causing her to lose her balance and stagger to one side.

"Try again."

She looked at Kaid again, ears tipped backward, eyes full of fear as she fingered the gold collar she wore round her neck. Light flashed within the heart of the green stone set in its center.

Kaid glanced back at Fyak, seeing him touch his gold bracelet. The bracelet! He was using it to control her! Then he felt the touch of her mind again. He knew that nothing either of them could do would improve his situation, but he could make things easier for her. He let his resolve not to cooperate leak from his mind, praying she'd pick it up.

She hesitated, and he knew she didn't want to betray him. "He will never yield, Liege," she said at last, her voice flat and emotionless.

Fyak sighed. "I'd hoped to be able to rely on you at least, Kaid. It seems, however, that none of the Brotherhood can be depended upon. That's a pity." From beneath the desk, the blunt shape of a stunner emerged.

Kaid spun round, leaping for the male nearest the door, hoping to use him a shield but the stunner caught him full in the back, felling him instantly. He lay there, his muscles convulsing as wave after wave of pain coursed through him. Once more his body was on fire with the agony of over-sensitized nerves, though this time, it was a hundred times worse than before.

"You know what to do," he heard Fyak say.

He was grasped firmly by the arms and hauled to his feet. The slightest touch brought fresh agony and he was unable to prevent a low whimper of pain escaping him. Incapable of standing, he was dragged through the main cavern and along the corridor to the entrance. There he was dropped on the ground and while one of them stripped him of his jacket, another bound each of his wrists with an individual cord.

Once more he was pulled upright, his arms held above his head while they tied them to the two metal rings set into the cavern wall. Then they released him. He hung there, toes barely touching the ground, his face pressed against the sandstone.

Already he was breathing in short gasps, trying to focus his mind on controlling the pain of inflamed nerves when he felt the searing cut of the lash across his back. As his body hit the wall, he gasped for air, trying to pull his wrist free, trying to twist himself out of the way of the next blow, but suspended as he was, he could do nothing.

The second cut flicked across his shoulder blades and under one armpit, catching his upper arm. Pain shrieked along nerves hypersensitized by the stunner, then exploded in his mind as he let out an involuntary yowl. He clamped his jaws shut, trapping the sound, trying to focus on at least remaining silent. He wouldn't give these bastards the satisfaction of hearing him cry out again. As the third blow fell and the rock wall in front of him began to spin crazily, he felt the hot blood running through his pelt.

The shock of being deluged by cold water made him gasp, bringing him round only to have the lashing start again. Twice more they did this to him, finally leaving him hanging where he was, barely conscious, blood slowly trickling down his back and legs to pool on the ground around his feet.

Through the fog of pain that held him in its grip, he heard voices approaching him. Hands that were rough but not unkind touched his back and his wrists, making him shudder as fresh pain lanced through him.

"The ropes are embedded in his flesh!" he heard the medic say. "If you wanted him dead, there are easier ways to do it, for pity's sake! What do you hope to achieve by doing this? Get him down from there immediately!"

"I want his cooperation, Anirra. Just get him conscious, I need to talk to him," said Fyak.

He was grasped round the hips and lifted up till the strain on his wrists was relieved. His teeth closed on a lip already bloody from being bitten as the ropes were cut through and his arms fell down by his sides. A low moan escaped him and once more he blacked out.

The sting of the hypoderm brought him to semiconsciousness. "That's the second dose, Prophet," said Anirra, his tone one of suppressed anger. "What else have you done to him? One dose of this stimulant should be enough. I need to know what you've done if I'm to treat him properly."

"He had to be stunned to prevent him killing anyone," said Fyak blandly.

"You use those stunners on too high a setting, I've told you that already. You're lucky he's still alive!"

Gradually the pain seemed to decrease a little and he surfaced to full consciousness again. He was lying face down on the ground, the cool stone of the cavern floor a comfort to him. He winced as the medic put a hand to his neck to feel for his pulse.

"He's conscious," said Anirra. "If you want him to live, get your talking over with and let me treat him."

"Watch your tongue, medic," snarled Fyak. "Remember, I

do the will of Kezule, not my own. Bring him round fully. He's too doped with your drugs to even think sensibly!"

"I can't give him another stimulant, Prophet," said Anirra firmly. "In his condition, it would kill him."

Fyak snarled and reached out to take hold of Kaid by the hair, pulling his head backwards till he was looking him straight in the eyes.

"Well, Kaid. Will you deal with me now?" Fyak demanded.

Kaid's neck was arched back, making breathing, let alone talking, almost impossible. He sucked air into his straining lungs before launching a few basic expletives at the prophet.

"You tree-climbing bastard son of a toothless krolla! You know what you can do with your proposal!" he hissed.

Fyak lashed out at him with his other hand, making his captive's head rock before he dropped it. Standing up, he aimed a kick at Kaid's side.

Anirra threw himself between them, protecting Kaid from any more blows.

"Prophet! Think what Ghezu will say if you hand him over dead! It could jeopardize your agreement! Revenge against this male isn't worth that, surely."

Fyak stopped, breathing heavily. He looked at the medic. "You're right," he said. "Take him then. See he doesn't die, but no more than that. I'll send word for Ghezu that we have him."

Lying there retching, Kaid was barely aware of Fyak's retreating footsteps.

"Get him up," said Anirra. "Take him to the infirmary, and try not to hurt him any more than you have to. He's suffered enough."

Every movement was agony as he was carefully helped to his feet. His head buzzed with the noise around him and the world seemed to swirl first one way then another in a sickening dance over which he had no control.

"You'll have to walk," said the young male at his left elbow. "I'll support you as much as I can."

Kaid nodded slowly as his arm was placed around L'Seuli's shoulders. Leaning on him, he painfully tried to put one leg in front of the other. His whole body was on fire and he could hardly move. On his other side, the second male matched what his companion had done.

"He'd no right to do this," the older one muttered. "A lashing is one thing, but to do it on top of a stunner shot is unforgivable. You're lucky to be alive, Kaid. The last two he did this to died."

Surprise at his criticism registered in Kaid's mind but it was all he could do to concentrate on remaining conscious for the moment. Something else was trying to force its way into his subconscious. Against his left arm, the younger warrior was tapping a fingertip in an age-old Brotherhood code. Too exhausted to interpret it, he found he suddenly knew what the youth was trying to tell him. A message, he thought. He had to send a message. He thought of the cargo of concealed weapons, then of Kusac, picturing Carrie beside him. The bracelet! They had to know about the bracelet and the collars! He was vaguely aware of the warrior starting in surprise but quickly managing to conceal it. At least they'd eventually know what Fyak was doing, and what had become of him.

CHAPTER 14

"It's been thoroughly picked over, Jo!" Davies had to shout to be heard above the sound of the wind howling round the wreckage of the Valtegan vehicle. "There's not much chance of us finding anything useful here!"

"Keep looking!" she yelled before turning back to the ruined consol. Davies was probably right, she thought, carefully moving the sections of electronic panels that hung by wires from the remains of the pilot's control array.

Inside the craft, despite the gaping split down one side of the hull, they were protected from the worst of the weather. While she picked her way through the controls, Davies was checking out the rear compartment where the cargo would have been stowed. She looked up again, squinting through the breach, checking to see if Kris was visible yet. The whole area surrounding the craft had been trampled down by people and animals dragging a heavy object. Kris, predicting a blizzard, had been quartering the surrounding area looking for clearer tracks. He wanted some idea of which direction the salvage party had been heading before the now leaden sky disgorged its burden of snow, obliterated the tracks and with it any chance of following them.

Squeezing past the seats, she stood to one side of the gap, narrowing her eyes as she tried to peer through the fast approaching twilight. A dark figure appeared over the ridge and just as it occurred to her it might not be Kris, she sensed his mental reassurance.

Their trip through the forest and up the lower mountain slopes had proved to be uneventful, the highpoint thankfully being the night they'd spent in the tree listening to the chorus of wild canines in the distance. Kris had relieved the boredom for them both by teaching her how to use her Talent to receive a basic telepathic message from him.

As he ducked to step through the gap, the first few flakes of snow followed him into the wreck.

"God, it's freezing out there," he said, unwinding his scarf from his mouth and nose.

"Any luck?"

He nodded. "They were headed southeast from here. To the nearest settlement I expect."

"How old are the tracks?"

He shrugged. "A day or two at most. They're still fairly sharply outlined." He stopped and half-turned to the gap through which myriads of snow flakes were now gusting. "I think we'd better see about turning this into a shelter for tonight at least, possibly longer if the blizzard keeps up. It's gotten too dark to see in here anyway."

She turned to look in Davies' direction. "Davies! We're calling it a night! Are there any pieces of wreckage back there big enough to plug this gap?"

He gestured for them to join him and pointed toward a tangle of debris that had once been one of the inner bulkheads.

As they manhandled the pieces into place over the breach in the hull, gradually the sound of the wind dropped and they were able to hear each other without having to shout. The temperature began to rise a little too.

Jo stood back and surveyed their handiwork.

"It isn't perfect, but it'll keep the worst of the wind out," said Kris as he adjusted the piece of metal he'd just propped against the hull.

Davies came up from the rear lugging a box about half a meter long by some thirty centimeters deep. With a groan, he carefully deposited it end up against Kris' panel. "It's locked, but I reckon it's a tool box," he said. "It's heavy enough to stop the wind blowing that section down at least."

"Good idea," said Jo. "Any more like that down there?"

" 'Fraid not. I think this ship was sent down on autopilot. There's none of the gear you'd expect there to be on a manned drop-vehicle like this. And no bodies," he added.

"No signs of blood either," said Jo. "With a crash of this nature, I'd expect the crew to have sustained injuries serious enough to kill them."

Kris walked up to the seats, leaning over them to have a look at the consol. "Is it a Valtegan vehicle?" he asked, reaching out to pick up one of the hanging circuit boards.

"Definitely. Look at the recessed key pads," Jo said. "They're not quite the same as the Sholan ones we used in the life pod on Keiss, but they're close enough. Sholans use their claw tips too, except theirs retract and the Valtegans' don't. If this was an automated craft, then we're not likely to find any maps or star charts."

Kris let the panel drop and turned away from the seats. "Let's get ourselves settled and fed, Jo. Anything else can wait for the morning."

"I agree. Davies, you can get that torch of yours out now. I don't think we're likely to be disturbed tonight. It's too damned cold for one thing, and we're at least twenty miles from the nearest town."

"How'd you know about my torch?" asked Davies as he went over to his pack and began unfastening it.

"I didn't, till now," she grinned as he pulled it out and switched it on.

A gentle glow filled the interior of the craft, making them all blink at its sudden brightness.

"You don't realise how dark it's getting till you put a light on," Davies said, placing the torch on top of his pack. He gave Jo a sideways look. "I brought a few fuel pellets, too. Shall I get them out? We could all do with a hot meal."

Jo sighed. "Yes, get them out! I'm too grateful that you have them to care."

Within half an hour, they'd spread their insulated cloaks on the ground and boiled enough hot water for a drink. In a pan over the makeshift stove, their dried meat ration plus a generous handful of dried vegetables, was simmering.

"What did you find out there?" Jo asked Kris as she held her mug close to her face, letting the vapor that rose from it warm her. She felt like she was finally beginning to thaw out.

"What we expected. The footprints of some half a dozen people leading off toward the nearest town. It looked as if the animals were dragging a sledge of some kind from the tracks they left in the snow." He leaned toward his pack, taking the map out of a side pocket. "Here, hold my mug, please," he said, holding it out to Jo. Once she'd taken it from him, he spread the map out on the floor between them.

"The tracks were heading southeast, toward the settlement here—a small town by the looks of it," he said, pointing to the place on the map.

"How far?" asked Davies.

"A couple of days walk at least for us, longer for them, but they've got a head start on us."

"Is it sensible to follow them into a town?" asked Jo, handing him back his mug. "We haven't much chance of finding whatever it was they took from here."

"The *Summer Bounty* should be in range, if not tonight, then tomorrow. We could delay leaving until we've spoken to Vyaka," Kris suggested. "Not that I think we'll have the option of leaving tomorrow. I reckon we're in for a couple of days of this blizzard."

"I want at least a day spent checking over this craft," said Jo. "I need to take rough sketches of anything that bears any Valtegan scripts or symbols. That control panel, for instance. The keys have Valtegan characters. There isn't much that hasn't been vandalized, but among the wreckage there may still be a few treasures we can find—items the Jalnians are too tech backward to recognize as being useful."

"I can live with that," said Davies, poking his knife into the pan to test the meat. "This is almost ready."

A chirring noise heralded the emergence of Scamp. Pulling himself out of Kris' sweater, he jumped lightly down to the floor and cautiously approached the pan of steaming stew. His nose wrinkled, the whiskers twitching as he began to sniff the air. With a flick of his tail, he turned and scampered back to Kris. Rising up onto his hind legs, he placed one paw on his master's leg, looking up hopefully as he made a series of tiny chittering noises.

Absently, Kris reached down to caress his head. "Yes, you'll get some too," he said, his attention still on the map.

Half an hour later, with hot food in their stomachs, they began to settle down for the night. After fastening her cloak together with the almost invisible seals the Sholans used, Jo had a pretty fair sleeping bag. Unlacing her boots, she began to haul one off when Kris leaned over and took hold of her foot.

"Let me," he said, giving the boot a tug.

"Thanks," said Jo, taking it from him, then putting her other foot into his waiting hands.

While she wriggled into her cloak-bag, Kris looked over at Davies. "I suggest we sleep close tonight. Our mutual body heat will help to keep us all warmer." He looked questioningly back at Jo.

"Fine by me," she said. "You're the field specialist."

"I don't think so," said Davies. "I was never into threesomes."

"Don't be daft," said Jo, folding her jacket up for a pillow before she lay down. "There's nothing sexual in Kris' suggestion. It's just common sense. Besides, I don't think you're his type!"

"Uh huh," said Davies, obliquely.

"If you've got a problem with it, then lie at our feet. I assure you, I don't have any worries," Jo said, curling up on her side. As she felt Kris settle down against her back, she heard Davies get up and move over toward them. A few minutes later, the torch was put out.

Carefully she stretched her feet down a few inches and felt the solidity of Davies lying there. With a small grin, she drew her feet up again. Kris had been right, she thought as she drifted off to sleep. Already his body heat was making her feel warmer than she'd been for many a night.

She woke with a start, aware of the weight of an arm across her body and a movement against her chest. Panic flared briefly until a feathery touch under her chin told her that Scamp had decided to sleep with her. He wriggled his way down into her bag, then, twisting round, curled up against her chest. Reaching up, she gently stroked him, feeling him begin to purr softly. A sense of well-being began to seep into her thoughts. With a small, contented sigh, she relaxed again as behind her, Kris stirred in his sleep and tucked her closer to him.

* * *

Ghezu arrived three hours later. His armored aircar landed just inside the cavern. As he emerged and looked around for Fyak, his personal guard of four Brothers joined him, one of them towing a floating stretcher.

Unhurriedly, Vraiyou came to greet them. He bowed, making a gesture of greeting, if not one of welcome.

"The Word of Kezule sends his regrets, but he is deep in meditation. I will take you to the prisoner. He's in our infirmary."

Ghezu gave a low growl of annoyance. "I didn't expect to collect an injured captive. This affects my own plans for him."

"He attempted to escape," said Vraiyou imperturbably,

turning away from him. "He was punished, as are all who
break our holy laws."

"You overstepped yourselves, not only by punishing him,
but by not informing me earlier that you had him in your
custody," Ghezu growled.

"I'm afraid you'll have to discuss that with the Prophet
himself. As to his punishment, no one can be above the law.
Isn't that why you want this male? Because he put himself
above your laws?"

Ghezu followed him to the infirmary, tail angrily lashing
from side to side. He wasn't in a position to argue with the
Head Acolyte and knowing that didn't sweeten his temper.
He'd wanted Kaid untouched. Apart from any other considerations, it was a damned sight more difficult to smuggle an
injured person on a floater into Stronghold, especially along
the tunnels.

"He should have been left for me to punish," he said
abruptly. "Tell that prophet of yours that the next time he
takes the law into his own hands when dealing with me, will
be his last. Our agreement will be over."

"I'll pass on your message, of course," said Vraiyou,
holding aside the curtain that covered the infirmary doorway. "However, surely mutual toleration for each other's
customs isn't too much to ask in a business arrangement?"

Ghezu pushed angrily past him and L'Seuli, his guards
and the floater following in his wake. "Just tell him," he
said, coming to a stop. "Where is he?"

Anirra emerged from his dispensary at the rear of the
ward. "You've come for Kaid? He's over there," he said,
pointing at the nearest bed. "The analgesics have made him
sleep. Fyak had him flogged. As for the stunner shot, I can't
tell you if there'll be any permanent neural damage. He's
obviously still in a great deal of pain. In fact, he's lucky to
be alive."

Striding over to where he indicated, Ghezu stopped and
stood looking at the inert form of Kaid. His body limp, he
lay face down on the bed, ears flat against his head, his pelt
dull and matted with dried blood. Over his back lay a large
dressing, its bloodstained whiteness a stark contrast against
his tan coloring.

Ghezu lifted a corner of the dressing, noticing the involuntary flinching of Kaid's back muscles as he did. Beneath it
lay a mass of bloody, swollen cuts that crisscrossed his back.

"He'll need continued medical care," said Anirra, handing a card to Zhaya. "That's a record of his treatment so far. I've washed the wounds, cut back the fur so they'll heal cleanly, and sprayed them with antibiotic sealant. It'll last till you get him to Stronghold but not much longer. His wounds are still bleeding just enough to prevent the sealant from holding. He'll need to exercise gently to make sure that when the scar tissue forms, it doesn't pull his flesh too tight."

Thoughtfully Ghezu let the dressing drop back into place. Perhaps this served his purpose even better. Because of his injuries, Kaid was now totally at his mercy. As he turned away, the glint of silver on Kaid's wrist caught his eye. He reached down to touch it, wanting to see the symbol on the bracelet. As he did, Kaid's hand clenched into a fist.

"You might wait till I'm dead before robbing me." Kaid's voice was slurred and barely audible. Slowly he opened his eyes and looked up at Ghezu. "Yes, it's Khemu's. We bonded before she died." He grinned, baring his teeth at his captor. "You still can't have her, Ghezu. She's beyond us both now."

"Damn you, Kaid!" Ghezu felt his ears folding in anger as he drew back from the bed. "Why you? Why did she choose you right up to the end?" He stopped as realization hit him. "By the Gods, she *was* Dzaka's mother! I had you and your son both in my hands for all those years and I never knew it!" He reached down and took hold of Kaid's arm, wrenching the bracelet off his wrist.

Kaid was unable to stop his low mewl of pain.

"She may have given it to you, but I have it now, just as I have you." He looked at the medic. "Where's the body of the female?" he demanded.

Anirra shrugged. "She was cremated when she died."

"Her possessions? She wore a bracelet. Where is it?"

"It went to the fire with her," Anirra said, turning away to pick up Kaid's jacket from where it lay on the end of the bed.

"You can't undo it by stealing her bracelet," said Kaid, his voice taut now with the fresh pain Ghezu had caused by reopening the wounds on his wrist. "She's my bond-mate before Vartra and the other Gods, even if she is dead. Dzaka witnessed it. He's legitimate now. He can claim protection from the Clan Lord."

As he wiped the blood off the bracelet before pushing it on his own wrist, Ghezu could feel the rage building inside him.

"He's still one of the Brotherhood, Kaid! I refused to release him from his Oath! There's a contract on him now—to bring him in alive. Then he can join you in the hell I'm going to create for you!" He turned to Zhaya. "Get him loaded on that floater! I want to leave here as soon as possible!" With that he strode angrily out of the infirmary.

Kaid lifted his head, gathering what remained of his strength. "Better finish me now, Ghezu," he called out after the Guild Master's retreating figure. "Because as Vartra's my witness, I'll kill you given the chance!"

Exhausted, he let his head fall back on the bed. Zhaya motioned the other two Brothers forward but Anirra stopped them.

"His wrist is bleeding again. I need to see to it before you leave."

Zhaya nodded reluctantly. "You have five minutes." He turned to the other two. "Wait for him and bring him to the aircar when the medic's finished," he ordered, and left to tell Ghezu about the delay.

Anirra lifted Kaid's head and slipped the folded jacket under it. "You won't want to be without that," he said, patting one corner of it before moving away to get swabs and the spray to treat his wrist.

As waves of pain coursed through him, Kaid vaguely wondered why his jacket should be important.

Anirra returned and squatting on his haunches, began to wipe the oozing wound that circled Kaid's wrist. "Her bracelet's in there," he whispered as he leaned across him.

Kaid looked up sharply, the sudden movement setting his head pounding again and forcing a low moan from him.

One of the Brothers moved forward. "What's up?" he demanded.

Anirra continued to swab the wound. "What d'you think?" he asked. "He's in pain!"

"Just get a move on," the Brother ordered. "Master Ghezu wants to get this renegade back to Stronghold."

"I'm no renegade." Kaid's voice was hardly above a whisper. "If you'd been in the Brotherhood longer, you'd know that. This is personal, between Ghezu and me."

"Be silent! We've been warned about you and your lies," snapped the other.

Kaid moved his hand, grasping hold of Anirra's fingers. "Keep the bracelet here for me," he whispered. Anirra nodded, slipping the jacket to one side, letting it fall to the floor. After spraying on the sealant, he stood up, nudging the jacket under the bed with his foot. "He's ready," he said.

The two Brothers stepped forward, pushing the floater till it was parallel to the bed. Each taking a side of the sheet on which Kaid lay, they lifted him onto the floater.

When they'd left, L'Seuli moved forward quickly, stooping to grasp Kaid's jacket before Anirra could stop him.

"Hey! Bring that back!" said Anirra.

"They forgot this," said L'Seuli, heading for the doorway. "I'll give it to them."

"But . . ." Anirra began, then realized he couldn't admit to keeping the bracelet back. "Damn!"

On board the aircar, Ghezu squatted down beside him and placed a hypoderm against his neck. "You're mine now, Kaid," he said softly. "I've decided I'm not going to kill you. No, you're going to live, but you'll pray for death before I'm done with you. Now, say goodnight. We don't want anyone at Stronghold knowing you're my guest, do we?"

Kaid's last view of Ghezu as he pressed the trigger of the hypoderm was of a pair of eyes too wide and staring for sanity. As reality began to fade, he wondered where, or if, he'd wake this time.

*　*　*

"Kaid's been seen at Chezy," said Rulla as soon as Kusac let him into the family kitchen.

"Was he all right?" asked Carrie, speaking the thought on all their minds.

"Fine. In fact, he was training Fyak's troops."

"Never," said Garras.

"Not Kaid," Dzaka said flatly. "You must be wrong."

Rulla looked at him briefly, eye ridge raised, as he sat down at the long table with them. "No, it's been confirmed. I heard the news before I left Stronghold. I wonder what he's up to."

"What were the circumstances, and how did they find out?" asked Kusac.

"There weren't any details, just wind-borne gossip from one of the Brothers who's recently piloted out grain to the tribes. He said he'd heard that Kaid had arrived at Chezy.

He'd been injured, and was bound as a prisoner—then a week later, there he was, training the troops."

"Fyak can alter minds," said Meral. "Look at what happened to the two telepaths at the medical center in town. He destroyed them. If Kaid's working for Fyak then it's not willingly, it's because his mind has been affected."

"I don't think so," said Carrie thoughtfully. "Much more likely he's playing for time—waiting to escape. It's what I'd do."

"That sounds more feasible," agreed Garras.

"Wait a minute, don't follow the wrong scent here! *I* don't think he's collaborating with them," said Rulla, looking round the little group. "You can mind talk, Kusac. Why don't you try to reach him, see if there's any way we can help?"

"There's an element of risk in trying to contact a non-telepath, Rulla," said Kusac.

"Especially if Fyak is targeting telepaths. Whoever is monitoring for them only needs to pick up Kaid receiving and he could be branded as a telepath," said Carrie.

"You've got a point," Rulla admitted. "How come this Fyak can alter people's minds yet you don't think he's a telepath himself?"

"We've no idea," said Kusac. "He obviously isn't, or else why would he want to abduct one from Laasoi? I'm afraid we've more questions than answers about Fyak at present. I do know if we interfere in his business, even to get Kaid out, we risk starting a civil war that could erupt out of the desert into these lowlands."

Murmurs of agreement greeted this, then silence fell. There was nothing they could say that hadn't been said already.

"Why the hell did you stay with Ghezu's lot, Dzaka? Why couldn't you leave like the rest of us?" asked Rulla.

Dzaka stirred and looked over at Rulla. "You didn't leave. Ghezu released you from your oaths. He refused me."

"Did you ask him? Did you think of disobeying him then? Even though you didn't leave, if you hadn't lashed out at Kaid like that, none of this would have happened," Rulla growled angrily.

"That's enough, Rulla," said Kusac sharply. "The matter's closed now. Over."

"Dammit, it isn't for me! Just because he comes back here

with his tail between his legs, says he's sorry and that he's left the Brotherhood now, doesn't excuse his past actions! He's the one responsible for Kaid being Fyak's prisoner!"

Dzaka flung his chair back as he leaped to his feet, glowering at Rulla. "You've had it in for me from the first, haven't you, Rulla? There's only one way to settle this as far as you're concerned, isn't there?"

"Fine by me," Rulla snarled, pushing his chair back and getting to his feet.

"Enough!" said Kusac. "Dzaka's here under *my* protection, and the wishes of Kaid, his father! I'll have no fighting over this, d'you hear me, Rulla? Dzaka?" He stood, looking from one to the other.

Dzaka, his eyes still on Rulla, nodded slowly, the tension going out of his stance.

Not so Rulla. Eyes glowing, he lunged across the table at him. An unexpected blow to the side of his head broke his balance and sent him spinning away from the table.

Kusac followed it through by reaching him within two strides, grasping him on either side of the neck by the collar of his jacket and slamming him hard against the wall.

"This is *my* home, Rulla! You'll not bring your fights in here, nor will you disobey my orders a second time!" he snarled, his teeth inches from Rulla's face and throat. "I'm in charge around here, not you, not Garras," he paused, "and not Kaid. Don't mistake me for *just* a telepath, Rulla. It might be your last mistake. Have I made myself clear?" He thumped Rulla against the wall once more to emphasize his point.

Rulla's ears were down, his eyes wide as he slowly nodded. "Yes, Liege."

"Good." Kusac relaxed his hold a little. "Dzaka is sworn to *me*—as you all are. He's not here on sufferance: I chose to have him. You'll treat him accordingly."

Kusac released Rulla and stepped back, watching while the other tugged his clothing into place, then tried surreptitiously to massage his neck. Turning round to resume his place, he was surprised to see Meral, T'Chebbi and Garras standing not far behind him. Carrie alone was untroubled. Catching the glance the males exchanged, Kusac waited for them to resume their seats before returning to his own.

"Garras, how're Vanna and the cub?" he asked, changing the topic to something neutral to break the tension.

"Fine," said Garras, "if noisy and always hungry are any-thing to go by. Zhiloma, the kitling Rrai's mother, is helping her. She'd be happy to see you again—and Carrie—any time you want to visit. Especially when Marak goes in for his op."

"I'm sure he'll be fine," said Kusac, knowing Garras didn't want to dwell on the subject. "Did my mother tell you she plans to open the nursery and have Zhiloma run it? When Vanna's ready to start work again, she could leave Marak there. He'd soon have company as Taizia's near her time, isn't she, Meral?"

Meral's ears flicked and his mouth opened in a wide grin. "Neither Taizia nor I can wait."

"Believe me, you can," said Garras drily. "Enjoy your sleep while you can get it because in a few weeks, you'll have forgotten what a whole night's sleep is like!"

"We won't mind," he said. "Taizia and a family of our own is a dream I never thought possible."

Garras snorted good-naturedly. "That's your hormones talking! You young males are all the same. All you want to do is breed! You'll feel differently in a few years time, take it from me."

Meral shrugged, but kept his grin.

Kusac sensed Carrie becoming edgy. Now just halfway through her own pregnancy, she was beginning to get fretful—a mixture combined of dread and impatience. As yet she hadn't been to see Vanna and the new-born for those same reasons. She'd go when she was ready, he knew that, and he knew that Vanna wouldn't be upset by her staying away for the time being.

"I think it's time we left for our dig," he said, getting up. "We don't know how much longer we'll have before the authorities discover what we're doing at the monastery."

"Liege, I've a message to pass on from Noni," said Rulla quietly. "She'd like to see you and Carrie today."

Kusac's face creased in a frown. "Noni wants to see *me?*"

"Yes. She was most insistent that you go too."

"How long will it take you to get ready?" Kusac asked Carrie.

"Only a few minutes," she said, carefully pushing her chair back from the table so she could get up.

Kusac was there to help her.

Hey, I'm not an invalid!

I know, but I want to help. "T'Chebbi, you and Meral

come with us. Garras, you and Jack will have to take charge of the dig. I've got a training session over at Nazule this afternoon so I won't be able to join you at all today."

Dzaka followed them into the hall, and seeing no one within earshot, called out to Kusac. "Liege, I'd prefer to come with you, if I may?"

Carrie glanced over her shoulder at him. "Is Kitra following you around again?"

Dzaka looked surprised but quickly righted his ears. "Yes. I don't mind her usually, but she's been over every day this week and I'd like a break," he said, keeping a wary eye on Kusac.

"I'm sure Meral would enjoy a day off with Taizia," said Carrie. "You don't have any objections, do you, Kusac?"

"None. Kitra can be a handful, especially now that Jinoe and Rrai have paired. They're spending more of their time training with Ghyan, and what little leisure they do have, they're not so interested in spending running wild round the estate anymore." He chuckled. "We shouldn't really be calling them kitlings. They're rather proud of what they see as their elevation to adult status!"

"We've all been there," said Carrie, looping her arm through her mate's. "And Kitra's not far behind them. She'll be choosing her first lover soon."

"I still think you're imagining it. At the most she's just copying Jinoe," he said. "We'll need two aircars, Dzaka, as Carrie will be coming back without me. We'll travel out with T'Chebbi."

"Yes, Liege."

"You didn't tell me Noni was going to be acting as birther for you," he said to Carrie as they headed up to their rooms.

"It just sort of happened," she said. "It's one of the things she does as the village healer, and she seems to have sort of adopted me since Kaid took me there. I don't mind. She doesn't seem so intrusive—not so impersonal and clinical."

"As long as you're happy," he said, placing his palm on the lock plate and waiting for the door to slide open. "Wouldn't you rather have Jack or Vanna, or even one of the human females with you?"

She looked at him with a mixture of horror and determination. *Noni* was all she sent, and he accepted it.

Now that there were not only considerably more humans on Shola, but also a large proportion of females, Carrie found that getting human-specific clothes like trousers was a lot easier. The local tailor they frequented had asked one of the human females to teach him how to make their clothing—but his variety of garments was still very limited.

While the house was warm enough for her to wear only the split-paneled long tunics, outside the temperature had dropped quite dramatically and she needed the warmth of trousers and a woollen tunic.

Kusac stood by the door waiting for her to change. The olive tunic she was putting on clung to her figure, accentuating her more generous curves. There was a rightness in the way she looked now, he thought, watching as she smoothed the tunic over her gently swelling belly before turning to pull a sleeved cloak from her wardrobe.

Once again he was there to help, holding it for her to slip her arms into.

"I'm not helpless," she said, a faintly reproving tone in her voice.

He settled the cloak round her shoulders, then turned her to face him as he sealed the center edges together. He slid his hands round her disappearing waistline till they met behind her back and he was holding her close.

"I know. I just want to enjoy helping you, enjoy the fact that you're carrying our cub," he said, his voice a quiet purr. "I'm no different from Meral in that." His tongue flicked out, caressing her cheek. "You've no idea how proud I feel," he began, then stopped as he heard her mind speak.

Oh, haven't I?

He laughed, his amber eyes glinting down at her as his hands slid back across the curve of her belly, lingering there for a moment. Reluctantly he let her go. "You're right. Of course you know how I feel. It's just that you, carrying our cub—it means so much to me. I can't find the words to say it properly."

She reached up and cupped his cheek in her hand. "You don't need to." Her voice was soft as she pushed her fingers gently across his cheek into his hair. "It's what I want too." She hesitated. "I'm sorry I can't go and see Vanna yet. I'm still a little frightened about this, afraid to see her cub in case . . ." She stopped, knowing her thoughts were conveying the words she couldn't say.

"He'll be fine. It's not a serious complaint and the Surgeons' Guild Master himself is doing the operation. He couldn't be in safer hands. Actually it might be easier for you to see Marak now rather than waiting for our own cub to be born," he said, "then she won't seem so strange to you."

"Maybe, but I'm not ready for that yet."

"When you are," he agreed. "Until then, I'm sure Vanna will understand how you feel. However, I do think you should keep her company when Marak is undergoing the surgery. He looks very like her, you know."

Carrie sighed. "I'm sure he does, and I have every intention of waiting with Vanna, and visiting Marak. Now, tell me what all that leadership bit with Rulla was about."

"They've always looked at Kaid as their leader, forgetting that *his* loyalty is to you and me. When he went missing, I began to realize that it was important for them to be reminded that they gave their loyalty to us."

"No matter what the trappings of civilization you wear, *Liege*," she said, reaching up to tweak his ear, "you're still my barbarian prince!"

"Imp!" he said, reaching out for her again, but she'd moved lightly away from him toward the door, grinning.

"Come on, we'd better get moving! T'Chebbi and Dzaka are waiting for us."

Garras rose and stood in front of Rulla, preventing him from leaving. "What happened between Kaid and Dzaka is their business, Rulla," said Garras. "We may have our own private feelings about it, but they remain just that: private. If Kaid can forgive him, then so can I. You'll have to do the same." His eyes took on a hard quality. "Like Kusac, I'll do what it takes to protect Dzaka, let there be no misunderstanding on this."

"But to lose Kaid because of Dzaka . . ." began Rulla, but Garras cut him short.

"We haven't yet. And even if we do, it was Kaid's decision to remain and let Dzaka escape, and we'll *all* respect it. Dzaka is worth having in his own right. Don't forget we've all been caught at one time or another by Ghezu's tricks, this was Dzaka's first time. His delay in leaving the Brotherhood only shows how serious an oath is to him, and that's no bad thing. You were lucky, Ghezu released you. Saying you'll leave and actually doing it is a very different matter, Rulla. Dzaka's life is at risk because of his decision. You were never put to the test, just remember that."

Rulla sighed. "All right, I'll admit I was wrong. I've never questioned Kaid's decisions before. I should have accepted that he trusted Dzaka."

"You still don't get it, do you?" said Garras, grasping him by the jacket front and hauling him closer. "You'll accept it because your Liege *orders* you to accept it!" He grinned, pulling his lips back to expose his teeth.

"I understand, Garras," Rulla said hurriedly, ears flat again, hands held open at shoulder level. "Kusac is our Liege. I'll not make the same mistake again. I hadn't realized how much of a warrior he'd become."

"To tell the truth," said Garras, releasing him, "even I'd forgotten how well he handled that Death Challenge on Keiss, and that was before he'd been trained to fight properly."

"Kusac's point was well made—to all of us," said Meral drily as he rose from the table. "He *is* our Liege."

"It's not one I'll forget again, I assure you," said Rulla, slowly lowering his hands. "He fought Guynor *before* he'd been trained?"

"Yes, before. You combine the ability to mentally acquire any skill with an intelligent mind, and the body of someone entering his prime, and you'll get a male *I'd* think twice about taking on," said Garras candidly. "What I said to Rulla goes for all of you," he added, looking round at them. "Make sure everyone realizes that. Our first loyalty is to our Liege. Even if Kaid returns."

It had been some time since Carrie had last left the estate, and that had also been to visit Noni. Now, as she watched the landscape unfold beneath her, she could see the effects of the changing season more clearly. The Taykui forest was a mass of gold and brown. Here and there, the stark branches of the trees that had already shed their leaves in preparation for the snows to come rose above the autumn colors. As they traveled further north, she saw that winter's breath had touched the tops of the mountains ahead.

Khuushoi sent the first snowfall yesterday, Kusac sent. *It's not deep, only a couple of inches.*

Khuushoi?

Goddess of Winter.

Do you realize this is our second winter together? Leaving aside that we aren't on Keiss, obviously.

We've been through a lot together. At least the worst is behind us now.

There's still the Fire Margins. Carrie's tone was somber.

Let's not worry about that now. We've a lot do to before that can happen. Finding Kaid is one of them.

Is there really no way to rescue him?

None. If we try, we'll make matters worse, I know it. The Forces are close enough that if he gets the chance to escape, they'll quickly pick him up. There's got to be a damned good reason why he's helping Fyak. As we said, it could well be the only way he can stay out of Ghezu's claws.

"Coming in to land," said T'Chebbi as she steered the craft toward Dzahai village.

Noni greeted them at the door. She pointed a gnarled finger at Carrie. "You, young Human, can just take yourself off with that T'Chebbi female to the village. It's market day. You're bound to find something to buy there. Your mate will send to you when it's time to return. Go on, spend some of that hard earned money of his. You deserve it!"

Carrie looked at T'Chebbi, a faint grin on her face. "Looks like we've got our orders, T'Chebbi," she said. "We'll see you later, then."

As the two females walked off down the dirt track to the village, they heard Meral landing, then powering down his vehicle. Within a few minutes he had joined Kusac.

"And you can stay out here," said Noni. "Don't hold with guards normally, but I suppose with him here," she jerked her head toward Kusac, "I'd better have you."

She turned and stepped back into her kitchen, beckoning Kusac to follow. Once inside, she closed the door and headed slowly over to the large table that, along with her double bed, dominated the room. She sat down, waiting for Kusac to come round in front of her.

Noni stared at him quite unashamedly, and he felt her mind touch the edges of his. He let her, remaining watchful, and when the sudden intrusive strike came, he turned it aside.

"Hmm. You'll do, I suppose. Sit down then. None of you young ones realizes what it's like for us old folks to have to keep staring up at you. Pain in the neck, that's what you all are," she said with a short cackle.

As he sat down, she poured him a mug of c'shar and pushed it across the table to him. "Next time you come, you

bring me some of that coffee of yours to try, hear me? I want
to know what all the fuss is about."

Kusac accepted the mug, picking it up and taking a drink.
"So you're Noni," he said. "Tell me why I should trust you
with my bond-mate? You're guildless, therefore unqualified
in all the trades you practice. You're domineering and full of
your own importance. What makes you think I want anything to do with you?"

Noni began to laugh in earnest. "Oh, you'll do. You'll
more than do, young Aldatan!" she chuckled. "You and Kaid
could be brothers, so alike you are in some ways."

Kusac frowned, irritated by her reaction but not prepared
to show it.

"There's not many prepared to say that to my face, lad.
You trust Kaid, yet he's guildless, isn't he? He's a trained
killer who held your lives in his jaws for several months
without telling you. Yet knowing that, you still trusted him.
Explain that to me, then I'll tell you why to trust old Noni!"

She *was* old, her hair a snow white plait, ears tufted with
age, her pelt liberally flecked with gray. Clear brown eyes
regarded him curiously, a glint of humor in their depths.

"You'll make a good leader for that new Clan of yours,
Kusac Aldatan, and a fine Liege for Kaid." She watched the
surprise on his face. "Yes, I know about that," she nodded.
"It's why you have to walk the Fire Margins, so those cubs
of yours—and his—will grow strong and free." She reached
into the pocket at the side of her robe and brought out a
comm crystal. "Here's what you want. I got one of the lads
up at Stronghold to put it on his comm then run me off a
crystal for you. Lijou's got a copy too."

Kusac picked up the crystal. "What is it?"

"You wanted all the records from each guild, didn't you?
Well, we know a damned sight more about what happened in
our past than either Stronghold or that Esken fellow down at
Valsgarth. In there are all the replays that have been experienced by us nonguild folk over the last fifty-some years, as
well as mention of those from further back. There's one or
two in there you'll not get from anywhere else."

"Thank you, Noni," he said. "How did you get hold of
them? What replays have you got that we haven't?"

"Ah, well, you'll just have to read them for yourself,
won't you?" she grinned, sitting back in her chair. "As to
how I got them, I experienced more than a few myself. Then,

some of the young ones in the village are sensitive enough to pick up the odd replay if they're in the right place at the right time." She paused, looking at him with amusement still in her eyes. "There's all the Brothers who visit me. They'll tell me what they keep hidden from Lijou up in that bird's nest called Stronghold. I'm not breaking confidences, now, you'll find no names attached to the files."

Kusac put the cube in his jacket pocket. "Thank you again, Noni. That's a gift we didn't expect. You know Kaid's been seen in the desert?"

She nodded. "Damn fool boy! Told him not to go there! He's put your Triad at risk. Still, he always did have a strange sense of honor. He had to do what he saw as right."

"Is there any way we can help him? Even get a message to him?"

Noni began to cackle quietly, eyes crinkling with humor. "You're asking me, a guildless, humble village healer? You, with your Guild-learned skills, know the answer to that one better than I do! You can do nothing but wait—and pray. It's Ghezu who wants him, not Fyak. He's just using Kaid's skills for now. When he's done with him, he'll hand him over to Ghezu, you'll see."

"There must be something we can do!"

"Told you. Pray to Vartra. He's the only one as can help you now. With your mental powers, you and that mate of yours can send your prayers to Vartra!"

Kusac decided to let the matter drop. Noni obviously hadn't any suggestions either. "Why did you ask to see me? You could have given the cube to Carrie, you didn't need me."

"I wanted to meet her mate. Needed to know if you could handle it."

Kusac frowned. "Handle what?"

"There you go again! The Triad, naturally!" She took a sip from her mug. "Can you remember you're Sholan and deal with it properly? Have you left adolescence behind?"

The look he gave her was cool in the extreme. "I'll handle it because it's Kaid."

Noni relaxed, resting her elbows on the table as she sipped her drink. "You're a strange one, right enough. Usually you males don't have the strengths we females are born with. But you, and Kaid . . . *You're* easy to understand, you get those strengths from her through your Link. They may be Human female, but they're close enough to us to make no real difference. Kaid baffles me. Always has, right from the time he was found at the Retreat. I don't know where he gets his strengths from. His mind's always so closed, even when I get him to open it up a tiny crack for me."

"You're as curious as Carrie," he said. "I don't need to analyze Kaid, he just *is*. I trust him, and that's it."

She nodded. "And you don't know why. Right?"

Kusac was getting exasperated, then he remembered the conversations about Noni he'd heard in the staff lounge when they'd all lived in the main house. It was his turn to grin. "You're good, too, Noni," he said softly. "Very good. Carrie trusted him first, and I trust her judgement."

"So?"

He shrugged, ears dipping in acknowledgment of a point scored. "So I trust you. Tell me about the replays you've had, Noni," he said, changing the topic. "I'll read the files, but while I'm here, you might as well tell me."

Noni snorted in disgust. "Lazy is what you are!"

"No, I *will* read the files, but you can save me a lot of time by telling me the points you consider important."

"Haven't you had the replays then?"

. He shook his head. "Carrie has them, not me, though afterward I do experience them from her perspective."

Noni raised an eye ridge. "Now that does surprise me," she said. "I was sure you'd have them as well."

"I did once, but they've stopped over the last couple of months."

"So, she's more tuned in to them than you. Why should that be, I wonder?"

"Tell me about the replays, Noni," he said.

*   *   *

Lijou and Yaszho were busy when Ghezu strolled into his office. He stopped in front of the desk, looking down at what the two males were working on.

"You really do intend to calmly hand over your Priesthood's files to Chuz's committee, don't you? I trust none of them pertain to me or my warriors."

There was an edge to his voice that Lijou didn't like. He looked up at him. "What can we do for you, Ghezu?"

"I said, are you really going to hand over your files?"

"I'd rather hand over what I've collated and edited, than

suffer the indignity of having the actual files collected by the Forces."

Ghezu smiled gently. "You know, you're actually cleverer than I thought. I have to admit that it didn't occur to me to give them what I wanted them to have. Quite subtle, Lijou. Worthy of a Brother."

"A compliment indeed," said Lijou, aware that Ghezu was trying to use his talent to charm him—and failing. His judgement, and his talent, was slipping badly. "Now, how can I help you?"

"The female, Khemu, is dead," said Ghezu, ambling over to the window. "Nice view you've got. Better than mine, I think."

Lijou put down his stylus and, clasping one hand over the other, sat back to watch Ghezu. "Oh? How did she die?"

"Her own hand. Poison, the medic said. Actually one of our drugs." He turned round. "Kaid gave it to her."

Lijou raised an eye ridge questioningly. "So Kaid went to her?"

"Yes. Fyak's people took him."

"Fyak's people? What would they want with him?" Lijou was puzzled as to why Ghezu was offering this information.

"Seems Kaid's got a new master, Lijou. He dropped us for the Aldatan cub. Now he's taken up with this desert prophet. Not only that, but I've had to put a contract out on his son now."

"Dzaka? What's he done?"

"He's broken his oath, Lijou." Ghezu returned to stand at Lijou's desk, towering over them. "He sent word he'd left the Brotherhood. He's hiding out on the Aldatan estate, but I'll get him, you needn't worry about that. Now I have all three of them. Khemu dead, Kaid a prisoner, albeit with Fyak, and Dzaka a walking corpse." He snarled the last comment, his eyes taking on a tinge of fanaticism that was quickly masked.

Lijou felt Ghezu's glamour slip, then as it returned, he sensed the subtle difference in it. The darkness he'd felt creeping across Ghezu's soul was echoed now in his gift. Lijou could feel himself being drawn toward the other's world of hate and paranoia.

"You were wrong, weren't you?" As Ghezu rested his hands on the desk and leaned forward, Lijou saw the glint of a silver bracelet on his right wrist.

"You thought you knew Kaid, that you could handle him. How does it feel to be so wrong, Lijou?" His tone now held a hint of gloating in it.

Lijou felt Yaszho stir beside him, reacting to Ghezu's dark glamour. He let his tail tip briefly touch the other male's leg and felt him start in surprise. He shrugged. "So I was wrong, Ghezu. What does it matter to us now? We have what we wanted, our Guild status."

Ghezu began to laugh as he walked toward the door. "You wouldn't make a politician, Lijou," he chuckled. "You miss the obvious. Without Kaid, the Aldatan cub has no chance of going to the Fire Margins! He's their third. Without him, they're ours! Members of the Brotherhood. I have my fighting telepaths, Lijou." Still chuckling, he opened the door and left.

A cold shiver ran down his spine. "I fear our esteemed Guild Master of the Warriors has finally crossed over that thin edge between madness and sanity," said Lijou. "We must get this news of Kaid and Dzaka out to Kusac immediately."

"It was so . . . seductive!" exclaimed Yaszho, flicking his ears in nervous reaction. "No wonder his bodyguards behave the way they do! I begin to wonder if remaining here at Stronghold is wise, Master Lijou. If you're right about Master Ghezu, and after this experience I'm sure you are, he could actually incarcerate you without anyone being the wiser—especially now he's had the whole complex fitted with psychic dampers."

"If I go, then all the Brothers in our Order are at Ghezu's mercy," said Lijou gently. "I appreciate your concern, but I cannot leave them at this time."

"You can't help them if you're dead."

"Nor can I help them if I'm not where they need me. You've done as you ought, Yaszho, warned me of the potential danger."

"There is an alternative," Yaszho ventured. "The tide of feeling against Ghezu and his guards is becoming stronger every day, among both the lay-Brothers and the Warriors. It would take very little encouragement for them to turn against Ghezu."

"Absolutely not, Yaszho!" Lijou was shocked at the suggestion. "Doing that will only cause Brother to fight Brother, and I will not be responsible for that! Now, how do we get the information out to Kusac?" he asked, trying to regain his composure. "In your opinion, is the comm link secure?"

"No, Master Lijou, I don't think it is. If your call was intercepted, Ghezu could claim you were acting against the Brotherhood interests by giving confidential information to non-Guild members."

"He could," agreed Lijou. "But we have to send the information nonetheless."

"We could encode it and send it direct to the temple at Valsgarth so they can see it's delivered to the estate. Or you can send it telepathically."

"Long range communication isn't easy, Yaszho. Apart from having the necessary degree of talent, it requires meditation and concentration. A little difficult when one's ears are freezing off on the battlements of Stronghold," he said, mouth opening in a gentle grin. He sighed. "It does seem the safest way, though."

"I see Master Ghezu has taken to wearing a bonding bracelet," said Yaszho, tapping his stylus thoughtfully on the desktop. "Hazarding a guess, do you think it could belong to the dead female, Khemu?"

"I think it very likely. And if Ghezu has it, then he must have been to Fyak's lair since she died."

"That was my thought. Likely he's also seen Kaid."

The two exchanged a glance. It was Lijou who voiced their common thought. "Kaid may no longer be with Fyak."

* * *

The infocube from the mountain clans living in the shadow of Stronghold was a bonus none of them had anticipated. That evening, Kusac copied the data, passing the original on to his father, and taking the other to Ghyan at the Shrine the next day.

Carrie was already there, poring over ancient books and more modern comm generated sheets while Ghyan worked at the other side of his desk on his personal comm unit.

The room was typical of Ghyan, Kusac thought as he stepped carefully round the piles of books that perched precariously on the floor. Books lined every available piece of wall space, saving only the niche where his friend kept a small statue of the God, the votive candle burning with a cold flame through the walls of its blue glass container.

The pale sunlight of early winter flooded the room, brightening the dark wooden shelves and their treasury of books, making them glow with a warmth that prevented the office from becoming dark and gloomy.

"Hi there," Carrie said. "We've been waiting for you."

Ghyan looked up from his work. "At last! What took you so long?" He stretched across the desk, holding out his hand.

"That's a fine greeting," said Kusac, handing over the cube.

"First things first," said Ghyan, fitting it into its slot in the comm. He waved his left hand in the direction of the hot plate. "Fresh c'shar, and coffee, over there. Help yourself."

"I will, don't worry," said Kusac, picking up Ghyan's and Carrie's empty mugs on his way.

The mugs filled, he placed Ghyan's on his desk, getting only a grunt in the way of thanks. Giving Carrie hers, he pulled up another chair and sat beside her. "How's it going?" he asked in a low voice.

"Fine. I'm actually working on historical records from Ghyan's books and files. I decided to work backwards from the present as it gives me a benchmark on their accuracy." She put down her stylus and sat back in her chair, stretching her arms. "Now you've arrived, I'll leave this and start working with Ghyan on Noni's data." She gestured at the second comm unit beside her. "That's linked in to Ghyan's so we can access the same data sources."

Ghyan continued to study his comm in silence for several minutes more before he looked across at them.

"I expect you realize the significance of what we have here," he said. "No one ever suspected that these stories and visions existed! If the data's accurate, and I've no reason to doubt it, at one stroke she's given us more information about the Cataclysm than is probably known by all the Guilds combined! You've obviously had the time to look at this last night. What did you make of it?"

"The replays," said Carrie. "Those at Stronghold differ from those here. I'd say they're location specific. The one I had at Noni's was obviously set in Stronghold itself as people record having seen it there for nearly a thousand years virtually unchanged, and it isn't one of those experienced at Valsgarth or Esken's Guildhouse."

"I agree," said Kusac. "There are common dreams of Vartra as a God from both locations, but the replays are different from the dreams. The ones that seem most significant

are those concerned with Vartra being seen in the lower corridors of Stronghold. Noni says that in those days, and for
many years after, Stronghold was mainly a subterranean base
for telepaths and the warriors who protected them. A safe
haven from a society that held them to blame for causing the
Cataclysm."

"Did she know why they blamed the telepaths?"

Kusac shook his head. "No. I think there are clues in the
stories, but that'll take longer to unravel."

"A thought, Kusac," said Carrie. "What about contacting
Kaerdhu, the storyteller, and asking him to interpret them for
us? It's his calling, after all, and we've all got more than
enough work to deal with."

"Good suggestion. It would present him with a challenge
he wouldn't want to refuse. He'd have to approach Noni herself to ask permission if he wanted to incorporate them in his
repertoire, though."

"Can you approach him regarding that?"

Kusac nodded. "If I can't, Mother can."

"Anything else catch your notice?" asked Ghyan.

"There are several scenes where Vartra is visiting telepaths suffering from a fever that appears to change them
significantly."

"Excuse me?" said Ghyan, visibly taken aback. "Do you
realize what you've just said?"

"Oh, yes," said Kusac quietly. "Vartra also visited telepaths with deformed or brain-damaged newborn cubs. This
seems to happen before he and his people relocate themselves at Stronghold."

"So they did live at Valsgarth first. But the cubs? How did
they come to be born deformed?"

"I assume the virus mutated them. What type of mutation
isn't mentioned in the replays or the folk tales."

"There's definitely a sense of responsibility in Vartra's
questions to our new Leskas," said Ghyan thoughtfully.
"Mention of lives lost, sacrifices . . ." He stopped. "Why am
I telling you? You know because you've experienced them.
Could Vartra somehow have been responsible for this hap-
pening? If so, how?"

"Genetic manipulation," said Kusac quietly, "could cause
that."

"The replay I had at Noni's is one regularly repeated
by the highlanders and the Brothers," said Carrie. "While

visiting Stronghold, Vartra told the folk there he wasn't looking for a solution, and one of the Strongholders answered that *no good comes of playing God, we were stronger before.* Before *what* isn't mentioned."

"A virus that swept through the telepathic community, rendering them weaker and unable to fight. A virus that contributed to genetic changes and damaged their cubs," said Kusac.

"And now, in our time, you meet Carrie, a telepath from another species, and when you return here, a naturally occurring Sholan virus caught by both of you mutates. It becomes an epidemic that leaves all telepaths, and those with any degree of talent, wild or otherwise, with enhanced abilities," said Ghyan slowly. "Could it be the same virus, lying dormant till it met new conditions that favored its growth? Those new conditions being our meeting the Humans. The thought is terrifying."

"If it is, it's already happened. Now we wait and see how it affects our cubs," said Kusac.

"But why Humans? Have we been acquainted with each other's species before?"

"I've no idea. It's one of the answers we may have to find in the Fire Margins."

"I heard Vanna's child has health problems."

"Only a minor one. A defect in the fourth heart chamber. He's due to have surgery within the week. Vanna's beside herself with worry for him."

"Our cub will be fine," said Carrie, filling the silence that followed. "I know it."

"I'm sure she will," said Ghyan quietly. "You have Noni to look after you, after all. Tell me, Kusac, how the hell did you get that stubborn old female to part with all this information?"

"I didn't," said Kusac simply. "She just put the cube in my hand and said, *There you are.* She actually organized the recording of the data specifically for us. It wasn't something she had anyway."

"I can't believe it," Ghyan said, absently picking up the spoon and stirring his c'shar. "It's so out of character for her. She hates the Telepath Guild, won't have anything to do with us, either as telepaths or priests."

"But she deals with individuals from the Brotherhood," said Carrie. "I think you'll find this has as much to do with

Kaid's disappearance as anything else. Look at what we're doing: carving our own future separate from the guilds. That's what she and the mountain folk have always done."

"Well, whatever her reasons, thank Vartra she did give us this cube! You and I are going to be busy, Carrie. Kusac," he said, looking over at his friend as he lifted his mug, "I suppose you're too involved with the dig to help?"

" 'Fraid so. We want to get as much information as possible before I have to hand it over to my father so the Earth archaeologists can be brought in."

Ghyan raised an eye ridge questioningly. "It's that important?"

"I think it could be one of the most important sites on Shola. Believe me, I'm not contemplating calling in the Terrans lightly, especially at this time," he said, reaching out to touch Carrie reassuringly. "But Carrie agrees with me. She says she can cope, and our circumstances are very different this time."

"Where will they stay?"

"We'll make a cottage available here in the village. They'll have to use our amenities, after all."

"What about security?"

"Ni'Zuhlu doesn't see a problem." Kusac grinned, showing his teeth. "Their cottage will be right beside the Brothers' accommodation, after all."

Ghyan laughed. "Neat. Very neat." He glanced at his wrist unit. "You'll have to excuse us, I'm afraid. I want to make a good start on this data and I've a service to take at fourteenth hour."

"I've got to get going, too," Kusac said, getting to his feet. "I'll see you at third meal," he said to Carrie, his hand touching her cheek before he left.

* * *

Several days had passed since Kusac's visit to Ghyan at the Shrine. The excavations had now reached the stage where he'd decided he had to call in his father. Though he didn't want Carrie involved in the actual digging because of her pregnancy and the danger of cave-ins, Kusac had no objection to her accompanying him and his father on their inspection of the ruins within the hillside. When Konis arrived, he had Kitra with him.

"I said I'd help make sure Carrie didn't do any digging," she said to Kusac, grinning up at her bond-sister as she greeted her with a hug.

"You're only coming because you think Dzaka's at the dig," laughed Carrie, tweaking her ear.

"Not true," said Kitra, flicking her ear free and dancing away from her.

The mound of earth and rubble that had been removed from the main chamber was the first thing Carrie saw when they arrived at the dig. It seemed almost as high as the hill itself. In that cavern, the picture that was beginning to emerge was one of a final pitched battle. The remains of ancient wheeled vehicles lay crushed and tangled where they'd been found, their sides riddled with holes and burn scars from projectile and energy weapons. Cavern floor and vehicles alike bore a scattering of Sholan and Valtegan remains. It had been a battle with few, if any, survivors.

Judging by the amount of rockfall from the ceiling of the cavern, Jack was pretty sure that a massive explosion had brought the roof down on defenders and attackers alike. Perhaps it had been a last desperate move to prevent them getting further into the complex.

As her father followed Carrie and Kusac up to the next level, Kitra saw Dzaka. He was working at a different place that day, near the Human physician, Jack. He looked up briefly as she headed over to him.

"Have you found anything interesting?" she asked, squatting down to one side of him.

"I'm helping Jack unearth this Valtegan soldier," he said. "Bits of his kit and uniform are still here so he wants me to try and get them out without damaging them."

"How different are they from the ones that were on Keiss? Do they have more primitive weapons, or are they like the ones we use now?"

"Difficult to tell," said Dzaka. "The weapons we've found have been badly eroded by the dampness in the cavern."

"Dzaka! Can you come over here a moment, please?" Jack called out.

"Excuse me," said Dzaka, getting to his feet and turning abruptly away from her.

Kitra stood up and reached out to grasp him by the arm. "Dzaka, what's wrong?" she asked.

"Nothing," he said, keeping his head turned away from her

as he gently tried to ease himself free. "Jack wants me, Kitra."

She refused to be moved. "I know there's something wrong," she said. "What is it?"

Dzaka could feel her concern. Unless he was prepared to hurt her, he had to say something. Schooling his mind to stillness, he lifted his head, looking directly at her for the first time that day. "Nothing's wrong, Kitra."

She gave a little gasp and reached out to touch the cut on his cheek. "What happened to you?"

He intercepted her hand. "Don't touch it, please. It hurts," he said. "I fell over something in the dark on my way home last night, that's all."

"It looks painful," she said sympathetically.

"A bit," he said, letting her hand go. "Now I must see what Jack wants."

"I'm coming too," she said.

He hesitated. If he didn't let her come, then the cowards who'd attacked him on his way home the night before had won. "If you want," he said.

"Hello, young lady," said Jack, beaming at Kitra as she and Dzaka approached the table he was using. Spread out on it were what looked like assorted lumps of earth. With the help of a small directional lamp and a rigidly supported magnifying lens, he was examining one of those pieces.

"I think this might be some kind of weapon. Come and see what you think," he said, pushing his chair back so Dzaka could get in.

Dzaka squeezed past him and peered through the lens at the object. Jack had managed to clean most of the soil from it, and some areas of small detail were visible. It was roughly rectangular, with various ridged markings on the face. There were the remains of what could be terminals at one end.

"More likely some kind of power pack," Dzaka said. "It's not like any I've come across, but that's my best guess. Where did you find it?"

"Actually, I found it," said a voice with a distinctive Human pronunciation to the words.

Dzaka looked up to see Mara standing in front of the table. "It was in one of the vehicles." She turned and pointed to a mass of crumpled wreckage not far from the entrance to the upper level.

"Can I have a look, please, Jack?" asked Kitra.

Dzaka moved aside to let her see.

"Of course, Kitra. Mara, keep with that vehicle and see if you can find any more of these," said Jack. "Better still, see if you can find what it fits into."

"Sure. Want to come and help me, Dzaka?" she said, looking over at him. "I can see where there's more of those, but some pieces of wreckage are in the way. I need them moved."

"I'm rather busy myself, Mara," said Dzaka, coming out from behind Jack's desk. "Why not get one of the others to help you?"

"They're all busy. I'm sure Kitra wouldn't mind finishing off what you're doing, would you, Kitra?" she said, smiling briefly at her. "I can't go any further until someone strong like you lifts those pieces out of my way."

Dzaka caught Jack peering over the top of his glasses at Mara, eyebrows lifted in surprise, before he glanced back at him.

He could feel Kitra's resentment of the Human female until she remembered to block it. Caught between the two of them, he compromised. "I'll lift the wreckage for you, Mara, but then I must go back to my own find. It's a little too delicate to leave to anyone else."

Mara linked her arm through his, drawing him away from the table. "Well, this type of work isn't for children," she said, her voice drifting behind her as they walked. "When she's older, I'm sure Kitra will be able to do delicate work too. You shouldn't really encourage her, Dzaka. It's not good for her to think she's more adult than she is."

Kitra realized Jack was looking at her and, swallowing her disappointment, she looked up. "Have you something I can be doing while Dzaka's helping Mara?"

Jack pushed his glasses back up his nose. "Actually, I have," he said, reaching down into a box that lay under the table. He pulled out a brush and trowel. "It's about time you had your own tools, Kitra, especially since you're helping out so often." He handed them to her. "How about you start working at the other end of Dzaka's skeleton? It'll be finished in half the time then, won't it?"

"All right," she said, accepting them without much enthusiasm. Not even Jack acknowledging her unofficial help by giving her her own tools could dispel the little cloud of gloom that had suddenly descended on her. As she turned away, Jack called out to her again.

"You make a start and before you know it, he'll be back," he said, keeping his voice low.

She nodded and went back to where Dzaka had been working.

Mara stood watching while Dzaka sat on his haunches examining the crumpled pieces of metal, trying to see where they overlapped or were crushed together. Making his mind up, he began to separate two of them.

As he pulled one piece free, he gave a yip of annoyance when a sharp edge of the metal cut into one of his fingers. Throwing the offending piece aside, he began to lick the blood off his finger.

"You've hurt yourself," said Mara. "Here, let me have a look." Taking a tissue from her trouser pocket, she stepped over toward him, reaching out and taking hold of his hand.

She pressed the tissue to the cut, dabbing the blood away so she could examine it.

Acutely uncomfortable, Dzaka submitted to her ministrations, all the while aware of the interest in him that she was radiating.

"You'll live," she said, smiling up at him, her touch on his hand becoming much lighter as she stroked the sensitive areas of his palm.

He snatched his hand back, moving away from her, aware his tail was flicking in agitation but unable to control it. "It's fine, thanks, Mara," he said. "I've got to get back to my work. Jack wants it as soon as possible."

"Are you sure you won't stay and help me?" she asked. "It can't be much fun having Kitra following you about all the time. It really is an awful imposition on your good nature. Stay for a while. She's bound to get fed up and go home eventually."

"Ah. No thanks," he said, backing off.

Almost at a run, he headed over to Jack's work table. "Jack," he said. "Sorry, but I've got to go now."

"Go? Go where?" asked Jack, continuing to peer through the magnifying lens at the object he was cleaning.

"Away from here. Home."

Jack looked up, surprised at the intensity in Dzaka's voice. "Why?"

"Mara—and Kitra!" He leaned forward on Jack's table. "I can't stay here with both of them like this!"

"That's what comes of being popular," said Jack drily. "Don't you feel flattered?"

"Ohhhh! You don't understand!" he hissed, pushing himself away from the table. "They're *both* trouble!"

"Then hadn't you better decide on which one you want?" asked Jack, peering over his glasses again.

Dzaka gave a low roar of frustration and spun away from him, heading out of the cavern.

The upward sloping tunnel that led from the lower chamber was clear all the way through to the entrance to the second cavern complex. There, the stark white of the lighting units illuminated what had obviously been a living area large enough to house some thirty people. This area had only suffered a light rockfall or two, probably the result of seismic activity over the last millennium and a half.

The metal skeletons of beds, their fabrics long since decayed, lined the walls. Springs so rusted that they disintegrated if touched showed where mattresses had been. Beside them, remnants of wooden night lockers stood in various stages of dissolution. Here and there lay the odd personal item, waiting for an owner long since dead. A brush, a jar of hair beads, and broken cosmetic containers were just some of the belongings that had fallen abandoned on the floor. Whoever they'd been, they'd left hurriedly with not enough time to collect all their possessions.

At one end of the dormitory, a narrow passageway through to the next chamber was blocked by a metal door that was amazingly still intact after so long. The other end was partitioned off from ceiling to floor by panels of wood, large areas of which had rotted away.

"Maybe this is the place Kaid described seeing in one of his replays," said Carrie, walking toward the partitions. "The one he listed as a training session."

"Don't touch them," warned Kusac, hurrying over to her. "Some of the panels are better preserved than others."

"I'm only going to look," she said, peering through one of the larger gaps. "Looks like a kitchen area." The disappointment in her voice was noticeable.

"It is," said Kusac, gently taking her arm and drawing her back from the partition. "I think you're right. This has the look of the place Kaid's book describes. That door, though," he said, flicking his ears toward the small corridor, "there has to be something important behind it for it to warrant such heavy security. That other replay of Kaid's, the one about Rezac and Zashou forming their Leska Link, it was in another cavernous area, wasn't it?"

As they approached the door, Carrie freed herself and walked a few steps ahead of him. Stopping in front of it, she examined the surface closely.

"Yes, it was. They were making notes—on paper, not comp pads, so they possibly didn't have such advanced technology as Earth or Shola has now," she said as she began to run her fingertips gently over the surface. "Or they no longer had access to it. Taking notes, compiling facts, waiting for results ... I wonder. Could they have been running data through a computer? And if so, what kind of data?"

"And why were they here," added Konis, joining them. *This is the first time I've seen Carrie work,* he sent to his son. *Interesting. I can feel her doing something that resembles probing, but what exactly ...*

"It is probing," said Carrie absently, unaware of the starts of surprise from the two males behind her. "They were hiding. Hiding from the Valtegans."

It unnerves me when she does that, sent Konis. *Even I can't listen in to private links!*

Her senses are extended while she's working. She's bound to pick up a lot more, replied Kusac.

"If you two stopped gossiping," said Carrie, moving over to the rock wall at the side of the door, "you'd be able to help me get in here. I'm sure there's a mechanism somewhere." She began to search the surface of the wall, trying to find any crevices or loose pieces where a switch could be concealed.

She gave up after five minutes fruitless searching. "Dammit! I *know* there's a way in somewhere around here!"

"Leave it for now, Carrie," said Konis, reaching out to gently draw her away from the enigmatic door. "The way in will be found eventually. If it isn't, then it will have to be forced."

"It shouldn't have to be forced! I know there's a mechanism, if I could only remember where," she said, pulling away from him to return to the doorway.

Kusac intercepted her this time. "No. You've spent long

enough looking. We should be leaving now. They've orders not to start work until we do."

As they began walking down the corridor back to the main chamber, high on the fortified walls of Stronghold, a gray-cloaked priest was standing with his Companion.

"You make it difficult for me to concentrate, Kha'Qwa," said Lijou as she came within his cloak to escape the biting wind.

"You'll manage," she said, leaning her head against his shoulder. "You were the one who asked me to meet you here. All I'm doing is supplying an alibi, not seducing you."

Lijou lowered his face till his cheek touched the top of her head. "Then since one of Ghezu's guards is coming this way, perhaps we should pretend to be taking a few moments for ourselves," he murmured gently in her ear before beginning to nuzzle it.

She sighed, relaxing her body against his and stretching her arms round his back and up onto his shoulders. "You never could act, Lijou," she whispered as they heard the approaching footfall of Kaibah, one of Ghezu's personal guards. Her face turned toward Lijou's and she began to delicately nibble at his cheek and jawline, sensing through her empathic talent his reluctant response.

Eyes half closed, he was peripherally aware of the guard passing them and his hands instinctively tightened on her shoulders.

Kaibah stopped. "Afternoon, Guild Master," he said. "Cold today, isn't it?"

"Go chase a tree-rhudda, Kaibah," growled Kha'Qwa, not bothering to turn round. "We didn't come here looking for an audience."

Lijou barely suppressed his grunt of surprise and interest as unseen, her hand slid through the opening of his robe and began to caress his thigh.

Her gesture had the desired effect on both males. Kaibah, seeing the expression on Lijou's face, realized why they were there and as his ears lay flat in embarrassment, he began to back away hurriedly. As for Lijou . . .

"You utterly unrepentant she-jegget!" he hissed, trying to keep his voice low while surreptitiously trying to remove the hand that was determined to become more intimate.

"What's wrong? You wanted us to take some time for our-selves," she whispered.

"Yes, but not this! My reputation will be in shreds!"

"You mean you haven't come up here before?" she asked, still managing to evade him. "In that case, it'll enhance your reputation among the males," she chuckled. "Not to mention some of the Sisters! Trust me."

Lijou gave up and instead pulled her close, swinging her round so her back was to the keep wall. "Since this is what you want," he began, but she stopped him.

"Now send your message," she said, her face deadly serious.

"Now?"

"Now. You'll find it easier when you have an incentive. Use that energy to send it. I've had lovers who were telepaths before. It worked for them."

Not quite convinced, Lijou began to visualize Kusac, reaching out to find the unique pattern of his mind. Within moments, he'd not only located him but sent the warning.

In the passageway, Kusac staggered slightly, reaching out for the wall for support.

"What is it?" asked his father.

"Lijou," said Carrie, steadying her mate.

"I'm fine," said Kusac, standing upright again. "He warns us that Fyak has Kaid and that Ghezu's put a contract out on Dzaka. He thinks Ghezu's finally gone over the edge. We're to watch out for him, and for Kaid being taken to Stronghold."

"I'll warn Nesul and the High Command," said Konis. "We'll have Ghezu monitored as best we can. I didn't realize our Head Priest was capable of transmitting over such a distance."

"He had help," said Carrie, a small smile on her face as her hand reached for her mate's. *You didn't tell him it all. Could Ghezu have Kaid already?*

Lijou thinks it possible, because of the bracelet. It could be that Ghezu's seen Kaid at Rhijudu and Fyak refused to hand him over. Lijou sent that Ghezu actually said Kaid was Fyak's prisoner. Let's not assume the worst.

We've got to do something, Kusac! At the moment we're doing nothing!

There's nothing we can do as yet! Kusac gripped her arm more tightly. *If there was, I'd do it!*

Then I'll do what Noni suggested. Go to the Shrine. Maybe Vartra can help, since He seems determined to be involved in all our lives!

It wouldn't do any harm, sent Kusac.

Back at Stronghold, Kha'Qwa grinned up at her lover. "See? Now you've had your alibi, we can go indoors, where we can continue this in comfort."

Lijou returned her grin as the wind whipped at his cloak. "Not quite. I haven't *had* my alibi yet."

"I wasn't exactly being serious," she said, trying to push him aside. "It's far too cold up here today!"

"You started it, Kha'Qwa," he purred, running a hand through her short ginger hair. "Kaibah will tell everyone why we were up here, and you don't want to make liars out of us, do you?"

"Lijou! I'll freeze to death out here!"

"No, you won't. I don't intend us to be here for that long. Then we can do as you suggested; go into the warmth and continue this little encounter in comfort."

"Did I really say you lacked imagination?" she murmured.

CHAPTER 15

He lay still, barely conscious, aware only of the fire that flickered through his limbs and tail before centering once more on his back. The slightest movement of his head exacerbated the throbbing behind his eyes. He could smell water nearby, and though his tongue was swollen with thirst, he knew he couldn't reach it.

How long he lay like that, he'd no idea. He thought he heard voices at one point, but they meant nothing to him. Then, like the last time, their cold hands touched his body, pressing and probing at him. The hypoderm stung his neck and he knew relief as the numbness spread along nerves that were inflamed and raw. Not quickly enough though, as the dressing on his back was ripped off.

He moved then, flinching as the fresh pain coursed through him, too weak to even cry out. That was when he realized just how ill he was.

"Why wasn't I called from the first?" a voice demanded. "I want him moved immediately to the infirmary. I can't treat him here under these conditions!"

"You'll have to," Ghezu said. "He's being held secretly because he has friends in the Brotherhood. My contract requires that I interrogate him. He was working for Fyak, training his troops. There's a lot that the High Council needs to know."

"That's your concern, not mine. You know the rules. All prisoners undergoing questioning must have a member of the Guild of Medics present! You've abused this prisoner by not bringing him to me on arrival! And you didn't tell me his wounds were in this state! They have to be cleaned—I'll need to return to my infirmary. In the meantime, has he eaten or drunk anything since he arrived? I thought not! Get some fluids into him immediately. I'll be back as soon as I can."

They made him get up and sit on the edge of the bed. He

was forced to drink water till it ran down his chin and started him coughing. Despite the analgesic, the pain was intense and he almost passed out. Then he was returned to the bed. Gratefully he sank back down onto his stomach, hands clutching the bed frame as he waited for the agony to subside.

The physician returned and began cleaning his wounds. Kaid lost consciousness almost immediately, and when he next woke, he was alone. He felt better—the effects of the stunner blast had finally gone. All that remained was the pain of the flogging.

One of the guards came in, bringing food and water. He was ordered to remain where he was, and for that one meal only, he was fed. Afterward, he slept till the physician woke him by removing the dressings and giving him more medication.

"You can get up when you feel ready," he said. "In fact, the sooner the better. I'm not replacing the dressings, those wounds need to breathe now. I don't need to tell you to make use of your back muscles, do I? Good. I'll see you in a few days, then."

Time settled down into a predictable routine. Day and night meant nothing to him as the overhead light was always on. His cell was in one of the disused basement corridors of Stronghold, one of those carved from the living rock itself. The room was sparsely decorated. An iron bed, a night table, and a wooden chair was his only furniture. The toilet was a closet at the rear of the room and consisted of little more than a seat over a long-drop down to the roots of the mountain.

The solitude would have affected most Sholans badly, but Kaid was used to it. His "day" consisted of eating and sleeping punctuated by short exercise periods when, mindful of the physician's warning, he did his best to stretch his aching back. Ghezu had refused to allow him any further analgesics so to escape the constant pain, when he wasn't sleeping, he recited his litanies and meditated, trying to boost his internal healing system.

Scabs had formed over his wounds, but every time he exercised, it caused them to split. Gradually, though, his back was beginning to ease.

Then Ghezu came, accompanied by another medic and two guards. Kaid stood patiently while his back was examined, the medic pressing here and there to check for swelling and sensitivity.

He suffered in silence, flinching when a tender area was touched, praying for the time he'd be strong enough to retaliate. It might cost him his life, but that was all he had left at the moment, save for the crystal Noni had made him keep. But, by Vartra, he'd take Ghezu with him when he went!

"Well? Is he fit enough?" demanded Ghezu at last.

"He'll do," said the medic. "I hope you realize the risk I'm taking administering this drug." He took an ampule from his medikit and loaded it into the hypoderm.

"You'll be rewarded," Ghezu said.

Kaid tried to step back from the medic. "No way are you going to . . ." He was cut short as one of the guards grabbed him by the arms and held him still.

The medic pressed the hypo briefly against Kaid's upper arm, fired it, then turned to leave.

"What the hell have you given me?" demanded Kaid, trying to pull free.

"Get him ready," ordered Ghezu, ignoring him. "We've only a few minutes before the drug takes hold."

Unceremoniously Kaid was dragged over to his bed where, with the help of the other guard, he was flipped down on his back. He began to struggle, then stopped as he realized it would only speed up his body's absorption of the drug.

While one held him still at gunpoint, the other quickly fastened padded bands round his wrists and ankles. His arms were drawn beyond his head to be secured to the bars there, then his legs were similarly secured by cords to the foot of the bed. Pulling against them, he tried to ease his discomfort, but found it futile. He was effectively prevented from moving anything but his extremities and tail. He had no option but to lie there, staring helplessly at the ceiling, waiting.

Ghezu ordered the guards to leave, then Kaid heard his soft footfall approaching. Anger and frustration rose in him as he realized that because of the angle his arms were in, he could barely turn his head to look at him.

"I told you, Kaid, that you'd pray for death before I finish with you. Well, the waiting's over," he purred, his voice soft and full of menace. "It starts now. I'm going to break you. I'll have you begging and groveling for a quick death." He stopped, moving his face into Kaid's view. From the front of his shirt, a torclike neck ornament fell forward, its inset green stone reflecting the light from the ceiling.

Kaid's eyes were drawn to it. Where had he seen its like before? Rhaid—the telepath Fyak had taken captive—she'd worn one. The stone had a hypnotic quality about it, making it difficult for him to look away. There was more, if only he could remember. . . .

Ghezu moved out of his line of sight, breaking the spell. "You should be beginning to feel the effects of the drug about now. A sense of well-being, of relaxation. Yes, I can see it's already begun," he said. "It won't last long, though." The footsteps stopped.

"In the next stage, your senses will become sharper. Every experience will become heightened. You'll be able to hear a beetle crawling over the floor in the next cell."

Ghezu walked down to the foot of the bed, testing the bonds to make sure they were tight. "The last stage, though, is in the lap of the Gods—or, as you would say, En'Shalla. You could see your deepest fears, or perhaps your wildest dreams. That's the problem with psychotropic drugs, they aren't predictable. And this one is a bit of an unknown quantity—it's from off-world."

Kaid could already feel the second stage starting. Ghezu's voice was beginning to boom in his eardrums. He folded his ears backward in an effort to lower the sound level.

"I didn't deprive you of an En'Shalla ritual after all, Kaid, did I? I'll leave you to enjoy the experience," Ghezu said, flicking the pads on Kaid's foot with a claw tip.

Each one of Ghezu's footsteps seemed to echo in the room and the door, when it closed, sounded like a peal of thunder. No sooner had silence returned when the light went out, leaving him in utter darkness.

He tugged at the bonds again, trying to twist free but the movement of the soft padding against his still raw wrists felt like grit was being rubbed into the wounds. Round his ankles, the displacement of his fur as he twisted against the cuffs felt like a thousand hot needles were being driven into him.

He became aware of the feel of the blanket against his injured back. The bindings not only held his limbs taut, but served to press him firmly against the bed beneath him. He could feel the woollen fibers being forced into the partly healed wounds, causing him even greater pain.

A rhythmic, pounding beat dominated his hearing, sending waves of panic radiating through him till common sense took hold of him again and he realized it was the sound of his own increased heartbeat.

Every instinct told him that he must break free, but fighting it physically was impossible. The slightest movement brought discomfort and pain. He forced himself to lie still, concentrating on breathing slowly and deeply.

Under his breath he began to curse Ghezu as he realized the sophistication behind his use of the drug. His anger and frustration built, and with it his pulse, until the beating inside his head again dominated every thought.

He gasped for air only to find that tiny particles of dust were scraping and burning their way down into his lungs. Reflexes started him coughing, and once again, the bonds restricted his movement. The small, jerking spasms that were all his body could make only added more pain. Panic began to rise in him again as he continued to gasp for air, trying to combat the pain by hyperventilating. Each breath only made catching the next one more painful.

Trained reflexes finally took over and he clamped his mouth shut, drawing shuddering breaths in through his nose. Gradually the spasms stopped, and his breathing eased.

Think, he told himself. *Use your brain! It's only a chemical reaction that's causing this. What did Ghezu say? That I'd see my worst nightmare or my greatest wish. If pain and panic creates fear, then somehow, I must remain calm.*

His breathing under control again, he began his relaxation litany, gradually forcing the tension to drain from each muscle group as he turned his focus deep within his mind. Having achieved that much control, he attempted the litany to banish pain, and instead of fighting against the drug, he tried to go with it, letting the sensations, good or bad, course through him without reacting.

It took time, but time was unimportant to him as he drifted in some limbo world between wakefulness and sleep. He felt his internal rhythms change in response to the drug and knew he'd correctly assessed the way it reacted to his state of mind. Where it found fear, it amplified it, triggering memories of terror and pain. Where it found calm, the memories were gentler.

Like a river in spate, the drug surged through him, driving fragments of images into his consciousness. He saw Lijou, lying asleep with his lover, then Noni, sitting at her table holding one of her crystals, concentrating on what she thought she saw within it. She stiffened, looking up suddenly at him. Her expression changed, becoming one of fear. She was speaking, but he couldn't catch the words. Her hand opened, showing him the crystal she held within it. Then the image was gone, swirling away in rainbow colors to be replaced by one of Dzaka sitting in a kitchen he didn't recognize. Kusac and Garras were there, arguing over something, then that, too, was swept away.

The smell of incense and of charcoal; the small statue of Vartra with the crimson curtain behind it. A slight figure running into the Shrine room, her body moving the way no Sholan's could. Carrie. She looked up at him as the priest joined her. Ghyan followed her gaze but was unable to see him. She reached out, so close he could almost feel her fingertips.

Suddenly, sickeningly, the world spun around him, flinging him back to his own body and the accumulated pain of lying tied to the bed for so many hours. Against his chest, he could feel the touch of her hand, feel it withdrawing from him till all that remained was the warmth of the crystal that lay in its leather pouch against the base of his throat.

The light came on, and blinking in its glare, he twisted one wrist experimentally. Where the binding held him, it was tender, nothing more. It was over, for now. He shut his eyes, letting his breath out in a long sigh. Then he thought of his crystal and prayed Ghezu wouldn't notice it

The door opened and Ghezu entered with two guards. The one he recognized as Zhaya bent over him and administered another shot from the hypoderm he carried. His arm was so numb, he was hardly aware of the sting.

As quickly and efficiently as they had bound him, he was released. He tried to speak but found his mouth so dry that his tongue was sticking to the roof. Painfully he pulled his arms down and pushed himself into a sitting position. He reached for the water standing on the night table by the bed, noticing that Ghezu and his guards had retreated until they were standing in the doorway.

The returning circulation sent pins and needles coursing through his limbs and his hand shook as he took several small sips from the mug before putting it down.

"Nice try, Ghezu," he said. "You almost had me there, till I worked out how the drug operates."

Ghezu shrugged and turned to leave. "No matter," he said. "That was only a foretaste, a gentle introduction if you like. This dose is stronger. Did I tell you its effect is cumulative? It stays in your system for several days, causing sudden and unpredictable periods of hallucinations. With what you've got in your system now, it should last well over a week. Pleasant dreams, Kaid, pleasant dreams."

The door closed behind them, leaving him alone again. Fear rushed through him. Was Ghezu lying? He'd only just managed to beat the drug, he didn't know if he could do it again it so soon.

Instinctively his hand went to the crystal. He could feel its gentle warmth even through the soft leather. The fear began to recede and as it did, he found he was able to think clearly again.

What did Ghezu hope to achieve by saying the drug's effect was cumulative? Make him afraid to sleep lest it started working while he was dreaming? Who knew what nightmares could come alive for him. He'd also be just as afraid to stay awake. Once again, Ghezu was using his own fear as a weapon. Even if it was a lie, sleep deprivation coupled with constant fear was enough to weaken him considerably, given his already vulnerable state of health. At least this time, he wasn't tied up.

He felt the drug beginning to course through his system again. Lying down, he pulled his blanket round himself, then curled up on his side, tail tucked close. A thought occurred to him, and reaching up, he tugged his fur over the crystal and its thong, hiding it from sight. Then, using the sensations of relaxation the drug was giving him, within moments he was asleep.

He dreamed strange dreams, drifting in and out of sleep and wakefulness as the drug controlled his every thought. The world beyond his mind seemed distant, removed from reality. Events that happened there seemed to take forever to reach him, his awareness of them arriving long after the incident had passed. Food and water he remembered, only because they made him eat. *You gave him too much!* Gradually the words penetrated and began to make sense, but it was of no importance, now.

Before him, scenes unfolded like the petals of a flower opening gradually. A sun-baked desert, the sky holding circling carrion birds that drifted lazily in the updrafts. A figure, his clothes mere rags, stumbling along the rocky outcrop toward the shade of an opening in the foothills. Staggering, his hands already blistered by the heat of the rocks, the gaunt male pulled himself into the opening to collapse in the shade.

The smell of water aroused him, and on all fours, he crept deeper into the welcoming coolness until he found the well. Choked by debris, the water now flowed sluggishly over the rim to the cavern floor. Scrabbling frantically, the gaunt one scraped a hole large enough to collect water to drink.

He drank deep, spitting out grains of earth. Thirst finally quenched, he collapsed once more, drifting into sleep.

Kaid watched as the shadows outside lengthened. The male within awoke. Refreshed by the water, hunger now dominated him. Rising to his feet, he surveyed the cavern, sniffing the air in the hope of something edible. Where there was water, there was life. His gaze fell on a clump of darkness at the far side. He staggered over to it, feeling the dampness of the ground under his feet.

He felt the gaunt one's surge of joy as he began ripping the broad, leathery leaves off the strange plant and cramming them into his mouth. *Be careful!* he wanted to call. *Don't eat it!* but it was already too late. His initial hunger satisfied, the male leaned back against the rock wall and began to examine the plant. A gleam from the earth caught his eye and scraping one-handedly at the roots, he pulled out a stone. Green it was, and though smooth, irregular in shape. Absently he licked the other hand where the juice from the plant had run down to his wrist—juice as green as the stone. As his hand closed on the colored pebble, he looked out to where the moon sent a shaft of white light into the cavern. As he did, Kaid recognized the gaunt face, and the eyes with the beginnings of madness in them. Fyak.

The shock of recognition sent adrenalin through his system, flinging him into a swirling maelstrom of sights and sounds that had him retching till his stomach and throat hurt.

There were vague memories of being taken down a passage to a room where he was held in a relentless stream of hot water. He struggled weakly against those who held him, gasping for breath, but they batted his hands away as if he were no more than a cub.

Someone rubbed him down, and pain flared through him as the towel tore at the scabs on his back and wrists. Flung back on his bed again, the smell of his room and the clean bedding on which he lay brought a sense of familiarity and he began to sink once more into the drug-induced stupor.

He should be over this by now! The voice was loud, enraged.

You gave him too much! I advised against using this drug—we don't know enough about it yet, no matter what that damned mad prophet of yours says!

Watch what you say, Medic, lest you join him! I want him conscious, and coherent! Now!

I can't work miracles! He's not excreting it, the toxins are remaining in his system!

Then do what you can, dammit! He's no use to me like this!

I can do nothing. You'll have to wait till he rids himself of the poisons.

Then came silence, and with it, a sense of urgency and self-preservation. He reached under his pillow, gradually pulling the sheet back till he could feel the mattress. Feeling over its coarse surface, his fingers searched for places where he could conceal his crystal. He found one, where a stud in the mattress had come free, leaving a small hole behind.

Reaching for the thong round his neck, he pulled it loose. Carefully he enlarged the hole with a claw tip, finally pushing his crystal, bag and all, under the top layer of material. Teasing the cloth over it again, he pushed the sheet back, finally pulling his hand free.

Willpower alone had kept the drug's effects at bay, now it coursed through him once more.

He dreamed of Fyak's lair. Khezy'ipik, the desert cavern carved from sandstone. A golden glow from torches held in sconces bathed the lower walls, glinting off the larger particles of quartz embedded in its surface. On either side of him as he walked down the passage, giant bas-relief carvings of people or gods lined the walls. The figures were seated, their limbs arranged in tidy formality. He stopped to look at their faces. Fear gripped the pit of his stomach then rushed upward making him lightheaded as he stared up at the shadowy reptilian faces of Valtegans.

Dragging his eyes away from them, he continued on down the corridor, alert now for the slightest noise. Rounding a corner, he saw a doorway ahead of him. On either side of it, carved pillars of flame reached to the ceiling some six meters above.

Cautiously, keeping to the shadows, he ventured forward till he was within a few meters of the doors. He stretched out his hand. No sooner had he touched one than it swung slowly open.

From within, white light flooded out, blinding him with its intensity. Automatically his arms went up to cover his face. He peered through the narrow gap between them, seeing opposite him a tall statue of a seated God. Round his feet, discarded weapons lay and in his hands he held a brazier of glowing coals. The face of the statue was Sholan. With a sigh, he released his breath. Then he frowned. Something wasn't quite right.

A figure stepped between him and the God, cutting out the worst of the intense light.

"Who are you to disturb the peace of Kezule?" a voice demanded in Sholan. "You have no right to be here. Leave, lest the wrath of Kezule strikes you down where you stand!"

He hesitated. The voice and the form were familiar.

The figure stepped forward, crimson robes rustling as he moved.

Kaid retreated as the priest continued to advance. Turning, he ran back the way he'd come, emerging at full tilt into another cavern—a cavern housing Valtegans the like of which he'd never seen before. He came to an abrupt stop, hardly able to believe what he saw. Short and squat, they were a parody of the soldiers. One lifted its head, looking toward him, the gold collar at its throat glinting. The face bore a look of such mindless hunger that when it began to raise itself to an upright position, terror freed him and he began to back out. Guards yelled and rushed toward him. Shock sent adrenaline rushing through his system. The world spun crazily, then suddenly stopped, leaving him reeling with nausea and the memory of groups of what could only have been large eggs lying on the heated floor of the small cavern.

Opening his eyes, he found he was lying on the prayer mat in his room at the new Shrine of the Valsgarth estate. He sat up, blinking and rubbing his eyes groggily. He couldn't be here, could he? Reaching out he touched the low table in front of him where the triple-wicked lamp still burned. It felt solid enough, but then, so had the cavern. He pushed himself up into a sitting position, looking round the room. Everything was where he remembered it. Had it all been a dream, then? Holding his hands up, he examined his wrists. The half-healed weals were still there. He flexed his shoulders. Pain shot through his back, making him gasp. Not a dream, then. Had Ghezu returned him to the estate, and if so, why?

Getting carefully to his feet he made for the door, opening it and stepping out into the corridor.

The cold made him shiver and he realized as he looked down at himself that he was still unclothed, as he'd been the last time he'd visited the Shrine room in the middle of the night.

The building was silent as he padded his way along the corridor to the entrance. Pushing the door open, he stepped inside. A figure wrapped in a cloak sat huddled on the steps of the dais at the foot of the statue of Vartra.

His hypersensitized sense of smell identified her at once. As he started down the hall toward her, she turned round. Her face was concealed by the folds of her cloak, but he knew it was her.

"We thought we'd lost you," she said, raising her hands to pull back her hood.

The flames from the braziers cast flickering light and shadow across her alien features. He stopped a few feet from her.

"How long have I been gone?" he asked.

"Just over six weeks now. We had news from Fyak's lair that you were there."

He shifted uneasily from one foot to the other. "When did I return from Stronghold? How was I brought here?"

She frowned, reaching out to touch his face, her fingers cupping his cheek. "You're really here this time, aren't you? Then you returned now, Kaid."

Hope began to rise in him as he covered her hand with his—it was warm flesh and blood. He stepped closer, putting his other hand against her throat, feeling her pulse beating under his fingertips.

Pulling her close, he buried his face against her neck.

Breathing deeply of her scent, he tried to reassure himself
with as many of his senses as possible that he was home.

"You're real," Kaid whispered, running his fingers through
her hair as he began to nuzzle her neck. "I'm really here, with
you." His tongue flicked across her cheek. As his mouth
touched hers, his teeth gently caught hold of her, tasting the
sweetness of her lips for the first time. Then he realized what
he was doing and released her.

"I'm sorry. It was just that . . . I didn't mean to . . ." he
said, backing away from her.

"Kaid!" she cried, reaching out for him as he saw her
begin to fade.

*   *   *

Carrie left the Shrine and headed for the room Kaid had
used when he'd stayed here before. It was still as Dzaka had
left it, the lamp burning in the hope that Vartra would guide
Kaid home. She closed the door behind her, leaning against
it as she sniffed the air. She *could* smell his scent! It couldn't
have been her imagination, could it? She reached out with
her mind, searching for the pattern that was Kaid, but once
more, she sensed nothing.

Turning, she left the room and headed for home. As she
walked along the main street in the gathering dusk, ahead
she saw and heard the bustle of people outside the Brotherhood dwelling. With a shock, she recognized the mental patterns of Humans. It was the group of archaeologists, a full
day earlier than expected. No wonder there was a commotion
outside the houses!

One of the Sholan guards standing helplessly watching the
confused Humans saw her and came hurrying over.

"Liegena," she said. "They weren't expected today! We
can't locate anyone who can key the door for them!
Everyone's at the dig trying to get as much done as possible
before the Terrans take over. You can fix the door, can't
you?"

"Me? I don't involve myself with Terrans," she said,
taking a step back as she sent to Kusac, letting him know he
was needed at the village.

*I'm on my way. Security informed me when they arrived.
You shouldn't have been out on your own!* he sent. *Leave*

*them till we get back. It'll only be another ten minutes. Keep
that guard with you until I return!*

"The Liege will be here shortly," she told the Warrior.
"He'll deal with them then. You're to remain with me."

Shayola looked at the group of Humans, then back to
Carrie. "We can't leave them there, Liegena. It's not an aus-
picious welcome for them."

Before she could answer her, one of the Humans who'd
seen them in conversation started walking over to them.

"Look," the woman said, stopping in front of them. "We've
just come from the Kysubi plains. We're tired and hungry, and
we don't need this kind of foul-up! We've been subjected to
the most ridiculous level of security checks to get onto this
damned estate in the first place, and now we've been left high
and dry out here in the street, in the cold, surrounded by a
group of armed guards! We've been treated like intruders! I
want to see someone in authority, and I want to see them now!"

*Dammit, Carrie! Get back home away from them! Tell that
Warrior to do her job and guard you!*

She's one of Ni'Zulhu's people, not a personal guard.

Still dazed after her experience in the Shrine, she was torn
two ways. Basic hospitality told her the Humans weren't
asking much, instinct and Kusac were telling her to run back
home, away from them, before they realized who she was.

"Please, Liegena! You can key the door lock and let them
in. The house is ready apart from perishable food," Shayola
was saying.

"All right, but you must stay with me as a bodyguard until
I'm back at the villa," she said before looking at the Human.

"I'll let you in," she said. "Someone will be along shortly
to show you round the house and tell you where everything
is. I'm afraid we weren't prepared for your arrival today, we
were expecting you tomorrow."

Carrie stepped past the woman and began walking toward
the house.

*I'm letting them in, Kusac, then I'll go home. We really
can't leave them standing outside.*

"Hey! You can't just walk off like that!" exclaimed the
woman, turning round to trail after them. "I want to speak to
someone in authority! I intend to lodge a formal complaint
about the way we've been treated!"

"Go ahead of me and clear them away from the doorway,

please, Shayola," Carrie said to the Sholan female. "I don't want to have to push through them."

"Yes, Liegena." She hurried off and began shouting orders to the other guards.

A hand grasped her by the arm, stopping her in her tracks. "I said don't walk away from me! I'm not done with you yet! I'm a professional archaeologist, here with my team at the personal invitation of the owner of this estate. I don't expect to be given the runaround by people like you! Now, I want to know your name, and I want to know it now! I intend to report you to your superiors!"

Carrie was peripherally aware of the shocked reactions of the woman's colleagues, and the estate guards with them, as the woman's frustration and anger flowed through her.

"Leave her alone, Pam," called out one of the men. "She's going to open the door for us. Let's just get in and relax till someone comes to sort this all out."

Carrie took the opportunity to move to one side, but Pam was having none of it and made another grab for her, catching her by the arm again.

"Oh, no you don't," she said, holding onto her.

Anger flared through Carrie, hers as well as Kusac's. As Shayola stepped forward to intervene, Carrie reached up with her free hand and pulled her hood back. Staring Pam straight in the face, she answered her.

"I am someone in authority. I'm Liegena Aldatan, and my bond-mate owns the estate. Now, I suggest that you release me at once." There was ice in her voice.

The light from the open doorway was behind Pam, ensuring that she caught the full effect of Carrie's feline eyes as they glowed in a way that was impossible for Humans'.

Shocked, Pam let go of her and began to back away. A dark shape came to an abrupt stop on the edge of the group, making them scatter in fright. Rearing up to his full height, Kusac stepped out of the bushes to Carrie's side.

"I apologize there was no one here to greet you," he said, putting his arm round his mate's shoulder and drawing her close. "We weren't expecting you. The security I'm afraid you'll have to get used to. It isn't normally so intrusive, but my people had to check your credentials, especially when you arrived so unexpectedly. Please, go into your lodgings. Someone will be here in a few minutes to show you round.

In fact," he said, looking over their heads, "here's someone now."

As they turned round, the small party of Humans was treated to their second sight of a Sholan transforming from a four-legged lope to an upright stance.

"I'll do it, Liege," said T'Chebbi, dusting the palms of her hands off on her thighs. "Dzaka's gone for attendants. Humans be here in fifteen minutes. They'll make it right."

"Thank you, T'Chebbi," said Kusac. "Tomorrow morning, at fourth hour, I'll join you here and brief you on our work at the site."

"I haven't keyed the lock yet, Kusac," said Carrie.

"I'll do it," he said, moving toward the door. He placed his right hand on the lock plate and the door slid back. The interior lights came on, their warm glow a welcoming contrast to the chill night air.

"Please, make yourselves at home," said Kusac, standing back so they could enter.

The rest of the group trooped past him, smiling and thanking him, but Pam would have none of it.

"I intend to protest about our treatment," she said angrily. "I demand to speak to the Clan Lord about this!"

"My father isn't in charge of this project, I am, and I've apologized for the inconvenience you've been caused because of your early arrival," said Kusac smoothly. "If you're of the same mind tomorrow, then by all means you can request a meeting with him."

"Pam," said a female voice from the doorway. "Leave it till tomorrow. Come in and get a hot drink. We're all over-tired after our journey."

"An excellent idea," said Kusac, looking curiously at the young woman.

"Mattie," she said. "Call me Mattie." She moved forward, reaching out to touch the older woman on the arm. "Come on, Pam."

"If you wish, on your comms you'll find the data regarding our discoveries so far at the dig," said Kusac. "You can brief yourselves for tomorrow. Now, I must go. T'Chebbi will stay with you until our Dr. Reynolds and Mara arrive to help you settle in."

He turned away, moving swiftly back to Carrie's side and drawing her away from the house.

Let's leave while we have the chance! Please don't go out

without one of our guards again, he sent. *I'm not saying it could have got nasty there, but I didn't like that older female's attitude at all. Accidents happen. All it needs is a small push and you could fall. Wrapped in your cloak like that, it's impossible to see you're pregnant.*

I should have called Dzaka when I was ready to leave. I wasn't expecting any strangers in the village.

I know you're safe here, among our own, but even if it's just across to Vanna's, take someone with you. You could fall, or one of the kitlings run into you and knock you over—it's not worth the risk, cub.

She sighed. "You're right, I suppose, but I think you worry too much."

As they approached the archway into the grounds of their home, Carrie, as usual, glanced up at the emblem set into the plaster. For some unknown reason, this time she really noticed it. "Why two suns, Kusac?"

He nodded in passing to the guard on duty. "Excuse me?"

"Why does the crest have two suns?"

He shrugged as he opened the door. "Don't know. Never really thought about it before."

"It isn't as if there are two suns," she said thoughtfully, stepping into the welcoming warmth. "How long have your family used that design?"

"For generations," he said, turning to help her off with her cloak.

"As far back as the Cataclysm? Yours is one of the oldest families on this continent."

"It could be. Mother's the one to ask about that." He handed her garment to the main house attendant who, realizing the Liege and the Liegena were home, had suddenly appeared at his side. Kusac flicked his ears in thanks.

"Let's go into the den. I've something I must tell you about," she said, linking her arm through his.

"I need a shower first, Carrie. I'm covered in earth from the caverns." He held out his arm and brushed his pelt against the lie of the fur.

"Then I'll talk to you while you shower," she said, backing away from the ensuing small cloud of dust.

"I won't be able to hear you over the sound of the water. Why don't you tell Zhala that we'll be ready to eat in half an hour and I'll join you downstairs?"

"Don't take too long," she said as he headed upstairs.

* * *

When they were through at the archaeologists' house, Dzaka accompanied Jack over to the village's medical center and labs.

"Don't go yet, lad," said Jack as they reached the pathway. "I haven't had time to talk to you about the other day."

"Talk to me about what?"

Jack took him by the arm and drew him up the path to the door, which as always, was open.

"Come in for a while. I think you need to talk," he said.

Dzaka hesitated. Jack was right, he did need to talk to someone, but who?

"Are they expecting you at the villa tonight?"

"Not till later," he admitted.

"Then there's nothing to stop you."

He followed Jack in, waiting beside him while the Human opened the door to his private quarters.

"You've not been here before, have you?" asked Jack, heading over to the kitchen at the far end of his lounge.

"No, I haven't."

Dzaka looked round in interest. Books lined the walls, the shelves almost groaning under their weight. In front of them were curios—a lump of rock here, a shell there, a small ornament or two. The desk, despite having the usual comm, was covered with papers, writing instruments, and more books.

The obligatory settee and couple of easy chairs were covered with brightly woven rugs of obviously Human make.

"Oh, they're from Keiss," said Jack, following his gaze from the kitchen doorway. "My possessions finally caught up with me. Sit down, Dzaka. Do you want coffee or c'shar?"

"C'shar," he said, lowering himself into one of the chairs.

Jack disappeared to return a few minutes later with a mug for each of them. Handing Dzaka his, he sat down opposite him.

"Now, how about starting by telling me what that bunch of no-goods were up to when I came along the other night," said Jack.

"A mistake, that's all," said Dzaka with a shrug, trying to avoid the other's piercing gaze.

"Mistake, eh? You didn't say that when I patched up your face and ribs."

Dzaka tried but couldn't control the flicking of his tail. "They thought I was someone else," he said.

Jack leaned forward, mug cradled in both hands. "Look, Dzaka, I know how difficult it is for you here. Your father is popular, people blame you for his capture, and you feel Kusac and Garras tolerate you for his sake, not through any care of you personally. There's no one you can really talk to, is there? That's why I'm offering. For you, not for them. I've yet to meet Kaid, so that makes me different from the rest, doesn't it?"

Dzaka nodded. The Human had got the problem by the tail.

"Has it something to do with Kitra?" Jack asked. "I've noticed how she's been following you around lately."

He nodded again, taking a mouthful of his drink, trying to delay having to answer. No warrior liked to admit to having been beaten up, whatever the reason.

"It wasn't a mistake, was it?"

He needed to talk to someone! All the anger and fear and frustration was building up inside him with no way to release it. "No, it wasn't," he admitted. "They were warning me away from Kitra."

"Warning you away from her?" Jack raised a questioning eyebrow. "Why?"

"Her age, the fact she's our Liege's sister, and because they think I'm trying to use her to get close to Kusac. Do you want any more reasons?" he asked, his voice low and angry.

"She's the one following you around!"

"I know," he said, looking up at Jack. "That doesn't matter. It's me they're warning."

"Kitra's mature enough. She's nearly a year older than Jinoe and Rrai. You only have to look at her coloring to see she's coming into her adult pelt!"

"I hadn't noticed," said Dzaka, looking back down at his mug.

"Have you told anyone about the attack? I'm sure Kusac wouldn't allow it to go unpunished."

"No, I haven't. It's not exactly the kind of thing I want known, Jack. I'm one of the Brothers. It shouldn't have been that easy for them." His embarrassment was acute.

"Come off it, lad! Four onto one isn't fair odds!"

"I should have been able to handle it."

"Not when they jumped you from behind, Dzaka! No one can cope with that kind of assault. They hit your skull pretty hard, you know. You're lucky not to have had concussion."

"I've a hard head," he muttered, taking another drink.

Jack sat back in his chair. "I heard you'd met your mother. What was she like?"

Dzaka looked up in surprise. "How did you know?"

"Carrie mentioned it. We go back a long way, Carrie and I. She was like you, you know. Trying to live up to her twin, forgetting that she was a totally different person and just as important to those who loved her."

Dzaka was intrigued. "I know nothing about the Liegena's past," he said.

"Ask her some day. She's easy to get on with."

"I know that, but . . ."

"Your mother. What was she like," interrupted Jack.

"Spirited," he grinned. "She didn't let Kaid get away with much."

"I heard you'd been given her family jewelry."

"I'll wear only the knife until he's home." Dzaka's face darkened as he remembered Kaid was still missing.

"I can understand why," nodded Jack.

"Why did I believe Ghezu? If I hadn't, if I'd gone to Kaid and told him . . . everything would be different now!"

"There's no point blaming yourself for it, lad. From what I hear, that's Ghezu's gift. Making people believe him."

"They blame me! She said it. She said I'd known my father for thirty years, so why was I believing Ghezu's lies rather than Kaid! And she was right!"

"It's easy to say that afterward, Dzaka, not so easy at the time. You'd been told too many new things, and thought because of what Ghezu said they were lies. I'd have done exactly the same."

He hardly heard Jack. "And now this allegation that I'm trying to seduce the Liege's sister to get close to him! Kaid will skin me for it when he gets back!"

"Why should he skin you for it?" asked Jack. "You haven't done anything. The fact that Kitra's interested in you should be a compliment."

"You don't understand! Relationships and work don't mix, Jack. They must be separate if you have a relationship at all. Kaid never mixed them!"

"You're not Kaid, lad," said Jack gently. "Don't try to be. Just be yourself. You have your own value."

Dzaka put the mug down and got to his feet. "I've got to go. They'll be waiting for me at the villa. Thank you for the drink."

Jack watched him leave, shaking his head. If Dzaka didn't let go of some of his feelings soon. . . .

*   *   *

Their den, located at the back of the villa, was a comfortable room that captured the sun for the larger part of the day. Built on two levels, the upper one had a working environment with a comm and a personal resource storage area. The lower level was designed for relaxation, with a large screen entertainment viewer and consol and several concave settees and chairs. Comp books and real ones were scattered on the low circular table within easy reach of all the seats. Like the more formal lounge next door, it had clear doors that opened out onto the garden beyond. At this time of night, they were closed and covered by dark crimson drapes.

The floor and walls were dark paneled wood, which, broken up as they were by brightly colored rugs and tapestries, gave the room a feeling of secluded comfort without being oppressive.

It was here that Kusac joined Carrie. Of all the day rooms in the house, this one had quickly become their favorite.

"Zhala says third meal will be ready shortly," she said as he came in.

"D'you want a drink?" he asked, heading for the dispenser.

"Got one, thanks." As she watched him, her mind began to wander. The run-in with the Humans had reminded her how ill at ease she was among them. Not so with *her* people. Even in Dzahai village, though they'd never seen her like before, there was a courtesy about their friendly curiosity: an acceptance that was lacking with the Humans.

Finished, he turned away from the unit then stopped, head cocked to one side, regarding her questioningly as his tail swayed leisurely from side to side.

The daily sight of Sholans was so familiar to her now that when she caught a glimpse of herself in the mirror, her own outward form seemed somehow alien. He was wearing his favorite olive tunic, she noticed with a smile. The soft material stretched more tightly across his chest and shoulders these days, a result of all the training. It fell to mid-thigh level, again showing the difference that hard physical activity had made to him. Naturally stronger than the Humans to start with, Kusac now looked—and was—as muscular as any of the Warriors or Brothers on the estate.

"What is it?" he asked, moving over to join her on the settee.

"Just that I think you need new tunics," she said, leaning against him as he sat down. "You've grown!"

He lifted his arm and put it round her, balancing the mug in his other hand as he did so. "I'm older. In fact, I reach official adulthood with my next birth day this spring."

"You're not an adult now?" This surprised her.

"Yes, and no. Telepaths and Warriors, and the Brotherhood of course, are all exempt from military service. We have to mature sooner—learn to control our aggression and our sexuality—because we stay on Shola where such behavior can't be easily redirected. So, from about twenty-five or so, we're considered mature enough to accept responsible positions within our guilds. However, thirty still remains the age of adulthood for the majority of Sholans. It's also when we males achieve physical maturity."

"Ah, I've found the memories now."

"You have it all there, somewhere. Now, what was it you had to tell me," he asked, lifting his mug to his mouth.

She chose her words carefully. "Someone came into the Shrine room while I was there. Someone who if it wasn't Kaid, was his double."

He sat up, almost spilling his drink. "What? You *saw* Kaid?"

"I'm sure it was him."

"How? Where is he? Why didn't you tell me sooner?" His questions came tumbling out one after the other.

"Let me tell it my way," she said, taking the mug from him and putting it on the table. "He came up to me and asked how long he'd been gone. Six weeks, I said. Then he asked when he'd returned. I couldn't believe he was really there, so I reached out and touched him. He was real, Kusac. Flesh and blood, I swear he was!"

"Go on. I believe you."

"He said he'd been at Stronghold."

"Stronghold! Not Fyak's?"

She shook her head. "Stronghold. He took my hand and said that I felt real so he must be here. Then, he just disappeared."

"Disappeared?"

"One moment he was there, the next gone. He seemed to fade—lose solidity—then he vanished."

Kusac said nothing, just looked at her.

"I went to the room that Dzaka keeps ready for him and I could smell his scent strongly there. I've no idea how or why it happened, but he really was there."

"But how? How did he get there, and why did he leave so suddenly? Why didn't he stay?"

"I've been trying to work that out myself. Remember when we were trying out all those skills in the encyclopedia? Maybe he teleported."

"But *how?* To do that he'd have to have a powerful talent."

"You do realize that he and Garras are the only ones who didn't tell us what their talents were," she said.

He gave a negative flick of his ears. "He said he was at Stronghold?"

"Yes. I remember that clearly because of Lijou's message. There was something else. He looked ill, and thin. And his wrists had been badly hurt. I'm worried for him, Kusac."

"If Ghezu's got him, so am I. At least we know he's still alive."

"But for how much longer? I know I shouldn't have, but I reached mentally for him, and I sensed nothing. Not a trace."

"He might have been asleep, especially if he'd just tele-ported here."

She made a derisory noise. "You don't believe that any more than I do! Now we know he's at Stronghold, not Chezy, what are we going to do about it?"

He said nothing at first, and Carrie watched as his ears began to flick with worry. Where his tail lay on the settee beside her, the tip was doing the same.

"We can't go running all over Stronghold looking for Kaid," he said at length. "Nor can we demand that Ghezu returns him to us. The fact that we know he's there could be enough in itself for him to kill Kaid."

"So what do we *do?* I'm sick of sitting here doing nothing!"

"No more than me. First we need proof that he's there, then we can look at our options."

"Our options will still be the same," she said. "Either we do nothing for fear Kaid gets killed, or we leave him where he is and he gets killed anyway! I know what he'd want us to do."

Kusac took her hand in his. "So do I, but he'd wait for the best time to be sure of succeeding. At least with him at Stronghold, we aren't risking a civil war."

There was a knock at the door and an attendant came in. "Third meal's ready, Liege, Liegena."

* * *

Kaid was still crying out as Carrie faded from his sight. His world had shattered only to resolve itself into an unfamiliar room. Hands grabbed him by the shoulders, slamming him painfully against the back of the hard chair in which he sat.

"So," said Ghezu, from his perch on the edge of the table. "How are you enjoying your visions? They seem to be displeasing. That's unfortunate."

Kaid struggled against the grip, trying to lift his hands only to find they were bound in front of him.

"You're not real," he said, relaxing back into the seat. "None of this is."

"Oh, I'm real, believe me," said Ghezu. "And I want some information from you."

Kaid raised an eye ridge. "I don't think so."

He watched Ghezu spin a small knife between his fingers. The overhead light flickered off the blade and the silver bracelet that he wore.

"What was it you saw, Kaid? I hear you were to be the third for the Aldatan brat and his alien female. Am I right?" He stopped, cocking his head to one side, watching him.

Involuntarily, Kaid's ears flicked back. Ghezu was touching him on a nerve that was very raw. It had seemed so real that he could still smell her scent.

"Yes." The word was drawn out, like a hiss. "Was it her you saw? Did she turn you down? Or perhaps she didn't. Maybe the dream was cut short, was that it, Kaid? Were you torn from her arms? Or perhaps her bed?" He stood, looking Kaid up and down. "No, not from her bed."

"It has nothing to do with you," Kaid snapped angrily, pulling away from the restraining hands. He didn't like being touched at the best of times. It was an intimacy he seldom invited and Zhaya's hands on his shoulders were becoming more than an irritant, it had become a physical problem.

"Hasn't it? I think you're forgetting the fact that you're my guest, Kaid. With you here, they can't have their Triad, and without you, they can't reach the Fire Margins and survive. Had you thought of that? Hmm? Then they'll remain members of the Brotherhood, and under my control." He walked round to the side of his desk, flicking the knife into the palm of his hand.

"Bring him here," he ordered Zhaya. "Yes, I can confidently say you'll never bed *that* particular female, Kaid, unlike that qwene, Khemu." He said her name as if he were swearing.

Zhaya grasped Kaid by one arm and pulled him over to the desk.

Reaching down, Ghezu pulled Kaid's bound wrists onto the surface. "Hold them there," he said.

Zhaya leaned against Kaid, pushing him forward against the desk, making him spread his hands out for support.

"I told you I want some answers, Kaid. I want to know the security codes for the Aldatan estate. I've got some unfinished business I need to attend to. You know Dzaka's there, don't you?" he said conversationally as Kaid glared up at him. "He's a renegade too. Like father, like son, eh? There's a contract on him and I want to see it's fulfilled."

"Go to hell," Kaid snarled, his lips curling back from his teeth in anger.

The knife thudded into the desk between the forefinger and thumb of his right hand.

"I said I want those codes!"

Kaid continued to stare at Ghezu as the Guild Master reached out and pulled his knife free of the wood.

"What kind of fool do you take me for, Ghezu? You're not just after Dzaka—you want Kusac and Carrie as well. With them gone, you think you can control the others. You'll get no codes from me. I'm no oath-breaker, unlike you."

Ghezu's hand lashed out, catching Kaid across the side of his face, making him reel.

Lifting his head, Kaid stared at Ghezu, ignoring the blood

trickling from the claw marks across his cheek. "What does that prove?" he asked quietly.

The knife point touched the underside of his jaw and as Ghezu lifted his blade, Kaid was forced to tilt his head up, exposing his neck.

"I want those codes, Kaid, and I want them now," snarled Ghezu, pressing the point harder against his throat till it just pricked the skin.

"You've had my answer. Go rot in hell, Ghezu."

The pressure under his jaw disappeared and as his head dropped down, he caught the flash of silver before agonizing pain from his hand exploded through him. The unexpectedness of it made him yowl in agony.

His knees buckled under him, but his fall was brought up short when Ghezu grasped a handful of his hair. As he struggled to stand, through the red mist of pain he heard Ghezu's voice.

"I told you it was real this time, Kaid. I will have those codes from you if I have to destroy you an inch at a time," he said conversationally. "Now, are you ready to talk yet, or shall I start on the next finger?"

* * *

Dzaka had no sooner entered the villa's grounds than he saw Kitra standing by the doorway, obviously waiting for him. He stopped dead and began backing away.

"Dzaka," she said, "don't go. I want to speak to you."

"I'm busy, Kitra," he said, still moving backward. "I'm going to the Shrine."

"I'll come with you," she said.

"Kitra . . ."

"I want to talk to you, Dzaka," she said.

"Oh, leave him alone, Kitra," came Mara's drawling voice from behind him. "You shouldn't be out at this time of night anyway."

Dzaka spun round and without a glance in her direction, headed toward the Shrine.

Kitra continued walking toward the archway, ignoring Mara.

"Goodnight, Kitra!" said the Human from her perch on the small ornamental wall outside the villa.

Kitra stopped and turned to look at the girl. "Why do you

want Dzaka to stay away from me?" she asked. "Why should it matter to you?"

Mara laughed. "Go home, Kitra. You're too young to understand grown-up matters."

"What's grown-up about this?" she asked, ears flicking and betraying her confusion. "What has it to do with age? You're a youngling, too."

With an exasperated noise, Mara jumped down from the wall, landing in front of Kitra. "You don't know anything about us, do you?" she said. "You should, especially with a bond-sister who's Human! We mature far earlier than you do."

"So?" Kitra frowned, no wiser.

"Dzaka wouldn't be interested in you, Kitra. You're too young for him. He's more likely to be interested in someone older, who's been with other males, not some kitling who's still wet behind the ears!"

"What has being wet behind the ears got to do with who Dzaka likes?"

"You really don't understand, do you?" Mara shook her head. "Forget it, Kitra. Just take my advice and go home. You're not in the running at all when it comes to Dzaka. If he wants a female, he isn't going to look to a cub like you!" She pushed Kitra aside and was about to head after Dzaka when she stopped, a frown appearing on her face. With an angry exclamation, she stormed off in the opposite direction.

Kitra had sensed Mara's Leska, Zhyaf, contacting her, telling her to return to the house they shared on the edge of the village. She sighed, glad that Carrie was so different from Mara. She didn't call her a child and exclude her from parts of her life any more than her brother, Kusac did. He was always pleased to see her. Maybe it was because Mara wasn't happy with Zhyaf, but Physician Vanna wasn't happy with her Leska at times and it didn't make her behave unpleasantly.

She realized with a start that she'd been walking, her feet carrying her of their own volition toward the Shrine, and Dzaka.

*   *   *

The den door opened and Dzaka stood there with a haunted look on his face.

Carrie put her comp book aside. "Come in, Dzaka. What's the problem? It isn't about Kitra, is it?"

The door slid shut behind him and he came over to her, ears back and tail swaying in apprehension.

"You know?" he asked as Carrie used her wrist comm to trigger the privacy lock on the door.

She nodded. "Sit down, Dzaka. There's no need to stand on ceremony with me."

Dzaka perched unhappily on the edge of the chair opposite her, noticeably trying to keep his face out of the light.

"What's happened?"

"Kitra!" The one word said it all.

Carrie tried hard to suppress a grin and failed.

"It isn't funny, Liegena," he said. "What do I do?"

"What do you want to do?"

He looked at her. "No offense, Liegena, but I want her to leave me alone! What else should I want?"

"What happened to your face?" she asked.

"Nothing, Liegena."

"I know when I'm not being told the truth," she said quietly. "Who did it? Was it Rulla? I heard about the last bit of bother you had with him."

"Not Rulla," said Dzaka. "I don't know for sure, but I think it was some of the estate workers—from the main estate, not here."

Carrie was furious. "They ambushed you? I'll see they don't get away with it, Dzaka," she said. "Where is Kitra at the moment?"

"At the Shrine. I spoke to Ghyan before she arrived and he delayed her so I could leave."

"What did you tell Ghyan?"

"Just asked him to keep Kitra busy for a short while so I could leave without her following me," he said, looking at the floor.

Using her wrist comm, Carrie called Ghyan. "Is Kitra still with you?" she asked.

"Yes, Carrie. She's in the Shrine room filling the incense holders for me."

"Find another reason to keep her there for at least an hour, Ghyan. Dzaka's sought sanctuary with me and we need to talk this over with Rhyasha."

"Will do. I'll offer her third meal," he said, his expression

and the set of his ears showing his complete understanding
of the situation.

"Thank you, Ghyan," she said, then cut the connection.
"You heard what's happening, Dzaka. I'm going to call
Rhyasha; she'll want to talk to you."

She saw the look of utter panic that crossed his face and
leaned forward to touch his hand reassuringly. "No, she isn't
going to be angry with you, nor is anyone else in the family,
Dzaka. Trust me on this. She needs to speak to you before
she speaks to Kitra, no matter what you decide. Actually, she
and I have been waiting for this to happen, so it's no surprise. You haven't said anything to Kitra yet, have you?"

He shook his head. "She's a child, Liegena. She can't
know what she's doing. How could I say anything to her?"

"Has she said anything to you?"

Again the negative head shake. "She tried, that's why I
went to the Shrine. It's how she's behaving—following me
around, anxious to touch me—you know what I mean. She's
just so *open* about it!"

"So that's why the other males were warning you away
from her," said Carrie. "You go to the kitchen and make a
pot of c'shar for the three of us while I speak to Rhyasha."

He got to his feet. "Liegena," he said, "where's the
Liege?"

"With his father up at the main house," said Carrie. "I told
you, there's no need to worry."

When he'd gone, she went over to the desk comm and
called Rhyasha.

"Would this have anything to do with the fact that Kitra's
staying for third meal with the priest?" she asked.

"Partly. Kitra's definitely chosen Dzaka," Carrie said,
"And he's feeling positively hounded by her. There's something else. Dzaka's been warned away from her by several
people. The other night four estate workers ambushed him."

"What! Was he hurt?"

"Some. A cut face, and judging by the way he's moving,
bruised ribs."

"That will be dealt with," said Rhyasha angrily, "I'll be
over shortly."

Settled with a mug of c'shar, Dzaka waited for Rhyasha to
arrive. Despite what Carrie said, he was worried. A lot of

people were waiting for the opportunity to find fault with him and this could well give them their excuse.

Rhyasha arrived minutes later, her long woolen robe swirling round her ankles as she swept into the den.

"It really feels like winter's here, doesn't it?" she said. "Let me see your face, Dzaka." She beckoned him over. "I won't stand for this kind of lawless behavior. I'll catch the culprits, never fear."

While Carrie poured Rhyasha a drink, Dzaka reluctantly went over to her. Taking hold of his chin, she examined his cut cheek. "Nasty," she said. "And your ribs?"

"Just bruised," he said, wincing as she ran her hand across his side.

"More than that, I think," she said, waving him back to his seat as she settled herself on the settee. "Do you know who they were?"

"No, Clan Leader. Clan Leader, I haven't done anything to Kitra," he said anxiously, still hovering in front of her.

"I know you haven't, Dzaka," Rhyasha said, taking her mug from Carrie. "Sit down so I can talk to you."

"I think I should leave this to the two of you," Carrie murmured, beginning to rise.

"No, stay, Carrie," said Rhyasha. "One day you'll have to do this for your daughter. You might as well learn about it now." She waited until Dzaka was once more perched on the edge of his seat.

"You're probably as confused as Kitra is right now, aren't you?" She saw his affirmative gesture. "It's quite simple, really. Females mature earlier, Dzaka, and that's what's happening right now to Kitra. Parents notice this, and start watching their daughters, as we did, to see which male she's drawn to. You, in Kitra's case."

"She's only a child, Clan Leader! I want nothing to do with her, she's far too young!" he exclaimed. The whole situation was ridiculous, couldn't they see that?

"She's old enough, believe me, Dzaka, or she wouldn't be coming into her first season," said Rhyasha drily. "She's going to chase the male of her choice, and she's going to pair with him, and nothing we can do will stop her, even if we wanted to! It's the way we are, just as you young males are driven with a need to father cubs. I take it you've never paired with a virgin before?"

Dzaka shut his eyes briefly. This couldn't be happening to

him! "No, I haven't. My lovers were all older than Kitra by several years. I lost my mate and cub on Szurtha, Clan Leader, and there's been no one since then." As he spoke, he felt their loss afresh.

"I'm truly sorry to hear that, Dzaka," said Rhyasha sympathetically, "but that doesn't deal with this problem. Kitra seems like a child to you now, but believe me, she'll change almost in front of your eyes when you're alone with her. My responsibility now is to see that the male she chooses will be sensitive to her needs and her age. As I'm sure you'll appreciate, the wrong lover at this stage in her life could do untold damage. So, now that you know my daughter's chosen you, and that I approve of her choice, what do you want to do about it?"

"Nothing! I want nothing to do with her, Clan Leader!" he said.

"Do you dislike her? Find her unattractive?"

Dzaka floundered, trying to find the right words. "I've never thought of her like that." He was beginning to feel as if he was trapped in quicksand. The more he refused, the more the Clan Leader was ignoring what he said.

"That's good. For a moment, Dzaka, imagine you have a daughter like Kitra. What sort of person would you like to be her first lover?"

"Someone who'll put her needs first, of course. Someone who isn't interested in only pleasing himself—but she isn't my daughter!"

"No, she isn't, but listen to what you've just said. You've just described yourself, Dzaka. An older male who has enough experience to please her, not himself. So wouldn't you agree that you'd make an ideal first lover for her?"

"Yes—No! Oh Gods! I don't know what to say, Clan Leader," he exclaimed, putting his head in his hands in desperation.

"One tiny, little word, Dzaka. *Yes.*"

"But Clan Leader . . . !"

"Yes, Dzaka," insisted Rhyasha.

Dzaka looked from her to Carrie. "Liegena!" The panic was audible in his voice.

"She's right, Dzaka," said Carrie. "Imagine if you refuse her and she goes to one of the estate lads—lads or males like the ones who jumped you the other night. She's chosen you. Don't turn her down."

"You're not going to help me, are you?" he said. "You'll let her plague me till I have to say yes, or refuse and hurt her."

"This isn't a long term relationship we're talking about, Dzaka," said Rhyasha. "What you do after tonight is up to the two of you, nothing to do with me."

"It isn't?" His ears began to right themselves. "Tonight?!"

"No, it isn't. Should you wish to stay together for a while, I have no objections."

"I think what Rhyasha means," said Carrie tentatively, looking at the other female, "is that she's pleased Kitra chose you out of the males available on our estates."

Rhyasha frowned. "Isn't that what I said?"

"No," said Carrie. "It isn't."

"Dzaka, I'm sorry," she said, ears flicking as her eyes widened in embarrassment. "I *am* glad she chose you. You're so . . ." she stopped, looking for the right word.

"Competent? Patient?" suggested Carrie with a slight smile.

"Yes!" said Rhyasha, relaxing again. "And kind. You've been so very gentle with her feelings, even though you've been victimized because of her."

"If Dzaka did agree to . . . ah . . . be with Kitra," said Carrie, "Wouldn't that make him even more of a target?"

Rhyasha frowned. "No. Dzaka and Kitra will accompany me to your dig site tomorrow morning, and I will make sure they all see that *I've* sanctioned their relationship."

Carrie nodded. "That would certainly help silence any criticism. Kusac, I'm sure, will do the same."

"You'll find our males are only too happy to leave these matters to us, cub! That's agreed, then," she said, a satisfied note to her voice. She picked up her mug for the first time and took a long drink from it. "Have you a guest room here that they can use? I think it better for them to be here than at home."

"Yes. There's a room next door to the nursery they can have," said Carrie.

"In which case," she said, finishing her drink and standing up, "I'll go and fetch Kitra, and you can show Dzaka the room."

Dzaka had given up protesting his lack of interest. Neither of the females was going to listen to him anyway so what was the point? Sighing, he leaned back in his chair, closing his eyes for a moment. At least after tomorrow, he'd no longer be a target for those who thought he was using Kitra. Then he remembered Mara. The knowledge that he'd chosen Kitra would make her leave the youngling alone, stop her trying to push Kitra away from him. That would be another weight off his mind.

About half an hour later, Rhyasha returned with Kitra. A rather subdued Kitra whom she left with Dzaka in the guest suite.

Dzaka suddenly found himself alone with her. He still wasn't sure how Rhyasha and Carrie had talked him into this. They stood there, trying not to look at each other, he under no illusions as to her feelings toward him because of his empathic ability. He watched her walk past him to stand at the window, looking out onto the inner garden.

He knew someone had to make the first move, and as the experienced one, it fell to him. Joining her at the window, he placed his hand on her shoulder, making her jump and turn round half in fear.

"It's all right," he said, taking a step back. "I'm not going to do anything you don't want me to do. We can sit and talk all night if you like."

"Can we talk?" she asked.

"Of course." He held out his hand to her and cautiously she took it.

They sat down, Kitra backing herself up against the armrest, he sitting a short distance from her. Gradually, he became aware of her scent. It brought back memories of Nnya. Hers had carried the same undertone of a female anxious to pair. The small hand he still held within his fluttered gently like a trapped bird, banishing the memories. It was more seductive than anything a mature female could have done.

"Do you mind me choosing you?" she asked, laying her ears back in embarrassment. "I didn't mean to cause you any trouble."

"You haven't caused any trouble, Kitra," he said, keeping his voice low. For the first time, he began to look at her as a lover would.

Physically she took after her mother, her pelt a light golden color. Carrie had been right, the darker banding of her childhood had almost disappeared. Today her hair was unbound, forming a pale cloud of soft waves that reached to below her shoulders. A pair of large brown eyes looked rather apprehensively at him.

He reached out with his other hand to touch her cheek, surprised at how soft it was. "I don't mind you choosing me, Kitra," he said, realizing as he moved slightly closer to her, that he was speaking the truth.

That night was one of discoveries for both of them. He realized her mother had spoken no more than the truth. Almost before his eyes, the kitling vanished, to be replaced by a young female.

As they lay entwined, her hands began to push through the longer fur on the front of his body, teasing him back to a state of interest. Rousing himself, as he leaned forward to gently nip her cheek, sensations that were not his began to gradually build in him until, shocked by their intensity, he lifted his head to look down at her.

Eyes almost closed, her breath coming in short gasps, she reached down till her hands circled his hips, pulling him closer. As she began to climax, her claws extended just enough to ensure he was there with her, sharing their combined sensations in a way he'd never experienced before.

His last coherent thought was to wonder why he'd ever thought Kitra was still a child. All she lacked was experience.

Then teach me, her voice said within his mind. *Show me what will please us both.*

With the touch of her mind, the ache of loneliness was washed away and frantically he sought her mouth, trying to keep his bites gentle. Across her cheek to her ear he went, feeling her shuddering in pleasure against him. He'd been alone for too long.

Then it was over, and he lay there with her clasped close within his arms.

Is it always that good? she sent, eyes large with wonder as she looked at him.

"It can be," he smiled. "It depends who you're with."

"Will you stay with me?" she asked anxiously.

"For a while," he said, stroking her cheek. "While you need me."

"A long while?" He could see her ears tilting apprehensively and against his leg, he felt her tail start to flick.

"A long while," he heard himself saying as he realized that was what he wanted too.

* * *

Sleep didn't come easy that night for either Carrie or Kusac. Carrie's dreams were dark with the sense of danger for Kaid. They culminated in her waking with a cry of pain and terror.

Trying to comfort her, Kusac experienced it through her memory and resolved that come the morning, something would have to be done, starting with contacting Father Lijou.

At first light, he contacted Stronghold only to be told Father Lijou was unobtainable till later in the day. Grabbing a quick first meal, Kusac left Carrie sleeping and headed across the road for the house where the Terran archaeologists were staying.

Zhyaf and Mara were waiting for him there. Mara was in her element again as their visitors, curious for information about the Sholans, quizzed her about her life on the estate and with her Leska.

Kusac briefed them on the work that had already been done at the site, then they all made their way to the dig.

While they were being shown round the first chamber, one of Ni'Zulhu's people came to him with a message from General Raiban's aide. Excusing himself, Kusac left them in Jack's care and headed for the aircar outside to take the call.

"Sub-Lieutenant Aldatan," said the aide. "I apologize for the short notice, but we have to act swiftly in this matter. General Raiban has issued you with an invitation to come to the Forces Headquarters in Sonashi. Some information has come to light through one of our field agents, lately based at Chezy, that will be of interest to you. If you could be here for the tenth hour, it would be appreciated."

"I'll be there," said Kusac.

If he was to get there on time, he had to leave virtually immediately. As he hurried inside to get T'Chebbi, he sent to Carrie.

I know. I picked it up from you, she sent. *Is it Kaid?*

Has to be. Don't contact Lijou in case it alerts Ghezu. If Raiban's had an agent in Fyak's camp, then they're bound to have up-to-date information on Kaid. Let's see what they come up with first.

All right. Keep in touch.

You'll know the second I do, he promised.

* * *

Konis and Rhyasha were finishing breakfast in the family kitchen when the main house attendant came with a message from the gatehouse.

"Guild Master Esken and Senior Tutor Sorli are requesting a meeting with you, Clan Lord."

Konis glanced at his mate in surprise. "Tell Ni'Zulhu I'll see them, Che'Quul. Bring them here when they arrive."

"Not here, Konis! This isn't the place for guests!"

Konis nodded to Che'Quul. "Here." He put his hand over his mate's and gently patted it as the attendant left.

"I've suffered a multitude of little insults from Esken over the past couple of months, Rhyasha. He obviously wants something from me, so now it's payback time."

"I object to you using my home like this, Konis," she grumbled, pulling her hand free and getting to her feet. "Choa!" she called as she headed off into the main kitchen area.

Konis cradled his mug of c'shar in both hands, mouth open in a gentle smile.

Esken looked disgruntled as he and Sorli followed Che'Quul into the kitchen.

"Forgive the informality, Master Esken," said Konis smoothly, getting to his feet. "Rhyasha and I were enjoying a late first meal. Please, sit down."

Esken lowered himself onto the end of the bench while Sorli, with a slight smile of amusement, stepped nimbly over.

Rhyasha came bustling in with Choa. "Master Esken, Tutor Sorli." She nodded to them, then turned to Choa to take from her the tray laden with an assortment of home-made cookies and pastries. These she placed on the table in front of them. "The c'shar will be ready in a moment. I hope you don't consider it too early to indulge in a snack, but I thought since we're being informal . . ."

Rhyasha! His tone was disappointed.

Konis! Hers was gently mocking as she turned to fetch plates from a cupboard.

Sorli leaned forward to look at the pastries, mouth open in a delighted smile. "They're homemade! I can't remember when I last had homemade pastries."

Esken gave him a withering glance which his assistant made sure he didn't catch.

As Choa returned with mugs and c'shar which Rhyasha began to dispense, Konis decided it was time to start talking. "What brings you out here, Esken?" he asked, helping himself to one of his favorite cookies. "How can I help you?"

Esken smiled briefly. "On the contrary, Clan Lord, it's we who have come to do you a favor. Sorli, the comp, if you please."

Sorli hastily put his pastry down and reached into his ample pocket. From it he produced a comp pad which he handed to Esken.

Esken took it from him with a faint look of distaste.

"Did I get crumbs on it?" asked Sorli unrepentantly, pushing the last of the sweet into his mouth. He leaned forward and attempted to brush them off with a hand that left more behind than it removed.

The Guild Master's ears began to twitch.

Rhyasha leaned forward and took it from him. "Here, let me do that," she said, wiping it with the cloth Choa had left. She handed it back to him. "There you are, good as new."

"Thank you," said Esken, his tone clipped. He put the pad on the table in front of him. "I know you're unofficially involved in collating the information from various sources regarding the Cataclysm. I'm also aware that you and your son probably have the most comprehensive database of dreams and visions experienced by telepaths—and I include those from the Brotherhood and elsewhere. It's because of this that I've come to you."

Konis maintained his mask of neutral interest with some difficulty.

"Ghyan owes his loyalty to Father Lijou as Head Priest of his Order, especially where religious matters are concerned," said Esken. "Dreams and visions of our God belong in that category, so there is little communication from him with me regarding these topics."

He stopped to tap the comp pad with a claw tip. "I have here a transcript of documents written by past Guild Masters, Konis. What it says, and what we've proved by collaboration with Ghyan, is, to put it mildly, frightening."

Konis stirred. "I take it you've handed this information over to the committee?"

"Not yet. I intend to do so, but first I've come to you offering a truce."

Konis raised an eye ridge. "A truce, Esken? Were we at war?"

Esken began to growl deep in his throat.

"If I might interrupt for a moment, Master Esken," said Sorli. "We're approaching you in a spirit of mutual cooperation, Clan Lord. Once our findings have been given to the committee, it is highly unlikely they will be made available to you or anyone else for fear of starting a global panic. However, Master Esken feels that the interests of Shola will be best served if you and he can agree to cooperate on certain issues."

Konis looked from one to the other of them. "What issues?" he asked, aware that his abruptness was almost an insult.

Sorli winced slightly as Esken's growl, which had subsided, grew again. "Master Esken and I feel that the contents of this transcript should be made known to you so that you can include it in the database you are compiling."

"And in return you want what?" asked Konis.

Sorli hesitated, looking back to his Guild Master.

"Get on with it," Esken growled.

"Access to the mixed Leskas."

"Ah," said Konis. He stretched out and helped himself to another pastry, then, as if remembering his manners, lifted the plate and held it out toward Esken and Sorli. "Do try one, Esken. Rhyasha made them and they're rather good, even if I do say so myself."

Esken waved them away but Sorli quickly reached for another.

Well, are you going to accept? Rhyasha sent.

It's not up to me, it's up to Kusac. I have no jurisdiction over him. Theoretically he's a member of the Brotherhood now.

"Stop quartering the undergrowth, Konis," growled Esken. "You're a fair-minded person. You know by rights I should have some involvement with those mixed pairs. *Our* guild has the teachers they need, the experience the Brotherhood lacks."

"You're still playing politics with the future of our world, Esken. If you believe this information is as vital as you say, and that including it with our findings is important, you shouldn't be withholding it from us."

"Your high-handed actions over the last few months have been nothing short of a campaign of . . ."

"Be quiet!" said Rhyasha, stunning both males into silence. "Esken, my mate is quite right. If this information is so vital, you shouldn't be using it to bargain with. Konis, it took a lot for Esken to come here and offer to deal with you. Considering the bad blood between you two, it was a noble gesture and should be treated as such. Having said that, Master Esken, the only person who can agree to you having any contact with the mixed Leskas is our son, Kusac. His people are living on his estate, under his leadership, independent of us. They belong to the Brotherhood of Vartra. Kusac is also the person responsible for the database, not us. He passes on his findings, but that's all. Your offer is being made to the wrong people, I'm afraid."

"Then where is he?" Esken demanded.

"I've no idea. Do you want me to locate him?" she asked, already reaching out for her son. "I have to say that if you continue to insist on a trade for this information, I have doubts concerning its importance."

"Just put my proposal to him," snapped Esken.

"My bond-daughter informs me he's unavailable today. He's attending to business in the capital."

Carrie, this could end the hostility between us and the Guild. The level of communication between you and Esken could be at your discretion. I don't need to tell you of the benefits of reestablishing friendly links with him, do I?

I'm coming over, Rhyasha. Kusac says he personally is not prepared to negotiate anything at this time, however I may act for him in the interim and he'll decide later on his course of action.

"Kusac has asked Carrie to join us and discuss the matter with you," said Rhyasha. "Why don't you have a pastry while we're waiting?"

Carrie, followed by Dzaka and Kitra, breezed in with fond greetings for Rhyasha and Konis. Dzaka and Kitra excused themselves while Carrie settled herself in a chair beside her bond-mother. She looked across the table to Esken.

"So, you want access to us. What degree of access are you asking for?"

"We need to know more about you. What you're capable of, your genetic make-up . . ." began Esken.

"Stop right there," said Carrie. "There will be no tests conducted by you, nor will any of our people attend the Guild for assessment or training. We have no intention of returning to the situation that existed when I arrived on Shola. We're in charge of ourselves now, Master Esken, and we intend to remain so. However," she said, cutting him short as he opened his mouth to speak. "However, we *are* prepared to make available to you the results of any tests we conduct on ourselves. I've been told to inform you that it would suit us to have the open hostility between you and our people at an end. It's going to be a long time, though, before many of us are prepared to trust you enough to set foot in the Telepath Guildhouse again."

"You're offering nothing!"

"On the contrary," said Carrie quietly. "We're offering a fresh start, with no restrictions for future relationships between ourselves and your Guild. All we're saying is that *we* are in control of our own lives, not you, nor anyone else. We've got a greater incentive to discover what's happening to us and why, and what the limits of our talents are than you have, believe me! On the basis of that, are you prepared to trade?"

Esken sat there barely concealing his anger.

"Your position over the last two months has been eroded, Master Esken," said Carrie. "You've lost us, very publicly, to another guild. You've been completely excluded from any involvement with us by Governor Nesul and the Forces. You've lost respect and support on the council because of this. If you can reestablish links directly with us, it'll be seen that you are still a force to be reckoned with. *You,* personally, have more to gain by accepting what we offer than we have."

"You said you can't make a firm commitment," said Esken between clenched teeth.

"Any deal Kusac agrees to will contain what I've outlined as a minimum, that I can promise." Carrie looked to her bond-father. "Konis, you can witness my agreement to that, can't you?"

"Certainly."

"Then I accept." The words were ground out grudgingly.

"No more attempted kidnappings? No more hostility from your staff toward us?"

"Agreed, if you start supplying us with information as soon as possible."

"This is legally binding, you realize that, don't you?" said Konis, looking at them both. "If either of you breaks the contract, you will be called before the Judiciary."

Carrie nodded.

"Agreed," Esken said.

"Then this proposed contract, agreed in principle, is to be ratified by both parties tomorrow. It is legally binding and will be registered as such from now," said Konis.

"Your comp," said Esken, pushing it across the table to Carrie. "If you need to know more, contact Sorli. He prepared the document."

"Thank you, Master Esken." She let it lie in front of her while the two Guild officials got to their feet.

"You and I should get together tomorrow, Esken," said Konis, also getting up.

Esken turned a surprised face to him.

"We've got to map out a policy of cooperation over the Mixed Leska Project."

"If I may contact you later today, Clan Lord, I'll be able to arrange that for you," said Sorli. "Without Master Esken's diary . . ."

"Speak to my secretary," said Konis as he escorted them from the kitchen.

Rhyasha let out a large sigh. "Thank goodness that's resolved! Being at odds with one's Guild is most uncomfortable, no matter how good the reason for it."

"The fewer enemies we have, the better," agreed Carrie. Reaching out, she picked up the comp. "Shall we see what this holds?"

"When Konis returns."

Chapter 16

As if the contents of Esken's transcript hadn't worried all of them enough, later in the day Kusac sent to Carrie saying he'd been able to speak to the agent working for General Raiban in Fyak's camp. His name was L'Seuli. He was one of the Brothers permanently attached to Intelligence and his news was mixed.

Fyak's power over the tribes relied on several factors. Once a tribe was subdued, the Elders were taken captive and sent to Chezy. The social structure of the tribes was then demolished so the people had no one to look to but Fyak and his Faithful. Fyak's gift of rhetoric and persuasion was what had initially drawn the people to him. Now fear held them; fear of retaliation if they disobeyed, and fear of the return of the demons that Fyak preached about so convincingly.

This last fear was justified by the tales Fyak's bodyguards brought with them from the heart of his lair. The inner corridors and the temple itself were decorated with carvings and paintings of the lizardlike beings who'd originally inhabited the complex. L'Seuli could testify to the veracity of the rumors, having seen for himself these images of what were undeniably Valtegans.

Despite all this, lately there had been a lot of grumbling against Fyak because of his increasingly violent rages. It had come to a near-mutiny over the issue of the warriors' wish to return to their villages and tribes to help them prepare for winter. Fyak had been compelled to back down and sanction a leave of one month commencing in two weeks time.

Fyak would then be at his most vulnerable as the majority of his troops left to plant winter crops in their villages, and the nomads moved to their winter quarters. Those who were left would be the ones who'd been under Fyak the longest— and they were thoroughly disenchanted with him. It wouldn't take much to turn them against him.

Because of the deaths of the two fighters who'd led the assault on Lassoi, L'Seuli and his partner Rurto had been promoted to the rank of inner bodyguards. While this had allowed L'Seuli to see the prophet at first hand, it had carried a price. Like the others close to the prophet, he'd had to wear one of the gold collars set with the green stones.

Before Kaid had been taken to Stronghold, he'd managed to confirm what L'Seuli already suspected, namely that the collars were controlled by a bracelet Fyak wore. It had taken all L'Seuli's training with the Brotherhood to be able to resist the effects of the collar long enough to remove it while fleeing from Fyak's lair and rejoining the Forces.

"I had to leave," L'Seuli said to Kusac. "The collar would have visibly compromised me when my contact next communicated with me."

"How?"

"My contact was a telepath. The collar monitors the brain waves of the person wearing it; if it identifies telepathic activity, then a circuit behind the stone lights up and triggers the release of the chemicals trapped within it. I couldn't even warn him not to contact me!"

L'Seuli went on to say he'd discovered that as well as supplying illegal arms to the desert tribes, Ghezu was also supplying Fyak himself with an illegal drug known as la'quo. It was the psychotropic plant extract that the prophet used to put himself into trances so he could communicate with his God, Kezule.

Fyak's original supply had come from a clump of plants found in the main cavern near the well that supplied their water. This had now been depleted and he'd had to look elsewhere. L'Seuli had seen Ghezu himself hand Vraiyou a box containing several phials of the drug. Little was known about it beyond the fact that its unauthorized use had been declared illegal by the Chemerians.

Kaid's deception concerning the training of Fyak's warriors had been discovered when Zhaya, chief of Ghezu's guards, had arrived with a shipment of arms. The punishment Fyak had inflicted on Kaid had been extreme and though L'Seuli said he'd been alive when Ghezu had taken him to Stronghold, he couldn't vouch for his condition now.

Raiban intended to arrive at Stronghold at dawn the next day, but she was giving them thirteen hours grace because of fears that Kaid might be killed when they arrived with the warrant to arrest Ghezu.

"General Raiban, I can't thank you enough for giving me this information and the opportunity to get Kaid out," said Kusac, "but I don't understand why . . ."

"We've had dealings in the past," said Raiban in a tone that made it clear nothing further would be said on the matter.

As Kusac rose to leave, L'Seuli stopped him, handing him a small package. "Give this to Kaid. I was able to retrieve it for him from the medic, Anirra," he said.

Once outside, Kusac sent to Carrie.
Get yourself, Dzaka and Garras over to Dzahai village. Whatever you do, keep out of sight of the Brothers. Go to Noni and explain the situation. I'll join you as soon as I return. I want Kaid out of Stronghold before Raiban's forces arrive at dawn.
Why's Raiban doing this for us?
She knew Kaid. Just thank the Gods she is! Tell Garras to take whatever he thinks we'll need in the way of weapons— and emergency medikits. The news about Kaid isn't good. I'll see you there.

In the aircar on his way to Noni's, Kusac opened the package. Within it lay a broad silver bonding bracelet. The engravings were worn but still visible as a scene of the Dzahai Mountains around Stronghold and Dzahai village.

T'Chebbi leaned over to look at it. "Kaid's. Wore it most of time."

Thoughtfully Kusac rewrapped it and put it into the inner pocket of his jacket.

* * *

"For the God's sake, if you need me after tomorrow, call me," said Vanna, handing Garras yet another case of analgesics from her store of drugs. "They're all clearly labeled, showing the different strengths."

She stopped, turning to look at him. "Are you sure you remember enough of your medic training to use these properly? Start with this type," she said, waving a blue pack at him, "and if he gets breakthrough pain, you can use these," she said, picking up a white pack, "every four hours."

Garras took the packs from her and put them in the medi-kit he was carrying. "Vanna, I'll remember, stop worrying. You've given me everything I could possibly need. By the time we have Kaid, we'll also be able to use Stronghold's physician and medic, as well as Noni." He put the case down on the countertop and wrapped his arms round her.

"I wish I didn't have to go now," he said, gently nuzzling her cheek. "I wanted to be with you while Marak's in hospital."

"I know," she sighed. "But he'll have the best possible medical care; Kaid won't. I'd be with you myself if it wasn't for that."

"Marak'll be fine," Garras reassured her. "Nowadays ops like that are commonplace, you know that."

"Yes, but when it's your own child and he's so young . . ."

"He'll be fine," repeated Garras, giving her a fierce hug. "We'll have a comm unit with us, you can contact me anytime. Now I must go." He released her to look down at the cub that lay sleeping in the carrier on her desk.

The little one lay stretched out on his side, the cover up to his arms. The fingers of the tiny pawlike hands lay open in relaxation. Garras reached out and touched his head gently, making his ears flick.

"You must have looked like this when you were a cub," he said, turning back to her.

"Hmm," she said, the tone mock-critical. "I think my markings weren't quite so dark."

Garras laughed, gently touching her cheek. "I have to go now. I'll call tonight if possible. Let me know as soon as you can how his op has gone."

"I will," she said. "*You* take care! There's no prizes for the worst injuries, you know."

He grinned, showing a flash of white teeth. "It won't be us with the injuries, believe me!"

* * *

Carrie waited impatiently for Noni to open her door. "We've found him, Noni," she said. "He's at Stronghold. Ghezu has him."

Noni looked beyond her to the two males then flung her door wide. "Get in, all of you. The fewer people who see you the better! And you, child," she said, grasping Carrie briefly by the arm, "you shouldn't be running about like this! Get you over to my table and sit down at once!"

"But, Noni," Carrie began.

"No *but Noni's* from you! Go and sit down," she growled.

Noni's living room seemed smaller by the time they were all seated round the table. The elderly Sholan looked across at Dzaka, narrowing her eyes. "Always thought you had the look of Kaid about you—and a bit of your mother." She looked over at Garras. "Aye, I remember you," she chuckled. "One of the livelier lads from Stronghold, you were."

Garras' ears laid back and his tail flicked in embarrassment.

"Always coming to me to get patched up after some brawl or another."

"Noni . . ."

"I'll say no more, never fear!" She looked at Carrie sitting beside her. "Now what's this you were saying about Tallinu being at Stronghold?"

"Ghezu has him. He's badly injured, Noni."

"Then you'll be needing me when you go for him," she said decisively. "I'm letting none of those medics touch him. What did this Fyak do to him?"

"He's been flogged," said Garras. "It happened just before Ghezu took him to Stronghold."

"There's no love lost between those two. Let's pray Tallinu is more important to Ghezu alive than dead."

"He's alive, Noni," said Carrie. "I saw him last night."

"*Saw* him?"

Carrie felt Garras' and Dzaka's minds flare in interest. "I was in the Shrine when he just walked in. I even touched him. I don't know how, but he was real, Noni."

Noni looked down at the table top, one claw tip gently tapping in thought. "I've seen him too. It was only a faint impression, like a pattern in smoke," she said. "Something's not right here. I don't know what Ghezu's done to him, but it's not good. Not good at all." She fell silent.

"We've got to get him out tonight, Noni," said Garras at length.

"We will, we will," she said, coming out of her reverie. "You need someone inside to let you in, don't you? That mate of yours, I take it he's joining us?"

"Yes. He's on his way back from Sonashi now. He's got T'Chebbi with him," said Carrie.

"Then there's four of you." She began to drum the table with all her fingers.

"If we can get someone inside Stronghold, they can open the internal door leading in from the tunnels," said Garras.

"You want to use someone who's already there," she said. "It'll attract less attention. That Lijou male, what's he like? Would he help?"

Carrie looked over at Garras, who nodded. "Yes, he would," she said. "He wants us to go to the Fire Margins. He's been collaborating a lot with our family recently."

"Right, here's what you do. Garras, I want you to go into the village, to the house at the end of the main street. It's painted white, you can't miss it. Knock and tell whoever answers that Rhuna has asked for Lokki to run an errand. It's dark now so you shouldn't attract any attention. We'll send Lokki in with a message for Lijou, one that'll make him contact me but won't get Ghezu, should he find out, suspicious."

"What's wrong with sending to him?" asked Dzaka.

"Dampers have been put in," said Noni. "The place is sewn up tighter than . . ." she caught sight of Carrie's curious look and changed her mind. "tighter than it should be. Even I turn off the damper most of the time! That one's up to no good, I'll be bound!"

"He's delivering weapons and drugs to Fyak," said Carrie. "That explains the dampers. He doesn't want any of the Brothers to know what he's up to."

"I've brought a portable comm with me," said Garras. "Why don't we use the most obvious way of contacting Lijou?"

"Try if you want," said Noni. "If you were Ghezu, wouldn't you have all incoming calls intercepted and monitored?"

"What's the message for Lokki, then?" sighed Garras.

"Let's see. Pass me the writing stuff out of that top drawer over there," she said, gesturing to the other side of the room.

Dzaka brought over the stylus and paper.

"I know what to put," she laughed. "He'll call us so fast, you won't believe it!" She scribbled a few lines, then passed it over to Garras. "You add the address of your comm."

Garras did as she asked, then pushed the paper back to her. Folding it, she returned it to him. "Give it to Lokki. They're used to him running around Stronghold with my potions and messages. He won't cause any concern."

* * *

The comm finally chimed and as Noni answered it, three pairs of eyes, all beyond the comm's pickup range, were focussed on her.

"What's this all about, Noni?" Lijou demanded. "What's this potion that you want collected by Kha'Qwa?"

"She visited me the other day, Lijou, asking me for a potion for what ails her belly. It's ready. She needs to come for it today."

"There's nothing wrong with her." He frowned. "Is there?"

"You'll have to ask her, Master Lijou," said Noni in an arch tone. "I don't discuss my patients with other folk!"

"Then why send me the message?" he demanded.

"Cos the lad knows you. He don't know your Kha'Qwa, that's why! Now, it's got to be picked up this evening. It won't keep."

"I'll pass the message on," he said tersely and reached for the comm switch.

"And Lijou!" she said, reaching over for Carrie's hand.

"Yes?" He was poised ready to cut the connection.

Noni pulled Carrie's hand briefly into view. "Don't let my work go to waste!" She cut the link.

"Why did you do that?" demanded Carrie.

"He had that look on his face," she said, closing the comm and pushing it back to Garras. "He wasn't going to come. Now he will."

"Wasn't that dangerous if the line's being monitored?" asked Garras.

"They'll have missed it, don't worry. It's the start of the call that'll interest them, not the end."

"Now what?"

"Now we wait for Lijou and perhaps even Kha'Qwa." said Noni, sitting back in her seat. She looked up at Carrie. "You're how many weeks on now?"

Carrie looked confused for a moment, then flushed. "Twelve."

"And you're still able to use your Talent?"

"Yes."

"No change in it, is there? It isn't becoming erratic or faint?"

"No!"

"That's good. We'll need to use that Talent of yours shortly."

* * *

It was a good half hour before a knock sounded at the door. Instantly, Dzaka, Garras—and Carrie—had their weapons out, the two males standing to the front.

"It's Lijou and Kha'Qwa," said Noni. "Don't be so fast off the mark!"

"I hope a time never comes when you're glad of our speed," said Garras, replacing his gun as he went to the door.

Noni eyed Carrie as she put her weapon away in the folds of the robe she wore.

"What you want with that, girl? The males can look after us."

"I prefer to be able to look after myself," said Carrie.

Lijou stood in the doorway looking at Garras with his mouth hanging open. Beside him stood one of the Sisters, anonymously wrapped in her grey cloak. Only her nose and eyes were visible.

Garras reached out and grasped Lijou by the arm, pulling him into the cottage. He turned to the female but she'd already followed Lijou in.

"It *is* you!" said Lijou, looking round the room. "You're here for Kaid, aren't you? I dreamed of him last night. Dzaka, Ghezu's got a contract out on you. I'd have thought you'd have the common sense to stay on the estate where you're safe."

"He's my father," said Dzaka. "I had to come."

"So you saw him, too," said Noni. "I don't like it. This has me worried."

Lijou turned to Garras. "You must get him out, Garras! I'm convinced that more than we realize depends on him."

"Kusac's on his way here. We're going to get him out, believe me, but we'll need your help."

"What can I do?" asked Lijou, perching on the end of Noni's bed.

"First I need to know what the situation is like in Stronghold now."

Kha'Qwa unwrapped herself from her cloak and put it across the end of Noni's bed.

"Security's tighter," she said, "but not what you could call unreasonable given the state of things out in the desert. Ghezu's had dampers installed in every public area till it's become quite oppressive, though we can still be comfortable in our own quarters," she said, glancing at Lijou briefly, "but our talents are useless for communication everywhere else. He said it was to make the telepaths who'd be coming to Stronghold feel more comfortable, but people like Vriuzu say there's no need for what he's done and they find it as oppressive as we do."

"What about incoming calls and visitors?"

"Ghezu has his own people on the comm line in the office, and yes, we do get visitors, once Zhaya's authorized them! We're gradually being cut off from the world outside."

"Why hasn't anyone reported him?" asked Carrie.

"To whom?" Kha'Qwa asked, looking over at the Human. "We're only just achieved Guild status. No one wants to lose it."

"I don't believe there's no opposition to Ghezu," said Garras. "The Brothers can't have changed that much in the last fifteen or so years."

"Talk, but nothing more yet," agreed Kha'Qwa, moving round to take the seat Dzaka offered her. "One or two of the senior tutors have approached Lijou, asking him if he'd be prepared to take control, but there's nothing really overt for anyone to complain about, that's the problem."

"There is now," said Garras. "He's been supplying arms and drugs to Fyak. In just over ten hours from now, he's going to be indicted for treason. We've got to get Kaid out before that happens."

"Ye Gods! Arming the desert people? And drugs?" She shook her head unbelievingly.

"I knew he was mad," said Lijou, "but I'd never have expected that of him!"

Carrie raised her head, looking over to the door. "Kusac's here," she said, moments before they heard the knock. Dzaka answered it.

Grim-faced, Kusac and T'Chebbi entered.

"Noni, I apologize for descending on you like this, but we needed . . ." Kusac began as he approached the table.

"Never you mind that," Noni interrupted. "You get on with your organizing. I'll see to getting something for you all to eat," she said, beginning to rise. "My attendant's gone home for the night but I can call him in if need be."

"No," said Kusac, looking across at Garras as he approached the group round the table. "Better if we don't eat first. I want to go in as soon as possible."

Garras nodded. "A quick in-and-out mission is best. My

bet is Ghezu'll have him in one of the holding cells in the basement level. They were hardly ever used even in my day. What do you think, Kha'Qwa?"

She nodded slowly in agreement. "Makes sense. He'd have to be somewhere off the main trail for none of us to be aware of what was going on."

"We need to get into Stronghold without being seen," said Kusac. "Suggestions? I don't know the territory."

"Kha'Qwa, do you know the upper tunnel entrance? The one that brings you in on the west side of Stronghold?" asked Garras.

"The one that was supposedly blocked off because it was unstable?" she grinned. "Who doesn't?"

"Can you get one of your friends to make sure that the door into Stronghold is open and our way in is clear?"

"I can do that."

"Where will it bring us in?" asked Kusac.

"The upper level back tunnels. They in turn lead to the floors above ground, or down to the basement levels."

"What can I do?" asked Lijou. "I feel partly responsible. I should have been aware sooner . . ."

Kusac put his hand on the older male's shoulder. "With the dampers on, how could you have known? Ghezu's the only culpable one. What I'd like you to do is gather a few of the Warrior Brothers you trust and be ready to help if need be. Should we end up in a face-to-face with Ghezu, we may need you to rally the Brothers against him."

"One other thing you might do," said Garras thoughtfully, "is get someone to disable as many of the damping units as they can without it seeming suspicious."

"We can do that," said Lijou.

"If you can, then we should be able to locate Kaid," said Kusac, looking over at Carrie.

"I'm coming too," she said.

"Carrie, you know . . ."

"An injury to you will harm me just as much," she said firmly. "If you want to guarantee my safety, you'll have to stay here with me."

Kusac made an exasperated noise. "Very well, you can come."

"You can make arrangements for me too," said Noni, glaring up at him.

"You wouldn't make it along the tunnels, Noni," said Kha'Qwa gently.

"In that case, I have to return with you, Lijou. This female of yours is more ill than you think, aren't you Kha'Qwa?"

Lijou frowned. "Yes, what's all this about her being ill? She'll tell me nothing!"

Noni laughed. "Got you worried, didn't it? Knew it would! You were out here as fast as a youngling in her first season, worried she'd got it wrong and was pregnant! There's nothing wrong with her, but you wouldn't be believing that now, would you? Kha'Qwa, you'll find your bottle of oil over on the chest behind me."

Lijou looked baffled. "Oil?"

"Sand fleas at Laasoi," Kha'Qwa said. "I got an allergic reaction to the bites and Noni gave me something for it when we came back. I needed some more, that's all."

"You're an evil old female," growled Lijou, frowning at her.

Noni continued to chuckle. "You just call Stronghold and tell them Kha'Qwa's been taken poorly and I need to nurse her. Get them to send an aircar for us."

"It's not a bad idea," said Garras. "It would explain why you came out here so hurriedly."

"No. We need Kha'Qwa and Lijou working on the inside for us," said Kusac.

"Then Lijou can find someone I can visit when he gets back," said Noni. "You're not going without me!"

Carrie took the old Sholan's hand in hers. "Wait here for him, Noni. We'll bring him back to you, I promise."

Noni pulled her hand away, grumbling under her breath. "I'll not have those butchers at Stronghold treating him!"

"They won't."

"Actually, keeping Lijou out of the line of fire would be better," said Garras. "He's no fighter, and as you said, he'll be needed to take over the Guild when Ghezu's arrested. Kha'Qwa can easily ask for a friend to come to her and set it up that way. Noni returning with them helps dispel any doubt that the visit here was genuine, especially as it's known she refuses to travel."

Kusac flicked an ear. "Very well. You've got a point," he conceded.

"Now that's sorted, you and me got some work to do first, girl," Noni said to Carrie, content now that her part in the

proceedings was secure. "We're going to try and reach
Tallinu using that crystal he has."

"You can't reach him, Noni," said Kha'Qwa. "I told you,
there are dampers on all over Stronghold."

"Stronghold's full of these crystals," said Noni, fishing
one out of her pocket and holding it up for them all to see.
"We'll reach him, never fear. Makes sense to try and locate
him first, though, then you don't have to go searching for
him." She pushed herself up from the table. "We'll go into
my bedroom," she said to Carrie. "It's too damned noisy
here!"

                            *   *   *

He was shivering, whether with cold or fear he didn't
know. He wasn't even sure he was awake as there was only
the darkness, and the pain. His scalp ached as did the side of
his face that lay against the cold floor. That was nothing
compared to how his right hand felt. It throbbed with an
agony that dominated his senses just as much as the flogging had.

He tried moving his arm, bringing it closer to his body for
protection. There was a strange noise. His ears tried to focus
on it, then he realized it was himself whimpering gently. He
was glad of the darkness then: he wasn't ready to see what
Ghezu had done to him.

Carefully he pushed himself into a sitting position.
Moving slowly, using his good hand, he felt around till he
located something solid—a metal strut. Recognizing it as
one of the legs on his bed, he inched his way over to it. By
the time he finally reached it, he was sweating with the exer-
tion. He hauled himself up against the side of the bed,
leaning against it with relief.

His recollection of what had happened after Ghezu injured
his hand was hazy. Had he told him the codes? He couldn't
for the life of him remember. *For the life of him,* he thought.
*What life? Ghezu's breaking every law of civilized behavior,
let alone the Brotherhood, in treating me like this! He's
insane, beyond reason!* His fear now was that Ghezu
wouldn't kill him. There were worse things than death: however painful it was, it *was* an end.

Unclothed as he was, he had no way to end the torture
Ghezu was inflicting on him. All he had was a mattress, a

blanket and a sheet—even his jacket had been taken from him. The walls, though roughly carved from the rock, had no projections onto which he could tie anything. His meals were served without knife or fork, he had to use his hands to eat.

The temporary warmth his exertions had generated had gone now and he began to shiver again. The movement jarred his hand, reawakening the pain he'd managed to push a little distance from the forefront of his mind. Death was preferable to this. One thing all warriors feared was dying limb by limb. Better a clean death than living with a broken or maimed body.

An inch at a time, he'd said. The words echoed inside Kaid's head and he felt the fear grow. To have the strength to make one attack! Even if he didn't take Ghezu with him, the guards would be sure to kill him. But Ghezu was keeping him weakened with pain and the drug.

Forgetting his new injuries, he clenched his fists in anger, coming close to blacking out with the agony it caused.

Tallinu?

Gods, I'm still hallucinating! he thought, lightheaded.

Tallinu, damn you! Listen to me!

His reserves were gone, there was no more fight left in him. He let the dream flow through him.

Tallinu!

The tone was familiar. *Noni?*

Vartra be praised! You're still alive! Where are you?

Where am I? Why was she asking that? *The basement cells. But you aren't real, Noni.*

They're here, Tallinu, and they're coming to get you out! Hold on for just a little longer, and for the God's sake, boy, use that damned crystal so she can keep track of you! Ghezu's got that place sewn up tighter than a high-lander's purse! We're real, never fear.

What's real, Noni? I can't tell any more. The drug . . .

Touch the crystal, then you'll know what's real. Trust me. Have I ever lied to you, boy?

I don't know that I can hold out any longer. The admission hurt.

The crystal, Tallinu. Hold it, then you won't be alone, she'll be with you. Only an hour, maybe two at most, and we'll be there.

She'd gone. His mind was silent once more. There was an inevitability about the dreams: once they had started, he had no choice but to follow where the storyteller led. Twisting round slowly, he reached up under his pillow and tugged his sheet back till he could find the hole in which he'd hidden his crystal. Probing through the stuffing, his finger finally touched the leather bag and pulled it free. There was no reason not to do what she'd said, but he didn't believe anything would come of it. Holding the neck between his teeth, with his left hand he poked the opening wider till he could reach inside and take the crystal out.

As soon as his hand closed around it, it warmed to his touch, releasing memories, not of their time at Noni's as he'd expected, but of the dream meeting at the Valsgarth Shrine. He could smell her scent, sense her presence. Then he felt her unmistakable mental touch. Embarrassed, he backed away, only to find his mind held by hers.

Kaid, we're here. We got your message. Ghezu has been indicted for treason. We didn't wait for the warrant. One of Lijou's people is letting us in through the tunnels. Just keep hanging in there, Kaid. We . . . I . . . don't want to lose you again.

His thoughts were too confused to be coherent even to himself.

I'm keyed in to you now, Kaid. Put the crystal back into its pouch, but keep wearing it, and don't give up. I promise you we'll be with you soon.

He sat there for several minutes before rousing himself to return the crystal to its bag and putting it round his neck. Then he waited for Ghezu—or the dreams—to return.

*   *   *

Carrie hiked her robe up yet again as it got tangled between her ankles.

"Damned thing!" she muttered. "Never could stand skirts!"

"Ground's uneven here," said T'Chebbi from in front. "Watch your feet, Liegena."

Reaching out for the tunnel wall, Carrie used it to steady herself as she cautiously picked her way among the fallen debris. T'Chebbi's torch shed enough light for her to see by and she silently thanked Vartra that she had functional Sholan eyes. Had she had Human eyes, the journey would have been virtually impossible for her.

The first part had been easy. While she maintained a light contact with Kaid through the crystal, Kusac had mentally checked the tunnel ahead. Though not that dependable a talent, it made them feel more secure. Garras entered the code Kha'Qwa had given them into the keypad set into the concealed entrance in the hillside.

The technically abandoned tunnel was kept clear—mainly by students who had overstayed the curfew—of any small rocks and rubble that broke off from the roof or walls. They knew they'd come to their turning when they saw a brick wall off to one side. Blocked off a generation ago, it only took the removal of the loose bricks that Kha'Qwa had told them about, and they had a space large enough to crawl through. But the floor of the tunnel ahead was littered with the debris of countless minor rock movements.

Suddenly Carrie collided with T'Chebbi, letting out a surprised gasp. Behind her, Dzaka came to an abrupt stop.

People ahead. Friends of Kha'Qwa, I think, Kusac sent as they all started moving slowly again.

Beneath her fingers, the wall was damp and, in places, slimy to the touch. With a shudder of distaste, she pulled away from it, touching it only with her fingertips. T'Chebbi's flashlight glinted off the veins of crystal embedded in the rock walls around her.

Up front, Kusac and Garras disappeared into the darkness. The gap between the two groups had gradually increased as Carrie had slowed down.

We'll check out who's waiting up ahead, said Kusac. *Take your time, Carrie. This ground's treacherous.*

I'll have to! I'm having difficulty maintaining any contact with Kaid!

Why?

His mind's still behind those barriers of his. All I can really do is keep track of where the crystal is.

If they move him, let me know!

I will.

They weren't far behind Kusac and by the time they arrived, one of the females was telling him that unless they took out the main power system, there was no chance of disabling all the dampers. A couple of people were going after a few selected key units, though. With any luck it would allow them to communicate with Lijou and the outside world.

Among the group of half a dozen Brothers was a telepath Kusac recognized from his father's description—Vriuzu.

Catching Kusac's curious glance, Vriuzu's mouth opened in a slight grin and he held out his palm in greeting.

"Didn't think I'd ever see any of the Telepath Guild again," he said as Kusac responded. "I know you're not with them now," he added.

"It's good to know you're safe, and that you've found peace with your talent," said Kusac.

"I owe the Special Operatives my life. I'll gladly do anything I can to help one of them."

Kusac nodded his thanks, then turned to Carrie. "Have you still got a fix on Kaid?"

"Just. As I said, it's more of a fix on the crystal than him now. I can barely sense his presence," she said tiredly, leaning back against a dry section of the wall.

You shouldn't have come, Kusac sent, looking over at her, ears flicking in concern.

You need me to find him. What I'm getting is so faint, I could never have picked it up from Noni's. Besides, we owe him. Without him that sniper could have killed us during my Challenge.

Kusac could feel her still raw memories of that day. "Where is Kaid?" he asked quietly.

"West of here, on this level," she said, waving her hand in the direction they needed to take.

"She's right enough," said Rhayna, the obvious leader of the group of Brothers.

"I've got contact with Lijou," said Vriuzu suddenly. "The dampers are down between us and him."

"Make sure no one overhears you," warned Kusac. "Keep him up to date. We'll let him know when we need him. Right, let's go, Rhayna."

Rhayna took the lead as they turned a corner and stepped through the heavy wooden door that was the entrance to Stronghold.

Suddenly the light came on. Kaid stayed where he was, having no reason to move.

The door didn't open immediately but when it did, Zhaya stood in the doorway. He was alone. Moving to the side of the open door, he gestured with his stunner. "Get up," he ordered.

Kaid leaned on the bed with his good arm, levering himself tiredly to his feet. Cradling his right arm and hand, he turned and moved slowly toward him.

"You know what this stunner can do," said Zhaya. "So let's keep this civilized, shall we?" Holding him firmly by the good arm, he dragged Kaid along the corridor.

Kaid tried to keep his mind blank, to think of nothing, but gradually the forgotten memories of his last visit with Ghezu began to seep through from his subconscious. As Zhaya opened the door, he remembered the smell of his own freshly spilled blood so strongly he could taste its metallic tang in his mouth.

His tongue flicked out to moisten his lips only to find he'd bitten himself again. He thrust the memories aside, forcing his mind to become still once more. Attempting to control the pain was difficult enough without remembering and anticipating what was to come. He needed to focus all his attention on now. When his moment came, he had to see it and take it: he'd never get a second chance to end this.

"He's been moved," said Carrie.

"Where?" demanded Kusac, turning back to her.

"I don't know. All I felt was a sudden flare from him, then silence again. He's in danger, Kusac, that much I did get."

Kusac looked at Vriuzu.

He shook his head. "My Talent's sending, not receiving," he said.

"Rhayna, where would they take him?"

"It could be anywhere. Depends what they're doing with him. It wouldn't be to any of the common areas of Stronghold, that's all I can tell you."

"Lijou says try the interrogation rooms," said Vriuzu.

"Where?" demanded Kusac.

"Here," said Rhayna. "This level's where the old holding cells and interrogation rooms are. They're never used now because their facilities are so primitive."

"Take us there. Carrie, for the God's sake, try to find him!"

She nodded, her face pale with concentration and worry.

Ghezu was sitting at the desk when Zhaya and Kaid entered. He looked up from his comp pad.

"Sit down, Kaid. I'll be with you in a moment."

The wooden chair was in the same place as before. Kaid found himself walking over to it as if it was part of a well established ritual. How often had he been here? Once—or more? The fact that he didn't know disturbed him profoundly. Silently, he sat down, watching Zhaya walk across the room to stand behind his chair.

Ghezu continued to study the pad for several more minutes before putting it aside and getting to his feet.

"How's the hand today?" he asked, coming round to stand in front of him. As he reached out toward him, Kaid pulled back.

"It's your own fault," Ghezu said. A flick of his ear and Zhaya stepped forward to grasp Kaid by the shoulders, holding him firmly against the chair back.

"All you had to do was give me the codes. I'm not unreasonable." Again Ghezu reached out for Kaid's hand.

This time he couldn't pull away. As Ghezu took hold of him by the wrist and pulled his hand forward to examine it, a low mew of pain escaped him, and for the first time, he looked down at his injuries. His hand was distended, the fur matted with blood. Agony lanced through it and up his arm when Ghezu touched the two swollen outer fingers. The fourth one, the smallest, was missing.

"Nasty," said Ghezu, ears flicking in false concern. "The whole hand's badly inflamed. Still, we did a good job of cauterizing that finger, even if I do say it myself."

His touch was light but it was enough to make Kaid cry out again and try to twist free. Ghezu let his hand go and turned to walk back to his desk. "The others are only broken, Kaid. They should heal, given time."

Kaid held his hand close against his chest, barely conscious, the room seeming to recede around him. Rather than holding him still, Zhaya was now holding him upright.

"Let's start again, shall we?" he heard Ghezu say. "We'll use your left hand today, give the other one a chance to heal. Remember what I said to you. If I have to cut the information out of you an inch at a time, I'll do it. It's a matter of how many fingers you're willing to lose. Bring him over, Zhaya."

Zhaya hauled him to his feet and dragged him over to the desk. His left hand was pressed down onto the desktop and held there as Kaid fought to remain conscious and on his feet. Between his spread fingers, he could see the bloodstained white scars already in the wood's surface. His blood. Once again, his senses began to swim.

Gods! It was too soon! He had to do something before . . . ! His mind veered away from that. Leaning forward, he took several large breaths, trying to focus his thoughts. Already he could feel the sweat starting to form across the back of his shoulders.

Suddenly Ghezu leaned forward to grasp the leather bag hanging from Kaid's neck.

"What's this? Why haven't I noticed it before?" he asked sharply, using the thong to jerk Kaid's head closer.

"Leave it."

"Something else she gave you? Maybe I should take it, too."

Kaid said nothing, just stared.

Ghezu twisted the thong round his hand and pulled sharply, breaking it. He let it dangle in front of Kaid.

"I'll take everything you ever had, or hoped to have, Kaid. I already hold your life, and Khemu's bracelet. Now this little trinket." He began to open it.

The pressure on his left hand had eased a little. Zhaya was as intrigued as Ghezu as to what was in the leather pouch.

Concentrating all his remaining energy, Kaid twisted round and swung the elbow of his injured arm backward, catching Zhaya hard in the pit of his stomach. As the guard released him and doubled over retching, Kaid, hardly able to see through the haze of pain the blow had cost him, staggered away from the desk. Sight didn't matter, he *knew* where Ghezu was. Regaining his balance, he dropped into a crouch, ready to leap.

"I wouldn't, Kaid," said Ghezu, pointing his energy pistol at him. "It won't work. I can stop you without killing you, but do you really want to lose a leg? Isn't one finger enough?"

With a cry of pain, Carrie clutched her head and stumbled into T'Chebbi, who just managed to catch her before she fell.

Kusac was at his mate's side. Taking her from T'Chebbi, he held her close.

"What is it? What happened, Carrie?"

Although she was still trembling, she'd already begun to recover. "The crystal. Ghezu took the crystal from him," she said, pushing him away. "We've got to get there *now,* Kusac! Kaid's trying to make Ghezu kill him! Go! We'll follow!"

Are you sure you're all right?
Go!

He went, followed by all but Dzaka and Vriuzu.

"Send to Lijou now, Vriuzu," she said, leaning against the wall. "Tell him to bring Noni. She'll be needed." She looked up at Dzaka. "Don't even think of following them," she said, her tone uncompromising. "You're here to protect me, not get yourself killed because of Ghezu's Contract." She held her hand out to him.

He took it, pulling her upright till she could lean on his arm. "I'll say with you, Liegena," he said.

"You don't need to like it," she said, aware that her tone had been sharper than she'd intended. "Believe me, I'd be there with them if I could, but I've got other responsibilities too."

Dzaka looked down at her, mouth opening in a small grin. "So we have, Liegena. Thank you for reminding me."

Her hand tightened reassuringly on his arm. "I'll know as soon as Kusac does, Dzaka. It's almost as good as being there. They'll be in time, don't worry."

As Kaid hesitated, the door exploded inward in a shower of splinters and smoke. Kusac and Garras appeared in the opening, rifles trained on Ghezu and the still retching Zhaya.

"We've got a warrant for your arrest, Ghezu," said Kusac, his voice cold and dispassionate. "High treason. I suggest you put down the gun and surrender quietly."

Ghezu moved swiftly, grabbing Kaid and pressing the pistol to the side of his head. "I think not," he said, backing away toward a door at the rear of the room. "You want your friend alive, don't you?"

The sound of running feet could be heard echoing in the corridor behind Kusac and Garras.

"Just keep your people under control and no one need get hurt," said Ghezu, stopping at the door. As he changed his grip on Kaid to fumble for the door handle, his gun knocked against his captive's injured hand. Soundlessly Kaid began to crumple, dragging Ghezu down with him. Dropping him, in one fluid move, Ghezu had the door open and was gone.

"Damn!" swore Kusac, running toward the door, Garras close behind him. "Where does it lead?"

"No idea. My bet is it joins the lower corridor," said Garras. He turned to the Brothers behind him. "Four of you double back and cut him off at the other end," he ordered. "The rest, come with us." A movement at the main doorway caught his eye. "Dzaka, stay here with Carrie and see to your father. T'Chebbi, see to Zhaya." With that, he was gone, hard on Kusac's heels.

Carrie ran across the room and knelt down beside Kaid. His injuries, past and present, were only too visible.

"Oh God," she said softly. "What has Ghezu done to him?" She looked up at Dzaka, who was obviously as shaken as she was.

"We need to move him. He can't lie here on the floor," she said.

"I'll see if there's anyone outside," Dzaka replied, straightening up.

"No need," said Lijou as he and Kha'Qwa entered. He glanced momentarily at the shattered doorway. "We can lift Kaid between us. Noni's not far behind."

Carrie got to her feet and looked hastily round the room. "The desk," she said. "I'll clear it if you lift him."

Running over to it, she picked up the comp pad and swept the rest of the clutter onto the floor. The pad she placed on the wooden chair.

As Lijou and Dzaka gently laid Kaid on the desk, Carrie saw the expressions on their faces.

Lijou looked up, meeting her eyes. "If I'd known what was happening , . ." he began.

Carrie reached out to touch his arm. "It's not your fault, Lijou. It was your warning that alerted us to the possibility of Kaid being here. There was nothing more you could do without risking your own life. Ghezu had the place damped. You weren't to know it was because of Kaid."

"There are times when I wish we telepaths *could* inflict pain, because as Vartra's my witness, if I could get my hands on Ghezu now . . ." he growled.

A small whimper of pain, quickly silenced, came from Kaid as he began to stir.

"I suggest we leave," said Kha'Qwa, touching Lijou on the arm to attract his attention. "For Kaid's sake."

Lijou looked up at her. "Yes. Of course. We have to see to the rest of the Brothers now. They need to be informed of what's happened. I'll call an assembly in the temple. You can handle Zhaya, can't you? T'Chebbi ought to remain here with them."

"With pleasure," said Kha'Qwa with a growl, going over to take him from T'Chebbi. Zhaya, still doubled up in pain, his wrists secured behind him, was unceremoniously dragged from the room.

Kaid's body spasmed, jolting him back to consciousness.

"Lie still," said Carrie, moving round till she was sure he could see her face. "It's over, Kaid. You're safe now."

Eyes more than half-covered by their inner lids looked blindly at her. She took his face between her hands, leaning closer, trying to catch his gaze. "Kaid, this is Carrie. This is real. We're here. It's truly over now."

Slowly his eyes began to focus on her. His left hand came up to take hers, carrying it to his mouth and placing her fingers inside. His tongue touched them, pressing them gently against the roof of his mouth.

Puzzled, she glanced at Dzaka.

"He's tasting your scent," he said quietly. "It's more sensitive than using our noses."

She looked back at Kaid as he removed her hand from his mouth.

"You're real this time, aren't you?" he mumbled, tightening his grip on her hand as he lowered it to his chest.

"It was all real, Kaid. Even the first time you saw me," she said, reaching out to stroke his forehead. "Noni will be here any moment. Rest for now."

His eyes flickered briefly, then he lapsed into unconsciousness again.

"Dzaka, see if Noni's out there yet," said Carrie, looking over to where he stood opposite her.

He shook his head. "I can't, Liegena. I've been told to remain with you. And I want to stay with my father," he added.

"T'Chebbi, you go, please," she said, fretting as she looked over toward the doorway.

Minutes later, T'Chebbi called out to her. "The Stronghold physician is here, Liegena."

Carrie looked up, torn between knowing Kaid needed treatment now and her desire to wait for Noni.

The physician solved her problem by ordering her to move. His examination was quick but thorough, and in short order, Kaid had been given the drugs he needed to relieve the pain and deal with any infection.

"I'm giving him a sedative too," he said, administering a

final shot. "If this Noni of yours is going to see to his wounds, it would be better if he wasn't conscious. Why you want to use an unqualified, guildless female, I've no idea," he said, packing away his instruments.

"Cos they got more sense than you have," barked Noni as she stomped in leaning on her stick. "If he's sedated, you could have brought him to me on one of those floater things," she grumbled as she made her way over to them. "I hope Kaid realizes I don't do this for just anybody. First time I've come this far to a patient in fifteen years!"

"I just hope you know what you're doing," the physician said, preparing to leave. He handed a small phial of bright green liquid to Carrie. "You'll need this," he said. "The drug should be out of his system by now, but if it isn't, at least I've got what's left from that damned medic of mine!"

"Drug? What drug?" demanded Carrie, catching hold of him to prevent him leaving.

"The drug Ghezu gave him." He indicated Kaid. "It's an off-world one he got for that desert maniac, Fryak, or whatever he's called—except that's the refined drug, and it's far more powerful than the sap. Ghezu wanted me to use it on your friend and I refused. It hasn't even been analyzed yet, we don't know what it does! In the end, Ghezu bribed my medic to use it."

"Who gave it to him?"

"I already told you, Ghezu, and my medic," he said, using his free hand to pry himself loose from Carrie's grip. "I know nothing more about it. Now, if you don't mind, I've got duties elsewhere. Finding my medic for one! I'll see he's expelled from the Medical Guild for this!"

"We'll sort it out, never fear," said Noni. She looked hard at Carrie. "So you've decided he matters to you and you're going to have him, have you? Huh! Might be the most sensible thing he's done in years, if you can get him to bed you!" she said, ignoring Carrie and Dzaka's outraged exclamations. "Now, both of you, get out of my way. Give me space to work. Go and sit down somewhere."

In the distance they heard the sound of an alarm.

"The meeting call," said T'Chebbi as Carrie and Noni glanced fearfully at the doorway.

The whole business of announcing Ghezu's dishonorable expulsion from the Brotherhood went a lot more smoothly than Lijou had anticipated. He was surprised to find how many of the senior, and some of the junior staff, supported the change. Kha'Qwa wasn't. With the help of Rhyaz as a stand-in for Ghezu, Lijou was now in sole charge of the Guild pending the appointment of a new Warrior leader.

Meanwhile, Kusac and Garras' chase after Ghezu had proved fruitless. Throughout the building and the surrounding area, an intensive search was mounted, but the Brotherhood's Warrior Master had vanished. General Raiban was not impressed when she heard the news. The search was immediately augmented by her people from the Forces, who also relieved them of Zhaya and his three accomplices.

For all her grumbling about medics and physicians, Noni had done very little for Kaid, mainly reassuring herself that his life was in no danger. She had him loaded onto a floater, then taken by aircar to her house.

"Garras, you and Dzaka are coming with me. Get in. The rest of you folk can stay away," she said from the doorway of the aircar before it took off. "You'll only clutter up my place. I need peace and space to work. You can see him tomorrow."

Several Brothers were relocated to ensure that Carrie, Kusac and T'Chebbi were found rooms as close to Lijou's as possible. Left high and dry as they were without any further news on Kaid's condition, it was some time before any of them was able to settle down for what remained of the night.

Despite the knowledge that the cottage was almost better guarded than Stronghold, Dzaka and Garras camped out in Noni's livingroom cum kitchen, determined that if Ghezu was still in the area, he'd get nowhere near Kaid again.

While he slept, with Garras' help, Noni had Kaid washed down with a special potion of antiseptic herbs.

"His back's healing," she said, gently testing the scabs. "But whoever caused these wounds knew what he was doing."

"Kusac said he'd been stunned on full immediately before being flogged," said Garras grimly. "I want not only Fyak, but the one who used that whip."

"Don't you go sinking to their level now," warned Noni as

she sat back in her chair, gesturing for him and Dzaka to turn Kaid over.

"I'll do what I have to, Noni," he said, gently easing his friend over onto his back.

"His back'll need massaging," she said, leaning forward to spread a clean cloth over the bedding beside her. Carefully she moved Kaid's damaged limb onto it.

As she gently felt over the swollen surface of the hand before working down to what remained of the little finger, Kaid began to mutter and twitch in obvious pain again.

"Hold him still," she ordered Garras. "I don't want him moving this hand while I'm working on it." She leaned closer to Kaid, beginning to croon to him as she carefully explored the extent of his injuries.

" 'Tis all right, lad. It's just old Noni. Rest easy, you're safe now."

As he began to quiet, she moved on to the next finger, taking it carefully by the sides and feeling along its length.

Again Kaid began to moan, trying to move his hand free but Garras held his arm firmly down.

"This one's shattered," she said, shaking her head as she moved to the next one. "A clean break here, Vartra be praised. Pass me the dish and those swabs on the table, Dzaka. I need to soak the blood off him before I can see how bad that stump of a finger is."

Dzaka released Kaid's shoulders and got up to fetch the shallow tray of antiseptic from the table.

Lifting his hand carefully, Noni immersed it in the greenish-colored liquid, gently dabbing at the injured fingers and the stump.

"Hold his arm again for me, Garras."

Gradually the water became darker as the blood began to dissolve from the matted fur.

"The towel," she said, lifting Kaid's hand out and letting the worst of the water run off back into the tray.

Garras handed it to her and, lifting the tray, passed it to Dzaka.

"Why did Ghezu do this to him?" Dzaka demanded, voice thick with suppressed fury as he returned from replacing the dish on the table. "Why torture him like this?"

"Have done with that anger, brat," snapped Noni as she gently dried Kaid's hand before replacing it on the cloth. "You should know better than to project in the company of telepaths! Didn't they teach you anything in that bird's nest up there?"

"Sorry," he muttered, flattening his ears in apology, tail twitching with embarrassment. "But how can anyone be callous enough to systematically smash someone's hand like that?"

Garras looked up at him. "You're a Brother and you ask that?"

"That's different," said Dzaka defensively. "We don't use torture. When we have to kill, we do it cleanly, without causing unnecessary suffering."

"There's many wouldn't differentiate between us and him, lad," Garras replied, turning back as he felt Kaid's arm twitch under his grip. "And yes, some of the Brothers know how to use torture, but not crudely like this." He looked over at Noni again. "Can you save the third finger?"

"Maybe, maybe not. It needs to be cut open and the bigger pieces of bone fitted back together. Once that's done, I can try healing it. It depends on how many large pieces are left. This needs cutting too," she said, indicating the stump. "It's been burned to seal the wound. It needs a pad of flesh and skin over the end, else the bone will keep cutting its way through. The third finger's easy. It just needs setting. The rest of his hand's intact, thank Vartra! It's only secondary swelling."

She sat back, closing her eyes and rubbing her temples. "Garras, I've changed my mind. You get that Ghezu for me. Get him good," she said, her voice harder than he'd ever heard it before. She put her hands down and opened her eyes, looking straight at him. "A person as brutal as him doesn't deserve to be treated any different."

"I'll get him, never fear, Noni."

"I want him too, Garras," said Dzaka.

Garras glanced up at the youth, seeing the bleak look in his eyes and the set of his ears. "We'll get him together."

"Dzaka, lad, brew some c'shar for us, please. I could do with a drink before I start cutting those fingers."

Dzaka nodded and went over to the old stove.

In the silence that followed, Noni gave a small cackle of laughter. "I forgot you young ones can only use dispensers! Garras, tell him what to do while I get my implements. When you're done, get some of that anaesthetic of yours from your bag of tricks. He'll need to be deep under for longer than I can keep him with my herbs alone."

* * *

Early the next morning, Kusac and Carrie arrived at Noni's to see Kaid. A strong antiseptic smell greeted them. They shared a worried glance before entering.

Noni and Garras were sitting at the table drinking c'shar. Dzaka lay curled up asleep in an easy chair.

"Early rising for you, late night for us," Noni said as Carrie came over to the table and Kusac continued to hover uncertainly in the doorway.

"How is he?"

Noni sighed. "Better. He's sleeping off my butchery."

Garras stirred, looking up tiredly at her. "Hardly butchery, Noni. You did a good job."

"Well, we'll see," she said. "Fetch yourselves a drink."

Kusac stepped over to the bed to look at Kaid. He lay sleeping on his side. His right hand, heavily bandaged, lay above the covers. Though now clean and free of the matted knots, his pelt was still dull. Glancing at Noni, Kusac said, "He looks bad."

"Huh! If you think that's bad, as well you didn't see him last night," she said.

Dzaka uncurled himself from his chair and stretched. "I'll get you both a drink."

"Thanks," said Carrie, sitting down.

"You just want to show off, now you can work my range," snorted Noni, glaring at him above her mug.

Dzaka's mouth opened in a faint grin.

"That's better," she said approvingly. "He's not going to die, lad. Keep that long face for those that need it. He doesn't."

Kusac joined them. "How is his hand?"

"Not as bad as I first feared," Noni admitted. "Only three fingers had been damaged. One was a straight break; one, as you know, had been removed and the wound badly cauterized; the last—well, we don't know yet. Garras and I spent most of last night taking out tiny splinters of bone and trying to rebuild what was left. If it starts to knit in the next twenty-six hours, I can encourage the growth of new bone to reinforce what's left. Luckily the joint wasn't damaged. He might even be able to use it again when it's healed."

"You found out what happened?"

"Mostly," said Garras. "What he couldn't tell us, we pieced together from his injuries."

"He was conscious last night?" asked Carrie.

"Unfortunately, yes. He came round not long after we operated on his hand. It took some time for the analgesics to work, he was feverish, and . . . he talked," sighed Garras, putting his mug down. "We were up with him all night, until a couple of hours ago."

"So what happened?" asked Kusac, glancing up at Dzaka with a nod of thanks as a mug of c'shar was placed in front of him.

"No. Tell us about his other injuries first," said Carrie, putting her hand on Garras' arm.

"His back's healing cleanly. With any luck, his pelt will grow back normally, leaving no scars. Likewise the rope cuts round his wrists. The ones on his face are superficial." He looked over at Noni, waiting for her to tell the rest.

"They used a drug on him, one that confused his senses. It was while he was under the effects of it that he managed to appear to us," said Noni. "It's one of those off-world ones, just as that physician said last night."

"How did he manage to come to us?" asked Carrie.

"I've no idea," said Garras. "He certainly hasn't. Part of the problem last night was that he didn't believe he was here. He was afraid to sleep lest he wake up back at Stronghold."

Kusac turned round to look over at Kaid again. "He looks peaceful enough now, Vartra be praised. How did Ghezu get hold of him?"

"We assume Ghezu made a pact with Fyak concerning supplying him with weapons and drugs if he would place a watch on Khemu's home. Kaid was supposed to be taken and handed over to Ghezu. It seems Fyak had other plans for him. He wanted Kaid to train his troops."

He stopped to take another drink from his mug. "The medic at Chezy kept Kaid unconscious there for two weeks while his arm finished healing."

Dzaka made a small noise of apology.

"When he recovered, he agreed to train Fyak's troops in the hope of gathering enough evidence against Ghezu before escaping, only he was found out. As you already know, Fyak had him flogged after personally shooting him with a neural stunner on full power."

"The pain must have been indescribable," said Carrie quietly.

"It's a wonder he survived it," said Kusac. "L'Seuli says he passed out several times. Then Ghezu came for him and he was taken to Stronghold, where he was tortured again." Kusac's voice was full of suppressed anger.

Garras nodded. "From then on we have a fair idea of the sequence of events, not the dates. Ghezu overdosed him with a drug that caused him to hallucinate. It was supposed to react to his state of mind at the time and alter his sense of reality. It also enhanced his senses, adding to his mental confusion. Each dream was experienced as if it were real and just as he began to believe it was, he was flung into another. It was during one of his semi-lucid periods that Ghezu took him into the interrogation room. Kaid made the mistake of assuming it was another dream. He had no way of knowing that a great deal of what had happened was real, that somehow he'd actually physically been to the places he thought he was dreaming about—like the Shrine when he saw you, Carrie."

"Was it bi-location?" asked Kusac.

"You'd know more about that than I would. There was no one with him to tell us if his body remained in the room at Stronghold while he talked to Carrie at the estate."

"Why did Ghezu torture him? Surely it wasn't all because of Khemu?" asked Carrie.

"Yes, and no," said Garras. "He wanted the codes for your estate security. Once he knew that Dzaka really was Kaid and Khemu's son, he wanted him dead. He also wanted you two dead so he could control the remaining mixed Leska pairs. With you gone, he knew the others would have to remain members of the Brotherhood. Kaid refused to tell him, so Ghezu began by cutting off one finger and, when he still refused, he went further, smashing two more fingers, probably with the pommel of his knife. Kaid said that's when he realized it wasn't a dream. Which is why he didn't believe you and Noni when you sent to him yesterday." He stopped, looking from Kusac to Carrie.

"You were right when you said Kaid was going to try and force Ghezu to kill him."

"But I told him we were on our way!" said Carrie.

"You weren't here last night when he was convinced that at any time, without warning, he'd find himself back with Ghezu. Believe me when I tell you that after seeing what he went through last night, I'm not surprised he has problems knowing what's real. I want Ghezu," said Garras, his eyes becoming as hard as glittering stones, and his voice dropping to a low snarl. "I want to rip him apart piece by piece till nothing remains."

"Do you think Kaid knows he's safe now?" asked Carrie, filling the ominous silence that fell after Garras finished talking.

"We won't know till he wakes," said Noni. "I couldn't touch his mind last night. If I'd tried, I'd only have made him worse. I'm afraid his mind will have to heal itself."

Kusac pushed his chair back angrily, getting to his feet and starting to pace the room. "Ghezu's got to be found," he said, tail lashing from side to side and ears folding back.

"What he did is utterly inhuman," said Carrie, her voice no less angry. "Someone that evil doesn't deserve to live."

"He won't," said Garras, lifting his mug again.

Noni slowly pushed herself up to her feet. "I've got to rest," she said. "So do Garras and Dzaka. Will you stay till the afternoon? We aren't leaving him alone in case he wakes and thinks he's still dreaming. There's a stew in the pot on the range. It only wants heating. Help yourselves."

"We'll stay," said Carrie. "You get some sleep. If he wakes, we'll fetch you."

Noni nodded. "You got blankets in your aircar?" she asked.

"Yes. Why?" asked Kusac, stopping in mid-stride.

"If you fetch them in, these two can bed down on the floor in my room so's they can get some peace. Reckon I'll be safe enough alone with them, more's the pity," she cackled.

"I'll fetch them," Kusac said with the ghost of a smile.

It was late afternoon before Kaid began to stir. Carrie was sitting at the table dozing, head cradled on her crossed arms while Kusac watched him.

Seeing him begin to move, Kusac got up and went over to sit on the bed beside him. Kaid's movements stilled but Kusac knew he was awake.

"Kaid, it's me, Kusac," he said quietly, reaching out to

touch his good hand reassuringly. "You're here at Noni's. Can I get you anything?"

Kaid's outer eyelids opened slowly and he turned his head to look up at him. The inner lids were still partly closed and Kusac could feel the pain radiating from him.

His tongue flicked out as he opened his mouth to speak. "Water, please," he croaked.

Kusac got up and fetched him a mugful from the faucet. He held it against Kaid's lips, but he made a noise of denial, moving his head aside before beginning to push himself up into a sitting position, his injured hand held close against his chest.

He took the mug from Kusac and began to drink slowly, his eyes never leaving the other's face.

There was an emptiness about them that worried Kusac. "I'll fetch Noni," he said, getting up.

"No!" said Kaid sharply.

Kusac sat down again. "All right," he agreed.

Kaid finished the water and handed the mug back to Kusac. "How did I get here?" he asked.

"Garras and Dzaka brought you here yesterday."

"Yesterday? How long have I been here?"

Kusac looked at his wrist comm. "Twelve and a half hours," he said. "You *are* here, Kaid. There's been two people watching you constantly since you arrived."

"Where's Ghezu?" The words were delivered in an emotionless voice that brought a chill to Kusac's heart.

"He escaped. The Brothers are still out looking for him. We're safe here, Lijou has the place surrounded, so has Raiban. She's after him for treason."

Kaid nodded, then lay back against the pillows.

"How do you feel?"

"Better than I have for . . ." Kaid stopped. His ears began to fold backward, then righted themselves.

"You've been at Stronghold for nearly two weeks," said Kusac compassionately.

"That long?" said Kaid.

They sat in silence for several minutes before Kusac spoke again. "I have something for you," he said, taking the bracelet from his pocket and handing it to him. "A bonding bracelet. Khemu's?"

A look of anger flashed across Kaid's face. "No. Ghezu

stole hers from me. This one's mine. Fyak's medic took it from her body and kept it for me."

"L'Seuli got it from him for you. He said she was dead. I'm sorry."

"Don't be. It was quick. I gave her a poison capsule. She used it when Fyak's men took us."

Kusac nodded, then reached forward to touch Kaid's left hand again. "I'm glad you're still with us," he said, gently tightening his grip. "Carrie was able to find you because of the crystal you're wearing."

Kaid closed his eyes, his hand responding with a tiny movement before he removed it from Kusac's grasp. "Ghezu took that too," he said bleakly.

"No. You're wearing it again, Kaid. T'Chebbi found it on the floor in the interrogation room. Noni tied it back round your neck before you left Stronghold. Let me go and fetch her," he said, getting up. "Carrie's at the table. You aren't on your own." He waited for a response but there was none. Stifling a sigh, he went to the bedroom to rouse Noni.

She stomped in a few minutes later, followed by Garras and Dzaka. Going to the sink first, she washed and dried her hands, then went over to the bed. Plonking herself down beside him, she reached for Kaid's injured hand.

"I'm going to look at your hand, Tallinu," she said. "Don't pull away! Garras, give him some more of that pain relief stuff of yours," she said, holding onto his wrist. "Dzaka, fetch my flat dish and mix two parts of warm water with one of my herb potions, same as you did last night," she ordered. "Carrie, stir yourself, girl!" she called out. "Get a fresh cloth, dressings and swabs from my cupboard over by the table. And the pot of ointment you'll find there."

Kaid opened his eyes. "There's no need to fuss over me like this, Noni. I'm fine."

"Fine is it!" she said as Garras stepped past her to administer the analgesic. "If that's the case, then humor an old female, lad." She took her scissors from the night table and began to cut the dressing free.

"It can't be that good if you're admitting to being old," said Kaid tiredly, closing his eyes again.

Noni snorted her contempt and continued with her cutting.

Carrie came over with the pot and dressings which she put beside the elderly Sholan. "Where do you want the cloth?" she asked.

"Spread it under here," she said, indicating with a flick of her ear where she was working.

Carrie did as she was asked, then joined Kusac at the other side of the bed, watching as Noni gently peeled the bandages back to reveal the wounds beneath.

Kaid heard Carrie's sharp intake of breath. It was still bad then. His hand twitched automatically, making him wince with pain.

"Now hold still, Tallinu. The dish, Dzaka," Noni said.

Dzaka placed it under his father's hand and retreated.

Noni supported Kaid's hand with hers, tilting it this way and that as she examined her handiwork. She reached for a swab, immersing it in the liquid then squeezing it out before she gently wiped the residual blood away from the wounds.

Kaid let out a low hiss, his hand twitching involuntarily again.

"Be thankful it does hurt," said Noni tartly. "At least we know there's no nerve damage."

Even as he growled in response, Kaid felt the pain begin to dissolve as the analgesic cut in.

"Well, the swelling's going down," Noni said at last. "It looks as if you might have got away without an infection." She looked up at him. "We might even have saved that finger."

Noni placed his hand on the cloth and, opening the pot, started to spread the ointment on one of the dressings.

Carrie leaned over to touch Kaid's shoulder. He looked round at her, opening his eyes tiredly.

"Don't worry. Your finger'll be all right," she said reassuringly.

His ears flicked once and, closing his eyes again, he looked away.

Noni finished bandaging his hand and turned to look at the wounds on his cheek. An application of her ointment and she was finished. She knew he was feigning sleep and took advantage of that to sign to Garras to give him a sedative.

As he felt the hypoderm a second time, Kaid's eyes flew open and he pushed himself up on one arm.

"No sedatives!" he said, a look of panic in his eyes as they began to glaze over.

Noni reached out and taking hold of the thong round his neck, cut it with her scissors, pulling it free. Opening the pouch, she took the crystal out and placed it in his left hand.

"Hold the crystal, Tallinu. You can't lose us if you hold onto it," she said. "Tell him, Carrie. Tell him it's his anchor to you."

Puzzled, Carrie looked from Kusac to Noni.

"Tell him!" Noni insisted.

Carrie reached forward and placed her hand over Kaid's, closing it around the crystal. "It's your anchor, Kaid. You can't get lost if you hold it," she said quietly.

The drug was rapidly taking effect. Kaid's hand opened enough for her fingers to slip through his into his larger palm alongside the crystal, then he closed it tightly, trapping both her and the stone in his grasp.

His eyes flickered, then shut as he slipped back down onto the bed, deep in a drugged sleep.

"Um. I can't get my hand free," said Carrie, looking up at Noni.

"Then you'll have to wait till his hand relaxes," she said. "Dzaka, Kusac, clear away all my stuff, would you?"

Carrie's arm was stretched uncomfortably across the bed to Kaid's hand. "Noni, I can't sit like this. Can't you open his hand for me?"

Noni's eyes fixed on her. "Your hand and that crystal are the only things keeping him sane at the moment," she said sternly. "And you want to move? No, girl, you hike yourself across that bed and sit this side! He'll let go of you soon enough when he relaxes. He's still afraid this is all a dream."

On you go, cub, sent Kusac. *It's little enough to do considering all he's been through.*

Carrie scrambled across to sit beside Noni, trying not to lean on Kaid as she did so. "Why me, Noni? Why should he see me as his anchor?"

"In a minute, child. Dzaka, take Kusac to my herb garden and show him the herbs I pick for my ointment. I need to make a new batch and if he's going to be about here for several days, he'd better learn where everything is. Garras, you go out to the aircar and call that mate of yours and have more drugs sent out here. Yes, I know I usually use herbs," she snapped, "but they take longer and he needs to be healed as quick as possible if I'm to save his finger!"

"I didn't say a thing, Noni," said Garras with a grin.

Noni waited until the males had all gone off on their separate tasks, then turned back to the human female.

"It's you he kept coming back to, Carrie. First time you

could only sense him, next time he was actually there. He's your third, with a link to you so you can bind the three of you together to walk the Fire Margins. No wonder he's drawn to you." She touched Carrie's face fleetingly. "He's been through a terrible ordeal in these past weeks, child. Do what you can to strengthen him. He's still disoriented, unable to tell what's real. I think there's still a residue of the drug in his system. He trusts you: you're the only solid, dependable person in his world at the moment. It isn't easy for him to know he's facing a fear he can't control."

"But why me, Noni?" she asked, a puzzled look on her face. "I'd have thought an old friend like Garras was a much more likely anchor than me."

Noni sighed. "Another one who needs to hear it confirmed before she'll believe! Because you matter to him, of course! The drug responded to his state of mind, and took him to you. Use your head, girl! Now, enough talk. The males are returning and it's time we ate."

Chapter 17

Two days had passed since Kaid had been brought to Noni's. Physically he was improving, but the psychological impact of his imprisonment would take much longer to heal. At times he still woke suddenly, not knowing where he was and whether what he saw around him was real.

It was midafternoon, and Kusac sat in the garden with Noni while Carrie showered.

"You leave her here with me," she said. "They need to pair to complete the Triad. It won't happen with you here too."

"I know," he said, keeping his eyes away from her. "It's just that . . ."

"Jealous? That's a rare emotion for one of us, but then, you aren't just one of us anymore. Listening to the Human side, are you? And you with a Human life-mate that's becoming almost more Sholan than you! Huh! Make me laugh, you do! Think Sholan, boy! That scrap of a youngling female loves you more than anyone yet born! Only ones she'll love as much as you will be your cubs, you can rest safe in that, young Aldatan!"

"You're right, of course, and I know it," he admitted, looking up at her. "Our bond is so close, Noni. I don't know how I'll feel when she . . ."

"What about that Vanna female you pair with now and then?" she interrupted. "Does your life-mate flex her claws and growl? Does she go into a *hunt* state, have hysterics? Does she insist on sharing it mentally with you?"

"No, of course not! But since Garras moved onto the estate . . ."

"Does your Carrie think you love her less for being with Vanna now and then, or does she grudge either of you a little of what you and she share?"

"No!"

"Then why should *you* have a problem?" she demanded.

"It isn't just anyone! It's someone you trust, someone you like! Just as she can let you be with Vanna, you'll find you can let her be with Tallinu. She's not going to love you any the less, you know."

Kusac looked away again, mentally squirming under her sharp comments.

She leaned forward, patting him on the hand. "Rest easy, boy. She cares about Tallinu, but not like she loves you. Be thankful it's him that's the third. He'll never cross either you or her."

"What about him? Does he care for her?" he asked.

"Ah, that's one you'll have to ask him. I will tell you he's afraid of pairing with her—partly because of his loyalty to you. You need to speak to him, but not now, after."

"After," Kusac nodded with a sigh, flexing his claws.

"Leave them alone here for a bit. Let them get easy with each other. They'll not pair first time out on the estate. She's never had a lover but you, she's afraid too. Go to your Vanna when the time comes—you'll know when. Meanwhile, Dzaka can bring her back every four days. I'll get Lijou to send someone to guard us while he's gone. I could do with her help anyway."

He nodded, then looked sharply toward the back door as Carrie came out wrapped in her toweling robe. "You shouldn't be out here," he said. "You'll catch a chill."

"I felt your concern," she said, going over to him.

Leaning on her stick, Noni pushed herself to her feet. "I've things to do before I go out," she said.

Carrie took her seat and they sat in silence till Noni had disappeared indoors.

"What's wrong?" she asked quietly, reaching out to put her hand in his. "Is it about Kaid?"

"We've never really talked about this Triad, cub," he said, tightening his grasp on her hand. "We try to avoid it. I think we have to talk now."

"Just before we leave for the estate? Wouldn't it be better left till we're at home?"

"We need to talk. I know I say this was a joint decision, but do you feel that I pushed you into agreeing to the En'Shalla rituals?"

"No, you didn't push me," she said. "It *was* a joint decision. I want us to be free, and like you, I'm prepared to do what it takes to achieve that."

"What about Kaid? Are you agreeing to this Triad just to please me?"

She glanced away.

He could feel her reluctance to discuss the subject, then he sensed her resolve harden as the inner strengths that had served them so well in the past came to the fore.

"To be with you, Kusac, I had to turn my back on everything I'd been taught, everything I'd been brought up with. It wasn't easy, but it was what I wanted to do. Humans have very little understanding of me and why I want to be with you, none at all of why I want to have your cubs." She looked up at him.

"Our daughter is who *we* are, neither Sholan nor Human, but both. What we want is worth fighting for, Kusac. Is it the Sholan you that's concerned, or your perception of my Human side? I asked myself that question. Hell," she grinned wryly, "I'm sunk already among Humans, no matter what I do! And Sholans don't care whether I've got a lover or not!"

He leaned forward, caressing her face with his hand. "Cub, the Sholan me feels no jealousy for Kaid, just sadness that he can only touch the edge of what we share. I hope he finds someone who'll bring to him everything that you've brought to me."

His hands sought hers as, standing, he pulled her up into his arms.

"My worry is that we're forcing this on him," she said, resting her head against his chest. "That he'll do this out of loyalty. If he does, I hope I never find out."

"I don't believe he will, though he keeps his mind so tightly closed it's impossible to tell." He rubbed his cheek against the top of her head, holding her as close as he could. "It's no different from the times I've shared with Vanna, cub," he said softly. "We've more control over our link now, we know it's not a problem if the lover is known and liked by both of us. The same will be true with Kaid, you'll see. Just remember, he's not like me, he has no Human side to him. What we take for granted, he won't know, and not being a telepath, he can't read from you."

"I'll remember." She looked up at him. "You want me to stay here, don't you?"

"You have to. Once this last link is forged, then we can go to the Fire Margins and gain our freedom, as well as finding the answers we need to so many questions. Kaid's imprisonment has reminded me how fragile all our lives are. Once we've been, we'll have bought the freedom of not only people like us, but untold generations of our children. We have to go there, and soon."

"I never saw myself as a seductress," she murmured. "I wonder how it's done."

Kusac laughed, picking her up and swinging her into his arms. "You don't have to do anything, cub! Just the fact that you exist was seduction enough for me!" He began to walk indoors with her. "You get some rest," he said, putting her down on the spare bed they'd placed in Noni's bedroom for her. "Don't forget, while Noni's got the damper on, I can't reach you, you'll have to come outside. Dzaka can bring you home tomorrow evening."

"Are you sure you'll be all right?"

"Sure. I've plenty of work to do on the data Esken brought the other day, and I want to see what Ghyan's made of it."

She clung to him for a moment. "Take care," she said before kissing him.

"Always."

* * *

Ahead of them, Jo could just see the lights of the town glowing against the darkening sky. They were all tired and cold, none more so than she with the wet hem of her skirt flapping against the short ankle boots she was wearing. A town meant hot water, hot food, dry beds and dry clothes!

"Almost there," said Davies.

Jo grunted, too tired for words. They'd been traveling through this fresh, loose snow now for two days, and she was heartily sick of it. It clung to her boots, making walking more like paddling with all the extra effort it entailed.

Gradually the lights got nearer until at last they were approaching the arched gateway into the town.

"What now?" muttered Jo to Kris. "They don't seem to be stopping anyone."

"Brazen it out," said Kris. "There's no reason why we shouldn't be allowed in."

To either side of the gate, on the stone wall, large torches flickered. The last of the field workers trudged toward the lights, following in the path of a couple of mounted nobles.

They fell in behind the workers, keeping an eye on the guards.

These worthies suddenly sprang to life and began bellowing at the straggling line of which they were part, telling them to get a move on lest they be shut out for the night.

"Obviously for the benefit of the riders," said Davies.

He was right enough, as when the riders passed beneath the archway, there was much bowing and scraping from the guards.

They were the last through, and behind them they heard the squeaking and grinding of the ancient mechanism that closed the heavy wooden gates.

"Strick said to carry on down this main road till we came to the third street on the left," said Davies. "Then along there till we see the sign for the Silver Tree Inn."

"At least they keep their streets clear of snow," said Jo. She was getting a second wind now that the going was easier.

On either side of them, grime-covered buildings, packed too closely together for comfort or safety, loomed toward the night sky. The roadway was wider here on the main street, but they still had to dodge not only potholes but piles of noxious garbage thrown down from the dwellings above.

Kris turned an amused look on her. "This is civilization, Jo," he said.

"I know," she muttered, hopping from one frozen rut to another to avoid a puddle of God-knew-what.

After the silence of the mountains and the forest, the bustle and color around them was almost too much. Strident voices called out to each other as shops began to close for the night, and the night trade began to come to life. The smell was indescribable, a mixture of stale ale and rotten garbage overlaid with cooking.

They wound their way through the bustle, finding their side street with little difficulty. This area was quieter and Jo found the tight band of pain that had formed round her head was beginning to ease.

"I'll give your neck a rub later," said Kris, glancing at her as they headed for the building boasting a swinging sign of a silver tree. "You've been picking up the mental noise of the town, that's all."

"Never used to bother me before," she muttered, easing her pack across her shoulders.

"Just set up your mental blocks so they're active all the time," said Kris, taking her by the elbow and steering her toward the brightly lit doorway of the tavern.

The heat cast by the log fire that blazed in a central open fireplace, was the first real warmth any of them had felt since leaving the *Summer Bounty*. Jo made straight for it, the other two close behind. She started to open her cloak and unwrap the scarf from round her head and face, reveling in the heat.

A large, burly man detached himself from the counter at the other side of the room and made his way over to them. He threw what appeared to be a bundle of animal skins on the floor to one side of the grate and began warming his hands at the blaze.

Kris immediately sensed his interest in them and as he took his cloak off, he kept a wary eye on him.

"Travelers, are you?" His voice was deep, yet surprisingly quiet.

Kris nodded, folding his garment and putting it down on the floor at the other side of the fireplace. "Yes. We've just come in off the mountains," he said.

"You'll be staying a while, then."

"We plan to," said Davies, cloak over his arm as he turned round to warm his rear.

"Name's Railin," he said, reaching out to snag an empty chair from a nearby table. He set it down it beside Jo, gesturing for her to sit. "You look like your bones could do with plenty of warming," he said.

Thanking him, Jo threw her cloak over the back of it, then sank down gratefully onto it and let her body soak up the heat.

Railin hauled another chair over to the fire, then proceeded to plant his large frame in it. "No one's going to complain if we sit here awhile," he said to Kris and Davies.

Kris fetched a couple more chairs from an unused table which he and Davies put next to Jo's.

A tavern girl came bustling up. "These friends o' yours, Railin? Hope you're all goin' to order somethin' worthwhile, or I can't be lettin' you sit in front of the fire like this."

"Come on, Jainie," said Railin, "you can see they's just arrived here. Look at them! Wet through and dead beat! Let them warm themselves a bit."

"It's all right for you to talk! You ain't got Mippik peerin' over your shoulder!" she retorted.

"It's all right," said Kris. "We want some food, a room for the night, and four ales."

"Get them some of your stew," said Railin. He looked at Kris. "Don't ask what it is, just eat it," he advised.

"Watch it, or I'll tell Mippik what you said of his wife's cookin'," warned the girl with a grin, happy now that a large order had been placed. "You fetch a table over and I'll bring the drinks." With a swirl of her long skirts, she was gone.

"Is the stew that bad?" asked Jo, a concerned look on her face as she bent down to pull another bit of her skirt hem round to the fireside.

"Not really." A grin split the large man's face, making his teeth flash against his weather beaten complexion.

He had to be around fifty, Jo reckoned, but it was difficult to judge his age when his face was concealed by the long greying beard and mustache that blended so well with his shoulder length hair. His blue eyes regarded her humorously as he pulled an ancient pipe and an oiled pack of some smokeable herbs out of his pocket.

Kris and Davies got up and fetched over the table that they'd denuded of chairs. They placed it beside Jo, allowing her to continue sitting beside the fire.

"You are joining us, aren't you?" said Kris, as he moved his chair to the other side of the table. "I ordered an ale for you."

"Yes, thanks, young man, I will," he said, rising up slowly from his chair and bringing it over to join them. "What brings you to Kalador? It's bad weather to be traveling the mountains."

"We're passing through. Our family's wintering in the lowlands and we're due to join them before they leave."

"Nomads," he nodded. "Pity you didn't arrive a day or two earlier. You'd have had a tale or two to tell round the campfires this spring!"

Jainie returned carrying four tankards which she placed in the middle of the table. "There you go," she said. "Food's almost ready. Mippik'll see to your room when you've eaten. We don't exactly have'em queuing up for one!" she said, indicating the customers of the tavern with an expansive sweep of her arm.

Kris fished out a handful of coins and held them out to her.

"Trustin', ain't he?" she said to Railin as she picked a few small coppers from his hand. "You told them yet about the happenin's here the other night?"

"Just about to," said Railin, picking up his tankard. "Just about to, Jainie."

"Right strange, it was," she said, putting her hands on her hips and leaning conspiratorially toward them. Her long ginger hair dropped over her shoulder, almost hiding her face as she spoke. "Bright lights in the sky, there were, then this almighty bang! They could have heard it all the way down to the plains, I tell you!"

"Jainie," said Railin gently, "you're spoiling my tale."

"Ooh, sorry, I'm sure!" she said, pulling a face at Kris and Davies as she stood up again. "Can't lose you your living, can I? I mean, ain't as if you has an honest trade, after all. You're only the storyteller! Who'd buy your ale if you didn't tell 'em stories!" She ducked the playful swipe he aimed at her and headed back to the counter.

"What was all that about?" asked Kris, sipping his ale carefully. He tried not to shudder as the bitter drink slid down his throat. "Bright lights and so on. We saw nothing as we came through the forest."

"Don't you go listening to her," said Railin, putting his pouch away and reaching forward to pick a small glowing piece of wood from the fire. He proceeded to light his pipe, sending small clouds of aromatic smoke upward to drift briefly over his head. That done, he threw the stick back into the fire.

"That was months ago. What did happen a couple of days ago was more interesting," he said, fishing something out of his pocket and handing it to Kris.

Kris took it from him, turning the small disk over in his hand before handing it back to him. "Strick said we'd meet someone who'd help us," he said quietly, "but I didn't expect it to be so soon."

"Nor so easy, I'll be bound," said Railin, returning it to his pocket.

"How d'you know it was us?" asked Davies. He took a long swig of his ale, then put the tankard down on the table.

"Told you. Travelers at this time of year are rare, even allowing for the late thaw."

"So what happened?" asked Jo. She'd had a small sip of the ale and decided water might taste better.

"Well, Jainie was right about the lights and the bang," said

Railin, putting his pipe to one corner of his mouth. He sat back in his chair and folded his hands across his ample gut, obviously getting settled to tell his tale. "But that happened in the deep of winter, when no one could leave the town, the snow was falling so thick. No one wanted to go out at that time of night even if they could. For all we knew it could be demons, or evil beings that live in the heart of the mountains at their dirty work, dancing round their fire and casting spells the like of which no decent man or woman wanted to know even existed! A group of us gathered on the town wall and watched the glow. Eerie it was, a strange blue light that flickered and shone for nigh on an hour before it died down." He stopped, as if recalling the scene to mind.

Power, or electrical circuits shorting and burning, Kris sent to Jo. So powerful were Railin's powers of recollection, that he could almost see the scene unfolding before his eyes.

"Anyway, there was nothing we could do till the spring. However, the thaw, when it came, didn't last, but it was long enough for us to get out to where the lights came from."

Railin stopped as he saw Jainie approaching with a tray of plates. These she put down in front of Jo, Davies, and Kris, again waiting till Kris had paid her.

"Don't you let him bore you stupid with his tales," she said before disappearing.

While they ate, Railin continued his tale. "Lord Killian, up at the castle there," he said, nodding to his right, "he gathered together his guard and some of us as volunteers and off we went into the mountains after whatever it was that caused the lights." He stopped to remove his pipe and take a swig of his ale.

"Well, I don't mind telling you, we were scared of what we might meet out there. We knew we'd get out in a day, but we wouldn't get back before dark, and the thought of spending a night up there among the mountain demons and monsters wasn't pleasant." He puffed on his pipe, taking it out to tap the herbs down more tightly.

"Go on," said Jo, spooning some vegetables into her mouth.

"When we got there, we found this metal-shelled carriage," he said. "I don't know what it was because I'd never seen its like before! It lay there with a gaping hole in its side, and out on the snow beside it was this . . . box!"

"A box?" asked Kris, opening his padded underjacket so

he could get Scamp out. As the jegget poked a cautious head over the top, Railin stopped talking.

"A box," said Railin, staring as Scamp eased himself out onto Kris' shoulder and sat there, looking around and sniffing.

"What kind of box?" asked Davies, sitting back, his plate clean.

"It was about the height of a man, and large enough to get one of these tables in," he said, still watching the jegget in fascination.

Bolder now, Scamp allowed himself to be enticed down Kris' arm to sit on his lap while he was fed pieces of meat from the remains of the stew.

"It was a strange, magical thing," said Railin. "It looked like it was made of glass, but it was like no glass I've ever seen. The light didn't shine on it, it kind of . . . slid off it. It was dark in color and when you touched it, it moved."

"It moved?" Kris looked up from feeding Scamp.

Railin nodded. "We had to wrap ropes round it to hold it back! It was so easy to move we were afraid it would run away with us. Lord Killian had three of the guard pull it with their horses, and the rest of us hung onto the ropes at the back to see it didn't go too fast."

Frictionless from the sound of it, sent Kris.

"Lord Killian had it taken to the castle," said Railin. "It's still there now, in a room on the ground level. He can't get it opened, and he's had nearly every wise man in the town come to look it over, but no one's been able to figure it out yet. He's even had a couple of spell-casters look at it, but their spells were as useless as everything else. You can hit it with an axe and it just slides off, doesn't even mark it."

"It's still there now?" asked Jo, leaning toward Kris with a small piece of meat for Scamp.

"Oh, yes. It's still sitting in its room. It's definitely from off-world," said Railin, "and Lord Bradogan down at the Port City, won't let off-world goods come to the likes of Lord Killian. He won't do what Bradogan wants, raise the food levy and the taxes, so we don't get any benefits of the off-world trade."

Railin leaned forward. "You'll be wanting to see this box, won't you?" he said quietly. "It isn't guarded. No one could steal it, it's too big. It can't be opened either, so he's no fear anyone can steal what's inside it either. So there it sits!"

"We need to see it," said Kris, watching as Scamp, with a small chittering noise, carefully climbed over to reach Jo.

"I can tell you how to get in," said Railin, "but that's all. I won't come with you. I got to live here, and I don't want to spend what days I got left shut up in a cell in the castle. You get caught, you're on your own."

Kris nodded. "Understood. Can you get us plans of the castle?"

"I can. It'll cost, though. I'll have to buy them myself."

"How much?"

"Five silver crowns."

Kris dug in his pocket for them. He'd been carefully eavesdropping on the man's surface thoughts since he'd joined them, and he was as straight as he seemed. He handed the coins as unobtrusively as possible to Railin.

"I don't know why you want to see it," he said, pocketing the money. "It just stands there, doesn't do anything. I don't like the feel of it," he said. "Eerie, it is."

Scamp was making up to Jo now. He sat in her arms, his front paws reaching up to touch her cheek as he crooned quietly to himself. Jo was stroking his head gently, making similar little noises back to him.

Jainie came bustling over and Scamp took one look at her before diving back to the safety of Kris' jacket.

"Mippik says if you all bed down in the one room, he'll only charge you two crowns a night, or ten for the week," she said.

"We'll take it for the week," said Jo. This time it was she who dug into her pouch for the money.

When Jainie had gone, Kris looked back at Railin.

"When and where will we meet you to get the plans?"

"I'm in here every evening," said Railin. "I'll join you after I've done my storytelling."

"You really are a storyteller?" said Jo, surprised.

He laughed. "Yes. Jainie had it right when she said it was my living. I tell the stories the customers want to hear and they pay me! The winter's long up here, and tales pass the time."

"Don't you ever run out of tales?" she asked curiously.

"No. I go down to the lowlands in the summer season to collect more tales, and I talk to travelers like you. Now, if you've a tale or two to tell me," he said, "maybe *I'll* buy you an ale for the telling of it!"

"You're on," said Davies.

Railin got to his feet. "Time for me to begin, I think. The tavern's filled up while we've been talking. Are you staying to listen?"

"I'm afraid not," said Jo. "I'm tired out. What I could really do with is a bath. I don't suppose . . ."

"There's a metal bath in each room. Jainie'll bring hot water up for you if you ask her," he said.

The room was basic, but at least it boasted four cots. Jo dumped her pack on the fourth bed, and began to take off some of the layers of clothing she was wearing to keep warm. A knock on the door heralded the arrival of Jainie— and Kris—with three kettles of hot water for her bath.

She lay soaking in the hot water until it was almost cold before she reluctantly got out and toweled herself dry in front of the small fire. Shivering, she hauled some clean, dry clothes out of her pack. When she was dressed, she bundled the damp and dirty clothing up, waiting for Jainie to return. She'd offered to have them washed and dried for her by the end of the following day.

Kris turned in before Davies. Jo lay with her face turned away from him as he washed and changed, so he could have some privacy. Scamp, not wanting to be anywhere near the wet stuff, had headed straight for her and was curled up under the bedding against her chest, purring happily.

"I'll leave a couple of candles on for Davies," said Kris as he climbed into the bed alongside hers. "If I don't, sure as fate he'll fall over us when he comes up."

"The light won't keep me awake," said Jo, yawning hugely. "I don't know where he gets his energy from! What do you make of this box Railin was talking about?"

"No idea. It definitely sounds as if it's frictionless. Something that large wouldn't be that easy to move otherwise. Beyond that, we'll have to wait till we see it."

Scamp had begun to move. He wriggled free of Jo's arms and scampered off to Kris. Jo could hear him chattering away happily for a moment or two, then with a small thump, he landed on her bed again, fussing round her face, snuffling at her neck before settling down beside her. He was purring loudly now, and one paw reached out to touch her face, patting it gently.

"Off you go, Scamp," she said, gently pushing him, trying to encourage him to get off her bed. He wouldn't be budged.

He curled his bushy tail round her neck, sending warm, gentle thoughts to her as he purred happily.

"Scamp!" she said, pushing gently at him again, surprised at how heavy he'd suddenly become. A small tongue flicked out, touching her cheek. Again he licked her, moving closer till he was tucked around her neck and face.

"Kris, I think you'd better come and get him," she said. "Much as I like him, I don't want to be suffocated in my sleep!"

Kris called to him, but the jegget was happy where he was, thank you very much, said his thoughts. Throwing back the covers, Kris stepped over to Jo's bed, squatting down beside her. He put his hands round Scamp's middle and tried to lift him, but his tail was firmly coiled round Jo's neck and he wasn't going to let go. He liked this nice person, his thoughts said. His friend did too, so why couldn't they cuddle up to her?

"Excuse me," he muttered. "I'm going to have to unwrap him." Kris reached for the offending tail and uncurled it despite the squeaks of protest from Scamp. As he did, his hand brushed Jo's cheek and he felt her flinch away from him at the unexpectedness of it.

"Sorry," he said, embarrassed by his little friend's behavior. "He's never been like this before. I'll make sure he doesn't get out again tonight."

"Just a minute," said Jo, sitting up and reaching out to pat Scamp before he turned away. "He's all right, Kris," she said. "Don't worry if he comes back over in the night. He's rather comforting to cuddle up to—so long as he's not trying to suffocate me!"

Kris mumbled some vague reply and climbed back into his bed, thanking the Gods that Jo wasn't a better telepath. Had she been, she couldn't have failed to realize that Scamp's affection was partly due to him. That would have been all they needed on the mission: Jo terrified of him coming near her. As he wormed his way down into the bedding again, and tucked Scamp up against his chest, he wondered what had happened to Jo out on Keiss that she was afraid to let a man come closer to her. Whatever it was, she kept it a closely guarded secret. Her surface thoughts didn't betray even a hint of her fears.

* * *

Kaid surfaced slowly from sleep. His body felt heavy and languid, the echoes of pain not far away: he'd been given analgesics then, strong ones. His senses still heightened by the psychotropic drug, he gleaned what he could about his surroundings before opening his eyes.

The scent of Noni was everywhere, but it was at least two hours old. He rotated his ears, flaring them wide, listening again for the slightest sound. There was none: he must be alone in the house. Opening his eyes, he looked around. As he expected, everything seemed real. That was the horror of the dreams—their apparent reality. All he could do was endure each one till it ended, taking him back to a world dominated by pain—and Ghezu.

Slowly he sat up, flexing his shoulders, testing his back. Bearable, and movement felt easier. His hands next. He looked down at them, feeling the room swim slightly about him as he did. His injured right hand was bandaged. It had been treated. And his left one hadn't been touched. Curious. He had vague memories of Ghezu about to use the knife on him again.

Cautiously he tried moving his unbandaged thumb and forefinger. They responded but the swelling of his hand restricted their movement. He tried his remaining two fingers. Barely dulled pain lanced instantly up his arm, making him break out in a sweat across his back and chest as well as the palms of his hands.

Not good, he thought. He collapsed back against his pillows, taking short, rapid breaths in an effort to still the pain.

It passed eventually, and, when it had, cradling his injured hand against his chest, he pushed himself upright again. Carefully, avoiding sudden moves, he pulled back the cover and lifted his legs over the side of the bed. Standing up brought the dizziness back but after a moment it, too, passed.

His first call was to the water faucet for a drink. He filled the mug twice before his thirst was satisfied. Leaning with his back against the sink, he looked round Noni's kitchen. Why was he here? What thoughts of his had generated this dream?

A slight sound from the partly open bedroom door drew his attention. His ears swivelled toward it, followed more slowly by his head.

Pushing himself away from the sink, he moved toward the door. His nose picked up her scent before he reached it—a sharp musk that he knew only too well. Pushing the door gently, he held onto the wall and looked inside. Against his chest, the crystal began to warm.

He knew now what had called him here. Carrie. He closed his eyes, resting his head against the wooden frame, ears folding back in distress. Once again his mind had betrayed him.

Vartra, why? Why does she dominate my thoughts like this? You know what I fear! You ask too much of me!

Her body moved restlessly in sleep, her scent growing stronger as it drifted toward him, burning like fire in his lungs, making it difficult for him to breathe.

She isn't even of our species, Vartra! She's alien— "... and she draws me like an insect to a flame," he said, his voice a bare whisper.

He opened his eyes, looking across to where she lay on top of the bed. The cover was dragged haphazardly across her, and her head was turned away from him. Beyond her, the window was open just enough to admit a gentle breeze that stirred her hair where it lay spread out on the pillow. It brought her scent to him once more.

Then he was beside her, with no memory of how he'd gotten there. One of her legs lay uncovered, pale against the blue quilt. On her thigh he saw the faint line of the scar. He saw his hand, of its own volition, reach out and gently trace its length with a fingertip. Against her bare flesh, his pelt of brown fur looked wrong, as if he were the alien, not her.

Hand trembling, he moved back. He wanted to touch her again, to feel the gentle swell of her firm muscles under his hands; to run his fingers through hair the color of sunlight, softer and finer than hair or fur that Sholans possessed; he wanted to hold her, let his tongue taste her sweetness again, his hands explore her, and hold her long, slim throat between his jaws as she accepted him as her lover. He wanted to be a million light years away from her!

A low sound of pain came from deep within him. He felt the crystal begin to come alive, to pulse against his chest in a rhythm that was echoed in the tide of his own heartbeat as it speeded up, sending waves of sensual arousal through his body. The God spared him nothing! Against his calves, his tail swayed, echoing his inner conflict.

I never wanted this, Vartra! To desire a female so much that it robs me of my senses even in my dreams! Why have

you done this to me? Why do I fear to take what I want most?
I have the right to ask her! I'm the third!

A dream! It was a drug dream! He shook his head, trying
to clear it, his ears rising as he realized the significance of
what he'd said. His thoughts might betray him in his dreams,
but he could also fulfill them. There was no harm in fanta-
sizing: perhaps it would even release him from the strange
hold she had over him. In a dream, he couldn't harm her—
and his secret would be safe.

He approached the bed again, this time from the other
side, slowly lowering himself till he sat beside her. Reaching
out with his good hand, he touched her face. Unbidden,
memories of the last drug-dream came to him: the flickering
flames of the Shrine at Valsgarth, the smell of incense—
and her.

Her eyes flickered open and she turned to look at him.
"You're awake."

"How long have I been gone?"

She frowned, sitting up and reaching out to touch his face.
"Some six weeks. I told you before. Are you all right, Kaid?"

He reached out and covered her hand with his. As before, it
was warm, flesh and blood, not mist. He turned his head,
taking her hand to his mouth, placing it against his lips. The
tip of his tongue fleetingly caressed her palm then released
her as he reached out to place his hand against her neck,
drawing her closer till he buried his face against her.
Breathing in deeply, he drank in the new-washed scent of
her body and hair before his tongue began to flick across her
cheek to her mouth.

"We did this before," he murmured before catching her
bottom lip gently between his .teeth. "You taste as sweet
now." As her lips closed on his, her hands came up to touch
his shoulders.

The intimacy of her Human kiss took his breath away.
Already sensitized to her, the wave of desire built in seconds,
sweeping downward through him, tightening the muscles in
the pit of his stomach and groin. Between them, the crystal
flared hot then steadied to a different rhythm, pulsing gently
in time with *her* heartbeat.

He broke away from her long enough to climb onto the
bed before gently urging her down beside him. Cupping
the back of her head in his left hand, he leaned over her,

lowering his face to hers, his mouth seeking hers, anxious to share another kiss.

Hesitantly, her tongue touched his lips, pushing gently past them till she touched his teeth.

He caught hold of her, pushing her tongue upward against the roof of his mouth, tasting her properly. Once more the tension built, flooding through him, triggering the release of his genitals.

Torn in two directions, part of his mind told him to leave now, before it was too late; the other to stay, it was only a drug dream, nothing could go wrong.

In that instant, what was left of his barriers collapsed as his mind exploded outward to hers, forcing a rapport, compelling her to accept the knowledge of what he was.

Images flickered in front of his mind's eye, images of what he'd been, what he'd done; images he knew she was seeing.

No, not this! Not again, Vartra! his mind cried out before she seized it, deftly taking control and slowing the memories till finally they stopped.

You sent! You're a telepath, Kaid!

The realization that this could be no dream hit him like an icy wave and he recoiled from her. As quickly as the rapport had begun, it was over, leaving him lying beside her, cursing himself as, once more, he retreated behind his barriers.

He waited for the anger and recriminations, but she was silent. Pushing himself up on his good arm, he risked looking at her.

"This is real, isn't it?" he said. "I thought it was like the last time, a drug dream. If I'd thought or known otherwise . . ." He left the sentence unfinished as he looked away.

She reached out for him. "You did nothing wrong."

He pulled away from her, angry with himself. "I had no right to touch you. I knew what would happen if I did."

"You thought it was a dream."

"That doesn't excuse me!"

"You don't need to be excused," she began. "Your lack of training . . ."

"Training be damned! I should never have let myself be talked into being the third! I should never have listened to Lijou and the others: they made me hope it would be different with you." He turned away, hearing the pain in his own voice, unable to face her or the truth about himself. Why was he denied the most basic of all Sholan companionship?

"Fine. Have it your way," she said coldly. "Blame me because you've actually had the nerve to approach me. Run and hide behind your anger when it doesn't go as you expected! Why should I care? After all, it isn't me who's hiding behind the fear of pairing!"

He turned angrily back to her, hurt beyond measure by her words. "Damn you, Carrie! You're *using* what you just learned against me!"

She sat up, eyes blazing. "Too damned right I am! What do you expect me to do when you behave like this? Have I rejected you? Called you a cold, callous killer like she did? When I shared your dream of the pack wars in Ranz, I didn't even *think* that! You'd rather run than face up to this fear!"

"I'm no coward!" His ears folded sideways with anger.

"I know that," she said, her tone softening as she reached out a comforting hand.

He pulled away, avoiding her touch. "What just happened to you, happened to Khemu—my mind swamped hers utterly, that's why she became pregnant. Whatever it is, I can't control it, Carrie! As long as I have a tight hold on my mind, I can block it, but when I pair . . . I have a rogue talent!"

She could feel his fear of being no different from the telepaths he'd hunted down for Esken's Guild.

"No, you haven't! And I'm not Khemu! She was a young and partly-trained telepath who reacted badly to the touch of your mind! *I didn't*. It's me you're with, not her! Don't forget that as well as having a Sholan side, I'm also Human."

He looked up, mouth twisting in a strange grin as his ears began to lift slightly. "I can't forget that, nor how Sholan you are."

"Listen to me, Kaid!" she said, taking him by the arm. "*You* might not be able to control it, but *I* can. I'm not some Sholan Telepath with all the inhibitions they have trained into them, and their fear of pain—other people's as much as their own. I can see your darker side and not turn away from it—because Kusac and I both owe our lives to that part of you!"

His ears flicked backward. He'd forgotten about Kusac, her Leska, his Liege.

"Friend," corrected Carrie. "He's your friend, as I am."

Letting his arm go, she reached out and placed her hand over the pouch that held the crystal round his neck.

He felt it respond instantly to her touch, beginning to flare again.

"I know what this does, Kaid. I understand why Noni gave it to you. We all knew this pairing between us had to happen, we all agreed to it. Kusac's with Vanna, and believe me, we're the last consideration on his mind just now."

The crystal was pulsing again, a rhythm deeper and older than time, vibrating through his body and dominating his mind. He closed his eyes, trying to suppress it, trying not to respond to her nearness again.

"You aren't making this easy for me, Carrie," he said, his voice barely audible.

"You're one of us, Kaid. Telepaths aren't supposed to live isolated from mental contact with others of their own kind. Because you've spent a lifetime suppressing it, whenever your barriers are low, your mind reaches out for companionship, that's all. We're at our closest to each other when we pair. That time for us is beautiful: it's sharing anticipation, sharing pleasure with each other." Her voice was pure Sholan, a low, seductive purr. "If you'll accept what you are and learn to live with it, it will never happen again, I promise you."

Her hand left the crystal and moments later he felt it touch his cheek, the fingers running downward till they closed in the hair that grew on the back of his neck. Before he could stop her, she'd pulled his head back by the scruff.

His eyes flew open as he froze, obeying instincts lost in a childhood spent on the wrong side of the hearth as a parentless cub.

"No," he said hoarsely, unable to pull away from her. "Carrie, don't. Not that."

He sensed her hesitation, then she released him. He lifted his head, seeing her about to move away. *No, don't go!* He couldn't let this moment slip by! If he did, he'd never have the courage to face her again. Reaching out, he caught hold of her, clumsily pulling her to his side with his one useable arm.

"You've seen the dark side of me, Carrie, you know what I am, the things I've done. I make no apologies for them. Do you still want me as your third, knowing all that?" he asked, his voice low and rough.

I chose you, Kaid, she sent, *because I wanted you.*

His arm tightened round her. "What happens if one day this forced rapport takes over and you're unable to stop me?" he asked, looking down into her eyes, unable to hide the hope in his.

"It won't happen. I can prove it if you let me."

"Then show me," he said, his voice barely more than a low growl as his mouth closed on hers.

Her hands came up to hold his face, gentle over his injured cheek. The kiss seemed to last forever as he responded in kind, his tongue darting across her lips then touching the soft insides of her mouth. Gods, he wanted her so much!

Vartra, let this not be a dream-within-a-dream! I'll do anything you ask, just let this be real!

The taste, the touch, the feel of her was all so new, not only because of the years of celibacy, but because she was so very different.

Then her hands touched his body, held him close to hers, and all thought of anything but *now* vanished. His breathing fast and ragged, he clenched his hand in her hair, pulling her head back, arching her long throat toward him.

He bit at her lips and tongue tip with a flurry of gentle nips, then his tongue was flicking over the soft underside of her jaw. Moving his head lower, he nuzzled aside her robe as his hand reached to undo the tie belt.

It fell open and with every sense he possessed, he drank in the sight and smell of her smooth, pale body. He could feel her mind alongside his as his mouth closed over her throat with a gentle yet firm pressure.

"Kaid." The word was no more than a whisper of her breath against his ears.

He released her and raised his head, looking directly into her eyes—Sholan eyes, the lids, like his, half-closed with desire.

"Tallinu," he said, his voice a deep purr. "Call me by my chosen name."

"Tallinu," she whispered.

He covered her face in tiny bites, his hand moving to push the robe off one shoulder, then the other. This time wouldn't end like the last, finished before it began.

Let your barriers down, she sent as he pulled the sleeves free of her arms. *Stop trying to control it, just share what you're experiencing.*

He tried, his hand running hesitantly over naked skin as silky as any Sholan's belly fur. He caressed her face, her neck, then his hand ran down her side to her flank, reveling in at last being able to enjoy the firmness of her body. Gradually, he was forgetting his fear, was getting swept into the pure sensual enjoyment of touching her.

His tongue travelled across her throat and shoulders, alternately licking and nipping at her flesh, loving her nakedness that enhanced his pleasure.

The need to anchor himself in the present, to feel the reality of *now* again, drove him, and finally the barriers behind which he'd hidden all his life dropped. Her mind touched his again, establishing an even deeper rapport. He pressed his injured right arm against her side, his tail flicking across her leg, twining round it in his need to hold her completely.

Let me feel what you feel, she urged.

Then he felt *her* pleasure, felt the fire start low in her belly, spreading outward till it licked at him. She arched her body against his, pressing his still-pulsing crystal between them.

He shuddered, his claws flexing out then retracting as he drew them down the soft skin on the inside of her thigh. His hand slid up over her hips, reaching for a tail that didn't exist, then he remembered and returned to explore the softness of her thighs. His tongue flicked lower, his hand following to caress the swell of her belly, sensing the new life that slept within her. There was a rightness about this moment, and he felt an inner peace. He realized then the irony and simplicity of the situation they'd all been placed in.

She reached down, pulling his head upward. *This is how it should be,* she sent, her mouth taking his in a kiss that was wild and fierce. Her hand closed on his naked flesh, sending a spasm of pleasure surging through him.

He gave a ragged moan and lifted his head as his hand grasped her wrist, holding it still.

Carrie, for pity's sake, don't! I'll be spent too soon!

She released him but the wave of tension that heralded his secondary phase had already started. Ignoring the pain in his injured hand, he turned her on her side, her back toward him. Pushing her legs forward, he grasped her by the hips and pulled her down onto himself. Not a moment too soon. As her warmth closed around him, he swelled inside her, then their bodies were moving to a rhythm as old as time. Suddenly her mind exploded within his, creating such closeness that their responses to each other were inextricably intertwined. Sensations belonging to them both surged through him, wave after wave of them as he was swept upward with her to their climax.

Slowly their minds spiraled down into a motionless peace. Then suddenly she felt his hand clench as he moved back from her, turning his face into the robe on which they lay. She felt the self-control he'd hidden behind all his life break, leaving him unable to cope with the emotions that were now flooding through him. She turned over, moving toward him.

"Leave me," he said, his voice barely audible, as he pulled his arm protectively round his head.

She ignored him, moving closer till their bodies touched again. Reaching out, she touched his head, stroking gently downward.

His ears flattened, almost disappeared within his hair as he began to shake.

Carrie gathered him close, insisting when he tried to resist her. His hand reached blindly for hers, pressing it tightly to his chest as he buried his face against her shoulder. The tears he shed hurt, but they were also the beginning of his healing. He clung to her, knowing only that with her he could let those barriers go completely, knowing that for him she represented a need so basic that he couldn't remember not needing her.

She held him close, gently rocking him, saying quiet words of comfort. Gradually he grew calmer. He lifted his head, wiping his forearm across his eyes, trying not to look at her. She reached for his face, a hand on either cheek, and brought him close till she could gently kiss first one eye, then the other, before she let him go.

He lay back, reaching out to touch her face with a hand that wasn't yet steady. As he began to open his mouth, her fingers were there first, briefly touching his lips.

No need for words, she sent. *You were there for me when I needed you.*

He held her close, feeling the years of mental isolation and fear of his talent at last start to dissolve. She'd been right.

He started to purr, then it turned into a shaky chuckle.

What's so funny? Her mental tone now sounded lazy, pleasantly satisfied.

Us. Vartra Himself arranged the timing perfectly!

Mm?

You're the only telepathic female who could know my mind and not recoil in horror at what I am. You're also the only one I couldn't mentally harm or overpower—and you're already pregnant so I didn't need to fear that . . .

I suppose He did.

He felt her begin to shiver. Sitting up, he slid off the bed, staggering slightly as he stood up. Instantly she was at his side to support him. "I should have remembered you've been bedridden for several days," she said solicitously. "I was surprised to see you in here."

"I'm fine," he said, leaning forward to pull the bed cover off. He started to put it round her. "Wrap yourself in this, you're freezing."

She did as he said, then sat on the bed looking up at him. "I ought to get dressed," she said. "Noni will be back shortly, not to mention Dzaka."

"Noni's been trying to get me to bed you since I first brought you here."

"Because of the Fire Margins."

"That's in the future," he said. "Let's leave it there for now." His ears were laid back slightly in apprehension. "I'd like to stay with you for a while, but not here, in the other room."

She stood and, reaching up to him, placed a finger against his lips. *I'll stay while you sleep,* she sent, and he knew she understood the fear he still had that this was no more than a drug dream.

He picked up her robe and threw it over a chair. "You can't wear that now. I'll lend you mine."

Automatically she picked up her silver-caged crystal from the night table where she'd left it before her shower, and slipped the chain over her head. She wore it constantly now, feeling naked without its warm weight between her breasts. Then she reached out and took his hand, drawing him into the main room.

Still dressed in his robe, she burrowed under the cover of the large bed in the kitchen. Almost hesitantly, he joined her. Carefully he slipped his good arm under her neck, and gathered her against him, feeling her warmth reaching more than just his body. Looking at her, her eyes heavy now with sleepiness and shared pleasure, he remembered the day he'd gone to the temple to collect the agreement between Kusac and the Brotherhood.

"You need to care what happens to them or none of you will return! Do you think you can learn to do that, Kaid?" Ghyan had asked sarcastically. *"Learn to care? You'll have to if she's going to accept you—if Kusac is."*

Ghyan hadn't realized the distress he'd felt knowing he could do nothing to stop Carrie's Challenge, knowing the risk she was taking and being unable to even express his fears to anyone.

Those days are gone now, she sent, touching his face with gentle fingers.

"There's so much to say that I don't know where to start," he said at length, his voice low and quiet. "As Vartra's my witness, I never intended that you should get inside my heart, Carrie. That's partly why I fought against the Triad for so long."

She lay there, her breath warm against his chest, listening.

"You don't realize what it was like, suddenly having feelings for a female after so long. I didn't know what to do . . . how to cope! I care about you both, but what I feel for you . . ." He broke off for a moment. "Feelings have never come easy to me. I learned long ago to live without them. I've never felt like this about anyone before."

"I know," she said, her hand reaching for his. "I guessed that might be the case when you took care of me when I was pregnant the first time. I knew for sure when you appeared at the Shrine."

"That was a dream," he said, gripping her hand so tightly his claws began to prick her skin.

"No. It was real, Tallinu. We don't know how, but it was. So is this, but in a different way. We physically brought you here," she said soothingly. "We are here, together for now. Ghezu was wrong. He didn't win, Tallinu, you did."

He sighed, letting his eyes close and his grip relax. "I know," he said, but deep inside, all the pain and the fear he'd suffered at Stronghold was a black pit, and he still stood on its edge.

Noni returned after dark. As she reached her door, Dzaka emerged from the aircar and joined her.

She glowered at him. "What you doing out here, brat?"

He frowned, disliking the word. "He's with her."

"Which her?" she demanded.

"The Human, Carrie, of course."

She nodded, pleased at the news. "Is he now? Good."

"Good?" said Dzaka.

"Your father's not a celibate, boy. He might have lived like one, but he isn't. It's long past time he had a lover, and they needed to pair. He's part of their Triad." She opened the door and stepped inside, turning back to him. "They're asleep. No need for you to sit out there."

Reluctantly he followed her in, going over to the chair at the far side of the room.

She activated the lights, keeping them low so as not to wake the sleepers. Going over to her stove, she put water on to boil for a brew of c'shar. That organized, she went to the bed, looking down at them.

He looked better, his face more relaxed than she'd seen it since they'd brought him here. His mind felt better too, some of the darkness, the brittleness, was going. She frowned, recognizing a difference in him but unable to pinpoint it. She glanced at the female. She felt well enough, content with her Leska and her approaching motherhood—and Tallinu.

He stirred, the light disturbing his eyes. He knew Noni was back, he could smell and sense her. As he looked across at her, they locked eyes.

"So that's the secret you've carried all these years," she said, nodding her head slowly. "Now you begin to make sense to me, Tallinu the Foundling. It's a wonder you survived Ghezu's drug." She held up her hand in a negative before he could speak. "I'll say nothing, never fear." Then she began to laugh quietly.

"What?" he asked, his voice drowsy with sleep.

"You three. What a Triad you'll make! Now you've finally paired with her, I can see that everything that's happened to you has just put your feet more firmly on the path to the Margins, Tallinu."

A movement behind her caught his eye. He raised his head to see Dzaka standing there.

Dzaka pointedly looked from him to Carrie.

"*My* life, Dzaka," he said. "The debt I felt I owed to Khemu is paid." He closed his eyes again, pain creasing his face as his recent activity caught up with him. "We need to talk when I'm better."

"Dzaka, the hypoderm. He needs a dose for the pain," ordered Noni.

He could feel Carrie's weight on his arm, against his chest: smell her scent. She was still there, warm against his body. Nothing had changed while he slept. Even the return of the pain was welcome. He knew without doubt he *was* here. He felt the slight sting of the hypo against his neck and allowed himself to relax into its welcome relief. He was asleep again before Dzaka had returned the instrument to its case.

* * *

Garras was away on his family estate for a few days so Vanna was pleased to have Kusac's company. When she woke to feed Marak, she found him standing looking out of the window.

"What's wrong?" she asked, leaning down to pick Marak up from his crib.

"Nothing."

"So it's happened, has it?"

"Mm?"

"It's happened."

He turned round, ears flicking in momentary confusion. "What?"

"The Triad. It's happened," she said, raising her voice to speak over the top of her son's sudden insistent yowling.

"That happened several hours ago, Vanna," he said. "Why should that worry me?"

"I just thought . . . that is . . . I mean . . ."

"Vanna," he said gently, walking over to her and touching her cheek, "I think you'd better feed him."

"Yes . . . I think I had," she said, unsure what else to say.

Kusac held out his arms toward her. "You're not really awake, are you? Come on, give him to me while you get back into bed and get comfortable."

She passed Marak over, surprised to see he knew how to hold the cub.

"Go on," he said, holding the little one close while supporting him under his rear. His eyes lit up with humor and his mouth spread in a grin that was very human. "I could do with the practice! As well as being an uncle to Marak, Taizia's cub will be born before long, then soon after, we'll have our own cub." She could hear the quiet pride in his voice.

Going back to the bed, she picked up the towel that hung over the head of Marak's crib. Settling herself comfortably on her side, she spread it over the sheet.

"Watch the cloth," she warned.

"I am, and don't worry, he's still clean," he said as he passed Marak back to her, making sure the cloth round the tiny cub's nether regions didn't fall off.

"That's a first," she said as he laid the cub down on the towel. She held him close against her breast.

Kusac knelt down till his head was level with the bed and stayed there, watching while the hungry cub clung to his mother, sucking lustily. Reaching out, he touched him gently on the head but Marak, with a small noise of complaint and much flicking of tiny ears, moved closer to Vanna, hands clutching tighter to her pelt.

"He's only got one thought on his mind just now," said Vanna, cradling her arms round her son.

"I know. I can feel it."

"You've never been this close to a newborn cub before, have you?"

He shook his head. "Never. I was staying at the Guild by the time both Taizia and Kitra were born. Are they all like this?"

"Hungry?" she laughed.

"No. This small and so determined!"

"Yes, but it doesn't last. You blink and they're grown up. I know that from watching Sashti's cubs."

"How's Garras coping?"

She reached out to ruffle the hair between Kusac's ears. "He's as fascinated by him as you obviously are!"

"Has he any cubs?"

"None. He never met anyone he wanted to share his cubs with."

Kusac sighed gently. "It's a damned shame you and he can't . . ."

"That's not necessarily true," she interrupted. "Since the ni'uzu epidemic there are quite a few people with the potential to be compatible with us, and Garras is one of them. We think that with a little help from the labs, it may well be possible for me to have his cub."

He lifted his head to look properly at her. "Really? That would be wonderful if you can."

"The only difference between him and us is that the changes haven't affected his reproductive system. He can't pass them on."

"We've several like that on the estate, haven't we?"

"One or two. Dzaka, his father Kaid, of course, and a couple of the one-time Brothers. If they were telepaths, they'd be prime Leska material. All it would need would be a trigger from a gestalt." She stopped and looked at Kusac. "Kaid."

He was watching Marak again. "Yes. He never did see you about taking that backlash from Mara and Zhyaf's gestalt, did he?"

"No, he didn't," she said slowly. "Dzaka and he fought that night. He was gone by morning."

"So he was. The cub Carrie and I lost, Vanna, did she look like this?"

"Yes. Yes, she did. Kusac," she said, her tone urgent. "I have a blood sample from that night which I never got around to checking."

"Leave it, Vanna. I already know the answer. You know, Marak may be small, but he's perfectly formed, isn't he?"

He'd reached out and was touching one small foot. The pads on the sole were bright pink and as he stroked his finger gently across them, the tiny curved claws were extended briefly then retracted. "He hardly seems to have been affected by the surgery."

"He was lethargic for a day or two, but now he's back to normal. Kusac . . ."

He looked up at her again. "There's nothing to talk about, Vanna." His voice, though quiet, was firm.

Vanna looked away. If he didn't want to discuss it, there was no way she could make him. Perhaps it was better left like this. She reached out to untangle Marak's hands from her fur.

"Will you hold him while I turn over?" she asked.

"Of course."

It was easier said than done as Marak, in common with all Sholan infants, was born with a tiny but full set of teeth.

She settled down again, this time at the other side of her bed. As Marak began to feed once more, she winced. "Thank

Vartra it's only for a few weeks," she said with heartfelt relief. "I don't know how the Humans do it for months!"

"Their young don't have teeth to start with," said Kusac, standing up. "Shall I get you your drink now?"

"That would be wonderful! I'll be finished in a few minutes."

"Don't hurry him, Vanna," he said, going over to the dispenser. "I'm in no rush. I'm not about to leave yet."

"You're staying till morning?"

"If you have no objections," he said, bringing the drinks over to the bedside and handing one to Vanna.

"None at all."

He couldn't settle and eventually he admitted to himself that he needed to see Carrie. Carefully he untangled himself from Vanna's limbs and slipped out of bed.

"Send to Noni before you go, Kusac," came the sleepy voice from the depths of the covers.

"I will," he said, slipping his arms through the sleeves of his robe. When he did, to his surprise, Noni answered.

I knew you'd call. Come if you must. She's in the back bedroom with me. There's too many changes these day, she grumbled. *You young ones aren't satisfied with the traditional ways any more!*

He leaned over Vanna, gently nuzzling her cheek.

She reached up and took hold of his robe to stop him from leaving. "Kusac, it's no different from what we share . . ."

"Vanna, I know," he said, trying to release her grip on his clothes. "I'm a fully grown adult male now. I'm life-bonded to a mate I love, and I've fathered two cubs with her. Believe me, I'm well past the adolescent stage!"

"I'm glad that my link to Brynne doesn't involve a love like you and Carrie share," she said. "I couldn't cope with it."

"I think too many people have taken too much notice of how a Human would react, and forgotten I'm Sholan," he said, a hint of displeasure creeping into his voice. "All this concern that I don't become jealous is likely to *make* me so! Let's leave it, Vanna. I don't have a problem."

"I'm sorry, Kusac. Just give her my love, and travel safely," she said, releasing him.

A false dawn lit the sky as Kusac nodded to the guards on duty outside Noni's cottage. As he touched the door knob, he stopped long enough to reach for Carrie. It was just as Noni had said. She was in the rear bedroom, and alone.

Closing the door behind him, he looked over to where Kaid lay. The older male was dreaming, and it wasn't a pleasant dream he realized, watching as his movements became more and more restless.

Suddenly Kaid's whole body spasmed and with an involuntary cry of pain, he was awake. Kusac could smell his fear and sense the agony radiating from his injured hand. In moments, he was at his side and before he'd realized what he was doing, he'd placed his hand on his arm and was reaching mentally for him the way he would for a fellow telepath. Too late to stop, he had to continue. Locating the nerves that were transmitting the pain, he carefully deadened their sensitivity until he knew Kaid was no longer in distress.

As he finished, Kaid begin to retreat from him behind sophisticated mental barriers.

"In Vartra's name, Kaid! You've been a telepath all along!" Kusac exclaimed. "How? *How* did you manage to conceal it—and still be a Brother?"

Kaid's gaze, though feverish, was steady. "I didn't realize I was at first. By the time I did, I'd learned to block it."

As the moment stretched, Kusac realized neither he nor Kaid had broken the physical contact. As he pulled away, Kaid reached for him with his good hand, catching and holding him.

"The Triad's complete, Kusac," he said quietly.

"I know. I felt an echo of it while I was with Vanna. Why did you take so long to approach her? You showed almost as much restraint as me," he said, in an attempt to lighten the moment.

"Fear of revealing my talent, and fear of the emotions she'd wakened in me." Kaid's gaze didn't waver.

Kusac nodded. "I was sure you cared for her. She was afraid you might be indifferent."

His grin was slightly twisted. "Never that. Vartra knows I was far from indifferent to her, no matter how hard I tried."

"You were Carrie's choice," Kusac said. "I don't think you realized those last few weeks before you left quite how often she was aware of your surface thoughts. I saw it happen a couple of times myself, that's what made me suspect you might have some telepathic abilities. She chose you because of what she felt in your mind, and because she trusted you. So did I, Kaid."

"You've nothing to fear from me, Kusac. I won't come between you."

"I know. Vanna's done a lot to help my mental balance and I'm hoping you can do the same for Carrie. You've had a steadying influence on her for some time now."

He stopped, watching Kaid's face, the set of his ears, his scent. "What do you feel for her, Kaid? I need to know, because our Triad has deeper implications than what you shared with her today."

"Don't look too deeply into the past. The Triad's complete now, that's all that's needed. I won't go to her . . ."

"No," interrupted Kusac. "Make no promises, even to yourself, Kaid. Carrie's free to take a lover if she wishes. If it's you, all to the good. I'd rather she turned to you than anyone else. The old laws are there for a purpose: I've registered the Triad at the temple."

"What!" Kusac felt Kaid pull his mind back under control. "That's hardly necessary," he said, releasing his hold on Kusac and beginning to shift restlessly again.

"Not yet," agreed Kusac, sitting back slightly to watch Kaid's reaction.

He froze, eyes once more focussed on Kusac. "You know?"

"We knew it was possible. I told you, Kaid. Her choice— and mine."

Kaid sighed, looking away again. "We've all come a long way since the spring. Then I was Guildless, making a living doing what little work came my way in Ranz. Now here I am, at the heart of a new era on Shola."

"A long way, as you say," said Kusac. "I'd like to think we became friends on the journey."

Again the strange grin. "If we haven't, it's not through lack of you trying. Gods, Kusac, you've no idea of the chaos you and your Leska have caused in my life! Both of you awakening feelings I'd long ago learned to live without."

"I've some idea," said Kusac, grinning back at him. "You still haven't told me if you love her."

Kaid looked helplessly up at him. "I can't put a name to what I feel, Kusac. I've nothing to compare it with. Your Link to Carrie means you know everything she does. You're more likely to know than me."

"I don't know anything about the time you shared. When Noni has the place damped, nothing gets out, or in. Even now, all I know is Carrie's asleep. Besides, even when she wakes, what you shared will be yours, not for me to know."

"Dammit, Kusac! Yes I care! I care in a way that'll never change, but I can't give that caring a name! Look for yourself, you'll see I'm telling the truth!"

"I don't need to, your word is enough, Kaid, it always has been." He reached out and touched his hand, turning it over to feel the palm. "You're feverish. We shouldn't have talked of this till tomorrow. Shall I get Noni?"

"No. Just some water, please."

Kusac helped Kaid to sit up, then lifted the mug off the nightstand for him.

"Are you sure you don't want Noni?" he asked.

"No. Let me sleep," said Kaid, lying back down. "I'll be fine."

"Very well." He got up and went over to the faucet to refill the mug. Replacing it on the nightstand, he reached out to touch Kaid's hand again, gripping it gently. "Good night, Kaid," he said.

Kusac padded quietly into the bedroom. Dzaka was sleeping on a mat in front of the window, and Carrie was curled up in the spare bed.

Quietly, so as not to wake the other two occupants, he removed his robe, then eased up the covers and slipped in behind Carrie. In her sleep, she turned to him, reaching out to hold him as he tucked her against his chest. All was now well in his world.

Nicely done. The tone was unmistakably Noni's. *You'll make a good Clan Leader yet, when the time comes!*

CHAPTER 18

It was some time before Kaid finally managed to drift off to sleep again. When he did, his dreams were once more troubled.

It wasn't Stronghold, that much he knew, but it was similar. Like the lower corridors, this place had been carved from the living rock. Everywhere, people were rushing around, shouting to each other, gathering equipment, papers, disks—just about everything that could be moved. There was a sense of urgency, panic barely controlled as, one bundle at a time, the packages were handed to a living chain and passed out of sight.

Obviously this was an exodus. The inhabitants were leaving, and obviously the need to leave was urgent. He alone seemed to be uninvolved, noticed by none of them. A passive observer to the scene, he watched for any familiar faces but found none.

He tried looking round, and to his surprise, found he could do so. Experimentally, he took a few steps, and again found he was able to move. He was actually able to interact with the scene! He made for the corridor down which all the equipment was being passed. It was just wide enough to accommodate him as well.

It led to another chamber, higher than the last, and full of vehicles. The three largest, nearest the entrance, were being loaded first, and as soon as one was ready, it left. Overseeing the operation was someone he recognized—the male who'd been training Rezac.

Having just sent a vehicle out, he was standing talking to a younger male while he checked items off on the board he was carrying. The younger one suddenly turned and looked straight across the cavern at him.

Grasping the other by the arm, he pointed in Kaid's direction.

"There, Goran! By the tunnel!"

Confused, Kaid backed into the shadows. The people in the tunnel didn't seem to be aware of him, so how had the one talking to Goran seen him? He risked a glance into the main chamber again. Goran and the other were arguing.

"You're getting jumpy, Tiernay," he was saying. "You've been jumpy since they arrived. Let's just focus on the work in hand, shall we?"

"I tell you I saw something move!"

Goran looked up again, and taking Tiernay by the arm, led him toward the tunnel entrance where Kaid was concealed.

"You aren't going to be satisfied till we look," he said, stopping in front of the chain of people.

"Anyone passed by here in the last couple of minutes?" he asked, raising his voice.

Heads were shaken all round. "No one," said one.

Goran turned back to him. "Satisfied? Now unless you feel feverish, I suggest you get on with the loading. Ready or not we leave in two hours."

Tiernay nodded reluctantly and headed back to the center of the chamber.

Goran took a few steps into the tunnel, looking round carefully. His eyes slid over and past where Kaid crouched behind an outcrop of rock.

"There's been too many shadows like this lately," Goran muttered to himself. "I'll be glad to reach Stronghold, glad when they leave." With that, he turned and headed back the way he'd come.

As Kaid breathed out in relief, everything began to fade until he was once more spinning in the blackness of limbo. Colored lines shot through the darkness, lighting it up briefly, then were gone. One touched him, sending a jolt through him like a static discharge. Stuck to it now, he was propelled onward at a faster and faster pace till with a sickening familiarity, he felt himself dropped to the floor.

He landed badly, grazing his knees on the gravelly floor of the cavern. It was empty now, save for the tall figure he'd come to associate with Vartra. He stood framed in the entrance to the smaller chamber where the equipment they'd been rushing to remove had been kept.

His vision was blurring. Raising his hand, he rubbed his eyes. He heard footsteps off to his right, and looked round to see Goran and two of his companions heading over to Varta.

"We have to leave now," said Goran. "There's no more time left, Vartra."

"We're coming," the tall one said, glancing over his shoulder. "Are our travelers safe?"

For an instant, his gaze seemed to meet Kaid's, then the scene blurred momentarily.

"Yeah, all loaded up like you said. Have you put the collar in yet?"

"We're doing it now."

Kaid took his hands away from his eyes again, trying to focus on the figures at the opening, but his vision remained blurred. He blinked rapidly, and in a single moment of lucid sight, saw a steel door slide across the opening before he was pitched into blackness once more.

He woke with a yell that brought everyone tumbling into the kitchen.

"What is it?" demanded Kusac, gun clutched in one hand as he looked round the room.

Kaid pushed himself up on one arm, still blinking, trying to clear his vision. "They left it for us to find," he said.

"Who left what?" Carrie stood framed in the bedroom doorway.

"There was a steel door—and Vartra. In a cavern," he said, pushing himself upright. "It's there! Waiting all this time!"

"Check outside," Kusac ordered Dzaka as he cycled his gun down to standby. Dzaka nodded and crossed the room at a run, pulling the front door open.

Going over to Kaid, he sat down on the edge of his bed, reaching out to feel his hand. "Your fever's broken," he said. "How do you feel?"

"Fine. I'm fine," said Kaid, pulling his hand away and reaching for the mug of water. "I was in a series of caverns. They were rushing to leave—loading all they could carry onto trucks. Goran was there, and one called Tiernay." He saw Kusac look over at Carrie as she started across the room to them.

"The caverns, Kusac! He doesn't know what we found there!"

"Go on," said Kusac.

He took another drink before continuing. "There was a door they were about to close, a steel door." He looked up at them. "You know where it is."

Dzaka returned, shutting the door behind him. "Nothing," he said.

"Yes, we know where the door is," said Kusac "On the estate, buried under the old Monastery. We can't get it open."

"I can," said Kaid. "They left something there for us to find."

"What?"

"They know about us," said Kaid. "One of them sensed me. Tiernay. No one else could, but he did." He corrected himself. "No, that's not quite true. Vartra knew I was there, too."

"Did he say anything?" demanded Carrie, sitting on the other side of the bed. "Are you sure it was him?"

Kaid looked over to her. "I'm sure. Goran called him by name."

"What did they leave?" asked Kusac.

"A collar."

Kusac drew his breath in sharply. "What was it like?"

"I didn't see it."

"Could it have been gold with an inset stone . . . a green stone?"

"Where did you see one like that?" Kaid demanded.

"L'Seuli had one. He brought it with him when he escaped from Chezy with your message."

"Khezy'ipik," Kaid corrected him. "All Fyak's senior people wear them. And Ghezu."

"L'Seuli left the day he was given his. Your warning confirmed what he'd seen the collars do to the others," said Kusac. "It's being studied now to find out exactly what it is and how it works. You say Ghezu wears one?"

"I saw one round his neck when I was at Stronghold," said Kaid. "Fyak wears one. I recognized them from somewhere . . ."

"Why would Ghezu and Fyak . . ."

"Let's just stop here a moment," said Carrie, drawing everyone's attention to her. "We've just been told that one of these collars has been left for us in the caverns at Valsgarth, somewhere around that steel door. Right?"

Kaid nodded. "I think it's in the concealed operating panel."

"Then Kusac, I suggest you call our people and stop the Humans detonating that door, as they plan to do this morning," said Carrie calmly. "Or had you all forgotten about that?"

"Gods! She's right!" said Kusac, getting to his feet. "The rest of you get ready to leave, I'll contact them from the aircar comm!"

Kaid pushed his bedding aside and, swinging his legs out of bed, attempted to get to his feet.

"You stay put," said Kusac. "You're not fit to travel yet."

Kaid stood up, staggering slightly. "You can't open it without me," he said. "I need to be there."

"He's well enough to travel," said Noni from her bedroom door. "If he can do what he did yesterday, he's fit! Mind, I'm not finished with you yet, Tallinu! You'll come back when I tell you, hear me?"

"I'll come back, Noni," he said. "Has anyone anything I can wear? I'd sooner not travel like this."

"I've a jacket you can have," said Dzaka.

Kusac shrugged. "I know when I've lost," he said with a slight grin as he opened the outer door.

Kaid looked over at Dzaka. "Aldatan colors?"

Dzaka flicked his ears and looked away. "I reckoned if it's good enough for you . . ."

Kaid nodded, reaching out with his good arm to hold him close. "I was never ashamed of you, Dzaka. You were always the son I wanted," he said quietly. "We'll talk later. Meanwhile, I'd be proud to borrow a jacket from you."

They flew straight to the hill, landing beside the hoppers. Kusac was first out. T'Chebbi was waiting there to meet him.

"I've got guards on the door, Liege. The Human Pam was all for continuing. She said they're in charge of operations, not us."

"She did, did she? We'll see about that."

"You've brought him back." There was a quiet pleasure in her voice.

Kusac turned round to see Dzaka helping Kaid from the aircar. He turned back to T'Chebbi. "Yes, we brought him back," he said, fleetingly touching her shoulder. "He's home now."

She nodded, then turned to lead the way into the hill.

As they entered the large chamber, Kaid stopped to look around at the ruined vehicles. "I don't understand why they're still here," he said, a confused note in his voice. "I was sure they'd all escaped."

"Perhaps they took what they could, then returned to fetch more," said Kusac. "Don't let it worry you."

Kaid was still weak from his injuries. The surgery plus the fever had taken their toll as well and they had to move slowly. When they reached the next chamber, it was with relief he saw the packing crates near the wooden screens. He hardly even noticed the Humans sitting there.

"Eight guards?" Kusac murmured to T'Chebbi. "Surely two would have been enough."

"Of course, Liege. No point in encouraging them to try their strength. They'd be hurt. Wasteful, that is."

The small group of humans got to their feet when they entered the chamber. One of them, an older female, came striding over purposefully.

"Look, you've no right to stop our work," she said. "Our remit from General Raiban says we're in charge of the digs. In fact, you shouldn't even be on the land, let alone in here!"

Kusac turned his head to look at T'Chebbi. "Which one is she, T'Chebbi? I'm afraid I have great difficulty telling the females apart."

"Pam," said T'Chebbi succinctly.

"Ah, yes. Pam." He looked benignly at her, mouth opening in a human smile. She was tall, topping Carrie by some six inches. Iron gray hair cut close to her head, gave her a very severe look. Pale blue eyes flashed angrily at him from a thin face.

"This land belongs to me, Pam. It's been in my family for a great many generations. Are you suggesting that we should vacate our homes so you may dig up my land at will?"

She looked flustered. "No. No, of course not, but you're not allowed . . ."

Carrie came forward from the rear. "I think if you check with General Raiban you'll find that the normal rules don't apply here," she said. "Now if you don't mind, we've work to attend to, and one of our number is far from well." She turned away and started over toward the steel door.

Pam looked from her retreating figure back to Kusac, who

was talking to T'Chebbi. "Dammit! You can't just walk in here with your armed guards and tell us what to do!"

Kusac ignored her. "Get a floater chair sent for Kaid. We'll be a lot faster if he's not having to walk," he said. T'Chebbi nodded and moved away from them to activate her wrist comm.

"Dzaka! Take your father over to the . . ."

"No," Kaid interrupted him. "I want to see the door now. If you don't let me, I won't use the floater," he warned.

Kusac felt his arm being grabbed and turned round to face Pam again.

"You don't treat me like this and get away with it!" she said angrily. "You've got a human wife! I know damned well you can tell us apart! What makes you think you can insult my intelligence like that?"

"Don't try to dictate to me what I can do on my own land!" snapped Kusac, reaching up to remove her hand from his arm. "This site touches us all in ways you cannot possibly comprehend! We called you in to help us, not to order us around. If a way can be found to open this door without blasting, we'll try it!" He turned and stalked off to join Carrie and Kaid at the face of the door.

Kaid was feeling round the edges with his good hand.

"I tried that," said Carrie. "I know there's a concealed panel or something, it's just as if I've forgotten it," she said, the frustration she felt obvious in her tone.

He looked up at her. "You, too?" then went on feeling round the seal while hanging on to one of T'Chebbi's guards.

"Not there," he said at last, standing up and looking upward then down round either side of the narrow tunnel entrance that led to the door.

"Did that as well," said Carrie, standing back, hands on hips, watching him.

"There's nothing there, you fools!" said the Terran woman as she came up behind them. "We've searched the whole damned thing using scanners, the lot! You'll need to blow that door open!"

Carrie turned her head to look over her shoulder. "Do be quiet," she said conversationally.

"Even *you're* saying there's nothing there," said Pam in a more normal tone. "Your Godforsaken damned felines don't know everything! *I'm* the specialist here—that's why I was called in!"

Carrie ignored her, turning back to watch Kaid.

Reaching out, Pam took Carrie by the arm and swung her round.

The hum of five energy rifles and two pistols cycling up from standby echoed round the empty cavern. But it wasn't that that stopped the woman dead and made her drop Carrie's arm. It was the snarling mask of fury inches from her face, and the clawed hand that held her by the throat.

"Don't dare to touch the Liegena," hissed Dzaka, tail bushed out and lashing furiously from side to side.

Kusac skidded to a halt beside Kaid, clawed feet gouging lines in the earthen floor. "He's fast, your son," he said.

Kaid straightened up, hand still on the wall. "I believe he had a good teacher."

"Let her go, Dzaka," Carrie said calmly.

Dzaka released her, stepping back a couple of paces. He continued snarling, though more quietly now.

"I'd like to think this was a cultural misunderstanding," Carrie said, "but I'm not sure it is. You see, this isn't the first time this has happened. No one touches a Telepath unless invited to do so."

"Telepathy among us hasn't been proved," said Pam, massaging her throat with one hand.

"That's your second mistake. Anyone wearing purple is a recognized Telepath. As you see, I'm wearing purple, so is my mate. The third mistake you made," she said, dropping her voice to match her anger, "was attempting to touch a *pregnant* Telepath!"

"Shouldn't you step in here?" asked Kaid.

"No, I don't think so," said Kusac thoughtfully. "She's facing her own fears, which she needs to do. A few months ago a confrontation like this would have been unthinkable."

"Where's Zhyaf?" Carrie demanded, looking round the cavern at the guards.

"In the main cavern, Liegena," said one.

"Fetch him! No, I'll send to him, it's quicker," she corrected herself.

"You're pregnant?" said Pam, looking slightly dazed.

"Yes, and our males get very protective, as you've seen!"

"Especially when it's our Liegena," snarled Dzaka.

Kaid leaned forward and touched his son lightly on the shoulder. "Enough," he said.

Dzaka visibly forced himself to relax.

"Stand down the guard, Carrie," said Kusac quietly.

A gesture from her and the guns were lowered, then cycled down. Beyond them, the other Terrans hovered uncertainly.

The sound of running feet resolved itself into Zhyaf who emerged from the tunnel like a cork from a bottle.

"Liegena," he said, sketching a hasty bow when he reached her.

"What the hell do you think you're doing, Zhyaf?" she demanded. "This female has accosted me for the second time! It was your responsibility to see that they were all integrated into our culture! That hasn't been done, and I want to know why!"

"Liegena, I've only had three days," he said. "There are six of them . . ."

"It's Mara, isn't it? Dammit Zhyaf, you'll have to learn to control her!" She turned to Kusac. *Speak to him!* she sent.

"Zhyaf, you and I will have words later," said Kusac. "If the job was too large for you, you should have mentioned it earlier."

"You weren't here, Liegen," said Zhyaf, ears flicked back in a mixture of apology and defiance.

"That is irrelevant," said Kusac, his tone icy. "Where matters of this nature are concerned, you know the procedure! Now go!"

"Yes, Liegen." He inclined his head briefly before he left.

Kusac looked at the Terran female. "I should have you sent back to your headquarters," he said. "I've reason enough! What you've done is tantamount to a physical assault in Terran law. Just keep out of our way until I've made up my mind what I intend to do with you!" he said, waving her back.

Pam stood there, rigid with shock and indignation.

From behind him he heard a soft click, followed by the sound of machinery that had lain idle for centuries jolting into life.

"Get back," said Kaid, bumping into them as he moved away from the steel door. "The air inside will be stale at the very least, if not foul."

Kusac grasped Carrie round the waist, lifting her bodily into the air as he moved aside.

"You found it!"

Kaid nodded as, at a reasonable distance, they watched the steel door gradually slide back into the tunnel wall. "And this," he said, holding up a flexible gold collar. The green stone inset in it reflected the light from the units spread along the chamber walls.

Kusac reached for it, but Kaid held it back. "No. Not until I know it's safe." It slipped from his grasp and he stooped to pick it up.

"I held the one L'Seuli brought out of Chezy."

"Khezy'ipik. The Valtegans called it Khezy'ipik, " said Kaid automatically.

"How do you know that?" asked Carrie.

Kaid looked confused for a moment. "I remember it being called that," he said.

"You're right. Sorli mentions the old name in the records he gave us, but how could you remember?" asked Carrie.

Kaid put his hand up to the side of his head as the cavern seemed to swim around him.

"Catch him!" said Carrie sharply. "He's about to pass out!"

T'Chebbi caught him as he began to stagger.

Carrie reached forward and took the collar from his grasp.

Kaid seemed to rally, making a snatch for it, but he missed. "No! You mustn't hold it, Carrie! It could harm you!"

She was already examining it, turning it so the light shone on the stone. As Kusac reached forward to take it from her, she moved aside.

"It doesn't affect me," she said slowly. "I can handle it in this state, but you and Kaid can't. I don't think any Sholan could."

"What do you mean?" demanded Kusac. "I won't have you risking our daughter over a damned torc, no matter how old or important it is!"

Carrie tore her gaze away from it and shoved it in her copious pocket. "It's safe with me," she said, her tone brusque. "If you want proof, look at Kaid." She nodded in his direction.

Kusac did, and saw that he was making an almost instant recovery.

"It hasn't done that to me," she said. "The door's open, by the way."

His attention diverted, Kusac looked over to where the steel door had been. He took a step forward, then stopped.

"No one's going in there till we've checked the air," he said. "We also need lighting." He turned to face the half dozen Terrans, his gazed fixing on Pam.

"We're supposed to be cooperating on this dig," he said. "So let's cooperate. We need lighting. Get the help you need from my people. I want the lights up and working within the hour."

"Can we count on your lot to help us?" demanded Pam. "So far, they've been of no use whatsoever!"

"T'Chebbi, you liaise for us, please."

"Liege," she said, flicking her ears before she joined the small group of Terrans.

Carrie turned to Kusac, drawing his attention away from the archaeologists. "Vanna's here," she said, looking uncomfortable. "She's brought the floater chair, food, and Marak."

"Exactly what we need," he said, looking over to the tunnel from which Vanna was emerging.

The floater was being propelled by Jack. In it was the food and a medikit. Vanna came straight over to them, casting a professional eye over Kaid.

"Just as I thought," she said, passing Marak to Carrie. "Here, you hold him while I see to Kaid."

"But Vanna," she said, looking in horror at the active bundle she'd had thrust upon her. "I don't know anything about cubs!"

"You'll have to learn soon enough," Vanna said firmly, taking the medikit and food basket from the chair while Jack parked it. "You might as well start now."

Vanna. Kusac's thought was reproachful.

Neither you nor she can go through the rest of your lives with you continuing to protect her from every little breeze! You need to be more robust with her at times! She's a big girl, you know. She used the Terran term.

I know, and getting bigger every day, he sent wryly, turning to watch his mate.

"Don't let the cloth round him fall off unless you want to clean up the mess," Vanna warned, glancing briefly up at her as she guided Kaid into the chair.

"Vanna!" wailed Carrie, as Marak purred and squeaked with delight over her long hair.

Kaid sat down with relief. "I'm not an invalid, Vanna," he said.

"No. You should still be bedridden," she said, checking his wrists and cheek. "But I know that's out of the question now. How's his back healing?" she asked Kusac.

"Fine."

"It doesn't hurt," said Kaid, leaning back and closing his eyes.

"Liar," she said, opening her medikit. "I can feel it the moment I touch you," she said as she unpacked a couple of ampules.

"Kaid, Vanna needs to know," said Kusac quietly, bending over him.

"I need to know what?" she asked, loading her hypoderm.

"I'm a telepath," said Kaid tiredly.

Vanna looked up sharply. "Since when?" Pushing his fur aside, she wiped him with an antiseptic pad before pressing the hypo against his upper arm.

"Always," he said briefly.

"Can you block, or will you need suppressants?" she asked, squatting back on her haunches.

Kaid opened his eyes. "I can block," he said with a small grin. "That's about all I can do."

Vanna nodded. "You're not going to run out on me this time, are you, Kaid?"

"Not if I can help it."

"Good." She stood up and nodded to Jack. "We'll move away from this entrance. You can do without the clouds of dust this lot will be kicking up when they start stringing lighting units everywhere."

Jack flicked the power back on and the chair began to rise until it floated some six inches from the floor.

"Do you want to drive it, or shall Jack?" she asked.

"I'll do it,' said Kaid, stretching his good arm along the armrest till his fingertips matched the recesses. Extending his claws, he turned the chair and floated it over to the pile of crates at the other side of the cavern where one or two of the Terrans still sat.

Vanna looked over to Carrie who had finally worked out that since no one was going to rescue her, she'd better make Marak comfortable.

"Coming?" she asked.

Carrie nodded and followed her over.

"Hey, he's cute," said one of the Terran males. "Hi, little fella," he said, reaching out to touch him between the ears. "Your baby?" he asked Vanna.

She nodded.

"Which one's your husband?"

"The one called Brynne," she said, looking him straight in the eye.

"The . . . Human . . . called Brynne?"

"That's right," she said. "You're looking at the first Sholan/Human child."

A female leaned forward to touch him. Marak, willing to play grab-the-finger at any time, happily reached out, snagging the digit with his extended claws.

"Ouch!" she said, wincing. "He's got sharp claws, but you're right, he really is cute."

Carrie pulled her head back to see him more clearly. "I suppose you're right," she said. "He is rather pretty."

She looked up at Carrie, Marak still attached to her finger. "I heard you say you were pregnant. Will yours look like this?"

Carrie glanced at Vanna in momentary panic, finding her friend regarding her composedly. "Well, answer her, Carrie," she said.

She looked back at the woman. "Yes. My daughter will look like this," she said, managing to keep her voice level and calm. At her side, a hand reached out to touch her elbow. She looked down at Kaid.

You're doing fine, he sent.

The woman laughed as Marak put her finger into his mouth and began to suck it. "He's just like my sister's child," she said. "I guess all babies are essentially the same. I'm Mattie by the way, and that's Greg." She indicated the male who'd admired Marak. I know you're Carrie, but I don't know your friends."

"Vanna, and Kaid," she said.

"Hi there." She smiled sympathetically at Kaid. "What happened to your hand? Did you have an accident?"

"You could say that," he replied, putting his good hand back on the chair arm.

"I'm sorry to hear that. I hope it's better soon." She looked up at Carrie again. "Don't pay any attention to Pam. She can be a pain to get on with, but she really knows her stuff."

"How did she get to be in charge of your team?" asked Carrie.

"Politics," said Mattie with a grimace. "When this dig came up, she demanded to lead it, and pulled strings to see she got what she wanted."

Carrie made a noncommittal noise as she sat down on one of the cases.

Vanna turned back to Kaid. "Feeling better?"

"A lot, thank you."

"I'll check your hand later. There's too much dust around to look at it here. Jack, would you hand me up the protein drink for Kaid, please?"

As she shared the contents of the basket around, she reached for Kusac.

Have a look at Carrie. I told you this was what she needed.

He looked. *All right. I admit it, you were right and I was wrong. You have to realize it's not easy for me, especially at the moment. All my instincts are demanding that I protect her from everything.*

I do appreciate that, Kusac. So long as you're aware of it, I know you'll manage. Come and get some food. You can't go in till they've got the lights up anyway.

She handed Carrie a small bottle. "Want to feed him?" she asked, pleased to see her son lying happily in the crook of Carrie's arm while she teased him with a lock of her hair.

"Yes, of course I'll feed him," she said, "but I thought that . . ."

"I can't always feed him," she said. "So every now and then he has a bottle. Just put it in his mouth, he'll hang onto it for you," she said.

It was a couple of hours before the lights were strung up and the cavern ready for them to enter. By that time, Kaid was looking and feeling a lot better. Jack had taken the rug out of the floater's back storage locker and spread it round him.

"It can be cold when you're sitting in just one position for several hours," he said.

Marak had been returned to his carrier and was peacefully sleeping off his feed.

"What do you intend to do about Pam?" Mattie asked Kaid as they made their way over to the entrance. "Quite frankly, we wouldn't miss her if she went! She's as unpleasant to us as she is to you."

Kaid set the floater to a height that matched his own when standing so he could answer her quietly.

"It depends on her. If she leaves Carrie alone, Kusac and she will probably tolerate her continued presence on the estate. If she doesn't, then she'll be sent away."

"Can they do that? I thought General Raiban had ordered . . ."

"You don't know the politics behind this," interrupted Kaid. "Briefly, Kusac's father is head of Alien Relations. Kusac was the one who first made contact with the Terrans on Keiss . . ."

"So he and Carrie were the first mixed Leska pair," she finished. "That part I had worked out."

"We've been on the cutting edge of the research into our past since the beginning, collating the various records of dreams and visions and suchlike . . ."

"Dreams and visions? You've based research on dreams and visions?" Her tone was one of disbelief.

"Yes, and they led us here, to this hill."

"You're kidding me!"

"I'll tell you the details another time," he said as they passed from one cavern into the other. "But to continue, because we've been so instrumental in the discoveries, Raiban isn't going to alienate us by keeping us out of this dig. She needs the information only we can provide."

Mattie shook her head slowly. "I still don't get it. Dreams and visions, for God's sake."

"Exactly," said Kaid. "Just stay around, you'll learn." He speeded the chair up a little to catch up with Kusac who was standing a few feet ahead of him.

"Just look at this place, Kaid," he said. "Think of the effort that went into outfitting it!"

They were in the central aisle of the room. To their right was a long wooden bench where various beakers and equipment had been left. A couple of notepads lay there, their writing long since faded. Carrie reached out to touch one and it dissolved in a small cloud of dust.

"Don't touch anything!" Pam's sharp voice echoed round the cavern.

Inwardly, Carrie growled her anger. She knew the older woman was right, but by Vartra, she was abrasive! Now she had an overwhelming desire to touch something else just to prove to Pam that she wouldn't be ordered around.

To the left of the room was a long rack of metal shelves. Wires dangled all over them, but the equipment they'd been attached to was gone save for one small screen which sat on top of a unit faced with small windows and keypads. Beyond that, at the far end of the cavern, sat a large boxed unit. The front had small glass bulbs set into its surface as well as units with horizontal slots obviously designed to accept some kind of physical object.

Pipes ranged along the upper walls, and in the far right hand "corner," was another tunnel mouth.

"It's a lab," said Mattie as she looked around. "A research lab." She walked past Kusac, stopping to look at the devices set on the shelves to her left.

Carrie had gone over to the large metal box at the end of the passage.

"Don't touch anything till we have a record of what's here," said Pam, pointing to Greg who carried a vid recorder. The recorder was running as he slowly panned over the bench, then moved on to the shelving behind it.

Mattie examined the unit with the keypads visually before cautiously touching it with the pencil she was carrying.

"Has anyone tried the power just on the off chance it's still working?" Bob called out.

A ripple of laughter greeted his remark.

"OK, so it wasn't my brightest idea," he said with a grin.

"Pity about the power," said Mattie, jotting down a few notes on her pad. "I'd swear this unit was part of an analyzer, and the one above would probably be linked into the main computer, wherever that is."

"Over here," said Carrie. "This has to be their main comp. It's huge! Almost as large as the one we had on the *Eureka*. In fact, they're pretty similar. See if you can find any data storage disks or crystals. I'm sure the slots are for putting in some kind of flat device for reading and recording data."

"It's possible that we still have computers capable of reading data stored that way," said Mattie.

"If you can't, Keiss can," said Carrie, turning away from the box. "And there are the Touibans whose speciality is comps of all types."

"There are Touibans in Valsgarth," said Kusac thoughtfully from where he was examining what was obviously a microscope of some kind.

They heard a scraping sound from behind the metal shelving where Dzaka had gone prowling.

"You were told not to touch anything!" repeated Pam, rushing around the corner.

"It's only drawers full of decaying papers," said Dzaka.

"Dzaka, look in the end unit, bottom drawer," said Kaid, maneuvering his chair down the passageway between the shelves and the stools that sat at the side of the long bench.

They heard his claws clicking on the bare wood, then he stopped. Again the squeaking of metal against metal.

"I think I've found what you're looking for." Dzaka's voice had a strange quality to it, part awe and part elation.

"Leave that where it is!" Pam's voice traveled loud and clear through the room. Moments later, Dzaka emerged carrying several flat objects which he took to Carrie.

Taking them from him, she examined them carefully. "They could be data disks," she said. "The casing's about to disintegrate, but I'm sure that can be got round."

"I'll take them," said Pam, holding out her hand to Carrie.

"I think not," Carrie replied, moving away from the computer to stand beside Kusac. She handed the disks to him.

"I'll get Father to set it up so we can bring the Touibans in to see this place. Once they've got an idea of the type of device that reads these disks, they can duplicate something, I'm sure."

"Those disks will be sent to our HQ for analysis, nowhere else," said Pam firmly. "I'm asking you to hand them over to me so the proper authorities can have them."

Kusac sighed as he pocketed the disks. "You just don't listen, do you? We *are* the proper authorities. We personally have the resources of not only of a whole planet at our fingertips, but those of another three species, one of which is expert in all aspects of communications and storing data. Yours is only *one* of the cultures we have helping us."

"I want those disks!"

"My son is quite right, Ms Southgate," said Konis as he walked down the passage to join them. "Those particular finds do not fall within your area of responsibility." He stopped beside Kaid for a moment, reaching out his palm in greeting. "It's good to see you back, Kaid."

Hesitantly Kaid returned the gesture, aware that Konis had welcomed him as a fellow telepath. "Thank you, Clan Lord."

"I thought I'd see how you're getting on," he said to

Kusac. *And bring Kitra over to see Dzaka,* he sent with a slight smile.

Kusac grinned as he glanced over to where his young sister was greeting Dzaka. *Looks like they've missed each other.*

She's been pestering us for news every day!

"Lord Aldatan," began Pam, squaring up to him as she stepped between him and Kusac. "*We're* supposed to be in charge of this site! My team and I cannot possibly do our job properly if crucial finds are withheld from us!"

"I trust my son's judgment, Ms Southgate," said Konis. "If he feels the Touibans are better equipped to handle the disks, then they will be given to them. The important factor here is recovering the data, not cataloging finds. You are here to help us achieve that end, not fulfil your personal ambitions. It might be better for you and your team to keep that point in mind, then you are likely to face fewer disappointments." He returned to Kusac. "When do you want the Touibans?"

"Today?"

Konis frowned. "Rather short notice, but I'll contact them and see what can be done. Where can they work?"

"At our lab," said Vanna. "We're not using most of those rooms yet. They can use the whole of the first floor for living space if they need it."

"Get your estate manager and main attendant to organize appropriate bedding and food. If they need advice, tell them to contact Che'Quul. He's dealt with all our Alliance friends at one time or another."

While they were talking, Carrie leaned over to speak to Kaid. "How did you know the disks were there?" she asked.

He raised one shoulder in a shrug. "I just knew. I don't know how." He tried to force himself to remember but he found it impossible to focus his mind on the subject.

"It doesn't matter," she said, touching his shoulder as she felt his distress. "We have the disks, that's what matters. We're in the new house now," she said, changing the subject. "I hope you'll stay with us. We need to talk about this, and the collar, later."

"Thank you," he said quietly. "I remember more, but it's from the time of the drug dreams and it's difficult to recall. I wish I knew what he'd given me!"

"The physician at Stronghold found a phial of the drug in the medic's kit. He gave it to us for analysis."

"He did? What have you found out?"

She shook her head. "Nothing yet. Jack's been working on it with Vanna's help. We'll ask them later." She stopped to study his face. "The drug dreams. We need you to record them. Are you able to cope with the memories?"

His face hardened, his eyes taking on a dead quality. "I can cope," he said. "Fyak uses the same drug, if my dreams are to be believed. It's a plant that grows in the caverns at Khezi'ipik. He found one of the green stones, like those in the torcs, among its roots. The stones and the plant are connected somehow."

"Why do you keep calling it Khezi'ipik?"

He looked away for a moment. "I remember it being called that. Khezi'ipik was the Valtegan name for those caverns. It was their hatching ground."

Carrie leaned against his chair as the blood drained from her face. "Oh, dear God, no! They were *breeding* on Shola?"

Kaid's hand closed on her arm like a vice as Kusac looked in their direction. "Send to him! Tell him you're all right before everyone knows!" he said urgently, keeping his voice low. "The hatchery was there fifteen hundred years ago, Carrie, not now!"

She nodded and did as he asked.

"He's not convinced but he's leaving it till later," she said. "How do you know all these things?"

"Drug dreams and memories from somewhere perhaps. Somehow I just remember it, Carrie. It's all confused and vague—all blended into one. Leave it for now. I shouldn't have mentioned it until we were alone."

Shortly after, Vanna ordered Kaid back to the main house to rest.

"You look awful," she said frankly. "Carrie, Dzaka, see he's put to bed and stays there. I'll look in later this evening and check on his hand." She handed her medikit to Kaid. "You might as well take care of your own pain medication now," she said. "Don't look for Fastheal, I purposely left it out!"

"I wouldn't touch it, believe me," he said.

"I'm not taking that risk after the last time!" she answered.

"I'll be home for third meal," said Kusac, giving Carrie a hug. "I've got to tie matters up before tomorrow. I think it'd be better if you weren't here when the Touibans arrive."

"If you're going to be unavailable tomorrow," said Kaid, "we need to see Ghyan tonight. We've matters to discuss that can't wait."

"Invite him over to eat with us," said Kusac.

"Let me understand this fully," said Ghyan, sitting forward in his seat. "Effectively you're saying that of these drug dreams Kaid had, we know that two of them can be proved to have actually happened."

"That's right," said Carrie. "I think you can also add a third. The dream he had last night concerning the lock for the steel door, and this." She placed the gold-colored flexible collar on the table. "They were exactly where he said they'd be. I think that somehow Kaid's managing to *physically* travel, not only to distant locations, but back in time."

"I don't think we can assume he's physically going back in time, Carrie," said Kusac, picking up the collar to examine it once more.

"No one in the cavern saw me," said Kaid. "A couple of them sensed I was there. I may only have been a presence in their time."

"We still need to know if, when you can be seen and touched, your physical body goes with you, or duplicates itself in the new location," said Kusac. "Would you object to there being vid surveillance in your room for the next few nights? If you have another dream, we'd at least know whether or not you were still present in your room."

"No problem. I'm rather anxious to know what's happening myself," said Kaid.

"Now, about these," said Kusac, waving the collar gently. "You said all Fyak's top people wore one, including Fyak himself?"

Kaid flicked an ear in assent. "And Rhaid, the captured telepath."

"L'Seuli said the same," he said thoughtfully, looking closely at the green gem set into the center of the device.

Playing a hunch, Carrie leaned forward, hand held out. "Can I have it, please, Kusac?" she asked.

Kusac kept running his fingers over the gem. "Hmm? Oh, not yet, Carrie," he said. "I'm trying to work out how it was made. It's a cunning piece of craftsmanship, the way they've managed to make it so flexible."

Her suspicions confirmed, Carrie sat back again and

looked at the other two males. "Is it just me, or does Kusac seem a little distracted?" she asked quietly.

"A little," said Ghyan with a slight frown. "Why?"

"You take it from him," she said. "Go on."

Obviously puzzled, but prepared to go along with her request, Ghyan turned to Kusac. "May I have a look at it?" he asked.

Kusac seemed to consider it for a moment or two, then with obvious reluctance, handed it to Ghyan.

"Now watch Ghyan," she said to Kaid.

It quickly became obvious that when it was being handled, it seemed to instill in the holder an unwillingness to part with it. The only one who seemed impervious was Carrie.

Kaid at first refused to touch it, then reluctantly took it from Ghyan. The effect on him was startling. He became lethargic to such a degree that Carrie hurriedly leaned forward and snatched it from his hands. His return to normal was slower than that of the others, but when he had, he was able to describe how he'd felt.

"I'm remembering again," he said. "They were pacifiers. The closing mechanism on that one's been damaged. Normally, once it's been put on you, you can't get it off without alerting the nearest Valtegan."

"Why? Did they put these collars on everyone?" asked Kusac.

"I'd rather know what you mean by *remembering*," said Carrie.

Kaid looked across at her. "I still don't know," he said. "I'm just aware that it's something I *used* to know but forgot. And no, the collars were worn only by telepaths. It was to inhibit their ability to mind talk. I don't know how it worked, but it was a Valtegan device."

"One which doesn't appear to affect Humans, if I'm anything to go by," said Carrie, picking it up again to examine the stone. "Where did you say Fyak dug up a stone?"

"In the soil at the base of the plant. In among the roots. It's the same color of green as the sap."

"The liquid in the phial the physician gave me was just this shade too," she said thoughtfully.

While the others discussed the two dreams Kaid had had of the caverns, Carrie continued to hold the collar and handle the gem. She knew there was a secret locked inside it, knew that it was up to her to find out what it was.

It felt soft, almost soapy, as she rubbed her finger over it. She thought she felt a slight crack in the surface. Putting it up to her mouth, she first ran her tongue, then her teeth across the surface before going back to rubbing it. She'd been right. There was a crack. She reached inside it with her mind, trying to identify with its composition so she could match its natural resonance.

It worked rather too well. Suddenly she was flung into a memory it had stored of the life of the wearer.

The room was bare and antiseptic, the temperature way too high for Sholans, but the Valtegans had little tolerance for the cold. She sat huddled in the corner, watching as the Valtegan guards came in. There were four of them. Two stayed at the door, one with his rifle trained on her, the other on Rezac, as the other two advanced on him.

Rezac had been pacing round the room, frustrated and angry that they'd been arrested so soon.

"It's too soon, Zashou. We shouldn't have been picked up for another month at least!" He banged his hand hard against the wall in frustration. "Dammit! We could lose it now, just because of this! All those risks, all those lives wasted!"

The Valtegans had only picked them up on suspicion. They hadn't known for sure they were telepaths until they did the pain test. Then they'd both reacted, her worse than him. She'd doubled up retching while he'd managed to maintain his front of insensitivity for several minutes before he, too, had succumbed.

She watched while the lizards took hold of him, placing the collar round his neck, then electronically sealing it on. He'd struggled, but it hadn't done any good. The Valtegans were stronger than them. Released, he'd been flung into a corner as they turned to her. They'd made the mistake of not activating his collar first.

She'd tried to sink back into the wall as they came for her but it had done no good. Cool hands grasped her, the nonretractable claws scratching her even through her pelt as they dragged her to her feet.

As soon as they'd touched her, he'd exploded with rage, the anger coupled with an empty stomach keeping the pain sensitivity at bay for a time. One held

her still despite her struggles, managing to collar her
while the other dealt with Rezac.

"Rezac, leave it!" she'd yelled, twisting in the Valtegan's grasp so she could see her Leska. "Don't! You'll
get hurt!"

He hadn't listened. Amazingly, one of his blows
floored the guard and suddenly he was attacking the
one holding her. Another lucky blow and that guard was
sent flying.

Rezac grabbed her collar in both hands, pulling at the
ends till it snapped and fell to the floor. That was all
he'd time to do before the stunner hit him full in the
back and he collapsed against her, unconscious.

She'd yowled in fear as they'd both tumbled to the
floor. Then everything went black.

She felt something ripped from her hands and a worried
voice saying over and over again, "Carrie, come back. Come
back to me."

Her vision cleared but she couldn't stop shaking.

"Carrie, come back. You're at home in Valsgarth. Come
back, Carrie."

Looking up she saw the fear in Kusac's amber eyes.
Reaching up with a trembling hand, she touched his face.

"I'm back," she said. "I saw Valtegans."

He held her close. "You keep doing this to me," he
growled in her ear. "Dammit, stop frightening me like that,
Carrie! What the hell were you doing?"

"I'll tell you if you let me go," she said, her voice muffled
against his chest. The shaking had begun to subside now that
she knew she'd left the other life behind.

"Sorry," he said, releasing her. "What were you doing
with that damned collar anyway? You seemed to drift off
mentally, as if you weren't there. Are you sure it's safe for
you to handle it? You seem to have had an even worse reaction to it than the rest of us!" He sat back on his haunches but
remained in front of her.

"I tried to tap into it, and succeeded rather too well," she
said. "Where is it?"

"I don't know," he growled. "I threw the damned thing to
the other end of the room. It's dangerous, Carrie."

"No, it isn't. I saw the memories it had stored from its last
owner."

"Who was it?"

"It was Rezac and Zashou again. Kaid was right. The Valtegans used them to inhibit the telepaths, and to identify them." A shudder ran through her again at the memory of the reptiles. "They were electronically sealed on so they couldn't be removed, but Rezac managed to rip this one off Zashou before they'd closed it properly. How it got here, I've no idea."

She reached out to hold Kusac's arm, looking over his shoulder at the other two males. "The Valtegans were there," she said. "They'd taken Shola just as they took Keiss. If we go back, we're going back to them! I don't know if I can do it, Kusac. Not if there are Valtegans there."

"We shouldn't be going anywhere near the Valtegans," said Kaid. "Vartra and his people are trying to avoid them. That much is clear from everything we've read and experienced."

"Shola was crawling with them, Kaid! You told us they even had a hatchery at Chezy! They were here to stay as far as they were concerned!" The black terror of her sister's death loomed in front of her again: the smell of blood and the feel of Valtegan claws touching her started her shivering once more.

The knock at the door came so unexpectedly that Carrie found herself starting in fear and crying out.

Vanna and Jack came rushing in.

"What's wrong?" Vanna demanded, moving quickly toward the little group. "What's happened?"

"Carrie's had a scare, that's all," said Kusac, leaning forward to hold her again. "She picked up memories from that collar Kaid found, memories of Valtegans, and it's started up her old nightmares. The knock on the door was the last straw, I'm afraid."

Vanna went round behind the chair and sat on the arm at her side. "Come on, cub. Everything's all right, you know it is," she said, reaching out to stroke her hair.

Carrie suddenly felt embarrassed by all the fuss and, forcing the memories to the back of her mind, she pushed Kusac gently away. "I'm fine now," she said. She turned to Vanna. "We've just discovered that back at the time of the Cataclysm, Shola was crawling with the damned Valtegans!"

"And they want you to go back to those days," said Vanna sympathetically. "I understand your fears, Carrie, but don't look on it as going back to a time dominated by the Valtegans, look on it as going back to a time where the knowledge you have now can help those people against them! Perhaps your going back helped them finally overthrow the Valtegans."

"That's probably where your memories are coming from, Kaid," said Ghyan. "You're remembering what you learned while you were in the past."

"You could be right," he murmured, keeping a watchful eye on Carrie.

Carrie was aware of his concern too, a quieter presence at the edges of her mind. "Hey, people," she said, rubbing her eyes. "I'm fine, really I am. It's Kaid who's the invalid, not me."

"Are you sure?" asked Vanna as she got up from her perch.

"Positive. It was just so real for a while, as if I was there with them, that's all."

Vanna nodded and went over to Kaid as Kusac got to his feet and turned to welcome Jack.

"Oh, I've just come over to bring myself up to date on what's been going on, and to let you know what we found out about that drug," he said, handing Vanna her medikit before heading for the nearest seat. Passing Kaid, he patted him gently on the shoulder. "Good to see you back," he said.

Kusac sprawled along Carrie's chair arm, resting his hand on her shoulder, needing the physical contact with her. "So what did you find?" he asked.

"It's a narcotic derived from a plant extract, not native to Shola, and it has strong psychotropic properties. All of this I'm sure isn't news to you, but we have something that is. When we evaporated some of the liquid off the drug, the residue formed a small green stone, similar to our Earth's amber."

"The stones in the collars," said Kaid. "No wonder they have mind-altering qualities! I'll guarantee that that's why Fyak uses them!"

"But where did he get them from?" asked Carrie. "Could he have found them in the caverns at Chezy?"

"Khezi'ipik," said Kaid grimly. "Don't let's forget that place is a Valtegan hatchery." He was aware that he was repeating himself, but somehow it seemed important, too important to ignore.

"Your hand, please," said Vanna as she hauled a small stool out from under the table and sat at his feet.

"If that collar could be left for Kaid to find, what's to prevent someone else leaving a large number of collars for Fyak to use?" asked Kusac.

"Nothing at all," said Ghyan, digging in his robe pocket for his comp pad. "I seem to remember a reference to the green seeds or something like that in the texts that Esken gave us." He punched in a search command and the relevant text appeared.

"Here it is. *Secondly, Bless all contrivances of ancient days, that they become Holy, for they hold the Green Seeds of New Regret.* If there were large numbers of these collars, or even large numbers of the stones around on Shola back then, likely there'll still be some out there somewhere in the ruined cities. *That's* why there are injunctions to be sure to "Bless" the old cities! Only by doing that can they be sure the stones have been destroyed!"

"Where's the one you pitched across the room?" asked Kaid as he sat patiently with his arm on Vanna's lap while she cut off the old dressing.

Kusac got up and went to look for it. "You aren't going to believe this," he said, coming back holding it carefully by the clasp. "The stone's shattered. They must be very fragile."

"Let me hold it," said Kaid.

"You're joking!" said Kusac, about to put it down on the table.

"No, let him," said Carrie. "It affected him most, so we'll easily be able tell if it's still working."

Reluctantly, Kusac passed it over to Kaid. Nothing happened.

He handed it back. "Looks like a minor blow is enough to break it," he said.

"It didn't break when Rezac ripped it off Zashou and threw it to the ground," said Carrie. "However, I did feel a crack in the surface after Kaid dropped it in the cavern."

"Maybe it has something to do with its age," said Jack. "After fifteen hundred years, I'd be somewhat fragile!"

"Well, we'll still treat it with respect," said Kusac, putting the collar on the table out of harm's way.

"Mind if I take it to the lab?" asked Jack, picking it up and examining it.

"Help yourself," said Kusac. "I think we've got all we can from it so far."

Carrie was aware of Kaid's sharp intake of breath as Vanna carefully removed the dressing from his injured hand. She looked over to him in concern. "How is it?" she asked.

"I'm impressed," said Vanna, giving the wound a quick visual inspection before getting her handheld scanner out and running it over him. "Noni's done a good job. I couldn't have done better myself. The fingers appear to be healing well. I can see the beginnings of new bone growth on the shattered one. If it keeps progressing at this rate, you should have a reasonable amount of mobility back in that finger, Kaid." She put the scanner down and began preparing a fresh dressing.

"I'll leave the scanner with you too. Just don't lose this one," she said. "I haven't quite forgiven you yet for your raid on my drugs and equipment!"

"I apologize, Vanna," he said. "I had to get out to Rhijudu as quickly as possible."

"No excuse!" she said, her tone belying the words.

"Kaid, I think we need to speak to L'Seuli regarding the dreams set in the caverns at Khezi'ipik," said Kusac. "He spent some time undercover there. If anyone can confirm what you saw of a temple and walls covered with carvings, it's him."

"He can't confirm whether or not I saw Fyak there at the same time as the Valtegans. The only way we can do that is for me to try to return next time I have a drug dream."

"I hate to put a damper on both your enthusiasm," said Carrie, "but I hope Kaid's dreams are finished once and for all!"

"We all do," said Kusac. "What concerns me is that not only we, but Esken and Sorli are sure there's a link between Fyak and the past."

"Fyak preaches against the *Demons of Fire,*" said Kaid, his voice sounding strained as Vanna began to put a fresh dressing over the wounds on his hand. "He may well be an agent for the Valtegans, but if he is, he doesn't realize it."

"I'm sure he's acting for them in some way," said Carrie. "His fanatical desire to destroy all telepaths fits in with the fact that in the past the Valtegans were marking them apart from the rest of Sholan society and using pacifiers to keep them under control. It's no coincidence that Fyak is using the same mechanism to control Rhaid."

"Then there's his social engineering with the tribes. He's breaking down the tribal ties and their interdependence on each other till all that remains is the individual and the Faithful, with Fyak at the top leading them," said Kusac. "It seems our decision to go to the Fire Margins is more important for Shola than we realized. Not only will we have won the right to set up our own clan, but we may get answers as to why we have close links with Humanity, and find out what the Valtegans and Fyak are up to."

"I've still no idea whether you'll actually have a physical presence in the past or not," said Ghyan, "but if what Kaid's been through is anything to go by, then it looks as if you are flesh not spirit. That being the case," he said with a sigh, "I suggest you consider taking the ritual as soon as possible, before Carrie's pregnancy becomes too advanced for her to go anywhere safely."

Carrie felt her stomach turn over in fear as he spoke. She looked first at Kusac, then at Kaid, seeing and feeling a mixture of grim determination and fear in their faces and the set of their ears.

"I think you're right," she said, surprised at how steady her voice sounded. "What's the latest I can safely go, Vanna?"

Vanna looked up from bandaging Kaid's hand. "Safely?" she asked. "Leaving aside that no one's ever survived the journey, how many weeks on are you now?"

"Thirteen."

"Given that your Talent will disappear at sixteen weeks, and by then you're so large that you're never comfortable, no matter what you do, I'd say you have to go within the next two weeks at the latest. After that, forget it until after your cub's born."

"I'll be ready," came Kaid's quiet voice as Vanna refastened the sling round his neck.

"Two weeks," said Kusac softly, his hand tightening on Carrie's shoulder.

When their gathering broke up, Dzaka helped Kaid upstairs to his suite.

"It's time to talk," said Kaid, sinking down with relief into one of the easy chairs in his lounge. "Will you get us a drink?"

"What do you want?" asked Dzaka, going over to the dispenser.

"Protein. I need to get back my strength as quickly as possible." He watched his son dial the drink for him, then another for himself before he rejoined him.

"Thanks," he said, accepting the mug and waiting for him to sit down. "I see you're wearing your mother's Clan jewelry."

"I waited till you'd returned before putting the torc and buckle on," Dzaka said. "They seemed . . ." He searched for a word, then shrugged. "pointless . . . if you weren't there."

"You want to know what happened."

Dzaka stirred in his seat, obviously uncomfortable about the forthcoming discussion. "It's not my business to know what went on between you and my mother."

"You made it your business," reminded Kaid, lifting his mug to his mouth. "Some of it I can tell you now, but not all. I'm still oath-bound to not talk of it with you."

Dzaka looked up. "To whom? Who could be so involved with what happened between you and her that they could demand such an oath?"

"That, unfortunately, is also part of the oath. At least you saw her, heard what she had to tell you, before she died. It's more than I had. I remember my mother only dimly, and my father not at all, but you know that."

"Then tell me what you can," he said.

"Khemu drew males to her like a flower attracts insects," he said. "Yes, she played us off against each other, but lightly, not seriously. She had a deeper relationship with about four of us, not sexual, but more intellectual. We'd talk a lot," he said with a small grin.

"Ghezu was one of the four. I forget now who the other two were, they weren't important. After a few months, it became obvious she'd choose between me and Ghezu. He and I had been friends up till them, as Khemu told you. The night it all came to a head, she asked me to accompany her home. Ghezu heard her and the rest you know. We left while the others from Stronghold who were in the tavern delayed him." He looked curiously at his son for a moment.

"Have you ever paired with a telepath?" he asked. "A Guild-trained telepath?"

Dzaka looked away briefly, ears flicking back then righting themselves in embarrassment.

"They haven't told you, then. Yes, Kitra. Kusac's sister. It nearly cost me my life," he said, looking up again. "She'd picked me as her first lover. While she was busy trying to get my attention, a couple of our people decided I was betraying the trust Kusac put in me. They already believed I was responsible for your capture and that just gave them the excuse they were looking for."

"So. What happened?"

"Jack came along and they ran off. I had to go to Carrie about Kitra eventually, and the Clan Leader came to speak to me." He closed his eyes, remembering the interview. "That has to be one of the most embarrassing moments of my life," he said.

Kaid began to laugh.

Dzaka looked at him in faint surprise. He heard a knock at the door and rose to answer it. Kusac and Carrie stood outside.

"We were passing and heard the noise," said Carrie, looking beyond him. "What's up?"

Kaid, his laughter beginning to fade, looked over at them. "Dzaka's just telling me about his audience with your mother over Kitra," he said.

"It must have been something to have heard," agreed Kusac. "Ask Carrie. She was there too."

Kaid caught Carrie's eye and began to laugh again.

"I think we'll leave you to it," said Carrie primly, "considering you're incapable of anything but mirth at the moment. Good night, Dzaka, Kaid," she said.

A coughing fit cut his laughter short and after Dzaka had provided him with some water, he calmed down.

"I'm sorry, Dzaka, but . . ."

"I suppose I can see the humorous side now," said Dzaka, obviously a little put out. "Believe me, there wasn't one at the time!"

"Oh, I believe you," he chuckled. "Getting a lecture on acceptable intimate social etiquette from Rhyasha would daunt anyone! However, I take it the answer to my question is yes, you *have* paired with a Guild-trained telepath. You'll understand, then."

"What's your point?"

"Khemu was the first telepath I'd been with. It wasn't till after we paired that I realized I might be too."

Dzaka looked at him in stark amazement. *"You're* a telepath? A *full* telepath?"

"Yes. Carrie confirmed it yesterday," he said, his gaze holding his son's eyes. "Because I'd hidden it even from myself for so long, when Khemu and I paired, my mind swamped hers, and she became pregnant with you."

He stopped to search in his jacket pockets for something. Not finding it, he looked over at Dzaka.

"Would you mind looking in the drawer unit in my bedroom to see if they brought my stim-twigs with the rest of my belongings?"

Dzaka reached into his own pocket and pulled out a packet, tossing it across to his father. "Have mine."

"I didn't know you used them," he said, pulling one out and beginning to chew the end.

"I think there's a lot we don't know about each other . . . Father."

Kaid nodded his head slowly. "It's time we found out, don't you think?"

It was Dzaka's turn to nod.

"Now you know what happened between us. As for the rest, the mental experience terrified both of us. She refused to see me or anyone else. When her family found out she was pregnant, they put around the tale that she'd died and imprisoned her on the estate for having a bastard cub—you."

Dzaka winced at the term.

Kaid leaned forward to take hold of his arm. "You're no longer a bastard. I saw to that! I owed it to both you and her. I knew she had conceived, but the first I knew for sure she'd *had* a cub was the night I found you outside the gates at Stronghold. She'd managed to escape the estate and took you with her. She stayed by the gates near you as long as she dared, then fled to avoid capture by her father. You could only have been alone a short while, Dzaka. She sent you to me to raise." He sat back. "And I did it the only way I could."

"Why did you have to conceal the fact that I was your son from Ghezu? I don't understand any of that."

"Ghezu and I were at each other's throats for months following that night, then suddenly, everything was all back the way it had been. I thought he'd got over it. He hadn't. When you turned up, Ghezu immediately suspected the truth, that you were my son by Khemu. Vartra must have been with me that day, because I refused to confirm or deny it. Ghezu made it plain that if he ever found out for sure you were our

son, he'd kill you outright. He'd wanted Khemu and not only
had I paired with her, but our pairing had prevented him
from ever having her. I think that even then, his mind must
have had the seeds of sickness in it. We heard later that she'd
died in a climbing accident."

"So you told everyone you wanted to foster me."

Kaid nodded. "Old Jyarti, the Head Priest then, got me
transferred to the religious side so I could legitimately
remain on Shola to raise you. I'm almost certain he knew
you were my son."

He sat chewing his stick for a moment. "The God knows,
Dzaka, I wanted to acknowledge you. I wouldn't have
wished illegitimacy on you if it had been in my power to
stop it. Having gone through it myself, I knew how it felt to
grow up the wrong side of another's hearth. I had no choice,
though. I did what I thought best."

The silence lengthened until Dzaka broke it. "So that's
why Ghezu has played me against you this last year. Because
he still thought I might really be your son. All the lies, her
death, your imprisonment . . . all of it because he wanted
Khemu?"

"Essentially, yes."

"Why did you get expelled from the Brotherhood?"

"That I can't tell you. I'm still oath-bound. Not for much
longer, though." His voice carried beneath it a low, angry
growl. "The day I kill Ghezu, my oath is over."

"I'll always remember that day . . ." began Dzaka.

"Forget it, I've had to," his father interrupted. "If I hadn't,
it would have eaten at me the way not getting Khemu has
eaten Ghezu."

"We'll get him, never fear."

"No! He's mine, Dzaka. I'll tolerate no interference on
this. He owes me—all your childhood, and the last ten years
of my life, as well as what I endured at Stronghold. *I* will
have him, Dzaka!"

"If he can laugh, he's healing," said Kusac as they went
into their suite. "I've been worried for him, cub. His eyes
have seemed so empty at times. How does he seem to you?
You've felt more of his mind than I ever have."

Taking her gun from her pocket, she laid it on their bed.
"He's still Kaid, whatever's happened to him," she said,
beginning to unfasten her robe. "Yes, I've seen his mind, all

the dark corners and the bright ones, because he sent it all to me."

She sighed, sitting down on the bed and looking up at him. "I don't know what's fair to tell you, Kusac. His inner strengths are unchanged, but he's never faced a fear like this before. He's coping with it by refusing to look at it for the moment. It won't pass till he's faced it, and for him, that means facing Ghezu."

"That what I thought," he said, stripping off his robe and throwing it over the bed. "Then Ghezu didn't break him?"

"No," she said, getting up. "He didn't."

"Thank the Gods for that," he said, heading for the shower.

Slipping off her clothes, she joined him.

He moved over, making room for her. As his hands touched her, she felt the familiar electric current of pleasure run through them and knew that he felt it too. She was drawn closer to him till their bodies touched and his face lowered to meet hers.

This is our time, he sent. *Ours alone.*

She reached up for the hair that grew at the side of his neck and pulled his face down till her mouth could reach his.

You're my Leska, my bond-mate, and my love, she sent. *This magic we share, nothing can match it, or you.* She knew the question he tried not to ask.

He's Tallinu, and Kaid. He's not you, just as I'm not Vanna. We have each other and this.

He lifted her bodily in his arms and stepped out of the shower. Opening the towel closet, he pulled the pile of towels out, letting them tumble to the floor as he knelt down.

Carrie began to laugh gently, then turned her attention to his neck and cheeks and ears.

Holding her close in one arm, he hastily spread the towels about and laid her down in the nest he'd made of them.

"Each time is as urgent as the first," he said, his voice and the purr mingling till she couldn't tell them apart. "I have to hold you, feel you touching me . . ." His voice tailed off as he began to lick and gently nip his way down her throat and across her breasts. His hand went to her belly, stroking the curve that held their cub.

They both froze at the same instant as Carrie felt a butter-fly movement within her. She held her breath and Kusac lifted his head to look at her in disbelief. The tiny movement came again, then a third time.

She's moving! he sent.

I know! Her own hands went down to touch her belly, waiting for it to happen again. It did, and she began to laugh and cry at once, her arms going round him and holding him close. "She's really there! I'm really going to have our child!"

"Of course you are," he said, confused by her reaction.

"You don't understand," she said. "She's not been real till now! Now I've felt her move, *I* can believe in her too!" She began to cover his face with tiny kisses, her hands pulling him close again. "Love me, Kusac. Just make love to me," she said as she gently caught at his lower lip with her teeth.

He didn't need to be asked a second time.

Unusually, it was Kusac who dreamed that night. At first he was only aware of the darkness around him. Gradually the faint noise grew, rising till it surrounded him, sounding like the quiet breathing of some huge sleeping beast. Growing louder, a new tone began to emerge—a gentle whistling that gained strength until it reached the point of a full-blown howling.

His hair, caught by the force of the blast, was whipped over his face, into his eyes, making him blink. He turned his face into the wind, letting it tug the wayward strands back. Cold was penetrating through his borrowed coat, touching him with its icy fingers as the wind gusted round him, making him sway with its rhythm.

The darkness was suddenly lightened as the twin moons swam out from behind the clouds. By their reflected light, he could see his surroundings.

"What are you thinking of?" a quiet voice asked him from behind.

"Them," he said. "My people. Those out there, beyond the moons. They're fighting our battle, one they must win, yet when they do, it'll condemn them to death or permanent exile. They'll never return home."

"They knew that before they left, Vartra," said Zylisha, joining him. "My sister and her Leska went willingly, as did all the telepaths."

"I should be out there with them on the plains, not

kept here out of harm's way!" There was anger in his voice.

"To what purpose? So you can be killed? No, we need you alive, Vartra. The people look to you, you have to live if we're going to succeed!"

"I've got no choice, have I?" He turned and pointed out three dark shapes. "They guard me like a prisoner!"

He lapsed into silence again, staring out across the forest to the plains beyond. In the distance, they could see sporadic flares of light and hear the sounds of explosions coming from the city of Khalma.

"Even I felt it begin," he said. "The signal came like a wave, gathering strength as it rushed toward us from space."

"I know," she said, holding onto his arm and pressing herself close to his side for comfort. "We all felt it." A small silence. "I thought I felt my sister's presence, and Rezac."

"I wouldn't know," he said morosely. "I'm not a telepath, only a sensitive at best." Then he thought of her. "Likely you did, Zylisha," he said, freeing his arm to put it round her shoulders. "Likely you did. They were the ones who had to give the signal to attack, after all."

From their left, the comparative silence was shattered by a deafening explosion. They swung round to look.

"The battle's been joined at Nazule," she said.

All around them now, the night was filled with the sound of dulled explosions and flares.

"Leave the fighting to those who know how," said Zylisha. "Finding people willing to fight and die for freedom from the Valtegans was easy. Finding a leader capable of taking us from the ruins and rebuilding us into a free nation once more, isn't."

"How many of us will survive?" he demanded. "I can do nothing if all the telepaths die! We need their talents to convince the survivors not to degenerate into looters and bandits! I'm only a figurehead, Zylisha, I can't do anything by myself—except send people out to die!"

She tugged gently on his arm. "We must go in. I can sense reports of Valtegans taking to the air. We're sitting targets out here."

He let her pull him round toward the monastery, then stopped dead. "Look!" he said, pointing upward. "What's happening? Isn't that the Valtegan warship?"

In the night sky, a point of silver light shot toward the

smaller moon, disappearing behind it. Moments later, a faint glow began to build until its light paled that cast by either moon.

"Tiernay sends that it was the Valtegan warship. The Leska telepaths on board couldn't take control and it crashed. All on board died."

"Dr. Vartra," a male voice said from behind them. "We need you below now. We've been warned to expect aerial attacks."

"I'm coming, Goran," he said, turning again and walking toward the monastery entrance.

They climbed the steps into the building, passing through the heavy wooden doors, then through the crimson curtain into the shrine itself. Ahead of them, the draft their entrance caused gusted smoke from the braziers to either side of the God's statue. The bowl of Living Fire in His hands flared, making shadows dance on the walls.

"Varza'll drink deep of those damned lizards' blood tonight," said Goran with satisfaction as he slung his rifle over his shoulder.

His vision seemed to blur, and feeling momentarily dizzy, he stopped, swaying on his feet. "He'll drink deep of Sholan blood, too!" he said as around him the shrine, the God—all seemed to fade.

Kusac was chilled to the bone and the blanket that was laid around his shoulders was welcome. Above in the clear winter sky, the two moons shone down on the balcony where he stood. He frowned, studying the smaller one. Something was different about it.

"Kusac, come in," said Carrie, touching his arm. "It's bitterly cold and you're frozen."

He hardly heard her, so intense was his concentration on the moon. Further along the balcony, another door slid open. Kaid stood there looking down toward them. Then he, too, looked up.

"The shape has changed," Kusac said. "The warship hit the moon and damaged it. The explosion would have blown chunks of rock and dirt into space."

"The Cataclysm," said Kaid, coming toward them. He stopped several feet away.

Kusac frowned, turning his head to look at him. "What?"

"A chunk of debris from the explosion must have hit Shola."

"The Cataclysm," said Carrie. "A time of fire and flood when the sky itself was on fire. It fits."

"It's what Fyak preaches," said Kaid.

"We both sensed your dream," said Carrie. "Now we know what happened."

"We know more," said Kusac. "We know exactly where we're going, and when."

"When?" she asked.

"We must arrive on the night of my dream, before the rocks hit Shola," said Kaid. "Once they do, all hell's going to break out. The debris thrown up could cause a cloud of dust to encircle the planet for months, if not longer. If it hits the sea, which sounds likely given the quotes about flooding, you'll have massive tidal waves, and earthquakes. The world they knew will cease to exist. They'll have to rebuild almost from scratch, probably without any advanced technology."

Kusak began to shiver. "Will you ask Dzaka in the morning to find out what he can about such a disaster? None of us should be out here any longer."

"I'll ask him," said Kaid, turning to walk back to his room. "Good night."

"Good night," said Carrie.

CHAPTER 19

Vanna was in the lab with Jack when Garras arrived back. "Hello there," she said, as he came over to her. "Did everything go well? How are your family?"

"Fine, to all your questions," he said. "I see we've got two sects of Touibans with us."

"You met them?"

"It wasn't me they were interested in. It was the Terrans!" His mouth opened in a slight grin. "They didn't know what to make of them. Why are they here?"

"We got the steel door in the upper cavern open," she said. "They were brought in to try and get the information off some ancient computer data recording disks we found. And, more important, Kaid's back on the estate."

"I know. Ni'Zulhu told me when I flew in. How are the Terrans getting on?" he asked in an effort to change the topic. Looking around, he grabbed the nearest stool to sit on.

"Fine. Garras, don't you want to know how Kaid is?"

He sighed inwardly. She wasn't going to let it go. Now he knew that Kaid was safe, the hurt over his lack of trust throughout all the long years of their friendship had returned. "How is he?"

"Oh, he's fine now," interrupted Jack. "He's recuperating over at the house with Carrie and Kusac. It's just a matter of time. I believe Dzaka's there, too."

"They resolved their differences then?"

"I believe so, Garras."

"Jack!" said Vanna.

"Not now, lass," he said. "Maybe you'd look at this, Garras," he said, holding out the collar with its broken piece of green stone still set into it. "Kaid found this collar in the lock-releasing panel for that steel door in the upper chamber," he said, putting the collar down on the bench. "This stone has some remarkable properties. It's resinous and formed from the sap of a plant—possibly an off-world plant. The stone and the drug both have psychotropic properties. When an electrical current is passed across the stone, or it's broken, it releases as a vapor the chemical trapped within it. That acts as a pacifier to any Sholan wearing the collar. Makes them lethargic, that kind of thing. As for the sap, its narcotic properties seem to allow the user to either teleport or bi-locate."

"Excuse me?"

"This stone," Jack said, picking up a small, sealed culture dish, "we grew from a sample of the drug Ghezu administered to Kaid." He placed the dish in front of Garras. "And that's the drug," he said, tapping the rack in which the almost empty phial of emerald green liquid sat. "We think it might be responsible for him being able to physically visit Carrie at the Shrine while he was actually in Stronghold."

Garras reached for the rack, lifting it up to examine the phial closely. "Is this the original phial?" he asked.

"Yes. Why?" asked Vanna.

"I've seen one like this before," he said. "I can't remember where. Give me a minute," he said, putting it down. "I'm sure it'll come back to me. That red banding round the top is quite distinctive."

"The stone doesn't affect us," said Jack. "I'm running comp simulation tests on the drug now to find out if we're also immune to it."

"Makes sense," he said. "Vanna, can you find out if we get any drugs from off-system companies? Not necessarily Sholan drugs."

"That's not a problem. I'll call the medical center at the guild. They'll have the details there."

Garras got up from his stool. "I'm heading home," he said to Vanna, reaching out to touch her cheek. "I want some breakfast. I didn't eat before I left."

"Aren't you going to call on Kaid?" she asked.

"Later," he said, turning to leave. He stopped by Marak's carrier to check on him on his way out. "He looks peaceful enough," he said.

"Little jegget should be!" said Vanna, watching him. "He kept me up most of last night!"

"See if Rrai's mother will watch him tonight," he said before leaving.

He'd just gotten outside when he stopped dead as he felt

the familiar touch of Kaid's mind, a touch far stronger than any he'd felt before.

I owe you an explanation, Garras. Will you come and listen to it?

The shock he felt rendered him incapable of replying, and as if in a daze, he turned and headed for the villa.

Dzaka met him at the door. "It's the Liege and Liegena's Link day," he said. "My father's upstairs. He's in the suite opposite the staircase. I left the door open, you can't miss it," he said.

"Father now, is it?" Garras asked.

Dzaka's ears flicked selfconsciously a couple of times but his eyes were steady as they regarded him.

"Yes, it's Father when we're not on duty. Because we both want it that way."

Garras nodded, then turned away and headed for the stairs.

Kaid was still in bed with his arm in a sling, he noticed as he stood at the bedroom doorway. An easy chair had been placed close to the bed for him to use.

"Thank you for coming," said Kaid, opening his eyes and pushing himself up against the pillows.

"Since when did you become a telepath?" Garras asked as he came over.

"I found out for sure two days ago. Carrie told me."

"Carrie did?" He raised an eye ridge, curious despite himself.

Kaid touched the remote unit set into the arm rest at the side of the bed. The outer and inner doors closed.

"We go back a long way, Garras. Let me tell it my way."

"Go on," he said. He sat down and listened while Kaid told him.

"If I'd told you at the time who Dzaka was, I could have placed your life in danger too," Kaid finished. "After you left, there was no point in telling you."

"And your refusal to be the third member of the Triad was due to that forced rapport with Khemu?"

"Yes. It . . . she . . . Carrie had become too . . . important to me to risk that happening with her," Kaid replied, unable to meet Garras' eyes.

"Had become?"

"The Triad's complete now, and before you ask, yes, it did happen with her."

"What did she do?"

"Showed me how to prevent it happening again." He looked up. "Do you remember when we told Kusac and Vanna why I was on the *Khalossa?* How Vanna reacted to your profession? Imagine that all you are and have been, everything you've ever done, was suddenly forced into Vanna's mind by yours, and you couldn't stop it happening. That's what I did to her, and to Khemu."

Garras couldn't prevent a shudder running through him at the thought. "Vartra's bones, Kaid, no wonder you were afraid of it happening again! So how does that leave you with Carrie? I'm not blind: I know you too well. I can see what she means to you."

"The one thing I'd forgotten was what made all the difference. She's not a Sholan Telepath who feels too much pain if she's near violence. It should have been obvious to me."

"With how you were feeling about her?" snorted Garras. "I've never seen you like that over a female. Wanting her so much and terrified to go near her at the same time!"

"It must have been quite amusing," he said dryly.

Garras leaned forward to put his hand on Kaid's. "No. Far from it. I wish I could have helped. Don't get me wrong, that wasn't a complaint. I would have done the same as you in the circumstances. And I understand your fears for Dzaka. You did what you thought right, I can't fault you for that."

Kaid turned his hand to clasp Garras'. "It was never lack of trust in you," he began, but Garras cut him short.

"Enough. It's in the past, leave it there." He gripped Kaid's hand again before withdrawing it from his clasp. "So what's the state of things between you and Carrie now?"

"Whatever we want to make of it," he said. "She's got what it takes to be one of the Brotherhood, I'll say that for her—so's Kusac."

"We knew that already."

"It only needed us to be together once, Garras. Now our minds have been joined, I can reach her easily."

"How does she feel about you?"

"I didn't ask."

Garras felt his confusion. "I expect you told Kusac that."

"Well, yes," he began.

Garras sat back in his seat with a noise of disgust. "Was that it? Just one pairing? Was that *all* you wanted?"

"Of course not!" he snapped. "What do you take me for?"

"A fool. If you won't ask her for yourself, I damned well will!"

"You damned well won't!" said Kaid, taking hold of the covers to throw them aside.

"Stay put," said Garras, reaching forward to prevent him getting up. "You need to rest. All I'm trying to say is this isn't only your decision. You haven't the right to make it alone. You have to ask her what she wants. You're always saying how Sholan she is, so why deny her the Sholan right to choose for herself? Unless, of course, she behaved in such a way as to show you she didn't want to be with you again."

"You're too damned clever at times for your own good, Garras," Kaid grumbled, relaxing back against his pillows. "You always were. No, she didn't. She behaved as if she were taking me as her lover, but she isn't Sholan! I can't assume she knew what signals she was giving me."

Garras gave him a long look before he spoke. "How long has she been with Kusac? Do you really think she's that naive? Stop kidding yourself. Ask her."

"All right, I will!"

"Good. Now do you mind telling me how you've managed to be a Telepath and fight? And how did you manage to survive what Fyak and Ghezu did to you? Any normal telepath would have been long since dead!"

"I've no idea, Garras. Right from the start I always had to fight for everything. I suppose I just got used to it. After the Brotherhood took me in, my training would have reinforced those childhood lessons."

"Sounds plausible, I suppose. Now, how about bringing me up to date on what happened yesterday? Vanna mentioned that you got the door open, and Jack showed me that collar, and the drug Ghezu gave you."

"They've got some of the drug? How much is left?"

"Virtually none. Why?"

"Damn! I need more of it. I've got some tests of my own I want to run on it."

"Vanna's checking at the guild medical center for suppliers of off-world drugs, Sholan or others. I recognized the band round the phial, but I couldn't remember where from."

"What was it like?"

"Red, with gold wavy lines on it."

"Chemerian," he said. "Definitely. Their authorities are trying to trace a black market trade in certain drugs, so they're labeling their legal ones very distinctively. I suspect they come from their undisclosed new trade area where the Valtegans sold four Sholan captives several months ago."

"This is news to me. Where the hell did you get that information from?"

Kaid grinned. "One of my sources. There's more. The world's called Jalna, and the Chemerians trade there with several species for items they describe as "species-specific." There's a recon unit on the planet now. Three Terrans. Jo and Davies from Keiss, and a Terran telepath."

"They've sent Terrans? Why?"

"The Jalnians look like them. They've gone down to investigate a Valtegan craft which apparently dropped something on the surface before it crashed while attempting to take off."

"So where do the four Sholans come in?"

"They don't, this time around. They were sold as slaves in the spaceport. The next expedition will be going down to get them out. They're planning to send Kusac and Carrie, but they haven't told them that yet!"

"Nice of them," growled Garras. "I take it that Carrie's pregnancy put their plans out a little."

"It did. That's why Kusac's on semi-active duty now. He's being trained up for the mission."

"Don't you think you should tell them?"

"No. The Fire Margins and their cub are enough for them to be concerned with for now."

Garras nodded. "You're right," he said.

"Going back to the drug, what Ghezu used on me isn't the same as what Fyak uses for his trances when he communicates with this Kezule. Apparently Ghezu got it when he was obtaining supplies for Fyak. I think it was responsible for me going to the Shrine, and back to the time of the Cataclysm."

"You're getting ahead of yourself, Kaid. All of what you're talking about is news to me."

"Wait. There's a Chemerian merchant trading in Valsgarth. Can you go to him—take the phial with you—and see if he recognizes it? And try to . . . encourage him to obtain at least another two doses."

"I can do that. Now, for the God's sake, tell me the news!"

The next day Kaid was up and about before anyone. He headed over to the Shrine where, some time later, Ghyan found him sitting at the foot of the statue of Vartra.

"I'd heard they'd brought you back to the estate," he said, coming over to stand beside him. "How are you?"

Kaid squinted up at him. "Not bad," he said. "It isn't a bit like Him, you know."

"Excuse me?"

Kaid pushed himself to his feet with his good arm. "Vartra doesn't look like this. Have you come across a reference to Varza, God of a Warrior priesthood that existed back then? The statue up on the hill was like this, like the one at Stronghold. He's your real God."

"A moment, Kaid," said Ghyan, reaching out to take him by the arm.

This time, Kaid made no effort to conceal what he was feeling from the priest, and no sooner had he touched him, than Ghyan drew back in shock.

"It's different when you feel for yourself the effect you have on others, isn't it?" Kaid said. "Perhaps now you'll see me, not what you think I am. It makes no odds to me, but it would make it easier for us to work together."

As he stepped over to the side braziers, he could feel Ghyan's utter confusion. Taking a piece of incense, he crumbled it over the coals, quietly repeating the ancient ritual. Having finished, he decided to take pity on the priest: he was just being over-protective of those he loved.

"I told you, Ghyan, we're both working for the same goals."

"Kaid, if I misjudged you, I apologize," said Ghyan. "If it's any consolation, after the last time you and I talked, Father Lijou held up the same mirror you just did."

Kaid raised an eye ridge in surprise.

"He'd read what his predecessor wrote about you. I hadn't realized you'd been attached to the priesthood for so long."

"I had Dzaka to care for, I needed to stay on Shola for him. It wasn't all religious work, though, I had secular duties as well during that time. That's how Garras and I became a team."

"With your telepathic talent, no wonder you became a Special Operative. It must have helped enormously in locating those with rogue talents, and in assessing whether or not they could be helped at Stronghold."

"You have been talking to a few people, haven't you?" said Kaid with a slight grin. "What's past, is past, Ghyan."

Ghyan's ears flicked in assent. "You mentioned Vartra. Have you seen Him?"

"We all did, but it was Kusac's dream. You'd best ask him."

Ghyan shook his head. "You tell me. What's He like? Those who've seen Him in dreams or visions never seem to see Him clearly."

"Tall, and slimmer than most. More like a priest, certainly no warrior," he said. "Plains born, with the narrower ears and a dark tan pelt." Kaid gestured to the statue. "Certainly not with muscles like those!"

"I don't understand you, Kaid. You've consistently had visions and dreams of Vartra, and you've spent years as a lay-Priest. Why do you still burn incense for Him if you believe He's only a person, not a God?"

"He did what the legends tell us," said Kaid, shivering despite the long woollen robe he wore. He suddenly felt bone-weary. He realized that coming to the Shrine had been too much for him. "He may have started out no different from us, but the things He achieved!" He shook his head thoughtfully. "*He* is the one who speaks to us in our Visions, Ghyan. Only a God can do that. I have no problems with *His* having been a mortal, in fact, I prefer it. Godhood should be earned, not conferred at birth. If Gods are born," he added as an afterthought. "We have to work closely now, Ghyan. We travel to the Fire Margins within a fortnight."

"I didn't realize you'd finalized it. I've studied the texts on the Pathwalking used for the Margins. I can handle it. I think we could all do with a couple of practices first, though."

"I know the Path, Ghyan. We'll need you here to guard us while we're traveling."

"How do you know the path? You couldn't have been there, surely!"

"All three of us have been there at some time," he said. "Whether it was a replay, or a vision, we saw His world. I'll describe it to you, and you can monitor us. When we travel, if need be, you can reinforce what I'm showing them. But not now. Not today. I'm sorry," he said, reaching out to hold onto the stone pillar for support as a wave of nausea and lightheadedness swept through him. "It's too soon after . . ."

"You don't look well. Let me help you," said Ghyan, slipping his arm under Kaid's sound one.

* * *

Carrie was in the den at the time. Sensing that Kaid was reaching the point of collapse, she went looking for Dzaka in the staff quarters. There was no reply when she touched the buzzer, so she went in, heading through the tiny sitting area to his bedroom door.

Dzaka lay sprawled across his bed, dead to the world. The lightweight cover was tangled round his limbs—and Kitra was nestled in against his side. Kitra had obviously stolen down from the main house to be with him, only to find she was unable to wake him.

Stopping at the foot of the bed, Carrie ran her fingers down the pads of Dzaka's foot, making him jerk in his sleep. Repeating it, she watched in amusement as he began to wake, then feeling the warmth of someone else beside him, discovered Kitra, then her.

He sat bolt upright, looking from one to the other, mouth open in an "Oh, my God!" expression.

She laughed at his confusion. He obviously wasn't used to being disturbed when he was sharing his bed. "Dzaka. Kaid's overdone it by going to the Shrine. Will you take the floater chair over and fetch him back, please? Once you've returned you can go back to bed if you want. You're not on duty till evening," she said, unable to hide another grin.

Dzaka carefully untangled himself, throwing the cover over Kitra once he'd gotten up.

"Sorry, Liegena, I didn't know she was there," he mumbled, rubbing the sleep from his eyes as he staggered over to his shower cubicle.

"It's not a problem, so long as Rhyasha knows she's here. I thought she'd been visiting less often."

"She has, now she's gotten things into their proper perspective. She's still a kitling, after all."

"True. I'll leave you to it. Let me know when you've got Kaid settled," she said.

Carrie had just finished organizing Zhala and first meal when Kitra came bouncing into the family kitchen.

"May the sun shine on you this morning, Carrie," she said, heading for one of the chairs in preference to the benches. "Can I eat with you?"

"Does your mother know you're here?" asked Carrie, pouring out some coffee for herself and Kusac.

"I always leave a comm message for her when I come to see Dzaka," she said archly. "And if it's night, then one of the guards brings me."

"You come here at night?"

Kitra frowned. "Why not? I don't disturb anyone, except perhaps Dzaka," she grinned.

Kusac came in on the heels of her comment and stopped to ruffle her hair before sitting next to Carrie.

"Kusac!" Kitra's tone was outraged. "I just did my hair, and it took me ages! Now I'll have to do it again."

"It's fine, kitling," said Kusac, reaching for the plate of freshly cooked meat. "I'm sure it had the desired effect on Dzaka. Where is he, by the way?"

"I don't know," she said, putting her hands up to try and smooth the mass of waves down again. "He wouldn't wake up when I came last night, and this morning he was gone when I woke." She sounded very disgruntled.

"Did you know your sister was coming over here in the dead of night?" asked Carrie, helping herself to some meat as well.

"No, but I don't mind so long as she doesn't come bouncing in to see us the way she used to at home," said Kusac. "Coffee, Kitra, or c'shar?"

Kitra's brows met in a frown. "You would remind me of that," she said. "I was only a cub then. I'm a lot more grown-up now. C'shar, please."

Kusac choked slightly on his mouthful of food.

I know it was only a month ago, but don't you dare *remind her!* cautioned Carrie, casting him a look that spoke volumes.

When he'd swallowed, he said, "So long as someone walks or drives you over, I don't mind. Someone does, don't they?"

"Of course. I just told Carrie that," she said, picking up the plate of meat and helping herself from it.

"Where is Dzaka?" Kusac asked Carrie.

"Fetching Kaid. He went to the Shrine this morning and it was too much for him. He'll come for his meal when he sees Kitra's not in his quarters."

True to her prediction, Dzaka arrived a few minutes later. "Kaid's settled upstairs, Liegena," he said, sitting down on the last of the chairs beside them.

"Help yourself," said Kusac, "if you can find anything my sister's left for you!"

"Huh!" was all she said, passing the single piece of meat left on the plate to Dzaka.

Carrie pushed her chair back and was about to get to her feet, but Kusac stopped her.

"I'll see to something for Kaid," he said. "You eat your own meal. You'll get few enough peaceful mealtimes in a couple of months time."

"You'll have more than a few disturbed ones yourself," she said pointedly as he got to his feet.

"Try stopping me," he said, his hand touching her cheek gently as he walked past her to the main kitchen from which Zhala ruled the household.

When he came back with more food, he glanced at the time. "I've got to go. I'll be up at the caverns with the Touibans all day, I'm afraid. My father's using their presence as an opportunity to accelerate the rest of my training in AlRel. He says the sooner I've got my final qualifications, the better." He smiled down at her as he picked up his mug.

"He did say that my practical experience with you was counting for a lot with the Board of Regulators. That's why he's had permission to speed up what's left of the field work."

"I always knew I had another purpose in life," she said with a sigh. "Field work. They might have phrased it a bit better."

He was still laughing as he left.

Carrie looked over to Dzaka and Kitra. "So what do you plan to do today?"

"Hunt," said Kitra firmly. "And visit Father and the Touibans."

"Hunt and visit the Touibans," repeated Dzaka with a shrug when Carrie looked at him.

"Kitra, do remember Dzaka may have things he needs to do in his off-time," she said, looking back to her bond-sister.

"You don't need to come to the caverns with me," Kitra said to Dzaka, "just so long as you do take me hunting."

"We'll go hunting," he said, reaching out to take the hand that lay on the table. "And I actually do want to go to the caverns later, if you're sure you don't need me to help with Kaid," he said to Carrie.

"No, we'll be fine. T'Chebbi's around somewhere and Meral's on duty today. You enjoy your rest day," said

Carrie, getting up from the table. "I've got a few things I want to see to myself today."

Konis had taken a hopper down to the Valsgarth estate village. As well as meeting up with his son in the caverns, he wanted to see how matters were progressing regarding Pam Southgate. He'd called one of his AlRel team in the day before and had him added to Kusac's people working in the dig. His job was to observe the Human and report back to him. He arranged to meet him at the village medical center.

"It's her personality that's the root of the problem, Master Konis," he said, using the informal AlRel title. "She's no different with the members of her own team. It's not a species problem, it's a personality one."

Konis put his elbow on the chair arm and rested his chin on his hand. "What do you suggest we do? Request someone else in her place?"

"We can't. She's got connections with the head of the Cultural Exchange back on Earth. She might be difficult to get on with, but at least her work is good." Falma spread his hands expressively. "Every now and then we all come up against abrasive people who get appointed to their positions because of their connections, she just happens to be Terran as well. We wouldn't send one of our own back for those reasons, so why should we do it with her?"

"You're saying our people need to learn to cope with her type in Human form."

He nodded. "If I might make a suggestion, it might be better for the Liegena if she stays away from the caverns while the archeologists are here."

Konis turned a chilly gaze on him. "My bond-daughter should not have to be careful of people living on her estate," he said. "There has to be another solution."

"Why not pair the archeologist off with one of our folk interested in learning their trade. Make sure they'll watch out for the Liegena as well."

"It might work," said Konis thoughtfully. "Perhaps her opposite number from my son's people. Thank you, Falma. What are you scheduled to do now?"

"Since I was coming here anyway, I've been asked to observe your son working with the Touibans for the examination board, so I'll be around for a few days yet."

Konis nodded. "You're staying in the Human's house, aren't you? Have you everything you need?"

"I'm fine, thank you, Master Konis," he said.

"Then I'll see you down there," said Konis, getting up.

* * *

Twelve Touibans in any one area made it seem crowded. Living their lives at a slightly faster pace than their Alliance allies, they darted about like glittering points of light, first here, then over there, with no apparent in-between. The trick was to not watch them too closely, otherwise motion sickness would set in very quickly.

Carrie had once told Kusac that they reminded her of the mythical human trolls. Just over a meter and a half tall, they seemed impossibly long-limbed for the size of their bodies. Their eyes appeared to be sunk in dark sockets, and their noses were thin and flanged with stiff bristles. A shock of sandy-colored hair sprouted from the crown of their heads and their chins. By Human and Sholan standards, they might be ill-favored when it came to looks, but that paled into insignificance by comparison with their dress sense.

No color or combination of colors was too loud or garish for them. The more, the brighter, the merrier seemed to be their motto. Then there was the jewelry.

Vartra help the Touiban who falls into a lake, thought Konis. *With the amount of gold chains, bracelets and rings each one of them is wearing, they'd sink to the bottom never to be seen again!*

The lab, as the cavern behind the steel door was now being called, was literally a hive of activity. The Touibans had had their own power source set up. While some were experimenting with the ancient machines, others had made room on the long bench for their own comms and scanning equipment.

Their high-pitched trills filled the air, varying in pitch and volume as they put the disks through all manner of scanning devices. A light and pleasing scent hung in the air: the scent of happily busy Touibans. A small group sat amidst the ruins of one ancient device, examining every component as they systematically took it apart.

In the midst of this sea of colorful activity, Konis could see his son sitting on the end of the bench talking to the

Touiban who was the designated Speaker for the two groups. This being's job was to communicate with their Sholan employers and make sure they understood exactly what was being done. This was achieved partly by their own design of translating device, which each of them wore, and partly because their minds could be read, and sometimes even understood—if the telepath were good enough and had the experience. This experience was what Kusac was aiming to gain over the next few days.

Konis decided not to disturb him and sent a questing thought toward his son, looking for an opportunity to send telepathically to him.

Kusac raised his hand in acknowledgment and continued listening to the Touiban. From the corner of his eye, he saw Pam heading in his direction. He sighed inwardly, knowing what was coming.

She stopped behind the Touiban, fixing Kusac with an angry look over the top of that person's head. "I don't know how you expect me to work under these conditions," she snapped. "Look at the place! These damned little people are everywhere! My folk can't move for them! Not just that, but . . ."

The Touiban turned swiftly round, aiming a brief, high-pitched riff of sound at her before turning back to Kusac. The air immediately behind the being was permeated by a harsh scent of displeasure.

As the Touiban continued his discussion with him, Kusac managed to keep one eye on the Human as she began to cough and choke on the scent. She began to back away, hastily pulling a handkerchief out of her pocket and placing it over her nose and mouth.

He wasn't too concerned about her, scent was only the Touibans' secondary means of communication and though not harmful, could be far more unpleasant than that which Pam had been subjected to.

Noticing a sudden tapping on his knee, he looked back at the Touiban, realizing he'd let his attention slip. He apologized profusely, using gestures that the Speaker in front of him understood, trying to explain that never having met his people before, the Human hadn't realized the iniquity of her interruption.

"As soon as our negotiations are concluded, Speaker, I will explain the etiquette to her," he assured him.

"Turns must be taken. Without turns who knows which being speaks when there are so many, many voices all to be heard. You instruct her on this then she can take her place and her voice will be heard as separate from the many. We need that they stay away from our workings and do not interfere with what we are using. Curiosity is acceptable as through that all beings learn but it must be asked through me as the Speaker. Only you may address our sect members directly, as their concentration on these ancient pieces of equipment is great and to talk to them breaks it. You see to this now so I may attend to what our sects need in the way of nourishment." With that, he inclined his head and vanished.

Kusac took a deep breath, and immediately regretted it as he began to cough. The scent message was still hanging in the air. He got up and hurriedly headed behind the metal cabinets. This was hard work, and he could only justify a few minutes break before going to find Pam and trying to not only calm her down, but explain the intricacies of communication with the Touibans.

With a grin, Konis turned away and ambled back to the other chamber. Large radiant heating units had been placed throughout the cavern, raising the temperature to one in which it was possible to work comfortably. Makeshift tables and basic chairs had been set up to provide not only working space, but also at the far end near a heater, a mobile kitchen and dining area.

Seeing T'Chebbi sitting there nursing a mug, he headed in her direction. Having been given his drink by the attendant, he sat down opposite her.

Immediately she sat bolt upright, obviously wondering how she could salute him as was his due while seated. She began to move but Konis shook his head.

"Stay in your seat, T'Chebbi," he said. "Consider us both off duty. What do you make of all this?" he asked, half-turning in his seat and indicating with a wave of his arm the heaters and the kitchen area they were in. "Isn't this going a little too far?"

"No, Master Konis," she said. "Only your second visit. We've done weeks in the cold and damp. Governor sent this. All major sites like this to continue working through winter."

Konis raised his mug to his mouth. "We're a major site, then."

"Yes," she said. "This is complete. The others are ruins."

"Everything low-lying shows evidence of having suffered massive earthquakes and flooding," said Kusac, coming round to sit beside his father. "We've some earthquake damage here, but nowhere near as much as the other sites."

"Our family seems to be fated to be at the center of everything," sighed Konis. "Still, it could be worse. At least I only have to get out of bed to be virtually at the site. Oh, before I forget, was Kitra with you last night?"

"Not with me, Father!"

"You know what I mean. Was she with Dzaka?"

"Yes. They've gone hunting and plan to join us here later today. She said she'd left a message for Mother."

"She did, but you know how your mother worries," he said. "Did I tell you she found out who attacked Dzaka? Well, she's dealt with it. I really don't think he'll have any more problems."

"I'm glad. Dzaka's beginning to fit in well with the rest of us now. He's getting himself straightened out slowly but surely, as is Kaid. They're both coming to terms with their new relationship."

Konis sighed, idly picking at a loose sliver of wood on the table top. "There was a time when no telepath would have anything to do with those in military careers, now look at us. The estates patrolled by guards, electronic surveillance all over the place, each of us with bodyguards, and my two daughters both with Companions from the Brotherhood of Vartra."

"We live in more dangerous times, Father," said Kusac. "At least you know both your daughters are safe even in sleep. Not many can say that."

"You're right," sighed Konis, looking up at him. "I'm beginning to sound like one of the elders. Let's get on with business. What have the Touibans discovered?"

"They're still discovering what the disks aren't. However, one small group is building, as near as they can, a duplicate device which they think is a reader for the disks. They're having a great time," he said. "They love a challenge, and one like this is unique. They say the joy of solving it will be payment in itself, provided, of course, they're allowed to make full use of whatever devices and information they find."

"That's too far reaching. I hope you didn't agree to it. We can't possibly negotiate the matter with no knowledge of the type of information we're discussing."

"I passed it over to the Governor's office," said Kusac. "It's well outside my negotiating authority."

"Best place for it," agreed Konis.

"What do you think of our site now? Kind of mushroomed, hasn't it?"

"T'Chebbi was telling me. If the Governor feels it's worth it, I'm not going to argue, especially when T'Chebbi indicated how cold it gets in here. At least with everything at the same location, you can work the day and night round if you need to."

Putting his mug down, he crossed his arms in front of him, leaning on the table. "I stopped off to talk to Falma. He tells me the problem is down to the personality of the female, Pam Southgate, herself."

"In retrospect it was naive to assume otherwise," said Kusac. "What now?"

"Falma suggests we team Ms Southgate with her opposite number among your people. That way there will always be one of us around if she has to deal with Carrie."

"We can't do that. Our expert is Jack and he's got his own research program with Vanna." He turned and looked thoughtfully round the cavern.

"No, Liege, not me! I'm one of the Brotherhood, not a soil-grubber!" T'Chebbi protested as his glance met hers. The look on her face was one of pain.

Kusac laughed. "Don't worry," he said. "I've got a better idea. Why don't you appoint someone from AlRel and tell this Pam they're from General Raiban's staff? She's always going on about her remit coming from the General. If she's got what she thinks is one of his aides working with her, we should have a lot less problems. She'll feel her interests are being looked after, and at the same time we've got someone there who can look out for Carrie."

Konis raised an eye ridge in surprise. "I'll speak to Raiban today," he said. "An excellent suggestion, Kusac." He'd make sure that Falma heard about this. It would count well toward his son's grades.

* * *

Half drowsing, Kaid sensed Garras' arrival outside his rooms.

Come in, he sent. *I hoped you might call by.*

From Garras he received a sense of communication being easier now than it had been in their past.

How do you think I kept up with all that was going on? he replied.

"You fraud," said Garras as he came through into the bedroom. "You mean to say that all along . . ."

"No, I don't mean that," said Kaid, turning onto his back so he could see his friend. "I did have good contacts, you know that. I also just *knew* things. I never could work out how, it just happened. What about you?"

Garras shrugged, then went to get himself a seat. "Who knows? You know I receive better than I send. Whatever it is, it's not quite telepathy. I can't send words, just the idea of what I'm trying to say. It improved after that ni'uzu epidemic, though, and now I can communicate reasonably well with Vanna."

"We were all boosted by that infection," said Kaid drily.

"How are you feeling? You still look exhausted."

"I am. I took a walk down to the Shrine and they had to send Dzaka to help me home."

"It's going to take a while to build your strength up again. You took one hell of a beating, so did your system."

"I never was a good patient," he said.

"It's time for second meal. Have you eaten?"

"Not since this morning."

"Carrie's bound to send something up. In the meantime, do you want a drink?"

"No, thanks. What brings you here? Apart from coming to wake me up and make sure I don't get that rest you've prescribed!"

"I saw the Chemerian trader this morning."

Kaid's curiosity was roused and he pushed himself further up against the pillows. "I take it you've got news."

"Some. I wish you'd been with me, you'd have enjoyed it. I started by throwing his two customers out and locking the door. That got him nice and paranoid. Then I told him about the drug problem his people are trying to solve. Naturally he had no idea of what I was talking about."

"Naturally," agreed Kaid, reaching for the half-chewed stim twig on his night stand.

"So I told him about the trade route to Jalna, and the other three species they traded with there. He became rather distressed at this point."

"Understandably so."

"As you say. This was where I suggested his Ambassador might not be pleased to hear about him importing off-world illegal drugs to Shola. He became even more agitated and happened to let slip that the drug was species-specific to Chemerians only. It was rare to start with and was no good to any of the other Alliance races as it gave them terrible waking dreams that lasted for a whole day at least. I showed him the phial. That's when I had to pick him off the ceiling."

Kaid raised an eye ridge. "Literally?"

"Well, figuratively," admitted Garras with a grin. "Once I'd helped him over his hysterics, he began . . ."

"How did you manage that?" asked Kaid. "Once they get to that stage they're usually incoherent for hours."

"I discovered that cold water works just as well on Chemerians with hysterics as it does on Sholans," he said. "Amazing, isn't it?"

"I'll have to remember that. How did you administer the cold water?"

"Stuck his head under the faucet in the back of the shop. After I'd done that, he was remarkably helpful."

"I'll bet. So what did you find out?"

"You'll love this," said Garras with a large grin. "He was partially right. It is species-specific, if you want an expensive and extremely rare Chemerian aphrodisiac!"

"What? You can't be serious! You are, aren't you?"

Garras nodded, a wide grin on his face as Kaid began to laugh.

"That's exactly what I did, much to the embarrassment of the Chemerian. I was able to settle a deal very quickly after that. You'll have two phials of the stuff, called la'quo, next week. He can't get it any sooner, I'm afraid."

"What did you trade?"

Garras shrugged. "Nothing much. Just a promise that I wouldn't make his people the laughing stock of every spaceport in the Alliance."

"It's almost worth passing the word to some less scrupulous persons," said Kaid. "The thought of those self-important, moralizing tree-climbers importing aphrodisiacs is one a lot of people would find amusing! If it's an off-system drug, why did I see Fyak eating the plant it comes from?"

"We know the stones come from the plant's sap, and we know there were a great many of those collars around on Shola at the time of the Cataclysm. Therefore there must have been some plants left behind in or around Chezy," Garras said.

"I know Fyak's had to augment his stock by buying the drug from the Chemerians through Ghezu," said Kaid. "Where do they get it from? If it's a Valtegan plant extract, then the Valtegans must be trading at Jalna."

"We've no proof of that. That's part of the reason they want Carrie and Kusac to go to Jalna as soon as possible," said Garras.

"You could be right," said Kaid thoughtfully. "You could well be right. Thank you, you've done me a great favor. I owe you yet again."

"Forget it. Our friendship was never based on favors."

The buzzer sounded on the outer door, then Carrie came in with a tray of food.

Garras got up and moved the chair away. "I'd better be leaving," he said. "Have you spoken to Carrie yet?"

"Spoken to me about what?" she asked as she came further into the bedroom.

"Nothing," said Kaid, looking warningly at Garras.

His friend took the tray from Carrie and laid it down on Kaid's lap before turning back to her.

"He wants to ask you something, but knowing him, he'll never get around to it," said Garras.

Carrie looked from one to the other. "You're being very mysterious."

Garras flicked his finger gently under her chin. "Get Kaid to talk to you," he said. "He promised me he would. If he doesn't, let me know. I'll see you later," he said to Kaid.

"Garras . . ." But he was gone. Kaid sat there fuming until Carrie spoke.

"You're projecting a lot of anger," she said. "Not a good thing to do. Apart from letting everyone know how you feel, it's not pleasant for the rest of us."

Instantly it stopped. "Sorry," muttered Kaid. "I'm not used to this telepathy yet."

"It was beginning to break through the odd time over the last couple of months," she said, sitting down beside him.

"Just the occasional flash, a sense of your emotions at the time, then it was gone."

He looked at her in surprise. "You didn't mention it."

"I was never completely sure it was there. Now, do you want to talk to me while you eat, or after you've eaten?"

"Neither. Garras has made a mistake, Carrie. He's just teasing you at my expense."

"Strange. It doesn't sound like him."

Kaid picked up his fork and began spearing chunks of meat from the bowl of stew she'd brought him.

"Do you mind if I get myself a drink?" she asked. "Do you want one?"

"Water, please."

He ate slowly, giving monosyllabic answers to her small talk. It was obvious she had no intention of leaving until he'd finished his meal, and had spoken to her.

As he set down his fork, she lifted the tray away, putting it on the floor beside her.

"Now talk," was all she said.

She sat within his arm's reach, and from the moment she'd entered the room, all he could think about was the velvet smoothness of her skin, and her heady scent. He sighed.

"Thank you for the compliments," she said quietly, making him start in surprise. "but I still don't know what you want to talk about."

He lay back against his pillows, closing his eyes, feeling boxed in by his promise to Garras, and Carrie's determination that he would keep that promise. He felt her hand touch his, and as he turned it over, her fingers crept onto his palm.

"I don't mean to pressure you, Kaid," she said quietly. "Leave it if you'd rather. I'll just sit with you for a while if you like."

He closed his hand round hers, glad to be touching her again. For several minutes he stayed like that, drawing strength from her presence.

"I told Kusac I wouldn't go to you again," he said, "but both he and Garras said I haven't the right to make your decisions for you. That you have the right to choose what you want to do. Do you realize that the way you submitted to me when we paired is the way a Sholan female shows that she's accepting you as her lover?"

"Yes, Tallinu, I knew that. I knew that is was what we

both wanted, and to offer less was to debase ourselves and our Triad. Yes, I accepted you as my lover that night."

Opening his eyes, he tugged gently on her hand, letting her know he wanted her to come closer. She moved forward until he released her hand and put his arm round her, clasping her against his chest. He could feel her warmth and her scent surrounding him. The darkness that had lived in his mind since his imprisonment by Ghezu began to recede once more, giving ground before her presence. This was all he needed for now.

Tentatively he touched the edges of her mind with his.

You're tired, he sent.

I know. Carrying the cub drains me at times. I usually rest in the afternoon.

"Rest beside me," he said, moving his legs aside to make room for her.

She stretched out beside him, lying on top of the covers. He turned on his side, his sound arm going protectively round her so she couldn't roll off the bed.

Kaid wasn't used to female company, nor did he envisage a time when he'd want a Companion in the traditional sense, but having her close for the moment was what he needed. Someone to hold, someone he had permission to touch and who would touch him in return: the most basic of all companionships—of any species.

Since he'd returned from Stronghold, the only night he'd slept well was the one night Carrie had stayed with him. The sedatives might make him sleep, prevent him dreaming, but he never felt rested when he woke. Now, lulled by her presence, he quickly fell into a deep, natural sleep.

* * *

"I'm a Warrior, Fyak! Not some damned weakling of a priest! I don't care who you worship, but don't expect me to join you!" snarled Ghezu. "None of the Gods are real anyway!"

"You think I'm a weakling?" Fyak's voice was deceptively smooth. "It takes more strength than *you* possess to control the sap through which Kezule calls me! But then, you must know this, having used the narcotic on that captive you wanted so much."

It dawned on Ghezu that perhaps his last comment had

been unwise. "I'm not speaking of you, Prophet. Only of the Priests of Vartra back at Stronghold."

Fyak turned to look at the female sitting on the floor at the side of his throne. "Well?"

"He lies," said Rhaid, her voice toneless as she answered her master, the green stone flashing at her throat. "He thinks you're weak, and ruled by insanity. He believe in no Gods, only himself. He hopes to persuade you to let him lead your people against the Brotherhood."

Fyak turned back to Ghezu.

There was no alternative but to bluff. "You're going to take her word for it? Don't make me laugh, Fyak! It's one thing having a tame telepath, it's another relying on what she tells you. Look at her!"

He strode past the throne to Rhaid. Reaching out, he took hold of her by the collar round her neck, yanking her to her feet. She gave a mew of pain, putting her hands up to protect her throat in a vain attempt to stop the collar cutting into the sores it had already rubbed there.

"Look at her, Fyak! She hates you—you can see it in her eyes! Oh yes, she'll tell the truth enough times to convince you to trust her, then she'll slip in a lie!" He threw her aside, not bothering to even look where she fell.

Fyak was regarding him thoughtfully. Vraiyou came forward and spoke to him in an undertone. The Prophet nodded once, then the head acolyte left.

"Vraiyou has made an excellent suggestion," purred Fyak, "one that will solve this matter of loyalty once and for all. We'll wait for him to return."

Ghezu cursed under his breath, making sure to shield himself from Rhaid. Why the hell had he forgotten about her? If he got the opportunity to speak to her alone, he'd make damned sure she knew what would happen if she pulled *that* stunt again!

"Fyak," he said at length, "how much longer do I have to wait here? I've important matters to see to, namely training your warriors!"

The Prophet leaned forward, placing his elbow on the ornate arm rest and propping his chin on his hand. "If I were you, I'd wait patiently for the return of Vraiyou," he said. "Remember that you're here on *my* sufferance, Ghezu. Out there beyond the desert boundaries, an army of people waits

for you, baying for your hide. Anger me much more and I
may just give it to them."

Ghezu felt the sweat start on the palms of his hands. Fyak
was mad enough to do just that. He remembered the condition Kaid had been in when he'd collected him and a cold
shiver ran down his spine.

Vraiyou, flanked by two guards and followed by his
youngling servant, returned carrying a small wooden chest.
He went right up to Fyak's throne, bowed, and presented
the box.

The prophet leaned forward and took it from him.

"It's time for me to commune with Kezule, Ghezu. I think
it only fitting that since you deny His existence, you should
take this opportunity to accompany me, don't you?" He
looked to the guards.

"Bring him over, Rrurto."

"Now just a minute," said Ghezu, backing away from
them and reaching for his side arm. Before he could, he felt a
sudden burst of heat from the torc round his neck. A lassitude spread throughout him, and with it a disinclination to
move. When the guards took his gun, then took hold of him
and drew him toward Fyak, he didn't resist—though a small
portion of his mind sat there observing his actions in sheer
terror.

Fyak opened the box and handed a small red-topped phial
to Vraiyou. "See he takes it," he said.

"As you wish, Prophet," said Vraiyou.

Everything was happening slowly for Ghezu. He saw
Vraiyou remove the seal from the phial of green liquid, saw
it coming closer to him, and with horror realized his mouth
had opened almost before he heard the command.

"Hold his mouth open, and tilt his head back," Vraiyou said.

While his jaws were held apart, Vraiyou poured the thick
liquid onto the back of his tongue, making sure it trickled
down his throat before ordering him to be released.

Fyak watched him slump to the ground before he turned
his attention to the box. Handing it back to Vraiyou, he lifted
out the second phial. Removing the stopper, he tipped the
contents quickly down his own throat, touched his gold
bracelet, then relaxed back in his seat.

Ghezu suddenly found he was back in control of himself
again. The aftertaste in his mouth was bitter, and falling
down to all fours, he began to retch. As he did, he thanked

the Gods that it was only the sap that Fyak used, not the narcotic he'd given Kaid.

"The bitterness is the price you pay to walk with the Gods," drawled Fyak. "It passes."

"Prophet, we should leave now," said Vraiyou, handing the chest to the youngling.

Fyak nodded, pushing himself to his feet. The drug was already beginning to affect him.

"Bring him," said Vraiyou, indicating Ghezu.

* * *

Something was wrong, Kaid could feel it. Darkness surrounded him, but as his eyes gradually accustomed themselves to it he saw it wasn't total. Ahead of him was a faint line of yellow light.

Limping carefully on three legs, Kaid moved slowly and quietly toward it, sniffing the scents, using the air currents that moved past his body to tell him what was ahead. For once, his drug-enhanced senses were an advantage.

Reaching the end, he stopped, checking again for scents, listening for sounds. Beyond the door he could sense one person, a Sholan, but there were traces of something else, something he wasn't so sure of. Standing up, he ran his fingers along the wall in front of him, then down the sides, feeling the draft. This was a door of some kind, but without an opening mechanism that he could detect.

His fingers found a depression at one edge. Cautiously he tugged. The door moved a fraction. Again he pulled, opening a gap of about three centimeters. Putting his eye to it, he looked through.

He saw a partial wall in front of him. Above that there was a glow of light—not bright, subdued. He frowned. The little he could see gave no indication of what lay beyond this first door. Listening carefully, he heard voices but they were too far away for him to make out what was being said.

Reaching up for the gap with both hands, he realized with a shock that his right one was still bandaged. He sat down hard as his senses began to spin and his heart beat faster. A drug dream! Gods, he thought he'd done with them! Why? What had called him this time? It couldn't be Carrie. He'd been holding her when they fell asleep. What had caused this one?

Is it a dream? his mind asked, *or is this the reality? Was the time I spent with her at Noni's and on the estate the dream?* The dark pit of uncertainly loomed in front of him, waiting for him to fall into it. Mentally, he forced himself back from the edge, refusing to be drawn toward it, turning his mind to what he knew had to be true. This was a drug dream, nothing more. Reality was back there, with Carrie, and his way back led through this doorway. Something had called him here, and until he'd worked out what it was, he wouldn't be able to return.

He stood up and cautiously inserted his fingers through the gap, curling them round the edge of the door. He pulled gently. Soundlessly the door slid back, letting the glow from beyond fill the passage he was in.

He waited, listening for any movement no matter how small. The only sound was the murmur of voices beyond the half-wall, otherwise it was silent. He risked a quick glance to either side. Nothing. Keeping low, he stepped through the gap, finding himself on the balcony of a large chamber. Above him on a ceiling the color of the night sky, stars were painted. Wooden beams crossed from wall to wall, supporting the vaulted roof.

From beyond the balcony, the scent of incense drifted up, confirming his guess that he was in a temple of some kind. Crouching down, he crossed the three meters to the balcony wall. The lattice of diamond shaped gaps that formed the upper portion of the wall provided an ideal way of looking down into the temple without being seen.

He saw that the main chamber had been divided into two sections, the larger one containing the statue of the God he knew would be called Vartra. The smaller one, beyond the crimson curtain that formed the divider, he couldn't see into because of his angle of vision.

The voices came again, one of them tantalizingly familiar. He glanced ahead, realizing if he made for the side section of the balcony, the chances were good that he could see not only who was in the main chamber, but also who was behind the curtain.

He made his way along to the end, then, checking round the corner first, he headed down there until he judged he was in the right position.

Looking through the lattice work, he could now see
the figures below. With a shock he recognized not only
Fyak, but at his side, still retching, was Ghezu! Pushing
back the anger that threatened to trigger hunt mode, he
took a few deep breaths and forced himself to look
toward the other side of the curtain.

What he saw and heard there before this world
exploded around him, etched itself into his memory.

* * *

Carrie woke feeling chilled to the bone. Kaid's arm was a
dead weight across her side and as she reached to move it,
she realized it was as cold as stone. She froze. Lightheaded
and heart pounding, she felt her stomach leap with fear. She
must have cried out mentally because within moments,
Meral came rushing in, rifle at the ready.

She watched him slow to a stop as he saw the situation. A
tiny noise of fear escaped her and he was instantly by
her side.

There was no need for her to say anything. It was obvious
that he'd assessed the situation. He knelt down till his face
was level with hers.

"I'm going to lift his arm, Liegena. When I do, I want you
to take my hand and slide off the bed. Do you understand?"

She made a tiny movement of her head.

Meral stood up and waited till she'd taken hold of his outstretched hand before carefully taking hold of Kaid's wrist
and lifting it high enough for Carrie to move.

Sliding out, she would have fallen had Meral's hand not
supported her. As she moved away from the bed, Meral
replaced Kaid's arm on the covers.

"Are you all right?" he asked, turning round to check on her.

She nodded, putting both hands over her mouth in an
effort to control her need to scream.

Meral pointed to the chair. "Sit down until I've checked
Kaid," he said, turning back to the bed.

Kaid was covered in a tiny mist of water droplets, and
when Meral touched his neck, checking for a pulse, the skin
beneath his pelt was cold. Though he kept his hand there for
a good minute, he could feel nothing.

"I'm afraid he's dead, Liegena," he said, turning back to her.

Carrie was still standing where he'd left her. She took her hands away from her face.

"He can't be dead. Try again. You've done it wrong!" Even she could hear the edge of hysteria in her voice.

"No, Liegena," he said, stepping toward her. "I really am sorry, but he is dead."

"He can't be, I tell you!" she said, her voice rising as she ran past him to the bed.

Pushing Kaid's arm clear, she pulled back the covers and felt his chest. "He's still warm!" she said, reaching up for his neck to check his pulse for herself.

"The fact he's still warm means nothing, Liegena. The body cools down after death. The covers will have prevented the heat from dissipating so quickly, that's all," Meral said. He reached out and took her by the arm. "Leave him, Liegena. I'll call Physician Vanna. You're distressing yourself. Please."

"I've got a pulse, Meral," she said quietly. "My God, I've got a pulse! Get Vanna! No, get me something to keep him warm!"

He leaned over her. "Let me," he said.

She pulled back enough for him to feel the pulse.

"You're right! I'll get Vanna and tell Zhala to fetch a warming blanket," he said, dashing out of the room.

Carrie replaced Kaid's arm at his side, then pulled the covers up to his chin. Taking his head between her hands, she reached mentally for him, trying to locate his consciousness and call him back. She couldn't find him. It was as if he wasn't there. Memories of doing the same for Kusac came flooding back to her. She'd succeeded then, she couldn't fail now; but there was nothing, no response.

Checking his pulse, she found it unchanged: slow, but definitely there. Perhaps his coldness was the clue. Leaving him, she ran to his shower and grabbed a towel. She began to dry off the moisture, then pulling the covers back again, began rubbing his arm and chest vigorously to try and speed up his circulation. After a couple of minutes she stopped and took his pulse again. She was sure it was faster. Not by much, but it was faster.

She kept this up until Zhala came running in with a heating blanket. With her help, they stripped the covers back and wrapped him in it, turning the setting to medium to avoid overheating him.

Again, she tried to reach his mind, but once more, it was as if he wasn't there. The front door opened and closed. She heard the sound of Vanna's feet taking the stairs at least two at a time. Then she was there beside her.

Carrie moved round to the other side of the bed, sitting as close to Kaid as she could while she told Vanna what she knew.

Her friend pulled the warming blanket away from him and threw it on the floor. "I know why you did it, but if he's had a stroke, that could be enough to kill him. It pulls the blood back to less vital organs," she said, checking his pulse and eyes before giving the rest of his body a quick check for swellings or wounds of any kind.

"He was covered in moisture? That's most peculiar," she said, finally running her scanner over him. She checked his brain readings twice before looking over at Carrie. Her ears were lying back in distress.

"He's alive, Carrie, no doubt about that, but his pulse is far too slow, and I'm getting no brain activity at all. How long has he been like this?"

Carrie checked her wrist unit then looked over at Meral. "How long is it since I called you?"

"Coming up for fifteen minutes now, Liegena," he said.

"That's all I know," said Carrie. "You could add on an extra five minutes at most as the time it took me to call Meral."

"He's got to be hospitalized. I need to do tests, have emergency equipment on hand in case he needs it," she said, getting up. "I suggest you call Kusac. There's nothing more we can do for him here."

Vanna was speaking to the medical center when there was a sudden exclamation from Meral. A gust of hot wind rushed through the room and Kaid, gasping for air, sat up, a look of sheer terror on his face.

Carrie grabbed hold of him, pulling him close and holding him tight.

It took Kaid only moments to realize where he was, then he clung to her as if afraid that at any moment she'd disappear.

"He's fine, Vanna," Carrie said over her shoulder. "It was a drug dream, nothing more."

"I still want him admitted . . ."

"No. He's fine. He's staying here," she said firmly. Gradually, the calming effect of her mind touching his and her arms around him had the desired result, and his trembling began to lessen.

For a moment more he rested against her, his face buried against her neck, his arm wrapped round her.

"Can you tell me what happened?" she asked, her hand gently smoothing his hair.

He nodded and began to pull away from her.

"You don't have to move."

"I need to lie down," he said. "I'm fine. Really."

She let him go and he moved away to lie back against his damp pillows.

"It was a drug dream," he said, looking up briefly as he felt Kusac arrive. "I was pulled back to the Cataclysm because there were two others there from our time. The Gods help me, I know what's happening. I know what Fyak's doing. It's all been planned, right down to the plant being left in the cavern for Fyak to find. He's using the sap as a drug to take him back to the Fire Margins. His God, Kezule, isn't a God. He's the Valtegan Commander in charge of the unit guarding the hatchery that was at Khezy'ipik, Fyak's lair."

CHAPTER 20

Carrie ignored the others' reactions to the news. "Go on," she said.

"Fyak doesn't know any of this. When he visits the Margins, he's pulled back to a temple where Kezule and his troop are hoping to weather out the arrival of the meteorite. I heard Fyak talk to the statue and call it Kezule. I saw the Valtegan, Kezule, reply to him through a translator concealed in the statue. Fyak thinks the voice comes from the God—his God."

He stopped for a moment. "This Kezule is the one pushing Fyak. He's rearranging our society so that when the Valtegans return to Shola, they'll find it vulnerable."

"You said there were three people there. Who was the third?" asked Kusac, coming forward to sit on the bed.

"Ghezu. He's with Fyak now."

"Ghezu! What's he doing there?" asked Kusac.

"Hiding from us. Why he's visiting the Margins with him is another matter. He was throwing up, which isn't surprising if Fyak made him take that sap," said Kaid, vague memories of doing the same coming back. "At least for him it'll only last a day."

"Do you think the drug, whether it's sap or the narcotic, is the key to returning to the Margins?"

Kaid shook his head. "I don't know. I think it's certainly a factor."

"You were still physically here, Kaid," said Carrie. "We thought you were dead. You had no pulse we could feel at first, you were as cold as the grave, and covered in dampness."

He looked at her in shock. "I was here? I couldn't have been! I was at the temple!"

"We know you were here, Kaid," said Vanna, sitting in the chair. "Unfortunately we only know what you saw at the temple. We've no proof you were physically there."

"You said I had no pulse . . ."

"That could have been trauma caused by either being in a deep trance, or your reaction to the dream."

"Then how do I know so much about Fyak and what he's doing!" Kaid demanded, pushing himself into a sitting position.

"I think we'll call it a night," said Kusac, getting up. "Kaid needs to rest. Vanna, we'll join you downstairs shortly. Thank you for coming so quickly."

Refusing to let the matter be discussed further, he waited till Vanna and Meral had left, then turned back to Carrie and Kaid.

"I'm not saying you weren't there, Kaid, but what you're telling us about Fyak, this Kezule, and the Valtegans, isn't substantiated by what you said you saw. I can't see why you're drawing the conclusions you are," he said. "Have you any explanation?"

Kaid threw himself back against the pillows angrily. "None you'd accept."

"Try me."

"I'm remembering again," he said, staring straight at him, daring him to disbelieve.

"If you're remembering again, then it's got to be because we've been back and learned what's going on," said Carrie.

"A possibility," said Kusac. "but only if we'd gone back already."

"I don't think it works quite like that," said Carrie. "Even if we don't go for another week, this will still be our past today, the past affected by the fact that we've been back."

Kusac shook his head. "Let's leave that one alone. For the sake of argument, we'll assume you were physically there, Kaid. If it needs three to go back, then how does Fyak manage, and you? And how did he *get* back in the first place?"

"You're asking me which came first. Fyak's return to the past after eating the plant, or this Kezule leaving some plants growing in that area so that Fyak could find them in order to go back in time! It's the same question as the last one, Kusac! We'll get nowhere like this," he said, obviously frustrated at his inability to explain what had happened to him.

"Well," said Carrie. "We do know we go back because we now have evidence that we did—Kaid's memories. Let's go forward from there. In actual fact," she said, shifting round so she could see both Kusac and Kaid comfortably, "what Kaid says tallies with the warnings from Esken. The priest with the ties to the past who'll bring the past to our future? If that isn't a Valtegan Commander trying to affect our future by using this mad priest, Fyak, I don't know what is!"

"You've got a point," conceded Kusac. "All right, I accept that what you say is correct, Kaid. That still leaves us with how the hell do you and Fyak go back on your own?"

"I don't know!" Kaid was sounding exasperated now. "Maybe that's why Fyak's mad—because he's gone back alone so often! Maybe that's part of why there needs to be three of us!"

"I'm more interested in how he manages to get himself back to the right time and place," said Carrie thoughtfully. "Does he just decide to go, and his arrival is reported to this Kezule? Or does Kezule call him, perhaps through the collar? How often did he go into trances while you were there, Kaid?"

"At least once."

"Say he goes back once a week, that's a lot of visits even since we've known about him. It depends over what time span he arrives in the past," said Carrie. "Any ideas?"

"We know that debris from the explosion caused by a Valtegan warship hitting our lesser moon caused the actual Cataclysm," said Kusac. "Dzaka's been checking out what would have happened to Shola when this debris hit us. The heat of its approach could have started forest fires. When it actually landed, there'd have been an immense explosion. If it landed in the sea, giant tidal waves. There would certainly have been massive earthquakes, and clouds of water vapor. The rubbish from the seabed as well as the meteorite would have ended up in our atmosphere. And it would all have to fall down again."

"That's a definitely a cataclysm," said Carrie. "How long would they have between knowing the debris was coming and it actually hitting the planet?"

"Maybe a couple of days at most."

"If there were any Valtegan ships capable of space travel, then you can bet that the Valtegans who could would have headed off-planet," she said. "Why did Kezule and his males stay behind?"

"Who knows? Loyalty? Stupidity? No ships? Any answer is as good as the next one," said Kaid. "Just as we may never know what caused Fyak to go back to the past the first time, unless we ask him."

"How do we pinpoint *our* return to the past?" asked Carrie. "That's more important to us than the why's or when's of Fyak."

"Each time you had a drug dream," said Kusac, "something or someone called you, didn't it? We know we've gone back, so perhaps those we're visiting call us there, because we told them to."

"Maybe. But I think an important factor we've forgotten is the other crystals. The ones that were used for the eyes of the statue in the monastery," said Carrie. "I still have the one I found. Maybe we could use the memories it holds to choose the right time."

"We can, but not the way you're thinking, Carrie. We've still got the traditional way," said Kaid. "The En'Shalla ritual has its own rules on how to reach the Cataclysm. It's been handed down for the God knows how long. It's something we haven't yet put into the picture we're building of the past, despite the fact that we've been planning to use it all along. We're probably avoiding it because we know we're going to have to use it."

"You're right," said Kusac. "We have forgotten about it. However, the people using the ritual didn't survive. Was that the ritual's fault, or the fact that, once there, they met Vartra the person and couldn't cope with it?"

"We'll use the En'Shalla ritual enhanced by what we've learned. I've been studying it in greater depth," said Kaid. "It works on the principle that a gateway to that time exists because of the energy produced by Shola herself during the Cataclysm. This power pools in certain places—places I've discovered have large deposits of those blue-white crystals in the ground. The Pathwalkers, or Travelers to the Margins leave from either Stronghold, or more commonly in modern times, from the temple at Valsgarth."

"We'd better start making plans now," said Kusac. "I suggest we look at leaving at the end of this week. Is your body in the past the same there as it is here? Do you still have an injured hand?"

"Yes," said Carrie. "When he came to the Shrine he had injuries."

"She's right," said Kaid. "The past feels just as it does

here. It's just as real, except when you leave and arrive. Those times can make you feel that all you want to do is die."

"Can we take anything with us?" asked Carrie.

Kaid shook his head. "Not even clothing."

"Where do these new bodies come from? Do we create them from our imagination? Does going through this gateway automatically create one?"

"I've no idea, Carrie. We can speculate all we want, but all that really matters is that we go back. We warn Vartra of what's going to happen to his world, and when we return, we can set up our Clan," said Kaid. "To be honest, I've never even seen a gateway."

"What about stopping Fyak?" asked Carrie. "Shouldn't we be trying to do something about that?"

"No. We can inform Raiban of what we know and leave it to her to deal with in our time," said Kusac firmly. "How do you feel now, Kaid?" He leaned forward to touch his hand. "You're not as cold as you were."

"I'm all right," he said. "When I was away, I felt fine. It was a shock to come back to a body that was so cold!"

"We'll need Vanna to watch us while we're away," said Carrie. "And Ghyan."

"Talking of Vanna, she's waiting for us downstairs. I suggest we go down and get a meal organized. Are you up to joining us, Kaid?"

Kaid nodded.

"Use the chair," said Carrie firmly.

Kaid exchanged glances with Kusac over her head.

"I'm no more fussy over you two than you are over me," she retorted in reply to their common thought.

* * *

All day Mara had been feeling annoyed. She'd tried to help the archeologists, but the old woman, Pam, had been very unpleasant.

"If you really want to help," she'd said, "then help by keeping out of our way! I've got enough on my hands trying to deal with those damned Touibans! The last thing I need is a kid like you getting under everyone's feet!"

That had hurt, and hadn't been justified. She'd only thought that because they were all Humans, they'd be as pleased to have her help as she'd have been to give it.

Angrily she'd stormed off down to the lower cavern where
several of the Sholans were still working on the vehicles.
They'd not been overjoyed to see her either. Well, damn
them all! She wasn't going to be told by anyone what she
could and couldn't do!

Going over to Jack's table, she'd collected a brush and
trowel from there and headed off to the place Dzaka had
been uncovering several days before. She squatted down in
front of the metal plate he'd been working on and had a good
look at it. He hadn't done any more since that day. Well,
she'd finish it off for him. With any luck he'd be in later.
She'd seen him the day before but Kitra had been hanging
around him, and there wasn't a lot she could do with Kitra's
father there as well.

She became quite engrossed in what she was doing and it
came as a surprise when she heard Dzaka's voice.

"What are you doing, Mara? That's the piece Kitra and I
were working on."

She looked up, pleased to find him on his own. "I thought
I'd help you," she said, sitting back on her heels. "Look, I've
uncovered another three letters."

"That's not the point, Mara," said Dzaka gently, bending
down to her level. "You know enough about the way things
are run here to know you mustn't work on someone else's
finds without permission. Working on this with me meant a
lot to Kitra. She'll be disappointed that you've done so
much."

"Oh, come on, Dzaka. She's only a child! She can find
somewhere else to dig, surely," she said, putting her head to
one side in an unconscious parody of a Sholan gesture.

"Why should she?" asked Dzaka. "Why couldn't you have
found somewhere else to work?"

Mara looked up at him, her mouth an *O* of surprise. "I
didn't realize that the feelings of a kitling were that important to you," she said, hearing the touch of anger in her tone.
"I'd have thought you were beyond playing nursery games,
but it seems I was wrong!" She stood up, and throwing down
her brush, stormed past him and out toward the exit.

She passed Kitra on the way and stopped to turn her
temper on the young Sholan as well. Taking her by the
shoulders, she pushed her back against the cavern wall. It
was all her fault anyway!

"Just you keep out of my way, Kitra! I'm sick to death of

finding you hanging round Dzaka every time I want to talk to him! Go and play with the other cubs and leave the grown-ups to get on with their own lives," she said, her face a spiteful mask of anger.

"Hey!" a voice yelled from the mouth of the tunnel. "Leave Kitra alone!"

Mara looked up to see Rulla heading toward her. She gave Kitra one last thump against the wall. "Remember what I said." Releasing her, she turned and ran out past Rulla.

Rulla ignored her, going instead to Kitra who was still standing there too stunned to move.

Dzaka was heading toward her at a run from the other end of the tunnel.

"Are you all right?" asked Rulla, skidding to a stop in front of her. "Did she hurt you?"

Dzaka pushed Rulla aside, reaching out to gather her close against him. "Are you hurt, little one?" he asked, touching her face gently, ears laid back in concern. "I didn't think she'd dare go near you."

"I'm fine," she said, her voice shaking as she took hold of his hand. "She told me to leave you alone. I think she wants you for herself. Why would she want that? Why is she being so unpleasant to me?"

"I don't know, Kitra," said Dzaka, resting his cheek on her head. He looked across at Rulla, his eyes challenging him to say anything. "Perhaps Rulla knows."

Rulla found himself looking at Kitra, and he didn't know quite what to say.

"Rulla and I'll talk about it later," said Dzaka, turning his attention back to her. "Don't worry, Kitra, we'll see someone speaks to Mara."

She nodded, moving closer to him. "Can we leave now? I don't think I want to stay here any longer."

"Of course. Where do you want to go?"

"The villa. I want to see Carrie, please."

His arm around her shoulders, Dzaka led Kitra past Rulla and toward the exit. He stopped a moment, turning to speak to the other male over his shoulder. "You have some responsibility for Mara, Rulla. Make sure she comes nowhere near my Companion again," he said with a low growl.

Kitra didn't want Dzaka to mention anything about the incident with Mara either to Carrie or her brother, but they did spend the rest of the day within the villa grounds.

Consequently Dzaka was unable to speak to Rulla about the matter and had to leave it till the following day.

The silence of the night was split by a shrill scream. Before he'd time to put on the light, Dzaka's bedroom door was flung open by T'Chebbi. Taking one look, she straightened up from her crouch and switched her gun to standby, the slight whining noise sounding unnaturally loud in the small room.

As Kitra put the light on, Kusac, closely followed by Meral, came running through the small lounge to stop beside T'Chebbi.

Dzaka removed his knife from Mara's throat and released her.

"Mara, what the hell are you doing here?" demanded Kusac, seeing to his gun as he came into the room. "Excuse me, Dzaka, Kitra," he said, remembering his manners.

Dzaka nodded to him and moved back to his bed, sitting down beside Kitra.

"Me?" said Mara, passing her hand across her throat to make sure it wasn't bleeding. "Me? What about them?" she demanded, pointing to Dzaka and Kitra. "She's only a child! He's seduced her!"

T'Chebbi began to laugh softly. Mara rounded on her.

"What's so bloody funny about it? Don't you care about that cub?" she demanded.

"More than you," she snapped back. "You attacked her in the cavern today!"

"What?" demanded Kusac. "Is this true, Kitra?"

Kitra looked from her brother to Dzaka.

"Yes, but Rulla and I were there almost immediately. Kitra wasn't harmed," said Dzaka, answering for her.

"Why didn't you tell me?"

"I didn't want to," said Kitra in a small voice, speaking for the first time.

"Liege, could you . . ." began Dzaka, picking up her distress at being disturbed in his bed.

"Of course," said Kusac, turning to Meral and T'Chebbi. "Out, you lot," he said amicably. "Meral, you go back on duty. T'Chebbi can stay to escort Mara home." He took Mara firmly by the arm and pulled her outside with him.

"I don't think that'll be necessary," said Meral, cocking

his ears backward as the faint sound of the door buzzer was heard. "I think that'll be Zhyaf now."

"See to it, please," said Kusac, shutting the bedroom door firmly behind them. He turned back to Mara.

"Have you any idea what trouble you've caused?" he demanded. "Kitra isn't a child, she's just entered adulthood, and your behavior could have spoiled what should be a pleasant time for her! The family knows all about Dzaka. We're all in favor of their relationship, and anyway, it's none of your damned business! You have a Leska, you don't need to try and spoil my sister's first relationship!"

"But . . ." began Mara, backing away in the face of Kusac's obvious anger.

"If you're interested in someone, you ask them! If they say no, you leave them alone! Did you bother to ask Dzaka if he was interested in you?"

"No, but . . ."

"Then you had no right to pursue him as you have! This matter isn't over, Mara. I'll be seeing you and Zhyaf tomorrow! Now get out of here and go home!"

Mara fled.

"See she reaches her home," Kusac ordered T'Chebbi. He knocked on Dzaka's door and opened it. "Kitra, I'm sorry you've had all this bother. You should have told me before now," he said, going over to sit on the bed beside her. He took hold of her hand, giving it a comforting pat. "This won't happen again."

"Liege," began Dzaka.

Kusac looked at him. "At this time of night? Don't be foolish, Dzaka."

"Kusac, if Mara could get in unnoticed, then we need to check the security," said Dzaka.

"We will," said Kusac. "I'm getting Ni'Zulhu onto it immediately." He stretched forward to stroke his sister's cheek. "I'll see you in the morning," he said, getting up. "Sleep well," he said, with a humorous look at Dzaka.

* * *

They'd passed on their findings concerning the drug and the green stones, along with Kaid's recent "dreams," to General Raiban. No trace had been found of Ghezu, and

Kaid's claim that he was with Fyak came as no surprise to her.

Back on his feet, over the next few days Kaid worked with Ghyan on the En'Shalla ritual, learning the different phases that led to the gate, and what the gate itself looked like.

He'd read the description himself some time before he'd been captured by Fyak's warriors, but now it held disturbing echoes for him.

"Twin pillars of flame between which are two wooden doors bearing the sign of . . ."

"A burning sun," finished Kaid. "I also saw it on the doors of the temple at Khezi'ipik, Fyak's lair."

"Is that doorway the Gateway? Will it take you there?"

"I don't know. There are three sites that I know of for the crystals, Ghyan. Khezi'ipik, Stronghold, and the ancient monastery up on the hill. All of them have something that represents pillars of fire at their entrances. Perhaps the other travelers arrived at the wrong temple, maybe even the one Kezule controls, and were killed by him."

Ghyan put the book down and leaned forward on his desk. "So how will you decide which is the correct one?"

"I'll know," said Kaid confidently. "I've seen the one at the monastery. I'll take us there."

"How? Will you change the nature of the gate?"

"As far as I'm aware, I didn't use a gate, but yes, I can try to make it look like that one."

"Kaid, what you did, what allowed you to travel back and return, won't necessarily work for Carrie and Kusac as well. All three of you have to travel together. Your way is untested. You were called. You didn't travel there voluntarily."

"I went there and returned alive," said Kaid. "That's better than any other traveler has done, isn't it? Yes, it's a risk, but so's the other way. I'm sure the two can be combined."

"What we need is the time to test your theory."

"Time's what *we* haven't got. This is a one-shot journey, Ghyan, we all know that," said Kaid, making sure his private thoughts stayed just that.

Ghyan sighed. "We don't have to like it, though. Incidentally, how is your telepathic training progressing?"

"It's going well. Kusac gave me the knowledge I needed and he and Carrie have been making me practice using my abilities whenever they can. It's hard work, Ghyan," he said, opening his mouth in a small grin. "I never realized how tiring it could be."

"Everything has it's price," said Ghyan.

"That, I do know!"

*   *   *

Toward the end of the week, Garras came round to the villa to see Kaid. He came across the back gardens and in through the lounge, heading for the family kitchen.

Second meal was not long over, and Kaid was still sitting at the table over his mug of c'shar.

"Where is everyone?" asked Garras, joining him.

"Kusac's around, and Carrie's resting. As for the others . . ." he shrugged.

"Good. I'm glad I caught you on your own." He reached into his coat pocket, pulling out a small box and handing it to him. "The la'quo. He could only get one phial, I'm afraid. Profuse apologies and all that, naturally."

Kaid picked it up, opening it to check. Wedged in protective packaging was a glass phial of the green liquid.

"Thanks, Garras," Kaid said, taking the phial out of the box. He'd been both dreading and anxiously waiting for it to arrive.

"What d'you want it for?" Garras asked, helping himself to the jug of c'shar on the table.

"Research," he said. "I've a couple of theories I want to try out and I need this to do it."

"Tell me more," his friend said, lifting his mug.

"Not a lot to tell. I could do with your help, though."

"In what way? Are you planning to give it to lab animals? See what happens to them?"

"Not exactly," he said, holding the phial in his palm. "There's a gate to the Fire Margins, Garras. One with pillars of fire outside it. The problem is, there are three temples like that, each one slightly different. I think the previous travelers may have gone to the wrong one, perhaps one where Valtegans were waiting for them. I saw the doorway of one of them through a dream that Kusac, Carrie, and I shared. It's the monastery on the hill. What I need to know is, can I use the drug to take us there?"

"Well, you said it responded to your state of mind, so I

expect you could," he said. "But I don't see how you can devise a test for that."

Kaid took the phial between his fingers and broke off the red paper seal.

Garras watched him, suddenly realizing what he was going to do. "You can't seriously be going to take more of that damned stuff, Kaid! For Vartra's sake, leave it alone!"

Kaid smiled. "It is for Vartra's sake, Garras," he said, taking off the stopper.

"No!" Kusac's shout rang through the kitchen.

Kaid and Garras looked up at him.

"You will *not* take that drug, Kaid," said Kusac, coming into the kitchen.

"I have to. We need to know if it can take us to the monastery, Kusac," he said, raising the phial to his mouth.

"I said no!"

A look of utter shock crossed Kaid's face as he realized his body was frozen, incapable of moving. Kusac's fear for his safety resonated through him and he realized what had happened. Helplessly he watched as Kusac strode over to him and took the phial from his rigid hand.

"You're right, Kaid, it has to be tested, but you've already got too much of it in your system. What's your plan? Try to make it take you to the monastery?" He swallowed it quickly, almost gagging as the thick liquid seemed to clog his throat.

He grabbed Garras' mug and took a large mouthful of the cold c'shar, then sat down heavily, releasing Kaid from his mental control.

"What happens now?" he asked, eyes glazing a little as he realized what he'd done.

Before Kaid could answer, they heard the sound of footsteps racing down the stairs.

"You fool!" said Garras, pushing his chair back as he leaped to his feet. "You forgot about Carrie! She'll share the effects! Kaid, is it too late to make him vomit?"

"Yes. He's taken the sap, not the stronger narcotic I was given. I'm not sure its effects are the same. I've seen Fyak take it and he reacted as quickly to it as I did."

"Dammit, Kaid! Why didn't you stop him?"

"I controlled his mind, Garras," said Kusac. "He couldn't move."

Carrie came running in. "Kusac, what have you done?" she demanded, stopping beside him. "What have you done?"

He took her hand in his. "We have to know if the drug will help us reach the past, Carrie. Kaid has too much of it in his system already. It's dangerous for him to take any more. That only left me. I've known for several days what he intended to do and I've been watching him. It had to be me. We'll know then if what Kaid's experienced is real."

"Kusac . . . Oh, God! What do I do with you?" she asked, taking his hand to her cheek.

Kaid stood and looked over at Garras. "Get him to his room now," he said. "He needs to be kept as quiet and as comfortable as possible."

Garras looked at Kusac. "Can you stand?"

"Yes," he said, getting to his feet. He staggered as he tried to turn round.

"He needs help," said Kaid sharply. "It starts almost immediately. Get him upstairs before he becomes hypersensitive!!"

Garras nodded, taking hold of Kusac and hurrying him from the room, Carrie following behind.

Kaid stood still for a moment. Light glinted off something on the floor. He bent down and picked it up: the glass phial. A low growl began deep in his throat and pulling his arm back, he threw the phial as far as he could.

"Damn you both to hell!" he roared.

Upstairs, Kusac stood like a giant lethargic child with no will of his own while Garras stripped him of his robe.

Carrie stood watching, feeling her fear pushed aside by the lassitude that was spreading through him and beginning to touch her. She resisted it, pushing it aside as she reached for the cover on the bed and pulled it off onto the floor.

Going to a cupboard she pulled out a fresh sheet, waiting while Garras led Kusac to the bed and made him lie down.

"The God help you, Kusac," he said, "Because when this is over, I'll damned well have a few things to say to you!"

Kusac looked up at him. Everything felt distant, removed from him—or he from it. He wasn't quite sure which, and it didn't really matter. He saw a sheet billow up, then settle over him. Something was missing: someone who was always there. Then he remembered. It mustn't touch her or the cub. He could isolate himself now, he'd been practicing over the last few days in case it came to this. Turning his head, he saw her and reached for her hand.

"I'll be fine. You look after our cub." He heard the door slide back and Kaid enter, but the lassitude had him in its thrall now.

"Garras, get the house emptied of everyone but us for the next two hours. He'll hear the slightest noise," said Kaid. "The drug amplifies the senses."

"If I'd known what you planned to do," began Garras, his voice low and angry.

"Later. Just do what needs to be done," Kaid snapped, moving further into the room.

It was different from what Kaid had described, Kusac realized. Probably because it wasn't the drug, but the sap. His senses were becoming heightened but with it, the room around him seemed to be draining of its color.

Curious. There isn't the sense of fear that Kaid spoke of. Then he remembered that their circumstances were very different. He was safe at home, with those he trusted around him. Kaid had been a captive in a violent environment.

He felt himself sinking downward into a gray mist that totally enveloped him, cushioning his senses from the outside world. Turning inward, he could hear his body rhythms, was aware of the slightest changes in his skin and pelt.

Gradually even the grayness started to fade into darkness. *The monastery. I want to reach the monastery,* he reminded himself as he began to try and build an image of it.

Carrie sat at his side, watching as his eyes closed and his breathing became shallower. Then their Link began to fade, getting weaker and weaker till she could barely feel it.

"This isn't the way it happened with me," said Kaid, sitting at the other side of his bed. "This seems far gentler."

"He's getting cold, Kaid," said Carrie, reaching out to touch Kusac's face with first her palm, then the back of her hand. She was frightened. It felt too like that time on the *Khalossa* when he'd turned to death rather than be without her.

Her lassitude had gone now, and as his mind began to still and their Link fade, real panic set in. She reached mentally for him and found nothing. Her hands went to the sides of his head as she tried again. Then the chill started.

With a cry of terror, she let go of him, looking at hands red with burns. Over Kusac a layer of frost had formed, each tiny droplet a perfect snowflake.

She screamed again, a shriek that pierced the air and echoed round the house. Flinging herself onto Kusac, she reached for him with all the power she could muster.

"Carrie! He's all right!" said Kaid, reaching for her, trying to pull her away from Kusac.

She could sense him, just beyond her reach. A little more energy, and she'd be there, she knew it. Then she felt Kaid's touch, and immediately she pulled on him, taking his energy into herself and sending it all toward where Kusac was.

Reality shattered into a thousand fragments as they were whirled into a maelstrom of sight and sound and smell. Helplessly, all three of them were pulled together, then sucked down and down till there was nothing but the sickening flashing of colors, a roaring that filled their ears, and the flames.

Caught between the two males, Carrie felt first one then the other almost torn from her mental grasp. It was so noisy, she could barely think. There was something she had to do, something important that involved all of them, if she could only stop the roaring long enough to think.

Let me lead! It was Kaid, his thoughts faint but unmistakable. *I know where we must go!*

Yes. He could lead. He knew the way, he'd been there before. She and Kusac would follow. Kusac. Where was he? She could sense him, closer than Kaid, but so confused by what was happening.

Which way? I need to know which way! he was sending. The drug was confusing him.

Why didn't he listen to Kaid? Kaid said he knew the way! Then the memory returned. She was their link to each other. They couldn't communicate without her, she had to join them all together. How? Dear God, how?

Fear leaped inside her and she felt it transmitted to Kusac. As it rebounded to her, she felt the gestalt gradually begin to wake inside her. Almost sobbing with relief, she grasped it, harnessing its power to strengthen the bonds between them. Slowly it built, reaching the point where it seemed to explode out from her to touch the minds of Kusac and Kaid, binding them to her. The power surged through their bodies, burning and searing the flesh from their bones till they were nothing: only their minds survived, linked together as one. Then, in one blinding second of light, suddenly they were three not one, and they were tumbling downward.

Garras heard her scream. Leaving everything, he headed back to the bedroom at full speed. He stopped dead at the door, holding onto the wall for support as he saw what had happened. The anger that had been simmering since he realized Kaid had intended to take the drug, exploded in one roaring shout of rage.

Minutes later, Dzaka, Meral and T'Chebbi were there.

"They've gone," he said, his voice hoarse, waving a hand at the three frozen bodies lying on the bed. "We need Ghyan and Vanna—get Ghyan first. And there's no need to rush."

"Tell Master Lijou," said T'Chebbi.

Garras looked at her in surprise as the other two left at a run.

"He and Ghyan know most," she said. "We may need beds for them. I'll get them." She turned and headed off downstairs.

Garras went over to look down at them. Kaid was half sprawled on the floor and against the side of the bed. Carrie had fallen across Kusac. He shivered, looking round the room. It was freezing. He went to the window, pulling the drapes aside but the windows were closed. What had caused the huge drop in temperature? He looked at them once more. There was nothing he dared do for now. Shaking his head, he went out to the lounge and activated the desk comm to call Lijou.

*   *   *

The yowls of terror from the temple penetrated through the heavy curtain to the lounge, making everyone look up in surprise. Tiernay was first on his feet and out into the corridor. One of the temple students in his grey homespun robe careened into him, almost sending him flying.

"Sorry," he gasped, continuing on his mad dash to the office.

Tiernay picked himself off the wall and pushed through the curtain into the temple. A small group of students stood between him and a semicircle composed of Goran and the three indoor guards, their rifles pointed at something on the floor.

Goran looked up at him. "Get blankets, Tiernay, and quick."

Tiernay doubled back to his room, returning with several. As he pushed past the students, he looked down to see what the fuss was about. What he saw defied belief.

He felt Goran twitch the blankets from him, then saw him kneel down to cover up the alien form that lay on the floor between two Sholan males. All three of them looked to be unconscious.

"Where did they come from?" he asked when he finally found his voice.

"According to the students, there was a noise like the wind blowing, followed by a blast of heat, then the air seemed to bend, and there they were," said Goran.

A squall from one of the females drew their attention back to the people on the floor.

"He moved! That one moved!"

Goran signaled to his guards. "Clear this lot out," he said. "Last thing these folk need is to see dozens of faces staring at them."

The guards moved toward the students who backed off, scuttling to their quarters to tell their less fortunate friends what had happened.

Kaid was the first to fight his way back to consciousness. He could feel Carrie's mental presence, and though not as strongly, he knew Kusac was there too. It wasn't enough. He had to see them.

Groaning, he pulled his good hand to his side and tried to push himself upright. Everything hurt, he discovered, as he managed to raise himself enough to lift his head and look from one side to the other.

Willing hands took hold of him, helping him sit up before putting a blanket round his shoulders.

At first his eyes wouldn't focus, then gradually the blurring passed and he saw that they'd all arrived safely. Someone, thank the God, had covered Carrie with a blanket.

There was a voice speaking to him, but he couldn't understand it at first. The aches and pains had resolved themselves now and he could tell that most of them were due to landing face first on the floor beneath him. He pushed the hands

away and reached out for Carrie. If she'd landed the way he
had . . .

He hadn't the strength to pull the blanket from her and
check she was all right. Looking up, he saw the person who
was doing all the talking. Why the hell couldn't he see that
she needed help? Angrily, he turned on him.

"In the God's name, shut up!" he said. "Check her! She
fell. She's pregnant!"

The talking stopped but there was confusion all around
him. They didn't know what to do. Then the one beside him
spoke.

"We have. We could see nothing obviously wrong with
her, but rest easy, a doctor is on the way."

"Kusac. How's he?"

"Your friend is unconscious. Has he been drugged at all?"

"Yes. La'quo. That's what brought us here."

"Not one we've heard of, I'm afraid. My name's Tiernay.
You're at . . ."

"I know where we are," interrupted Kaid. "We've come to
see the one called Vartra."

"I'm afraid you'll have to wait," said Tiernay. "We don't
know who you are or where you came from. You're a security risk at present."

Kaid was beginning to feel more alert by now and as he
looked around, his eyes lighted on Goran standing there,
rifle at the ready.

"I know you," he said. "Goran. You trained with Rezac.
Where is he? Has he been taken yet?"

Startled, Goran and Tiernay exchanged glances. "Taken?"

"Carrie saw it. She read it from the collar they tried to put
on Zashou. Has it happened yet?"

"How do you know about Rezac and Zashou?" demanded
Goran, stepping forward.

A wave of lightheadedness swept through Kaid and he
began to sway. Tiernay caught hold of him before he fell.

"Look, we're not from now," said Kaid as nausea began to
hit his stomach. "We've come back to warn you. The moon. It
was hit by the warship. A meteorite is coming," he said,
clutching hold of Tiernay's arm as the room began to darken.

"He's passed out," said Tiernay, making a grab for him
before he fell. Carefully he laid him on the ground again.

"Mad, that's what he is," said Goran, pulling a stim-twig

from his pocket and sticking it in his mouth. "Here's the doctor. I'm keeping them under guard here. I don't trust them. Two males and a pregnant female alien turn up out of nowhere? Smells to me, that does. Mark my words, the Valtegans are at the back of this."

Both doctors came running across to them. "What's happened?" demanded Nyaam, kneeling down beside Tiernay. "Let me see him."

"They appeared out of thin air, if the students are to be believed," said Goran.

"Dr. Kimin," said Tiernay, looking up at the female Sholan, "Will you look at this one? She's pregnant and one of the males is afraid she may have hurt herself."

Kimin nodded and moved round to the side of the female. Pulling back the blanket, she let out a cry of disbelief.

"What is it?" demanded Nyaam, breaking off his examination of Kaid to see what had caused his colleague to cry out.

"She's an alien," said Goran, pushing his twig to one side of his mouth. "A furless one."

"So I see," said Kimin, her voice a little faint as she began to check the unknown alien for any obvious signs of injury. "She seems all right, but I don't know where to start with her! I want her up in the infirmary and settled into a bed," she said, standing up and moving to the third body.

"They stay here for now," said Goran. "That one hasn't moved."

"They can't stay here!" exclaimed Kimin. "They need to be treated!"

"Then bed them down here," growled Goran. "I don't like the way they suddenly arrived, nor what that first one knew about us."

Kaid surfaced again about an hour later. He looked across at the camp beds beside him and saw Carrie and Kusac were also there. With a sigh of relief, he sat up. They were still in the temple, and an armed guard sat watching them. When he saw Kaid moving, he got to his feet and, going to where the crimson curtain had been pulled back, he opened the door, speaking briefly to someone outside.

While he was doing that, Kaid got up, pleased to find that this time he was steady on his feet. He padded over to Carrie's bed and quickly checked her pulse for himself. As he did, her eyes flickered and with a groan, she began to move.

"It's all right, Carrie," he said quietly. "We've arrived safely. I'm just going to check on Kusac."

Another groan and, as she pushed herself up, she opened her eyes. "Gods, if this is what time travel does to you, I don't think I'll do it again," she moaned, putting a shaking hand up to her forehead to push her hair back. "I feel awful, Kaid! How's Kusac?"

"I'm just going to see," he said, leaving her side and padding over to Kusac's bed.

"Hey! Get back into bed," ordered the guard.

Kaid looked over at him, raising an eye ridge questioningly. "Or what? Don't be so damned stupid. You can see I'm only checking on my friends. It isn't as if I've got anywhere to conceal a weapon!" He turned his back on the guard and continued to check Kusac.

Meanwhile, wrapping her blanket around her, Carrie had got up and was now standing beside him.

"Can you sense him?" asked Kaid.

"Yes, thank God," she said, reaching out to touch her mate's face. "Not like it was back at home." She looked at Kaid. "I'm sorry, Kaid. I know it was my fault that we all traveled, but I couldn't bear to be alone. Not being able to feel his mind in mine terrified me. I wasn't thinking."

Kaid gave a lopsided grin. "You're pregnant. Pregnant females aren't expected to be logical in what they do," he said.

"How is he?"

"Your friend's unconscious," said a voice from behind them. They turned round to find themselves face to face with a female who was obviously a medic.

"My name's Dr. Kimin," she said, mouth opening in a friendly smile.

"He isn't my friend," said Carrie. "He's my Leska and life-mate. We know he's unconscious. Is there anything else wrong with him?"

The doctor's jaw fell further open in shock and she looked from one to the other of them.

"Please," said Carrie. "I want to know how he is. He'd taken a drug . . ." she looked to Kaid.

"La'quo."

"That one, before we left. How is he?"

"Ah, I've never . . . That's a new one to me," she said. "Your . . . Leska is fine. He should waken any time."

As Carrie turned back to Kusac, Kaid decided to try once more. "We've come here to see the one called Vartra. Is he here?"

"Yes, Dr. Vartra is here, but he can't come to you at the moment," she said. "You haven't told me your names yet."

"I'm Kaid, the Human is called Carrie, and her Leska is Kusac," he said.

"When you say Leska, what exactly do you mean?"

"You know what a Leska is, Vartra's been working on and with them! What else could I be talking about?"

"But she's not Sholan! She can't possibly have a Sholan Leska!"

"Tell her mate that! Look, it should be obvious to you that we aren't from your time. We've only just met the Humans, of course you've never seen them before! We need to talk to someone in authority here, preferably Vartra!" Kaid turned as the door open and a tall, slim male of middle years entered.

"I'll talk to them, Dr. Kimin," said the newcomer.

"You're Vartra," said Kaid.

"I am. How can I help you?" he asked.

"My name's Kaid. This is Carrie, and the third member of our group is Kusac, her Leska," said Kaid, suddenly feeling tired again. He lowered himself down onto his bed.

"Surely she can't be his Leska," said Vartra. "No offense, my dear, but you aren't Sholan," he said, looking over at Carrie who had looked round at the mention of his name.

"No, but if I'm right, you're the one responsible for the fact that I'm carrying a Sholan cub," she said. "We're from your future, fifteen hundred years in your future."

Vartra's ears flicked backward in shock as he looked from her to Kaid. "That's impossible!"

"Which?" asked Kaid drily. "That we came back fifteen hundred years, or that my friend is carrying the second cub to have one parent Sholan and the other Human?"

The silence was broken by the sound of Kusac coming round.

"He's going to throw up," said Carrie, her attention on Kusac again. "You'd best get him a bowl or something."

Kimin moved quickly, but not quickly enough. Kusac just managed to get his head over the side of the bed before throwing up. By the time he'd finished, he was feeling and looking better. One of the students came to clear the mess up, and mumbling apologies, Kusac gratefully took the mug of water Carrie held out to him.

"Are you all right? Our cub didn't get hurt, did she?" he asked anxiously as he reached out for Carrie, holding her close. "Why did you come too?"

"I couldn't be without you," she said, relaxing against him. "As far as I know, our cub is fine." She looked over at the doctor.

"I could see nothing obviously wrong with you," she said. "But I know nothing about your people."

"You say you've come back to warn us. Warn us of what?" asked Vartra.

Kusac had swung round and was sitting on the edge of his bed, facing them, Carrie sitting beside him.

"Did the fighting start tonight?" asked Kusac. "Did you stand outside here with Zylisha and hear the blasts from the cities? See a glow in space where the Valtegan warship hit the lesser moon?"

Vartra looked at Kimin, ears going back in surprise then righting themselves. "Yes, I did. Why?"

"The debris from the moon will collide with Shola two days from now," said Kaid.

"It'll will cause global destruction," said Kusac. "Tidal waves, earthquakes—clouds of thick dust that will stay in the sky for months, cutting out sunlight. A Cataclysm that will reduce this civilization to virtually nothing. But before that happens, the Valtegans that haven't already left Shola will discover you here."

"How did you know that the Valtegans have been leaving? That isn't public knowledge yet!" demanded Vartra.

"We know a lot," said Carrie. "This hill is full of crystals that are storing the events that are happening now. I shared the experiences of Rezac and Zashou when they went down with the fever that changed their genes. You had to put them together, pack ice round them to bring their temperatures down, didn't you? And you," she pointed at Kimin, "you argued with Nyaam over putting them together and releasing Rezac's restraints."

Kimin looked at Vartra, her ears laid flat in distress as she looked for a seat to sit down.

"They know it as if they were there!" she said.

"And you blame yourself because they took the vaccine too soon," Carrie finished, pointing to Vartra.

"How do you know these things?" asked Vartra. "You can't possibly, unless . . ."

"Unless what we say is true," finished Kusac.

"You have to leave here," said Kaid. "And as soon as possible. If you saw the explosion on the moon tonight, you have to be in Stronghold within two days or you'll never make it because of the Cataclysm. You'll be cut off here till the floods subside."

"You'll be safe at Stronghold. There's villages nearby for food and other supplies, and you'll have the Brothers to protect you," said Kusac.

"Brothers?" Vartra looked like a person who had heard more than he could take in.

"You're a God in our time," said Carrie gently. "The Brotherhood of Vartra is a semi-religious Warrior cult based at Stronghold. They'll guard the telepaths at a time when your people will blame them for the Cataclysm."

Vartra shook his head. "This is utterly unbelievable, but it has to be true! What you know about us you could never have learned. It's as if you were there."

"All very interesting," drawled Goran, walking into the temple. "I don't believe you yet. I'm not convinced. How do we know you didn't lift what you've told us from our minds? Give us a good reason to trust you."

"You're a telepath," Carrie said looking at Kimin. "Touch my mind. You'll see that we're telling the truth."

Kimin tried but after a minute or two had to give up. "You're just too alien, I'm afraid," she said.

"Try mine," said Kusac.

"Get Tiernay," said Goran to the doctor. "He's good at this."

Kimin returned with Tiernay.

Kusac lowered his shields, sitting patiently while he felt Tiernay's mind touch his. Carefully he guided him, letting him see the memories of their world.

"He's told the truth," said Tiernay at length.

"Him next." Goran pointed to Kaid. "They could have conditioned the other one's mind. The Valtegans are good at twisting people like that."

Kaid looked over at Carrie and she could feel his panic. She reached out to touch his hand. "You'll be fine," she said. "Just lower your barriers and sit quietly, concentrating on keeping them down. Let him do the hard work."

Reluctantly Kaid stilled his heart rate and began to recite the litany for clear thought. He concentrated on lowering his barriers, sensing them go down one at a time until he sat there feeling vulnerable and exposed. He felt Tiernay's touch. It wasn't subtle or gentle, but the young male was able to look at his memories.

Gradually he felt his mind become numb and hazy until he almost fainted. Someone was holding him, telling him to wake up. He blinked, trying to focus, and eventually Kusac's face swam into view. He frowned, and put his hand up to rub his eyes.

"What happened?" he asked.

"You nearly passed out," said Kusac, letting him go. "How do you feel now? Are you all right?"

Kaid nodded slowly. "I'm fine," he said, looking beyond him to where Vartra was talking to Tiernay and Goran. "Do you have your proof now?" he asked.

"Yes," said Vartra, coming toward them. "Dr. Kimin will take Carrie and try to find some clothes for her. If you two will come with us, we'll see what we can find in the way of clothing for you."

Half an hour later, they met on the way into the common room. All three of them stopped dead just inside the doorway, looking over at the log fire crackling and spitting in the corner.

"The old ties of family have broken down and we must survive as best we can" Kaid quoted. *"Your loyalty can only be to each other, no one else. Those of you who survive . . ."* He stopped, having forgotten the rest.

Tiernay leaped to his feet as soon as Kaid began to speak. From the other side of the room a small female came forward and with a noise of surprise, reached out to touch him.

"Rezac?" she said, then pulled back. "You can't be, but you're so like him!"

"Where did you hear that?" Tiernay demanded as they came further into the room.

Carrie stopped by the young female. "He isn't Rezac, I'm afraid. He's called Kaid. Thank you for lending me the clothes," she said.

Jaisa nodded, watching them come into the room.

"I heard it in here," said Kaid, moving toward the seats

round the table. "We call them replays because though they come to us as dreams, we know they've really happened."

"Tiernay, I've spoken with them, so has Dr. Kimin. We're convinced that what they've told us is true. There's no other way they could have learned what they know," said Vartra. "Like the quote just now. It's of so little consequence, why would anyone know about it unless they were there?"

Kaid looked up at Vartra. "You knew I was there," he said. "You felt me." He looked to Tiernay. "Within the next few days, you'll sense me again in the caverns while you're loading the vehicles to leave here. You'll point me out to Goran, but he won't be able to see me."

"There's hot food over there for you, and c'shar if you wish it," said Vartra, breaking the mood. "Please, help yourselves."

"This is getting so weird," said Tiernay, going back to his chair. "I don't know what to make of it."

"We're going to have a meeting tonight," said Vartra, taking a chair near the fire. "Goran will be here. We'll listen to what our visitors have to say, then decide what to do."

Carrie, sent Kaid. *I remember this place! It's familiar to me.*

She looked sharply at him. *You can't, Kaid. You've seen it so often in replays and dreams, that's all. Don't let yourself get confused.*

He didn't reply.

"You do realize you're talking about a journey of over thirteen hundred miles, don't you?" said Tiernay. "It isn't a short hop you know. Driving nonstop, even with several drivers in each vehicle, you're looking at a whole day!"

"I know," said Vartra. "Goran and I have discussed it before now. We're well aware of the distance and time involved."

It was late when the meeting broke up, but by that time all the questions had been asked and answered to the best of everyone's ability. What was left was a sense of purpose. They were moving to Stronghold, and they'd start packing in the morning.

Goran, Tiernay, and Vartra were last up.

"Look at it this way, Goran," said Vartra. "From the viewpoint of this coming cataclysm alone, we can't afford to remain here and be cut off from any sources of supplies.

We're bound to be in the center of flooding because we're right on the coast. We aren't self-sufficient, we're dependant on Nazule for just about everything. It's a very different picture at Stronghold." He paused. "We should have realized this could happen when we saw the warship explode."

"I still think we're trusting them too easily," grumbled Goran. "But from a defense point of view, we're definitely safer at Stronghold. I've been saying that for some time now."

"We also don't need to move all the equipment," said Tiernay. "Their lab is at least as sophisticated as ours."

"More so," said Vartra. "I'll need those facilities if I'm going to be correcting the work I've done."

"What do you make of Kaid?" asked Tiernay. "Jaisa put her finger on it earlier when she said he looked like Rezac."

Vartra frowned. "I don't follow."

"He is like Rezac. And I told you what I saw in his mind. It's uncanny just how like him this Kaid is. The odd movement as well as the way he stands. Just every now and then I could have sworn it was him."

Vartra patted Tiernay on the shoulder. "He's not Rezac," he said with a grin. "He's too quiet, not impulsive enough, thank the Gods! One of him was enough."

"But we haven't got one of him, have we?" Tiernay reminded him.

Vartra looked away. "That had occurred to me already," he said quietly. "Let's leave it for now and see what happens."

The three of them had been left to sleep late. When they rose, it was Jaisa who took them to the student's dining room for first meal. That over, they joined everyone else in the lab cavern to help pack.

It was strange to see the caverns in use when all they'd seen previously were the ruins. There was the kitchen area, and the chamber full of beds.

"We've been sleeping here for the last month," said Jaisa. "The Valtegans are getting too good at finding telepaths. We think they have several of our people helping them."

"Why don't you use dampers," said Kusac, fascinated to see the lab equipment actually working.

"They're still experimental," she said, "and huge. We have

one or two in use, down here for instance, which is why we're all sleeping here."

"Let me see what they're like," said Kaid. "I might be able to help."

"Sure, but we won't have time to do that until we've moved to Stronghold."

Tiernay saw them and came over. "We could do with your help," he said. "Come with me and I'll show you what needs doing."

"What about me?" asked Carrie.

"I think you're a little too pregnant to be doing much," said Jaisa as tactfully as she could.

Carrie looked down at herself. "I'm sure I didn't look this large yesterday," she said.

Jaisa laughed, linking her arm in the Human's. "My mother always said that once the cub moved and you know it's real, then you begin to look really pregnant!"

"You might be right. Where is your mother now?"

"She's dead." For a moment, the sun seemed to leave Jaisa, then she recovered with another smile.

"We can take some of the lighter items down to the vans, if you want," she said. "I've been asked to keep you company today, just to see you're all right. Did you really come from that far in the future? Shola must be very different."

"I don't know. I haven't seen anything outside the temple yet," she said. "It is really strange to see this place when all I know of it are the ruins."

A table had been set up for the fragile items. The older members of the community, and the two or three children who seemed to be everywhere at once, were ferrying those down through the tunnels to the vans.

After a couple of trips, Carrie was beginning to feel tired. Her back ached, and her arms; the small box of paperwork she was carrying seemed suddenly a lot heavier. She really wanted to sit down. She half-turned to Jaisa in the corridor.

"Can we take a break after this trip? I'm beginning to ache."

"No problem," said Jaisa. "Hey! Watch it!" she yelled as two of the children hared past her.

The lead one turned to look at her and crashed into Carrie, sending the papers flying everywhere. Staggering backward, Carrie caught hold of the youngster by the arm.

"Watch out," she said, then almost fell as his mind

touched hers, flaring into a rapport that one so young shouldn't have been able to achieve.

Shocked though she was, Carrie had enough presence of mind to grab the cub's other arm and hold on to him.

"Kusac! Kaid!" she yelled, pulling the youngling closer till she had her arms wrapped firmly round him.

"What is it?" asked Jaisa. "Carrie, what is it?"

Strangely, the cub wasn't struggling to escape. Instead he reached out to touch her.

"Pretty," he said, running his fingers through the blonde hair that cascaded over her shoulders.

"I know . . . Kaid . . . Kusac, I need to see them now," she stammered.

"Put the cub down and we'll find them," Jaisa said, obviously concerned.

"No. No, I can't let him go," said Carrie, picking him up. "You don't understand . . ."

Jaisa took her by the arm and led her the few feet back up to the upper cavern. "I do understand," she said quietly. "We wanted to see if you would."

Carrie was totally confused. "What?" she asked. "What are you talking about?"

"Just wait," Jaisa said, steering her over to a table by the kitchen area.

Kaid and Kusac came across the cavern toward her at a run. As he got closer, Kaid seemed to stagger slightly, then slow down. Seeing it, Kusac was torn between the two of them.

I'm fine, see to Kaid, Carrie sent.

He stopped, turning back to his friend, helping him cross the rest of the space between them. Kaid stopped by a table a few feet from them and refused to come closer.

"What is it, Carrie?" Kusac asked, keeping an eye on Kaid. "Who's this?"

"Touch him, Kusac," she said. "Tell me who he is."

Puzzled, Kusac did as she asked.

The cub was indifferent, preferring to play with Carrie's hair.

"He's familiar, I don't know how, but that's all."

"It's Kaid," she said. "He's not from our time, Kusac. He's from here!"

"What?" Kusac looked from the cub to his friend, now sitting at the table resting his head on his arms.

"She's right," said Jaisa. "This is Rezac's son. We don't call him Kaid, though."

"You call him Tallinu."

Jaisa looked surprised. "You know? He must have remembered that much at least."

"No wonder he could bring us here," said Kusac.

"That explains his memories, too. Last night he sent to me that the monastery was familiar, he remembered it," said Carrie.

"I think you should let him go now," said Jaisa, reaching out to touch the cub. "Your friend's suffering too much. It can't be a pleasant experience being in two bodies at the same time, even worse when you're in the same room. We'll try to see Tallinu is kept away from him."

"How did he get to the future? Kaid definitely grew up in our time," said Kusac.

"We must send him forward," said Carrie. "He has to go, otherwise we can't be here to save the telepaths. But how did you know?"

"Tiernay saw Kaid's childhood in his mind, just before he nearly passed out. That's how we knew you were telling us the truth."

The cub solved the problem by squirming off her lap. With a flick of his tail, he was off, stopping briefly to look up at Kaid.

As he left the cavern, Kaid raised his head and looked over toward them.

"Rezac and Zashou patched up their differences then," said Carrie.

Jaisa smiled. "Not really. She couldn't accept what Rezac was, what he'd been. If it hadn't been for their Leska link that allowed them to hide nothing from each other, they might have had a chance. The cub isn't Zashou's. It's a child Rezac never knew existed. The Valtegans took them before the lad was sent to us from Stronghold. His mother died of the fever that changed us. Before she did, she gave him to someone to bring to Rezac, not knowing he'd gone. She was some female from Ranz that he knew, someone he visited just before the Valtegans arrived."

Carrie got up. "I'll go to Kaid," she said to Kusac. "You speak to him later."

He nodded, reaching out to touch her face before she left.

Jaisa watched her go, then looked back to Kusac. "It's

good to know that all Vartra's tinkering will lead to what
you and she share," she said. "We were Vartra's control
group. The only Leska pair that developed among us was
Rezac and Zashou, and they had it rough," she sighed. "She
was just so damned prissy! If it had been me, now," she
grinned up at Kusac. "Before all this, I was training in the
warrior skills, but the changed genes put an end to that. Can
you still not fight?"

Kusac pulled up a chair and sat down. "Until Carrie and I
bonded, no, I couldn't, but our Link changed all that. Tell
me, was Tallinu born before or after the virus?"

"Before. He hasn't caught it yet. Why?"

"Because Kaid's able to fight, and he doesn't have a
Human Leska. He caught the virus in our time, but it only
enhanced his abilities, nothing more."

"You need to tell Vartra that," said Jaisa. "The DNA of
you three could be crucial to his project. He's determined to
correct the mistakes."

"He will," said Kusac.

Kaid was beginning to feel better but he didn't want to
move in case the nausea came back. He watched Carrie come
over and sit beside him.

"I used to wonder," he said, "about the parents I'd never
known. Wonder why I'd been abandoned, who to blame." He
raised his head, giving Carrie a very strange Human smile.
"Now I know. I also know why I feel about you the way I do.
It's come back, Carrie," he said. "Everything was founded
on these few minutes when I first met you. The dreams of a
cub!" He felt empty and alone.

"Don't be so damned stupid," she said, reaching for the
hair on the side of his neck and pulling his face closer.
"What about you and Garras? The lives of telepaths that
would have been lost, what about these people here? Their
future depends on a cub of what age, Tallinu? Two, or is it
three? Their future is in the hands of the cub you were. Stop
being so damned sorry for yourself! Yes, you were a bastard
cub, but look what you are now, what you have!"

Releasing him, she stopped for a moment, searching his
face. "So you fell in love with me when you were two. How
do you feel about me now you know that? Do you feel different? Cheated because meeting me today meant you carried my image in your mind all these years?"

He looked beyond her. Kusac had gone, so had Jaisa. With his good hand he reached out and grasped her neck, pulling her closer still so he could kiss her. Lowering his mental barriers, he let his open mind touch hers, sharing what he felt for her.

His mouth moved, nipping at her cheek and jawline till he reached her throat. "What do you think?" he asked, beginning to lick her till he felt her responding. *Do you still want me as your lover now you know who I really am?*

She tried to laugh, to say yes, but with her throat pulled back, she couldn't.

Don't speak. I can hear your answer in the way your body talks to me. His jaws closed on her throat and this time, she was aware of the full crushing power behind his bite, then it was gone and he was grinning at her.

His finger flicked her nose lightly. "So Sholan," he said. "So help me, if we were at home . . ." He left the rest unsaid as his hand closed on hers. "You've given me the strength I need for what I have to do," he said more seriously.

"You're at peace with yourself," she said, sounding surprised.

He nodded. "I know now the goal I set myself wasn't unrealistic, it was obtainable," he said, twining his fingers round hers and lifting them to his mouth to nibble. "I have to get back to work," he said. "Wait here and I'll find Jaisa for you." He let go her hand and got to his feet.

Carrie nodded, then her face creased in pain and she clutched her belly.

"What's wrong?" he asked, concerned as he sensed some of her discomfort.

"Nothing. I'm sure it's nothing," she said, the color returning to her face. "I'll wait here for Jaisa, you go on."

When Jaisa came, she took her immediately up to the infirmary to see Dr. Kimin.

Carrie patiently submitted to a thorough examination, made easier by the fact that up there a damper had been installed.

"As far as I can see, everything is fine," Kimin said at last. "If it's as you say, a Sholan gestation, you've only another eight weeks to go."

Carrie pushed herself up. "I've got ten weeks left," she said.

"Well, you know when you conceived, but to me it looks

like you're further on than you think. Of course, it could just be that you have a large cub."

"And the pains?"

"Twinges, nothing more. The cub pressing against a nerve," she said, turning to rummage in one of the boxes her nurses had been filling when Carrie and Jaisa had arrived.

"I don't have all the supplements you need," she said, "but take these. It should keep you going while you're here."

Carrie took the two boxes of pills Kimin handed to her. "Thanks."

"My advice is to stay well out of the way of the move," she grinned. "Get Jaisa to organize you a place on the best transport out of here, then stay at Stronghold once you get there. Leave it to the males. You're working hard enough growing that cub! You don't need any extra duties."

Carrie laughed. "I'll do what you say, don't worry."

The lab had been emptied. All that remained was to seal the door. Kaid, knowing he would be there again, waited outside with Goran, Carrie and Kusac. It was Jaisa who took the cub, Tallinu, to Vartra.

"Show him how to use the lock," she said, then drew from her pocket a damaged collar of the type the Valtegans used on telepaths. "This was for Zashou. Put it in the lock recess. He's to find it one day," she said.

"Where did you get it from?" he asked.

"One of our people was in the center that day. He got it from the holding cell when they took them away. It was sent to me as her friend." She looked up at Vartra. "It's hard knowing I'll never see either of them again. We don't even know where they were sent."

"Where they could do the most damage," said Vartra, his hand cupping her cheek in comfort. "You can depend on that. If ever there was a team that could manipulate themselves to the very seat of the Valtegan Emperor himself, it was Rezac and Zashou."

She nodded. "I know."

Holding Tallinu by the hand, Vartra went over to the lab entrance. Picking the cub up, he showed him where the collar went, then put him down so he could seal the doorway. The steel door slid slowly shut, sealing off the chamber that would lie undisturbed for over a thousand years. This one act, more than anything, brought to Vartra's mind all the strange little happenings over the last few months. As much as the cub at his side, he could hear the inexorable step of destiny behind him.

Each of the three vehicles was taking a slightly different route. In their vehicle was Vartra, Zylisha, Jaisa, Goran, and two of his people, and the cub under heavy sedation. That way it was possible for Kaid to be nearby without too much discomfort.

They were in one of the large delivery vans and with them was the bulk of Vartra's research. They'd tried to duplicate his data on each vehicle, but that hadn't always been possible. There was also a fair amount of medical supplies and equipment on board as well as food for the journey.

They were using three shifts of drivers. Goran was taking the first leg, driving through the night as he was the most experienced.

"What about the fighting?" asked Vartra as they set off.

"Our people know we're coming. There will be an escort wherever possible in the territories we control. Latest word is that the majority of the Valtegans have left, there's only isolated pockets now. Worst part is at Chiyak, in the plains between the Ferraki hills and Dzahai Mountains."

"That's where you said the main temple of Varza is."

"That's so," said Goran, steering the vehicle down the slope toward the forest below.

"Strange to see my family's land," said Kusac. "I don't think it's changed that much."

Zylisha looked curiously at him. "Your family's land?"

"I'm not talking about now," he said hastily.

"What's your family name?"

"Aldatan."

"That explains, it," she said. "We're of the same family."

"I wondered why your mother resembled Zashou so much," said Carrie. "Even down to liking the small braids."

"Your mother wears her hair like that?" Zylisha sounded pleased. "It's good to know something of my sister will live on."

"Just make sure you keep that land in the family," said Kaid. "Your future depends on it!"

"It does rather, doesn't it?" she said.

"Goran, we need to stop at Chiyak," said Kaid. "It's the third gateway."

"No way. We go straight through to Dzahai."

"Then we have to go back before the floods start," insisted Kaid.

"You can do what you like once I've got my people safe to Stronghold," said Goran. "You're not my responsibility."

Kaid subsided into silence. He wasn't coping well with the presence of himself as a cub. It was making him feel ill and irritable. Part of it, he had to admit, was probably because Carrie kept the cub close to her. He curled up inside the pile of blankets and tried to sleep.

The space inside was limited, and Kusac was also lying on his side, curled round Carrie, trying to cushion her from the jolting of the truck. She rested against his chest, holding the sleeping cub in her lap.

"For someone who didn't want to even see Vanna's cub, you've certainly taken to this one."

"No, it's not because it's Kaid," she said, picking up his thought as she stroked the little one's head. "At least, not directly. When he leaves his own time, Kusac, we know what kind of life he'll face. Surely there should be a few gentle memories for any cub?"

"There should," he said, reaching for her ear with his tongue. "And no, I'm not jealous. I don't think you're going to have many problems with our cub. Will it matter that she doesn't look like you?"

"No, she'll be ours, that's all that matters," she said, turning her head to smile up at him.

Kusac looked down at the sleeping cub again. "You know, he is rather . . ."

"Don't you dare!" said Kaid, lifting his head up to look at them.

". . . cute," said Carrie with a grin.

Kaid growled deep in his throat and turned his back on them.

Sitting in the back during the journey, there was little to interest them. Goran was in radio contact with various resistance cells along the way, giving him updates on safe routes and fuel stops. The bulk of their journey was through forested land and the few towns they passed through hadn't commanded much of a Valtegan presence.

The road blocks which had restricted travel under their rule, were no longer in force; the barriers now broken and deserted. Stops were kept to a minimum for refueling, calls of nature and changing drivers. Then they hit the more populous Kysubi plains that led to the city of Chiyak.

Carrie had spent much of the journey asleep. The cub was now been kept lightly sedated by Jaisa, who also saw to it that he was fed plenty of fluids and high protein liquid foods. Kusac also spent much of the time lulled by the motion of the vehicle but when he was awake, he listened lazily to the conversation around him, noticing that Jaisa was chatting to Kaid in an effort to make him forget his discomfort.

Chakku was driving as the message came in. He had Goran roused to deal with it since it involved a route change.

"We're taking a detour," Goran finally announced after some heated discussions on the radio. "Seems that they're still fighting in Chiyak. There's a unit of the Emperor's Faithful taken the Temple of Varza. They're using it as a base to try and take control of the city. We're going to travel alongside the Ferraki hills till we're level with Stronghold, then cut east across the plains. It'll take a couple of hours more, but it's safer."

There was a general moaning from everyone.

"Hey. This is no holiday for us either," said Goran, hanging over the back of his seat. "There's looting and fighting going on as well. Best we steer clear of it."

"The leader of the Valtegans," said Kaid, sitting up, "is he called Kezule?"

"He is. How'd you know?"

"He's the one we have to find."

"You're welcome to him! He's one of the trickiest bastards around, so I'm told. His unit were originally posted to the desert, Varza knows why! They came into the city a couple of days ago according to my sources."

"Did you ever stop to wonder what they were guarding that needed the Emperor's top unit?" asked Kaid.

"No. Didn't concern me. Not my territory," said Goran.

"You should have been concerned," said Kaid. "He was guarding the hatchery."

The van swerved sharply and Goran turned to shout at Chakku. "Watch it!" He turned back to Kaid. "A hatchery? They had lizard eggs on Shola?"

Kaid nodded.

"Where the hell are they now?"

"Maybe off-planet, maybe in the temple with Kezule. That's why we've got to get there."

Crafty, Kaid. Very crafty, sent Kusac.

I thought so.

"I'll see what I can find out," said Goran, his tone grim as he turned back to the radio. "We might just be able to get you some help when you go there."

Won't the flood destroy them and any eggs? asked Kusac.

Maybe. Would you take the risk?

They continued on through the night, Carrie giving them all a fright when once again she was gripped by pains in her belly for which there seemed no cause.

At last they stopped and the engine was turned off. The silence and the stillness was profound. Then the radio burst into life.

"Skyhawk Two to Traveler. Come in Traveler."

Goran flicked on the radio. "Traveler here. What's with the Skyhawk Two?"

"Hold fire. I repeat, hold fire. The craft approaching you is ours. Do you understand, Traveler?"

"We understand. What craft?" he asked as they all heard the high-pitched sound of an airborne vehicle approaching.

"The one about to land beside you, Traveler. You folk want a lift up to Stronghold?"

A ragged cheer went up as they heard the vehicle getting nearer.

"Thank Varza for that," said Jaisa with heartfelt relief. "I was dreading the journey up the mountains!"

They began to stir, passing boxes behind them until they had cleared a path to the rear doors. Jumping down from the tailboard, one by one they staggered onto the roadway, looking upward to find the aircar.

Last off, Kaid passed Carrie down to Kusac, then jumped down himself. The night air was cool, a contrast to the heat in the vehicle. Carrie shivered. The Sholan clothes she wore weren't adequate for a furless person.

"Where's the cub?" she asked.

"Zylisha has him," said Kusac.

The sound of the aircar grew louder as it hovered overhead, then gradually settled to the roadway a few meters ahead of them. A door slid back and a group of half a dozen armed Sholans jumped out and came over to them.

"Dr. Vartra," said their leader, "I'm glad you made it safely. It must have been a grueling journey for you. We were told you had guests."

Vartra indicated where Kusac stood, Carrie wrapped in a blanket beside him. On her other side, was Kaid.

The male approached them. "I'm Khyim, head of our community at Stronghold. Your presence is well come." He held out his palm for the greeting.

Kusac introduced their little group in return, then Khyim turned to business.

"I suggest all of you, save one or two, return with my pilot to Stronghold. Meanwhile we can be unloading your cargo, ready to take it with us on the second trip."

Goran barked out a few orders then turned to Khyim. "My guards will stay," he said. "I'll accompany you up to Stronghold."

Carrie was beyond caring what happened now. She just wanted to sleep in a bed that didn't move. She was stiff and cold, and her back ached abominably.

Kusac swung her up into his arms. "We should have left this till after you'd had the cub," he said. "I'm sorry. We shouldn't have come."

"We had to do this before she was born," she said, putting her arms round his neck as he walked over to the aircar. "She couldn't be completely En'Shalla if we hadn't come now."

"I know, but just the same, I feel responsible for your discomfort." He ducked as he stepped inside the aircar. "You feel heavier," he remarked as he set her down beside the seats.

"It's the weight of the blanket," she said.

CHAPTER 21

During the trip up to Stronghold, Vartra elaborated on the quick briefing he'd given Khyim the morning after the three travelers had arrived. When they landed in the courtyard, they were ushered through the wooden doors into the main building. Off to one side, Carrie glimpsed two metal braziers flanking double wooden doors.

People were everywhere as old acquaintances were renewed and arrangements made for meals and sleeping. The first to be whisked off was the cub, Tallinu, which helped Kaid no end.

In the hubbub, Carrie went over to the doors and gently leaned against one. It opened easily, allowing her to see into the temple beyond. At the far end, against His crimson curtain, stood the statue of Varza, holding in his hands the glowing brazier.

"You can't go in there!" a voice called out.

Carrie turned round to find all eyes focussed on her. "Why not?"

"Only those who follow Varza may enter the temple," said the brown-robed figure that stepped out of the crowd toward her.

"I do," said Carrie.

"You can't. You're not Sholan."

Within moments, Kusac and Kaid were at her side.

"She does," said Kaid, preventing Kusac from stepping forward. "I'm a priest. I witnessed their life-bonding, performed because she's carrying a Sholan cub. If the God blesses them, who are you to deny her entry to the temple? Do you put yourself above the Gods?"

"Vangan, you're being both foolish and discourteous to our guests," said Khyim, joining the small group at the doors. "I will not have you haggling like a market seller over who has the right in your eyes to approach the God. You're completely out of touch with the needs of my people!"

He took Carrie by the arm and led her into the temple. "All are welcome here, Carrie. You're free to worship or meditate as you wish. If Vangan should try to stop you again, let me know," he said.

Carrie looked up, opening her mouth in a Sholan smile of thanks. "I meant no harm," she said. "I just wanted to see what the temple at Stronghold was like."

"As you can see, it's very plain in comparison to the one at Chiyak. There they've made use of the beautiful crystals mined from these mountains to decorate the entrance. When you see the pillars on either side of the God, it's as if you see him between pillars of living flame!" He sighed. "It's a pity that the Valtegans hold the temple."

We have to go there! sent Kaid. *It's got to be the main gateway!*

We will, came the answer from both Carrie and Kusac.

"Thank you," she said. "Perhaps I could return tomorrow? The journey really has exhausted me."

"Of course. We'll see to getting a room and food for you and your mate immediately," said Khyim, escorting her out into the entry hall again.

Their rooms were adjacent to each other—in corridors that all three of them recognized only too well.

"Are you going to be all right, Kaid?" asked Carrie, concerned lest this return to Stronghold after what he'd been through with Ghezu, would prove unsettling for him.

"I'm fine," he said, standing at the door to his room. "The place isn't quite the same as it is in our time. For one thing, there's only one level above ground."

"We'll see you in the morning," said Kusac. "Good night."

He'd no sooner closed the door than there was a knock on it. Opening it, he was surprised to see Jaisa standing there with a large tray of food.

"Hungry?" she asked. "I thought you might like the company. I couldn't face a dining room full of people tonight either."

"I don't know that I'm that hungry," he said, standing back so she could enter.

"Neither am I, if I'm being honest, but we can pick at it. Don't shut the door," she said, going over to the center of the room and placing the tray on the floor. "There's a jug of c'shar out there!"

"I'll get it," he said, stepping out and bending down to pick it up. He stood watching her in surprise as she pulled the bed covers back to get the pillows.

"For the floor," she said, throwing them down, then promptly sitting on one. She looked up expectantly at him. "Well, shut the door."

Rather nonplused, he did, then walked over to join her.

Leaning forward, she picked up a small piece of meat. "You're not used to female company, are you?" She held the plate out to him.

Kaid took a couple of pieces of meat from it and began to chew one. "Not really," he said. "Is it that obvious?"

"Yes, it is," she said frankly. "Apart from anything else, I can pick your unease up mentally."

"I didn't know you were telepath."

She raised an eye ridge in surprise. "You *are* new to all this, aren't you? You mean you didn't realize you were a telepath?"

He shook his head. "Things are different in our time. It never really occurred to me I was because I could fight, and everyone knows telepaths can't fight."

He could feel himself beginning to relax at long last. The journey had been bad enough, but coupled with the fact he was there twice . . . And he realized he was hungry as he reached for some bread and the cheese.

Jaisa was good company, keeping the conversation going with her easy, amusing chatter. Soon all the food was gone and they were sitting in companionable silence.

"Well," said Jaisa, "I suppose I'd better leave you to get some sleep."

Impulsively, Kaid reached out to touch her hair. "Those curls have been fascinating me for the last hour," he said, letting one curl round his finger then roll off.

She turned her face so her cheek touched his hand. "I don't have to leave," she said quietly. "I'd like to stay."

There was no need for him to be alone that night, unless he wanted to be. He turned his hand, letting it stroke her cheek. "That would be nice," he said as she moved closer and he felt her mind tentatively touch his. "You knew Rezac, didn't you?"

"Yes," she said, as her tongue gently touched his cheek. "Is that a problem?"

"No," he said, letting himself enjoy the sensations she was waking in him. "You must have felt the touch of his mind."

"Yes." Her hand was playing with his hair now, first smoothing it then teasing out individual locks. "Why?"

"You knew about his time in the mountains, didn't you?"

"Yes. So what?" She stopped and pulled back from him a little.

He watched her green eyes flick thoughtfully across his face, then take in the bandaged hand and his wrists. "You're sending yourself forward, aren't you? You must, or you wouldn't be here now. Did you go to Ranz, too? Are you *that* alike?"

"His Leska, you said she was prissy," he began, but she cut him short.

"No, I'm not going to freak out about your past," she said, "No more than I did with Rezak. Now will you *please* stop talking!"

Taken aback by her vehemence, Kaid wasn't quite sure how to react.

Jaisa reached out and took hold of him by his ears. "Look, I want your body and your mind, Kaid, not your damned life story! At least, not right now," she amended, letting him go.

Kaid couldn't help but laugh as he pulled her into his arms and began nibbling at her ears in retaliation.

Much better, she sent, beginning to project what she hoped they'd shortly be doing.

* * *

"Here's Kaid and Jaisa now," said Kusac, nodding toward where they were threading their way through the tables to the meal counter. "He looks better today."

"He's well pleased with himself too," said Carrie. "I think he had company last night. I'm glad. I was worried about him being alone here of all places."

"He'll find his own way now," said Kusac, reaching across the table to touch her hand.

"The meteorite will hit today," said Kaid when they joined them at the table.

"I know," said Kusac. "We have to go to Chiyak now."

Kaid nodded as he began eating. "When do we meet with Vartra?"

"As soon as we've finished eating," said Carrie.

Kaid looked up sharply at her, frowning. "Are you all right?" he asked. "You look a little pale."

"I'm fine," she said, closing her mind to them.

Kusac sighed. "I've already been through this with her. She won't go to the medic and get a checkup."

"What does En'Shalla mean?" she asked, looking from one to the other of them.

"In the hands of the Gods," said Kusac, his tone baffled.

Kaid nodded agreement.

"Fine. Leave it to the Gods then," she said, pushing herself back from the table and getting up. "I'll see you at Vartra's lab." With that, she walked off.

"She had those pains again last night," said Kusac in response to Kaid's questioning look. "And she does look pale."

"I hate to butt in, but isn't she a bit . . . er . . ." began Jaisa.

". . . larger?" finished Kaid.

"I think so, but she'll have none of it. The cub's still moving. We can both feel her, mentally and physically, so I suppose they must be all right," said Kusac morosely, looking at his mug of c'shar.

"See how she does today," said Kaid. "With any luck, we'll be home in a few hours. Incidentally, how are you? You don't seem to be suffering any more effects of the drug."

"I'm fine. How did you feel when you were in one of these situations?"

"Fine, until I was dragged out of it to the next one." Kaid stood up. "Let's get going. We've got to get to Chiyak as soon as possible."

The lab was small in comparison to the one at the monastery, but it was warmer. Again there were the ubiquitous work benches complete with their clutter of equipment. At the far end, a couple of people were setting up one of the analyzers that had been brought with them from the monastery. Carrie was already there and Vartra was in the process of taking a blood sample from her.

"What were you originally trying to do with the genes?" Carrie was asking.

"I was trying to improve the abilities of telepaths," he said, "and to increase the number of Leska pairs to enrich the gene pool. Then the Valtegans arrived." He withdrew the syringe and passed her a wad of sterile wool. "Press that against it for a minute or two," he said, handing the hypo to one of his lab assistants.

"What happened to your program then?"

"At first I could continue uninterrupted, then the Valtegans began to shut down all the research establishments. We had nothing to use against them; they just walked over us," he said. He looked over at Kusac. "You next, please."

He picked up a fresh syringe and began swabbing the inside of Kusac's arm. "That was when it was suggested that telepaths with enhanced abilities could give our resistance fighters the edge they needed. Only it didn't work out that way. This brave but foolish group of mine," he said, looking over at Jaisa, "used the serum before it was ready. It wasn't stable enough. When the virus carrying it took hold, we lost so many of our talented—young and old—through high fevers and convulsions. We've been trying to find a way to correct this, but so far, no luck. The main problem is that none of the other teams can repeat my results!"

"Well, they couldn't, could they?" said Carrie, examining her arm to make sure it wasn't bleeding. "You're manipulating the results mentally, making the experiments do what you want them to do, whether it's possible or not."

"I beg your pardon," said Vartra, looking at her in surprise. "What did you say?"

Carrie looked up, and realized from the looks on the faces around her that she'd obviously said something that hadn't gone down well. "I only said that you're mentally manipulating the experiments to make them do what you want rather that what nature will let them do. Psychokinesis."

"It would explain why no one else can duplicate your work," said Jaisa.

"I'm not a telepath," said Vartra. "I can't possibly be affecting my experiments!"

"There are more Talents than telepathy," said Carrie. "That's something your people are going to forget, which is why the Brotherhood will be able to gather all those Talents into their membership. Which is another reason why you have to be based here."

"I tell you, I'm not manipulating my results!" Vartra exclaimed angrily, rounding on her.

"I saw you doing it when I came in," said Carrie apologetically. "I'll grant you don't realize you are, but that's probably why the genes that you're working on are unstable. Nature never intended them to exist in that form or combination."

"Playing God," said Kaid. "Making what you want to happen, happen. That's why we're compatible with the Humans, Kusac. That's why Vanna can't explain it."

"Then I'm responsible for *your* Link and all those deaths? Oh, Gods! What have I been doing?" said Vartra, his face taking on a pinched look as he leaned back against the bench behind him. "What have I done to you all? What can I do to correct it?"

Carrie leaned toward him, a look of panic on her face. "Don't change it, Dr. Vartra! If you do, then my cubs will never have been conceived. For God's sake, leave things the way they are!"

"I can't!"

"You must," said Kusac, removing the syringe from Vartra's slack grasp. "If you don't, you'll change the future."

Vartra looked at him. "You're changing the future right now by being here!"

"We're making sure it happens the way it should," said Kaid. "When a Sholan combines with a Human in a Leska link, they get back the ability to fight. What you've been trying to do to combat the Valtegans *will* work—in the long term. Your research enhanced our talents and gave us back the ability to fight. I told you there are no Valtegans on Shola in our time. That's true, but we're still facing them in space!"

"You didn't tell us that," said Jaisa accusingly.

"We can't tell you everything," said Kusac. "There's so much that trying to choose what you need to know is almost impossible."

"Look, we've got something we have to do right now. You have more time than us to work on your problems. We've probably only got today," said Carrie. "We have to get to the temple and deal with this Kezule. He has to be stopped. What he's getting Fyak to do is going to destroy our world if we don't act now. We've explained all this to you."

"More importantly, we need to take the cub with us," said Kaid. "I've got to send him . . . myself . . . forward."

"You've decided then," said Jaisa.

Kaid nodded. "I have to, because I'm here."

"You haven't the right to . . ." began Vartra.

Kaid cut him short. "Yes, I do. I'm the only one who *does* have the right to decide! He comes with us."

"Have you any idea how you're going to send him forward?" Jaisa asked.

"Yes. The gateway is in that temple. It'll take the combined power of all three of us, but we can do it."

"We need help, though," said Kusac. "We need weapons and fighters. And we need to use the aircar. Without it, there's no way we'll make it there before the meteorite hits."

"What about coming back?" asked Jaisa.

"We'll be leaving through the gate, too," said Kusac. "If we don't go through today, we may never get back."

Vartra looked at Jaisa. "Send someone for Goran, then go and get the cub. Bring him here. Be as quick as you can."

Reluctantly, she went.

"Tell me," said Vartra, almost afraid to hear the answer as he looked from Carrie to Kusac. "Are you content? Are things well between you? You're two different species— have you enough in common to be happy?"

As Carrie began to laugh gently, Kusac put his arm round her.

"Yes, we're content," he said. "I'd choose no other for my Leska. We're alike enough for many of our people to find happiness together, even without the Leska Links."

"Why is she laughing?" asked Vartra, a puzzled look on his face.

"Every new Leska pair will hear you say words similar to those, even fifteen hundred years from now!" Kusac indicated the room with a sweep of his arm. "This mountain is full of crystals that can record sounds and images. In years to come, they'll replay them. Those words will bring comfort to a great many people, Dr. Vartra. That's probably yet another reason why you'll come to be seen as a God."

"Don't talk like that," he said. "It makes me shudder every time I hear you say it."

"When the Cataclysm is over, there will be very little technology left. You'll have to rebuild from the ground up," said Carrie. "Just remember the guilds."

"The guilds?"

"That's all," she said.

Kaid's ears dropped flat against his head and he sat down suddenly. "Gods, I hate this! Being in the same place twice is awful."

"Kaid, you said you remembered nothing about this life until a few months ago," said Kusac. "If that's the case, then your memories can't be left. They need to be removed."

"I know. Like father, like son," he said with a sigh. "Khemu did that to Dzaka."

"What I'm trying to say is, I can do it safely. I've worked in the medical unit at Valsgarth, treating illnesses of the mind. Do you want me to remove the memories for you?"

Kaid rubbed his sound hand against his leg, trying to wipe the sweat off it. "Yes. You'll have to do it nearer the time, though."

Kusac put his hand on Kaid's shoulder. "When we reach the temple."

Kaid nodded and got to his feet.

As the males left to join Goran, Jaisa arrived with the cub.

"I'll take him, Jaisa," said Carrie, bending down slightly till she could lift Tallinu up. He stood waiting for her, arms held up, mouth open in a grin.

"Hello," he said as she held him in her arms. "You playing with me?"

"Yes, love. We're playing a very special game," she said, her eyes meeting Jaisa's over the top of his head. "One that will last all day."

A tiny hand reached up to touch her cheek. "Tears. Why?"

* * *

"Their condition's unchanged," said Vanna. "It's Carrie I'm worried about. Her pregnancy is definitely accelerating, Garras."

"What can you do about it?"

"There's drugs that will slow the development, but I don't know if I should use them. I don't know what to do!" she said, pacing round the kitchen.

"Then leave it. Let nature take its course."

"Nature?" she said, stopping beside him. "This isn't natural to begin with!"

"Then I don't know what to suggest. Why not go and talk to Noni, or ask Jack what he thinks. They may be able to help."

"You don't seem at all concerned," she grumbled. "If you had to go up there and watch them the way Chena and I have, you'd think differently about it."

"Vanna, there's nothing I can do. I found them, have you forgotten that? Do you think I want to go back up to the bedroom? They look like damned corpses! I don't know how you cope, and you have all my admiration for doing so," he said, catching hold of her. "Let me take you over to Jack's."

She hesitated. "All right," she said.

*　*　*

They got the help they needed. Overnight, Goran and Khyim had decided a raid had to be mounted against the Valtegans in Chiyak. When Vartra, having tasted freedom from Goran's restrictions for the first time in a month, insisted on accompanying them, so did Jaisa. With the aid of one of Vartra's concoctions for his stomach, Kaid was better able to control the constant dizziness and nausea caused by the proximity of his childhood self.

"We'll set down as near to the temple as possible," said Khyim. "Then the aircar will take off again, staying within radio contact. I can't afford to risk this craft on the ground. It's the only one we have."

There were ten of them in all, each of them armed, even Vartra. As they looked down on the city below, they could see it was in the throes of a war that had little to do with the Valtegans.

"It's been like this since they left," said Khyim. "Anarchy. Too long under the repressive rule of the Valtegans made them go mad as soon as they caught the scent of freedom."

Overturned vehicles littered the streets, forming road blocks and barricades behind which the various factions took shelter as they hurled everything from bricks to energy bolts at each other. Gangs roamed around, smashing store fronts so they could help themselves to the goods inside. Plumes of smoke and flames licked the air as fire swept unchecked through houses and stores alike. It looked like the battle zone that it was.

"It's brought out the worst in these people," said Khyim. He turned to the pilot. "Fly past the temple courtyard," he said. "I want to see for myself what they've got there. That's it coming up now," he said, pointing through the haze of smoke to the building ahead.

It was squat and ugly, not at all what they'd expected for the main temple. A flight of stone steps led up to the red facade in which were set two heavy wooden doors. In the courtyard, under the watchful eyes of a dozen Valtegan guards, sat two massive troop carriers.

"They're dug in to stay," said Goran as the aircar banked sharply in the opposite direction. "You really want to go in there?" he asked.

"Not want, need," said Kusac, one arm round Carrie, holding onto the bulkhead in an effort to keep his balance.

"Land us in the park by the river," Khyim said. "We'll go in that way. It looked pretty clear as we came in over it."

"River?" Goran queried.

"The city's storm drains and sewers all run into the river that flows past the Temple. There's a labyrinth of tunnels there that the Valtegans haven't had the time to find out about. We're going in along them, and coming out in the heart of the Temple itself. There's an access tunnel in the kitchen area."

Almost before the craft settled on the grass, Khyim had his people out providing cover for the rest of them. It was airborne again the minute the last person was clear.

"Head for the bushes," said Khyim, pointing toward the undergrowth that flanked the bridge ahead.

Carrie took the cub by the hand, intending to tow him after her but Kusac bent down and scooped him up under one arm while, with the other, he hurried Carrie along. Kaid followed with Goran, giving them cover.

Once among the bushes, Khyim sent one of his people ahead to scout the entrance to the tunnels.

As they waited impatiently, Kusac shook Carrie's arm, pointing toward the horizon. High above them, a second sun was glowing red in the sky, shining brighter by the minute as they watched. Behind it, like a vapor trail, were the smaller fragments of debris.

"Goran," said Kusac. "Look up."

Goran glanced up. "The meteor," he said.

"The double sunburst," murmured Carrie.

Kusac nodded. "You're right. We haven't got long now."

"How long?"

"An hour or two, three at most before it hits."

Goran nodded and passed the word up to Khyim.

The scout returned to the arch of the bridge, signaling that all was clear.

In pairs, they sprinted over to join him. Ducking under the archway, they edged sideways along the narrow path that led to the drainage tunnels. Kusac was still carrying the now protesting and squirming cub. As he and Carrie reached the safety of the entrance, he put the cub down with relief and stepped over to where Khyim was talking quietly to his scout.

Aware that her mate was getting irritated, Carrie took charge of the cub. Squatting down as best she could, she put herself at eye level with him.

"Look, Tallinu, you've got to understand that you must do as you're told. We're trying to sneak into the Temple up above without the Valtegans seeing or hearing us. We can't do that if you're making a fuss because you have to be carried."

"A game!" he said with relish. "I can play that!"

"Er, not exactly a game," she said, casting a glance over at Goran and Kaid. "It's more serious than that. Did you ever play hide?"

He nodded solemnly.

"Good. This is a game of hide. We mustn't let the Valtegans find us, so we have to move as quickly and as quietly as we can. Understand?"

There was an impatient noise from behind her and an arm reached forward to grasp the cub by the tunic front, lifting him bodily into the air.

"Hey!" said Carrie, pushing herself upright again and turning to confront whoever it was.

Kaid was holding him at arm's length while the cub, ears back in terror, held onto his hand like grim death.

"Do you want to grow up to be a warrior like us?" Kaid demanded.

The cub nodded.

"Then you've got to follow orders, starting now. Understand?"

Again the cub nodded.

"She's in charge of you, so do everything she tells you, or else . . . !" He left the threat open as he returned him to the ground. Immediately the cub clung to Carrie's leg, looking up at Kaid with huge eyes.

"I know," Kaid said with an embarrassed shrug. "Tell me who wasn't a brat at some point in their life!"

She laughed, reaching out to stroke his cheek before taking the cub by the hand and starting up the tunnel after Kusac.

Dank and dark though the tunnels were, the smell was nowhere near as bad as Carrie had feared. Her makeshift foot coverings were sodden, but at least it was only stagnant water. A halt was called when they reached a grating that blocked their way forward.

"What are we going to do now?" Carrie asked Kusac. "You realize this is one of the worst places to be caught during an earthquake or flooding, don't you?"

He nodded. "So do they," he said, indicating Goran and Khyim who were checking round the bases of all the metal rods. "They're hoping to find some loose ones."

"Let me," said Jaisa, pushing to the front. "I might be able to help."

Kusac raised an eye ridge at Kaid, who shrugged in response.

Intrigued, Carrie stepped forward, the cub held firmly by one hand as she watched what the young Sholan female was doing.

"I don't know what you hope to achieve . . ." Khyim began, but Goran cut him short.

"Don't underestimate our telepaths, Khyim, nor our females," he said. "Jaisa here, she was doing pretty well at Warrior training before this all started. She's still good," he added.

Kusac looked at Carrie. *What's she doing?*

She's vibrating the molecules! Shaking them loose! I didn't know that could be done.

They might not be able to fight, sent Kusac, *but if the others are like her, they've a few tricks we could do with learning.*

Tiny puffs of dust were coming up from the cement that held the bars in place, but they could see by the strained set of her ears how much it was costing her.

Standing behind her, Kusac put his hands over hers. "Draw on me," he said.

Startled, Jaisa lost it for a moment, then Carrie felt Kusac push some of his energy to her. Within moments, the bars came loose in her hands.

"Hey! Well done!" said Khyim, slapping Jaisa on the back as she stood there with a surprised look on her face and a steel bar in either hand.

Goran took them from her and laid them down at the side of the tunnel. "Let's keep moving," he said, stopping to say "Good work," to Jaisa as he climbed through the gap.

"Nice trick," said Kusac. "We'll have to remember it."

"I couldn't have done it without the boost from you," she said as she stepped through after the others.

"Yes you could, it would just have taken longer," he said, turning round to pick up the cub and hand him through to her. Carrie he swung up into his arms, and ducking, carried her through.

"How are you coping?" he asked quietly, setting her down on her feet again.

"I'm fine," she said, leaning against the grill for a moment or two. She gently massaged the top of the lump that was their daughter. She was so tired, and her insides felt bruised with all the kicking. Pinning a grin on her face, she said brightly, "We'll soon be home now anyway. Another couple of hours at most."

Jaisa came over, Tallinu in her arms. "I'll keep him for a bit," she said. "We're not likely to need my rifle skills down here."

Carrie nodded her thanks, and, holding onto Kusac, started walking.

It wasn't long before Khyim called a halt again. Shining his torch upward, he pointed to a drain cover above.

"That's it. We're under the Temple kitchens. It's coming up to second meal, so there's likely to be people up there now."

"If the Valtegans are in charge, the kitchens will be empty," said Carrie. "They prefer freshly killed meat. With warm blood in it if possible," she added.

Khyim looked across at her. "We've had them here for over a year. I think we should know about their eating habits by now."

"We had them ruling our colony, Keiss, for ten years," said Carrie. "Where our people lived and worked beside them, yes, they made a pretense of cooking their food. Not on their bases, though. Not there. The kitchens were nothing more than slaughter houses."

"Ten years?" said Goran, mouth hanging open. "How did you get free of them?"

"That's another story," said Kusac. "However, Carrie does know about the Valtegans, believe me."

"Kusac, there's an easier way to check," she said. "Let's search for them. It's what we did before."

"Search?" asked Vartra, ears pricking up.

"I can read their minds on a basic level. At least, I could do it with the ones in our time," she amended.

"Give us a little space," said Kusac, putting his arm round Carrie and drawing her over to the ladder. Putting his foot on one of the rungs, he turned her round so her back was leaning against him, partially supported by his leg.

Just relax. We can do this as easily as falling off a branch.

Carrie wasn't so sure. *Maybe. That officer on the Khalossa was very different from any of the other Valtegans we met. If they still react to my Sholan mind, we could get nothing. Worse, we could alert them to our presence.*

Just try, we can't do more, he sent encouragingly.

She closed her eyes, trying to slow her breathing until she felt his mind completely synchromeshed with hers. From then on it was easier, as she was able to concentrate on reaching out to find the nearest mind while he controlled their body rhythms.

If she'd been asked to describe what she was doing, she couldn't have. It felt like a focussing of energy in the front of her mind, and a reaching, a projecting of that energy outward until it found what she was searching for.

Then she sensed it; the movement of thoughts, a life force. Latching gently onto it, she drew on Kusac and together they examined the mind she'd found. It was Valtegan, but it was different from any Valtegan mind she'd experienced on Keiss or the *Khalossa*. With a quick mental thrust, she'd penetrated his mind and insinuated herself into his thoughts at a level too deep for the Valtegan to be aware of.

Looking through his eyes, she saw the inside of the temple. He was bored, and kept flicking his gaze from place to place, never still long enough for her to get a good mental picture.

He knew they were only marking time here until the General's other pet arrived, but this was boring, no fit job for a warrior people! Once he'd been and gone, then they could leave for the mountains till this damned meteor strike was over. After that, it was their time! He looked forward to it. There would be fighting enough for all of them, even the hatchlings, safely in their shells at present. They'd be old enough to make their first kills by then.

His eyes stopped on his nest-comrade. At least he didn't have to keep company with the stinking mammals! His nostrils flared in disgust. He could smell the mammal from here. It wasn't his place to criticize his superiors, but why the General had to keep this slave when all the other treacherous mind readers had been slaughtered, he had no idea!

The mammal was looking at him now. He was glad that the slave wore one of the new collars! His mind would be safe from that one, doubly so since *he* was wearing one of the controller devices. A pulse against his wrist made him look more closely at the slave. The stone in his collar *was* glowing! How dare he look at his mind! A loud hiss escaped him as he triggered not only the pacifier circuit, but the pain one too. The mammal gave a cry of pain, and, clutching at his collar, fell writhing to the ground.

Carrie backed off hurriedly before her presence was detected by the Sholan telepath above. She shuddered as she returned to her own mind. It had never been pleasant to look inside Valtegans.

You weren't found, all's well. Kusac's thoughts were soothing, a balm to her mind. She felt exhausted now.

"Kusac, he was . . ." She started to tell him what she'd found but he hushed her.

"You were speaking his thoughts, cub. We know what you felt," he said. "You did well."

"So he's got a tame telepath up there," growled Khyim. "And worse, hatchlings! Kezule plans to wait the cataclysm out up in the mountains, does he? Then they'll just come marching down and take over!" He looked over to where his two fighters stood with their backpacks. "Chelgo, you got enough flexi and detonators to blow this place?"

"If I can put it where I want, yes. No problem."

"We need to take out their transport too," said Goran. "The hatchlings could be on board already."

"Eggs," said Kaid. "And they'll be somewhere warm to incubate them."

"Have they got females that sit on them?" asked Nyak laughingly.

"No. Believe me, you don't want to see the females," said Kaid with a shudder.

"You've seen them?" asked Vartra. "What are they like? Why haven't we seen them before now?"

"There's only five on Shola—or there were," he corrected himself. "All I had was a quick glimpse. They're larger than the males, heavy, and built for violence. If their Emperor has his top unit guarding the hatchery, my bet is that all the eggs but those Kezule stashed away left Shola. Obviously he stayed behind for reasons of his own."

"We're wasting time," said Kusac. "We know the kitchen is empty now so let's go while we can."

"You're right," said Khyim, gesturing them out of the way.

When he reached the cover, he very carefully lifted one edge of it, peering out into the kitchen beyond.

"It's empty," he confirmed quietly. "I'm going in."

Sliding the cover back to one side, he flipped his rifle round, ready to use, as he climbed up the last few rungs into the kitchen.

They waited impatiently till they saw his face blocking out the light.

"All clear," he whispered. "Move up!"

Once they were all up, Nyak opened the door and slipped into the corridor beyond. He was back in moments.

"I heard two voices in the office, just to the left of here," he said. "Likely that's Kezule and his senior officer. Ahead of us is the curtain through into the main temple. The other side of that is where the telepath and the two guards are."

"There's a passage that leads up onto the rear of the balcony," said Kaid. "If we can get someone up there, it'd be like picking off the weak in a herd of rhaklas."

Khyim looked at Chelgo. "He's right. I'd forgotten about that passage. I remember using it when I was here as an acolyte. We can get there from down below. I know the way."

"Jaisa, you think you can mark one?" asked Chelgo.

She nodded. "I can take out one, two if I have to, then the pain they'll broadcast will affect me," she said apologetically.

"Then go for kills," said Kusac. "Think of it as saving them the pain of an injury."

"What a novel approach," she murmured. "I'll try it."

"Lift the route from my mind, Jaisa," said Khyim, "then you'd better get going. Send to Kusac when you're in place."

"Make it tight beam," Kusac said as she turned to go back down the ladder. "One word only. We'll get it."

"When you're in place, we'll tell you when to take out the guards. If you need to, kill the telepath as well," Khyim said. "The four of us will hit the office, the other two will head into the temple to back you up. When you're done, get down here as fast as you can."

Chelgo and Jaisa nodded, then began their descent back into the tunnel.

Carrie found sacks of flour and vegetables in the store room and decided to wait there, as even a lumpy seat was a seat. As luck would have it, the pains in her belly struck just as Jaisa put her head round the door.

Before she knew it, she'd become the center of concern for Kusac, Kaid, and Jaisa.

"I'm fine," she said angrily. "It was only a momentary pain. It's gone now. Your fussing is worse!"

Khyim came in to see what was happening, and when he heard, insisted on feeling her belly.

"It won't do any good," she said, refusing to let him near her. "You're not a medic, what can you tell?"

"I could tell from the feel of you whether your cub's about due," he said. "I've got four of my own at Stronghold! From the look of you I'd say you've got three, maybe four weeks to go, which if you're having pains, means it could be any time in the next ten days or so."

"I'm not a Sholan though," she said. "And my cub's not due for another nine weeks!"

Khyim shrugged. "It's your cub. Let's break this up and get back into the kitchen. They shouldn't be much longer."

She could feel Kusac's fears for her and his worries that their cub could be born too early.

"Stop worrying," she said, pushing herself up from the sack. "I'll last the course. Kashini won't be born too soon."

"Her freedom's not worth her life or yours," he said. "We shouldn't have come till after she was born."

"I think her freedom *is* worth the risk," said Carrie, looking him straight in the eye. "You ask Kaid if it's worth dying for. You know he'll say yes."

With a low, rumbling growl, he waited for her to precede

him into the kitchen area. About to follow her, he stopped in
midstride. "They've reached the balcony."

"Good," said Khyim. "Goran, you and Kusac take the
temple, Kaid, you, me, and Nyak will go after the two in
the office."

"Wait!" hissed Carrie. "Someone's coming! It's the
telepath!"

There was a general flurry of movement as everyone went
for the nearest cover, except Carrie.

"Move!" hissed Kusac, reaching out for her.

She batted his hand away. "Surprise! He'll be thrown
when he sees me!"

Then it was too late as the door handle began to turn.

Halfway into the room, he saw her, and froze in shock.

"Hello," she said, raising her gun and firing. Her voice
was the last thing he heard.

She sidestepped as he crashed to the ground, then moved
as quickly as she could to close the door. "He's only
stunned," she said as Khyim leaped across to check him.

Carrie! What in the God's name were you thinking of?
Kusac demanded, coming out from behind the food warming
cupboards.

*Stop treating me differently, Kusac! If you're too protec-
tive, you'll lose the ability to make quick decisions—you'll
be too busy looking out for me instead of dealing with the
situation!*

The unconscious Sholan was dragged into the store cupboard and the door hurriedly jammed shut by ramming some
cutlery underneath it.

"Goran, Kusac, get going and alert Jaisa."

They left, heading quietly toward the curtain.

"Carrie, you and Vartra stay here with the cub," said
Khyim as his group prepared to leave.

Silently they ran across the hallway toward the curtain,
stopping where the wall of the office ended. Heart pounding,
Kusac kept a watch over his shoulder till he saw Khyim
signaling.

Jaisa, now! he sent.

They waited till they heard the faint whine that accompanied an energy discharge, followed by the sound of a body
hitting the ground. Pushing the curtain aside, they ran into
the temple, heading to the right and left of the statue.

The guard on Kusac's side of the statue was down: Chelgo had taken him out. The other emitted a loud shriek of pain as Jaisa's shot seared past the side of his face, scoring his cheek.

A shot from Goran and he fell like a stone.

Up on the balcony, Chelgo threw his rope over the side and slid down. Slipping off his backpack as he went, he began digging the flexi explosive out and breaking it into chunks.

Jaisa followed him down, then ran over to join Kusac.

"There's bound to be guards outside," said Kusac, pointing to the doors ahead of them. "Keep an eye on the doorway while I check on Khyim."

They'd been aware of the sounds of scuffling, and as he headed for the curtain, Khyim and the others emerged, dragging the Valtegan General. Khyim held him from behind, an evil-looking knife pressed firmly against his throat.

Kaid sprinted to the far end of the temple to fetch the rope. Awkwardly, he sliced through it with his knife, trying not to use his damaged hand. He returned with more than enough to bind Kezule's wrists.

It's safe now, sent Kusac, waiting anxiously with the curtain held back until Carrie, Vartra, and the cub joined him.

They headed for the statue of Varza as the only place capable of giving them any cover. Once she'd found them a reasonable spot, Carrie left them to join Kusac who was now among the group round the General.

"How many more fighters have you got in the temple?" Khyim was demanding, but the Valtegan refused to utter a word until he saw Carrie, then he began to hiss, his rainbow-colored crest rising in anger.

Remembering the officer on the *Khalossa,* Carrie moved till she was standing in front of him.

"You don't want to see me, do you?" she said in Sholan. "I offend you. A female, in public, and worse than that, a breeding one." She shook her head making tsk-ing noises as she reached out to touch his mind. He stiffened, a look of terror and disgust mingling on his otherwise bland face.

"You're emitting fear scents," she said. "That's bad. Your guards out there had better not smell that, had they? You wouldn't last long with them. That's the way it is, isn't it? Kill the one who shows any weakness."

As she'd been talking, the others had moved aside to give

her room, except for Khyim who continued to hold onto the General by the arm, and Kusac who stood, gun trained on the Valtegan, watching for the slightest aggressive move toward Carrie.

She stepped closer. "Shall we take you to the door and throw you out to them, bound and helpless as you are, reeking of fear? Maybe not. Maybe we will keep you alive—if you help us."

His green skin was pallid now, the color of dough, and of his crest, there was no sign.

"I can take the information I want, Kezule, but that would further dishonor you, wouldn't it? Tell us, and I'll release your mind. I won't even try to touch you," she said. "Now that's generous of me. If I were you, I'd accept before I change my mind."

He hissed loudly, tongue flicking out at her. "You stinking mammal! May your offspring rend you with their teeth even as they hatch!"

"Words, Kezule. Only words," she said, walking slowly back and forth in front of him. She stopped abruptly, mentally reaching out again, this time to take control of his mind.

"I can hold you so you can't move," she said, gradually releasing his muscle control back to him. "Shall I do it again? If I do, this time I'll touch you," she said, moving even closer.

He took a step backward, oval eyes blinking slowly. His temper was under control now. "Do what you will. If you can take what you want, why ask?"

"It saves time, Kezule. We'll forget the guards for the moment. Hatchlings." She stopped, appearing to be listening to something. "Ah, not hatchlings. Eggs. Where are they?" A look of surprise came over her face. "The *kitchen!*" She looked across at Kusac. "The eggs are in the food warming cabinets!"

"You stole those words from me!" he hissed. "You are no better than your vermin-ridden allies! Mind-stealers!"

"No, you sent those words to me as thoughts, Kezule," she said, aware of Goran and Nyak heading back to the kitchen.

"Another question. You have a pet. He comes to you from another time, a time when there are no Valtegans on Shola. In fact, you're expecting him soon, aren't you? Tell me when, Kezule. Tell me when, and how you call him."

He hissed angrily, tongue flicking out at her.

"Khyim, put the knife to his throat again," she said. "I wish to touch him."

Grinning, Khyim placed his knife once more at the Valtegan's throat.

"Kill me then. I'll tell you nothing," he said, his crest flaring briefly upward.

Carrie reached for his wrists, pulling them round so she could see the control bracelet he wore. He flinched, but otherwise remained still.

"How does it work, Kezule?" she asked. "Tell me what to do."

He said nothing, continuing to stare ahead, his eyes blinking slowly.

She examined the bracelet, finally finding the catch. Releasing it, she slipped it off his wrist.

"It controls the pacifiers, doesn't it?"

"Get the collar off the telepath back there," Khyim said to Jaisa. "Maybe when our lizard's wearing it, he'll talk."

Carrie handed the device to Kusac, moving away from her captive to concentrate her efforts on pushing back the mental block that the Valtegan had somehow managed to put up.

His mind was quite different from the one she'd read earlier. It was more complex, capable of blocking her attempts to penetrate below the surface level.

I can't get any more without force. If I do that, he'll be of no use to us, she sent to Kusac. *Can you understand the device?*

Not in the time we've got left.

She looked over to Khyim and shrugged.

Jaisa came running back with the collar and handed it to Goran.

"You think that will work?" sneered Kezule as they fastened it round his neck. "Think again!"

"I didn't damage the terminals," said Jaisa. "It should function properly."

"Give it to me," Goran said to Kusac. "I've seen one before. It was damaged, but we got a fair idea of what should happen."

Watching their captive closely, Goran tried punching a couple of the indentations with his claw tip to no effect. Then he tried the grouped keys.

The sneer on Kezule's face froze as his body stiffened.

Still in a light rapport with him, Carrie was instantly aware of the result.

"Pain and dizziness," she said. "It's creating some of the effects of the drug directly into his mind!"

Goran repeated the sequence and they watched as their captive's breathing became faster and the protective membranes began to cover his eyes. His skin took on a slick, oily quality and he began to sag in Khyim's grasp.

"The traveler," said Carrie. "When is he due?"

He jerked his head away at the sound of her voice.

"Hypersensitivity," said Kaid. "No more, Goran, or he'll be incapable of answering you."

Carrie reached out and took Kezule by the jaw. "When does the traveler arrive?" she repeated.

Eyes rolling and nostrils flaring in obvious distress, his mouth opened and he began to mumble incoherently. Then he suddenly crumpled, unconscious, against Khyim, who let him fall heavily to the ground.

As Kezule collapsed, Kusac felt rather than heard the sound from behind. Swinging round, he looked toward the pillars flanking the steps up to the statue of Varza. The subsonic noise rose in pitch until he was sure they could all hear it. Ears plastered flat to his skull in an effort to cut the sound out, he yelled a warning to Vartra.

"Vartra! Move away from the statue!" Staggering backward, he tried to see what was happening. He was aware of his mate's confusion but the noise was vibrating right through him now, setting his teeth on edge, making his whole body ache.

Vartra grabbed the cub and ran.

The sound peaked into the audible range as the pillars began to flicker with a rose glow that steadily deepened. All around him, he could feel the energy swirling, being pulled by the crystal pillars toward the space between them.

He watched as the air seemed to shimmer briefly, then a tan-colored body suddenly materialized, dropping to the floor in front of him. The flickering in the pillars stopped abruptly as if it had never been, but the body on the ground remained.

It moved, groaning softly as it tried to push itself upright.

Kaid launched himself toward it and would have been first there had Kusac not had the presence of mind to leap out after him.

"Get him! It's Fyak!" he said, struggling to keep a hold
on Kaid.

At the other end of the hall, alerted by the noise, the doors
parted and three Valtegan guards rushed in, energy rifles
spitting fire in their direction as soon as they realized what
was happening.

Chaos ensued as people dived for cover, returned fire, and
tried to grab their hostages.

Taking Kaid down with him, Kusac raised his rifle and
opened fire on the guards, taking one of them with his first
shot. A cry of pain from behind him signaled one of theirs
had taken a hit.

Not me, sent Carrie as she crouched behind the statue with
Vartra and the cub.

A shower of crystal shards sprayed over him as a beam hit
one of the pillars. Kaid took that guard out with his pistol.

"The pillars! They mustn't hit them again or we're
stranded!" yelled Carrie.

A burst of fire from Goran took the other at the knees, his
second shot killing him as he fell. Then it was over, the
silence intense after all the noise and confusion.

Slowly they picked themselves up, looking around to see
who had been hurt. It was Jaisa, but Khyim as the nearest
was already seeing to her. Tearing a strip from his tunic, he
bound up the gash along her forearm.

"Shallow flesh wound, no more," he said. "You'll live."

Around the nose, Jaisa was gray with pain. She nodded
slowly as he helped her to her feet.

They all felt the slight movement beneath their feet at the
same moment. Frozen to the spot, they looked at each other,
fear in their eyes. It came again, a faint trembling of the
ground that continued, growing stronger and stronger, till
above them the wooden beams began to creak and plaster
began to flake off the vaulted ceiling, falling down on them
like rain.

Kaid and Kusac exchanged glances then headed at a run
for Carrie and the cub. Kusac reached his mate first and
pulled her with him toward the crystal pillars.

"Stay there," he said, darting back for the unconscious
form of Kezule.

"Bring Fyak to us!" Kaid yelled to Goran as he picked up
the cub and sprinted toward Carrie. "Get the gate working!"
he said. "We have to go now!"

"How? I don't know what to do!" she said helplessly.

"The ritual! Remember the ritual," shouted Kusac, depositing Kezule like a trophy at his mate's feet. "Carrie, touch the pillar! Use your mind to key the crystal—match its resonance and draw the energy from the earthquake!"

"Oh, God, I don't know what the hell I'm doing," she moaned, hurrying over to hold the nearest pillar. The crystal was cool beneath her touch but she could sense the echoes of the gateway deep within it.

Kusac ran to the other, looking at Kaid. "Send the cub first! You know when he has to arrive, we don't!" He turned to the pillar and began to reach with his mind into the heart of the crystal column.

Standing between them, his younger self in his arms, Kaid could feel the energy between the pillars starting to build. He had no idea what any of them were doing, but he knew they had to succeed.

"We haven't erased his memories!" said Carrie, turning a frightened face in his direction. "You'll have to do it yourself!"

He held the cub at arms' length, looking down into his own terrified eyes. There were things he-the-child had to remember! Thinking back to one of his earliest memories at Dzahai Village, he began to reach for his own immature mind. It was easier than he thought to link with him, but then their minds were the same, after all. He saw the beginnings of memories of this day's work being stored. They had to go, and ruthlessly, he took them. Those of himself went, as did those of Kusac. That left images of Carrie. He backed away from them, turning instead to those he knew he must leave, and create. The door in the cavern, the collar—adult memories from *his* mind, not belonging to childhood. What he was doing was brutal and harsh: he had no time for subtlety, even had he known how. Carrie's images came again, and as he reached for them, he, the adult Kaid, began to remember her touch, her scent, the sound of her voice, the feel of her hair.

"Kaid!" she yelled, breaking his concentration. "Now! Send him now!"

He looked ahead and almost fell back in terror at what was before him. Between the pillars, the very air itself seemed to be melting as it bent and folded tortuously back on itself. From the center, a wind began to blow, the current of air pushing at him, forcing him backward from the gateway. In his grasp, the cub began to whimper in fear.

He knew where he-the-cub had to arrive. In his mind he built an image of the statue at the Retreat. "Remember, Tallinu! Vartra go with you!" he said, then threw the cub into the center of the maelstrom.

The cub hit the spiraling vortex and was sucked instantly into it. A high-pitched scream, almost above the level of Sholan hearing, split the air. Abruptly it was cut off, as from the heart of the gate, colored light flared brightly then died, leaving him shaken and blinking, unable to focus. He fell to the floor as under his feet the ground began to heave and buck like a living beast in agony. He staggered then fell, unable to keep his balance. Pushing himself onto his knees, he rubbed his eyes with his good hand, peering through the choking dust for Carrie and Kusac. They were still there, hanging onto the pillars for dear life. Between them lay the huddled shapes of Kezule and Fyak.

"We have to leave!" yelled Goran, running over to help him to his feet. "You did whatever you came to do! Now come with us before this place falls about our ears!"

"No! We have to go back!"

"You can't! Look around you! The pillars are beginning to break up! They won't stand much more of this!"

Kaid pulled away from him. "Go! Leave us here! Get your people to safety!"

Goran hesitated a moment, then grasped Kaid by the forearm in the Warrior's grip. "Good fortune," he said before leaving at a run.

Kaid watched them leave through the doors at the far end of the hall. Vartra stopped and turned to look back at them, standing framed in the doorway. Between them, the flames leaped, rising higher as the temple began to burn. Then he was gone.

Kaid turned back to his friends. Kusac was still leaning against the pillar.

Take Carrie's place. She needs to be between us.

He went, stepping over Fyak on the way. A hand closed on his ankle, the claws penetrating as he was pulled up short.

"You!" hissed Fyak, trying to tighten his grip. "I should have known! How dare you violate the sanctity of Kezule's temple! You have no right to be here!"

Kaid tried to pull free. "Let go, Fyak. I've no time to waste on you!"

"You've destroyed His temple with your blasphemy! You'll burn in hell for this!" yowled the prophet, clutching at Kaid with his other hand as he tried to pull him down.

"Now, Kaid!" Carrie shouted.

He bent down, swiping at Fyak's head, sending him flying across the floor to crash headfirst into the pillar opposite Carrie. "Later," he muttered.

As he reached Carrie's side, she took him by the arm, placing his injured hand against the column.

I'll show you what to do, she sent, then he felt her mind touch his, guiding it into the crystal, finding its rhythm, its unique pulse of energy. *Keep hold of that and match your mind to it. When I call you, come to me and bring Kezule. Understand?*

He nodded, unable to speak. Her touch had been the final trigger that released all the memories that had been hidden— by himself scant minutes before. Reaching up, he touched her cheek.

"I remembered your tears," he said softly. "The echo of them, the memory of you—even though I didn't know who you were—kept me going during those dark days after I arrived at Vartra's Retreat."

"We'll get home safe," she said, touching his fingertips to her lips. Then she was gone.

He did as she told him, trying to ignore the sound of the debris falling around them. The crystal warmed to his touch as his mental contact with it strengthened. Against his chest, he felt an echoing pulse from the one he still wore.

Instead of the rose tint, it began to flush red, brightening and darkening till it glowed the color of new-spilled blood. Overhead he could hear the squeal of tortured metal. He risked a glance upward in time to see the roof begin to crumble as giant blocks of masonry and metal beams crashed to the ground just meters from them. Fear leaped into his mind to be instantly caught and stilled by Carrie. He looked at her, a tiny figure standing between the flame red pillars, their reflected light washing over her like blood. Before her, the vortex was building again, and he could feel the energy she was drawing through him and Kusac from the ground beneath their feet—the ground that still heaved and bucked.

Now! she sent, calling them to her side. Kaid was there,

holding her right hand as the air gusted toward them from between the pillars, blowing her hair backward, plastering her robe against her body. His right hand gripped Kezule by the scruff, the body of the unconscious general lay slumped against his leg.

At her other side, Kusac grasped her firmly by the hand, his other holding on to Kezule. His last coherent thought was fear for their unborn cub. He suddenly knew the medic at Stronghold had been right. He felt her triggering their gestalt in one mighty outpouring of energy directed at the gateway. Above them, the sky was ablaze as glowing cinders from the meteor's tail rained down through the vanished temple roof. Flames flared upward as fuel lines underground fractured and caught light from the blaze already engulfing the far end of the temple. The crystal pillars cracked then shattered, unable to bear the weight of the beams. The power of the vortex began to falter as its heart took on a dark, ominous glow. Shot through with purple, roiling streamers of energy flicked toward them as it began to shrink and pulse.

The gateway! It's collapsing! sent Kusac, fear making him tighten his grip on her hand.

As the shards exploded outward in every direction, the gases within the temple ignited. The noise of the eruption was heard throughout the city. For a moment the Temple of Varza seemed to rise in the air before its walls were blown asunder.

* * *

The castle loomed in front of them, a darker shape against the blackness of the night sky. There was no moon tonight, a fact for which Kris had been extremely grateful. Jo crouched beside him, comfortable at last in her grey trousers; she hated wearing skirts. Concealed behind the low clumps of undergrowth, they waited silently for Davies to return. Around them the snow had been churned to almost nothing with the constant traffic of people and carts in and out of the castle. At least they didn't show up against the muddy background, Jo thought.

A small stirring of air, the faint outline of a moving shape, and he was back beside them.

"All clear," he whispered. "It's just as it's shown on the map and I couldn't see any guards."

Kris nodded, and crouching low, he and Jo followed Davies round to the side of the building.

They stopped in the lee of another clump of bushes, crouching low while Jo pulled the rope out of Kris' backpack.

The castle was built on similar lines to those of Earth. A series of buildings either backing onto the inside of the outer walls, or free standing within them, provided housing and protection for the Lord's family and retainers. The barracks for his small army of guardsmen was there as well. Lord Killian's castle was unusual in that it had an extended rectangular building on one side. Built outward from the curved walls, this was the main keep, or dwelling for Lord Killian. With its thick outer walls and the protected castellated sentry walk, it formed part of the outer defenses. This was where they planned to go over.

"Here," whispered Jo, handing him the coiled rope. Kris took the grapple from the clip on his belt and quickly tied on the rope.

In his gray clothing, they could hardly see him as, keeping low, he ran toward the wall. Stopping a few meters away from it, he sized up the distance and readied his grapple. It arced up into the night, then began to curve down toward the top of the wall. Jo held her breath. If it missed, it could clatter off the wall on its way down, alerting the guard. It caught first throw!

Jo let her breath out in a rush. First stage out of the way. She watched as Kris shinned up the rope, pausing to check the sentry walk. They'd spent a couple of nights just watching the castle, getting to know the sentries' rounds and their shift changes. Their entry had been carefully timed to coincide with the changing of the guard when this area was unguarded for at least ten minutes.

Kris stuck his head through the crenellations and waved for them to follow. Doubled over, Jo ran toward the dangling rope, Davies close behind her. He took hold of the end, giving her a boost up.

The rope was knotted but even so, climbing up wasn't easy. By the time she reached the top and grasped Kris' outstretched hand, she felt as if she couldn't have climbed another foot if her life had depended on it.

Davies swarmed up like a monkey, pulling the rope up behind him. He recoiled it and when Kris turned round, put it back in his pack, handing him the grapple.

Clipping it back on his belt, Kris crept along the walkway, keeping in the dark shadows close to the wall. Ahead of them were the rough wooden steps that led down to the castle courtyard.

The sound of harsh voices calling out orders drifted up to them from below. Kris signed for them to stop, and flattening themselves to the walls, they waited, barely daring to breath, until they heard the sound of marching fade.

Kris signaled them on again, letting Jo know mentally that it was only the interior guard changing shift.

Are you sure the area we want won't be guarded? she asked.

Shouldn't be, he replied, filing away for later the fact that she was getting better at communicating mentally.

They crept toward the stairs, checking that the courtyard was indeed deserted. Like shadows they made their way down the steps, doubling round immediately to hide underneath them.

"Where now?" whispered Davies.

"Across the front of this building and round to the other side of it," said Kris, mentally checking through the remembered details on the map. "There's a small side entrance, one that leads to the stillroom. Lady Killian uses it when she's been out collecting her herbs. We'll go round the front of the building one at a time. Go straight to the section next to the outer wall and wait for me. You first, Davies."

Davies nodded, and in single file, they crept out from under the steps to the corner of the building.

"Wasn't there an easier way in? One that didn't go past the front door?" muttered Davies, carefully peering round the corner.

"No. Now go as soon as you can! We've only a few minutes left," said Kris.

Davies hesitated, then left at a run, keeping low until he rounded the corner and disappeared from sight.

"You now, Jo."

She nodded and carefully moved out, keeping close to the wall. She wasn't going to run like Davies, she preferred to slowly edge her way round, only dashing past the doorway when she had to. Slowly she inched her way along, freezing to the spot when she heard loud voices approaching. Crouching down, she curled into as small a shape as possible, pressing herself so hard against the wall that she was

sure she'd fall through it. There was a gust of warm air, then
the area in front of the door was flooded with light as
someone stepped out. Calling back over his shoulder to the
person still within, he walked straight past her. The door shut
again with a loud, hollow bang.

She waited, listening to the retreating footsteps as he
walked across the courtyard to the barracks. Another door
opened, then shut, and silence returned. Cautiously she lifted
her head up and peered around. It was clear again. Getting
carefully to her feet, this time she ran like the devil himself
was on her heels and arrived round the corner, almost knocking Davies flying as she crashed into him.

Staggering, he caught hold of her arm, bringing her to a
stop and preventing her falling over. "Got you!" he whispered. "Though he'd see you for sure!"

"Me too," she whispered, trying to catch her breath as she
pulled away from him.

Kris arrived, slewing to a stop in the slushy snow.
"Where's the door?" he demanded. "Have you checked it?"

"Waiting for you," said Davies, turning and walking round
the last corner to the small wooden door. He took hold of
the round metal handle, giving it an experimental twist.
They could hear the grating of the latch moving up on the
other side.

"It's open," he said, surprised.

"Why lock it in a castle this well protected," said Jo with a
faint smile. "Besides, locks will be expensive in this tech
level society. They'll be used for important things."

"Like strange gray boxes," muttered Kris. "Let's get
moving, people. We not only have to get in, we've got to try
and get out."

Davies pulled the door open a crack, checking to see that
the corridor was empty. "Hey, you check it out, Kris," he
said quietly. "Carrie used her telepathy for that when we
worked together on Keiss."

"Got a point," he murmured, sending a quick mental probe
out to check the way ahead. "Clear, as you said. I don't like
relying on it, though, it's too easy to depend on your mind
and forget your other skills."

Privately, Jo agreed. Relying on hunches was one thing,
but a fear of self-delusion was one of her constant worries.
Briefly she envied Carrie with her certainty that what she
sensed with her mind was true and accurate.

Closing the door behind them, they crept along the passageway. It was dimly lit by the spillover of light from the main corridor ahead of them. All was quiet. The normal number of lit torches in the wall sconces had been halved. With the Lord's family and retainers asleep for the night, there was no need for costly illumination. This was to their advantage.

A short way along the main corridor was a junction to their right. The room at the bottom of this passage was where the box was kept, according to Railin's information.

"Last leg," whispered Kris. Once they were in the room with the box, they'd be safe for a while at least. "Davies, you go first."

As they made their way carefully down this last passageway, Kris drew their attention to fresh score marks in the walls.

"Whatever it is, it's solid enough to gouge marks in stone," he whispered.

"This door will be locked, Davies," said Jo quietly as they came to a stop outside it. "I'd take money on it."

"No deal," said Davies, bending to examine the handle. "There's a keyhole right here." He reached into his pocket and pulled out a small roll of waxed cloth. In it were his collection of lock-picking tools.

"Hold that," he said, handing the open roll to Jo. Turning back to the door, he carefully inserted his piece of wire into the lock.

As Davies gently twiddled it, Jo began to fret.

"You'll only make him nervous," said Kris quietly, bending toward her so his mouth was close beside her ear. "Then he'll get clumsy."

She grunted in reply, shuffling her feet in an effort to keep warm.

The click, when it came, sounded far too loud for safety.

"We're in," said Davies, grinning up at them as he pushed the door open.

Jo closed the door behind them, looking in awe at the alien object that Kris' torch illuminated.

"What is it?" she asked of no one in particular.

Kris began to walk round it, reaching out gingerly to touch the surface that seemed to defy light itself.

"It's solid," he said, coming back round to his starting point. He blinked, trying to focus on it. His eyes seemed to want to look away, to slide off the surface. The faint light from his torch flickered across it, only to be bounced off the wall alongside them. "It's also very much here, it just doesn't look like it!"

"Davies?"

"Beats me," he said, running his hands over the surface in front of him. He bent down to look at the lower edge. "This is way beyond our tech level, Jo, and the Sholans, too, I'm betting. Aha! What have I here?"

"Well?" she demanded.

"The base has controls set into it. Let's see what it's like on the other sides."

He crawled round the cube, prodding and poking at the base unit, but leaving the control depressions alone.

"Well, it's Valtegan, going by the look of the recessed controls. They match others we've seen on Keiss and in the crashed ship," he said, looking up at Jo and Kris. "I'm not sure what the controls do, though. That's going to be a matter of trial and error, I'm afraid."

"Just don't touch anything without my say-so," Jo said quickly. "We don't want to go setting off any alarms that could be built into it."

"Hey, folks, I've no more wish to get caught than you," he said, lifting his hands up to show his good intentions.

"Kris, try a mental probe. See if you can find anything."

Kris nodded. "Stand clear, Davies," he said as he handed the torch to Jo. Putting both hands on the surface, he began to concentrate, trying to find the natural resonance of the object.

"Jo, give me a boost," he said quietly. "This one's a toughie. It's taking more energy than I thought."

"What do I do?" she asked.

"Just hold my hand and relax," he said, taking one hand off the cube.

Though she felt rather foolish, she did as he asked. She couldn't feel anything happening.

"Hush. Stop thinking so loudly," Kris murmured, squeezing her hand gently. "There's something inside it," he said. "Organic, but no life signs—no mental activity. And things," he said.

"Things," said Davies. "Very descriptive. What kind of things?"

"Various. This is still an inexact science, Davies. We're

writing the rules as we go along. Ah. Interesting. Electrical activity."

"Electrical?" queried Jo.

"A device. Hold on. With a little more energy from you, I might just be able to . . ."

Jo felt a sudden surge followed by an overpowering sense of exhaustion, then Kris' hand fell open and he slumped against her. Stumbling backward, she fell against the wall, Kris landing at her feet. She recovered her balance and bent down to help him up. Dazed and blinking, he stood there rubbing his eyes.

"Hey, you've activated it!" said Davies. "Look!"

As they watched, the lights along the base unit flared into life, beginning to hum gently. Gradually, the sides of the cube began to waver, becoming more transparent until they could see through them.

"God! There're people inside! Sholans!" said Jo.

Kris watched fascinated as the sides began to recede until they could plainly see the two Sholans standing frozen within. The taller figure stirred, gasping for air as his arms clutched protectively round the female held with them. He staggered, about to fall. Kris leaped forward, grasping hold of him, calling out to Jo.

"Jo! Catch the female! She's not breathing!"

Jo ran to his side, reaching up to take hold of the female Sholan as Kris pulled the male's arms free of her. She collapsed limply against her, her weight pulling them both down to the ground. Kneeling beside her, Jo put her cheek to the female's face, praying for a breath from her, but there was none.

Kris was having problems with the male who was still struggling to catch his breath and was beginning to suffocate.

Jo glanced over at him, realization dawning. "They're Leskas, Kris! Start resuscitating!"

She spilled her Sholan onto the ground, quickly stretching her limbs out and tipping her head back. Sealing her nose and opening her mouth, Jo began to force her own breath into the female's lungs.

It was hard work, but at last she began to cough. Raising her arms, feebly she tried to bat the Human away.

As Jo sat back exhausted, she looked over at Kris and the male. He'd recovered and was attempting to sit up.

Leaning over the female, she pushed the blonde braids

back from her forehead. "It's all right," she said in Sholan. "You're safe. Your Leska's fine. He's right beside you."

Her eyes flew open, taking in the alien face and the Sholan words as she tried to sit up. Jo helped her, an uneasy feeling of deja vu gripping her as she looked into the amber eyes.

"We're friends," repeated Jo. "Alliance Allies of Shola."

The male pushed Kris aside and tried unsuccessfully to get to his feet.

"The Valtegans, where are they?" he croaked.

Taken by surprise, Kris didn't know what to say.

"Gone," said Jo, reaching out to touch the collar she'd noticed round the female's throat. "That's pretty."

"Gone?" echoed the male.

Jo nodded.

He grinned, showing his teeth as he crawled toward his Leska and took hold of her collar in both hands, wrenching it apart. He threw it against the far wall, then reached up to do the same with his own. Lifting his head, he gave a roar of defiance, his call deafening in the small room.

"I told you we'd be free of them one day," he said, his hand closing on her arm. "I reached for home, telling them of our success and our survival, and was answered."

"It looks like the guard was right. I do have off-world visitors," said a voice in the common language of Jalna. "Touching as this rescue and reunion is, I want to know just what you think you're doing breaking into my home, and opening my property without permission!"

Kris looked up to see three crossbows trained on them. "Oh, shit," he said.

The male lunged for the floor of the base unit, trying to reach a pistol that lay there. Kris reached out and stopped him.

No, don't. He'll have us killed before you reach it. You're weak from being inside that cube. You both nearly died. Wait for now.

Chapter 22

T'Chebbi was first on the scene when she heard Vanna's cry of terror. She took in the empty beds and said one word.

"When?"

"I don't know! They were here an hour ago! They can't just have vanished," Vanna wailed.

Walking further into the room, T'Chebbi put her hand on the main bed. It was warm. Frowning, she moved her hand beyond the depression caused by the body. That was equally warm. Quickly she checked the other beds, ignoring Vanna's tearful monologue, grateful when Dzaka arrived and took charge of her.

"Stay here. I'm going to Ghyan," she said and left hurriedly.

"What shall I tell Konis and Rhyasha?" Vanna asked Dzaka as he tried to comfort her.

When told of the disappearances, Rhyasha and Konis made straight for their son's home.

"I don't believe they're dead," said Rhyasha, pacing the floor of the den. "If they'd died, none of this would be here! None of them would have been! And they have, Vanna, we *know* they have!"

"Then where are they?" Vanna asked.

"I've no idea, but they have to be somewhere!"

"They could have come back to the wrong time!" whimpered Vanna.

In Vartra's name, Konis, send someone to fetch Garras to take her home! I'm having enough of a problem coping without dealing with her grief, too!

Konis raised an eye ridge at her and she made a gesture of apology but remained adamant. He rose and left the room for the comm in the lounge.

The message sent to the dig, he sat for a moment looking

at the screen, then punched in Ghyan's code. He, like a great
many other telepaths these days, was learning to listen to his
instincts.

The screen resolved to show Ghyan had company—
T'Chebbi.

"Just going to call you, Clan Lord," said Ghyan. "Can you
come over? We think we know where they are."

* * *

A cold so bitter it burned gusted round her, and she could
feel ice crystals forming on her body. It spiralled outward,
clutching at her, grasping and tugging her toward its heart.

No! Not yet! Every sense she possessed shrieked a
warning. Her Companions' fear flowed through her as they
fought to remain steady by her side. Between her breasts, she
felt the crystal eye of Varta flare, sending a wave of energy
pulsing through her body. An echoing beat so faint she
almost missed it, came to her from Kaid.

The crystals! sent Kusac. *Use the crystals you and Kaid
wear!*

Unasked, she felt Kaid open his mind, letting the power
from his crystal flow through him to her. Grasping it, she
drew on its energy, combining it with hers till it blazed like a
beacon within their minds.

Before her the vortex flickered, the air roiling as it poised
on the edge of collapse. Carrie reached for it, throwing the
energy of the crystals directly into its heart. Blue fire
exploded, flooding across the vortex, returning it to stability.

Now! she sent, as the cold wind once more howled round
them, sucking them toward the icy heart of the gateway.

As they leaped into the swirling maelstrom, behind them,
the temple exploded. Wind so hot it seared their lungs
howled round them, blowing stinging fragments of crystal
against their bodies. It felt as if the explosion itself had propelled them forward. Blackness shot with coruscating colors
dazzled their eyes, surrounded them while the wind howled
and buffeted and tore at them, robbing them of their breath.

Only just conscious, Kaid at last sensed the ground
coming up to meet him. Releasing his hold on Kezule, he
curled up, landing in a roll that let him stumble into a
crouching position.

It was a new day here. In the distance, the sun glowed

orange as it began to climb above the horizon. Rrurto stood looking at them, mouth open in shock. Kaid glanced to either side; he could see the prone bodies of his companions and their two prisoners.

"Wait, Rrurto!" he said, aware that the guard was about to call for help. "We've come from the Fire Margins. We found Fyak there."

"Cover me," Rrurto ordered his partner before cautiously stepping closer. He looked from Kaid to the bodies still lying prone on the sand "That's Fyak, right enough. And the Aldatan youth and his human Leska," he said, then pointed to the fifth body. "Where d'you find that one? His likeness is all over the inside of the corridors and the temple!"

Moving slowly, Kaid got to his feet. "He's a Valtegan. His name is Kezule. He's a General in the Valtegan army."

Rrurto studied him. "Kezule, you say."

Kaid nodded. "He was the leader of a unit of the Emperor's elite guards. His job was to protect the hatchery on Shola—the hatchery that would populate our world with his Emperor's heirs."

"And Fyak?"

"The drug he uses lets him travel back to the time of the Cataclysm, where he met with the Valtegan he thinks is his god, Kezule."

"He's talking treason, Rrurto!" the other guard called out. "Don't listen to him! When the Prophet wakens, he'll have our hides for listening to these lies!"

"Be quiet, lad," said Rrurto. He thought furiously. The caverns would still be quiet. It was too early yet for the next watch to be up and about. This might be the chance they'd been waiting for. If he could alert the Elders and his own tribe without disturbing Vraiyou and the few Faithful that remained in the camp, then maybe . . .

"They haven't been with Fyak! Can't you see they're lying?" demanded the young male. "I'll wait for the Prophet to wake, then do what *he* tells me! You can risk a flogging if you want, not me!"

Rrurto turned angrily on him. "Then where'd they come from?" he demanded. "They all arrived together!"

"Fyak never moved! He's exactly where he was when we started this vigil!"

"No," said Rrurto. "He's not where he was." Of that at least, he was sure. He'd seen the unconscious body of the priest seem to flicker and fade, only to reappear where he now lay.

A noise from the priest drew his attention. He was beginning to stir.

With a groan of pain, Fyak sat up, his hand going to touch his scored cheek. His eyes fell on Kaid. "You disbeliever! You defiler of Kezule!" Fyak snarled, looking from his bloodstained hand to Kaid. "You dared to raise your hand against *me*—Kezule's chosen! *You* destroyed His temple with your blasphemous actions!" Scrambling to his feet, he looked over at the two guards.

"Shoot them!" he snarled, pointing angrily at the small group lying around him on the sand. "They have defiled Kezule's temple in the other world by daring to lay violent hands on me!"

Rrurto raised his rifle to point directly at the priest's chest. "You have your proof, straight from Fyak's own mouth, and the wound on his face," he said to the young male. "Go to the cavern. Wake my father and tell him our time's come." Something very strange indeed had happened here.

Eyes wide with fear, the younger one left at a run.

"What do you think you're doing?" Fyak took another step. "Are you mad?"

"Stay where you are," growled Rrurto. "You taught us to hate the demons, so why do you deal with them?"

"Demons?" Fyak looked genuinely confused. "What demons?"

"Him!" Rrurto pointed toward where the Valtegan was beginning to stir.

Fyak swung round to stare aghast at the General. Kezule's arms moved and he began to push himself up from the sand.

"Do something!" Fyak said. "Shoot him!"

"Why don't you call on your god to deal with him, Fyak?" said Kaid sarcastically. "Surely he can deal with one demon!"

"Yes, call on Kezule," said Rrurto.

The Valtegan looked groggily over to the source of the voice that had spoken his name. "Who are you? Where am I?" he asked in slurred Sholan as his eyes blinked in the sunlight. He caught sight of Fyak and sat back on the ground, tongue flicking out as he hissed in anger.

"Don't you recognize him, Kezule?" asked Kaid, squatting down to look across at him. "Do you know where you are?"

Kezule sniffed the air, tasting it with the tip of his tongue as he looked around. "Khezi'ipik," he said, obviously uneasy. "We must leave. The meteor will hit soon. This area will be flooded." His clawed hands went to his throat, pulling at the gold collar he still wore. It remained firmly fixed despite his efforts. He hissed his anger.

"The meteor hit Shola over a thousand years ago, Kezule," said Kusac as he began to sit up. "We've brought you home with us. To our time."

Kezule hissed loudly. "You lie!"

Kusac didn't bother to answer. Still on all fours, he padded the few steps over to where Carrie lay unconscious on the sand.

"Kill him!" said Fyak, his voice rising in panic as he began to back farther away from them. "Kill the demon!"

A warning shot raised a small cloud of dust at his feet. He stopped dead, looking at Rrurto in shock.

"Stay where you are," the older male warned. "I'll shoot you if I have to."

"Why? I warned you of the return of the demons, and here they are! Why don't you believe me? Kezule has kept His promise to us!"

"He *is* Kezule, Fyak!" said Kaid. "He's your god in the flesh, only he's a Valtegan! He's been using you to destroy our telepaths because they're the only weapon we have against them! That's right, isn't it, Kezule? Sholan telepaths destroyed your worlds, didn't they?"

Kezule hissed angrily, getting to his feet. "Our people will never forget what you have done! You repaid our trust with treachery!"

"You're lying!" said Fyak, ears laying flat in rage as the hair around his face and down the center of his back bushed out to twice its volume. "He's not Kezule!" Then he remembered the bracelet he wore. Reaching for it, he began to press the buttons.

Kezule clutched his neck, roaring in agony, desperately trying to pull the collar free.

"Stop him!" yelled Kaid, running toward him. "He'll kill him!"

Spinning round, Fyak let out a howl of anger and rushed at Rrurto. "I told you to kill them! I don't have to stand here and listen to their lies!"

Rrurto stepped back, avoiding the Prophet's mad rush. Kaid launched himself after Fyak, his claws scrabbling to get a hold on the priest's back as he brought him tumbling to the ground. Fyak howled again, trying to twist round and snap at Kaid's hands and arms.

Stepping forward, Rrurto delivered a sharp crack with his rifle butt against the side of the priest's head. Fyak fell limply to the ground.

"That should keep him quiet awhile," he said, slipping his foot under the priest's chest and flipping him off Kaid.

"Thanks," said Kaid, scrambling to his feet. He grabbed hold of Fyak under the arms and dragged him back to where they'd originally been sitting.

Kezule lay on the sand panting, his tongue flicking as he recovered from the pain caused by the collar.

Rrurto was unwinding his head covering. He threw it over to Kaid. "Might be an idea to tie that Kezule up. He's more use to us alive than dead." He reached up to his own neck, fingering the collar he wore. "So that's what Fyak's collars do, is it," he said. "I'm beginning to like this prophet less and less. I'd take that bracelet from him as well. How do you get these collars off?" He tugged futilely at his.

Kaid picked up the cloth. "With cutters, I suspect. Wait till you have Vraiyou under guard. Trying to remove the collar triggers a warning to anyone with a bracelet." Crouching down behind Kezule, he pulled the Valtegan's hands behind him, securing them firmly with the twisted cloth rope.

"The only bracelet around here is his," said Rrurto, pointing to Fyak.

"Have you some water?" Kusac asked. "My mate needs to drink."

As he walked across to them, Rrurto pulled a canteen free from his belt. Unscrewing the top, he handed it to Kusac. "The sun's too strong for her to be exposed to it," he said. "She needs to be covered."

"I know," said Kusac as he raised her head and placed the canteen to her lips. "Clothes don't travel with us, though."

"Fyak's robes are over there. I'll get them for you," he said.

Kusac gratefully accepted them. He wiped Carrie's face with a corner of the robe first, then as she began to cough up some of the dust that had lodged in her lungs, he held her close till she'd done. As he did, he noticed that the crystal she wore was crazed and shot through with purple and black streaks. He touched it, watching in shock as it disintegrated into a fine dust. The early morning breeze caught it, whipping it up into the air and blowing it out to the desert beyond. If the power she'd been controlling for the gateway had done that to the crystal, what had it done to their unborn cub? Ruthlessly he pushed his worry aside. This was no time for new fears.

"More water," she said, oblivious to what had happened. He held the canteen to her lips again. She took it from him, drinking deeply before she handed it back. "Thanks."

He helped her to her feet, holding the robe for her as she slipped her arms into it. As he was passing her the wide waist tie, he stopped, turning his head in the direction Rrurto's companion had taken. "Four people, coming this way."

"It'll be the lad with Chaamga. I sent for him because he used to be the chief Elder of the tribes," said Rrurto.

"Are you ready now to be done with Fyak and his alien ways?" asked Kaid.

Rrurto lifted an eye ridge, glancing pointedly at Carrie. "Alien ways, you say? Well, the Humans haven't done what Fyak has. They don't make us kill our own." He sighed, thinking for a moment. "What do you plan to do now?"

"Take Fyak and Kezule to your people, tell them how they've been used."

He nodded. "They need to know. Evil, that's what Fyak is. I was a fighter with the Forces. Fyak's way was never for me. More I saw of it, the less I liked it. Every day, there's plenty more that think like me."

"I know," said Kaid.

Rrurto gave a short bark of laughter. "Happen you do! L'Seuli and I watched you, we did. Pity about the lad. I liked him. Don't suppose you know what happened to him, do you?"

Kaid nodded. "He's back with Intelligence. His testimony helped get me out of Stronghold, and damned Ghezu."

"Ghezu's here now. He hasn't been the same since Fyak took him to meet the God! He must have taken him to that temple you were speaking of. You'll want him personally, won't you?"

"Yes." Kaid's voice was a growl of cold anger.

"We'll see what the other Elders say. You're lucky. We've only a couple of hundred warriors here at present. The rest have been disbanded for the month to see to their holdings or to move camp to winter quarters. Those of us that're left have had Fyak's brand of religion longest. Like I said, we'd had enough anyway. I can see his god's as false as he is."

The guard, accompanied by three older males, came into view.

"What's going on?" demanded the tallest of them. "What's all this insane tale of people materializing out of thin air?" He stopped dead as he caught sight of Kezule. "Where did *that* come from?"

"They were waiting for Fyak at his god's temple," said Rrurto. "Only Kezule isn't a god. That's him there," he said, pointing with the tip of his rifle toward the captive alien. "One of those who built this place. A Valtegan."

"A Valtegan?" echoed the elderly male.

"Yes, Chaamga. A Valtegan from the time of the Cataclysm," said Kusac, stepping forward with Carrie by his side. "We've been to the Fire Margins, and returned. We bring Vartra's blessings for our people, and proof that Fyak is a false prophet. This alien is General Kezule, lately of his Emperor's warrior elite and he was guarding the hatchery here at Chezy."

Chaamga looked toward the bound Valtegan. "*He's* Kezule?"

"The drug Fyak took allowed him—and us—to travel back to those days. Kezule used Fyak to try to destroy our civilization so that when his people returned to Shola, we'd be unable to defend ourselves against them. They may be returning already, Chaamga; it was the Valtegans who destroyed Szurtha and Khyaal."

Chaamga looked from Kusac to Rrurto who nodded. "I believe them. They arrived together, appearing out of nowhere, riding on a wind as hot as the breath of hell itself. Fyak seemed to fade, only to reappear with the others. When Kaid called the Valtegan by the name Kezule, he answered. We've been used, Chaamga. Used by enemies worse than the other tribes ever were!"

"It seems we have," said the chief Elder slowly. "Our people must hear of this." He turned to his nearest guard. "Go to my encampment and tell my warriors to call a meeting of the tribes. Tell them to do what's necessary to ensure we have no trouble from Vraiyou or the Faithful. Send a messenger when you're ready."

"Tell our tribe to send us an escort, Father. I'm not risking our lives while we wait," said Rrurto.

Chaamga nodded. "Do it." He moved closer, finding a rocky outcrop on which to sit down. While his companions did the same, he turned his attention back to Kusac and Carrie.

"You actually walked the Fire Margins?"

Kusac nodded as he found somewhere comfortable for Carrie to rest. "Kaid, the third member of our Triad, is a priest. He can tell you about it better than I can," he said, returning for Kezule. As he took hold of the Valtegan's bound wrists, his captive protested.

"My capture is worthless," he said. "Unless we leave immediately, we're all dead!"

"Look at the sky, Kezule," said Kusac, yanking him upright. "There's no sign of the meteor, is there? No fire in the sky. Your world and everything you knew has long since gone."

"Then what use am I to you?" Kezule hissed as he was dragged over to the chief Elder.

"We'll find a use for you, never fear," Kusac reassured as he made him sit in front of Chaamga. Leaving him there, he looked round to check on Fyak. One of the other Elders had given Kaid his headcovering and his aide was now binding the unconscious prophet's wrists.

"You want Ghezu," said Rrurto. "You can have him, but Fyak and the others are ours."

Kaid looked up at him, hesitating, unsure what to say.

"They're yours," said Kusac. "Provided as well as Ghezu, we have your word that this will be the end of the tribal wars, and that you'll disband and return to your homes. Aid and rehabilitation teams must be allowed into your territories."

Rrurto looked at the other three Elders. There was general nodding of heads and agreement.

"We won't turn down the help this time," said Chaamga. "We've more need of it now."

"Have you got the clout to make this agreement stick?" asked Rrurto.

"Yes."

"We've been to the Fire Margins," said Kaid quietly. "That alone gives us the authority." He handed him Fyak's bracelet. "This controls the collars you and the others wear," he said.

Chaamga nodded his thanks, taking it cautiously from him and handing it to Rrurto. "You were going to tell me about your journey," said Chaamga. "Now would be a good time."

Their escort arrived shortly. Kaid recognized them. Ten of the best veterans in what had been Fyak's army. He glanced curiously at Rrurto.

"My warriors have always been well-trained," Rrurto grinned. "It helps that I'm an active fighter myself. Gives them a high standard to achieve before they begin."

By the time a runner arrived from the Lair, Chaamga had been appraised of the main details of their journey.

"To have met Vartra . . ." Chaamga found it difficult to continue. "To have met Him while He was working among our people, pulling them together after the Cataclysm!"

"We met him before the Cataclysm hit Shola," corrected Kaid.

"No matter! That is an irrelevance! You still met Him and received His blessing!"

"He's blessed us in many ways," Kusac murmured, drawing Carrie closer to his side as they rose to their feet.

"We'll take Fyak," said Rrurto. "You can bring the Valtegan."

Kaid nodded. "Where's Ghezu?"

"Detained," grinned Rrurto.

As they walked into sight of the main camp, there was a general disbelief and hush among the fighters gathered there. They watched and waited, seeing what their Elders intended to do. Fyak's teachings had only gone flesh deep, respect and obedience to the traditional Tribal leaders had been bred into them from birth. As well as that, though they'd heard of the Valtegans, very few of them had even seen a vidicast of one, or of Humans for that matter. The presence of two aliens among them was enough to make the most volatile silent for the moment.

"They're too quiet," said Kusac, keeping his voice low.

"Stop worrying. They're assessing the situation," said Kaid, tightening his grip on Kezule.

"A bit slower, please, Kusac," said Carrie. "I can't keep up any more."

Rrurto looked at Kusac. "Take your bond-mate into the cavern," he said. "It's better she's not in front of our fighters in such an advanced state of pregnancy. Our own females are kept indoors from the time they reach their twentieth week."

Kusac nodded and they veered to one side, heading for the caverns.

"The cheek of it," Carrie muttered, limping across the hot sand.

"No," said Kusac. "It's for sound reasons, Carrie. The heat in the desert is really fierce for a large part of the year. Pregnant females would be more comfortable indoors."

Carrie muttered under her breath as they made their way through the entrance. She stopped dead, looking up at rings set high in the wall.

Kusac's arm was round her shoulders. "I know. It's past now," he said, urging her on.

A short way further on, she stopped again, refusing to go any further.

"No, I've walked far enough," she said, sitting against an outcrop of rock. "Go and join Kaid, I'll rest here."

"Can I get you some water?"

"Water would be wonderful," she said. "Please."

He made his way down to the cooking area where the only two females he'd seen so far were seated.

"Have you some water, please?" he asked.

One got up to fetch him a mug. The other's stare made him turn round.

"Liegen Aldatan! It *is* you!" she said. "Vartra be praised! Don't you recognize me, Liegen? I'm Rhaid!"

"Rhaid! Yes, I remember you," he said, leaning forward to look at her more closely. "What happened to you? You're so thin!" He reached out to take hold of her chin, turning her head to the light. "Who's been beating you?" he demanded, the rumble of anger audible in his voice.

"Fyak. He made me his property," she said, keeping her voice low. She looked up at him. "What's happening, Liegen? What brings you here?"

"It's too complicated to explain now, Rhaid, but you'll hear about it, I promise. Fyak's been taken prisoner. The tribal Elders are taking over again. I'll see you're picked up by our people as soon as possible."

"Vartra be praised! Her, too. She's a Warrior, taken like me from Laasoi."

He looked at the other female as she handed him the mug. Every line of her body spoke of her defeat at the hands of Fyak's troops. "Both of you. You have my word on it. Will you sit with the Liegena? I must join Kaid."

"Of course, Liegen," Rhaid said, getting to her feet and taking the other female by the arm. "We'll sit with her."

Kusac headed back to Carrie and gave her the water. "I've asked the telepath, Rhaid, to sit with you till I return. Are you sure you'll be all right?" he asked, catching her free hand in his.

"I'm fine. You worry too much," she said, taking her hand back and stuffing it into the ample pocket of the robe. "Go."

He flicked her cheek with his finger before leaving.

Once he'd gone, she leaned back against the wall, hands clenched tight against the pain in her back and belly. Now she really was afraid, but she couldn't let him worry when so much was at stake. They'd all been right, her cub had been growing too fast, and even she could no longer ignore it. She could still feel her moving—the butterfly sensations as well as the kicks. She winced as another one came. This daughter of theirs felt more like a kangaroo than a cub! That was the other thing. Her talent hadn't diminished at all. She tried not to think about it. There were so many factors that could have harmed her baby over the last few days—and fifteen hundred years.

"Liegena, are you all right?" asked a concerned female voice.

Opening her eyes, she saw Rhaid and the other female. "I'm fine, just tired," she said. "Let me sleep here till the males return."

"As you wish, Liegena."

It was over an hour later when she opened her eyes.

Rhaid was shaking her awake. "Liegena, we've been called to the meeting to hear the Elders pronounce a sentence on Fyak and Vraiyou. This warrior will stay with you till we return."

Carrie nodded. "Go. I'll be fine," she said.

Mildly curious, she listened in through Kusac to what was happening. His mind was tightly controlled, unusually so for him.

You don't want to watch, he sent. *He's been sentenced to death. So has Vraiyou. The females have demanded they be involved carrying out the sentence as they suffered under his rules too. They're tying him to the banner-pole now. Many of the females are in a hunt state.*

He thrust her from his mind as she saw the foremost female—Rhaid's companion—advancing on their terrified victims. The silence was suddenly broken by a loud chorus of hunting cries, audible even as far away from the meeting place as she was. The images kept coming, though, broadcast by the enraged minds of the desert tribesfolk as, using any instrument that came to hand, they hacked their false prophet and head acolyte to pieces.

Carrie leapt to her feet with a cry of pain and disgust as she tried to block out the awful images. Then someone held her close, shielding her mind and murmuring comforting words.

"It's all right, Liegena," soothed Rhaid, smoothing Carrie's hair comfortingly. "I couldn't stay either. It's only what he deserves though," she added, her voice taking on a hard quality that made Carrie pull back.

"How can you say that?" she demanded. "No one deserves such a fate!"

"I agree. Not even the telepaths that he had torn to pieces, nor those whose minds he destroyed." Rhaid's voice was implaccable. "He was shown as much mercy as he gave. He betrayed these people, Liegena."

A disturbance at the cavern mouth claimed their attention. Ghezu was being dragged toward the entrance, where his wrists were lashed to the rings in the wall where Kaid had been flogged.

"What's happening?" she asked sharply. "What are they doing to him?"

"Nothing, Liegena," said Rhaid, "only securing him so he can't escape. He's to return with you so he can be handed over to the proper authorities for trial."

Tiredly, Carrie leaned back against the rock, content to let her argument with the telepath drop. She waited for Kusac and Kaid to appear. When they did, she knew instantly all was not well between them.

Kaid wants to kill Ghezu now, sent Kusac, his mental tone furious. *I've told him he has to go back for trial.*

You can understand why.

I can't allow that in front of the Tribes! I have to keep the

laws we want reestablished here! Kaid refuses to see it that
way! He put me in a position where I had to uphold the law
against him!

There was nothing she could say. She watched them come toward her, their anger only too apparent in the set of their ears and tails. As they passed Ghezu, the situation exploded.

"Well, if it isn't my one-time guest, Kaid! And the Aldatan brat!" Ghezu said, twisting round till he could see them.

Just that bit taller than Kaid, his feet touched the ground, allowing him more freedom of movement, and he was making full use of it.

"Hey, Aldatan! Has he had your mate yet?" He laughed. "You should have heard his drug ravings! What he was going to do to that little female of yours doesn't bear thinking about!" He laughed again. "How'd she like your scars, Kaid? She into that? Cripples?"

It was Kaid who had to hold back an enraged Kusac who roared his hate and anger as he tried to reach Ghezu.

"Leave him!" Kaid said, pulling Kusac close enough to wrap both arms around his, pinning them to his side. "He's trying to goad you, and he's succeeding! It's all lies, you know it is!"

Ghezu began to laugh again. "Got you riled? Shame!" He looked beyond them to the approaching group of Tribal rulers.

"I demand justice, Elders!"

Kaid took his chance to haul Kusac back out of Ghezu's line of sight, giving a yelp of pain as Kusac's struggles hit his injured hand.

Carrie pushed herself to her feet and in a couple of strides, was standing in front of them.

"Kusac! What the hell do you think you're doing?" she demanded. "How *could* you behave like this!"

He ignored her, twisting in Kaid's grasp, trying to get free.

Carrie reached out, grasping him by the ears and pulling his head down. He yowled in pain, but it brought him to his senses and made him look at her.

"Kusac, stop it! How can you shame me like this! You lend truth to Ghezu's lies by reacting to them, and you've hurt Kaid's injured hand!"

His eyes were black with anger but he forced himself to calm down, to leave the hunt state behind. Gradually he relaxed his muscles till Kaid felt it safe to release him.

"Now you've tasted *my* anger," said Kaid, facing him. "You tried to do what you denied me! What am I, Kusac? Friend—or liegeman?"

There was no opportunity for Kusac to answer as from behind them, the topic of Ghezu's argument became clear.

"I have the right to trial by Challenge," said Ghezu, pulling at the ropes that bound him to the rings above. "You can't deny me that right!"

"You can request it at your trial," growled Chaamga. "We'll return you to the Forces at the Nyacko Pass when we meet with them tomorrow."

"I have the right to be heard now!" Ghezu howled, enraged by their refusal. "I hold the rank of Guild Master! I demand a speedy settlement!"

"He has the right," admitted Rrurto.

"We've no Warriors here to accept the Challenge," said Chaamga, turning away. "The matter is closed."

"You have two," said Ghezu, dropping his voice to a gentle purr. "You have the Aldatan brat standing there," he flicked an ear in Kusac's direction. "Don't be put off by him being a telepath, he's a member of my Guild now. He trained at the Warrior Guild. And there's Kaid."

Carrie stood there hardly believing what she heard. Pain gripped her again, but she couldn't let it show. Wrapping an arm across her belly, she stepped in front of the Elders.

"Don't listen to him! His Talent is to charm people into believing him reasonable! He's not! He's guilty of treason, and of torturing a prisoner! He deserves the public humiliation of a trial!"

The Elders looked from one to the other, muttering among themselves.

Ghezu laughed. "You'd listen to a pregnant female so close to her time? I ask you, how rational can she be?"

"I'll give him the Challenge he wants," said Kaid, stepping forward, casting a long look at Kusac. "It has to be me. Kusac risks three lives if he fights. I only risk my own."

"No!" shrieked Carrie. "You damned-fool males with your cockeyed sense of honor! You fight between yourselves, then threaten everything I hold dear! You will *not* fight him, Kaid! I forbid you!"

Kusac reached out for her, taking her by the arm and thrusting her behind him.

"Well, Liegen Aldatan? Do you permit your liegeman to fight?" asked Chaamga.

Kusac stood looking at Kaid, still holding onto Carrie who was now beginning to weep. "Kaid," he began, then he saw Kaid's chin tilt up and his eyes darken.

"My friend is free to do what he must," said Kusac. "He's a member of my house, the third in our Triad, not a liegeman." He watched Kaid relax, his ears giving the smallest of flicks as he acknowledged the public recognition of their friendship.

Chaamga nodded. "Then release Ghezu under close guard and let him prepare himself for the Challenge. You have half an hour."

Chaamga turned away, leading his party deeper into the cavern. Ghezu was cut down and taken within as Kezule was brought past, bound and heavily guarded. Gradually the area cleared. Finally Kaid came over to them.

"Thank you," he said to Kusac, watching his friend's eyes, studying his face as if for the last time. "I don't intend to lose, that's not why I'm doing this."

"I know," said Kusac.

Kaid could hear and feel the tight control it was costing him to speak at all. He looked at Carrie, who refused to see him. Reaching out, he took hold of her face in his good hand.

"Carrie, you know I have to do this," he said. "You've seen my inner fears. You know I must face them. This is the only way I can do it."

She nodded.

Carrie, I have to! If I don't, he's broken me! Kaid's sending was full of the emotions he could barely admit to himself, and it cost him dear to mindspeak it to her.

She lifted a trembling hand to his face. "Just don't lose," she whispered. Her hand dropped to the leather bag that held his crystal.

"I'll try not to," he said, mouth opening in a smile.

"It stayed with you again," she murmured. "Part of me goes with you."

He put his hand on top of hers, pressing it gently before she stepped back from him. As he turned to move away, Kusac stopped him.

"You lose, and he won't live, Kaid, no matter what the law says!"

Kaid grasped Kusac's arm. "Then I have double the reason to win; I would not have you dishonor your family name."

He left them, going into the cavern and walking deeper and deeper through the tunnels till he came to the temple. Hesitating, he pushed the door open and walked in. It was deserted but the lights were still on. Going over to the altar, he put his hands on it, feeling the coolness of the rock absorb some of the fires of anger within him. Flexing his injured hand, he winced a little at the pain, realizing for the first time that for the last two days he'd been using it almost as if it were uninjured. Lifting it up, he tried to remove the bandage but he needed two hands for that. Using his teeth, he cut through the seal, then carefully pulled it off.

Underneath, the skin had healed completely and there was very little swelling. His pelt had even begun to grow back. Strange. He tried flexing the fingers again and found he had some movement back in them, particularly in the one that had only been broken. The other still felt painful, but at least he could bend it. It was as if they'd had weeks to heal, not days. Then the realization hit him. Time. They'd traveled in time and it hadn't left them untouched. Carrie must be near full term whether she admitted it or not, and his hand had healed beyond any expectation given that they'd only been away four days.

Sitting down with his back to the altar, he realized worry about Carrie and fear of how he'd manage with his damaged hand was not what he needed before a fight. He began to quiet his mind, reciting the litanies to Vartra that still brought him comfort, inner peace and clear thought. Relaxed, he began to drift, confident now that he could cope with the coming Challenge.

So, a now familiar voice said within his mind. *Should I be less because you've met me in the flesh?* The voice faded to nothing as someone shook his arm.

"It's time," said Kusac, holding out his hand to help him up. They stood eye to eye for a moment before embracing.

"Just see you win," said Kusac again.

"I'll try. If I don't, would you go with Dzaka to the Arrazo's estate? He'll tell you why. It's a promise I haven't had the chance to keep."

"We'll go together," said Kusac as they began to walk

down the corridors to the cavern mouth. "I've a robe for you.
Do you want to put it on?"

"Keep it for afterward."

Now that Fyak's hold had been broken and the false priest
was dead, many of the remaining fighters had left to return to
their tribal lands. Little of Fyak's army was left now. Riders
had been sent to the Nyacko Pass to deliver the message
Kusac and Chaamga had written to Governor Nesul during
the last half hour: the letter that offered the Forces Kezule as
the tribes' gesture of atonement.

"Carrie refuses to watch," said Kusac. "Understand that
she had to watch me fight a Death Challenge on Keiss. She
won't go through that a second time, she said."

"I understand."

"We've been loaned an aircar. We're leaving for home
after your fight."

"Good."

Kaid walked out into the sunlight, blinking slightly as they
headed toward the area that had been set aside for the Challenge. They made their way to the awning that had been set
up for the Elders, and waited beside them for Ghezu's
arrival.

Kusac glanced at the arena. "They're bringing Ghezu out
now," he said.

Kaid nodded and stepped out to meet him.

Like Kaid, Ghezu had opted to fight unclothed because of
the heat. "Think you can beat me, Kaid?" he asked, beginning to circle slowly round him. "How's the hand?"

Kaid said nothing, moving just enough to keep Ghezu in
the center of his sight.

"Do you still get the drug-dreams? Dream of her a lot, do
you? That's as close as you'll get now, Kaid," he said, still
pacing slowly round him. "Inch at a time, that's what I said.
I didn't get the chance to finish it, but I will today."

Kaid watched and waited. He felt nothing for Ghezu now,
he couldn't afford to. Rage and anger had been put aside
during the half hour he'd spent in the temple.

Kusac watched, afraid for his friend. He knew Kaid wasn't
ready to face Ghezu yet; he was still weak not only from the
torture he'd undergone, but from their journey to the Fire

Margins. It had left them all weaker. If ever Kaid needed a god to answer his prayers, now was the time!

Kaid himself had no illusions about his physical state. He knew that Ghezu had the edge on him. He was also insane, with the added strength that gave him.

He's nothing to lose, Kaid thought dispassionately as he continued to watch him.

Tiny telltale movements warned him Ghezu was about to leap, but when he did, Kaid was no longer there. Dropping down on all fours, he shoulder-charged Ghezu, timing it perfectly and catching him just as the other landed. As Ghezu fell to the ground, Kaid reared up to his full height and spun round to face him again.

As he rose, overextending his reach, Ghezu lashed out at him, his claws catching him across the chest, lacerating his flesh. Kaid leaped back; it stung, but nothing more and he knew the cuts were only shallow. As Ghezu continued coming toward him, Kaid pivoted to one side, landing him a vicious kick in the ribs. He felt something give beneath his foot and knew he'd caused some damage.

With a grunt of pain, Ghezu staggered back and stumbled to the ground. He pressed his hand to his side, trying to catch his breath as he stood up.

Warily Kaid began to circle, trying to keep on his opponent's injured side, but Ghezu followed him.

Carrie sat on the step of the aircar, clutching herself as another spasm gripped her. Sweat was running down her forehead, stinging her eyes. It passed and, shaking, she wiped her face on her forearm. It was taking all her concentration to block the pain from Kusac. There would be time enough to tell him when the fight was over. She was also terrified Kaid might pick it up and be distracted.

Like the sighing of the wind, she heard the sudden reaction of the crowd. Starting to her feet, she began to walk along the line of riding beasts toward the arena. She didn't dare use her mind to find out who'd been hurt, and she had to know. The pain was gone now, and wouldn't come again for another ten minutes or so. She had time enough to look.

The expected leap came, but with it was a cloud of dust and sand. Effectively blinded not only by the dust but by his inner eyelids, Kaid backed off, arms coming up to protect his face and throat from further injury. Then Ghezu's weight hit him full in the chest and he fell to the ground, hard. His arms were dragged from his face and slammed down on either side of him as Ghezu landed astride his chest.

Ghezu's breath was hot on his face. Kaid blinked furiously, still trying to clear the sharp particles of grit from his eyes. He could see his enemy hazily: his face was only inches away.

"You and me, Kaid. That's what you wanted, wasn't it? One on one—a chance to kill me." His voice dropped to a low malicious snarl, lips pulling back to reveal his teeth. "You're finished now. You've lost it, Kaid. I said I'd break you and I did. I knew I had the moment you tried to make me kill you at Stronghold." He began to laugh, edging his left hand along Kaid's arm toward his injured hand.

Kaid did the only thing he could: he brought his head up sharply and hit Ghezu in the face. The blow stunned him, too, and he lay there momentarily dazed.

With a yowl of pain, Ghezu released one of Kaid's arms, sitting back to put his hand up to his nose. He sneezed and snorted as blood began to flow from it.

Still dizzy, Kaid reached up and grabbed hold of him by the scruff, extending his claws into the loose flesh as he twisted it tightly, jerking Ghezu to the side. The unexpectedness of his follow-through caught Ghezu unaware and he tumbled sideways, taking Kaid with him.

Releasing his grip, Kaid found himself sprawled across Ghezu. Seeing his opportunity, he lunged for the exposed throat. Ghezu was quicker, and forcing his hand between them, he managed to hold Kaid off. He still had hold of Kaid's right hand, and shifting his grasp, he managed to trap it within his.

Kaid yowled in agony, pain lancing through him as Ghezu began to crush his damaged fingers. Slowly, painfully, he inched his free hand up, trying to grasp Ghezu by the jaw.

Carrie stood there, almost hidden among the desert fighters, her fist pressed to her mouth as she watched.

One of the males standing beside her looked down. His hand reached out to touch her shoulder gently. She looked up at him, eyes wide with fear.

"Vartra will protect him, Liegena, never fear," he said.

With a sob, Carrie turned and, clutching her belly, stumbled back toward the aircar. As she rounded the outcrop of rock between the riding beasts and the vehicle, she had to stop as another spasm wracked her.

Ghezu's hand reached frantically for Kaid's throat but met his teeth instead. Biting down hard, Kaid felt his canines puncture the flesh, and grate through the bones till his teeth met. Blood spurted into his mouth, almost choking him, making him swallow convulsively.

The screech of pain from Ghezu almost deafened him and the pressure on his damaged hand was instantly removed. Opening his jaws, and releasing his grip on Ghezu's neck, he pushed himself back, scrambling to consolidate his position on Ghezu's chest. The pain in his own hand hadn't diminished, but he pushed it aside as best he could.

Beneath him, Ghezu twisted and bucked, trying to throw him off, trying to protect his mangled hand. It had to end now, Kaid knew. Ghezu's neck arched back momentarily. Clenching his good hand, he struck at Ghezu's larynx, crushing it, feeling the spine beneath snap.

Ghezu went instantly limp. Eyes dilated, he stared up at Kaid, making small gurgling sounds as blood from his larynx and nose began to flood down into his lungs.

"Who broke whom, Ghezu?" Kaid asked softly, reaching for Ghezu's right arm and pulling Khemu's bracelet free. Taking his time, he put it back on his own wrist, where it belonged.

He could feel Ghezu's helpless rage turn to horror as he realized he was dying. He wasn't prepared to experience the dissolution of his enemy's mind, the gradual extinction of his senses, his memories, and finally himself.

Sickened, Kaid got to his feet, turned and walked away.

Kusac ran across the arena to meet him.

"Are you hurt?" He touched the oozing claw tracks across his friend's chest.

Kaid shook his head slowly. "I had to kill him that way." He needed Kusac to understand, and was afraid he wouldn't. Part of his mind told him that this was what feelings did to one.

"I know," said Kusac, looking briefly over to where Ghezu lay gasping and wheezing. He held out the robe for him to put on. "Is it over now?" he asked, searching Kaid's face.

"Yes. It's over," Kaid said, closing his eyes and swaying slightly.

Kusac caught hold of him.

"I'm fine, just drained now it's finished," Kaid said, righting himself.

"Let's go home," said Kusac, helping him into the robe and tying the sash for him. "Carrie's waiting. You got Khemu's bracelet?"

Kaid nodded.

The warriors parted for them as they headed toward the line of tethered animals. When they reached the rock where Carrie had stopped, Kaid held Kusac back.

"Wait," he said. His inner lids were partially closed and his face had a pinched look about it. Leaning against the rock for support, he began to vomit blood.

"Kaid! What the hell's wrong?" demanded Kusac, leaning over him. "Where's the blood coming from? You *have* been hurt! Have you got internal injuries?"

Kaid grasped hold of his arm, holding onto him as his retching began to lessen. At last he straightened up, wiping a trembling forearm across his face. "I'm fine. It's Ghezu's blood, not mine."

Kusac reached out and put his hands on his friend's shoulders. "You frightened me, Kaid. I thought we really were going to lose you this time."

Kaid's grin was uneven—part Sholan, part Human. "Not yet," he said, his good hand going up to cover Kusac's.

He hesitated a moment, then looked down at his injured hand. Once again his fingers were swollen and hurt when he tried to move them, though it didn't feel as if they'd suffered any worse damage.

"I saw him get your hand," Kusac growled, watching while Kaid examined it.

"I don't think it's that bad. Kusac, my hand had healed," Kaid said, looking up at him. "Time acted strangely on us while we were in the past. We've aged by several weeks. It's done the same to Carrie. She's closer to having the cub than we thought."

Kusac glanced round at the aircar, worry written in the set of his ears. He began to run, Kaid close behind him.

Carrie was sitting resting quietly when they arrived. She opened her eyes and smiled at them.

"I knew you were all right," she said.

"Carrie, how close are you to having the cub?" asked Kusac, squatting down beside her.

"Several weeks yet," she said, reaching out to stroke his face. "Don't worry, we're fine."

"Kaid's hand healed faster than it should. You're further on than you think."

"We're going home. I'll see Vanna as soon as we get there, I promise," she said.

"Are you sure?" he asked, taking her hand in his.

"Positive. Now let's leave," she said.

"I'll drive, you sit with her," said Kaid, slipping into the pilot's seat and sealing the door.

"I'll call home first," said Kusac, moving to sit in the front.

He punched in the number and to his surprise, found the call diverted to the Shrine.

"Thank the Gods you're safe," Konis said, the relief evident on his face. "You're at Chezy?"

"How did you know?"

"T'Chebbi. She worked out you'd arrived back at another temple. Ghyan pinpointed it as Chezy. Raiban's forces are already on their way out for you." He hesitated. "Did you. . . ?"

Kusac nodded. "We walked the Fire Margins, Father, and we're all safe."

"What about the situation out there? How did you persuade Fyak to let you go?"

"Fyak's dead, so's Ghezu. It's a long story, Father. I'll tell you when we get back. Have you been told about the Valtegan yet?"

"What Valtegan?"

"Contact Raiban. We brought Fyak's God Kezule back with us."

"What?" Konis' confusion showed in the set of his ears. "You've brought back a Valtegan?"

"One from the old days, before they were so afraid of us. You should be able to get a lot of information from him, even if it's one and a half thousand years out of date." Kusac could feel the tiredness descending on him like a weight. "Talk to Raiban, Father. Tell Vanna that Carrie's near her time. We'll need her when we arrive."

Konis frowned. "Carrie's all right, isn't she? She wasn't due for another couple of months."

"It was going back in time that did it. The cub isn't premature, don't worry."

"I thought she was going to Noni."

Kusac shrugged and grinned. "She wants to come home."

"I'll tell Raiban you're on your way," said Konis. "Travel safely."

"We'll see you soon," said Kusac, signing off.

The presence exploded within their minds, stunning them all with the force of its sending. They could almost hear the roar of victory that preceeded it.

We succeeded, and we live! Tell Vartra that his experiments worked!

They all saw the darkened cellar, and the indistinct forms of three Humans before it was replaced by an image of a female so like Rhyasha that it defied belief.

It was Carrie who responded. *Rezac?* She felt the affirmative rather than heard it. *Trust those with you. They'll bring you safely home.*

Then a sense of danger filled her as she saw the force gathered against them. *Take care! We'll come for you, I swear it!*

As suddenly as it came, the sending was gone, leaving them feeling drained and confused.

"Who was it, Carrie?" demanded Kusac. "Where were they?"

Shaking, she put her hand up to her eyes, trying to rub the tiredness from them before answering.

"It was Rezac and his Leska, Zashou. I don't know how, but they seem to be in the same place as Jo and Davies."

"Are you sure?"

"Positive. We've all seen them before in replays."

Kusac let out a long breath as he looked at Kaid. "They're still alive," he said. "*Your* father!"

Kaid made a dismissive gesture. "I'll believe that when I meet them," he said. "Let's get Carrie home."

They'd barely been traveling for more than quarter of an hour when Carrie, unable to hide the fact she was in labor any longer, began to moan.

"What is it?" asked Kusac, immediately concerned as she doubled up, clutching her belly in obvious pain.

"Stop the aircar," she said, barely able to talk.

"Stop?" he repeated, confused by the sensations of pain that were starting to flood through him.

"Oh, God," she whimpered. "Land it, Kusac! The baby's coming!"

"I'm landing," said Kaid, dropping the aircar down to look for a likely site. "We're not clear of the hills yet, it's not going to be easy."

Carrie felt her barriers weakening but she was in too much pain now to care.

Kusac watched his mate in panic, trying to put his arms round her while at the same time experiencing the same abdomen-wrenching pains. "Kaid, land this 'car now!" he said. "She's broadcasting her pain!" He looked at Carrie, trying to use his own blocks to keep her agony at bay. "What do we do?"

"I don't know," she said, tears running down her face. "No one told me! There were supposed to be weeks left yet. It hurts, Kusac!"

"There should be a medikit on board," said Kaid, glancing round.

Her pain had stopped for the moment and Kusac was able to slide out from his seat and look at the locker fronts. One of them bore the Medic Guild's symbol on the front. "Got it," he said, opening it and pulling the medikit out.

"See if there's analgesics in it. And psychic suppressants," he added, feeling an echo of Carrie's pain himself.

Kusac sat down beside her again. She was beginning to uncurl and looked a little better as some of the color returned to her face. "Everything'll be fine," he reassured her as he began to fumble in the bag. Various sealed bandages and dressings began to fall out as he searched for the drugs. Finally he pulled a pack out.

"Got some analgesics and a hypo," he said, as Carrie once more doubled up. The pain hit him again too, low in his gut, making him double over in shock.

"Kaid! Get this thing down! I can't help her when we're like this!"

She was making small mewling noises of pain as she rocked herself back and forth in an effort to ease the agony.

"I'm trying," said Kaid, aware of the pain both of them were suffering. He reached inside himself, building the barriers he'd lived behind until now. This time there was a real need for them. "Don't do anything till I've landed," he warned. "I need to check the drugs myself. Try and find those suppressants! This is the craft Anirra used to use when he had to accompany them on a raid. There's got to be some on board somewhere!"

He flew lower, searching for a clearing. Some almost forgotten bit of knowledge from his days in Dzahai village came back to him.

"How far apart are her pains? The closer they are, the nearer she is to giving birth. And the membrane round the cub, has it burst yet?"

"They don't stop," Carrie whimpered as the contractions continued. "And yes, it burst while you were fighting."

"Kaid," said Kusac, his voice taut with pain as he dropped the medikit and tried to comfort Carrie, "In the God's name, land anywhere!"

"Got somewhere," Kaid said, circling over a small clearing before beginning to descend.

No sooner had he switched the engines off than he was out of his seat and round beside them.

"We need to move her," he said. "There's no room to treat her. Carry her down to the rear. Her pains have eased off, you should be able to cope for a few minutes."

Wrapping his arms around her, Kusac picked her up carefully and eased his way off the seat. While he was doing that, Kaid was opening all the lockers to get what blankets and pillows he could, as well as trying to locate the suppressants. He only came up with two blankets.

Kusac was squatting with Carrie held across his knees, unwilling to lay her down on the bare metal floor. Kaid opened the blankets out, then reached over and handed them to Kusac.

"Make her as comfortable as you can while I check the drugs," he said, going back to where the medikit lay on the floor.

"Kaid! I don't know anything about this! Come back!" said Kusac, looking up the aisle at him.

"Neither do I!" Kaid replied, reading the instructions on the pack.

Kusac threw one blanket down on the floor then placed Carrie carefully on part of it, covering her with the rest. Quickly he folded the other, placing it against his knees. He drew her closer, resting her head on his lap, gently stroking her with one hand while she held onto his other.

She began to laugh hysterically, tears of pain running unchecked down her cheeks. "Oh, God! Here I am, in the middle of nowhere, the first Human woman to have a Sholan cub, with two males who don't know the first thing about childbirth as birthers!"

Her laughter turned into a cry of pain as the contractions intensified and she began to moan again, gripping Kusac's hand so hard she was hurting him.

Waves of her pain hit both males full force this time, bringing Kaid to his knees and making Kusac double up and nearly collapse on top of her.

She cried out again, pulling away from him this time in an effort to push herself up onto her knees. The pain was unremitting now as her insides contracted, determined to expel the child that had become such a part of her.

"Don't sit up, cub," said Kusac, pushing himself upright again and taking hold of her in an effort to urge her back down beside him.

"Leave me!" she snapped, almost falling as she bent over, holding onto her belly again. "It helps," she moaned. And it did. The next few spasms weren't so intense as gravity itself seemed to help pull her cub lower.

Terror gripped her in its claws. Was the cub really coming too early? Dear God, no! They'd both wanted her so much . . . loved her from the first. She couldn't lose her now, not again! With a cry of anguish and pain, she collapsed back against him, her fear echoing throughout the small cabin, and the minds of the two males.

"Forget the drugs, Kaid!" said Kusac, holding onto her as all three of them suddenly felt the cub's mind flare to wakefulness. "Come and help me!"

"I've got the suppressants!" said Kaid, scrambling forward as he hurriedly loaded the drug into the hypo.

The pain eased off again, but not Carrie's fear. "Leave me alone!" she shrieked, trying to pull away from them as both males reached for her. She backed off toward the rear bulkhead and stayed there, doubled forward on her knees.

"Carrie, it's only a suppressant," said Kusac, trying to keep his voice calm as he held out his hand to her. "We need to stop you broadcasting your pain and fear. We can't help you if we don't."

"No! Stay away from me! You're not giving me anything

that'll hurt my baby! I won't let you!" Her voice was hoarse, her throat scraped raw with crying out.

"Think of the cub, Carrie," said Kaid. "What's your pain and terror doing to her? Have you thought of that?"

She looked at him. "She can feel it?"

"Of course. She's closer to you now than we are."

Slowly she forced the fear back, and uncurling herself, crawled toward Kusac, lying her head on his lap and starting to cry.

They felt her mind taking control, felt her pain gradually recede, taking the fear with it until it was gone. Both males breathed a silent sigh of relief.

"Kaid," said Kusac, his voice still shaken from the pain he'd experienced, "I really could do with your help." He gave a strangled yowl as Carrie clutched at his leg.

Dropping the hypo, Kaid scrambled over to them and squatted down at Carrie's side.

She was vaguely aware of her hands being taken and held by Kusac as the need to push down overwhelmed her.

"She's coming now, and I can't stop her," she sobbed, twisting and turning as she tried to escape her mate's hold on her.

"Then let her come," said Kaid, reaching out to take hold of her chin for a moment. His brown eyes regarded her calmly. "Your body knows better than any of us what to do, let it."

"What if something's gone wrong?" she moaned, tightening her grip on Kusac's hands as Kaid helped her curl up on her side. "What if we need help? Medical help. Vanna did!"

"We're all of us En'Shalla now, Carrie. *In the hands of the Gods.* Trust in Vartra to have got it right. He's not done badly so far, considering he only had one Human blood sample to work with."

"I'd forgotten about that," said Kusac quietly.

Once again they felt a tiny presence flare within their minds.

"In the God's name, see what's happening," Kusac hissed urgently as Carrie cried out again.

His Brotherhood paramedic training taking over, Kaid untangled Carrie's legs from the heavy robe and pulled it aside. He was just in time to catch the small, damp bundle of newborn cub as she emerged into the world.

"Oh!" he said, looking down at the tiny unmoving body that lay in his hands.

The two males exchanged worried glances as Carrie lay exhausted and panting between them.

Kaid looked away first. Putting the cub down onto the blanket, he pulled the waist sash free of his robe and began carefully cleaning her cub's face, checking that her mouth and nose were clear of the remains of the membrane.

Her sudden sneeze seemed to echo loudly in the silence as both males began to breath again themselves. As she began to whimper, they felt her mental presence begin to steady and search for her mother.

Kaid offered up a silent prayer to Vartra.

Carrie began to push herself up but Kusac's arms were instantly there to help her. She peered down at Kaid who had just finished wiping the cub.

"I want her," she said, holding out her arms. "I want my cub."

"Her pelt's still slippery," he warned as carefully he lifted her up and moved forward to place her in Carrie's arms. "And she's still attached."

Carrie held her in the crook of her arm while, with her other hand, she gently touched her daughter's face. Though her cub's eyes were squeezed tightly shut, a tiny hand reached unerringly for her, wrapping itself round her finger. Carrie felt the cub began to gently vibrate.

"She's purring!" she said in surprise, looking up at Kusac.

"She is," he agreed, a slow grin spreading across his face. With their daughter's birth, his link to Carrie no longer brought pain. The joy he felt was enhanced by hers. Reaching for his own sash, he pulled it free, holding it out to her.

"Wrap her in this," he said. "We don't want her getting cold."

"You'll help me, won't you?" she said, her eyes shining up at him in the dim light of the aircar.

He leaned down to gently lick her cheek. "You try and stop me," he said.

Kaid decided now was a good time to make his retreat. "I'll go call Vanna for some advice."

"Vanna, Kaid here."

"Kaid! You're all safe! Thank the Gods for that! What's

this about Carrie being nearer to having her cub than we thought? She's not going into premature labor, is she?"

"Not exactly, Vanna," he said. "It's an effect of travelling back to the Margins. She's just had the cub and they're both fine. I'd like to know what the hell do we do now?"

Vanna began to laugh hysterically.

Half an hour later, they were on their way again. Carrie and Kashini were wrapped comfortably in the blankets, both of them lying curled up at the back of the aircar with Kusac. He sat there, Carrie held in his arms, watching their daughter having her first feed. Reaching down, he gently ran his finger across the curve of Kashini's cheek. With her tiny ears still folded close to her head, and her short blond pelt, it was easy for him to see the Human in her.

"She's our daughter," said Carrie contentedly, "and she's beautiful."

"She certainly is. You know, we've really got a lot to thank Vartra for," he said, transferring his attention to her.

"But not the way everyone else means it," Carrie said, grinning up at him.

THE CATFANTASTIC ANTHOLOGIES
Edited by Andre Norton and Martin H. Greenberg

☐ **CATFANTASTIC** UE2355—$6.99
With fur fluffed and claws unsheathed, they stalk their prey or stand fast against their foes . . . with tails raised and rumbling purrs, they name and welcome their friends . . . with instincts beyond those of mere humans, they ward off unseen dangers, working a magic beyond our ken. . . . they are Cats, and you can meet them here in stories by C.S. Friedman, Mercedes Lackey, Elizabeth Ann Scarborough, and Ardath Mayhar, among others.

☐ **CATFANTASTIC II** UE2461—$6.99
Far more than nine feline lives are portrayed in this delightful romp along the secret ways known only to those incredible cats. With stories by Elizabeth Moon, Susan Shwartz, Nancy Springer, and Andre Norton, among others.

☐ **CATFANTASTIC III** UE2591—$6.99
SKitty, unflappable space traveler, makes a triumphant return, as does Hermione, who gives another detailed report on the serious duties of a respectable familiar. Join them and new feline friends in stories by Charles de Lint, Mercedes Lackey, Lyn McConchie, and Ardath Mayhar, among others.

☐ **CATFANTASTIC IV** UE2711—$5.99
Meet wizard's four-footed helpers, a feline with a most discerning taste in jazz, some Japanese cats talented enough to improvise a Noh play, among other fabulous felines in stories by Mercedes Lackey, Jane Lindskold, Elizabeth Ann Scarborough, and Andre Norton.

☐ **CATFANTASTIC V** UE2847—$6.99
Twenty-four sleek new tales about cats of the past, cats of the future, and cats only too ready to take matters into their own paws! Stories by Mercedes Lackey, David Drake, Barry Longyear, Ardath Mayhar, and others.